# The Misfortunate Maiden

## A Fates of Emvarr Novel

### Mary J Nichols

Emvarr Publishing LLC

Published in the United States of America by

Emvarr Publishing LLC, Michigan

The Misfortunate Maiden/Mary J Nichols

ISBN 978-17374523-6-2

Cover Art and Map Art by Erica Hogendyk

Dear Reader,

This story takes place in a fictional medieval world that contains adult content some might find difficult to read. Such as: language, sexual situations, act of violence (sword fights, harm/brutality toward men and women, attempts/mention of sexual assault, and attempts to cause a miscarriage), deaths, and use of fictional narcotics and alcohol.

## **Characters**

<u>Thylaina Zorlias</u> (*Thī-lā-na Zor-lī-us*) – Niece to the king of Etharell.

<u>Breydon Colmstad</u> (**Brā**-don **Kalm**-stahd) – First Captain of Caerabis.

<u>Arhgrim Momestid</u> (**Ar**-grim **Mō**-mu-sted) – Marshal of Caerabis.

<u>Bramn Jalfiasin</u> (**Bramn** Jah-**fī**-uh-sin) – Knight in Caerabis. Breydon's closest friend.

<u>Brenlyr</u> (Bren-**leer**) – A notable knight in Caerabis.

<u>Gavrel Kedanier</u> (**Gav**-rel **Ked**-a-neer) – Soldier in training for the knighthood; a Dubight.

<u>Katjina</u> (**Kat**-ye-na) – Thylaina's handmaiden in Caerabis.

<u>Mikan Thornsalin</u> (**Mī**-kin **Thorn**-su-lin) – High priest at the temple of Valorius in Caerabis.

<u>Nadiera</u> (**Nā**-dē-eer-a) – Arhgrim's and Tesesra's daughter.

<u>Telsia</u> (Tel-**sē**-a) – Arhgrim's and Tesesra's youngest daughter.

<u>Tesesra</u> (Te-**ses**-ru) – Arhgrim's wife, the Lady of Caerabis.


## **The Divine**

<u>Fynthiar</u> (**Fin**-thē-ar) – Creator of Emvarr. Known as the Father of All or Fate.

<u>Bryric</u> (**Brī**-rik) – God of the elves.

<u>Chaos</u> (**Kā**-as) – Demigod. Lord of Darkness.

<u>Grestin</u> (**Gres**-tin) – Demigod. Chaos' brother.

<u>Lessindra</u> (Le-**sin**-dra) – Goddess of Love, Mercy, and Forgiveness.

<u>Valorius</u> (Va-**lor**-ē-us) – God of humans favored by knights and warriors.

<u>Vynia</u> (**Vin**-yu) – Earthen goddess. The Healer.


## **Places**

<u>Alohrius</u> (*U-**lōr**-ē-us*) – A human country overseen by the Three Marshals.

<u>Emvarr</u> (***Em**-var*) – The world created by Fynthiar.

<u>Etharell</u> (***Eth**-a-rel*) – The Elven kingdom ruled by descendants of Bryric.

<u>Caerabis</u> (***Kair**-a-bis*) – Knight City in the southwest of Alohrius.

<u>Haevaun Balaeus</u> (***Hā**-vahn Ba-**lā**-us*) – Capital city of Alohrius.

<u>Haevuan Flameral</u> (***Hā**-vahn Fla-**meer**-al*) – Capital city of Etharell.

<u>Karvorn</u> (***Kar**-vorn*) – Seaport in southern Alohrius.

<u>Kilstra Forest</u> (***Kil**-stra*) – Yeuroth's and Etharell's largest forest. Home of the Kilstra Xilys.

<u>Monsor</u> (***Mahn**-sōr*) – Knight City in northeastern Alohrius.

<u>Ormiana Forest</u> (*Ōr-**mē**-**a**-na*) – Forest in southeastern Etharell. Home of the Ormiana Xilys.

<u>Rhigowan</u> (*Rī-**gow**-an*) – City north of Karvorn.

<u>Warstchia</u> (***Wars**-chē-a*) – Walled Knight City in western Alohrius.

# Southeast Alohrius

# Chapter One

Lord Rhomasyn's laughter sent a shudder of piercing thorns and revulsion throughout Thylaina. Her hair plucked out one strand at a time was preferable torment than enduring him for the rest of her days. If only she could escape her betrothed's irritating cackles as easily as she avoided his company this night. It took little to circumvent him amid the hundreds of guests gathered in the Royal Garden for the Harvest Moon celebration. The gloriously bright moon's early arrival provided a gorgeous evening and promised an exceptional harvest. Rhomasyn, however, was not the only one to ruin this joyous event for Thylaina. Emptiness devoured her heart as two lines from her brother's letter passed through her mind once again.

*'Rhomasyn is to be your husband—something neither of us can change... Embrace your destiny just as the rest of us have.'*

Embrace her destiny, indeed! A forced betrothal in which she had no say was not her destiny. For Neldrid to insist she accept it, when he was free to choose *his* bride, was ludicrous.

How had it come to this between them? Why did her need for his presence and the knowledge he still cared about her push Neldrid farther away? Thylaina closed her eyes to hide the building tears as another line from the letter surfaced.

*'I love you, dear sister, but I am happy with my path. I will not return to Haevaun Flameral at your every request just to please you.'*

He knew not what love meant if he believed it was about pleasing her. Love was more than broken promises and unwanted gifts. But that letter had broken her heart. More bitter words came to mind, sending her back into the fray against the urge to sob in front of the surrounding guests. Thylaina scanned the dozens of faces around her. People who smiled at her because she was of the royal bloodline, who looked to appease her like Neldrid did, but cared not about *her*. She was finished with them all.

Throat constricting, she pressed through to where the crowd thinned. Around the corner proved a place of solace, for none bothered to view the dead allotment. Deep breaths eased out as she stared at the viny branches of the tree, shining silver under the moonlight, the only lovely feature of the otherwise unattractive garden. Solitude offered no comfort to decades of painful memories involving her brother, most of them recent.

During the last few years of his visits, Neldrid had neglected Thylaina while he focused on a future bride. So she interfered. Without invitation, she joined him and his prospects for walks in the Royal Garden, enjoyed lovely meals with them on the terrace, and sat on the other side of the frustrated maidens during feasts so she could impose on their conversations. She ignored his many glares and jerks of his head, indicating she should leave. Of course, it was all poor behavior, but Neldrid's lack of attention was rather awful.

Ten years had elapsed since his previous return home, eight years since Thylaina had received a message. To regain his notice, she sent him reminder that she still lived. Not two days had passed when a messenger placed Neldrid's reply into her hands. Her brother often claimed there was no time to come see her, all while he was less than a day's ride from the city. Since breaking that seal, Thylaina had re-read the letter five times, but had no response. He no longer wanted her in his life. Their fragmented relationship left her a husk.

"Are you hiding from me, darling?" Rhomasyn slipped his arm beneath her waist-length hair, glided his hand to the curve of her buttocks.

She jerked, almost dropping her goblet. Such a shame he had not found a different maiden with whom to spend the evening. A slow breath pushed down the rising nausea and suppressed the sorrow afore she faced him.

His thin lips brushed her pointed ear. "You are difficult to find amongst these... guests."

Phony smiles were easy to learn while living in the palace, and she had mastered them since her cousin's exile nine years ago. Presenting one of those smiles now, she said, "I promised to assure everyone felt welcomed."

"That is not your duty. The queen—" Rhomasyn's eyes darted to a passing maiden as he combed his fingers through his long brown mane. He had not the courtesy to hide the desire to throng another woman. Not that it mattered, for no vows had yet been spoken. "The queen has servants to do such tasks."

"I enjoy speaking with the people." Thylaina hated lying, but the dead bushes of this small garden could offer better company than these pretentious idiots and her future husband.

"They do not deserve a moment with you."

True. But neither did he.

Rhomasyn guided her to the terrace stairs. "I want to be alone with you."

Thylaina searched the passing faces for a rescue. Raised goblets and bobbed heads were the only recognition received as a path cleared. Misery accompanied every thudding step. This was not good. How could she escape this unwanted fate with him in her suite?

Thylaina lay still, wishing the echoes of his touch and moans would fade faster. Even his scent offended her. If only he would leave. Gods! If she could convince him to break the betrothal.

Their arrangement made no sense. Even Neldrid had appeared puzzled when Father announced the accepted proposal. What a politically fit marriage: the Lord Advisor's son and the Second General's daughter. Thylaina and Rhomasyn shared no love while growing up in the palace. He was a pompous highborn lord who treated those of lower status poorly, and he showed little sympathy toward her family when Mother passed. In fact, while comforting Thylaina, Rhomasyn had grabbed her breast. Although the incident happened almost one-hundred-fifty years ago, she never forgot.

She fought the need to shudder as his finger glided along her shoulder.

*'Rhomasyn is to be your husband—something neither of us can change.'*

Pah! Thylaina would not suffer this man. To make a marriage vow she did not mean afore the Goddess of Love was wrong, and Thylaina refused to insult Her. Tonight's event offered the perfect opportunity to blend amongst the several groups moving about the garden and escape this dreaded future with Rhomasyn. However, his presence in her bedchamber brought that plan to a standstill.

Rhomasyn licked his lips. "I would like a drink."

That pretentious man! Wait... She held her breath as a new scheme formed. A drink would do wonderfully. Thylaina grabbed her robe and headed toward the table. "I have just the blend to finish the evening."

He sounded a moan as he rested his head on the pillow. "Shall it take long? I desire your warmth."

At least he could not witness the disgust passing over her face. "To experience the full flavor, you must be patient."

Thylaina stopped at her box of herbs, oils, powders, and combinations of them for remedies she had learned from her uncle and healing teacher. A skilled healer had the ability to remove ingredients from their box without looking. Thylaina could complete the task even while blindfolded. The necessary bottles snatched, she viewed the wine decanters for the best selection.

A glance confirmed Rhomasyn remained comfortable, his eyes closed.

Brief prayers to the Earthen Goddess accompanied the quick combining of herbs in a small bowl: a pinch of ashrych to ease Rhomasyn's body into a mild numbness, a dose of camiol to put him to sleep, and dried crueberry powder to mask the flavor. Thylaina poured the concoction into a golden goblet with the drink, then breathed its fragrance. The spiced redberry and plum wine veiled any hint of the sleep poison.

The idea of continuing with the next step brought a hesitation. Could Thylaina walk away from family? But *they* had left *her*. Every one of them. A better life could be found outside of the palace—outside of Etharell.

"My mouth remains dry," Rhomasyn snapped.

*Breathe. Relax. Try not to throw the damn bottle at him.* She tilted her head in his direction. "Forgive me... love." Great Bryric, that word tasted foul.

An extra dose of camiol floated into the cup to ensure an undisturbed slumber. The mixture should promise a mind too groggy to recall much of anything when he awakened.

Rhomasyn sat up at her approach, his gaze lowering to her breasts. "Take off your robe."

"I am chilled." Sitting on the mattress, Thylaina offered the drink. It proved a challenge to keep her excitement and anxiety at bay while he sipped.

His nostrils curled. "Is this not your brother's? He always offered this blend to me."

For twenty years, Rhomasyn had complained about his father's many praises of Neldrid. The sneers behind her brother's back and silent loathing added blackness to Rhomasyn's already dark eyes. Even when her brother was not present, the jealousy continued. How many times in the garden had her betrothed forced kind words through gritted teeth when pressed to discuss. This resentment might benefit Thylaina's plan.

She guided the cup back to his lips. "Imagine how displeased Neldrid shall be to find it gone upon his return."

His eyes darted upward as he snorted. "Your brother is not coming back." The chamber filled with his dreadful snigger. "Neldrid's only love is power. And with an army behind him, the man thinks he is untouchable."

Logs snapping in the hearth faded beneath the heavy thumps of her heart as rage heated her face. How dare he speak about her brother like that! As First General, Neldrid endangered his life to protect Etharell. Rhomasyn did nothing but live off his father's accomplishments.

His cheek reddened as a burning sting spread from her fingers to her palm, and the dark-red wine spilled on the bedding. "Do not insult him again," she said, her throat dry.

Eyes widening, Rhomasyn touched where she had struck him. The golden goblet flew across the room, leaving a spiderweb of cracks on a decanter. His painfully tight grip around Thylaina's wrist yanked her closer. "Never raise your hand to me!"

Instinct took over. While gliding two fingers across his forehead, Thylaina spoke a word of magic. "*Falashia.*"

The pain in her wrist eased as his hold loosened. His eyelids fluttering, he wavered. "Wha—? What are you... doing?" Rhomasyn dropped to the mattress, his chest rising and falling evenly. The combination of potion and sleep spell should bring a longer slumber. When he awakened, a clouded mind and foul mood would likely accompany confusion as to what had happened. Hopefully, he would not remember the spell.

Yet Thylaina gaped. If the king learned—if anyone discovered—she was capable of divine magic, she knew not what would happen. Thylaina had never shared about the power's emergence shortly after her sixteenth birth-day. Not even with Mother, who had also received this divine gift from their god, Bryric.

Worry muddled her thoughts as she paced beside the bed. Although Thylaina had decided a few hours after reading Neldrid's letter to leave Etharell, moving forward was different. She was ready to change her life and take control of her fate. Was she not?

She stared at Rhomasyn, her future... if she did naught to change it.

*'Embrace your destiny just as the rest of us have.'*

Anxiety jumbled with urgency as Thylaina placed pouches and vials of healing herbs and powders in the travel satchel. She gathered precious jewels and gems, along with various roans, and a wineskin. The untouched red satin gown and silver cloak in the wardrobe would finally serve a purpose. Not her typical colors, but having something unusual prompted Thylaina to accept the suggestions from the local seamstress. After dressing, she fixed her black curls into a single braid.

The garden festivities could last into the early morning hours, which might be to her advantage.

Thylaina tucked a yavlar leaf down the front of the dress, pushed the satchel beneath the cloak, and entered the corridor.

The Royal Guard straightened her back and stared forward. "Is all well, my lady?" she asked. "I thought I heard something break."

Thylaina offered a polite smile. "All is fine. Lord Rhomasyn is exhausted and wishes his sleep to be left undisturbed."

"As you wish, my lady."

Thylaina hurried toward the massive landing, but paused outside Neldrid's chamber door. Although he was not present, sentries stood guard: one at the bedroom and one at the connecting cabinet entrances. She approached the guard at the cabinet door. "I wish to enter."

"He is not—"

"I know," she snapped. Thylaina lowered her head and sighed. "For only a moment. You can leave the door open."

He exhaled loudly, then unlocked the door. "No need, my lady." He removed a candle from the nearby sconce and lit four atop the dark room's hearth. The guard closed the door behind him when he left.

Thylaina stood at the fireplace, her gaze fixed on the painting above. Golden curls framed a delicate face of pure beauty, and green eyes stared back. How often she had wished to have inherited those golden locks and lovely irises. But like Neldrid, Thylaina had Father's black hair and rare copper eyes.

She drew in a trembling breath. "Mother... I am—I am leaving. Please do not be angry nor ashamed of me." Tears surfaced as she imagined her mother's displeasure, yet understanding. "This is not the life for me. I *cannot* marry Rhomasyn. And I do not believe I can ever come to love him." She fidgeted with the satchel strap. "So this is my farewell." She met the unmoving gaze. "I miss you so terribly much. It hurts."

There was nothing more to say. If Thylaina lingered any longer, she might lose the conviction to free herself from a life of misery.

"Please pray for me, Mother."

She hurried downstairs to the terrace, slowing as she returned to the gardens. Head down, she accepted a glass of wine and mingled amid the dozens of remaining guests. Meandering to the allotments nearest the exit, her gaze flicked toward the Royal Family and their guards. Thank Bryric! One of the smaller gardens was empty of guests, so she slipped within its thick foliage. It took little time to ensure everything was in place, and that the hood shadowed her face, particularly her eyes. No other family in the capital city boasted copper irises. The guards might question the raised hood, but hopefully, her plan would work and they would think nothing of it.

A small party of seven sauntered past, pausing just beyond the allotment's entrance to view the orange blooms within the brush.

Thylaina spoke an incantation upon the yavlar leaf to speed its release into her system, then she sucked on it, nearly gagging from the foul taste. As the group resumed toward the Royal Garden's gates, she trailed. The pungent essence of the leaf soaked into her tongue and slid down her throat, prompting a queasiness in her stomach. She dragged the leaf from her mouth and dropped it. By the time the group reached the gates, cramping pains pierced Thylaina's roiling stomach. The evening's meal of roasted rabbit and steamed vegetables churned with acid, lurching up to her throat. Slouched forward with one hand on her belly and the other over her mouth, she rushed forward, bumping into the others.

"My lady, are you well?" the nearest guard inquired. He reached for Thylaina's arm, but she stumbled aside, her body wracking.

"F-forgive me," she managed in a whisper. "I-I am not feeling—" Vomit splattered bits of meat and vegetables at his feet.

Jumping back, he yelled. The commotion caught the attention of a few nearby guards, one rushing over to assist him.

Still hunched, Thylaina wiped the cloak sleeve over her lips. "Forgive me."

"Move on afore you spread your illness." The guard waved her through as he dragged his boot on the grass. "Go now."

Thylaina shuffled behind the nobles hurrying through the gate and scattering from her path. "I am so sorry," she said. Others avoided her, many crossing the perfectly bricked street or rushing toward the carriages near the fountain.

A few blocks from the castle, and after a couple more bouts of retching, she took to the shadows. Trembles lingered as Thylaina drew in a deep breath, then washed her mouth out from the wineskin. It would be some time until she ate rabbit again.

Now to leave the city without notice.

Merchants traveled to and from Haevaun Flameral throughout the day, some preferring the quiet nights compared to the busier roads of the sunlit hours. Thylaina needed to find one such wagon.

Wakale, Yeltar, seemed the perfect destination. The humans of Yeltar had an outstanding reputation with Etharell. Perhaps she might find a new life in Wakale, a great seaport where many elves had settled for more than two centuries. Maybe Bryric would lead her to a proper husband.

Thylaina traveled to the northern end of the city, which put her in the correct direction. Unfortunately, no merchants left by that path. She hastened to the southern road. It took almost forty-five minutes to reach Flameral Way through the side streets while avoiding city patrol. Two wagons had already faded into the night, but just off the path, a merchant had set his foot on the coachman's steps.

"Pardon me," Thylaina called, dashing to him.

He halted from lifting to the bench and faced her. The merchant appeared a hundred years beyond middle age, not yet considered an elder. "My lady?" He stiffened, then bowed. "Forgive me. I had not realized a noblewoman addressed me."

Thylaina waved his comment aside. "I seek travel arrangements."

Brows arched, he scanned the area, a heavy breath following. "I know not what you attempt to escape, but I cannot be a part—"

She raised her hand, revealing a large ruby. "This should pay for a ride in the wagon and for your silence."

His wide eyes broke from the gemstone. "I have several stops on my way to New Portes."

"Can you reroute to Yeltar?"

"Afraid not. However, I have patrons in Aubrasna. We can part there."

*Our distant kin.* Thylaina smiled. "That would be lovely, sir."

"My name is—"

"I think we best keep our names to ourselves." She gave him the ruby.

The moonlight glinted off the facets as he examined it. "I agree, my lady."

They traveled the main roads of Etharell through the night until reaching a trail leading through southern Ivory Forest and to The Narrow. The path took them on the outskirts of Mystier, Neldrid's army city. Thylaina had gripped her skirt, her gaze on the tree line encircling the city, praying none of the guards would stop the wagon. The merchant had assured her that travel on this route was common, for no other way reached the Narrow more swiftly. She did not relax until Mystier was at least a hundred yards behind, and there were no signs that anyone followed. The merchant promised they would find rest at a village soon, but Thylaina insisted they travel until the next evening.

"Such a feat should not be taxing on us nor the horses," she said.

He eyed her for a moment. "No. It would not," he mumbled. "I suppose with your payment for services, I can accommodate your request."

After that, Thylaina spoke little to the merchant, fearing he might turn her over to the nearest xilys post if he grew suspicious of her behavior. The last place she wished to be was back at the palace, which would likely cause enough commotion to gain Neldrid's attention, if not Father's.

The village was only a dozen buildings within a modest clearing in the thick forest, and only two miles from the Narrow. Sleep was little, for dreams about Neldrid arriving with soldiers and dragging her home kept her awake. Desperation to escape her dreadful fate intensified, and she urged the merchant to break fast on the road.

It would surprise her if Uncle Yasontler had yet to send out search parties. In fact, the king might contact Neldrid soon, if he had not already.

To ease the worry, Thylaina took delight in the fresh air, vibrant trees, and colorful wildflowers. Over sixty years had passed since she last left Haevaun Flameral, most of her healing lessons kept within the capital city since Prince Valraahn was amongst the pupils. Their instructor, Master Eidryn, disregarded the king's demands to keep within Ivory Forest while training the prince, and still took his students to different regions of Etharell to identify and gather healing plants and treat patients. Some of those people came from the neighboring countries.

Thylaina had never traveled Etharell for pleasure. Neldrid once vowed to take her to Mystier, but never made good on the promise. After Mother's death, Thylaina remained stuck in the palace, surrounded by people who often forgot she was there, especially after Uncle Yasontler exiled his only son. Incessant arguments over foreign matters often left the king infuriated with Valraahn, but pride and ego were their true downfall. Then Valrae had a decade-long tantrum over losing her brother, demanding her parents' full attention. It was easy for everyone to forget Thylaina.

However, the neglect from Mother's family had naught to do with her leaving. To marry Rhomasyn was to endure a doomed life. It could not happen—to live each day consumed by loneliness and heartache, only to eventually mean nothing to a man who did not love her. The sun up, the moon fading, each month lost to centuries of hollowness. If Thylaina *had* married Rhomasyn, she would have refused the fertility potion. But might a child have brought her some joy as it had Mother?

Tightness in her throat made it difficult to swallow. She blinked tears away and focused on the Narrow: a five-mile-wide stretch of lush pasture between the Ormiana and Kilstra Forests. The xilys remained unseen, but Thylaina felt the elven border guards' gazes as travelers rode or walked to the border shared with Alohrius. She kept her hood up, for it was possible many of the xilys knew Neldrid. Some of those observing from the trees might even know her.

If her recollections were correct, two close friends served in the Ormiana Xilys: Aarosyn and Rainsala. If they caught Thylaina leaving Etharell, they would likely force her to return to the life she did not want.

The merchant cleared his throat. "We shall find rest in Ormiana."

She jerked her head in his direction. "No. We ride into Alohrius."

"I should like to—"

"We continue," she snapped. "I wish to arrive in Alohrius today."

He sneered, yet did not redirect the horses southward. "Very well."

Dusk approached as they neared the border, the descending sun illuminating an orange hue on the armor of the Alohrian knights standing near the turrets. Their rugged faces came clearer, scrutinizing the few elves and carts crossing into their country.

Head down to avoid catching their notice, Thylaina held her breath, praying the knights would not halt the wagon.

"Good evening," the merchant said, continuing between the turrets the other travelers passed through. The humans said nothing; and Thylaina breathed.

Beyond the towers and knights, the merchant smiled. "Welcome to Alohrius, my lady."

The knights had let them pass. No xilys came from the woods for her. She was free. Thylaina grinned as she viewed the foreign country.

Alohrius appeared quite flat, but the villages seemed lovely... at first. The communities farther from Etharell were no longer quaint, but simple. Filthy. The merchant did not stop at any of them but rode on until reaching a hamlet a few miles outside of a walled city, where he acquired rooms.

From conversations within the tavern, Thylaina learned the nearby city was Warstchia, a place with a dark and bloody history. Elves rarely spoke about the horrid event that had taken place there more than a thousand years past. Appetite waning as she thought about the hundreds of lives ended in Warstchia by enraged demigods, Thylaina nibbled on the mediocre supper.

No other elves were present, but many human eyes fixed on her, most revealing lustful musings. A group of knights muttered over their meal at a table next to the hearth. A red-haired man amongst them caught her notice as his fierce blue gaze constantly settled on her. Disdain skewed what should have been a handsome face.

"You gain far too much attention," the merchant mumbled. "I do not like it."

Nor did Thylaina, but there was naught to do about it. Discomfort ruined any desire to finish the bland stew, so she excused herself to her room.

What was Thylaina to do? The bastard left. She was no soldier in the army nor a xilys warrior, therefore had no fighting skills, no means to protect herself. Except magic, which she dared not use for fear the humans might discover her bloodline and take possession of her.

Staying in the room to continue weeping was not an option, for the innkeeper's wife knocked several times, demanding Thylaina leave. So, she gathered her gold and jewels and went to the tavern. There had to be someone willing to take her to Yeltar, but none of the faces seemed trustworthy. Not even the knights. Too many human men looked at her with carnal interest, their thoughts openly displayed on their faces.

Afore the day grew too late, she hurried to the stables, losing another gemstone in a bribe for a horse. It was a dreadful thing to do, stealing someone's mount, but Thylaina had to get somewhere safe, wherever that might be. Not Warstchia. Conversations at the tavern warned about an illness plaguing those within the walled city. She knew not which way led north to Yeltar. The merchant gave her no course at all.

A plea to Bryric for guidance passed Thylaina's lips as she commanded the horse onto the road.

# Chapter Two

If Thylaina had stuck to the plan, she would not be in this cold, dark cell. All she had to do was collect apples from the orchard behind a mansion, then sneak out just as quietly as she had moved into the city. But while rounding the buildings, she noticed a massive garden; more food for her and the poor horse. While picking vegetables, she was drawn to tall stalks—taller than wheat—with something large wrapped in leaves jutting from them. Perhaps they would be delicious. Curiosity had her standing there for too long, contemplating whether to break one of the mysterious bundles off. Now, she shivered while loathing stared down upon her.

"A bloody thief." The man's nose wrinkled, lifting toward pinched brows and condemning blue eyes. Shadows from the torchlight shifted on the wall, making him appear enormous. It would not have mattered if he was twenty-feet tall, the fury in his gaze and his gritted teeth frightened her as it was.

Thylaina had never faced such hostility. When he had stepped from the darkness and neared the cell, Thylaina retreated from the bars. Now she trembled beneath his hatred as those words echoed in her ears. A thief? Her?

"Have you nothing to say?" His voice was low. Intimidating.

"I..." She swallowed to wet her throat. None of the days and nights alone in this wretched country had brought her to feel the amount of fear as she had that very moment. "I am *n'ei* a thief," Thylaina whispered.

"No?" His lips twitched. There was something familiar about him. "You stole a dubight's horse."

His eyes... She recognized them.

"You took the property of several farmers—"

"Food."

He gripped a cell bar and leaned closer, the sleeve of his leather jacket creaking from the motion. "Not *your* food."

She had seen few humans with red hair, and his short locks appeared a fiery color in the torchlight. Just like the man at the tavern her first night in this awful country.

"I was hungry," Thylaina said.

"Then you should've offered services! Not steal property from the Marshal and the Lady of Caerabis."

Somehow, Thylaina had traveled southward instead of northeast. What mattered most now was getting free from the cell and this dangerous man. Surely, humans felt compassion for those who struggled.

"From a garden," she said, her voice breaking. "I am starving."

"And what of the horse?" He straightened, his fingers sliding down the bar. "We can't save him from the death your actions have brought."

The poor animal had barely eaten the past five days. Afore finding this city, Thylaina came upon bushes with dark berries on a livestock farm. The horse ate two handfuls, then retreated. Shortly afterward, his steps slowed and grew erratic, his hooves sometimes dragging. Thylaina knew not what to do—she cared for people, not animals.

Acid churned in her empty stomach. How was she to know humans would grow poisonous fruits alongside their homes? "I am sorry. I-I thought the berries were fine for him."

He squinted. "What did you feed him?"

"Captain," a man barely noticeable in the shadows said. "We should send for the marshal."

A captain. This did not bode well for her.

He turned to the one addressing him. "You question my judgement?"

"No, sir." The other moved further into her view. He appeared younger than the redheaded beast.

"Then why send for the marshal?"

"Well... because she's an elf, sir."

The captain faced Thylaina. "She's a thief. And all criminal matters are for me to attend, are they not?"

"Yes, sir. But—"

"You said she had other items."

The younger man looked down at something. "This case, sir. Along with a pouch of roans and gemstones."

"Likely stolen." The captain reached for the healing satchel.

Gods! Leather rubbing against itself had never made her eardrums feel brittle as it did now. She cringed every time the men moved. Glancing at the nearest torch, she focused on the flames' soft crackles and sizzles from burning through the fuel.

The captain opened the satchel. All the herbs Thylaina had gathered afore leaving Etharell and during her travel were in there. He moved some bottles aside, then took out a few stems of lavender and xarflas; items she collected in the fields three days ago, blessed to have found the latter. Xarflas held properties for several ailments and was of great value to the elves. They had yet to grow it successfully in their own soil. The items returned to the satchel, he removed two bottles: crushed xarflas leaves and bossel powder—her only vials of each. He shook them. Shrugging, the captain let them slip from his fingers. The shattering of glass deafened the fire and leather. Tiny pieces of green mingled with white powder, spreading over the bricks and filling the cracks between them.

"N'ei!" Thylaina lunged forward, reaching through the bars.

He twisted from her grasp. "I find the contents rather dangerous."

"You jest." The younger man stepped forward. "Even I can see they're herbs!"

"They're more than that." The captain squinted, his gaze sharper. "Get the stick."

The young man blanched. "No."

Face darker, the captain's brows dipped lower. "That's an order, Gavrel."

Using an innate elven ability to charm or calm a lesser race, Thylaina entwined a soft melody into her voice as she spoke. "I intend n'ei harm to anyone. I only sought food and water." Both men stilled, their eyes locked to hers. She continued. "Please release me, and I will leave Alohrius. You shall never see me again, *Shapele*."

They had seemed entranced until she spoke the last word, Elvish word for *Captain*. The red-haired man jerked his head to the side and lowered the case.

"Get... the stick," he commanded.

"I don't agree with this," the younger man, Gavrel, said.

"It matters not!"

"No!"

"I'll do it myself. And you..." The captain's nose grazed Gavrel's. "You'll face insubordination charges for this."

The satchel landed atop the mess of glass and ruined herbs, and keys jingled in the captain's hand. A click, then the cell door wailed open.

Heart racing, Thylaina backed to the wall, then cowered on the floor. How had it come to this? She was in a jailhouse, and this man meant to do something awful to her. Warm tears trailed down her cheeks as she curled into herself.

He thrust his hand into her defenses with skilled practice, gripped her wrist, then yanked her up. Thylaina's resistance was in vain as he dragged her through the cell opening, forcing her to stumble. "Move!" he ordered Gavrel.

Gaze wide, the young man shuffled from his path. Thylaina reached for him, barely grasping his arm, but he only watched, growing distant beneath the flickering torchlight.

At the end of the hall, the captain threw a door open and shoved her into a small room. Wood rattled against the doorframe with a resounding crack. He pushed her into a strange chair. A flat and narrow surface stood upright on hinges from one of the arms. It came down fast with four leather straps, two each on the front and back, hitting her.

Frantic, Thylaina tried to hunch forward to keep her hands close to her chest, but he was too strong. While he fastened one of her wrists within a set of straps, palm up, she clawed at his arm. Her nails did nothing to the leather sleeve, but left trails of torn flesh on the top of his hand.

"Enough!" He slapped her hand away, almost striking her nose. In a swift motion, he had her other wrist to the vacant straps.

Shrieking, Thylaina attempted to break his hold, but he tightened it too quickly. Goosebumps rising, her breath came in quick gasps, and her head spun. Then the words formed. Magic surged through her veins, growing as the strap end fitted through the buckle, but no matter how much she wanted to, Thylaina could not cast a spell. To do so would reveal whom he held captive.

He stormed to a table on which various items rested. In seconds, the long jacket hung on the wall, and he was rolling his blouse sleeves. Tears blurred Thylaina's vision while she desperately tugged against the bindings. He grabbed something from the table, inspected it. The flesh beneath the straps burned from the quick and hard jerks as fear grasped her spine, sending shards of ice throughout her nerves. She froze as he returned with a thin, flat stick, the edges sharp. Not enough to slice, but meant to break skin.

"Open your hands," he commanded.

Acid burned up her throat. The words of the spell returned, but it was too late. Her hands were bound. "P-please."

"Open your hands." His nostrils flared with each labored breath, disgust an ugly mask, a force pushing him to act. He struck the curled fingers of her left hand, right over the knuckles.

She screamed as pain jolted to the bones and a thin layer of skin gathered, blood oozing.

"Open it!" He brought the stick down again. More flesh bunched on her fingers.

Body quaking, Thylaina cried out.

The captain dug his fingertips beneath hers to expose her palm. The stick rose high and came down like a lightning bolt.

Everything distorted and whirred in the same dizziness she had experienced upon Mother's death. Her lungs emptied of air, blood rushed to her head, and an unending fall happened all at once.

The stick struck twice more, then was high again.

"Breydon!" a man shouted from the doorway. "What are you doing?"

The stick now at his side, the captain straightened. He slowly turned and bowed his head. "Performing my duties, sir."

Thylaina sobbed over her trembling hands. Fear of causing more pain halted her from closing them.

The man stepped nearer, revealing Gavrel behind him. Sorrow overtook his tone as he said, "This is unacceptable, Captain."

"She's a criminal."

"She's an *elf*. Our ally."

The captain tossed the stick onto the table. "She's a bloody thief. And if I recall correctly, you put me in charge of all criminals brought to Caerabis... sir."

Still tugging on the straps, she sobbed. "Please... I was hungry."

The newcomer was older than her tormentor, his face displaying compassion as he looked from her to the captain. "Breydon—"

"She took the property of the dubight, farmers, and *you*!"

The marshal of Caerabis stood afore her. Was mercy possible after committing a crime against one of such power?

He gestured at Thylaina. "Breydon, you should've brought this to my attention!"

Nodding once toward Gavrel, Breydon replied, "I see he's not the only one who questions my judgement."

"This situation isn't normal." Disbelief wrinkling his brow, the marshal shook his head. "You should've informed me, especially since it involves our allies. You don't know whom she is."

"She's a bloody thief!" Breydon's face shaded crimson. "You've never doubted my judgement before. I'll not have it mistrusted now."

Thylaina pulled against the straps again. "Please."

The dense silence kept distance between the two men, amplifying Thylaina's heartbeat in her ears.

The marshal nodded slightly. "With the elves, I believe I must now question you."

Jaw working side to side, Breydon looked away.

"Release her," the marshal said. The captain's solid shoulders remained unmoving. A heavy sigh filled the small chamber as the marshal motioned to Gavrel. "Please take her to the temple."

"Yes, sir."

The quiet ensued while Gavrel gently unbuckled the straps. He lifted the narrow slat, then assisted Thylaina to rise.

She did not look at the captain, yet his gaze felt as rigid as the tension in the room. It weighed her progress to the door, each of her steps scraping the floor.

"The priests will tend to you, my lady," Gavrel whispered as they crossed the threshold.

"M-my satchel."

He smiled reassuringly. "I'll retrieve it once you're at the temple."

Further down the hall, Thylaina caught the beginning of a conversation from the chamber behind them.

"Your behavior is appalling, Breydon. I don't know what to do about it."

"Grim..." A loud breath sounded. "You've always trusted me. I don't know why you..."

Their voices faded while Gavrel walked her through another doorway. The distance from that dreadful room increased, lightening Thylaina's steps as the captain's hatred slipped from her shoulders.


Three priests presided over the temple. Mikan, the high priest, washed and wrapped Thylaina's hand, but offered no healing remedies nor prayers to Valorius, the Alohrians' favored god. Although not a healer like His mother, Vynia, Valorius could still have granted His Favor. Throughout the minimal care provided, Mikan's expression was unreadable, especially while he inquired about Thylaina's presence in his country. She did not answer, but asked if the temple provided a room of devotion to Vynia, of which there was none. Humans held little regard for the Earthen Goddess.

"Do you have a prayer room for Lessindra?" she asked.

An exceptionally handsome man in his middle years, Mikan smiled politely, his clear-blue eyes showing intrigue. "Of course. She *is* Valorius' lover. I'll escort you to the chamber shortly."

Humans always referred to Lessindra as such. She was more than His lover. The very Love of Fynthiar formed Her. No race gave as much honor to Lessindra as the elves. She was a part of their daily lives: peace, marriage, reunion after death, and above all, love, mercy, and forgiveness. Elves held great loyalty for Bryric, particularly the Royal Family since He was their ancestor. Vynia received their prayers and sacrifice for the earthen gifts that brought beauty and healing, and Lessindra gave them a view of Emvarr no others shared: appreciation for life. But to these idiot humans, She was simply Valorius' lover.

If the Alohrians believed they honored Lessindra by providing a meager worship room, they were terribly mistaken. No wonder they bore so much anger and unhappiness. It was a shame they made no room for Her in their hearts. What brought Thylaina to pause, her mouth agape, was a statue of a half-naked woman. Lovely artwork, yet insulting. She gave little attention to the face, for her gaze fell upon breasts larger than her head. Appalling.

Mikan beamed at it. "Beautiful, isn't she?"

Blinking to free herself from the statue, she faced him. "Who is this?"

He arched a brow. "Lessindra, of course."

Heat consumed her face. How dare he. And how dare the man who sculpted this rubbish! Calm and annoyance strained her voice as she pointed at the statue. "Lessindra has never revealed Herself to a mortal." Hand falling to her side, she huffed. "She has only given the vision of one object to represent Her: the beautiful Raizzia Tree. Not this—this grotesque thing!"

Mikan tilted his head. "This offends you?"

"*S'yai!* And likely offends Her as well!" High priest or not, the desire to slap him had her fingers twitching. "Have you men any knowledge of Whom She is? What She represents? Other than *Valorius' lover.*"

His expression reflected that of Rhomasyn's when displeased. "Of course we do."

"You must remove this."

"We shall not."

"You insult Valorius by insisting this represents Lessindra."

Mikan brushed his long blond hair aside. "And you assume too much. I'll now give you a moment to pray." He left her in silence.

A scream fought for release, but Thylaina did not want the priest to return, so she stomped her foot and sneered at the horrid statue instead. It offered a sense of calm. She sat on a small stone bench and closed her eyes. *Lessindra, forgive me for my wrongdoings. And please, show mercy to these men and their... lack of respect. They* are *humans.*

Several minutes of prayer passed, disrupted by Thylaina nuzzling her injured hand. Mikan's minimal work left her palm still throbbing. It was near midday, so he had no reason to rush. To have expected better results was foolish, since humans were not as skilled as her people. Once they returned her satchel, Thylaina would take care of the wounds properly.

Gavrel arrived, his eyes downcast. "Forgive me, my lady, but Captain Colmstad still has your items."

Her shoulders sagged. How ridiculous! "I do not understand."

The young man scratched the back of his neck. "He wants the priests to inspect the contents further. Marshal Momestid conceded."

A cry swelled in her chest. No. She would not show further weakness. Chin set, she asked, "What of me now?"

"Marshal Momestid invites you to supper." A crooked smile formed, his deep, earthy eyes brightened, and his freckled cheeks glowed. "I'm to escort you to his home."

A place of worship should have brought comfort, but escaping the half-naked statue was a relief. Thankfully, the priests were too busy to say farewell.

The dizzying agony now absent, Thylaina admired the enormous building's excellent craftsmanship. Tall pillars supported a rounded arch above a set of elegant double doors. Carved on each was a tall knight with a sword crossing his chest. Four colorfully glazed windows along the length of the building reflected the Harvest Sun, forcing her to squint. Lowering her attention, she took in the many structures ahead.

Outside a few of many large cottages across the cobblestone street, women and children watched Thylaina descend the temple steps. She flashed a smile in their direction, then followed Gavrel to a walking path of rose, gray, and brown stones along the street. Men in leather armor led or rode horses, while others moved with purpose, all of them heading in each direction. They slowed or stopped, gawking as Thylaina continued with her escort.

"Thank you for helping me, Sir Gavrel," she said.

His head jerked as he looked at her, a breathy laugh escaping him. "Oh, I'm not a knight. Not yet, at least." The freckles darkened over his reddening cheeks as he bowed. "Gavrel Kedanier, Alohrian soldier, at your service."

With natural grace, she curtsied while slightly lifting the right side of her skirt. "I am Thylaina."

He moved to take her injured hand, but lowered his arm. "If Captain hadn't..." His gaze met hers.

She swung her right hand forward. "I have an unharmed one."

Chuckling, he brought it to his lips, kissed softly, then straightened. "It's an honor to meet you, Lady Thylaina."

Gavrel appeared near twenty years, by human standards. His eyes offered the warmth of soft soil beneath the sun's light, and thin lips spread in a wider grin above a dimple set deep within a round chin. He was pleasant.

The pace to their destination was slower than when first leaving the temple. "I'm sorry for Captain Colmstad's behavior," he said. "I've never seen him like that before."

Captain Breydon Colmstad. Thylaina knew not the order of authority in the Alohrian knighthood, but hopefully, interaction with that man had come to completion. The thought of being in his presence caused a shiver down her arms, like the first time she encountered garden spiders and root grubs while collecting herbs.

A blue dress with white lace hung behind a shop window across the street, and she paused to admire it. Mediocre compared to the elven seamstresses, but these were simple people.

"I hope Marshal Momestid spoke some sense into him." Gavrel sounded a quiet laugh. "Please don't tell anyone I said that."

"I shall say nothing." The dress forgotten, Thylaina continued walking with him.

"I appreciate that."

For the first time in days, a sense of safety eased through her. At that moment, she wished to hug Gavrel's arm. He had saved her from a horrible punishment, showing compassion when his captain failed. Thylaina had heard the Alohrian knighthood was dying, but maybe men like Gavrel could salvage it.

She inched closer as they strolled along the stony path. "Shall you be joining us for supper?"

"Me? No. I'm only a soldier—a dubight. Certainly not one to sit at the marshal's table."

"What *is* a dubight?"

Pride shimmered in his eyes. "We're soldiers fortunate enough to be accepted into training for the knighthood." He looked forward and shrugged. "Of course, to be knighted, we must still accomplish all that's expected of us." Gavrel glanced at her, then ahead.

There was something awkward in that brief eye contact. Something... telling. As if she should already know more about him.

Captain Colmstad's voice echoed in her ears.

*"You stole a dubight's horse..."*

Rattled, Thylaina stopped. "It was your horse."

Gavrel regarded the colorful stones at their feet. After a moment, he nodded. "I had... I tracked you here."

Although his horse would likely die because of her, Gavrel had halted her punishment.

"Why?" Thylaina asked, her voice small.

"During your confession before he arrived, you said your guide abandoned you, and that you were starving after days of travel alone." Gavrel finally raised his eyes to her. "I imagined how frightened you must've been. Looking at you, I can see you don't know how to hunt, work a farm, nor do much at all."

A retort poised upon her lips, Thylaina stepped back. But he was correct; she was no laborer. "I did not know what those berries were, nor that they would harm the horse."

"I understand," he said. "And I did not mean to insult you, my lady. Forgive me."

Ashamed that *he* had offered an apology to *her*, she lowered her head. "It is I who offended you. And now you may lose your friend."

"My frie—?" He grinned. "I see. Although the horse has met its end, I will get an Alohrian stallion upon my knighting."

Tears immediately formed and fell. "He is gone?" Thylaina's lips trembled. "I was wrong to have taken him from you."

Gavrel's hands grazed her shoulders, then dropped to his sides. "I forgave you, and I told Marshal Momestid as much."

Perhaps some humans felt more compassion than she had been taught. "Thank you, Gavrel."

It was as if no other walked around Thylaina and Gavrel, glancing at them while they stared at each other.

He blinked and stepped back. "You're welcome, my lady. Now, I must get you to the marshal."

Upon arrival at a three-story mansion, a woman swept Thylaina from Gavrel's company and led her through the large foyer and up the staircase to the left, across from the entry door. She spoke speedily, making it difficult to understand what she said. In a sizable bedchamber on the third floor, a young maiden measured Thylaina for garments, then took her back toward the main level. A set of marble stairs were at each side of the long, curved landing that stretched half the length of the circular chamber, and at least five doors were on each of the three levels. It was hard to see how many rooms for certain, since the handmaiden had rushed Thylaina back to the foyer, which was quite an exercise after an exhausting start to her day.

The maiden guided her past a corridor beside the stairs and down a hall lined with several more doors, stopping at the fourth on the left. Inside was a round bathtub full of steaming water. A bath. A glorious and much needed bath.

Thylaina drew in a deep breath of the damp air, tasting rosemary and lavender. *Thank You, Vynia!* Although a large tub, it was small compared to the bathing pools in the palace. If only she could add bossel powder to heal the minor wounds and soothe the aching muscles.

The servant undressed Thylaina with care, especially around her hand, then assisted her into the tub. Thylaina gave in to the desire to sink into the water, air bubbles floating to the surface with her hair.

Hands gripped her arms, hauling her upward. "M'lady! Are you well?"

Wiping her eyes, Thylaina caught her breath. "S'yai."

"Goodness, you frightened me." The handmaiden's soft voice wavered.

Thylaina contemplated asking why she seemed nervous, but assumed the young woman had no experience tending an elf. Who knows what stories humans told each other about her people. Questions and assumptions slipped away while the woman bathed Thylaina, her touch perfect. If only it had lasted ten minutes more. But Thylaina would not complain now that the pain had eased from her muscles, and the grime from the road and the jailhouse were washed away.

They returned to the bedchamber, which would have been spacious had it not contained so much useless furniture. Two sofas of different lengths, three plush chairs, and two tables were afore the large fireplace, and a few feet from those was another table against the wall, holding a variety of wine decanters and goblets. The oversized bed beckoned from beyond the longer sofa, but that would have to wait. A vanity with a mirror twice its size reflected light from the nearby window and a tall candelabra, and a three-drawer chest stood between that and a massive wardrobe. Heavy brown drapes threaded with gold hung from the lovely canopy bedposts.

The maidservant guided Thylaina to the chair at the vanity. "In my nervousness, I've forgotten to introduce myself," she said, as Thylaina sat. "I'm Katjina, and tonight will determine if I remain in your service."

A handmaiden was not at all what Thylaina had expected.

Katjina lifted a brush from the table. "I'm from the scullery, a position I abhor. But when I heard you were here, I begged Her Ladyship to allow me a chance to prove my abilities." A small smile tugged at the corner of her lips. "I'm already blessed to have earned a position in Lady Tesesra's household. So if I fail this, at least I'll still work for her."

Her touch remained tender. When she put the brush to Thylaina's hair, it was with care. Several knots slowed her progress, but she showed patience. Not a complaint passed her lips, only compliments. "I've never seen such thick and lovely hair. Is it like this for all elven women?"

Thylaina shrugged. Truth be told, she never paid mind to the other maidens' hair. More important things held her attention.

"After you're dressed, I'll weave this into a beautiful braid. At least I hope—"

"Keep it down."

Katjina lowered the brush. "Forgive me. I didn't realize you're wedded, m'lady."

Nose scrunched, Thylaina turned in the chair to face her. "What?"

The handmaiden motioned to Thylaina's black curls. "To leave it loose signifies you're a wedded woman."

That could not possibly be true. But as Thylaina stared dumbfounded at Katjina, the idiotic custom was right afore her. The handmaiden's light-brown hair draped over her shoulder in a braid. Recollections from earlier brought visions of the women at the houses across from the temple and their loose hair. Obviously, mothers watching over their children while their husbands performed their duties. On the way to the mansion, there had been several young maidens with their hair braided, and many women with their hair down. Great Bryric, these humans were ridiculous! Surely rings were not too difficult to provide for one another.

Head tilted back slightly, Thylaina said, "In *my* country, marriage does not dictate how we style our hair."

"I see." Katjina set the brush on the table. "However, it might give the men here the impression that—"

"I care not!" Thylaina pointed to her hair. "You will lift the sides. Nothing more."

The handmaiden nibbled on her lip, then nodded. "Yes, m'lady." She walked to the wardrobe and opened one of the doors. "First, let's dress you."

She presented a red gown, but after holding it to Thylaina, she sent for a new one. While waiting, Katjina applied facial colors. "Red is not right for you, nor are the other colors in the wardrobe. I've never seen copper eyes before."

Red was Neldrid's favorite color, and he often wore it to feasts... on the rare occasion he attended. But the woman was correct. The color had never suited Neldrid. In fact, it contrasted with his eyes, which were just like Thylaina's. She giggled while envisioning him in a red blouse, his eyes afire.

Katjina paused dabbing color on Thylaina's cheek. "Did I say something amusing?"

The moment of joy faded as quickly as it had arrived. Thylaina missed her brother, yet he could not have felt the same, not when his messages had grown scarce. Although he *was* the First General of Etharell, the nation was not at war. He could have visited. No, Neldrid did not miss her. Devotion bound him to the army and Etharell. And there was his heartbreaking letter that may as well have said farewell forever.

"Forgive me," Thylaina said. "I was reminiscing."

The handmaiden stared for a moment. A smile graced her lips as she resumed working. "I hope I please you, m'lady."

She did splendidly. The light-green on Thylaina's eyelids and soft pink on her cheeks and lips accented her pale complexion. At least the dress was decent. Thylaina could not fault humans for their lack of elegance in clothing. Especially in a city that appeared to house a military and their families.

Families.

Shame plagued Thylaina for stealing from the city. She had believed the occupants would miss nothing from such an enormous garden or the orchard, but it was for their families.

"M'lady, you look sad again." Katjina finished tying the laces at the front of the dress, forming a perfect bow just above Thylaina's chest.

How could she speak to this stranger? This human might not care about what she felt: the guilt, anxiety, and fear.

Worry filled Katjina's hazel-green eyes. "I've wronged you."

"You have not." Thylaina looked down at her hands. Tears distorted the painful ugliness now marring her left palm and fingers. Someone would have to apply fresh wrappings. Thylaina could not bend her fingers without whimpering.

"Oh dear." A soft cloth glided along Thylaina's cheek, drying it. "Things will improve," Katjina said. "Marshal and Lady Momestid are wonderful people. You'll see."

Thylaina raised her eyes to Katjina, a young human who had already treated her better than her own royal handmaidens. "I am sorry I was harsh toward you about my hair."

The grin resurfaced as Katjina shook her head. "No worry, m'lady. I suppose if I get to keep this position, I'll have much to learn about you."

"How long am I to be here?"

"That, I don't know." Katjina motioned to the chair again. "But let's finish with your hair before we've no more time."

A woman appearing near her third decade arrived shortly after, and stood at the door, grumbling about having to wait. Katjina introduced the woman as Ardella, the head of the house servants. Face reddened from beneath a white wimple, Ardella's dark eyes narrowed.

"Her Ladyship will definitely hear about how slow and lazy you are," she said, pointing at Katjina. Pressing her fists to her hips, she tilted her head back, her upturned nose wrinkled. "Think you'll work with *my* maidens, kitchen slop? Think again!"

Through the mirror's reflection, Thylaina frowned at the sour woman.

Katjina only smiled. "Don't be angry, Ardella. Marshal Momestid will understand."

"Those knights want to eat when the food's hot. Not when you're done pinning hair!" Ardella stomped her foot on the floor, as if her thin-soled shoes added emphasis to her ire.

A flowery wooden comb now fixed in place within Thylaina's thick locks, Katjina stepped back. "Doesn't she look lovely?"

Ardella did a once-over of Thylaina. "Good, good. Let's move on then."

Thylaina held Katjina's gaze. "Are you not taking me?"

The young woman shook her head. "I do hope to see you in the morning, m'lady." Katjina curtsied. "Enjoy your evening."

"Thank you, Katjina."

The joy Thylaina had found in the young woman's company quickly dissipated as she followed Ardella. The head-handmaiden griped down each flight of stairs, while worry prodded Thylaina's mind. Captain Colmstad had deemed her a criminal, yet now she was a guest at the marshal's home. What awaited her in the feast hall? Freedom or more condemnation?

At the end of the stairs, she glanced around the entrance hall, noting two guards at the front door across the way. There was a hall to the left and two more to her right—the bathing room somewhere down the furthest.

Ardella continued into the first corridor on the right. The woman's hurried steps forced Thylaina to keep up. "I don't know how you *elves* behave at supper, but there are certain manners we *humans* don't tolerate." She scowled at Thylaina. "It's best you keep your foreign mouth shut. Especially if you speak your silly words."

Thylaina stopped listening, her thoughts too busy to mind the rude servant. The scent of roasted meat wafted in the hall, along with delicious aromas of bread, cinnamon apples, and—She paused. *Seared trout!* The thought of such a feast had her salivating.

"M'lady!" Ardella half-twisted from a standstill. "Why've you stopped? We must—"

"S'yai." Thylaina increased her pace, now forcing the woman to keep up with her.

Ardella pointed to a door on the left. "Slow down! That room there!"

Thylaina halted. Eyes closed, she relaxed. It was time to be the perfect guest and show the marshal she was no danger to Alohrius.

Ardella opened the door and stepped in ahead of her, bustling to a table large enough for a dozen diners, but only two people were present. Thylaina slowed when Captain Colmstad's gaze met hers. Her heart tumbled to the bottom of her stomach as he rose from his seat.

Marshal Momestid stood as she neared. Captain Colmstad bowed, the leather jacket he had worn earlier that day creaking with the motion. The marshal blinked a few times then followed suit. Perhaps Thylaina's beauty caused the latter's pause. It would not be the first time a man hesitated in her presence.

Smiling wide, Marshal Momestid spread his arms. "Welcome to my home, Lady Thylaina."

A clearer view of his face in better lighting revealed he was likely in his third decade, even with the scattered silver in his black hair. Yet he was no doubt at least ten years older than his companion.

He walked around Captain Colmstad and reached for Thylaina's hand, lowering his own upon seeing the bandage. "I-I have it correct, don't I? Gavrel told me Thylaina was your name."

"S'yai."

"I am Marshal Arhgrim Momestid." He gestured to the captain. "And you have met Captain Breydon Colmstad."

Thylaina refused to look at the captain. "If that is what you call enduring his torture, then s'yai, we have met."

Breydon released a long breath, gaining her attention. He darted his eyes to Arhgrim.

"I hope we can put that event behind us," the marshal said. "As awful as it was."

What an appalling request!

"Is it so easy for humans to overlook your cruelty toward others?" she snapped. "To *my* people?"

A hint of annoyance passed Arhgrim's face as he motioned to the chair beside Breydon. "Please."

Sit next to the beast who injured her palm? He could not mean it.

The captain pulled the chair back, creaking leather offending her ears. "My lady." He absorbed her glare with a smug grin.

The desire to hurt a person was a new feeling. An unwanted one.

"Are you not hungry?" he asked, the menacing tone from the jailhouse replaced by a softer, pleasant one.

The cruelty within this monster reminded Thylaina to be wary of anything he said. Certain men knew how to charm others, or make them feel relaxed enough to let down their guard. Stomach growling protests to the idea of walking out of the room prodded her to appease it and the men, so she lowered to the chair; they also sat.

Arhgrim draped a dinner cloth over his legs. "I hope Mikan or Raylen were able to tend to your injury."

Thylaina displayed her bandaged hand on the table. "They were not."

The marshal scowled, and Breydon barely afforded a glance.

Afore Thylaina could say anything more, five servants entered from the door at the far end of the room, two of them carrying trays. One of the tray-bearers set a plate with two slices of bread to the left of the large platter in front of each diner, along with a small dish of butter. A second servant bore a tray with three bowls of satiny beef broth, which she placed on the platters. Mushrooms and carrots floated within.

Thylaina scrutinized it, then sniffed a spoonful.

"I promise, my lady," Arhgrim said, "you'll find it accommodating to your palate."

One brow raised, she lowered the spoon.

"I've entertained many over the past several years, including elves," he continued. "I assure you, my cooks are splendid."

Thylaina had better manners. After a small smile, she sipped the broth. It was quite pleasing indeed. Fresh, earthy flavors blended well with the beef. Nodding, she dabbed her lips with the dinner cloth. "It is fine, Marshal. I appreciate theirs and your thoughtfulness."

He bowed his head. "Excellent."

Breydon buttered a slice of bread, then dipped it in the broth. A sloppy idea. When he bit into it, broth slid over his bottom lip. He caught the drippings with the bread, leaving crumbs gathered in the stubbles on his chin.

Thylaina broke a few pieces from a slice on her plate and dropped them into the bowl. Once absorbed, she scooped one up with a mushroom and enjoyed. It was less messy than the men's method. Rosemary accented the flavors, making each helping more satisfying than the previous. The broth was more delicious than she had first believed.

"Are you pleased, my lady?" the marshal asked.

"I am, Marshal Momestid."

"Wonderful." He sat back as a servant removed his empty bowl. "I'm shocked Raylen hadn't been able to tend to your injury. I know they've the means to heal wounds."

Thylaina regarded her hand, still fearing to move her fingers. "I did not meet Raylen. However, it appeared Mikan did not wish to exhaust his services on my..." She flitted her gaze to the captain, who frowned at her. "On my injury. However, I *had* the capability to treat the cuts, but Shapele Colmstad deemed it dangerous."

Eyes forward, Breydon straightened, his shoulders pulling back as his jaw tightened. Each motion was accompanied by the creaking of that damn jacket.

Thylaina slammed her spoon on the table. "Must you wear that while we eat?" Her voice was louder than she had intended, yet could not drown out the leather. Memories from the jailhouse had her heart racing: Breydon dragging her down the hall, forcing her into the chair, then fastening her wrists to the slat, all while wearing that bloody jacket!

Lips quirked, he glanced down at the sleeve, then at her. "You wish me to remove this?" he asked, tugging at the collar's corner.

She turned her head away, squeezed her eyes shut, wanting badly to silence the entire room. "If it is not too much to ask of you, Shapele."

His chair juddered along the stone floor as he stood, removed the jacket, then slung it over the chair's back. Breydon sat and grinned at her. "Better?"

If only she could slap that pompous smile. Thylaina lifted the spoon instead and resumed eating the broth. At least she would not have to endure the sound of the leather the rest of the night.

Arhgrim cleared his throat. After a silent moment passed, he resumed their conversation. "Perhaps our priests might have a remedy for your wounds."

Control prevented a scoff. Alohrians did not know the benefits of xarflas, but like most Yeurothians, they often used bossel roots as their primary healing remedy. "I doubt it," Thylaina said. "However, do your priests possess bossel powder?"

The captain sneered. "Why would we grant any of our healing supplies to you?"

She did not want to converse with him, let alone look in his direction again. His pompousness was more than she could tolerate, yet his question deserved a response. Thylaina squinted at him. "Because you shattered my best healing vial on the jailhouse floor."

Arhgrim regarded him. "Breydon, is this true?"

Motioning for the servant to collect his empty bowl and bread plate, the captain said, "I didn't know what she carried in that case. Like many items, it could've been harmful."

Thylaina gaped. "Harm—? You did not ask. You broke it because you wanted to frighten me."

He spun in the seat, his face nearly as red as his hair. "I broke it because you're a bloody criminal!"

"Breydon!" Arhgrim's fist thumped on the table.

The tears had formed afore the marshal spoke, but Thylaina willed them away. She would not crack in front of the captain. Not again.

"This is no way to treat our guest," Arhgrim said.

"Guest." Breydon scoffed as he turned to the marshal. "I thought she was our prisoner."

The men stared at each other.

The elder shook his head, then looked sadly at Thylaina. "Forgive me, my lady. The captain hasn't been himself this past year."

Brows dropping low, Breydon stiffened. He forced the chair back again, mumbling, "Good night."

"I insist you stay," Arhgrim said.

"I'm no longer hungry." The captain grabbed his jacket and headed for the exit.

"Viya made cinnamon apples for you."

"Good night, Grim!"

The chamber door slammed shut.

Thylaina remained still. She had not meant to cause an argument between the two men. But honestly, Breydon Colmstad was a dreadful human. His uncomfortable stare, just like the man at the tavern, observing her with distrust—Thylaina's breath caught. That *was* Breydon in the tavern the night the merchant abandoned her. What had she done to deserve his ire then? The death of Gavrel's horse weighed upon her, and she continued bearing the captain's hatred as well.

"Forgive me, Marshal," she whispered. "I did not intend to—"

"Nonsense." He waved away her unfinished apology. "The captain *is* a fine man. He'd not be at my side otherwise."

Servants entered with three trays. One of them halted when noticing Breydon was gone. She looked at the marshal, then left. Arhgrim motioned for Thylaina's meal to be set in the absent captain's place. Thylaina moved to the recently vacated seat. A blackened silver trout sizzled on a large flat bread. Butter melted over the vegetables covering the fish, soaking into the bread beneath.

She smiled at the unique serving method, then at the fish. "I believe these are native in Lake Wynland."

Arhgrim nodded. "One of my servants rode tirelessly to retrieve it for your supper. Another shall ride out in a couple of days to fish for more."

The man really did know how to entertain an elf.

Thylaina cut into the fillet, moaning as the aroma of thyme, garlic, onion, and mushrooms filled her nostrils. It smelled fantastic. Just as the cooks from the palace would have prepared it.

"I'm glad you're pleased, Lady Thylaina."

"I feel like I am home."

"No doubt a noble home." Those words came forth as if he knew the truth.

Thylaina almost dropped her fork, yet managed to disguise the falter as eagerness to eat the delicious fish. If she revealed to the marshal whom she was, he might send her back to Etharell, if he was the decent sort. If he was not, Thylaina feared what he might do. Arhgrim considered Captain Colmstad a fine man, so he might not be trustworthy.

"You carry yourself like a noblewoman," he continued.

It would be an easy lie for her, hopefully, brief time in Caerabis. He need not know she was royalty.

"I am, Marshal." Thylaina enjoyed another bite of trout.

"Why are you here?"

Golden wine sparkled within her crystal goblet. To wet her throat and gain a few seconds to consider the answer, she sipped the wine. The truth... to a point. "It was a choice I made."

He regarded her over his plate of steaming meat. What animal it was, Thylaina knew not. But the way he stared at her was with familiarity. "I'm not privy to your reasons," he finally said.

She inwardly sighed with relief. At least the marshal was not a prying man. "How long am I a guest here, Marshal Momestid?"

He paused from eating. "Forgive me, Lady Thylaina, but Breydon was correct with his questioning." Disappointment overtook Arhgrim's visage. "You *did* break Alohrian laws. Therefore, you must face punishment for your crimes." He raised his hand to halt Thylaina from speaking. "Although you suffered the captain's fury, there is more for which to pay."

She unwrapped her left hand, exposing the welts, cuts, and swollen flesh. "Was this not enough?" There was no stopping the tears from falling then.

His shocked gaze lingered on the wounds. Scowling, he blinked several times, then pushed the meal aside and lifted his goblet. "It was wrong, my lady. But it doesn't eliminate your punishment."

"I was starving!"

"I know. But we help each other in this region of Alohrius. Not take from one another."

No. Marshal Arhgrim Momestid was not a decent man.

Appetite lost, Thylaina shoved the bread-plate forward, nearly knocking the wine glass over. She crossed her arms and stared at the empty seat across from her. "Just what more must I endure?"

A heavy breath rushed through his nostrils. "A year of servitude in the very gardens you stole from."

Thylaina jerked her head in his direction. "What?"

"Just in Caerabis. The farmers on the plains will receive compensation for their losses."

Working in the city gardens was not so terrible. Thylaina often got her hands dirty while digging for herbs. But there was the punishment over Gavrel's horse.

"And the dubight's mount?" she asked.

The marshal nodded toward her hand. "I believe there's nothing more to be done. Besides, Gavrel forgave you."

"Will I stay in the jailhouse?"

Arhgrim laughed, the tops of his cheeks rosy and the deep green of his eyes growing more noticeable. "The vault? Of course not."

Thylaina rested the back of her left hand on her lap, palm throbbing. "Then where?"

"It's best you remain here, to be cared for and watched." He tilted his head slightly. "I'll send for your case. Hopefully, you still have a remedy for your wounds."

"If your priests send bossel powder, or roots for grinding, I can create a healing ointment."

Intrigue brightened his face. "Very well." Arhgrim signaled for a servant from the corner behind him, instructing her to call for a priest and Thylaina's satchel, "with all contents inside." Then he relaxed in his large chair. "Shall we resume with our meal?"

Thylaina moved the bread-plate back in place. "Seared trout tastes better when it has just cooled. It brings out the flavor."

"I didn't know that."

"What do you call this?" She motioned to the bread beneath the meal. "Do I eat it afterward?"

"A trencher. You may eat it if you wish. Or we'll give it to a less fortunate outside the city."

Thylaina straightened. Perhaps she was mistaken about the marshal, and he *was* a good man. He seemed to care about the people he oversaw. "That is a wonderful thing to do, Marshal Momestid."

They enjoyed their meal while speaking about the gardens, orchards, and herbs.

Afterwards, Ardella returned for Thylaina. In the bedchamber, she barely had the ties of the dress undone afore yanking the sleeves down, her knuckles knocking into Thylaina's wounded hand. She did not apologize, nor did she seem to care.

"You elves are pompous," she grumbled.

Thylaina held her breath. How dare this servant reprimand her! Yet this was not the palace in Etharell, so she did not respond.

Ardella, however, continued as she tugged on the garment, almost tripping Thylaina. "You've no idea what the captain suffered. What your kin did to him and his."

The dress pooled at Thylaina's feet, Ardella *humphed* as she stomped from the room, leaving Thylaina confused.

*What my people did to him?*

Considering his treatment toward her, it must have been terrible.

# Chapter Three

The aching throb prevented Thylaina from any decent sleep. Pink light glowed through the cracks of the thick curtains, yet a priest had yet to arrive with the satchel. Despite her suffering, Ardella cursed at her until she got out of bed, then dressed her in gardener's clothing. What an awful start to the day! Not just because Katjina obviously did not get the handmaiden position, but because Thylaina had to work in the gardens immediately, and in such a heavy dress. Instead of the free-flowing cotton of house servants, the gardeners and orchard caretakers wore thick wool. Although it was the third week of the Harvest Month, autumn's colors barely touched the foliage of the bushes and trees, yet the air had chilled early this year. The brown skirt and dark green blouse might hide the dirt Thylaina expected to gain while laboring in the gardens, but it would also attract the sunlight.

She looked atrocious in the garb, yet she could not ask for clothing fit for royalty. Thylaina turned to Ardella. "How *am* I to work when my hand is still—?"

"You whine too much!" The handmaiden's eyes rolled upward as she clicked her tongue. "You've an uninjured hand, don't you?"

Thylaina held her left hand to her bosom. "You are a horrible woman."

Ardella's nostrils twitched as she pointed to the vanity chair. "Sit. I must braid that dreadfully long hair of yours."

"I do not wish—"

"This is how it'll be, *prisoner*. Sit or you'll not eat at all."

Eyes closed, Thylaina breathed deep and focused on something other than her pain and annoyance with the servant. Prisoner, not guest. It would be best to do as she was told.

Ardella roughly handled Thylaina's hair, tugging and pulling while weaving it into a long plait. She even tied the wimple too tightly.

"Now let's go before it's too late to break fast." The woman stomped out of the room.

There was not a second of serenity to be had. Sighing, Thylaina followed the nasty handmaiden to the dining chamber.

Marshal Momestid was in his seat, and at the foot of the table was a woman with wavy blonde locks. She appeared near her mid-twenties in age and several months pregnant. Next to her sat a young girl of approximately six or seven years with the same hair as her mother. The two seemed petite compared to the stout marshal, and their hair contrasted his dark mane. Upon seeing Thylaina, the girl gasped and widened her eyes, which were deep green like her father's.

Thankfully, Captain Colmstad was absent. Thylaina had not the energy for the man's ire, especially after Ardella's hostility.

Arhgrim stood as she approached the seat to his right. "Good morrow, Lady Thylaina. I hope you rested well."

After Thylaina sat, Ardella left without pushing the chair in.

With a cocked brow, the marshal's gaze swung from the door the handmaiden just escaped through to Thylaina. "Are there troubles, my lady?"

Thylaina hated lying, but living in the palace and being around a family who made her feel unwanted had conditioned her to lie when necessary. Again, Caerabis was not Haevaun Flameral, and the mansion was not the palace. Yet the idea of suffering Ardella for a year, alongside Captain Colmstad, was a depressing thought.

"Her hesitation speaks." The pregnant woman smiled wryly.

Heat flushed Thylaina's cheeks as she looked down at her bandaged hand. "I do not wish to cause trouble amid the servants. I am but a prisoner."

"However, we demand better respect for you," the woman said. "Particularly from the head of my staff. Now tell me... has Ardella been unkind?"

"This is the Lady of Caerabis, my wife, Tesesra." Pride brightened Arhgrim's eyes. "You may speak truthfully with us without worry of retribution."

Thylaina sat back as a servant placed a bowl of fruit and a plate with a large sausage and sweet-smelling bread afore her. Once all the servants left the chamber, she lifted an apple slice, noting Arhgrim and Tesesra still awaited a response. "Despite my crimes, you take fine care of me. I have n'ei right to complain."

Tesesra tilted her head. "You'll fulfill duties for your crime, won't you?"

"Of course."

"And you're staying here during that time."

"I had expected to remain in the—"

"Keeping you in the vault wouldn't do." Tesesra frowned, yet sympathy flooded her countenance. "You were starving, and no one can blame you for seeking food."

"You're an elf," Arhgrim said, "and we'll not treat you as a prisoner. Except, as Captain Colmstad suggested this morning, you'll have an escort. For your protection."

"I understand," Thylaina whispered.

After adding three spoons of sugar to her tea, Tesesra said, "Grim tells me you're a healer."

"I am trained with using Vynia's Gifts."

Arhgrim chuckled, then shoved a chunk of sausage into his mouth. "Aren't you what the elves call a Vynist?" he asked, the meat forming a lump inside his cheek.

Her heart aching, Thylaina dropped the apple on the plate.

He glanced at his wife. "Forgive me, Lady Thylaina. I hadn't meant an offense."

"It is not that," she said. "My..." Her eyelids felt heavy as tears built beneath them. "My brother often spat that word at me as if it were vile." Thylaina shook her head, hearing Neldrid's voice laced with loathing.

*"I do not trust Eidryn nor the other bloody Vynists!"*

Her brother never seemed to understand that *she* was a Vynist, as were many of the elite healers serving in the armies and xilys. He trusted *them*.

"I could never fathom why he showed hatred toward something so good," Thylaina added.

"For some, it's a lack of understanding," Arhgrim said. "People emit aggression toward what they can't comprehend." His gaze darted to her bandaged hand. "Were you able to tend to your wounds last night?"

What small amount of comfort he provided had faded. "My satchel nor the bossel roots arrived."

"You jest."

"N'ei."

Frowning, he sat back. "We'll take care of that matter immediately."

Arhgrim thumped a wooden object on the table twice, which promptly had a servant in the room and at his seat to receive instructions for the temple. "Tell them if the items aren't here by the time I finish breaking fast, I'll retrieve them myself."

The servant bobbed his head once, then hurried to the door.

Thylaina tipped the strange wooden item's handle in her direction, then the opposite way. Scratches crisscrossed the bottom of the worn rounded base, grooves on the handle provided an easy grip, and the wood appeared smoothed with wax. The item was lovely, but harsh on the ears.

"My grandsire gave it to me," Arhgrim said.

Thylaina straightened it and lowered her hand. "I was only curious as to why you do not use a bell or something more pleasing."

He grinned. "They might not hear a bell."

"Then why not keep servants in here?" She swept her hand over half the expanse of the room, where none were present other than the family and her.

"Because we sometimes like to keep our conversations private." He looked at his wife, whose response was an arched brow.

"Nadiera, finish your porridge," Tesesra said, stroking her daughter's hair. The sunlight streaking through the narrow windows touched upon the girl's head.

"Now, about Ardella." Tesesra's blue eyes locked on Thylaina. "I understand you may not want to make trouble, but I'd like to know if any exists between you two." Leaning in Thylaina's direction, she added with a softer voice, "Is *she* causing a fuss?"

Thylaina swiftly searched her mind for a polite answer. "I believe we are not a fine fit for one another."

The corner of Tesesra's lips lifted.

"That's a kind way of saying you're not fond of her," Arhgrim said.

Tesesra winked at her husband. "Lady Thylaina is being amiable."

"That she is." He drank from his steaming mug.

Tesesra sighed into her teacup, then sipped. "I must find a suitable maiden for—"

"Katjina and I are quite agreeable." Thylaina's cheeks heated again as the marshal and his wife stared at her. "Please forgive my interruption."

"Katjina?" Face scrunched in confusion, Tesesra looked at her husband. "Who's Katjina?"

Nadiera tugged on her mother's sleeve. "She's a kitchen maiden. A nice one."

"From kitchen to handmaiden?" Tesesra laughed. "It just won't do."

"She dressed me for supper last night," Thylaina said.

Realization widened Her Ladyship's eyes. "Oh, yes. The poor girl nearly dropped her vegetable basket while begging for the opportunity. She had promised to impress."

"She did superbly." Arhgrim smirked. "Even Breydon held his breath upon seeing Lady Thylaina."

"Did he?" Tesesra giggled behind her hand. "That speaks well of Katjina's skills. Nadiera, stop scowling and eat your porridge."

Mouth slacked open, Thylaina forced her gaze from Tesesra to the little girl, finding the child glaring at her. It took a few seconds longer to break from the shock of what the marshal had said. Honestly, it was hard to believe Captain Colmstad had had such a reaction to seeing her the prior evening. Thylaina closed her mouth and swallowed to wet it.

"We'll have to increase Katjina's wages," Tesesra continued the conversation with her husband.

"And speak with Ardella." He looked at the opening door. "Mikan has arrived, and with Lady Thylaina's case."

The high priest strolled into the room with the satchel over his shoulder, and his hard gaze rising above Thylaina. "Forgive me, Marshal. When the messenger arrived last night, we were in prayer. Your request slipped our minds by the time we finished."

Appalled by the obvious lie, Thylaina frowned. This man was the leader of their temple, who likely knew not how to commune with his god.

Eyelids lowered to a slit, Arhgrim shifted his jaw from side to side. "Yet it seems my request hasn't interfered with your morning prayers."

The priest's steps scraped the stone floor. He half smiled. "We answer to Valorius, not marshals."

"As true as that may be," Arhgrim relaxed within the large chair, "marshals are Valorius' superior knights. Or has that changed?"

The priest glanced at Thylaina. "We were following orders from—"

"*My* orders, Mikan. Not Captain Colmstad's."

After a brief bow, the priest raised the satchel. "I brought it, haven't I?"

Arhgrim gestured to Thylaina. "It belongs to her."

Mikan's chest expanded as he turned, laying the leather case on the table. He slid it toward Thylaina. "My lady, it is a pleasure to see you again."

She grabbed the strap and pulled it the rest of the way, nearly knocking a goblet over. The satchel now in her arms, the familiar scents of dried herbs brought some comfort.

"Did you remember the bossel roots?" Arhgrim asked.

The priest smiled condescendingly at Thylaina. "Of course. I placed them inside." He turned to Tesesra while grabbing something below his throat. "How are you feeling, my lady?"

Beaming, she glided her hand over her round belly. "Very well."

"Excellent." The priest faced Nadiera. He hesitated, his eyes flitting between the young girl and Thylaina. Bent in her direction, Mikan whispered in a loud voice, "Lady Nadiera, did your porridge get too cold?"

The girl jumped in her seat, then stirred the porridge as if she had not been casting hateful glares at Thylaina a few seconds ago.

A thin fog seemed to overtake the room. A sudden chill filled the chamber, yet the sun still heated through the windows. It felt like a coverlet of tiny lightning bolts spread over Thylaina's flesh and tongue and danced in her nostrils. The only time she had known similar sensations was in her uncle's presence when he used magic. But that was not possible here.

Hand still clutched around an object—a pendant?—Mikan straightened as he spoke to Arhgrim. "Is there anything more the temple can do for you, Marshal?"

Arhgrim smiled, his eyes glistening. All signs of annoyance had transformed into joy. "We're grateful for all you do."

"By serving our knights, we serve Valorius." The mysterious item tucked beneath his robe and blouse, Mikan raised his arms outward and bowed. Faint murmurs passed between his lips. He glanced Thylaina's way, the whispers just out of reach of her hearing, yet weighing on her ears. Goosebumps rose on her arms, and her chest tightened.

Standing tall, Mikan said, "Blessed day to you all." Then he left the chamber, the haze leaving with him.

Able to breathe easier, Thylaina looked from Arhgrim to Tesesra. Peace filled their bright faces. It must have been a spell. What had the priest done to them? And how?

The gleam still in his eyes, the marshal motioned to the satchel. "Are your belongings intact?"

She blinked, unsure of what had just happened. Perhaps the pain and hunger fooled her mind. It was not possible for a human to cast a spell. She looked at the door, certain that was exactly what Mikan had done.

"My lady?" Arhgrim said.

This was not the time. Thylaina could not accuse the high priest to his own men. They would never believe her. Best to avoid him as much as possible until she left Caerabis.

Thylaina opened the case and inspected the contents. Not only were all the bottles and herbs accounted for, but Mikan added three *freshly* dug bossel roots, including the dirt. Thylaina released a heavy breath. Fighting the urge to weep, she dropped a root on the table. "None of them are ready. They need at least a fortnight of drying afore I can grind them."

Tesesra moved to the empty seat beside Thylaina. "Grim, isn't there something you can do?" she asked, patting Thylaina's back.

The euphoric expression disappeared while Arhgrim regarded the filthy roots. He slid his plate forward. "The temple might've given their prepared herbs to the soldiers I recently sent out."

No. This was an act of cruelty by the high priest.

A man in fine leather armor entered the chamber, his stride even. Confident. His gaze darted to Thylaina as he neared the marshal, a slow smile forming. After whispering in Arhgrim's ear, he straightened and waited, attention fixed on Thylaina.

"Good morrow, Sir Bramn," Nadiera said.

Grinning, he bowed slightly. "It *is* now that you've graced it," he said in a relaxed drawl hinted with arrogance, yet his voice was pleasantly mild. "I imagine my day can only get brighter."

The girl giggled.

Thylaina's tears dried as curiosity about this knight arose. She pushed the case aside, regaining his interest.

Sir Bramn's sandy-brown hair was bound at his nape, keeping clear of his handsome face. He held himself as someone with a disciplined upbringing. A nobleman. And he studied her as if viewing something he had only heard about.

"Please excuse me, my ladies." Arhgrim stood. "I've a meeting."

"Of course, love." Tesesra smiled while he kissed her forehead. "I'll tend to Lady Thylaina. She'll not work in the gardens until her hand's healed, and this will give me time to know her."

"Sounds like a grand idea." Arhgrim bobbed his head once to Thylaina. "Have a fine morning, my lady."

"My ladies." Sir Bramn bowed to Tesesra and Thylaina, then Nadiera. Intrigue showed in his deep-blue eyes as he glanced at Thylaina once again as he followed the marshal from the chamber. Many humans might look at her like that until they grew accustomed to her presence.

"Now," Tesesra said, "is there anything in your case that might help?"

Thylaina swung the draping strap. "N'ei. I had only one vial of potent healing leaves, but it was destroyed yesterday."

Tesesra reached for the satchel, pulled her hand back, then reached again. "May I?"

"If you wish, Your Ladyship. But you shall find nothing strong enough for the wounds."

"Are they so terrible?" Tesesra breathed a laugh that did not quite sound like a laugh. "Are you finished with your porridge, Nadiera?"

"Yes, Mother." The girl skipped from the foot of the table to the head and plopped into her father's chair.

There was a comfort with the Momestid ladies, and although Tesesra was more than two hundred years younger, she had a mothering quality toward Thylaina.

Tesesra removed lavender and xarflas from the case, frowning as small clumps of dirt landed on the tabletop. "Oh. I wonder why Mikan did this." She took out three pouches of dried herbs, then slid the vials from within, one at a time. Two olesa oils followed by dried berry brush, lavender, crueberries, bossel powder, crushed xarflas leaves, ginger root, and feverfew.

Thylaina straightened and stared at the vials of bossel and xarflas. "How?" She lifted the tubes. "I had only packed one of each."

"You must've packed more." Tesesra shrugged. "Now, what do you need of me?"

Praises to Vynia! During her swift preparations, Thylaina must have placed extra vials in the case. But she was certain she had had only one of each prepared at the palace.

"Warmed water and a bowl," she said.

A pleasant smile amplifying her loveliness, Tesesra turned to her daughter. "Darling, please send a servant for—"

Nadiera was already running for the door at the corner of the room. She threw it open. "Mother wants a bowl and warm water now!"

"Nadiera!" Tesesra scolded over her shoulder. "That's not how we speak to them, and you know it."

"I want them to hurry." Nadiera rushed back to the table, but now stood behind Thylaina's chair, peering over. "Can I help?"

"I'm uncertain what you can do." Tesesra untied the bandage, then carefully unwrapped it. The gashes, welts, and bruises revealed, she swiftly covered them with the cloth. "Nadiera, go to your lessons."

"It's not time to—"

"Now." Tesesra kept her eyes down as they welled with tears.

The young girl sighed heavily as she trudged to the door. "You never let me do anything."

By the time the door closed, the other opened and two servants entered, delivering a kettle and a bowl.

"Leave them on the table." Tesesra's voice cracked. She still had not moved.

Not wanting to cause any further pain, Thylaina remained motionless as well.

The chamber now empty of all but Thylaina and Tesesra, silence fell like a thick blanket. Dust particles danced together in the sunlight, swirling to the floor while Tesesra built the courage to continue.

She wiped her eyes, then lifted the bandage. "Breydon did this?" she whispered. Shaking her head, she set the cloth on the table, a teardrop skimming down her cheek. "I don't understand. This... This is unlike him." Her elbow on the table, she wept into her palm.

It bothered Thylaina to see Tesesra ache over the actions of the dreadful captain, and she knew not how to comfort the woman nor what to say.

Tesesra recovered surprisingly fast. After a few breaths, she wiped her face, then asked for instructions.

Xarflas and bossel root had no scent, a favorable characteristic of the healing herbs. No natural perfumes meant no stinging, and mixing them with warmed water produced a soothing ointment. Vynists always carried bossel powder and xarflas; however, the latter was not often obtainable.

Tesesra proved attentive and made the healing balm, then spread it just as Thylaina directed. The warmth worked into the open wounds, soaked into the bruises. While she wrapped Thylaina's hand with a clean bandage from a small compartment in the satchel, the ointment cooled, giving relief. By afternoon, the pain should ease significantly.

"I'm terribly sorry for what he did to you," Tesesra said.

"However, the apology means little spoken from you." A horrible thing to say, but truthful.

"I understand." Tesesra tied the bandage, then held Thylaina's other hand. "Breydon is a good man. I swear to you."

What it took to withhold laughter. "Forgive me if my opinion of him is not the same."

Nodding, Tesesra dumped the dirt from the case, then returned the vials. "I understand," she said again.


Relief eased every tense muscle throughout Thylaina when Katjina entered the bedchamber, announcing she was taking Ardella's place. Celebratory wine nearly filled a couple of glasses, but the recently promoted handmaiden said they were to head to the city gardens to, "help you become familiar with them." If Katjina's smile had not been genuine, Thylaina would have believed the woman was mocking her. Such was not the case. So they left the mansion with an escort of two armored guards.

The fence surrounding the several plots of vegetables reached Thylaina's shoulders. The mysterious tall stalks dominated the center of the garden, and in the daylight, she could now see the strange plant clearly. Encased within the bundle of leaves and ivory hairs was a long, yellow, and bumpy vegetable. Having never seen anything of the like afore, she wondered how humans prepared it and what it tasted like.

Several smaller yet long gardens framed in wood surrounded the large middle plot, each one elevated above the ground and containing a different vegetable plant. A dozen gardeners walked amid the aisles, some bearing buckets of weeds or water, others bore baskets of crops. The men wore floppy hats, and the women donned light-colored wimples to protect them from the high sun. One man moved amongst the garden, calling out orders while he consumed an apple. He halted, his expression shadowed beneath his wide-brimmed hat as he stared at Thylaina.

Uncertain as to his thoughts, she cleared her throat and pointed at the tall stalks. "What are those?" she asked, interrupting Katjina's string of chatter.

The maidservant's smile also had not disappeared since they hugged that morning. "Do elves not eat corn?"

Shaking her head, Thylaina forced a brief laugh. "I had never seen it until two nights past."

"I've no doubt you'll take delight in it." Katjina swung her arm in an arc, gesturing to the other plots. "Do you recognize any of these?"

What a silly question. Then again, the maiden knew nothing about her charge. Thylaina glanced at the man in the hat, who squinted at her. "I am familiar with herbs, not vegetable plants."

"Then let's resume." Katjina stepped into an aisle with three plots on each side, explaining which plant was what and why they were in specific locations of the gardens. The master gardener had an effective system for a thriving yield.

Thylaina followed Katjina toward the other block of plots, some of them bare of plants. The handmaiden explained they were for the next summer's vegetables. "That's why there's two empty gardens." She nodded to the bare plots. "Beans grew in that one this summer past. They'll plant them in that plot there next spring." She pointed to another gathering of empty gardens.

"Why change?"

"To lessen the risk of disease," a man said from behind Thylaina. Gasping, she spun, meeting an annoyed expression from beneath a wide hat. He looked from her to Katjina. "Is this the thief they sent work with us?"

A mix of anger and humiliation burned Thylaina's cheeks.

"Once she's mended, Escany." Katjina shrugged. "I'm showing her the garden to—"

"I don't like it." He glared at Thylaina. "She steals from our hard labor and gets naught more than a—"

"It doesn't matter what you think." Katjina's pleasant smile remained, yet her eyes hardened.

Escany straightened. After a few seconds of silence passed, he snorted at them, then returned to the laborers, snapping orders.

Katjina spun southward and pointed, stepping ahead of Thylaina. "There are more farmsteads outside of Caerabis from where we acquire other crops, as well as flour from the miller. And to the west are more orchards."

Either the handmaiden was daft, or she purposely acted as if Escany's interruption had never happened. Yet she had handled his complaint favorably. Thylaina smiled. Katjina was perfect for her.

A tight grip on her arm jerked her backwards, forcing her to keep balance as someone dragged her from the garden. Thylaina looked over her shoulder, catching sunlight on red hair. Captain Colmstad. The guards who had escorted her and Katjina did not interfere as he hauled her around the fence to the front of the building next door.

He whirled her until her back slammed against the wall. Crimson splotched his freckled cheeks, and his blue eyes were intensely bright as he leaned close, his breath hot upon her face. "Who do you bloody think you are?" His voice was low. Rough.

"I know not what—"

He smacked both hands on the wall, trapping Thylaina. "I've already endured Grim's chastisement, and now Tes?"

Thylaina attempted to square her shoulders, but his proximity prevented it. "I-I assure you, Shapele, I knew not she—"

"There you are, Breydon," a familiar and pleasant voice drawled. Sir Bramn. His gaze flitted between the captain and Thylaina as he neared. "I thought I might find you here."

Lowering his arms, Breydon straightened, and Thylaina breathed a little easier. "What does that bloody mean?" the captain sneered.

Bramn gestured at Thylaina. "Only that I believed I'd find you in the company of the woman who's captured your heart."

Hands formed into fists, the captain clenched his jaw as he leered at Bramn's smug expression. "There are often times I find you amusing," he said. "This isn't one of them."

Bramn shrugged. "Often is better than never."

A brief silence stood between them afore Breydon glared at Thylaina, then stomped toward the mansion. Maidens hurried from his path, shaking their heads at his back.

Closing her eyes, Thylaina rested against the wall and drew in a deep breath.

"He's a good man," Bramn said. "He truly is."

"I have heard." She sighed, then frowned at him. "Yet it does not change my opinion of the beast."

His eyes darted to her hand, then back to her face. "Breydon's angry about something that has naught to do with you, but he'll blame you because you're an elf. He wasn't like this before."

"It matters not to me."

"I suppose." Bramn stepped closer. "Are you well?"

"Do you care?"

"You are my charge, so yes, I do."

Surprised, Thylaina hesitated, opening and closing her mouth. "Marshal Momestid chose you as my guard?"

Bramn scanned the area. "Is your handmaiden nearby?"

"In the garden."

"Her name?"

"Katjina."

"Let's get her, shall we?" He gently grabbed Thylaina's elbow and walked her back to the garden's entrance.

Thylaina spotted the handmaiden standing near the cornstalks, searching.

Katjina saw them and rushed to where they waited. Gaze fixed on Bramn, she slowed and curtsied. "Sir."

"Greetings, Katjina." He flashed a stunning smile, then guided them to the shade of the building next door. "Now, ladies... I need you to wait here for a moment while I speak with someone over there." Bramn pointed at a group of knights standing near a triangular-shaped structure. "I'll only be a minute or two. Can I trust you to do as I say?"

"Where am I to go?" Thylaina snapped.

He grinned. "I promise I shall be brief." Bramn bowed partially, then strode to the other knights.

Exhaustion suddenly weighing upon Thylaina, she leaned against the wall.

Once he was ten feet away, Katjina grasped Thylaina's good hand. "What happened? You were right behind me, then you were gone!"

"Captain Colmstad," Thylaina whispered.

"Oh. I don't know why he's—"

"Sir Bramn sent him off," Thylaina said, preventing another acclaim for the captain. "It appears Marshal Momestid has appointed this knight as my guard."

"Truly?"

They watched as Bramn handed a folded parchment to one of the other knights, then shook hands with them all.

"Lovely indeed," Katjina said, her cheeks pink.

"Is *he* a fine man?"

"Oh, yes. Sir Bramn's a very fine man. He comes from a wealthy family." Katjina smiled crookedly. "But he's a breaker of hearts."

Thylaina stepped from the building's shadow, her focus on the knights while they looked in her direction. "He certainly put a stop to Captain Colmstad's assault. Does he hold authority?"

"Not that I'm aware of. Captain Colmstad's the First Captain, the second-in-command of Caerabis, so only the marshal is above him."

That made no sense. If Bramn had no authority over Breydon, why did the latter retreat?

Bramn approached, bowing his head to several maidens who called his name. "Lady Thylaina, let us return to the mansion." He motioned to the street, where many passersby busied with their day.

Katjina hooked her arm around Thylaina's and talked about the gardeners' routines. However, Thylaina barely heard, for the worsening plight with Breydon troubled her.

Thylaina and Katjina sat beneath an apple tree behind the mansion, enjoying hard cheese, sliced apples, and wine. The orchard's sweet aroma added more flavor to their small meal. Now and then, a fruit dropped from the crooked branches. The women jumped and giggled at the sudden thuds, anticipating a thump on the head. Thylaina moved her satchel against the tree behind her to keep it safe. It had been many years since she had last enjoyed an afternoon meal with someone. Strange how it was now a human.

Katjina continuously glanced at Sir Bramn, who leaned against an apple tree ten feet away, enjoying one of its fruits. He was not always watching Thylaina, his attention often shifting to anyone passing the orchard.

"He's so handsome," Katjina whispered.

An undeniable truth.

Bramn had changed from the leather armor he had worn that morning into a white blouse, black leather pants, and knee-high leather boots. The broadsword remained at his side. His hair was bound back with a strip of dark-blue cloth matching the color of his eyes. He had laced the shirt strings to just above his chest, revealing a hint of smooth flesh within the opening, and the sleeves clung to his muscular arms.

He looked their way, bowed his head.

Had he heard Katjina? No. It was not possible.

"It's a shame he'd never consider a servant for a wife," Katjina added, her cheeks rosy.

Offering a sympathetic smile, Thylaina squeezed the handmaiden's arm. "People who come from wealth bear expectations upon their shoulders. Some embrace those expectations." She thought briefly about her brother, then sighed. "Others suffer them like a duty." Others, like herself.

Bramn looked at them again, but now with a solemn expression. An understanding.

Thylaina's heart beat faster. His reaction revealed he had heard her, but he was a human, lacking the keen hearing of an elf. She would have to be cautious around her guard. Or...

"Katjina, I must change my bandage." She raised her left hand. "Please fetch some heated water."

"Yes, m'lady." Katjina rose, swiped some dirt and loose grass from her skirt, then headed to the banded scullery door at the back of the mansion.

Bramn's gaze did not leave the handmaiden until she vanished inside. He took a large bite of the apple, then dropped it to the ground while scanning north of the orchard, where soldiers walked to the barracks. His jaw flexed with each chew as he turned his head slowly. The knight was a fine actor.

Thylaina dumped Katjina's wine, then refilled the glass. "Sir Bramn."

He swallowed. "My lady?"

Smiling, she raised the glass. "Please join me."

The corner of his lips twitched. "I must decline."

"You need not pretend to guard me while your true intent is to spy." She set the goblet beside hers and patted the spot Katjina had previously occupied.

The tip of his tongue peeked out for a leisure lick over the center of his bottom lip. "Am I that obvious?" His heels dragged over the ground as he approached. "I shall have to improve on my spying."

"I am astounded at your ability to hear from such a distance."

"Not more than ten feet."

"A whisper?" Thylaina huffed a laugh. "Nearly as keen as an elf."

Bramn's cheeks tinged pink. "You flatter me with such a compliment." He lowered beside her, yet did not take the wine. "But I'm not nearly as gifted as the elves."

Thylaina must have mistaken his mannerisms for arrogance. The knight declined the compliment, refused to drink wine while on duty, and still minded their surroundings while speaking with her. No, he was not arrogant. Sir Bramn was devoted.

She lifted the plate of cheese and offered it to him. Chuckling, he took two chunks, tossed one into his mouth.

"How does a human learn to hear so well?" she asked. "Especially with the commotion of a city."

He shrugged. "Xilys taught me."

That was not possible. Xilys endured more strenuous training than the soldiers of the armies, honing their skills to give them an advantage over any threat toward Etharell. They protected the Elven Nation's borders without others knowing they were present. They were extraordinary warriors.

Amusement fading, Thylaina straightened. "When was this to have happened?"

"Three years ago." Looking upward, he nodded. "Yes. Three years. And now Marshal Momestid puts my skill to use as a scout for the Caerabis army. And now to spy on you."

"To give reports to him. Or is it the shapele?"

"Shapele?"

"*Captain*," she nearly spat. But if he and Breydon had spent time with the xilys... "However, I imagine you knew that. Perhaps other Elvish words learned from the xilys as well."

A crooked grin and a wink were his response.

An annoyed huff expelled, Thylaina sipped more wine. "How could the xilys teach something that is innate for elves? Our hearing is far superior."

"It may be innate for them, but when one is in certain environments, there's the discipline of concentration. Breydon and I had spent nine months between Lake Wynland and the Graunis Mountains with Ormiana Xilys, learning how to focus and how to ignore distractions."

Thylaina scowled. Neldrid might be furious to learn those meant to defend the border had trained foreigners, including one who despised elves. "That is difficult to believe."

"I'm no liar." Nor did he *not* appear offended. His expression softened, then he laughed. "I see. You mean Breydon." Bramn tugged a weed from the ground. "As I mentioned earlier, he was different then. Before his brother was killed."

That might partly explain the captain's behavior.

Neldrid returned to her mind. The thought of losing him completely was a pain reminiscent of the ache of Mother's death. "What happened, if I may ask?"

"It's not my place to tell. Even if—" He looked to the north, from where a man walked toward them, carrying a box wrapped in burlap. The knight's expression hardened. "Soldier."

"Sir Bramn. My lady." Gavrel nodded once to the knight, then to Thylaina.

"Gavrel!" She smiled wide at him. "What a pleasure to see you."

"Thank you, my lady." His blush accentuated the freckles on his cheeks. "The pleasure is mine."

Bramn's glare remained. "What's the reason for your being here?"

"To see how Lady Thylaina fared." Gavrel raised the package. "And I have something for our guest."

"As you can see, she's well," Bramn said, his tone lacking any kindness. "Leave the box and be on your way."

Thylaina frowned at him. "Sir Bramn."

The scullery door closed, gaining his brief attention as Katjina returned with a steaming kettle.

"Oh." The handmaiden halted, her gaze darting between the two men. "Are more joining us for afternoon meal?"

"No." Bramn rose. "Gavrel's leaving now."

"I should like him to stay," Thylaina said.

"Thank you, my lady." The dubight smiled.

"I'm certain he has more training to attend," Bramn snapped.

Gavrel shook his head. "Captain Eilisar said I earned the remainder of the day."

The knight squinted. "Is that so? Perhaps I should ask him."

"If you feel it necessary, sir. I'm not lying."

"Is all of *this* necessary?" Thylaina asked. "Sir Bramn, please go... guard."

Hurt passed over his face. "Yes, my lady," he grumbled, then tramped back to the tree he had leaned upon earlier.

Now that his overbearing hostility no longer dampened her meal, Thylaina grinned at Gavrel and gestured to the spot beside her. "Please sit."

"I didn't want to cause trouble."

"N'ei trouble on your part." She patted the ground again. "I want you to join me."

Once he sat beside her, she noted sweat beading along his hairline, suggesting he had come directly from training. Her gaze darted to the burlap-covered box.

"You look lovely today," he said, regaining her attention. "As every day, I've no doubt," he added in a whisper.

Thylaina huffed. "In these drab garments?" She lifted a pinch of the skirt. "There is no joy in this color."

"But the green shows your eyes. Truly enchanting."

The dubight was bold. Bramn seemed to think so as well, for he snarled from beneath the tree.

"Thank you," Thylaina murmured. "You are kind." She offered the plate of cheese. "Would you like something to eat? Or some wine?"

"I'm not hungry," Gavrel said. "I just wanted to see you—how you are, that is. And give you this."

She set the plate down to receive the item. "I am to remain a prisoner for a year."

His brows lowered. "I'm sorry."

"But I do not have to stay in the jailhouse." Thylaina tugged one end of the twine binding the cloth to the box. "The marshal insists I remain here with his family and under the care of one of his knights."

Gavrel glanced at Bramn. "One of Captain Colmstad's friends, I noticed." He placed his hand over hers, halting her from untying the twine. "Wait until you're alone. Please."

Curious, Thylaina tilted her head toward her shoulder. "If you wish." Then she looked in Bramn's direction. "One of the captain's friends, you say?"

"I wonder who assigned him. The marshal or Captain Colmstad?"

Katjina cleared her throat. "My lady, did you want—?"

"Forgive me." Thylaina set the package down and pulled the satchel forward. "I must change this now, and again tonight. Katjina, will you please assist?"

"I'll help," Gavrel said.

"If you are certain."

"Every knight should learn some mending skills." He nodded at the satchel. "Teach me. Maybe one day, I'll save a comrade's life."

What a wonderful thing to hear someone, human or elf, say. "N'ei better reason to teach someone."

She instructed Gavrel on how to make the simple healing balm of ground bossel root, pinch of xarflas, and heated water. Once it was ready, she presented her bandaged hand. It took longer for the wrapping's removal than she had expected, since he seemed extra cautious. But when the wounds came into view, he froze. Gavrel blinked several times, as if hoping what he saw might change. The bruises had lightened, and the swelling had lessened since that morning. The flesh around the cuts, however, was still red.

"This is..." His gaze met hers. "I'm sorry, my lady. I should've stopped him."

Thylaina palmed his cheek. "You need not bear guilt for what he did."

"But I could've—"

"Gavrel, you brought the marshal." She nodded. "You stopped that beast from doing further harm, and I am grateful."

He looked down at her hand, then held it atop his fingertips, as if it was fragile. "He *is* a beast." Gavrel lowered his head, kissed a cut.

She almost tugged her hand free, but stilled herself. "I-it does not hurt as much now. Lady Tesesra helped tend to it this morning, and there has been improvement."

"Show me what to do."

After spreading the paste on the more serious wounds, Thylaina handed him the bowl. Gavrel was attentive to the task, his touch surprisingly soft. The dubight was a fine student. After wrapping her hand with a clean bandage, he kissed it.

Her face warmed. "Thank you, Gavrel. Your kindness has been more than I deserve after what I have done to you."

He looked at the branches above, squinting from the sunlight breaking through the leaves. "You needed to find someplace safe." Eyes lowered to her, he added, "Your life is more important than a horse's."

"My lady." Bramn stepped closer. "Afternoon meal has ended."

It was a shame to return inside, but Thylaina had much to learn about the mansion and the Momestids. She nodded. "Very well, Sir Bramn."

Gavrel was quick to his feet and offering his hand. "I hope we can find more time together."

"That would be lovely," she said. "Thank you for your help... once again."

"It shall always be my pleasure, Lady Thylaina." Gavrel bowed, then headed down the eastward path.

"You'd do well to avoid the company of soldiers," Bramn said.

Thylaina gave the satchel to Katjina. "Please take this to my room."

"Yes, m'lady."

She then turned to Bramn. "Despite my offense to him, Gavrel has been kind to me. And he *did* save me from that dreadful captain's cruelty."

A brow arched, he glanced in the direction the dubight had headed. "My suggestion remains."

"Suggestion or command?"

A smirk curved his lips. "A strong suggestion beneficial for you to heed."

After drawing in a deep breath, Thylaina released it. One reason she left Etharell was to escape people telling her how to live. "Are knights the only company I am allowed while a prisoner here?"

His eyes darkened slightly. The darkest blue she had ever seen. "Gavrel is under strict training, my lady. He must remain focused. You're a distraction."

And Bramn claimed he was not a liar. Perhaps he spoke the truth, but there was something more he did not share. Fine. She would play along. Thylaina strolled slowly to the scullery door. "Because he is a soldier currently training for the knighthood, Gavrel may not be social with anyone?"

"That's not what I said."

She stopped and scowled at him. "Then he may not be social with me. Is it because I am a prisoner?"

"There is another reason. One you're not privy to know."

Some things never changed. It seemed Thylaina was not yet free from the control of others, for she could not even choose her own friends. She tried to relax the muscles in her neck. The tension encouraged pain, and she did not want a headache from all this contemplating.

He pushed open the scullery door. "After you, my lady."


Thylaina slouched in the chair afore the small hearth. The busy day had left her physically and mentally worn. During supper, she had borne the weight of Captain Colmstad's glares from across the table. She dared not look at him. The only reason she knew he had been staring at her was because Nadiera fought for his attention. When he did not give it to her, the child mumbled, "I wish Father would put that *elf* in the vault." No one at the table other than Thylaina had heard her. The only time the captain's gaze broke away was when a young man arrived to deliver a message to him, then sat at a tiny table in the corner to eat a meager meal. After viewing the missive, Thylaina fell victim to Breydon's heavy glares again.

What a horrible end to the day. Two people in Caerabis disliked Thylaina, and she had done nothing to them.

*Three. Escany dislikes me as well. And not only will I have to endure him in the gardens, but Ardella as well.*

"I had not intended for Her Ladyship to send Ardella from the mansion." Thylaina looked at Katjina. "I only wanted you as my caretaker."

"It wasn't your fault, m'lady." The handmaiden smiled sweetly. "This was of Ardella's doing alone. She had been pushing her authority with Her Ladyship for the past year. You were... How shall I say it?" Katjina scrunched her face in thought. "A test of sorts. Ardella failed. Now Her Ladyship has someone better suited in her position."

"But now she labors in the very place where I am to serve my punishment." Thylaina sat forward and rested her head in her hands. "Did they not think of that?"

"I understand your concern. Perhaps I can mention this to Her Ladyship."

"N'ei." Thylaina straightened. "It is not my place nor yours to insist a change on my behalf."

"But Ardella will be cruel to you. Not to mention Escany." Katjina knelt afore Thylaina. "The Momestids won't like that at all."

So she predicted the same outcome. This handmaiden truly paid attention to detail, an appreciated skill.

"What is done is done," Thylaina said. "I shall serve my punishment with honor, for that is what my parents taught me." She nodded once. No more was to be said on the matter.

"Very well." Katjina stood and retrieved the box from Gavrel off the table. "I've been curious all day about what he gave you."

Worries whooshed away as Thylaina set the gift on her lap and untied the twine. "It seems more curious than I." She giggled. "To be honest, I had forgotten about it throughout the day."

The burlap fell away, revealing a shoddy box, as if it had been quickly built. Gavrel must have nailed the wood slats together to fashion it. But fastened around the box were two leather straps, their ends nailed at the bottom and buckled on the top. Her mouth dried as she recognized not only the straps from the chair Breydon had forced her into at the jailhouse, but that the chair's wooden slat formed the container's base.

"Is something wrong?" Katjina asked.

Hands trembling, Thylaina unfastened the buckles. It took longer than it should have for the memories of the captain's torture resurfaced. Even the crack of the edged stick sounded in her ear. But to see that very item within the box stole her breath.

"M'lady?"

Thylaina licked her lips as she pulled a slip of paper from beneath the stick.

*Lady Thylaina,*
*I can't bear the thought of these items being used again on an innocent*
*person, or one who sought relief. Burn these, destroy them, or do what*
*you will. This is our secret.*
*Gavrel*

She looked at the hearth. As much as she wanted to do it herself, Thylaina could not stomach touching the stick. A teardrop skimmed her cheek as she lifted the box to Katjina. "Please put these into the fireplace."

"If… If you wish." The handmaiden took the container and turned to the hearth. She looked back. "Are you certain? Gavrel gave this to you."

Thylaina flashed a smile, gratitude toward the dubight encouraging another nod. "Please." She sat back and watched the handmaiden carefully toss the entire box into the fire. Releasing a long breath, Thylaina closed her eyes. "I must think of a way to thank Gavrel for his thoughtful gift. And tell no one about this."

"Of course, m'lady." Katjina touched Thylaina's cheek. "You look exhausted."

"I would adore some tea."

The handmaiden smiled. "I'll get some chamomile."

"Thank you."

Katjina closed the door quietly behind her, leaving the room in silence.

Thylaina relaxed in the chair and stared at the burning box. No one else would suffer that horrible captain's cruelty. She looked to the empty seat across the small rug. The logs and wood cracking from the flames' fury were the only sound. Knowing the stick was burning helped ease Thylaina's muscles and coaxed her mind to release all the worries gained over the course of the day. She imagined Neldrid sitting in the vacant chair. In years past, at moments like this, she and her older brother drank tea together while laughing over events that had irritated them throughout the day. It was their way of letting the menial things go. Family meant a great deal to Neldrid then. But now…

The door opened. Had so much time passed while she reminisced? Thylaina wiped her cheek, drying a teardrop. "Either you move swiftly or I lost the time."

Ardella closed the door. "Do you have any idea what you've done?"

One enemy after another.

Thylaina gestured to the chair. "Katjina shall return with tea. Please sit and have some with me."

"Katjina?" Ardella stomped toward her. "You replaced me with kitchen slop?"

Thylaina jumped up and hurried around the chair, using it as a barrier. "You and I were not a match. We—"

"I've never had trouble until you arrived!"

"Perhaps you should treat your guests better!"

"You're a bloody prisoner!" Ardella's face turned a deep red.

"She's correct, you know?" a man said from the chamber's entrance.

Both women looked to the doorway, where Captain Colmstad leaned with his arms crossed.

Thylaina froze, her heartbeat thundering in her ears. He must have followed the woman, or he knew about Gavrel's gift.

"You're a prisoner, not a guest." His gaze shifted to Ardella. "However, you shouldn't be in here anymore."

The woman shook her head. "She's ruined me."

"She's no longer your concern." Breydon stepped in farther, clearing the way for her to leave. "I understand your duty is elsewhere now."

Ardella glowered at Thylaina. "It is," she said between her teeth. "In the damn gardens."

"Go on then. Leave the mansion," he commanded.

Gripping the top of the chair, Thylaina pressed her wounded hand to her chest as she watched Ardella storm from the room.

Breydon did not move after she left. The man's hatred could stop a draft better than a wall tapestry. Thankfully, he did not look toward the hearth.

Courage finally built, Thylaina said, "Thank you, Shapele, for... coming to my aid."

He released a heavy breath. "Don't thank me for anything." The captain walked out.

Four seconds later, Katjina entered with a tray holding a teapot, two cups, and a few other items. "I don't know what just happened," she said, "but Ardella almost knocked this from my hands, and Captain Colmstad seemed in a hurry from here."

Thylaina stared at the steam rising from the teapot's spout, no longer wanting any. Tomorrow would be another day of torment under Captain Breydon Colmstad.

# Chapter Four

A few days passed without further occurrences involving Ardella, nor the captain, for that matter, thank the gods. During meals, Breydon did not look Thylaina's way, but conversed with Arhgrim and Bramn, and ordered the young man, whom she learned was the captain's squire, Arlin, to run errands. In fact, it seemed the marshal and Bramn kept Breydon occupied while in her presence, making the meals less stressful. The awful tension eased, Thylaina spoke more with Tesesra and Nadiera.

While breaking fast this morning, the young girl sat closer to Thylaina, her face shining as continuous questions about the Elven Nation dominated the dining hall. Sour expressions accompanied complaints about contradictions from her instructors regarding some elvish traditions. Nadiera announced her instructors must have erred, for an elf would know better. A smile lifted the corners of Arhgrim's lips, despite him rolling his eyes, and he said nothing as Thylaina continued educating his daughter. When Nadiera grew bored with the lessons, she inquired about the forests. Descriptions of colorful blooms and ancient trees of Thylaina's home took over the conversation, some of the latter so wide a score of elves could hold hands around them and stare to the tops a hundred feet up.

"It sounds enchanting," Tesesra said. "Why did you leave?"

Sorrow from the loneliness that had engulfed her life in Etharell struck as Thylaina slid her fingers down Nadiera's braid. "After my brother joined the military, I rarely saw him. Years passed, and I—"

"Your brother's in the army?" Breydon paused passing a parchment to Arlin. The chamber fell silent as all stared at her. Eyes hard and cutting, Breydon handed the scroll to Arlin, glanced at Arhgrim, then back to Thylaina. "Which one?" he continued as the squire hurried from the chamber.

"It doesn't matter," the marshal said. "They're allies."

"Unless he's a renegade," Breydon retorted.

Bramn nudged him with his elbow. "Since when do we question their alliance?"

"Shapele, I know not what you are suggesting." Thylaina pushed the remaining porridge to the other side of the bowl with her spoon.

"I think you do." He nodded once. "You're a bloody spy."

A gasp complemented Tesesra's frown. "Gods, Breydon."

Sighing, Bramn sat back and shook his head.

Thylaina pressed her lips together, but a giggle sputtered out.

Breydon scowled. "What do you find amusing?"

"You." She lowered the spoon.

Bramn smirked behind his friend; Arhgrim rested his chin on his palm and watched; and Tesesra moved to the empty seat to Thylaina's right.

Breydon's fierce expression remained unchanged. "I've just accused you of—"

"I heard your ridiculous accusation, Shapele." Thylaina drank some cider to wet her dry mouth. "You wish to know why I left Etharell? I shall tell you."

Bramn now sat forward. In fact, all of them waited for her to continue.

Even as Thylaina chose the next words carefully, what Neldrid had written in his last letter passed through her mind:

*'Embrace your destiny just as the rest of us have.'*

She sipped more cider, then cleared her throat. "As Marshal Momestid surmised the other night, I am of noble upbringing. My father betrothed me to a dreadful elf lord. This unwanted fate was unacceptable, so I left."

"How awful," Tesesra whispered.

The muscles of Bramn's jaw tightened as he minded his hands.

A chuckle sounded from Breydon, then it grew into laughter. "Of course. Is that not how it is for you women?"

He truly was an awful man.

"Breydon." Tesesra's brows lowered.

Disgusted, Thylaina shook her head. "I gave up everything, and you mock me."

"I think you're lying." His gaze darted to Tesesra, then back to Thylaina. Waggling his finger at her, he added, "And knowing your brother is in the elven military makes you more untrustworthy."

"Enough," Arhgrim said.

Breydon stiffened, then slowly turned to the marshal, his fingertips on his chest. "Will you not address my concerns?"

Arhgrim's eyes revealed a patient annoyance. He did not agree with what his captain believed, yet he knew not how to convince the young man. There was sympathy and love in that gaze. Arhgrim drew in a deep breath, then bobbed his head once. "I shall after breaking fast."

"Why not now?"

"I'll not make a display of it. This is no court."

"Shall I be present?"

"No." Not a hesitation at all in that response. And Arhgrim's stoic visage relayed to all at the table that his answer was final.

Dropping his attention to his hands, Breydon huffed a laugh. "I see."

This was terrible. The accusations, hatred, unhealthy attention... Thylaina wanted no more of it.

"She stays in a comfortable room in the mansion," the captain said, "gets a handmaiden, and dines like royalty compared to most in this city. All while being a prisoner."

Arhgrim cocked a brow. "The decision is mine."

The heavy thump of Breydon's palms striking the table happened so quickly, Thylaina jumped. Such loathing stared at her while he slid his chair back and stood, hunched forward as his hands remained flat on the surface. "Then I'll prepare for departure."

"That would be best," the marshal said.

The captain's leering tried to penetrate the shield Thylaina raised to protect the truth. He pointed at her face. "We'll learn whom you are."

"Breydon, please." Tesesra cradled Thylaina's wounded hand. "Haven't you done enough?"

Shock slapped the interrogator's façade away as he straightened, staring at Tesesra.

No doubt she referred to his torturing Thylaina, an event too recent to forget. Although Thylaina no longer needed the bandages nor ointment, it still ached to close her fingers or grab heavy items. She practiced, just as Master Eidryn would have instructed.

After swallowing the obvious hurt from Tesesra's words, Breydon pivoted on his heel and left. No stomping or hurrying out. Just walked, as if wanting to linger.

Bramn stared at Thylaina with intrigue and curiosity.

"Why is Breydon angry all the time now?" Nadiera asked. "And always with Lady Thylaina?"

"Go to your studies," Tesesra said.

"But—"

"Sir Bramn," Arhgrim said. "Please take Nadiera to her instructors."

"Yes, sir." The knight finished his glass of goat's milk, then stood. "Come, my dear."

Joy flushed away Nadiera's frown, and she skipped around the table to take Bramn's hand. The two left the chamber, the young girl's cheerful voice fading behind the closed door.

Tesesra turned to Arhgrim. "We must address—"

"I'll tend to it." He smiled assuredly. "I promise."

She rose, stilling to rest against the table. Eyes squeezed shut, breaths passed slowly while she held the underside of her stomach.

Thylaina stood and rubbed Tesesra's back. "Is it the babe?"

After a few more breaths, Tesesra nodded. "This shall pass." She huffed. "It always does."

"Is there pain?"

"Some. I'll rest before starting morning duties." Her Ladyship forced a smile.

"How long into your pregnancy?"

"Seven months." Tesesra barely looked at Arhgrim. "This is the longest since Nadiera."

Concern interrupted Thylaina's heartbeat with a skip. Recovering, she pressed on. "How many have you lost since your daughter?"

Anguish wrinkled Arhgrim's forehead as his gaze fell away from his wife, and grief moved in while he addressed Thylaina. "We needn't speak about this."

"Forgive me, my lord. I only mean to help." She looked at Tesesra, someone she would now do her best to care for. "I suggest you rest for the day, and relay all tasks to your handmaiden. I imagine she is capable."

Head falling back slightly, Tesesra giggled. "Oh, Bethlyn has been wonderful in Ardella's stead."

"Excellent," Thylaina said. "Then she will do all that needs accomplished today."

Frowning, Her Ladyship opened her mouth to argue, but winced. "Very well."

Three solid thumps sounded from Arhgrim's seat as he hammered on the table with the servant-caller. Thylaina and Tesesra jumped, the latter moaning and holding her stomach again. Three servants entered.

"One of you, send for Bethlyn," he said.

"Yes, my lord." The youngest woman hurried out.

"You two may clear the table." A hint of relief showed in his eyes as he faced Thylaina. "Bethlyn shall escort Tesesra to her bedchamber. I'd like to speak with you in my office."

Tesesra returned to her chair, waiting for her handmaiden. "This will be a long day."

Thylaina followed the marshal from the dining chamber, down the corridor, and into the entry hall. He then led her to the second floor and across the landing to the opposite end near the other staircase, stopping at a door where a guard stood.

"Sir." The guard bowed slightly. "Two messages arrived while you broke fast, one of them taken to your desk by Captain Colmstad only moments ago."

"Very good." Arhgrim opened the door and gestured for Thylaina to enter.

She halted upon finding the room empty of luxury. Only items of necessity took up space in the chamber: a large desk with a fine chair behind it and three facing it, and a few tables—one to the side of the desk and one behind it, both with neatly stacked papers and rolled parchments, and the last near a set of opened balcony doors, the sun shining upon the decanters and crystal glasses. Perhaps not all humans were as greedy as Uncle Yasontler had often claimed.

Thylaina approached the open doors and continued onto the small balcony overlooking the city. Near the rounded end stood a large range-viewer on three legs. Thylaina had seen one of these in Dragostros during the only visit to Father's army city he ever permitted. Although elves had excellent vision and could see great distances, a contraption such as this expanded their view even farther. Thylaina stood beside the range-viewer and took in Caerabis below. It was larger than she had realized.

Numerous streets crisscrossed throughout the city. Small buildings lined most of them, opposite larger ones, all appearing to be homes, for they were simple and uniform. Scattered amid them were taverns and shops, and other structures two stories tall. Farms with crops and livestock lay beyond the city to the south, where in the far distance stood a grand windmill, and more orchards lay to the west—as Katjina had mentioned. Rectangular buildings were to the south of the mansion, and nine more bordered the city in the north, east, and west. Thylaina had learned these were the barracks. At each of Caerabis' corners were triangular buildings: the guardhouses.

"Why are there no walls?" she asked.

Arhgrim stood just within the threshold. "Caerabis has never needed walls, my lady. Does your city have them?"

Prying. He would not get the answer he sought.

Thylaina turned and leaned on the balcony rail. "Has the shapele always been listening to me? Even while he is in conversation with others?"

"As has Bramn." The marshal shrugged at her sigh. "We still don't know you nor why you're here."

"I told you why."

"But you're guarded as to whom you are."

"The other night, you said you were not privy to know." Thylaina moved to one end of the railing as he neared.

"I wanted you to know you're safe."

"How can I believe that with Shapele Colmstad near?"

Gazing upon the city, Arhgrim nodded. "Breydon has his reasons. I'm not saying they're good reasons, but they're his." He released a heavy breath. "And I am trying to resolve this, my lady. I don't want this hostility."

She looked to the gardens, where she would begin working in a few days. "I am n'ei a spy."

"I must make an effort to prove him wrong." He motioned into the chamber. "Please, come sit."

Thylaina chose the middle seat of the three.

Arhgrim sat in his chair and presented a friendly smile. "Why are you in Caerabis?"

Bryric! She must answer this bloody question again. But then, the marshal was not present when she had first confessed at the jailhouse.

"As I had said at the table, I left Etharell to avoid an unwanted marriage."

"Betrothals happen all the time," he said. "Tesesra's father and I arranged my marriage to her. She wasn't pleased at first, yet she came to love me."

Thylaina's shoulders lowered and her back curved against the chair. "Why do fathers do this to their daughters?"

"We often know what's best."

She knew not whether to laugh or cry. "My father? He did not know me, yet he agreed to a marriage for political reasons."

One of his brows arched and his head tilted slightly, as if he caught on to a truth not quite revealed. Damn it to Darkness! She had said too much. His voice rose a slightly higher octave as he said, "Is that so?"

She could easily draw his speculations away from her truth. "I have not seen my father in nearly twenty years. My brother in twelve." Another crack forming in her heart, Thylaina shook her head. "Neither wanted me in their lives, and they were willing to marry me off to a man who treated me with n'ei respect." She met the marshal's inquisitive gaze. "Can you imagine spending hundreds of years with someone with whom you share n'ei love? None at all in a home without warmth. That was the fate those men decided for me. I would not have it."

Arhgrim nibbled on his lip. "Hundreds? My lady, I can't imagine three years." He rested his arms on the desk and leaned forward. "Why did you come *here*?"

"To be truthful, Yeltar was my destination." Thylaina forced a laugh, although her situation held no humor. "But the merchant with whom I traveled abandoned me in a village near Warstchia. I knew not my way in this strange land and became lost and hungry."

His face scrunched as he relaxed back. "That was foul for one of your own to do."

"I believe I brought undesired attention."

"No doubt. I'll not deny you're an exceptional beauty. Unlike any woman I've ever seen." Thumb tapping on the desktop, his gaze hardened. "Which makes you a perfect spy."

"You jest!" Thylaina scooted to the edge of the seat. "I am not a woman with ill intent. I am a healer. And I just want to start a new life."

His expression softened, and silence ensued for a moment. "Those questions you asked Tesesra about... about the lost babes, are you concerned?"

She shrugged faintly. "I know not your wife's history with the other pregnancies, but it would be helpful to learn afore determining if there is a concern."

"I see." He stared at his winding thumbs for a moment, the noise outside the mansion invading the chamber. "We lost four after Nadiera—all while Tesesra was in her fifth and sixth months." Tears welled in his eyes. "I'm afraid of losing *her* one of these times."

"Did not the midwife find answers?"

He breathed in, clearing his nose. "No. After the second loss, we brought in a new midwife and Mikan. When it happened again, we knew it wasn't their fault."

A tremor coursed through her. "The priest?" Disdain escaped in her tone.

Squinting, Arhgrim pointed at her. "He's a high priest of Valorius. Any implication you're making right now—"

"I make none." Thylaina lifted her hands to calm him. "My encounters with him have not been... agreeable."

"Mikan has had little dealings with elves. If he's said anything offensive, I assure you, it wasn't intentional. Our high priests serve Valorius, and in doing so, honor Lessindra."

Arhgrim must have never seen that disgusting statue in the temple.

Thylaina's thoughts went to how blinding oneself to titles was dangerous. The priest's behavior when returning her satchel was questionable. Then there was the unlikely possibility he cast magic. She must be careful. If she accused their high priest and was mistaken, she might never leave Caerabis. One thing was certain: she needed to gain the trust of these humans.

"I hope that during my time here, I can prove myself useful," Thylaina said.

"And once you are free?"

"I shall join my kin in Yeltar."

He nodded.


Tesesra did not join them for supper, so Thylaina asked to see her afterward. With Arhgrim's approval, Bramn escorted her and Katjina to the bedchamber. It was on the third floor, at the top of the southern stairs—now that Thylaina had seen the city from above, she had a better sense of direction. A maidservant bade them to sit and wait in the connecting suite. In front of a small fireplace were a sofa and two cushioned chairs, snug around a large brown pelt and a low table. Above the hearth hung a painting of a burly man standing beside a dead bear. It was grotesque and, no doubt, the very animal Thylaina walked upon as she approached a chair. Bramn sat in the seat opposite her, while Katjina lowered onto the couch.

Thylaina tried not to look at the painting, nor the animal rug at her feet, but there was nothing else. Except Bramn, who grinned. "Is there something you find entertaining?" she asked.

"This bothers you." He bobbed his head toward the rug.

"I do not appreciate the slaughter of animals for pleasure."

He looked at the portrait. "That's Marshal Momestid's father."

"I care not."

"The bear was quite a prize."

Thylaina's stomach turned, and her flesh warmed. "The poor animal," she whispered.

"That poor animal had killed a family traveling through Ullios Forest." Bramn sat forward. "Lord Aerhis Momestid lived not far from where the attack happened and felt it necessary to protect his young family and others nearby. So, whom do you feel sorry for? The bear or the family it slaughtered?"

She would not explain the family had likely crossed into the bear's territory or drawn too close to its cubs. Bramn might not listen anyway.

"Her Ladyship will see you now," the maidservant said from the bedroom door.

Bramn followed Thylaina, and Katjina trailed a few feet back. As they neared the bedchamber, Mikan exited, forcing Thylaina to retreat as he walked past, leering at her. She watched him until he was in the corridor.

Bramn released his sword hilt and smirked. "After you, my lady."

He was ready to protect her... from their high priest. Thylaina would inquire about that later. Right now, Tesesra needed her attention.

The bedchamber was enormous—larger than Thylaina expected. A fire in the great hearth offered the room's only source of light, yet left the other side dim. Once Thylaina's vision adjusted, she took in the details. Directly across from the door was a tall four-poster bed, and a small table on each side with unlit lamps. Between the two windows, where heavy drapes hung, stood a five-drawer chest with a dressing screen beside it. A cozy chaise and a large chair were near the fireplace. Against the wall adjacent to the hearth was a three-drawer vanity with a large mirror, and in the corner from there was a door with intricate flowers painted on it. Hanging on each side of the door were glass bowls with ashes, and burnt sage above.

Thylaina followed the maidservant to the bed.

A sheen of sweat dampened Tesesra's pallid face, darkness puffed beneath her eyes, and her breaths came labored. A middle-aged servant sat beside her, dabbing the perspiration from her cheeks.

"This is Bethlyn," Katjina whispered. "She resumed Ardella's duties."

Thylaina neared the handmaiden. "How long has Her Ladyship been like this?"

Bethlyn blew loose strands from her face, then shook her head. "She didn't eat afternoon meal, and very little of her supper," she said. "Mikan brought tea to help with the discomfort and pain."

"What tea?"

The handmaiden pointed to a cup on the table on the opposite side of the bed. "Mikan's doing his best to help. I don't know what more *you* can offer."

Thylaina squeezed the woman's hand. "Perhaps more."

She rounded the bed, where Bramn now stood lifting the teacup. Once he gave it to her, Thylaina closed her eyes and breathed deep through her nose, catching every scent possible. Honey, chamomile—No. Feverfew. Strange choice of herb. But there was something else. Something with a scent so faint she could not identify it. She tipped the cup and dipped her tongue into what remained, catching only a few drops. A fruity tang mixed with the honey. Definitely feverfew.

Worry etched lines on Bramn's forehead. "What ails her?"

"I know not." She looked at Bethlyn. "Did Her Ladyship complain about headaches?"

"No. Why?"

"N'ei reason." Maybe Thylaina was mistaken, and it *was* chamomile, but the fruity taste in the drink said otherwise. Perhaps Mikan thought feverfew might relieve stomach pain.

Thylaina sat on the side of the bed and inspected Tesesra: dilated eyes, tongue a bit swollen, and heart racing. She had never encountered a pregnant woman, nor anyone, with these inflictions at the same time. Dilation of the pupils and quickened heartbeat impressed something affecting Tesesra's mind. The woman had not chewed raw feverfew, so Thylaina doubted the swollen tongue resulted from that. However, the plant might have caused the other two problems. Considering feverfew's main purpose was for terrible headaches, of which Her Ladyship had not complained, Thylaina focused on other effects, drawing information from memory. One particular fact struck, and she straightened, her stomach suddenly tight. Feverfew could cause the womb to contract, leading to another lost babe or an early birth, which was also risky.

Hopefully, she was incorrect about the herbs Mikan used, but to be certain, she turned to Bethlyn. "Do you know what was in the tea?"

Shaking her head, the handmaiden shrugged. "No, my lady."

*Damn it to Darkness!* It made no sense. "Katjina, please get my satchel."

"Yes, m'lady." Katjina hurried from the room.

Bramn knelt and clasped Tesesra's hand. "Can you help her?"

Thylaina forced a smile. "S'yai."

His concerned gaze revealed he was not convinced.

Conditioned to lie, and exceptional when the moments deemed it necessary, she struggled to succeed now. Thylaina turned from him and instructed Bethlyn and the maidservant to prop Tesesra in a seated position. The older handmaiden did not appear happy with the request, but did as was told. By the time they finished, with Bramn's assisting, Katjina returned with the satchel.

Different remedies passed through Thylaina's mind while she took inventory of the ingredients, but it was a feeble effort without knowing all that Tesesra had consumed.

"What is it?" Bramn asked. All the man did since entering the bedchamber was ask questions.

"I must... create a potion."

He lifted her hand from the satchel and held it between his. "You'll do fine." He kissed her scarred knuckles, then let go. "I have faith in you."

No one else in Caerabis did. In fact, Thylaina had believed he felt the same about her as Captain Colmstad did: that she was a thief and a spy, and was unworthy of trust. But Bramn's handsome smile, the confidence in his eyes, and the uplifting tone of his voice gave her hope. The man had gone from worried to trusting in mere seconds.

Thylaina took the case to the vanity, using light from the fireplace to see the vials better. Tomorrow, she would organize it so she could blindly remove items. Selecting a xarflas leaf, a vial of olesa oil, the pouch containing camiol, and a rounded bottle, she put the rest back.

Bramn was beside her again. "Please tell me what you're doing, so I may relay it to the marshal."

This was about building more trust with them.

"I am using olesa oil as my potion base," she said, setting the vial down. Thylaina opened the pouch. "This is camiol. It helps one to sleep. Lady Tesesra shall rest well for the night."

"All right."

"The leaf is xarflas. It is a potent healer."

"Heal?" A scowl marred his face. "Are you suggesting someone harmed her?"

"I fear for the babe. It could very well be because Her Ladyship has had difficulty in the past." Thylaina uncorked the round bottle and poured a quarter of the oil inside. She dropped in two pinches of camiol, handed the xarflas to Bramn, then returned to the bed. Praying she had made the right decision with the herbs, Thylaina sat.

"Bethlyn," she said, gaining the handmaiden's attention. "Please open Her Ladyship's mouth. Sir Bramn, give me the leaf." Once she had the xarflas, she chewed it just until tasting ginger, then pressed the leaf on Tesesra's tongue. "Close her mouth."

Bethlyn looked questioningly at Bramn. After he nodded, she shook her head and closed Tesesra's mouth.

Swirling the bottle, Thylaina wove her pinky on Tesesra's chin to form a leyena flower, the five petals joined to the stem gliding down her throat, all while whispering a supplication to Vynia. The woman's brows drew together for a moment. "Open it. Now!" Thylaina commanded.

Bethlyn tugged on Tesesra's chin, parting her lips wide. Thylaina tipped the bottle, making certain the oil washed slowly over the xarflas. The moment the leaf moved, she snatched it, dragging it over Tesesra's tongue.

Tesesra swallowed, then grimaced. Breath slowing, she relaxed.

Fingertips to the woman's wrist, Thylaina felt the heartbeat, finding it had eased as well. "Light a candle and bring it here."

Once ten minutes passed, Thylaina reached for the candleholder from the younger maidservant. The dilation of Tesesra's eyes and her tongue's swelling had lessened. Thylaina then felt Tesesra's stomach and concentrated on the heartbeat within. Strong. Relief lowered her shoulders as she smiled at Bethlyn. "Her Ladyship should be ready to break fast in the morning."

The handmaiden stared, then suddenly threw her hands into the air. "Thank you! Praise the gods! Thank you!"

Katjina clapped, and Bramn smiled wide.

Exhausted, Thylaina looked at the empty teacup. What had Mikan given Tesesra?

Gentle shaking stirred Thylaina from a fitful sleep. A smile brightening Katjina's face was the first thing she saw, the handmaiden's pleasant visage chasing off nightmares about Tesesra and her babe.

"The marshal wishes to see you in his office." Katjina bobbed her head once, then perused the dresses in the wardrobe.

Thylaina sat up and stretched, pausing upon the sweet fragrance touched with a hint of raspberry. A vase with a spray of small red flowers was on the bedside table. Mayrb'ea were amongst her favorites, and she often visited the few allotments where they grew in the Royal Garden. "Did you bring the flowers?"

Cheeks turning pink, Katjina hung a purple dress on the changing screen. "I believe Sir Bramn's taken a fancy to you."

"I hope not." Thylaina eased out of bed.

"You'd be the only maiden in Caerabis. So many are trying to gain his favor… *and* Captain Colmstad's." The handmaiden giggled.

Just hearing Breydon's name soured Thylaina's morning. The flowers may well have wilted. Certainly, the captain was handsome, but his cruelty revealed his true ugliness. She could never find him attractive. Let the other maidens gain his attention. Thylaina did not want any more of it.

At least Bramn was a pleasant man. A gentle man, or so it seemed. The memory of his preparing to defend her from Mikan resurfaced, which left her considering Katjina's assumption. But could the man have already developed strong enough feelings toward Thylaina? Unlikely. However, it did not mean a swyve with the knight was out of consideration.

She slid to the edge of the bed and stared at the red blooms. "I shall have to thank Sir Bramn."

"How is your hand this morning, m'lady?"

The scabs on her palm were gone, pink lines showed instead of red, and the bruising was barely visible. With all the flexing and massages Thylaina had performed, the progress was no surprise. Master Eidryn would be proud of her. "Much improved."

She washed her face, then sat at the vanity. "Although red is not a suitable color for me, I should like to wear some of these flowers in my hair today."

Tittering, Katjina removed the dress from the screen. "Something green and gold, then, instead of violet."

This pampering was undeserved. Thylaina *was* a prisoner, yet they did not treat her like one—except for the constant guard. A handsome knight. One who gifted flowers.

Such silly thoughts to have, and ones she should have discarded. No plausible reason to ponder an affair with a human existed. Especially for *her*. Tainting her bloodline was unthinkable, even if Bramn was of noble upbringing. But he would not leave her mind.

"What is it, m'lady?" Katjina asked while brushing Thylaina's hair. "You're frowning."

"It is nothing of which to be concerned." *Just ridiculous fantasies.*

"Very well. Let's get you dressed so you can meet with the marshal before breaking fast."

Katjina braided a few of the mayrb'ea into Thylaina's hair, bringing the long coil over her shoulder, where she could see the blooms. The flowers accented the dark-green dress the handmaiden had chosen. Gold thread streamed from the neckline, sleeve cuffs, and hem. For a human, the handmaiden had a fine fashion sense.

Bramn waited outside the bedchamber door. A grin spread over his fine lips when he saw the flowers in Thylaina's hair. "You look stunning, my lady."

She curtsied. "Thank you for the mayrb'ea."

He scrunched his face. "What are—? Ah. That is what you call the flowers."

"What do you call them here?"

Eyelids lowering halfway, he whispered, "Virgin's Lust."

Thylaina caught her breath. "Why?"

A devious smile was his only reply.

She cleared her drying throat. "Why the flowers?"

Chuckling, he glanced at the floor between them, then stared into her eyes. "You don't know?"

His laughter and smile should not have sent a hint of a stirring within her, yet it did. Taming the desire, she entwined her fingers behind her and nodded. "I suppose I do. Thank you. They are lovely, and I adore their fragrance."

"You're welcome." Bramn gestured to the other end of the landing. "Marshal Momestid awaits."

Katjina walked behind Thylaina and Bramn, seeming to keep her distance while they took their time strolling to the southern end of the long hall.

"Has Her Ladyship awakened?" Thylaina asked.

Bramn's head fell back as he laughed. "With quite an appetite, I've heard."

"That is grand news."

"It is." He stopped and took her hand. "We're all grateful. More than you can imagine." His lips were warm on her fingers, the kiss soft. "Lady Tesesra is like a sister to Breydon and me. We love her dearly."

God, the captain again!

Thylaina gently tugged her hand away. "I pray last night does not repeat itself." Which was not a lie. There was still the mystery of the one ingredient Mikan had put in the tea, and why he added feverfew.

They resumed to Arhgrim's office.

Unfortunately, Captain Colmstad stood behind the marshal. A shame his excursion did not keep him from Caerabis longer. However, he bowed his head respectfully to Thylaina. Perhaps he might no longer be an overbearing ass.

"Wait outside, Sir Bramn," the marshal said.

"Sir." Bramn left.

Strange how the room felt different without his aura. The comfort he exuded was gone, as was his scent, which Thylaina had not noticed until that moment. A mild fragrance of leather and sage trailed toward the door. The herb must have been infused in his soap.

"Please sit," Arhgrim said, his eyes bright.

Thylaina lowered to the middle chair. Arhgrim sat, and Breydon remained standing at the back corner of the marshal's seat.

"Sir Bramn told me everything that transpired last night," Arhgrim began. "I'm deeply grateful for what you've done."

Breydon nodded once.

Glad to have possibly prevented something dreadful from happening, Thylaina smiled. "It was fortunate I could help her."

All joy faded from the men's faces.

"How do you mean?" Breydon asked.

He had not sent for her, the marshal had, so why was *he* asking questions?

"Only that I worry about her condition, and I mistrust Mikan's care for—"

"How dare you!" The captain stepped around the desk, pointing at her.

"Breydon." Voice firm, Arhgrim raised his hand, halting his friend. "I'd like to hear her reasons."

Thylaina glanced at Breydon. "I will not speak with Shapele Colmstad present."

He spun to the marshal, swinging his arm in her direction. "This is preposterous!"

"Please, Breydon." Arhgrim gestured toward the door.

Disbelief and hurt skewed the captain's face as he straightened. "Yes, sir," he snapped. Unlike the last time he had been upset with the marshal, he stomped to the door, slamming it shut behind him. Hushed talking from beyond started between the two knights, but Thylaina did not focus on it.

Arhgrim shifted his gaze from the entrance to Thylaina and sighed. "You're difficult with him."

Thylaina huffed a laugh. "*I* am difficult with *him*? After all he did to me, and how poorly he treats me?"

He waved her complaint aside. "Forgive me, you're correct. I believe I'm still trying to make excuses for him. A habit I've developed this past year." Arhgrim appeared worn. "Breydon truly is a—"

"Fine man." Arms crossed, Thylaina tried to keep her tone steady, but her face heated with each word. "I have heard plenty of times, and know not why everyone attempts to convince me."

"I see." Scratching the crown of his head, Arhgrim sat back. "I'll not keep you from breaking fast for long, but I'd like to understand what you mean about Mikan. Are you implying foul deeds?"

To make an accusation without proof could worsen her situation in Caerabis. Thylaina did not need more humans in the city holding her captive to think vilely of her. Especially those who might cause trouble, such as Captain Colmstad and Mikan himself.

"I only wonder if your priests are as learned in herbs as someone such as myself," she said. "Mikan may have used an herb for Her Ladyship's pain without realizing its danger toward her and the babe."

Arhgrim's brow twitched downward. "Is that so?"

"It is commonly used to ease headaches. He might have believed it would—"

The marshal raised his hand, silencing her. "I thank you for your thoughts, my lady. I assure you, Alohrian high priests know how to use herbs. We have an herbal priest who grows them and makes potions as well."

These men would never listen to her. It might take a death before they truly heard her warnings.

Thylaina sank against the chair. "S'yai, my lord."

"I do appreciate your concerns. Above all else, I thank you for caring for my wife."

"You are most welcome, Marshal Momestid." Although sincere, the words came out in a mumble.

He stood and motioned to the entrance. "You may break fast."

Frustration hastened her steps to the door. Stubborn men like Arhgrim were nothing new. Her uncle was the same, and that was why her cousin, Valraahn, left Etharell. Men in power do not listen. When she stepped through the threshold, Bramn and Breydon stared at her, appearing annoyed; Katjina was gone. Thylaina had not been listening, so knew not if they were still talking afore she opened the door.

The captain brushed past her, slamming the door shut again. His voice rose enough for her to hear. Likely for Bramn as well.

"At what point during her imprisonment will she begin her punishment, sir?" Breydon asked.

"You needn't worry," Arhgrim replied. "She starts tomorrow."

"Come, my lady." Bramn offered his arm for the first time. "Katjina awaits in the dining hall."

Cheeks warming, Thylaina accepted. His muscles hardened beneath her hand for the briefest moment as they smiled at each other.

"I want Bramn replaced," the captain said.

Stilling, Thylaina and Bramn looked at the door.

Arhgrim chuckled. "Enough, Breydon. I trust him."

"She's enchanted him!" Breydon boomed.

Bramn guided her to the stairs, flashed a charming smile. "I'll not deny that."

"Why would the shapele say that?"

"Because I defended you." He stopped in the hallway, then glanced both directions. "And I questioned Mikan." Their bodies nearly touched as he neared. "You were worried last night. You still are."

Sage smelled fine on him.

Thylaina nodded the slightest. "S'yai."

"And Breydon's a fool." He resumed leading her to the dining hall.


Thylaina spent the day in the garden, dodging the laborers while memorizing the different plants' locations. The rich soil and dedicated work brought forth a fine yield thus far. One gardener explained the frost should arrive in four weeks, so harvesting and planting were crucial until then. That meant there was plenty for Thylaina to do. At least Captain Colmstad left her alone. Or maybe Bramn guarding the entrance prevented him from approaching her again.

Sir Bramn... His kindness, care, and lingering gazes left her cheeks heated and heart thumping. How long had it been since a man treated her with equal fondness? Aarosyn Basylla. Gods! That was over a hundred years ago. Although the bond with her dear friend was special and deep, it was not love. Thylaina had never truly *loved* any man, yet she did not regret sharing Aarosyn's bed nor giving her purity to him. She missed him, just as she missed all her friends who left to serve in the armies or xilys.

The sorrow diminished as Thylaina wiped sweat from her nape and stared at Bramn while he turned southward. Did intimate thoughts like hers entertain the handsome knight while he gazed toward the farmsteads?

During the remainder of the afternoon, while walking aside each other, his fingers often grazed Thylaina's, and the smiles were constant. This relationship was blooming quickly.

On the way to sup, Thylaina visited Tesesra first. Bethlyn appeared surprised at her arrival. Nadiera sat next to her mother, her feet beneath the covers. Flames flickered in the lamps on both bedside tables, and the logs crackled in the hearth.

"Blessed evening, Sir Bramn." Nadiera's cheeks shaded pink.

"Blessed evening, my lady." He grabbed a chair from near the window and moved it to the bedside. A smile stretched as he gestured to it. "Lady Thylaina."

She sat, one corner of her lips rising. Nadiera sneered.

"How do you feel, Your Ladyship?" Thylaina asked Tesesra.

Sighing, Tesesra ran her fingers through Nadiera's hair. "I want out of bed. But I understand *you* insist I continue resting."

"I did."

"I'm not a child!" Her Ladyship sputtered through her pursed lips, then giggled.

"But something was... terribly wrong." Thylaina watched every movement Tesesra made. "And you need time to recover."

Nadiera stared at Thylaina as she wrapped her slender fingers around her mother's wrist.

A snort sounded from Tesesra's nose as she sank slightly and nodded. "There is... just so much to do." She tittered.

Thylaina frowned at the odd behavior. "And many here to help you."

"I'm the one who's... who's in control." Tesesra offered a stern expression, but then laughed so hard, her belly bounced up and down.

Thylaina moved to the edge of the chair and held the woman's chin. Her Ladyship's eyes were dilated again. "Did you drink something tonight?"

Bethlyn straightened her back. "Mikan brought a soothing tea."

Desire to yell tight in her throat, Thylaina glared at the handmaiden. She looked at Bramn, who scowled. "You let her drink more after last night?" she asked Bethlyn, then scanned the room. No cup tonight.

"I insisted," Tesesra said. "And there's no pain. I'm certain I ate something last night that caused my distress."

Yet it had not been distress.

Thylaina pulled Bethlyn to the vanity. "I trust nothing the priest gives her."

"My lady," the handmaiden hushed. "That's a dreadful accusation."

"I would rather be wrong than correct." Thylaina hesitated when Bramn joined. No. She trusted him. She had to. "Please send for me afore giving Lady Tesesra anything the priests bring. I care not if it offends them or upsets her."

Bethlyn's knuckles whitened as she bunched her apron. "Does she look as she did last night? No. She's fine. Mikan takes care of her."

"Please trust me." Thylaina rested her hands on the handmaiden's shoulders. "Her Ladyship has lost too much. We cannot risk losing this babe... nor her."

Bethlyn nibbled on the corner of her lip as she regarded her charge. After a silent debate, she nodded. "Very well."

# Chapter Five

Thylaina ignored her growling stomach to see Tesesra prior to breaking fast. The sun's pink glow shone through the curtains, presenting a calm aura to the room. Her Ladyship complained of a terrible headache, so Thylaina sent for a bowl of warmed water. She poured bossel powder into it, leaving very little of the ground root in the vial. With help from the servants, Tesesra moved to the chair next to the bed. Thylaina set the bowl on the poor woman's lap, draped a towel over her head and the steaming bowl, and instructed her to breathe deeply. While changing the bedding, the chambermaids watched, their work slow. Fists on her hips, Bethlyn snapped at them to stop gawking and finish their duties. No doubt gossip about the city's most intriguing prisoner would spread throughout the mansion.

By the time the bed was ready, Tesesra's treatment was complete. She hooted when Thylaina lifted the towel.

Thylaina giggled. "You must feel improved."

"I do. Although it was uncomfortable."

"Let us get you back into bed."

Bramn stepped forward to assist. "Your color looks perfect, Your Ladyship."

Snuggled under the covers, Tesesra stretched her grin. "Oh, Sir Bramn, you make me blush."

Gods! The man's handsome smile made Thylaina's breath catch. When Arhgrim entered the chamber, Bramn straightened, his grin wider. "Marshal."

Arhgrim ran his fingers along his wife's damp hairline. "Is something wrong?"

"N'ei." Thylaina patted the drier side of the towel along Her Ladyship's face and hair. "I was treating her aching head."

"Did it work?"

"Yes, my love." Tesesra grabbed his hand and sighed. "And I'm starving."

"I'll tend to that, Your Ladyship." Bethlyn exited the chambers.

"Very good." Arhgrim gave a grateful nod to Thylaina. "Do remember you begin in the garden today."

The moment of joy deflated, Thylaina curtsied. "Of course, my lord."

He narrowed his eyes. "You may break fast."

"Come." Bramn motioned for Thylaina to follow him.

Her steps were small on the way to the dining chamber. "Why can I not serve in here? I am better suited to helping Lady Tesesra."

A low chuckle sounded in his throat. "Because you stole from the garden." Sometimes, that drawl made it difficult to know whether he was being serious or pretentious. That damn attractive drawl Thylaina had come to adore.

On the way to the dining hall, maidservants tried to gain Bramn's notice, but he replied with a nod or a, "Good morrow." The women's cheeks tinged rosy. He continued walking beside Thylaina, his gaze forward. The man had no notion of how much they longed for his attention; however, it seemed Thylaina had it instead. To test whether her suspicion was true, she released a loud sigh.

He looked at her. "Does something trouble you, my lady?"

Mind whirring with a quick response, she uttered nonsensical noises afore sputtering, "Tesesra!"

"What about her?"

Damn it to Darkness! The test of whether Bramn's interest was solely in her left her struggling for a quick lie.

"My lady?"

"What if I am needed while I am in the garden?" That should do it.

He grabbed the large, curved door handle of the dining hall and stared at her, appearing thoughtful. "That's an awfully long run from the garden to tend to Her Ladyship. Perhaps we'll see how she feels this evening."

They entered the hall; the chamber felt odd. Stifling. As they neared the table, the pressure on Thylaina's chest increased.

Captain Colmstad was there, but the seat next to him was not vacant for Bramn; Mikan kept him company while enjoying porridge and fruit. The priest regarded Thylaina, then Bramn. Breydon smirked.

Mikan lowered his spoon and sat back. "Good morrow, Sir Bramn," he said. "I wish you'd join Captain Colmstad at the temple for morning prayers. You all could use the blessings."

Bramn pulled back the chair across from the priest for Thylaina, then bowed. "Valorius' Blessings upon you, Mikan." As Thylaina lowered to her chair, he sat beside her, across from Breydon. "Like many others these busy days, I say my prayers at home before first light."

"Why not at the temple? Come to me and gain further graces." Mikan's gaze shifted to Thylaina.

"Lessindra's Gifts are what those in Caerabis need most," she said.

The captain slammed his cup on the table, spilling milk on his hand. "How dare you."

Still staring at Thylaina, Mikan patted Breydon's arm a few times, curled his fingers over it. "All's well, Captain. I'm not offended by the bountiful gifts Valorius' lover bestows upon us. I often go into Her temple to... enjoy viewing them." He hummed a chuckle.

Thylaina envisioned the awful statue, and by the priest's snicker, so did he. "You are foul."

Breydon's fist pounded on the table. "Cease your disrespect!"

"Sir," Bramn said, failing to draw his friend's attention.

"Come now, my lady." Mikan rested his elbow on the chair's arm, then his chin on his hand. His eyes appeared icy. "There is no reason for such hostility."

"Why the feverfew?" she asked. "And what else are you adding to Lady Tesesra's tea?"

An unreadable mask overcoming his face, he blinked slowly. "Like you, I'm a healer."

"Then you know it will harm the babe."

The priest squinted as he slid his fingers down his throat, like a silent threat.

"I tire of your lies." Breydon's voice was the lowest she had yet heard. Rumbling.

Mikan suddenly laughed. "Elves are terribly misinformed about herbs."

Thylaina stood and leaned forward. "My master and my uncle know more about Vynia's Gifts than you idiot humans who care so little of what She offers. I have seen how you destroy the beauty She provides!"

The priest rested his arms on the table and clasped his hands. "Tell me, my lady... who are your master and your uncle?"

Thylaina straightened her spine and set her chin. Hopefully, she presented an unreadable mask of her own as she sat.

"Answer his bloody question," the captain spat.

"*Sir*," Bramn said again.

"What?" Breydon yelled.

"You have milk," Bramn slid his finger side to side between his nose and lip, "there."

Everyone looked at the captain, who glowered at his friend. There it was, the slightest line of white just above the edge of his upper lip. It seemed to glow as his face darkened.

Thylaina turned her head, doing her best to hide a breathy laugh behind her hand. Once composed, she looked at the men. A hint of amusement shone in Mikan's eyes, but Breydon and Bramn continued staring at each other, the latter smiling.

The captain's chair groaned against the floor as he stood, wiping his mouth with his arm. He then pointed at Bramn. "One day, I'm going to beat that grin off you."

Tilting his head to the side, Bramn shrugged.

Mikan rose, bowed to Thylaina. "Have a blessed day." He left, with Breydon following.

The air was easier to breathe, the room less suffocating. Thylaina turned to Bramn, finding concern had conquered the gaiety in his eyes.

"Something's not right," he said.

"Mikan never answered my question about the herbs." Thylaina grasped his hand. "My first morning here, I had felt an odd sensation when he delivered my healing satchel... and just now."

Bramn's gaze darted to her, then to their hands. "I might be an idiot human, but I know my friend... my brother. Breydon's ire grows worse when he's with Mikan."

Regret for her choice of words in a moment of anger left her faltering, and she slid her hand from his. "Sir Bramn, I... I did not mean you—"

"I know what you meant." The knight smirked. "I tease." He kissed her hand. "Now, shall we break fast?"


While Thylaina worked in the garden, Bramn spoke to the marshal. Thankfully, he promised to keep matters concerning the high priest between them. Now was not the time to bring accusations against Mikan to Arhgrim, who trusted him too much. She and Bramn would have to approach the marshal together once they obtained proof of Mikan's wrongdoing. Thylaina prayed the time would come soon, for she did not wish to wait for something terrible to happen to Tesesra. Not to mention, it appeared Breydon's behavior troubled Bramn more than he first admitted. He just was not telling Thylaina.

Escany assigned Thylaina to pull weeds. Some were real bastards, too stubborn to leave the ground. A few times, Ardella bumped into her, once successfully pushing her into a plot full of leafy plants. By the time afternoon meal arrived, Thylaina's aching fingers were red.

All the laborers sat against the wall, taking refuge in the shade as they took salted meat, cheese, and bread from baskets. Thylaina had hoped Katjina or Bramn would bring her a fitting meal, but neither arrived. A slice of bread landed on Thylaina's lap, then bounced onto the dirt.

"That's for you, criminal." Escany chuckled.

The sun's brightness forced her to squint as she tilted her head back to address him. "Then I shall like a fresh slice."

He squatted, his nose wrinkled in a sneer. "Think you can do to me as you did to Ardella? You can't. They can't replace me." He spat a glob of mucus onto the bread, then stood. "Eat that or nothing." A small plume of dust rose from beneath his heels as he stomped across the garden. Escany must have felt a sense of importance by treating her like that.

"Here." A woman sitting a few feet away offered pieces of meat and cheese.

Salted meat was not Thylaina's favorite, but it was better than filthy bread. "I am grateful."

There was no livestock within the city, so the meat must have come from a southern farmstead. Beyond the salt, it tasted like rabbit. Hunters, then. She chewed slowly, thinking of her last night at the palace. The memory of vomiting rabbit in the Royal Garden left her feeling queasy, so she put the meat in her pocket and drank water offered by two children carrying buckets.

Gavrel strode through the gate, bearing a small sack. He nodded to some of the laborers as he headed to Thylaina. "My lady," he said, then glanced toward Escany, who watched. "Katjina told me you were here."

Sighing, Thylaina stood. "Beginning my punishment."

Sadness flickered in his eyes as he viewed her from head to skirt. "You look miserable."

"I am." *And hungry.* However, his presence encouraged a smile. "Why are you here?"

"I brought something for you." He lifted the sack. "I came upon this plant while patrolling the plains with my squad."

Interest piqued, she took the sack and opened it. Xarflas. Delighted—no, thrilled—Thylaina released a breathy laugh. "Thank you, Gavrel. This is wonderful."

"I'm glad." He grinned broadly. "I feared to have made a fool of myself if I had brought a useless weed."

It was sweet of him to have gathered something for her at all. Resting her palm on his cheek, she said, "I would have appreciated that as well, for you wished to do a kindness for me."

His skin warmed beneath her touch. "I think I'd do anything for you," he whispered.

Bramn entered the garden, his gaze southward. It seemed to fix on the massive mill in the distance afore he scanned the laborers, finding Thylaina and Gavrel. Hopefully, his arrival meant she had finished for the day. He frowned as he joined them. "Let me guess, Dubight, Captain Eilisar gave you the remainder of the day again?"

Gavrel's spine stiffened. "I just returned from plains duty, sir."

"That means little to me when you're interrupting *her* duties."

Thylaina huffed as she looked from Bramn to Gavrel. "We are breaking for afternoon meal, Sir Bramn. He interrupts nothing."

A hint of a smile lifted the corner of Gavrel's mouth.

"I'm dismissing him, just the same." Bramn gestured to the gates.

The dubight bowed to Thylaina. "I wish you a blessed day, my lady."

"Thank you." She held the sack close. "This is a wonderful gift."

He opened his mouth, a question lingering, but then his eyes darted to Bramn and he appeared to think better. Perhaps about the first gift he gave her: the container, straps, and terrible whipping stick now burned to ashes.

Thylaina nodded once. "I appreciate both gifts immensely."

A deep blush bloomed beneath his freckles as he smiled and bowed his head. "You're most welcome, my lady." Gavrel left without showing courtesy to Bramn.

Thylaina did not blame him. It seemed the knight had ill feelings toward the young man.

Bramn sighed heavily. "You decided not to heed my suggestion."

"It was hardly a suggestion." She clutched the sack. "And I am not allowing anyone to tell me whose company I may enjoy."

He regarded her for a moment, as if contemplating her words, then appeared to understand. Clearing his throat, he viewed the garden and laborers. "How do you fare?"

"I am miserable." She showed him her hand, blisters already forming.

Bramn inspected the slightly bubbled, discolored flesh. It seemed minutes passed beneath the sun as he stared, unmoving. "That looks... awful." Bramn curled her fingers closed, but did not let go. "Come."

They walked to the nearby structure outside the garden walls, which she learned was a storage building. Bramn looked southward several times during that brief stroll, where there was nothing but the farmsteads and the windmill. When he faced Thylaina, guilt marred his handsome face.

"I am staying here, am I not?" she asked.

"And I am with you." His voice was unusually soft, the drawl barely noticeable.

As his head lowered, his thumb grazed over her palm. This was the first time Bramn had seen the damage Breydon had done.

She slid her hand free of his easy hold. "This is not of your doing."

"It was wrong."

"Have you ever stopped him from doing this to another?"

Bramn blinked, looked to the south again. "It's not the same."

"The bloody Darkness it is not!"

Silence. He looked down and kicked a rock aside. Lashing a prisoner's hand must be a common punishment.

After a controlled breath, Thylaina nodded. "I best return."

The knight followed her to the garden, keeping less than forty feet back while she worked. Strange that Escany and Ardella did not display poor behavior toward her while Bramn was present.


Thylaina did not join the Momestids for supper, but stayed in her chamber with her hands in a bowl of ice-filled water. What a blessing humans also had ice houses! She had believed only elves were ingenious enough to bring ice from the coldest mountain peaks. While humans kept it stored in cavernous rooms beneath the ground, Haevaun Flameral kept its supply in a marble building near the scullery. The reigning Elf King maintained its temperature with a spell cast during the coldest day of the Cold Moon. Wagons used to retrieve the ice from the Cliffshield Mountains remained in that same room until its next journey, usually taken in the fall.

Although her hands numbed amid the floating ice, the water felt wonderful. She wiggled her fingers, the ripples bobbing the slowly melting pieces on the surface.

"Are you certain you don't wish to eat?" Katjina asked.

"I am." Thylaina removed her hands, let the water trail off until it dripped.

Katjina stretched a towel and gently patted Thylaina's palms. "I'm sorry if this causes pain."

It hurt an awful lot. Thylaina's left hand had just recovered from Breydon's assault, and now it throbbed again.

"Will your balm work?" the handmaiden asked.

Thylaina did not have enough bossel powder. And the roots Mikan provided still needed at least another week to dry. "N'ei."

A knock sounded.

"Lady Thylaina," Bramn called. "I brought supper."

Katjina's face brightened. "He brought your meal," she whispered. "I told you he was fond of you."

Thylaina had not spoken to him since her outburst that afternoon, nor did she have much to say now. Perhaps he wished to make amends. She motioned to the door, then sat on the chair by the small fireplace while re-wrapping her hands in the towel.

"Greetings," he said after entering, yet remained near the door.

"Good night, Katjina," Thylaina said.

"Good night, m'lady. Sir Bramn." The handmaiden hurried from the room.

He looked odd holding a tray, and Thylaina could not help wondering if he had ever bore one afore.

"They served poached trout tonight. Although I don't like it, I understand you might've enjoyed it immensely." Bramn set the tray on the table beside her chair.

Dill, along with something tangy, wafted in the air. Spiced potatoes, a thick piece of yellow, porous bread, and a glass of wine accompanied the fish. While she ate, Bramn relaxed in the chair across from her and shared about the menial chatter during supper. Everyone had expressed their concerns about Thylaina, but he assured them she was only exhausted. He did not say whether Breydon had inquired. Thylaina doubted it.

Supper was delicious, especially the bread, which Bramn explained the cooks had made from corn. It was difficult to imagine humans could be as skilled as the cooks at the palace scullery in Haevaun Flameral. To have made such sweet bread out of that strange vegetable? Amazing!

Once she finished eating, he pulled his chair closer and sat forward. "Show me your hands."

"There is naught to see."

His gaze fixed on hers. "You struggled to eat—to hold your fork."

She hesitated, but held out both hands, palms up.

For such a powerful man, Bramn showed tenderness. His fingers caressed the backs of her hands, then over her aching palms. Suddenly, he rose. "There was little I could do with the marshal, but I shall speak with Tes." Bramn smirked. "I doubt she can resist my charm."

If he managed to free Thylaina from garden labor, she doubted *she* could resist his charm much longer.

"I would be obliged," she said.

He did it! The next morning, Bramn convinced Lady Tesesra that Thylaina was better suited serving her punishment in the mansion. The sudden change displeased Arhgrim, and Captain Colmstad was furious. Breydon's shouts carried from beyond the closed cabinet doors, filling the landings and entrance hall where servants bustled and guards stood. Glances darted toward Thylaina as she followed Bramn and Katjina from the third floor to the first.

"We can't trust her!" he bellowed. "The elf's using her beauty to trick others into doing what she wants. And she's a spy!"

Everyone in the mansion would surely think the same of her as Breydon did.

Not Bramn. His eyes brightened and his smile stretched when he looked at Thylaina. She could not wait for them to have a moment alone to thank him properly. Now she no longer had to endure Escany and Ardella. Besides, the scullery might be an interesting experience, and Thylaina might have helpful advice about the herbs.

Breydon's rage faded as they walked further down the corridor leading to the scullery. The heat of humiliation, however, remained.

The scullery bustled under the leadership of the head cook, Viya, who kept her nine maidens on the task of preparing afternoon meal and supper. A tight red bulge of hair peeked from beneath a small head covering, and her brown eyes constantly darted throughout the chamber and at the scullery maidens. She was a thick woman of strength, standing nearly six feet tall. Viya handled the brunt of the cauldrons' weight, even with two scullery maids helping to move them from table sides to one of the three large hearths; she carried bulky sacks of potatoes; and pushed aside the tables topped with a variety of cooking items and tools. Nothing stood in her way. She shouted commands, preventing anyone from remaining idle for too long, even those who fought for Bramn's attention. And the scullery maids seemed to love her.

They smiled while responding to her orders, giggled when she snapped at them, and a few even called her, "Auntie Viya."

Katjina interrupted Viya from rubbing herbs on a pig's head and side slab to introduce Thylaina.

The head cook's brow furrowed. "What good are you in the kitchen?"

Thylaina looked away from the animal's decapitated head and beady eyes to give Viya her attention. "I-I... Well, I am familiar with herbs."

"All of us know herbs. What can you cook?"

"I am n'ei a scullery maid."

Viya sighed over her shoulder at Bramn. Facing Thylaina, she asked, "What good are you to me, then?"

"I am an excellent pupil."

"I've a full kitchen and no room to teach anyone else, just as I told Her Ladyship!"

Wonderful. Another enemy.

Katjina stepped forward. "Lady Thylaina truly understands herbs. She helped when Her Ladyship fell ill two nights past."

"I heard about that." Clamping her teeth on the corner of her lip, Viya viewed Thylaina from head to skirt hem. "I heard you shoved a leaf into her mouth."

Thylaina caught Bramn bobbing his head once. She nodded. "I know many healing remedies."

"So do we." Viya set her greasy, herb-covered hands on her hips and released a heavy breath as she scanned the large kitchen. "I don't know where to put you."

"I can gather herbs and other items from the garden."

"The very place you were just removed from?" Viya laughed. "Oh. You elves sure are queer."

Bramn covered his mouth, hiding his laughter; the women near him giggled. One offered the knight a fruit.

"Please put me with someone who will teach more about your people and foods," Thylaina said. "I am fascinated to learn."

Viya regarded her. "Very well." She turned to a young woman rolling dough beneath a solid, cylindrical piece of wood. "Panya, teach this elf how to top a pie!"

"Damn," a young woman muttered.

"You were a fresh daisy here once before." Viya laughed again. "You might be getting better, but you're not leading a kitchen yet. Now do as I said."

Panya sighed, then mumbled, "Yes, Viya."

Thylaina bowed her head. "Thank you."

"Don't thank me just yet. You might regret it." Cackling, Viya walked to the back door, barely grunting as she pulled it open. Steel bands reinforced the heavy door. Five feet from the bottom was a peek-door, also reinforced, but with small bars just outside the opening.

Bramn approached Thylaina. "She's a lovely woman."

"Pleasant indeed."

He grinned. "Better than Escany."

"My lady!" Panya called. "Best come here, or Viya'll learn. And you don't want her wrath. Trust me." The other women nodded.

"I best return to the chamber and prepare for this evening." Katjina curtsied to Thylaina and Bramn, then left.

Thylaina neared Panya, pointed at the dough she flattened. "Why do you do that?"

"This?" She raised the wooden item. "I'm rolling the pie crusts flat."

"I see."

"Let's get to work, shall we?"

Although she had seemed reluctant to have Thylaina as a pupil, Panya was a delight once she learned Thylaina would handle none of the food. Thylaina's hands had improved from the previous night's icing, yet they still ached, so she observed how the scullery maids performed their tasks, and studied the large chamber to learn what was where. A few of the women sang songs together, others gossiped, and two desperately attempted to gain Bramn's attention.

Twenty minutes later, four pies had been topped, and Viya returned with a basket full of corn.

"Are you making some of that delicious bread tonight?" Thylaina asked.

The head cook raised a brow. "Goodness, you're daft! We don't make it with fresh corn." She laughed again and walked to the other side of the kitchen, plopping the basket onto a large table against the wall.

Cheeks flushing, Thylaina frowned.

The maiden beside her elbowed Thylaina gently. "Viya doesn't mean any harm. Honestly. She had a terrible instructor. Her mother. Always called her names."

"It does not mean she can—"

"She doesn't know any different," Bramn said. "I hear she's improving."

"That she is." Panya laid the flattened dough over slices of apple glistening with melted butter, cinnamon, and another spice with which Thylaina was not familiar. "There, last one."

Bramn pushed a small mound of flour with his finger. "It's time to leave, my lady."

Thylaina tilted her head. "What do you mean?"

"Your duties for the day are complete. You were only meeting the others and finding your place in the kitchen."

"Oh."

He smirked. "Besides, you can't eat supper with us while in here, can you?"

Thylaina removed the apron, glanced at the pies. She looked forward to trying one. "Have a fine day, ladies."

Some maidens waved, although likely at Bramn. Others were too busy to acknowledge she had spoken. Viya huffed.

By the time they reached Thylaina's chamber, Katjina had just hung a marigold dress outside the wardrobe. "Do you wish to have a bath first, m'lady?" she asked.

"Please."

"Of course, m'lady." Katjina left, humming a song.

Although it seemed like so little had taken place today, joy from gaining a position in the scullery encouraged Thylaina to dance. Bramn had lingered in the doorway, apparently awaiting an invitation. The words poised upon her lips, but he entered, closed the door, and leaned against it.

"That was an exhausting day," he said.

She laughed into her palm. "I know not how you survived with n'ei reinforcement. Honestly, Sir Bramn, the scullery maids nearly had you surrendering."

His smile widened. "That's what Breydon's for." The gleam in his eyes faded. "Or... he once was."

What a shame to see him downtrodden.

Thylaina reached out with both hands, wiggled her fingers. "I must thank you."

"For?"

"Taking care of me. You do more than is required. I do not deserve your kindness."

Bramn gently grabbed one of her hands and kissed her fingers. "You deserve better."

"Dance with me."

"Dance?" A nervous laugh escaped him. "I-I know not that—"

"Please?" Thylaina tugged, catching him off guard and pulling him closer. At least, he wanted her to believe as much. "Although tired, I am delightfully happy because of you."

"Ah, yes." He raised her right arm and walked a circle in the same direction. "No more Escany and Ardella."

Thylaina giggled as he lowered her hand, then lifted the left and circled the opposite way. "And n'ei more bastard weeds."

"My lady." He paused, feigning shock. "To hear such a word from you."

"Have *you* ever pulled those bloody weeds?"

"No, but I saw your hands."

Laughing, they spun faster.

"No more days in the unbearable sun for either of us," he sang. What a horrible voice. Bramn should never sing again. He grabbed her hips and twirled twice; she emitted a playful yelp. Feet gently returned to the floor, their nearness remained, as did his touch. Desire lit his gaze. Perfect. Bramn felt the same as she, and they could sate their need.

Pressed against his hard body, Thylaina slid her hand up his nape, delving her fingers into his hair. She raised to her toes and brushed her lips over his.

The force with which he pushed away sent her back a few steps. "Don't. Don't do this."

Heat spread over her cheeks as she blinked. "Sir Bramn, I—"

"I was speaking to myself." He glanced at her. "It's not you. It's me." His shoulders expanded, then lowered, his breath released. "You're a temptation of which I cannot indulge."

It should not have hurt, but the words stung, leaving her empty. Embarrassed. "Is it because I am a prisoner? Or because I am an elf?"

He stared at the charred logs. "Neither of those reasons deters me." Bramn finally looked at her. "But that my heart belongs to another."


A few men joined in the feast hall for supper; knights Thylaina had yet to meet. One of them introduced himself as Captain Miryl Eilisar, and Thylaina paused upon hearing his name. Gavrel had mentioned him in the orchard. Amongst his other duties, Captain Eilisar handled most of the training with the dubights, of which there were few. He was also third in command of the city. Shortly after the meal began, so did the political discussions.

Thylaina barely heard them as the afternoon's events consumed her thoughts, leaving her perplexed. Although Bramn spoke now and then, adding an occasional laugh, his eyes revealed an occupied mind. The judging glares from Breydon only agitated Thylaina's confusion. She had said nothing to him, yet he ate, drank, and stared at her as if he wished to damage her right hand. Then again, his upset about her punishment changing probably prompted a desire to crack the edged stick over her palm. The man enjoyed hurting her. Thank Bryric the stick was no more.

And Bramn had misled her. The flowers, the nearness, the gazes... he had done everything but outright express fondness. Thylaina was such a fool. All she had hoped for was an exceptional thronging afore supper. Thylaina was no dolt. She could not love a human, but laying with one was a different matter. Not that she had ever lain with one. Yet Bramn did not want to be with her. Thrice he had hesitated to turn away her offer to share ortia louvres. In the end, his devotion to a farm girl overcame desire. And why? He was unwedded. Most elves shared open relationships prior to marriage, and it surprised her that humans did not.

Bramn patted her hand and whispered, "Are you trying to break the arm off the chair?"

Thylaina's knuckles had whitened. She relaxed her grip and slid her hand from beneath his. "I know what I wish to break."

Breydon arched a brow.

"That's unkind." Bramn laughed softly as he grabbed his goblet. "I had explained well enough. I expect you of all people to understand."

He had a point. His mother had been attempting to force him into one marriage after another to noblewomen he did not love. And despite his admittance that he was smitten with a farm maiden outside Caerabis, his mother did not cease her efforts. She refused to acknowledge his wish to court and marry Einasa because she was not from a family of wealth, despite that her father owned the flour mill. If Bramn continued the forbidden relationship, his mother would sever him from the family. For the past eight moons, he had kept his distance from the maiden, sending messages when possible. However, Einasa had yet to reply.

After he shared all of this with Thylaina, he asked, "How did you do it, my lady? How did you leave everything? It terrifies me to do such a thing."

She had been too upset and overwhelmed to answer.

Now, as she pondered what Bramn had shared with her, Thylaina regretted holding anger toward him. Releasing a deep breath, she squeezed his hand. "Forgive me. I had not been a friend when you needed. Perhaps we can speak further about the matter later."

Gratitude accompanied a relieved smile. "I appreciate that." He kissed her hand, then resumed eating with a hearty appetite.

Feeling better, Thylaina lifted her fork to satisfy her growling stomach, but when she turned to ask Arhgrim about Tesesra, Breydon's glower shifting between her and Bramn caught her notice. The captain did not hide his hatred, which nearly snuffed the candles between him and Thylaina. The question forgotten and appetite ruined, she returned to poking her meal with the fork.

Captain Colmstad no longer touched his supper, but just stared and drank.

"Breydon," Nadiera called, thankfully drawing his attention.

The shadows immediately fled, permitting light upon his face and into his eyes, showing a brilliant blue as he faced the child. The ugliness was gone, revealing a truly handsome man.

"Yes, Nadi?" The adoration in his voice matched what shone in his gaze.

The young girl looked from him to Thylaina. "Are you angry with her?"

His brows lowered briefly as he blinked, and the corners of his lips twitched.

"That's an inappropriate question," Arhgrim snapped.

A scowl marred Breydon's face as he lifted his cup, barely glancing in Thylaina's direction. He did not appear angry, but confused.

Watching him, she tilted her head. Had he any inkling of his behavior a moment ago?

Supper continued without further occurrences from Breydon, ending with a slice of the delicious apple pie. It was nearly as wonderful as the sweet dishes from home.

Exhausted from a physically and emotionally taxing day, Thylaina wished to retire, but Bramn was having a heated discussion with Captain Eilisar about men he called the Three. Katjina had mentioned the Three Marshals once while bathing Thylaina. That was when Thylaina learned there were two other captains in the city, Breydon being Caerabis' First Captain.

"The Three needn't push for something over which they have no control," Bramn said. "They must answer to someone, and that's what the Council is for. If the Council falls, those three men will do whatever they want."

Breydon frowned Bramn's way.

Miryl shook his head. "Why should commoners have any say in what the knighthood does?"

"Because we serve the commoners." Bramn chuckled in obvious disbelief. "Or have you forgotten?"

"Of course I haven't. But they shouldn't rule us."

"The Council doesn't rule us." Bramn refilled his goblet, then lifted it. "They maintain an order to prevent corruption."

"Do you realize what you're saying?" Contempt saturated Miryl's tone. "To suggest the Three Marshals might lead us from Valorius' Ways is blasphemous."

"Why?" Bramn snorted. "They're not gods. Don't forget that."

"Enough." Breydon stood and straightened his leather jacket, the material's creaking a slight offense compared to a week ago. "You'll not speak of the Three with disrespect, Sir Bramn."

Arhgrim's gaze shifted from one man to the other, ending on Thylaina.

She placed her dinner cloth on the bare pie dish. "I am ready to retire."

Bramn rose, then stretched. He hesitated upon Breydon observance. "Sir?"

The First Captain nodded once to Arhgrim, then strode for the exit.

"I'll take my leave as well." Miryl smiled as he bowed to Thylaina. "Your presence brightens this chamber, especially with Her Ladyship absent."

"Thank you, Shapele Eilisar."

His cheeks tinged red as he chuckled. "My, the way you say my name is musical." He looked at Bramn. "Rest well, my friend."

"Good night, Captain."

"Marshal." Miryl bobbed his head to Arhgrim.

"Captain."

Bramn and Thylaina wished a blessed evening to the marshal, then headed to the door. As they neared it, a servant approached.

"Pardon me, m'lady, but Viya sends for you."

Curious. There was only one way to learn why the head cook would summon Thylaina. With Bramn at her side, she followed the servant.

A few scullery maidens were cleaning tables and washing crocks, pots, ladles, and spoons. Viya stood at her tall table, sweeping the surface with a bundle of berryless knee holly. Tiny leaves scattered, which she swiped away with another pass of the shortened branches. She rested her arm on the table, the bundled brush standing upright, and her other fist on her hip. "What're you staring at?"

Thylaina straightened. "I am curious as to why you use knee holly to clean your table."

Viya viewed the bundle as if seeing it for the first time. "Is that what you elves call it? Well, here we call it butcher's broom. As you can see, it does a fine job clearing the tables' tops. But it does more." She extended her finger upward. "It removes the nasties to prevent illnesses from spreading."

"Nasties?"

Bramn cleared his throat, but Thylaina heard a chuckle as well.

Lids half lowered, Viya leaned on the table and sighed. "I didn't realize I was giving lessons to a woman I believed already educated."

Humans were so bloody rude. Thylaina had a mind to educate her.

"It's a simple word I use for the simple-minded help," Viya said. "Germs, m'lady."

Thylaina stared at the knee holly. It was not possible. Surely the humans concocted this, for Master Eidryn would have known. "Why butcher's broom?"

"Because it wor—Oh, the name, you mean?"

Thylaina nodded.

"I had sent for you to tend to another matter, but maybe this happened for a reason." Viya pulled a tall chair to the table and sat. At that moment, she appeared older and tired. "Butchers in Rhigowan and Karvorn used this to clear their blocks once their shops closed," she said. "After a few years, they discovered illnesses had lessened. Priests studied the plant, learning it cleaned germs left on the blocks by the fish and meat. Naturally, manor kitchens began using the brooms as well." She wiped sweat from her forehead. "What do you elves use it for?"

Thylaina smiled. "We use it to help people who struggle to release their bowels."

Laughter belted out from Bramn, and Viya scrunched her nose.

"Truly?" the cook asked.

"S'yai."

"To help someone have a shite?"

Bramn laughed louder.

Thylaina sighed.

"Interesting," Viya said. "I never would've thought."

"The reason you called for me?"

"Oh... Yes, m'dear." Viya scanned the scullery. "You girls leave now. I'll finish up."

The maidens dropped filthy rags into a bucket near the archway leading to winding stairs, talking as they headed up. "Good night, Sir Bramn!" one called back. Focused on Viya, he did not appear to hear the young woman.

The three of them now alone, the head cook leaned closer to Thylaina and Bramn. "I'm concerned about Her Ladyship."

"Why?" he asked.

"Mikan had a kettle of hot water sent to her." Viya shook her head. "But the chambermaids said Her Ladyship had suffered no pain today."

Fear clutched at Thylaina's heart, stilled it.

# Chapter Six

Thylaina paced afore the hearth, her entwined fingers lowering and rising. Helplessness was a feeling she wished to never to know again, but it now engulfed her. She wanted to rush to Tesesra's room and throw out the window whatever it was Mikan forced down Her Ladyship's throat. But Thylaina could not do that. Not even Bramn could do that, and he was close to the Momestid family.

The young knight sat in the chair, staring at the low fire in defeat. He *had* gone to Tesesra's chamber to speak with her, but Breydon was at the door, like Mikan's bloody guard dog, and refused Bramn entry.

Halting, Thylaina threw her hands up. "We cannot sit here and wait for something dreadful to happen!"

"What do you want me to do?" Bramn snapped. "He's standing guard."

"We go to the marshal." She knelt in front of him and grasped his hand. "I witnessed his distress at the thought of losing Lady Tesesra and the babe. He must listen."

"It doesn't mean he will."

"I wish I knew what Mikan added to her tea." She rose and faced the hearth. "I should know."

Bramn released a heavy breath as he stood. "I'm getting some rest. You should find sleep as well. You've had a long day."

Thylaina lowered to the chair he had just abandoned. "I cannot possibly sleep."

"Do nothing foolish." It appeared he wished to say something more, but he nodded once and headed for the door.

She watched the flames dance until she could no longer keep her eyes open.

Thylaina sat up. The orange glow from the fireplace gave enough light for her to adjust to the room's dimness. Concentrating, she stared at the door and waited. It had seemed a dream, but someone might have—

Two knocks rattled the chamber door.

"M'lady?" a woman called, her voice unsteady. "You're needed with great urgency."

*Vynia, please not Tesesra and the babe.* Thylaina hurried to open the door. The younger maidservant from Tesesra's bedchamber stood there, her eyes rimmed red. "What is it?" Thylaina asked.

"Her Ladyship... Sh-she's bleeding."

There was no time to worry, for it was important for a healer to remain calm and controlled. A role Thylaina had mastered decades ago. Without waiting for the servant, she snatched the satchel, then rushed into the corridor and up the stairs to the third floor. The wide-open door to Tesesra's chambers provided immediate access. Bright candlelight flickering from the bedroom revealed the empty, dark suite. No priest, no captain. In the bedchamber, two maidens darted about, following Bethlyn's orders. From in front of the opened window, the handmaiden spoke with a hushed voice, instructing a maiden to position more candles near the foot of the bed, where at least ten were already lit atop small tables and floor candelabras. Then Bethlyn moved to the bedside, wrung out a cloth in a bowl of water, and placed it on Tesesra's forehead.

Thylaina's gaze fell on the Lady of Caerabis.

Perspiration darkened her golden hair, and her gown clung to her curled body as she panted and moaned. Worse, blood saturated the bedding, mattress, and Tesesra's gown.

Upon seeing Thylaina, Bethlyn gave the maidservant who had sought help an annoyed glance. "Thank Valorius you're here," she said to Thylaina. Her tone was all but thankful.

The maidservant ran from the room, weeping.

Thylaina sat on the edge of the bed and looked at Bethlyn. "What are you doing?"

"What does it look like? I'm preparing for the babe."

"That may not be necessary." Thylaina placed her hand on Tesesra's stomach. Focusing, she ignored the mother's moans and pain. So much distress. The child was barely alive. Blinking tears back, she asked, "What happened?"

The handmaiden swiped the cloth from Tesesra's forehead and wetted it. Wringing the water out, she said, "Her Ladyship had trouble sleeping. No position eased the hurt."

"When did the bleeding begin?"

"Only twenty minutes past." Bethlyn shook her head. "But the pain grew awfully fast."

"What did Mikan give her?"

The woman's eyes hardened. "He cares about Her Ladyship."

"He must have given her something harmful. Perhaps without intent." Thylaina grabbed the Bethlyn's wrist and held her glare. "But I cannot help without knowing what it was."

The younger maidservant returned, her cheeks raw from rubbing and her eyes beginning to swell from the constant weeping. "He comes."

"The priest?" Thylaina asked.

"Marshal Momestid." The young woman moved the large chair beside the bed.

"You sent for him?"

Bethlyn yanked her arm free from Thylaina. "He's her husband."

"And he might make it difficult to tend to her." Thylaina bit her lip. These women did not know better. Or Arhgrim might have demanded to learn of any complications. "We must try to keep him out of the way."

"Tes?" Too late. Arhgrim stood at the entrance, his face pale. He rushed to kneel beside the bed. "Love?" His gaze shifted to the blood. "Please, not again."

Despite the reactions she had received thus far, Thylaina had to take a chance. She rested her hand on his shoulder. "I came earlier to help, but was denied entry. I must learn what Mikan puts in her tea."

"Enough!" He drew in a few scant breaths through gritted teeth. "Now's not the time."

"I only wish to—"

"I'll not have you question our high priest!" He stood and spun, his face now red. "Leave!"

Tears filled her eyes as control slipped away. Thylaina looked down at Tesesra, the poor woman groaning and weeping. "But the babe—"

"Leave now!"

Quaking, she grabbed the satchel and hurried from the room. Upon reaching the suite door to the landing, someone called out.

"M'lady!"

Thylaina continued. She did not want to be there when those bloody humans failed.

Leaned over the railing to breathe, cool air from below swept over her face. Thylaina closed her eyes and let the teardrops break free.

"M'lady, please." It was the maiden who had called upon her. She glanced toward the room, then whispered, "Go to the kitchen and ask for Panya."

Confused, Thylaina shook her head. "For what?"

"The teacup." The maidservant backed toward Tesesra's chambers. "I gave it to Panya." She closed the door.

Tesesra cried out, then Arhgrim yelled to Valorius.

Thylaina remained still, contemplating what the servant had just said. Someone other than Bramn trusted and believed her. "Bramn," she murmured.

Time was crucial, so Thylaina sped down the stairs and to the front door where two guards stood. One of them glanced up at the third floor, concern wrinkling his brow.

"My lady?" the other said.

"You must send for Sir Bramn."

"Not our duty."

The worried guard snapped his attention to his partner. "What?" Huffing in obvious disbelief, he looked at Thylaina. "I'll send for him."

The other sneered. "It's not our duty."

"Don't you hear Her Ladyship?"

Hoping to relax them, Thylaina wove a melody into her words. It did not matter if the charm rhymed, just that she maintained a calm note and a steady voice. "Time is short. Sir Bramn is important. Please send him to the scullery."

The guards quieted, their expressions eased into peace. "Yes, m'lady," the less friendly one said. "We'll get him for you."

"In haste," she said.

"Of course."

Thylaina palmed their cheeks. "I am most grateful."

They bowed. The kind and concerned guard opened the door and stepped outside.

Thylaina headed to the scullery. It was empty. Not knowing what to do, she sat and waited.

After a few minutes, she began pacing between tables. She stopped and approached the glowing embers beneath the cauldron. At least, there should have been embers, but there were two half-burnt logs still afire. Foolish, considering the scullery was part of the mansion. In Haevaun Flameral, the cooks performed their duty in a separate building to prevent fire spreading in the palace, should one happen. But humans were not as intelligent.

Twenty-five frustratingly slow minutes passed when Bramn entered, his loose hair framing his worried face. "I heard Tes when I entered the mansion."

"The babe is in danger, and I know not how much time remains."

"What can we do?"

"Do you remember the scullery maiden, Panya? She showed me how to top pies."

"I do. But that's the extent of my knowledge about her."

"Bloody Blackening. I need her now."

Bramn nodded toward the archway where stairs ascended. "That leads to their quarters. I'll get her." He was swiftly up the stairs, bellowing, "Panya!"

Six minutes later, a young woman came down with him, clutching the collar of her beige shift. "What is—?" Upon seeing Thylaina, she froze. "It's Her Ladyship, isn't it?"

"How did you know?" Bramn asked.

"Quaiy said the elf maiden would come to me if something terrible happened."

Thylaina stepped forward. "Is Quaiy the maidservant from Her Ladyship's chamber?"

"She was frightened," Panya said. "Asked me to hide something for her and give it only to you."

"A teacup." It had to be.

"Yes."

"Where is it?" Bramn asked.

Panya hurried between the tables, squatting at one away from the fireplace. She moved three crocks aside, then rose, holding a small cup. "I didn't want it too close to the heat, fearing it'd dry what remained."

Thylaina drew in a rush of air and held it. Reaching out, she neared the woman. "Vynia, please," she whispered. Her inspection with the lowlight revealed less than a swallow.

"Did I do well?" Panya asked.

Thylaina nodded. "Hopefully, I can learn what he has done. A spoon, please."

Panya rushed to a table against the eastern wall and selected a long-handled spoon.

Bramn looked over Thylaina's shoulder. "I pray there're answers."

She took the spoon from Panya, who then sat on a nearby chair and watched. "As do I, Sir Bramn," Thylaina said. She gathered a taste on the end of the spoon. Eyes closed to help focus, she placed the tea on her tongue. Lavender still accompanied the other flavors: honey, feverfew, and something she could not identify. But she *knew* it. Master Eidryn insisted his healers tasted everything, even poisonous plants. This unknown ingredient was bitter. Thylaina looked at Bramn. He frowned. She drank the remaining tea.

"No!" He took the cup, but she had already finished. "What if this hurts you?"

"I shall be fine." Thylaina closed her eyes again and leaned against the table, centering every thought on the bitter taste. Feverfew could have caused the bleeding, but she did not believe it was the primary culprit. Mikan used honey and lavender to mask this unknown herb. Something that would cause Tesesra to lose her baby. This one... and the previous two. What plants could have caused the loss?

The answer came as soon as the question finished, turning Thylaina's flesh cold. "Insh weed."

Panya blanched, her fingers pressed to her lips. "No."

"We must go now." Thylaina grabbed the satchel and ran for the door. Bramn followed, but Panya remained behind, her sobs growing distant.

"What's insh weed?" he asked, his voice cracking.

Thylaina shook her head, her mind racing on how to counter the deadly effects of the plant, for it was not a subject Master Eidryn had touched upon. It was a painful way to end an unborn's life. There was healing offered to the woman afterward, but saving a babe that had consumed insh through its mother had never been attempted.

Although life was precious to elves, who were naturally infertile, some preferred to wait afore beginning a family if they were not blessed with a babe shortly after their marriage ceremony. Several couples waited a hundred years, then tried again, for it suited their life-plans. To avoid the harm and pain caused by using insh weed, Master Eidryn had developed a preventative oil from it. Disregarding the king, he shared this safer method with those outside the Elven Nation, for a fee, of course. Master Eidryn *did* have to fund his studies. But humans did not like parting with their roans. So, many of the women returned to the old method: eating the weed's bulb. When Uncle Yasontler learned about their using the plant in its potent form again, he blamed Master Eidryn for being greedy. In Etharell, it is forbidden to consume insh weed. Thylaina knew of no elf who had ever attempted it. Because her teacher had taken his pupils near the borders to learn some of the foreign ailments, Thylaina had helped human women recover from the insh weed's effects.

But how was she to save Tesesra's babe?

"My lady?"

She had halted on the second-floor landing, tears rolling down her cheeks. "I-I know not how to convince him," she whispered. "Marshal Momestid will not listen. Even after seeing the blood."

Disbelief, then worry contorted Bramn's face. "Tes is bleeding?"

Thylaina nodded. "She will lose the babe."

He grabbed the hair at his nape. "Might Grim know what this insh weed is?"

That was the first time she had heard Bramn call the marshal by his nickname.

"*You* did not," she said. "So I doubt he will."

He gestured back toward the kitchen. "Apparently Panya did."

"As do most women." She rested against the rail and massaged her temples. "How can I help Lady Tesesra if the marshal will not permit me in the room?"

"We get him out."

But nothing would pull Arhgrim from his wife's side.

"It will not work." Thylaina groaned into her hands. "The candle burns far too low, my friend. Not only must we get inside her room, but I must think of how to save the babe."

"Then let's make a plan." Bramn grasped her hand and led the way to her bedroom.

Time truly was too short, and while they paced between the bed and the fireplace, Thylaina contemplated magic. Bramn suddenly stopped and released a roar, making her jump.

"What was that for?" she asked, her hand pressed to her chest, as if that might calm her rapid heartbeat.

"I'm lost." Hands formed into fists, he stared at the flames. "I can't fight what's happening to her. To them." Running his fingers through his hair, he stomped to the water pitcher. "I need a drink."

Drink. Why was Thylaina thinking about spells? She had the means right there. "I have an idea."

He stopped and spun. "What do you have in mind?"

"We need not make the marshal leave." Smiling, she shrugged. "I can make a sleep potion."

"How do we get it to him?"

"Panya."

"I'll get her." He headed for the door. "You make your potion."

Bramn was gone afore Thylaina could respond. There was nothing to say, really. The plan was in motion, and she had a potion and healing sphere to make.

Thylaina started with the sphere, something she and Aarosyn Basylla had created while training under Master Eidryn. They had impressed their mentor and peers by displaying their capability to concoct a remedy of their own. But it was Aarosyn who had approached her with the formula, although a faulty one. Thylaina filled in the two missing ingredients: olesa oil and buraily leaves. So she gave the credit to Aarosyn for his ingenuity. At times, Thylaina believed he was a more accomplished healer than she, which said much, considering he was not of the Bryric bloodline.

Aarosyn's sweet smile, blue eyes, and handsome face passed through her mind as his voice whispered in her ear the instructions of mixing and forming the medicinal ball while she prepared it. She missed her dear friends so terribly much. Blinking the sorrow away, Thylaina focused on the task. She poured a tablespoon's worth of olesa oil into a dish, rolled the ball in it, then covered it with three buraily leaves. Certain they affixed to the sphere, she set it on a different plate and began the sleep potion, using the same ingredients as she had with Rhomasyn.

Images of that dreadful man began to form, but she quickly pushed them aside. He deserved none of her time, especially now.

Ashrych and camiol went into a shallow bowl, and half a spoon of crueberry powder mixed in with them. By the time she had the powders blended, Bramn returned with Panya.

"She's agreed to help." He stopped beside Thylaina, then pointed at the leaf-covered ball. "What's that?"

"A healing sphere."

One of his brows arched. "I've never heard of it."

Panya peered around him to view the table and its contents.

"Every ingredient within is a healing herb," Thylaina explained. "The powders, oil, and the leaves." She handed the plate with the sphere to Bramn. "Once the marshal is asleep, I must wet this in the oil and force it down Her Ladyship's throat."

"Wait." Scowling, he took a step back. "You're what?"

"This is the fastest and most effective way to get potent healing to the babe." Thylaina sighed. "And we have already lost too much time."

Bramn and Panya stared at the sphere as if having second thoughts. Then he met Thylaina's gaze. "I trust you," he said. "Panya brought fruzae for Grim. With the state he's in, I think he'll drink to calm his nerves."

"How will you give it to him?"

"I'll offer it." Bramn smiled wryly. "Grim won't question it from me."

Thylaina nodded. This *would* work. It must.

"Once this is all finished," he continued, "we'll speak with Breydon. He must learn about what's happening."

That ruined Thylaina's hope. Breydon would surely throw her into the jailhouse, and Arhgrim would no doubt agree. But to avoid further delay, she said, "As you wish, Sir Bramn."

Outside Tesesra's chambers, Panya poured fruzae into the glasses Bramn bought from Thylaina's room, while Thylaina placed the dish holding the sphere and the shallow bowl with the oil on the floor. She then looked from one glass to the other, then at the knight.

"With which hand do you drink?" she asked.

He raised the right glass.

After she administered the sleep mixture into the left cup, she retrieved the sphere and oil. "Marshal Momestid must drink that within the next five minutes, or the alcohol will alter the effects."

"Right." Bramn released a heavy breath, then nodded at Panya. The scullery maid opened the door.

Bramn and Thylaina entered, then Panya followed, closing the door behind her and locking it. They halted upon seeing Breydon in the suite, warming his hands at the hearth. His curious expression shifted to a frown as he noticed Thylaina. She stepped behind Panya.

"What're you doing here?" he asked, his voice low.

"I'm... bringing a drink for Grim." Bramn raised the glasses.

"Panya, take these." Thylaina handed the plate and bowl to the scullery maid. Bramn hurried for the bedchamber door, and Thylaina moved ahead to open it.

"Stop!" Breydon charged at them. "Why's she in here?" He pointed at Thylaina.

Bramn continued into the bedroom.

Thylaina closed the door as soon as he stepped inside, then faced the captain. When he made to push her aside, she flattened against the door. "Please, Shapele. Sir Bramn only wants a moment with them."

"Move it, woman!"

Panya suddenly tugged on his arm, pulling him off balance, and he stumbled backwards. "My lord, you must—"

He spun and slapped her. "Hands off me, kitchen slop!"

Appalled, Thylaina ran to the dazed Panya. "How could you?"

Breydon pointed at her. "You shouldn't be in here," he then motioned at Panya, "and neither should she. What are you *doing* here?"

"Sir Bramn wanted to bring something to help Marshal Momestid relax." Thylaina darted her gaze from him to Panya, back to him. "Is that wrong?"

He stared at her. Watched her for five long seconds that left her cheeks burning and her heart pounding. "You're lying."

When he started for the door again, Thylaina sprinted into his path. Breydon's hand slammed into her chest with such force, she struck the doorframe and rattled the door. It pushed the air from her lungs and sent a jolt of pain through her back, not to mention her head hit the frame. Warmth flared on her scalp, as if bleeding. Thylaina gasped for a breath, but it hurt to try. She slid to the floor, tears blurring her vision.

Panya jumped on the captain's back.

"Get off!" he bellowed.

This was not right. It was not supposed to happen like this.

*Vynia, please help me reach Tesesra and save her babe.*

The door thumped against Thylaina. "What's going on out there?" Bethlyn shouted from the other side.

Thylaina rolled onto her hands and knees, then crawled away, trying to avoid Breydon's trampling as he fought to get Panya off him. The poor scullery maid clutched her own arm, which braced around his shoulders, doing her best to hold tight to the captain.

The bedchamber door swung open, and Bethlyn gaped at the scene. "What the bloody Blackening is happening?"

Bramn appeared at the handmaiden's side, then lunged forward to grapple Breydon, who had just broken free of Panya. "Go, Thylaina!"

The tears wiped from her vision, Thylaina rose unsteadily. She looked at Bethlyn. The handmaiden's low brows shot upward, and she moved to slam the door shut. Thylaina thrust her arm in the way, crying out as the handmaiden trapped it between the door and the frame. She pushed on the door, but Bethlyn held fast.

"Stop, Breydon!" Bramn shielded the captain's oncoming fists with his hands. Breydon knocked them aside with one arm and jabbed a punch to Bramn's nose with the other fist.

Thylaina returned her focus to the door, confused that Bethlyn refused her help.

The handmaiden squealed, then Thylaina stumbled forward as the door swung open. Quaiy stood over a shocked and outraged Bethlyn.

"Come, m'lady!" The young maidservant waved for her to hurry.

Thylaina made to bolt forward, but she stilled. What had Panya done with the healing remedies? "Panya!" she called. "Where are the sphere and oil?"

The scullery maid scanned the floor. Vynia no! The girl had lost them. Crawling on the floor, Thylaina dodged Bramn and Breydon while they threw punches at each other, both men succeeding.

Even though Panya had already latched the bolt to the landing door, she pressed against it as it rattled.

Breydon lunged into Bramn. They tumbled on the sofa, shoving it a few inches back. Bramn tried to lock his arm around his friend's head, but the captain would not stop moving.

"There!" Panya pointed under the sofa.

Thylaina lowered until her cheek touched the cold stone. The scullery maid had hidden the items beneath the sofa, which rocked from the men's fighting. It tipped. Thylaina snatched the bowl and plate and slinked away.

The sofa crashed back, narrowly missing her, and the men grunted with the impact. Breydon's head snapped in her direction, and he reached for her. His fingertips curled within her sleeve, but she twisted free and climbed to her feet. Thank Vynia, she kept the items balanced.

"Hurry!" Quaiy shouted from the bedchamber.

Thylaina ran into the room, tripped on Arhgrim's outstretched legs, but caught herself on the bed by slamming against the post. However, she dropped the plate, and the sphere rolled a few feet away. Panting and ignoring the pain, she snatched it, then looked it over. The sphere was filthy. "I need water."

Quaiy was pulling Bethlyn's hair while pinning the woman's arms with her knees. "Panya!"

More shouts, cursing, and furniture moving sounded from the suite.

The scullery maid sprinted into the room; however, she did not avoid Arhgrim's legs and tripped, smacking her face into the bedframe.

"Panya!" Quaiy released Bethlyn to help her friend.

Crimson splotched Bethlyn's cheeks, and her rage-filled eyes shimmered different shades of blue as she huffed loose hair away. "Get away from her," she said through clenched teeth.

Thylaina considered her options. Unfinished fruzae was nearby, but she knew not if it was Bramn's or Arhgrim's. Giving the remedy with a drink already altered would likely cause more damage to Tesesra and the babe. Besides, Thylaina had never used a healing sphere with liquor and knew not what it might do. The water pitcher was behind the approaching handmaiden. Only one option remained. Thylaina put the leafy ball in her mouth and rolled it with her tongue until it felt clean enough, and did this while evading Bethlyn. Unfortunately, the handmaiden grasped the end of Thylaina's braid, which nearly forced the sphere down her throat.

"Let her go!" Quaiy pushed Bethlyn aside, causing Thylaina's head to jerk.

Thylaina spit the ball into her palm, disregarding the dirt and dust gathered in her teeth and on her tongue as she yanked her plait free from Bethlyn's grip. She dropped the ball into the olesa oil and headed to the frightfully pallid Lady Tesesra.

Breydon stepped into the doorway. A few places on his face swelled red, and a blood seeped from splits on his lip and above his left eye.

Thylaina left all worry about Bramn at the back of her mind and moved. *Bryric, help me!* She removed the sphere from the oil and stretched her arms for Tesesra. Breydon charged. Just as she reached the bedside, Tesesra opened her mouth to draw in a sudden breath. Bryric truly had sent aid, for the timing could not have been more precise. Thylaina shoved the sphere into Tesesra's mouth. Panya spilt water as she halted at the other side of the bed with the pitcher. Taking it from the scullery maid, Thylaina poured some into Her Ladyship's mouth, then placed her hand over the woman's lips and nose. *Swallow.*

An arm wrapped around her waist and pulled her over Arhgrim's legs.

"N'ei!"

Tesesra coughed, trying to spit out the sphere.

"N'ei!" Thylaina fought Breydon's hold as he dragged her back to the suite.

Panya placed her hands over Tesesra's mouth. "Swallow, m'lady. It'll help your babe. We promise," she said, her voice calm despite her panting and obvious pain. One eye was swelled shut with a red line showing over it, and blood ribboned from her apparently broken nose.

Just as the captain hauled Thylaina from the room, Tesesra removed Panya's hand and swallow. Breydon spun her until her back hit the wall, his fingers immediately gripping her throat. "What did you do to Tes?"

She clutched his wrist and hand. Dug her nails into his flesh and scratched as she fought to breathe.

"What did you do?" he shouted.

Breydon's head lurched forward, his grip slackened, and his eyes rolled back. He collapsed between Thylaina and Bramn. The latter's crooked nose bled, and the swelling of his cheeks nearly forced his eyes closed.

Bramn dropped a log as he stepped over his friend, reaching for Thylaina. "My lady, are you well?"

Rough coughs scratched her burning throat as she tried to regain control of her breathing. Nodding, she pointed to the main door, from where thuds sounded.

"Open this now!" someone bellowed.

"Miryl." Bramn hurried to allow the captain entry.

Thylaina lowered to examine Breydon's head, finding a gash atop a quickly forming lump. "Right the sofa," she rasped.

Bramn ordered the guards accompanying Miryl to straighten the furniture while the captain continued into the bedchamber. Once the sofa was upright, Bramn and a guard placed Breydon on it.

"What happened in here?" Miryl called from inside the bedroom.

"That bloody elf tried to kill the marshal and Her Ladyship," Bethlyn cried.

Thylaina met Bramn's annoyed gaze and sighed

# Chapter Seven

They had straightened Arhgrim in the chair as best they could, then sent the maidservants from the bedchamber, except Bethlyn. She remained to share with Miryl and Tesesra her side of what had transpired. In the suite, Quaiy paced outside the bedroom door, often scowling at it. Panya sat in a chair afore the fireplace, her nose straightened and bossel ointment on it and around her eye. Bramn slouched in the other chair with his head leaned back, nose also reset, and balm covering his face. Four guards stood sentry at the exit, two inside the room and two on the long landing. Arlin arrived a moment ago with another squire, Kimmy, who served Bramn. The young man had just returned that night from holiday to visit his ill father. Arlin stood behind the couch, his full attention on Thylaina while she pressed a poultice to Breydon's head, the bossel ointment already spread on the captain's face. She now waited for Katjina to return with more wraps, for Thylaina had used those from the satchel.

Quaiy stopped in front of the door, her brows furrowed. "Bethlyn's been in there for an hour. I wish we could hear what lies she spews."

Bramn turned his head in her direction, then back. "We'll have our chance to speak the truth."

Katjina returned with the wraps, followed by Viya and several scullery maids carrying trays of food to break fast. Great Bryric! Morning had already arrived. Viya took a large tray bearing several steaming plates to the bedchamber, while the other scullery maids offered a light meal to those in the suite. Although exhausted, all but Thylaina partook; she was too occupied caring for Breydon's wounds. Katjina promised to have hot water prepared for a bath, then left with the scullery maids. Arlin nibbled on a scone while he watched Thylaina wrap the captain's head to hold the poultice in place.

Panya also observed from the chair, her fingers curling and uncurling over the edge of a bowl of porridge. "After what he did, how can you help him?" she asked, her voice trembling.

Thylaina tied the ends and tucked them beneath the top layer of the wrappings. It scratched her throat to speak, so she whispered, "He needed aid."

Ire dwelled in the young maiden's eyes. "But he hurt you."

Bramn looked at Thylaina, his gaze darting to Breydon then Panya. "I know he hurt you as well, but Captain wasn't himself," he said, wiping his hands on a cloth.

Arlin and Kimmy glanced at each other, then at the maidens. It seemed the young men read each other's thoughts, for a shameful expression overtook them as they stared at their First Captain.

The bedchamber door opened, and Miryl stepped out. "Lady Thylaina, please come in."

Bethlyn walked past him, hatred loosing from her eyes like arrows at Thylaina. She continued to the main door, but Bramn called to Miryl.

"Sir, shouldn't Bethlyn stay until you've heard all accounts? Just in case you must ask further questions."

"You're correct, Sir Bramn." Miryl's tone did not sound grateful, but annoyed. "In fact, I didn't tell Bethlyn she could leave. Give your seat to her."

"Yes, sir." Bramn rose, then bowed with a touch of exaggeration as he offered the chair to the red-faced handmaiden. "My lady."

Thylaina pressed her lips together to avoid laughing, for the balm on his face made him look foolish. Panya, Quaiy, and the squires, however, could not help themselves, and giggles and snickers issued from them. Bramn winked at Thylaina as she turned to follow Miryl into the bedchamber, the satchel strapped over her shoulder.

The sun's yellow glow shone into the room, and birds sang beautifully outside. Too bad it did not reflect the mood within the chamber. An irritable and frustrated Tesesra sat against the elaborate headboard. Gesturing at her husband, who snored softly, she asked, "When will he wake?"

"I know not, Your Ladyship." Thylaina walked around an empty chair beside Arhgrim's. "I have never used the sleeping elixir with liquor."

"Is he well?" Tears brimmed the woman's eyes.

"He is. I assure you."

Miryl motioned to a lone chair near the end of the bed, facing Tesesra, the sleeping marshal, and the empty seat. "Please sit."

Thylaina did as he said, resting her hands on her lap; he lowered to the empty chair beside Arhgrim. She looked from the captain to Tesesra.

Her Ladyship wasted no time. "What did you put inside me?"

Miryl closed his mouth, his inquiries set aside for the moment.

"A healing sphere formed of herbs," Thylaina said. "A comrade and I created these decades ago for dire situations."

"Dire?" The captain rested his elbows and his knees and bent forward. "Are you suggesting Lady Tesesra was in danger?"

"The babe, s'yai. Without doubt."

"Why did you put my husband to sleep?" Worry wrinkled Tesesra's forehead. "Why go through all of this... this chaos you've created? Bethlyn assures me you've poisoned us. He and I!"

Thylaina nearly jumped from the chair, but maintained enough control to only scoot to the edge. "I would never."

"Why would she lie?" Miryl scowled. "Bethlyn has served here for five years and has been a faithful handmaiden."

"Do you feel ill?" Thylaina inquired of Tesesra. "Has the pain not eased?"

Placing her hand on her belly, Tesesra drew in a deep breath, then released it. "I do feel improved."

"Then please trust my concern is your babe. And I am not the only one who fears the safety of your unborn."

Miryl straightened, glanced at Tesesra. "What are you saying?"

"I have made my worries clear to Marshal Momestid," Thylaina said. "I fear someone is trying to harm the babe."

"Mikan," Tesesra whispered.

Thylaina nodded.

Nose scrunched, Miryl leaned forward. "You think our high priest is trying to kill the marshal's unborn child?"

"Other servants in the mansion have grown concerned," Thylaina said. "With the aid of... some, I learned a dangerous plant had been added to her tea last night and had likely caused the bleeding."

Teardrops trailed down Tesesra's cheeks, lingering on the edge of her jaw afore dropping to soak into her gown.

Myril straightened and crossed his arms. "You're making a serious accusation against our high priest."

"I had believed some herbs he chose were with good intentions," Thylaina said. "However, when resistance met my concerns, it felt wrong—that he was desperate to give you this tea he makes." She looked at the door, as if the handmaiden stood there. "And I believe Bethlyn assists."

Tesesra shook her head. "She is loyal to me. And you're mistaken about them both. You *must* be."

"You do not deny the pain is gone, the bleeding has ceased."

Her Ladyship stared at Thylaina, tears welling again.

"Tes," Arhgrim whispered.

Everyone turned to the marshal, a collective sigh of relief sounding from them all.

He stretched his neck left, right, then rubbed it. Repositioning in the chair and wincing, he looked at his wife. "The bleeding stopped?"

A partial smile appeared as she released a single breathy laugh and reached for his hand. "It has, my love. As has most of the terrible pain."

Arhgrim kissed her fingers. "I am relieved. And so bloody groggy. What happened?"

"That's what I'm trying to learn, sir," Miryl said.

The marshal rubbed his temples. "My head's throbbing."

"An effect of the elixir mixed with the fruzae, I am afraid," Thylaina said. "I can make a drink to ease the pain, my lord."

He nodded slightly, cringing from the small act. "Please."

She rose, set the satchel on her seat, then grabbed the kettle and headed for the door. Upon opening it, she took one step out and called for Quaiy. "Please fill this with hot water."

"Y-yes, m'lady." The maidservant snatched the kettle and hurried from the room; Panya followed.

Movement at the wall behind the sofa caught her attention. Breydon and Bramn stood nearly nose to nose, their squires attempting to get between them. Thylaina's breath caught, and she immediately touched her throat, feeling the First Captain's grip. The dried balm had turned light blue, paling against the brightness of Breydon's eyes as he charged toward her.

Thylaina retreated into the room and tried to close the door, but he put his shoulder into it. She stepped back until bumping into Miryl, who guided her to the end of the bed.

"Captain Colmstad." Miryl nodded once.

"Captain Eilisar."

Miryl, Arhgrim, and Tesesra gawked at Breydon, whose full attention was on Thylaina.

"Breydon... What's on your face?" the marshal asked.

"What?" He blinked several times, his gaze shifting downward. He slid his finger over his cheek, then inspected it. "I don't know. No one will tell me."

"Bossel ointment," Thylaina murmured, lifting the teapot from the bedside table. "T-to heal your wounds."

He sneered at her, then stomped to the washbasin and splashed water on his face. After he dried, remnants of the ointment remained along his hairline and near his ears. The cuts on his left eye and lip had already healed, and the swelling was gone.

"You look improved," Miryl said from the door.

Breydon neared the bed, his expression softening. "Are you well, Tes?"

She smiled briefly. "I am. What happened to your head?"

He touched the bandage, glanced at Thylaina. "We'll discuss that later."

Someone knocked. Sighing, Miryl opened the door.

"Forgive me, m'lords." Quaiy lifted the kettle. "Lady Thylaina requested hot water."

Thylaina had been gripping the teapot so tightly, she feared she might have cracked it. Thankfully, it was sound. Once Quaiy filled the teapot, she left, and Thylaina prepared feverfew in hot water.

"What's your plan?" Breydon asked Miryl.

"I'm questioning everyone about last night's events."

"And Lady Thylaina's making a drink for my aching head." Arhgrim stood, flinched, then returned to the chair. "That wasn't ideal."

"This shall not take long, my lord," Thylaina said, stirring the drink.

Breydon pointed at her. "Taking anything from this woman isn't ideal, Grim."

She stilled. Thylaina was tired of the First Captain's hatred, accusations, and was truly just exhausted. Ever since Quaiy woke her up, she had not a moment of rest. Honestly, she cared not what Breydon thought about her. Saving Tesesra's babe mattered most.

Ignoring the First Captain, Thylaina offered the drink to Arhgrim. "You shall find this helpful, my lord." Without giving a glance to Breydon, she returned to her chair.

"Captain Colmstad, shall you stay for the remainder of the inquisition?" Miryl asked.

Thylaina touched her throat where Breydon's fingers had squeezed, and opened her mouth to protest, but the First Captain had already answered.

"I am."

"Good." Arhgrim sipped the feverfew tea, released a breath.

"Do you wish to take the lead?" Miryl asked.

"No." Breydon did not remove his gaze from Thylaina. "I was a part of this mess. But I wish to hear all sides of what happened in here before I share what happened out there." He jerked his head in the direction of the suite.

"Very well." Miryl looked from Breydon to Arhgrim. "To reiterate Lady Thylaina's claims, she used a healing sphere to counter the dangerous herbs she claims Mikan put in Lady Tesesra's tea, which—"

"Not this again." Arhgrim stared at Thylaina like an impatient parent. "I said I'd hear no more of it."

"It's ridiculous," Breydon added.

"Yet because of what I experienced," Tesesra began, "I want to hear what she has to say."

The three men regarded her, then faced Thylaina. Miryl resumed summarizing Thylaina's beliefs. Arhgrim grimaced at the completion.

"Bethlyn?" he asked.

Thylaina wrung her fingers. With Arhgrim conscious and Breydon present, it would be harder to accomplish what she believed was possible with just Tesesra and Miryl. "S'yai, my lord."

"Those two are only in contact when he comes here," Breydon snapped. "To suggest—"

"Are you always in their presence?" Thylaina asked.

He clamped his mouth shut and glared at her. Miryl arched a brow and shrugged.

She gave her attention to Tesesra and gestured at the woman's stomach. "My lady, please allow me to feel how the babe is. Just to show that the sphere's success was not only what *I* had hoped, but the hope of those who helped me."

Tesesra looked at Arhgrim. He nodded.

Thylaina moved to the other side of the bed, where there was more room. She lowered the coverlet just below Tesesra's stomach, then lifted the woman's shift to expose her large belly. Blood covered the lower half of the nightgown. All three men blanched and swallowed hard. Arhgrim grasped his wife's hand. Thylaina asked them all to remain quiet while she concentrated, her hands gliding over the rise of Tesesra's stomach.

A solid, quick beat thumped against her palm. She smiled at Her Ladyship. "You must calm yourself. Your heartbeat is too fast and making it difficult for me to find your babe's."

"I shall try," Tesesra whispered.

"Long and easy. With me." Thylaina breathed in deep, then released it slowly. She did it a few times more, finding her patient followed along. "Perfect. Now relax completely."

Tesesra loosened her muscles, all tightness fading from even her face.

"Good." Thylaina closed her eyes and moved her hands while she prayed to Vynia. As much as she wanted to use magic to aid her, it was not possible with witnesses, so prayers would have to do. She focused beyond the others in the room, Tesesra's heartbeat, and her own breathing. Nothing. Frowning, she continued. *Vynia, please help me find their child. Please... I must have succeeded.*

"Something's wrong," Arhgrim said. "I can see it in your—"

"Silence, please." Thylaina moved her hands down Tesesra's right side. Thought she felt something. She paused. Waited. Moved further down, then toward her hip, then up again. A soft thumping grew stronger. A small heart beating, although too fast.

Thylaina smiled. Opening her eyes, she let out a breath. "I feel the babe's heartbeat."

"Oh, Grim!" Tesesra wept. "Thank Valorius, our babe is fine."

The joy left Thylaina, for that was far from the truth. "Forgive me, my lady, but it is not yet safe."

Breydon's smile transformed into a scowl. "What do you mean?"

"The babe is in distress. Her Ladyship needs more attention." Thylaina lowered the gown, then moved the coverlet back in place. "She shall not leave this bed."

"That's not possible." Tesesra shook her head. "I've a household to run."

Arhgrim nodded. "Which you'll do from here. Just to be cautious."

"Bring a chamber pot in here. N'ei more using the privy," Thylaina said. "You stay in bed."

Tesesra pointed at her. "I'm not using a chamber pot!"

"And n'ei more excitement."

"Then you should leave," Breydon said.

Arhgrim stood, stretched his arms out. "Forgive me, Breydon, but I don't agree." He arched his back and groaned. "My head feels better already. Thank you, my lady."

"Grim," Breydon said, "we can't—"

"I'll not risk my wife nor babe."

Thylaina built the courage to say the most important part of her demands. "N'ei priests." The room silenced as the humans stilled, their wide gazes on her. She kept a solid posture as she continued. "To lessen the risk of harm befalling Her Ladyship and the babe, the priests should *not* be in the mansion. A-and you remove Bethlyn as well." Her voice trembled as much as she did. "Quaiy takes her place as Lady Tesesra's handmaiden."

"You've a lot of bloody nerve," Breydon said, his voice awfully low.

Miryl shook his head in noticeable disbelief.

"It's not possible," Arhgrim said.

"I only ask for seven days." Thylaina moved around the bed. Her head suddenly felt light, her eyelids heavy, and the room distorted. "Give me..." She grabbed the footboard to keep balance as black spots invaded her vision. "Give me seven days to prove my claims. If I am wrong, then you can return me to the jailhouse."

"We should return you now," the First Captain mumbled.

"Breydon, that's enough." Arhgrim stared at her. "You're asking me to insult our high priest."

"I ask you to protect your wife and unborn." Thylaina's weary body wavered.

"My lady, are you well?" Miryl asked.

Breydon inched toward her.

"I am only tired, Shapele." She forced a smile for Miryl, then turned her head to Arhgrim. "Marshal Momestid?"

He looked at Tesesra. "Love?"

Tesesra's hands moved continuously over her stomach. "Seven days isn't much, is it?"

Thylaina felt might fall backwards, so she gripped the footboard tighter. Her mouth went dry.

"If Lady Thylaina is of any danger to me," Tesesra continued, "we'd know immediately, wouldn't we?"

"True." Arhgrim scratched his head. "Very well, Lady Thylaina. We'll meet your demands. You may take over the care of my wife while still under Sir Bramn's observance."

Wonderful! Stress easing off her shoulders, Thylaina relaxed her hold on the footboard.

"But know this," the marshal resumed, "if you harm her or the child, you'll face a reckoning unlike—"

She collapsed. However, she never hit the floor, but landed in someone's arms.

"I've got you," Breydon whispered.


A *crack!* stirred her awake. Nauseating memories of a stick cutting her knuckles and into her palms followed the abrupt sound. Thylaina opened her eyes to a gray brick ceiling above. The warm coverlets of her bed offered a sense of security. No new injuries existed, so Captain Colmstad must not have had the opportunity to commit harm afore they returned her to her chamber. With that worry cast aside, she sat up and stretched, accompanied by a soft moan. The trouble with pushing herself until exhausting all her energy was that a fog now drifted in Thylaina's mind. There was so much to do, and she needed Bramn's help. First, she must wash.

Thylaina tossed the covers off, then raced over the stone cold floor to the washbasin. At least the washbowl was near the fireplace, and the bricks there were warm upon her feet while she splashed her face. She then began lifting her shift.

"My lady," Breydon said.

Heart hammering, she let the nightgown drop as she spun toward the fireplace. The First Captain slouched in Bramn's chair, the bandage gone from his head. Thylaina must have been sleeping for at least five hours for the wound to have healed.

Gaze lowering from her face to the shift, he leaned forward, then looked at the hearth. "Forgive me." There were many things he should have been apologizing for, but the lack of clarity left the words hollow to her.

Thylaina grabbed her robe from the dressing screen and put it on. "What are you doing in here?"

"Watching over you."

Furious, she wiped her face with a towel, dropped it on the floor. "Where is Sir Bramn?"

"Sleeping." Breydon finally looked back at her. "Like you, he's bloody exhausted."

"And Katjina?"

"In the kitchen until the maiden who attacked me has also recovered from fatigue." He frowned.

"Panya was protecting me." Putting distance between them, she returned to the bed and sat. Thylaina grazed her throat, the memory of his choking her too fresh to forgive. "I am surprised you did not finish what you had begun."

He narrowed his eyes. "I'm following bloody orders."

"Pah!" Thylaina shook her head. "And if you had your freedom to do as you wished?"

The captain scoffed as he relaxed in the chair. "I'm not a murderer."

"You fooled me."

"You think you know me?" He bolted from the chair, taking a few steps toward her. "You elves are the murderers. Not me!"

Thylaina rushed around the bed, a spell ready. This time she would not dawdle if he came closer. "Unlike you humans, we value life."

"Value life?" Laughing sardonically, he combed his fingers through his hair. "Do you even know your people?"

Confused, she scowled at him. "Of what do you speak?"

"Your invisible warriors murdered my brother."

She shook her head. "Invisible warriors?"

"The elite xilys!"

Thylaina huffed. With his past interaction with those who protected the Etharell borders, Breydon already knew the truth. "The xilys *are* elite!"

"Don't be coy with me. You know of whom I speak." He began pacing between the hearth and chair. "They can't be seen, heard, nor smelled—even if they're right behind you."

The *Unseen*. This group had impressed her father and brother. They *were* exceptional warriors from an already superior force. The Unseen's training went beyond what they had endured to become xilys. Even other elves had difficulty spotting them.

In the war room three years ago, Thylaina had learned about several parties of knights and soldiers from southern Alohrius targeting villages of their own people, Etharell, and neighboring countries. Taking on the name Southern Brigands, they pillaged, raped, and destroyed. After three villages in Etharell suffered attacks from groups of these men, the Kilstra Xilys' commander formed the Unseen from both his forest and Ormiana to hunt the Southern Brigands. Less than a year later, the bandits were no more, and the Unseen disbanded, returning to their normal duties.

Thylaina would not tell Captain Colmstad the latter information. Let the humans believe the 'invisible warriors' still existed. Let them fear.

"Shapele, xilys do not murder people."

"They murdered Kreysin!" Breydon turned from her.

She stiffened from his pain-filled outburst. Bramn had mentioned Breydon's brother died, but not how. And then there was the admittance that Breydon would blame her for something that was not her fault.

His heavy breathing slowed as he looked down, then shook his head. "If they don't murder people," he faced her again, "then tell me why they'd hunt a group of knights and slaughter them."

The only explanation Thylaina could fathom was that his brother must have been a Southern Brigand. Apparently, Breydon wanted to blame everyone for his death. Arhgrim, Bramn, and even Ardella had hinted about his hatred toward the elves. What if Kreysin was not a Brigand, but a victim? Thylaina did not know the truth.

"I am not military, Shapele," she said. "I cannot speak of their reasons. Perhaps you can share with me—"

"You don't care."

"I cannot answer questions if you will not tell me."

Brows low, he regarded her in silence. His shoulders sunk and his expression softened. "Change your clothes." Breydon turned his chair toward the fireplace and sat with his back to the dressing screen.

There was no convincing him to respond. She still needed clean garments, so Thylaina selected a simple yellow gown from the wardrobe. She wanted to change as quickly as possible, while simultaneously learning as much as she could.

"Tell me about your brother, Shapele Colmstad," she said from behind the screen. Flames danced, logs popped and crackled, but he did not answer. "Please?"

Another few seconds of silence passed, then he cleared his throat. "We were twins."

Thylaina stilled while untying the dress' ribbon. Breydon must have been close with his brother. Now her curiosity grew even more.

"Tell me about yours," he said.

Her anxiety heightened as it always did when he questioned about her family. But Breydon had given a little information, so she would do the same. "He is older than I by forty-three years."

"That... That must've been hard. I imagine you had little in common."

She pulled the dress over her head, straightened it, then tied the ribbon in the front. "We were close until he joined the army," she said, stepping from behind the screen. "Then I rarely saw him."

"How often do nobles join the armies?" He kept his gaze on the fire.

"My people are dedicated to our nation." The bow finished, she sauntered to her chair, which faced his profile, and sat. "I know so little about the invisible warriors, Shapele Colmstad. Military matters were not my concern."

He rubbed the back of his neck. "Kreysin was a knight."

"Did he rise in the ranks like you?"

"No." Breydon's jaw shifted side to side. "Who are you?"

Thylaina kept a calm demeanor as she smiled. "A healer."

He tilted his head enough to meet her gaze. "Can you save Tes' babe?"

*Bryric!* She fell back into the chair and groaned. Waking up with Breydon in the chamber had thrown off everything.

"What is it?" he asked, concerned.

Looking toward the window, she tried to determine the time. "What hour is it?"

"Shortly past the fourteenth."

"I must tend to Lady Tesesra." Thylaina headed to the table to restock her satchel.

He walked to the door, grabbed the knob. "I'm to remain with you until Bramn is ready to resume."

That would not do. She needed Bramn to accompany her to the temple.

"You're troubled," he said. Her expression must have revealed her displeasure, and like Neldrid, Breydon read her like a scroll. He was dangerous.

"I-I need your help, Shapele."

"I'll do anything for Tes."

How was Thylaina to convince him to turn against his high priest? *Courage.* After a controlled breath, she said, "To prove Mikan is harming her."

One side of Breydon's mouth tugged upward. "You want me to dishonor my high priest." His hand fell from the doorknob. "Woman, you're foolish."

"Damn you."

His amusement changed to indignation. "You listen to me—"

"*You* listen, Shapele Colmstad." Thylaina neared him, then poked his chest with her finger. "This is beyond us—you and me, Alohrius and Etharell. It is not about our problems with each other. It is about the babe."

He straightened, licked his lips, then drew in a deep breath. That solid chest brushed Thylaina's finger, which still pointed at him.

"If I am wrong," she continued, "then I will walk to the jailhouse without resistance." She lowered her hand, readjusted the satchel's strap on her shoulder. "However, if I am correct, then *we* have a chance to save the babe. But I need your help."

Breydon closed his eyes and stretched his neck back. Looking at her, he smiled. "Very well. However, if you're wrong, *I'll* escort you to the vault. Now let's tend to Tes, then we'll go to the temple." He opened the door and gestured to the landing. "Shall we?"

Tesesra was still resting, and the babe's heartbeat remained the same. There was naught more to do but go to the temple. Breydon silently escorted Thylaina, ignoring the young maidens calling for his attention. The dour expression on his face had several clearing from his path. Thylaina could not fathom how people believed he was a fine man when he exuded intimidation. She prayed Bramn would wake up soon.

A temple had never appeared so foreboding. Sunlight flashed off the glass windows, hiding the colors, and shone on the engraved knights' feet on the doors. No warm invitation welcomed Thylaina. Hand resting on the left doorhandle, shaped like a sword hilt, Breydon looked at her, his visage softer and daunting aura fading. A few light bruises were all that remained on his handsome face from the previous night's fight.

What was she thinking? With his less than aggressive behavior, the ugliness dwindled to reveal a hint of the man everyone else had spoken so fondly about.

"Are you certain?" he pressed.

Her thoughts back to the matter at hand, Thylaina nodded. "We must learn if the herbal priest has the weed or not, and if Mikan acquires it from him."

"Fine." Glancing at the carved knights, Breydon pushed the left door open. It swung inward silently, alerting no one of their arrival.

Thylaina had not been here since the captain tortured her. Under distress then, she had not noted the surroundings. A short corridor opened into a grand foyer, that much she remembered. The rest had been a whirr of doors and hallways. A dark-green carpet took up much of the floor, likely to muffle the heavy steps of knights often walking in and out of the temple. Those in prayer would not like the disruption. Ten feet from the entrance was a door, which opened as Breydon and

Thylaina neared the hall. A young man dressed in the simple robes of an acolyte stepped out.

"Greetings, Captain." His gaze darted to Thylaina then back to Breydon. "Are you here to see Mikan?"

Breydon shook his head. "The lady seeks special herbs from Raylen."

The acolyte looked at her again. "Does she?"

Breydon advanced on him. "Is there trouble?"

"No. No, sir." The acolyte raised his hands defensively. "Forgive me. I'll take you to Raylen immediately."

Thylaina opened her mouth to thank him, but Breydon grabbed her hand and jerked. She frowned at the captain. Upon him shaking his head, she allowed him to escort her after their guide.

The young man led them into the large vestibule. Sconces along the perimeter of the walls remained unlit, for the sun's glow had reached the eight round windows of the domed ceiling, revealing intricate carvings of knights on the smooth stone beams separating each window.

A gentle pull on her arm drew her attention to their path, and she nodded appreciatively to Breydon.

Their steps whispered on the lush carpet, taking them past the main worship room. Mikan's voice carried through the gap of the ajar double doors. "When duty calls to you men, you will answer with the devotion that fills your veins."

The acolyte slowed just beyond the chamber's entrance. "You could join them, Captain."

A slight smile curved Breydon's lips. "Perhaps once I've finished matters with the lady."

"Of course." The acolyte gave Thylaina a disinterested glance.

Ignoring the disrespect, Thylaina continued beside Breydon. A touch of fear the captain's reply to the acolyte was sincere left her gut quivering. He just might reveal to Mikan her intentions. *Bryric, please let not my trust be a folly.*

Down a dim, cool, and narrow hallway, they passed several doors afore stopping at the last one on the right side. The young man removed a candle from the sconce, then motioned for them to follow him into a tight chamber. Lighting a lantern on a long table in the small room, he said, "Wait here." Then he walked behind the table and left through another door. On each side of that exit were three shelves lined with labeled jars.

Normally, Thylaina would have indulged in the many wonderful scents surrounding her, from floral, earthy, and sweet, to acrid and burnt. Instead, she hurried around the waist-high table and read the labels on the bottom shelf to the right of the door as swiftly as possible.

"You shouldn't be back there," Breydon whispered.

"Listen for them."

"What?"

"I understand you hear nearly as good as an elf." She looked over her shoulder. "Listen for them."

Annoyance accompanied his sigh as he tramped to the door, then pressed his ear to it.

The names of several common herbs read clearly on the labels, many found in a kitchen, such as rosemary, mint, ginger, and parsley, and there were bossel roots in full form in a taller jar. '*Hemlock*', however, brought her to pause. These priests were foolish to believe they could properly administer such a deadly herb. Master Eidryn only permitted a few of his pupils to do so. Thylaina was one of them, but she did not keep poisonous plants in her possession.

"Do you see anything?" the captain asked.

"Not yet." She moved to the other side of the door. No insh weed. Thylaina could not see beyond the first shelf, nor could she ask Breydon to leave his post to help. But it did not matter.

"They're coming," he announced.

He and Thylaina hastened back around the table, then breathed slowly a few times to calm themselves. At least the cool chamber helped.

The acolyte stepped through, followed by a priest, a man Thylaina had only glimpsed the day Breydon thrashed her hand with the edged stick. He was barely taller than she, his dark hair feathered to the side, and his brown irises fixed on her from beneath relaxed eyelids.

Upon seeing her, he gestured at the door. "You may leave," he said to the acolyte. Once alone in the room with them, the priest tilted his head and smiled. "My lady, your return is a lovely surprise." He did not hide his appraising of her. "One I welcome."

Crossing his arms, Breydon snorted.

"Captain Colmstad, it's uncommon to find you in my herb chamber." The priest cocked a brow.

To draw his attention, Thylaina stepped forward. "I beg your forgiveness, but I do not believe we became acquainted my first time here."

His robes whispered as he leaned on the table, his grin spreading. "We did not." He raised his hand and waited until Thylaina rested hers within. "I'm Raylen. Second to Mikan."

"I am honored." She forced a blush for him.

"The honor is mine." His warm hand held hers as he walked to the end of the table, away from Breydon, then pulled her closer. "What is it I can do for you, Lady Thylaina?"

A quick scan of the jars still did not reveal the presence of insh weed.

"Dreadful headaches have inflicted some women at the mansion," she said. "I promised Her Ladyship I had a remedy, yet I am without the necessary herbs."

Raylen eyed her person again. "I don't see your case, my lady."

Thylaina curled her fingers tighter around his and giggled. "I-I had gone through it, desperately searching for—" she slid his hand upward from her bottom "—feverfew, but found none."

Breydon cleared his throat.

"Must you stay, Captain?" Raylen asked.

"Yes," Breydon snapped.

Thylaina turned the priest's head back to her. "With the amount of roans I possessed to purchase these herbs, Marshal Momestid insisted Shapele Colmstad accompany me."

"What does 'Shapele' mean?" Raylen's arm wound its way around her waist, and his scent of sandalwood now mingled with the herbs and powders in the room.

"I-it means, Captain."

Crow's feet formed at the corners of the priest's eyes as he chuckled. "I adore the way that word rolls from your tongue."

"Can we return to our purpose of being here?" Breydon barked. Raylen did not jump from the sudden outburst, but Thylaina did.

"Of course, Captain." Raylen winked at Thylaina, then kissed her hand.

Disgust twisted her stomach, but she collected herself to speak convincingly. "As I mentioned, I left everything out of my case so I could replace the herbs in order." Thylaina brushed her cheek over his fingers. "That is, if you are kind enough to part with some of your supply."

Gaze lowering to her mouth, he licked his bottom lip. "Is feverfew all you require?"

Thylaina craned her neck to view the jars again. "I-I am uncertain what you—"

"Send Captain Colmstad away," he whispered in her ear. "Let us honor our gods together."

A shiver shot down her back, and her heart thudded. This was not going as planned. Not only that, Breydon apparently heard the priest and was moving toward them.

"Hemlock!" Thylaina nearly hollered, desperation overtaking control. Breydon halted, his eyes wide.

A smirk raised the corner of Raylen's lips as he straightened. "My lady, you've got my intrigue." A rush of air brushed Thylaina as his hands slipped away, permitting her heated cheeks to cool. He tapped his chin.

Had she said something wrong? Perhaps it was her reaction to his proposal. Damn it to Darkness!

"That is a challenging herb," he said.

Breydon glanced at Thylaina.

"It is." She tucked her hair behind her pointed ear. "One must be careful with such a powerful herb. A shame such a lovely plant is so dangerous."

"I agree." Raylen sauntered behind the table and removed the jar from the shelf. "I'm a fool for keeping it this low, but only I distribute them." He set the container down and slowly uncorked it.

"Are you the primary healer?"

"Mikan truly holds that role. Yet he doesn't put as much effort into preparing the herbs, which is no bother to me. I enjoy this. The time in here alone—to think, pray, and enjoy the fragrance of each plant," Raylen smiled, "I consider a gift. Especially the knowledge granted to me."

"It *is* a gift." A peek in the jar revealed a small amount of the herb. "Not much in there."

"Poison is not something I keep too much in stock. At least hemlock has its better uses." Raylen eyed her. "How much do you believe you'll need? How many women?"

"Three."

"Then I have plenty."

While he weighed the hemlock, Thylaina continued perusing the jars. "Do you have ashrych?"

Wrinkles waved along his forehead. "Isn't that native to Etharell?"

"I was uncertain if it grew elsewhere."

Breydon coughed.

Thylaina did not look at him, but the priest did. She drew in a shaking breath. "Might you help us with another matter?"

The captain's heat was suddenly against her back, and the scent of leather mingled with the herbs.

"What's that, my lady?" Raylen asked.

"A maiden at the mansion has... Well, she found herself with child."

Hemlock still within the pincher, Raylen stiffened.

"Do you have something that might," Thylaina shrugged, "remedy th-the complication?" Fynthiar, forgive her for referring to a pregnancy as such.

"Many of what I have might, as well as what you carry, my lady."

She flashed a smile. "I mean immediately."

The hemlock dropped into a black velvet pouch, he gathered more. "Why?"

Maybe Thylaina was mistaken. Raylen might have no part in what Mikan had been doing to Tesesra. But she had to find out. To continue the performance, she grabbed Breydon's arm. "Shapele Colmstad, the poor fool, could not resist. And now he is in a dire situation from which he must relieve himself afore anyone else learns."

Breydon's head whipped in her direction, and he gave her the most horrific scowl. Crimson bloomed on his freckled cheeks and his eyes burned with anger.

Raylen snickered. "He wouldn't be the only one to have given in to his desires, my lady." The last of the hemlock now in the pouch, he tugged the strings, closing the herb in darkness. "I always put the more dangerous ones in black velvet."

Thylaina took the hemlock. "I appreciate it."

"As for your other predicament, I'm uncertain how I can help." He sat on the table and addressed Breydon. "Can the maiden make her claim?"

Muscles flexed in the captain's clenching jaw.

Thylaina elbowed him. "Do not be sullen, Shapele. You got yourself into this. We shall do what we must." She hated this. Pretending and lying for pleasantries was different, but this... Acting as if a life meant nothing was dreadful.

Breydon bobbed his head once.

"Hemlock mixed with feverfew will do the trick," Raylen said. "But you already know this."

Thylaina shook her head. "It could harm the mother."

"What do you want from me?"

"Insh weed."

The light in Raylen's eyes dimmed slightly, and his smile lessened. "Insh?"

Thylaina moved between his legs until her chest was near his chin. "I need something that acts swiftly and does n'ei harm to the mother."

"But it *does* harm the mother," he whispered, his gaze softening as he stared into her eyes. "Gods, you're so beautiful."

Thylaina breathed deep, her breasts brushing him. "The mother shall feel some pain, but you and I know she does not suffer beyond that."

What. A. Lie.

More disgust roiled in her belly as he looked at her bosom. Why did she put herself in this position? *For Tesesra's babe. All of this is for them.*

"It's, uh... It's not one I keep in the open," Raylen said. "However, I have the bulbs for consumption. Although, I also remove the spikes to provide as a drink." He slid his hands up the sides of her thighs, stopping at her hips.

A chill invaded her flesh, although not from his touch, but from knowing he possessed the awful plant.

"You'll need to steep a full bloom's worth and have her drink it all," he said. "It'll do the same as eating the bulb, but you can add another herb to improve the flavor."

Breydon turned his back to them and cursed.

Body tense and brows low, Raylen looked his way. "Is something wrong?"

Thylaina directed his head toward her. Using her melodious voice to charm him, she hoped to guide the answer for her next question without resistance. "Has Mikan acquired some from you?"

The priest's muscles eased, and the worried expression fell away. "The spikes for tea. For more than a fortnight. Along with other herbs to mask the bitterness."

Rattled, she stepped back. As much as she had wanted to be correct in her summations about Mikan to avoid ending up in the jailhouse, it still made her nearly vomit to know the high priest was poisoning Tesesra.

"Do you know to whom he has given it?" Thylaina pressed, her voice shaking.

"A maiden he's taken pleasures with." Raylen shrugged and nodded in Breydon's direction. "Like many knights, Mikan is a man with needs. The young woman wanted to ease into the loss without anyone knowing. So she has been drinking a tea with a small amount of insh, preventing anyone from knowing she had been with child. Or so he has told me."

Breydon sneered. "And you believed him?"

Awareness cleared Raylen's eyes, and he blinked several times, freeing his mind from Thylaina's hold. Nose wrinkled, he said, "Why wouldn't I believe our high priest?"

The captain bore down on him, fury distorting his face. "Because he's killing Lady Tesesra's babe!"

Thylaina raised her hand to calm him, but he crushed her into the priest.

Raylen used her as momentum against Breydon, pushing them both forward, then whirled around the table. "Leave."

Breydon's grip on her arm hurt as he guided her back.

A soft grunt emitted from her throat as she twisted from his hand and turned to the priest. "Now that you know the truth, will you aid us?"

Squeezing the back of his neck, Raylen walked to the other end of the table, then dropped his hand with a heavy sigh. "I told you nothing. Do you understand?"

Revulsion fueled the anger filling her chest. "You are as foul as Mikan."

"If I was, you'd never leave." He glared at Breydon. "Take her from here, now."

His touch gentler, the captain led her to the exit.

Thylaina stared back at Raylen. "You are a part of this—of Mikan's harming good people."

The words did not strike compassion in the priest, for he did not react as he corked the hemlock jar and returned it to the shelf.

Urgency pushed Breydon to hasten down the corridor. His reaction in the room revealed enough to her to know he no longer supported Mikan. With his help, it should be easier to convince Arhgrim of the truth, and swiftly.

Two voices came from the worship room: Mikan's and another. Thylaina halted, catching Breydon off balance. Looking both directions of the hallway, she found no others were present. A quick prayer raced through her mind as she pulled the knob. Thank Bryric, no sound emitted.

"What are you doing?" Breydon mouthed.

Thylaina put her finger to her lips, then looked inside. The two men stood alone at the right end of the room, so she moved in and behind a statue. Breydon followed. The decoration was a sconce of a leveled shield held in place between the wall and a sword with the hilt tilted outward, supporting the shield's end. Six candles lined along the center of the shield, reaching a large gold lantern on the wall, light flickering behind the golden-glazed glass. Breydon crouched, watching from beneath the shield, and Thylaina pressed against the wall.

Her hearing was not nearly as good as a xilys warrior, nor her brother's, but she focused on Mikan.

The priest mumbled a few words as he cupped the knight's ears, then he placed his palm on the man's forehead. "May you find guidance throughout the day. Be true to the faith. Come to me if…"

*Which faith?* Since her arrival, Thylaina had yet to see actions true to Valorius' Ways.

"Bow your head," Mikan instructed. The young man closed his eyes and lowered his head. More words flowed in a hushed voice as the priest lifted a cup from a table behind him and poured red dust from a small vial into the goblet.

Stiffened muscles slowed Thylaina's hand as she covered her mouth to silence a gasp. The gods damn them, especially Raylen, for keeping this powder in stock.

Her eyes watered as Mikan removed a black stone pendant from beneath his robe. That was what he had touched the other day. Perhaps the eerie feelings Thylaina experienced in his presence came from that stone. Again, she froze, her heartbeat pulsating in her head as he dipped the pendant into the cup. She rested her hand on Breydon's back for support, barely feeling his tensed muscles. The priest tucked the pendant into his robe, and a dark mist rose from the goblet, fading into nothing.

"Drink," he said.

A warning stuck in Thylaina's throat as power from the black stone silenced her. It could not have been magic, but something darker. Something beyond her.

The knight swallowed several gulps. Finished, he wavered and dropped the cup. Mikan grabbed his arms, steadying him. The initial haziness of the poison passed, and the knight drew in a deep breath, then opened his eyes. Blood trailed from his nose—a dangerous sign.

Teardrops fell. "Vynia, n'ei," Thylaina whispered.

Breydon pulled her from the chamber. When she tried to protest in the domed vestibule, he hushed her. The eyes of several knights now present remained on them as they walked to the exit. A few men muttered Breydon's name and bobbed their heads, but none offered a friendly smile to Thylaina.

Out the doors, down the steps and across the street, Breydon finally let go of her arm. She rubbed where the pressure from his fingers lingered. Now and then he glanced back as they continued to the mansion.

Safety of the mansion in view, he said, "I'll meet with Grim. You do what you must to save Tes' babe."

Pressure of that demand only added to her overwhelmed and scrambled mind. Not only did she have no remedies available, but Mikan's ritual revealed more than Tesesra's babe needed saving.

# Chapter Eight

Thylaina read by the firelight. Even while scanning the entries from lessons and experiences with past patients, she scoured her memories of Master Eidryn's teachings about countering insh weed. Nothing surfaced.

Exhaustion coaxed her eyelids to lower, but worry kept her from sleeping. Thylaina tucked the journal against the chair's arm and rose to view the healing items on the table. Amongst them was a small pouch with a note beneath it. The contents within smelled divine, lavender more distinct. Tea leaves by the feeling through the pouch. She read the note.

*Lady Thylaina,*
*I understand you enjoy tea. This is a special blend from Rhigowan,*
*my home. My mother used to drink it every night before bed. I hope*
*you find it as helpful as she had. And I hope we might find some time*
*together again. I miss your companionship.*
*Your friend,*
*Gavrel*

Tea sounded perfect. The thoughtful gift from the dubight—her friend—might be just what she needed, so she placed the kettle over the fire.

With a steaming cup of tea, she sat in the chair, repositioned the journal, and sipped. It was delightful. Thylaina stared at the fire while she drank, her thoughts jumping from Tesesra's babe to Mikan's pendant, then to Gavrel and his kindness. In the midst of everything that had been happening, she lost count of the days since last seeing him. Thylaina did not want to lose another friend, having lost contact with those in Etharell decades afore leaving home. Aarosyn was the only one who had sent an occasional letter, often inquiring if she discovered new healing remedies or sharing his own. Of course he asked after her well-being, but most communication centered on their skills. Limitations likely prevented what he could write, considering he was a xilys warrior and camp healer. But the others—Rainsala, Leisyn, and Maelene—forgot about Thylaina. Strange really, when the former two had often spent time with her at the palace, mostly in attempts to draw her brother's notice. Maelene served in Neldrid's army as his healer, and therefore, was likely occupied with duty. Must it be that way with Gavrel? If so, Thylaina *would* lose another friend.

Those painful thoughts set aside, she finished the tea, then rested her head back. Just as she was about to drift into a dream, a knock startled her. She looked to the window to determine the hour, but was too groggy to care.

When Thylaina and Breydon had returned earlier that evening, she discovered Arhgrim had sent Katjina back to the scullery, deciding there was no purpose in wasting her time if she was only going to return there. That showed how much faith the marshal had in Thylaina. Breydon ordered Arlin to stand outside her door until after he met with Arhgrim, but it seemed a few hours had passed. Perhaps the captain had finally returned with news.

Despite how much she wanted to hurry to the door, Thylaina's feet dragged, the slippers making barely a sound. Rubbing her sore neck, she opened the door, slightly deflated to see Bramn. At least he looked well improved from the fight with Breydon. Barely any bruising showed on his face, except beneath his eyes and near his nose. Those bruises would take a little longer to fade, although faster than normal thanks to the bossel ointment. He even brought supper, which caused a painful rumble in Thylaina's stomach. She was famished.

"Well," he said, "I'm sorry to disappoint you."

Frowning, she shook her head. "What do you mean?"

"Apparently, I'm not whom you'd hoped for." He looked beyond her and nodded once. "Might I bring your meal inside?"

"Forgive me, Sir Bramn," she said as he entered. "I had expected—"

"The captain?" He chuckled as he set the tray on the table near the window.

Cheeks warming, she closed the door harder than she had meant, then crossed her arms. "Shapele Colmstad said he would return after meeting with the marshal."

"Come sit." Bramn removed the heavy linen from over the food, releasing a billow of steam. "I imagine you're hungry."

"That, I am." She placed the journal on the table, then sat to a meal of pheasant, roasted carrots, and that delightful sweet cornbread. "What hour is it?"

"Shortly after the twenty-first."

Thylaina hesitated from lifting the savory and buttery fowl leg. "Truly?"

"Yes." He leaned against the wall and stared out the window, which faced the orchards below. It was a strangely warm night for autumn.

"I slept two hours then," she whispered. "That explains my neck's ache."

"Chairs can do that." He smirked.

The warm meal was delicious, and she did not bother with conversation until she almost finished. Bramn remained quiet, appearing lost in his thoughts. Wiping her hands on the provided linen, Thylaina looked up at him. "What is it, my friend?"

His head snapped in her direction, his face brighter in the low firelight. "Friend? I appreciate that greatly."

"I mean it." She approached him, noting the concern in his eyes. "You seem troubled."

"If you're correct about all of this, I..." Bramn released a heavy breath. "I wonder what might happen. It could shake the knighthood." Brows dipped low, he chewed on his bottom lip. "Why has Mikan murdered Grim's unborn?"

Her meal churned in her stomach at that question. Walking back to her chair, she recalled Arhgrim telling her that Mikan had taken over Tesesra's care after their second loss. Had the priest also given her insh weed with the losses that followed? Tears blurred her vision as she gazed at the fire, praying she was wrong.

"I must go to Lady Tesesra," she said. And she still needed to concoct something to counter the damage Mikan had caused.

Upon arrival, she discovered Tesesra asleep, so Thylaina focused on the baby. The heartbeat was still too rapid. Quaiy promised to have followed the instructions left for her that afternoon, and was doing her best to keep Her Ladyship comfortable and entertained. Worry etched on the handmaiden's face as she stared at her charge. Thylaina gave Quaiy's shoulder an assuring squeeze, then left the bedchamber.

Some sort of order had been restored in the suite. No table had yet replaced the one Bramn and Breydon broke during their scuffle, but the sofa and chairs were back in their respective places, as was the horrible bear rug. Bramn greeted a guarding knight as Sir Amdronus, who appeared a few years older than he. The two men shook hands and smiled, but shared no conversation. The evening was late for everyone, except Thylaina. She had more work to do, so they descended to the second floor.

"He's a good knight," Bramn said.

"Who?"

"Sir Amdronus. He trained under Grim, so I'm not surprised to see him guarding Tes."

To hear those words eased some of the tension throughout her body, and she hugged his arm. "Thank you."

He patted her hand. "I didn't want you worrying. Did you notice his sword was at the ready?"

"I did."

"Then you know he'll keep Tes safe. As will every knight Grim assigns at her door."

In Thylaina's chamber, Bramn sat in his usual chair and she headed directly for the journal on the table. Ambling to her seat with her nose already in the book, she flipped through the pages. Thylaina sat, rested the book on the arm of the chair, and stopped on the chapter about pregnancies. In the index, she found the pages regarding herbs near the end. It had been at least twenty years since she last assisted with a pregnancy. Uncle Yasontler never let her help at the palace, and the priestesses at the temple believed the Vynist ways were untraditional, so refused her aid.

"What are you reading?" he asked.

She did not look up. "My healing journal."

"I thought you had your answers."

Sighing, she met his curious gaze. "I have never seen a pregnant woman suffer from the effects of insh weed like this. It was always after intentional consumption."

He tilted his head slightly, slowly nodded, then sat back. "So you don't have an answer."

"Please be silent."

"Forgive me." Bramn did not move while she read.

Thylaina reviewed what Master Eidryn had taught, what she had learned from treating Alohrian and Vhormon women, and what her peers had shared from their experiences. Unfortunately, none of them had encountered a situation such as this. She noted the herbs often used with pain and healing, but knew not if they might help Tesesra's babe.

"Sir Bramn, would you kindly bring the quill and inkwell to me?"

He retrieved the items, holding them while she dipped and wrote a new chapter in the journal. This one recording the current event with Tesesra Momestid.

"You're brave," he said.

She glanced at him. "I know not of what you speak."

"I mean..." He looked to the window, then back at her. "What it must've taken for you to leave everything."

Thylaina finished the final sentence, reiterating the uncertainty she could save the babe. "I know not if others consider that bravery or foolishness." She blew softly over the page. "For I *did* leave everything—my family and the status I once held."

He stepped back as she rose, then followed her to the table, where she lay the book open to finish drying. "I'm about to lose the most important person in my life because I'm afraid." He slammed the inkwell on the table, spilling some of the precious liquid into the surface's cracks.

Other than Neldrid, Bramn was one of the most confident men she had ever known. This side of him was strange to witness.

"What do you fear, Sir Bramn?"

He stared at her for a moment. Drawing in a breath, he looked down as he wiped his sleeve with a cloth he snatched from the tabletop. "Losing my family if I go against my mother's wishes." A groan rolled in his throat as he thrust his fingers into his hair. "But I'm losing Einasa."

Thylaina grabbed his hands and lowered them. "I love my father and brother, and all of my family," she said. "I did not leave because I was not the center of their attention, but because I could not give false vows to my betrothed under Lessindra's witness. And I was *truly* miserable."

His fingers curling around hers, Bramn inhaled a shaky breath. "I lose *everything* if I pursue her," he whispered. Shoulders dropping, he continued in a normal tone. "For a year, I've sent messages that expressed my love and devotion, yet promised nothing, and had yet to receive a response. This evening, one arrived." Tears surfaced in his eyes. "Her father insists she considers proposals from the men who've approached her the past several months. Einasa can't grow old waiting for my decision, and I can't blame her for moving forward." Bramn dropped his gaze, a few short, heavy breaths following. "Yet it splits me apart knowing the joy we could've shared."

When he first told Thylaina about his farm maiden, he had revealed vague details. Despite how much strain the man bore within, he always exhibited a strong, confident, and happy presence. Now, Thylaina saw him at his weakest. Bramn was terrified and unsure.

She squeezed his hands. "I refused to permit others who did not know me decide what was best for me. Marrying a man whom I did not love, who was not the foundation of my mortal joy, would subject me to a life of misery. My fate would be my own to determine, not theirs. It was difficult to do what I did—to leave Etharell and all I loved. But I tell you truthfully, I have known more joy these past three weeks than I have for the last fifty years."

A curious frown met her. "Gods, my lady. Staring at you while you say fifty years as if it was nothing is... profound. You look my age. Besides, you've been treated awful here."

"Trust me, the last five decades were not nothing." Thylaina laughed. "And despite some of the horrible things I have endured since leaving home, I feel a sense of purpose here. That I am needed." She palmed his cheek and stroked the top with her thumb. "This life is your only."

He straightened, contemplation weighing his brows lower. "I see. I understand." A smile formed slowly over his lips. He lifted Thylaina and whirled her around, then put her down and hugged her. "Thank you."

"Sometimes," Breydon said from the doorway, "I just don't know what I'm to think about you two."

Still laughing, Bramn and Thylaina separated. Irritation—or was it jealousy?—remained on the captain's face.

"There's nothing to think," Bramn said.

Breydon combed his fingers through his unkempt short, red strands as he closed the door.

Renewed energy added a spring to Bramn's steps as he approached him. "I request leave from the city at dawn."

"For what purpose?"

"To ask for Einasa's hand."

Breydon regarded his friend with a surprised yet pleased expression. "Truly?"

"Lady Thylaina has convinced me it's time to shape my destiny." Bramn's face glowed in the hearth's flickering light.

"You realize what your mother will do?"

The heavy sigh Bramn released faded as he smiled. "I can't live without Einasa."

Thylaina clasped her hands and waited. Surely, this request would not be denied.

Smirking, Breydon nodded. "Granted."

Bramn pulled him into a hug, thumping Breydon's back. "Thank you!"

"I... I'm sorry, my friend, for what I've done," Breydon replied.

The two men parted enough to look at each other.

"You're forgiven, my brother." Bramn grinned. "I thank Valorius you've returned."

They hugged once more, thumping each other's backs.

Giggles escaped Thylaina, and she swayed in place to satisfy the overwhelming urge to dance with joy. To see these two reconcile after a horrible fight was wonderful. Their friendship was on a solid mend.

Faces red from laughing, the men parted.

"If you're leaving at dawn, I suggest you sleep for the night, if you can." Breydon squeezed Bramn's shoulder, his eyes brighter. "You don't want to appear at her home looking exhausted."

"But Lady Thylaina—"

"I'll stay with her." Breydon bobbed his head toward the door. "Go on."

Bramn returned to Thylaina and kissed her cheek. "Thank you again, my friend."

Since her arrival at Caerabis, she had never felt so happy. Her elated heart swelled and her spirit soared. "Rest, my friend."

In his hurry, Bramn slammed the door shut. Breydon and Thylaina laughed. Gazes locked, their smiles slowly faded.

"How was your meeting?" she asked.

"I didn't want to discuss it in front of him." Breydon gestured at the door. "Bramn wouldn't repeat what I share, but it's still no matter for him to know yet."

"Understood." She sat in her chair, then held her breath for a second when Breydon sat on the arm.

"Grim sent me to arrest Mikan," he said.

Lip caught under her teeth, she knotted her fingers.

He tilted his head, his brows arched. "What?"

Would Breydon understand her insistence? She had to try. "Shapele... there is something I believe you must take from him. And please trust me."

It hurt to see the lack of faith, even after what they had been through that afternoon. So Breydon did not yet trust her. It should not shock Thylaina, for in his eyes, she was still a thief.

"What is it?" he asked.

She hesitated, staggered he took another step forward with her toward healing. "He wears a pendant, the one he dipped into the wine at the temple—"

"Yes." He rubbed his forehead, then scowled at the hearth. "I took it when I arrested him."

Her shoulders lowered, relaxed. "Thank you. However, I should like to study it."

"We'll see what Grim says about that." Breydon then chuckled, his head turned to the hearth. "Mikan was furious with me, to say the least."

She would tend to that matter later, especially now since the pendant was out of Mikan's grasp. At this moment, it was time to refocus on Tesesra and her babe. And that meant bringing up the high priest again. "Sir Bramn reminded me that Mikan had cared over Her Ladyship with the last two pregnancies, and that she had lost those babes as well."

Tears welled as he watched the flames. He swallowed, blinked, then looked down at his hands. "I forgot."

"I know not if he caused the other losses, Shapele, but I can try to learn." To offer him comfort, she lay her hand over his. "But first, I must try to save *this* babe."

A stillness followed as he stared at her hand atop his. His fingers bent around hers, then he kissed them. "You will. I know you will."

Thylaina's hand slipped free and lowered slowly to her lap.

Breydon trudged to the door. Gripping the handle, he said, "I'd like some wine. You?"

He had kissed her left hand—right over the knuckles left scarred by him.

"Lady Thylaina?"

She jerked her head up, meeting his gaze. That was the first time he had spoken her name.

"Would you like some wine?"

Unable to find her voice, she nodded.

"I'll return shortly."

The door closed. She tried desperately to piece together what had just happened. That was not the same man from the dark morning hours. The man who had tried to choke her. What in Bryric's Name was happening?

Breydon returned twenty minutes later with spiced redberry wine—elvish wine—a taste of home. How delightful.

"Have you learned how to help Tes?" he asked while filling the crystal goblets.

"Not yet." Thylaina received the offered glass. "Do you think servants are still in the scullery?"

"Possibly." Sipping, he sat in the chair across from her. "Why?"

"I need bossel roots ground, and I do not have the means to do so."

"Then let's go before Viya retires for the evening." He stood, took Thylaina's glass, and placed them both on the table beside the journal. Breydon lifted the book, his brows gathering as he scanned the page.

Thylaina neared him. It was not possible he read it, for she had written in Elvish. Yet his expression gave the impression he could. No. He was likely impressed with her elegant script. She took the journal, closed it, then set it back on the table. "My notes. This contains everything I have learned and continue to learn about herbs and healing." She lifted her cup, brought it closer to her lips. "I have not yet tasted it." Eyes closed, she focused on the flavor of redberry, cinnamon, and cloves settling on her tongue. It seemed ages had passed since she last tasted such a fine wine. "That is delicious."

"I believed you'd enjoy it."

"Where did you get it?"

"Etharell." He headed for the door.

Once again, this man confused her. Breydon held anger and hatred toward her people, yet interacted with them. Spiced redberry wine was not available at border villages, nor was it sold from merchants' wagons. Only wealthy elves acquired it. So how did the wine come into the captain's possession?

He opened the door. "Let us go before Viya leaves."

Thylaina placed the dried bossel roots into a wool pouch, then followed him to the scullery, where she hoped the humans worked efficiently.

Viya could not let the simple request pass without making her own suggestion. Of course, some cooking herbs benefited certain ailments, but this was a serious matter, and she was not a healer.

Thylaina shook her head at Viya's offer. "I would appreciate if your maidens grind all the roots." She gestured at the dried leaves and flowers of an unknown herb. "This is not necessary. I have never used ver... What is this?"

"Vervain." Viya thrust the sack of bossel roots at one of her girls. "And you can't deny something just because you don't know its usefulness." Huffing, she looked at Breydon. "Can you believe we know something the elves don't?"

He chuckled, and Thylaina sighed.

"I'm just as worried about Her Ladyship as you," Viya continued. "Likely more! All of us are." The few maidens present nodded while they cleaned.

Thylaina sniffed the jar of vervain and wrinkled her nose.

"It tastes quite bitter!" Viya laughed.

"What does it do?"

"Many of us use it before and during our monthly bleeds. Forgive me for speaking as such, Captain." Viya did not seem as bothered as he did, for *his* cheeks shaded pink, not hers.

"How does this help Lady Tesesra?" Thylaina asked.

"We also use it at the end of stagnant pregnancies, to help push 'em along."

Thylaina gestured at the bossel roots in the process of being ground into powder. "Those are all I shall need."

"I'm not finished!"

"I do not need to force Her Ladyship into having her baby," Thylaina snapped. "They need healing."

"There is more." Viya crossed her arms and tilted her chin up. "It heals inward infections and eases pain and swelling. Even headaches and burning throats."

"Inward infections?" Thylaina arched a brow. That *was* something more.

Nodding, the cook patted her lower abdomen, then just below her ribcage.

Thylaina lifted the jar again. "Is it best used in a tea?"

"Yes. But it's an awful flavor."

"I have something for that." Thylaina gave the jar to Breydon while thanking Viya.

Once the bossel powder was ready, she and the captain hurried back to her room. She spent the next two hours measuring the powder into vials, then distributing the vervain into separate tubes as well. Finished, she placed two of each in the satchel, along with camiol, xarflas, lavender, mint leaves—the latter also from the scullery—and feverfew. Thylaina closed the satchel, set the remaining vials on the table, then grabbed her journal, the quill, and inkwell. She sat in her chair and began writing notes about vervain and what Viya taught her, using the fireplace for light.

"Do you have any new plans?" Breydon asked.

More questions, yet the same.

To ease his worry, Thylaina did her best to offer a comforting answer. "I believe I do, Shapele. Tomorrow I shall begin a new treatment."

"Good." He slouched in the chair and closed his eyes. "I'll pray it works."

All information recorded, she placed the book afore the hearth to dry. Thylaina knew not if she could slumber with the captain present, but the last two days had been terribly draining. She went behind the screen and changed into the beige shift. The robe donned, she stepped out and toward the bed.

"Lady Thylaina?"

She halted. To hear him speak her name was still strange, yet he had said it with tenderness. "S'yai?"

"That red powder Mikan put in the goblet at the temple... you recognized it."

Thylaina ambled to stand behind her chair, squeezed the back cushion, and gazed at the flames. "S'yai." She turned her attention to him. "Those who make and sell it call it Divine Wrath."

A fearful expression washed away the curiosity. "Why?"

"They convince their buyers it gives the strength of the divine." She sat and pulled her feet up, curling her toes over the edge. "My master tended to some overcome with insanity by the mind poison, those who had suffered its rage. Without us pupils ever being near one such victim, he taught us with the best of his knowledge of how to *try* to help them."

"Why would Mikan do this?"

Thylaina shook her head at the thought of a high priest bringing harm to those he was to guide in their faith. "Those who take the red dust willingly do so because they believe they have nothing to lose or they want to forget their pain. Mikan may have convinced his victims with these lies." She lowered her brows in thought. "But what has he to gain? I imagine part of the answer depends on the number of men he has poisoned." Dropping her shoulders in defeat, she sighed. "But he dipped that black pendant into the drink as well, which was strange."

Thylaina looked at Breydon. "I have never seen someone affected by Divine Wrath, so I know not what they are like compared to my master's teachings."

"You have." Guilt overtook Breydon's visage. "Your first night here, the morning you broke fast with Mikan and me, and last night... when I tried to choke you."

# Chapter Nine

The next morning, while Thylaina tended to Tesesra, Breydon stayed in the suite with the current knight guarding Her Ladyship. Nadiera slept soundly next to her mother, who drew in a few deep breaths.

"Are you well?" Thylaina asked.

"Some pain." Tesesra rubbed just below her belly button.

Thylaina placed her satchel on the table by the window, using the sun for light. She then sat on Tesesra's other side. "I am sorry for everything you have endured. All of it. The pain, sorrow, and the stress of the claims I have made, which forced you and your husband into making difficult decisions. But I want you to know life is something elves value, especially us healers. I will do everything within my knowledge and power to help you and your babe." And she meant it. If Thylaina had to use magic, she would.

Tears shimmering in her eyes, Tesesra nodded. "After seeing the care you provided to Breydon, I believe you."

"Thank you, my lady." Thylaina held her hand to offer further comfort. "Now, I shall prepare a special tea for you to begin the healing within the womb."

Since she did not want Tesesra birthing yet, there was very little vervain blended with crushed xarflas and grated camiol in the tea mix, and Thylaina added crueberry powder for flavor. While it steeped in hot water, she asked, "Your

Ladyship, I should like to learn more about something, and hoped you would impart your knowledge."

Tesesra petted her daughter's hair. "I shall try."

Thylaina hesitated, for inquiring about personal tragedies was not a habit. Breydon had shared some information, more than she had expected, but there was more to know. She looked toward the door and listened. He was having a conversation with the knight. "Can you tell me about his brother, Sir Kreysin?"

Tesesra regarded her with surprise. "What did Breydon tell you?"

"Shapele claims my people killed him."

Still stroking her sleeping daughter's hair, Tesesra released a soft sigh. "I will let you know this much... it isn't yours, the elves', nor Breydon's fault, yet it's a guilt he bears that was always Kreysin's. And it breaks my heart to see him change because he refuses to accept his brother's choices had consequences." Teardrops rolled down her cheeks as she rested her chin atop Nadiera's head. "They were close, yet Kreysin envied Breydon and how well he advanced in the knighthood while he struggled. And because he didn't fare as well as Breydon, he was left behind. Unfortunately, they grew distant, and Kreysin gained friendships with unsavory knights. The brothers rarely talked without fighting. Then during Breydon's weakest moment, when he needed him most, Kreysin turned away." Tesesra smiled sadly. "Yet Breydon forgave him."

Thylaina removed the diffuser from the cup, then stirred the tea.

"Losing Kreysin was the last grief Breydon could suffer," Tesesra continued. "It was like a bowed stick finally snapping from beneath heavy weight. No matter the love Grim and I have shared with him, that this darling girl gives, Breydon is lost to us."

That was why Mikan poisoned him, making him controllable. But why did the high priest wish to control the First Captain of Caerabis, along with a dozen select knights and soldiers?

"He was taken." Thylaina faced her. "Mikan found him fragile, then he struck. But I am trying to help him."

Lips trembling, Tesesra shook her head. "I wasn't Mikan's only victim?"

"There are more." Thylaina offered the steaming tea. "But that is naught for you to worry. Now, drink this slowly. After examination, you shall rest, then I shall return afore afternoon meal."

Sipping the tea, Tesesra wrinkled her nose. "It's not delightful, but it's not awful."

Thylaina woke Nadiera and had her move to the chair, then she instructed Tesesra to lie flat. Palm on the woman's stomach, she focused on the babe, distress and the rapid heartbeat still worrying her. Hopefully, the tea would bring quick healing.

"Quaiy is to perform every task you need." Thylaina pulled the gown down to Tesesra's thighs, then replaced the coverlet. "Understand?"

"If you insist." Tesesra's eyelids drooped as her daughter snuggled in her arms.

"To ease your worry about Shapele Colmstad, he is letting that burden go." Thylaina squeezed Her Ladyship's hand. "You shall see your old friend return to himself."

Tears broke from the corner of Tesesra's eyes. "That is wonderful news."

"Rest, my lady." She glanced at Nadiera, finding the girl watching her.

The men silenced as Thylaina entered the suite, Breydon's gaze brightening. A flutter in her chest had her catching her breath.

"How does she fare?" Breydon asked, gently guiding her toward the door.

"Her Ladyship sleeps."

"That doesn't answer my question."

"She is at ease and resting well," she said as they stepped onto the landing. "I shall return at afternoon meal."

Breydon gently placed her hand in the crook of his arm. "What now?"

Shocked by this behavior, she fumbled with her response. "I-I must see how this dosage performs for Her Ladyship."

"Then let's break fast. I'm starving."

A meal sounded perfect, and she increased their pace to reach the hall sooner.

Arhgrim sat at the table, his food barely touched while he read from a large tome. He hardly looked up when Thylaina and Breydon approached. The marshal sounded a soft grunt, thumped the wooden caller on the table twice, then returned his attention to the book. "How does my wife fare?"

Breydon pulled the chair next to his seat from the table and motioned for Thylaina to sit. While she did so, she said, "Her Ladyship is well and resting, my lord. The babe, however, is my concern."

Relaxing against the chair's back, Arhgrim rubbed his eyes, then looked from Breydon to Thylaina. "Is there anything I can do to help?"

Excellent. The question she had hoped for, and she prayed the marshal would agree to her demands. "For the babe's sake, I must have full control of what happens in that room, my lord."

His forehead wrinkled and his brows lowered further. "What do you mean?"

A maidservant entered with a tray. She placed porridge and pork strips afore Thylaina and Breydon. The captain requested a cup of coffee, and Thylaina asked for tea. A web of honey decorated the surface of the porridge, which Thylaina broke with her spoon. The warmth felt good moving down into her belly.

"Are you eating that?" Breydon tapped her plate of pork with his spoon.

Smiling, she pushed it closer to him. When she returned her attention to the marshal, his grin swiftly disappeared. Thylaina fought the urge to giggle at his assumption.

"My lady," Arhgrim said. "What do you mean you must have control of Tes' chamber?"

Thylaina scooped more porridge. "The servants follow my orders."

"Now wait a—"

"I do this for the babe's sake," she said. "I have never faced such a difficult situation, my lord. Full cooperation from *all* the servants from the chamber to the scullery is necessary."

Arhgrim's eyes locked on her while she ate, and he slid his thumb and middle finger over and under each other. His gaze went to Breydon as the maidservant returned, setting down the steaming cup of dark liquid for the captain, then the teapot and cup for Thylaina. "Breydon?" he said.

The cup at his chin, Breydon shrugged. "Don't have a choice, do we, Grim?"

"I could say no."

"It's a great risk." Breydon sipped, then grimaced. He set the cup down and lifted a pork strip. "If Tes was my wife, I'd trust Lady Thylaina."

Arhgrim waved a hand in her direction. "What if she's wrong?"

"Again, what choice do you have?" The captain bit into the chunk.

She stared at him. Breydon's complexion was brighter and his eyes were clearer. No harshness touched his tone anymore. The man had changed, and so quickly. But that should not have surprised her, not after their conversation the night afore and everything she had learned about his consuming Divine Wrath. Sipping the tea, she thought about what the captain had revealed to her.

*"I was lost after Kreysin's death. Weak and angry. Mikan assured me the red dust would help me recover and return to duty as a stronger man. Each time he gave it to me, the more I believed I truly needed it." Breydon had looked at her then. "Over the past nine moons, Mikan administered it twice each month... until your arrival. After my admittance to finding you—" He lowered his eyes and licked his lips. "I admitted to finding you attractive. Then he started giving me smaller doses every other night, claiming I required the red dust to fight your enchantments." Grimacing, Breydon squeezed the back of his neck. "I can no longer blame the elves nor myself for the choices Kreysin had made. It's a guilt I'll no longer bear." He took her left hand, his fingers caressing the scars. "And I'm terribly sorry for hurting you."*

Thylaina stirred the tea, remembering what had followed. Disbelieving that she found it in her heart to forgive him, Breydon wept. She had assured him she understood why he carried a burden that was never his to bear. Love often did such things to people when they lost someone dear to them. Thylaina could not blame him for seeking a way to ease his pain, nor for believing someone he trusted would lead him down a path of devotion, only to be betrayed. Breydon then released a great breath, as if freed from beneath an immense encumbrance. He met her gaze and smiled—a truly dashing smile. She could not help returning it. Holding hands, they had stared at each other and grinned like fools. Until she asked him if he had experienced any nose bleeds after drinking one of Mikan's poisoned wines. Breydon admitted to a bloody nose after the last two drinks.

Now, she worried about what injuries *he* suffered, and if the remedy for Tesesra and her babe would help him... should it be successful.

"Very well." Arhgrim's voice cut into her thoughts. "What do you need, my lady?"

Thylaina pushed to the back of her mind that the man beside her confessed to having an attraction to her. Setting the spoon on the small plate, she said, "Her Ladyship requires absolute bedrest. Quaiy must follow my orders and Lady Tesesra must obey. Is that understood?"

Smirking, Breydon raised an eyebrow.

Arhgrim grunted. "Go on."

"You and Lady Nadiera may visit once a day, but n'ei longer than an hour, and only if you keep Her Ladyship free of stress."

He chuckled in disbelief. "If I wish to see my wife—"

"My word stands," Thylaina said. "And I will hear n'ei disagreement. The visits are limited unless I say otherwise."

The chamber fell silent. Even Breydon stopped eating, his attention shifting between the marshal and Thylaina.

Cheeks crimson and eyes darker green, Arhgrim leaned forward. "Can you assure me that—?"

"I promise nothing, my lord." Thylaina lifted her cup and met his fierce expression. "But is not the life of your babe worth trying?"


Tesesra attempted to argue, then impose her authority, but none of it worked, not with Breydon reiterating Arhgrim's command. Thylaina ignored Her Ladyship's scowl and began making the special tea while awaiting Viya's arrival. It was the same dosage as that morning: very little vervain, crushed xarflas, grated camiol, and crueberry powder for flavor. This evening, she intended to lessen the vervain and increase the xarflas. Perhaps Thylaina might add mint instead of crueberry.

Viya arrived shortly after Tesesra finished the tea; Thylaina sat at the bedside with the cook and Quaiy and went over what foods Her Ladyship could eat. "She may have porridge with n'ei honey, app—"

"No honey?" Viya appeared appalled.

Thylaina kept a solid posture. "N'ei honey *at all*."

"Well... there goes any delight in eating."

"As I was saying." Thylaina looked from Viya to Quaiy to Tesesra. "*Only* porridge with n'ei honey to break fast. Apples may accompany it. For other meals: mushrooms and carrots in broth, boiled cabbage and carrots, roasted squash, and even some of the tasty cornbread—"

"I make that with honey." Viya raised her brows.

Sighing, Thylaina looked at Tesesra. "Forgive me, my lady, but you cannot have the cornbread."

"Damn it to Darkness," Tesesra snapped.

"Bloody Blackening," Viya muttered.

Quaiy's eyes widened.

Thylaina resumed the instructions. "N'ei raw honey, nor wine, mead, ale, or beer. And she absolutely cannot have fancy drinks, like that coffee from Myndrose. Only the tea I provide, milk, and water *I* bring." It was time to purify Her Ladyship's drinking water as well.

Scowling, Tesesra opened her mouth, but Thylaina raised her hand to silence any protests. Her Ladyship crossed her arms and huffed.

"Do we have an understanding?" Thylaina asked.

Viya stood. "What if there's trouble with delivering the meals?"

It was hard to imagine anyone giving this woman difficulty.

Leaning beside the bedroom entrance, Breydon said, "I'll ensure you and... Panya is the name of the other kitchen maiden permitted to help?" He arched a brow; Viya nodded once. "You both shall have a trusted guard present at all times to make sure nothing happens to Tes' meals."

Thylaina stared at him. This was more than she ever expected. "Thank you, Shapele."

He bowed his head, his expression revealing it displeased him to even have to assign guards concerning Tesesra's food.

"I must examine Her Ladyship." Thylaina gestured to the door. "If you do not mind, Shapele..."

Breydon kissed Tesesra's forehead. "We do this because we love you," he whispered, then left; Viya followed.

Thylaina performed an examination, then pressed her hand to Tesesra's stomach. There was still a sign of distress, yet the babe's heartbeat was stronger than that morning. Not as alarming this time, but it did not mean all was yet well.

"Do you enjoy needlework?" she asked, while Tesesra sat up.

"That is what we're forced to do to entertain ourselves, isn't it?"

Thylaina tried not to laugh, yet a titter escaped. "I suppose." She pushed a lock of hair from Tesesra's temple. "You shall have time to make something lovely."

The woman groaned.

"I will return afore supper," Thylaina said.

Quaiy giggled as she sat beside her charge. "I have some wonderful needlepoint ideas."

Breydon spoke with the guard at the landing door. The knight silenced, then approached Thylaina.

"My lady." He blinked several times, concern dominating his visage. "Is there anything further I—I mean, we—can do to help Her Ladyship? I'll pass your orders on to the other guards."

The love for Tesesra was absolutely beautiful. Delighted with the dedication of those around her, Thylaina smiled wide. "If possible, make certain Her Ladyship does not get out of bed. And none are to upset her."

"If I hear any commotion," he nodded toward the bedroom, "I'm in there."

"There are other orders, such as who shall bring her meals."

"Captain Colmstad has informed me of those details." The guard stood tall. "I'm your faithful servant."

"Thank you."

Breydon took the satchel from Thylaina, grinning at her curious expression. He hooked the strap over his shoulder and began escorting her back to her chamber. "Grim chose fine men," he said, as they entered her bedroom. "Trustworthy men."

"It pleases me greatly."

Breydon placed the satchel beside Thylaina's journal on the table, then turned and crossed his arms. "His family is too fine to me," he said. "It amazes me such nobles would befriend a poor bastard knight."

Appalled, she stood beside him. "Why do you call yourself such a dreadful name?"

"That's what I've been branded since joining the knighthood." He shrugged. "It doesn't matter that I've proven myself a knight's offspring and became a leader. I'm still a bastard knight."

Understanding, Thylaina nodded. "You know whom your father is, yet he does not claim you."

Breydon shook his head. "Even as he stared at his reflections, he denied us both. But it didn't matter when the Council saw Kreysin and me standing beside him. They permitted us into the knighthood to begin our training."

She tilted her head, squinted. "You cannot join the knighthood unless you share the blood of a knight?"

"No."

What a horrible way for a country to limit its strongest military power; basing it on bloodline alone. Unbelievably senseless.

"It is sad he denied you," she whispered, deciding it was best not to insult his people's traditions.

"I admit back then I had hoped he might embrace us as his sons." Breydon lowered his arms and faced her. "But months afterward, when I sparred against his rightful heir in the arena, and saw my father with his family, I understood why."

"Yet did he not love your mother?"

Gaze lost in the dancing fire of the hearth, the captain chewed on his lip. "My grandsire told us the man adored our mother, and often came to the farm to see her. But once he learned she was with child, he ceased. She died minutes after birthing us. Everything I learned about her was from what my grandsire and grandmother shared."

Thylaina's heart ached for him. For herself. "I sometimes wonder if it would have been best to have never known my mother, for many of us were left empty after we lost her. She was a glorious presence in our lives."

"Then you were blessed to have known her." His warm hand pressed to her cheek, his thumb smearing a teardrop dry. "For she must've left an impression on you—formed a part of you—just as those I had loved left an impression on me."

Breathing deeply, Thylaina met his gaze and rested her hand on his. This moment revealed a connection they shared in their losses. "What was your mother's name?"

The corner of his lips rose just the slightest. "Elianna. And your mother?"

Mother had passed well over a hundred years ago, so it was unlikely he would recognize the name. Heart thumping hard in her ears, she said, "Alihean."

His smile grew. "Both beautiful names."

"They are." Thylaina leaned into him, hoping she returned the same warmth and comfort he gave.

Breydon's fingers slid gently from her cheek, down the side of the neck, over her shoulder, forcing her arm to lower as they glided along the length of it until he held her hand. He pressed his nose into her hair and inhaled. Placid, they remained unmoving for a long moment, breathing together. A soothing sway began. She tilted her head back enough to feel her cheek brush his jaw, her lips grazed his earlobe. Her breathing grew deeper, shaking, as his hand moved to her waist, then her back, pulling her nearer. Breydon's heat enveloped her. Thylaina had never felt so bonded with someone. Frozen in that warmth, she did not want to move nor speak, but remain close to him for as long as possible. Which was only a few seconds more, for a knock startled them apart.

The door opened and Katjina popped her head inside. "My lady!" The handmaiden entered, excitement lighting her face. "Marshal Momestid has returned me to your side. Isn't that wonderful?"

"He could've waited a few minutes more," Breydon muttered.

Thylaina smiled as she hurried to hug Katjina, her face now cooling. "I am happy to have you back."

"I suppose you don't need me any longer." Breydon headed for the door.

No. He could not yet leave. She needed him near. "Shapele."

He immediately spun on his heel, as if he had hoped she would call him.

Cocking her head toward her raised shoulder, Thylaina asked, "Shall we not share supper together?"

Cheeks now ruddy, he bowed. "I'd be delighted to sit beside you, my lady."

"I-I mean... if we could dine alone."

Breydon raised a brow. "I would like that."

"Wonderful. We shall eat after I visit Her Ladyship." Thylaina then looked at Katjina. "I think in the orchard would be perfect since the weather is still agreeable."

"Lovely idea, my lady," Katjina said.

The captain grinned and partially bowed. "As you wish."

Thylaina and Katjina watched him leave. Once the door shut, Katjina slowly faced Thylaina, her eyes widening. "Captain Colmstad?"

Nothing could restrain Thylaina's smile as she slipped her arm from the handmaiden and returned to the table. "What of him?"

Following, Katjina said under her breath, "'What of him?' she asks. What happened? I never imagined you'd willfully share any meal with the man."

Thylaina slid her hand down her long braid, curled her fingers within the hair beneath the tie. "I have finally met a hint of the fine man of whom several of you have spoken," she said, her cheeks warming again. "I should like to know him more."


Katjina and Arlin stood under the apple trees, the setting sun's orange blaze glowing on their sides. Breydon squinted and blinked an awful lot, averting his gaze from the burning hue. He had eaten nothing and his wineglass remained full. Plate pushed forward, he rested his elbows on the table, then rubbed his earlobe twice. Arlin inched toward him, then stilled, concern showing in his eyes. The captain could not seem to focus on any one thing, not even Thylaina. Had the moment in her chamber caused the same unsettled feeling for him as it did for her? Not that the closeness shared with Breydon disturbed Thylaina, for it had not, but confusion overwhelmed her while she freshened up for the meal. She could not stop thinking about the First Captain of Caerabis.

"Shapele, does something trouble you?"

Eyelids squeezed shut, he pinched the bridge of his nose. "No." An unsuccessful lie.

"You do not look well."

"I'm fine." He sipped from the wine cup, then grimaced. Pain or disgust?

"Are you certain?"

"My head aches." He offered an assuring smile. "Only a little."

"The fresh air should do you well."

Thylaina spread goat's cheese combined with rosemary and garlic on a piece of flatbread. The flavors blended perfectly together. Breydon still had yet to eat. So while he rubbed his eyes with the heels of his hands, Thylaina viewed the space between the orchard and the mansion to distract her mind with something other than the captain. She envisioned knee holly bordering each side of the walking path from north to south. The bushes would be lovely in each season—white star-shaped flowers in spring and red berries from late summer through winter—while providing valuable healing herbs year-round. In fact, the mansion's back wall was perfect for repenia vines. To have the leaves available for olesa oil would be beneficial. Even for a short stay. The vines could easily be collected from Ormiana Forest where they flourished. Enjoying another bite, she imagined more herbs growing behind the mansion.

Breydon snatched a slice of bread from his plate and bit into it. After swallowing, he dropped the remainder atop his untouched meal. "Forgive me, my lady." He stood. "I fear I'm terrible company this evening."

"What is it?"

"I'm not feeling well." Breydon blinked several times again. "I must retire."

"Do you wish me to—?"

"No. Tes needs your attention." His forced smiles were not as handsome as the real ones. "Good night."

Breydon did not wait for a response; he was already on the northern path, Arlin following. Strange how the air seemed to chill after his departure.

Setting the bread on her plate, Thylaina sat back. He was obviously not feeling well, but it seemed something else trouble him. Perhaps, like with Bramn, she misunderstood Breydon's feelings toward her. Whatever the emotional turmoil, this food could not go to waste. Thylaina motioned for Katjina to sit and share the delightful meal with her. Pickled silk wyrs from Vhormos were a real treat for Thylaina. No one prepared the flying fish from the Silver Sea like the Vhormons. Katjina, however, passed on the sea fare. They finished the meal quickly, for the night grew colder as the sun faded.

Once inside the mansion, Thylaina asked a guard to escort her to the marshal's cabinet to make a request for an herb garden.

After the meeting, Thylaina came upon Bramn in the entrance hall. Elated, he spun her until she was dizzy. "Einasa joins me in a fortnight!" He held her arms while she regained her balance. "But we shan't plan the wedding until the babe is born. Besides, I sent a message to the high priest in Warstchia to preside the event." He began walking her to her chamber, whistling a light tune reflecting the merriment in his gaze.

"Why from Warstchia?"

"Because Mikan can't do it." Bramn chuckled. "I wouldn't want him to, anyway. And this priest is dear to me."

Upon entering her bedroom, Katjina took Thylaina's shawl and hung it up, then motioned her to the chair afore the hearth.

"Tell me what happened, my friend." Thylaina gestured to the other seat.

Bramn's face brightened as he pulled the chair closer to hers and sat. "Einasa's father wasn't pleased at first."

Thylaina lowered her brows. "Why not?"

"Understand that poor Einasa has waited a year for me to come to my senses. He's protective."

"I suppose."

"After I told Grim, he sent my request to my Uncle Haltrin, asking him to oversee the wedding."

"Your uncle is the high priest in Warstchia?"

"He is." Bramn looked down at his palms. "He stepped forward when my father died."

Thylaina had never heard about his father's passing. "I… I am sorry, my friend. But I am glad to know your uncle was there for you."

"Thank you." He smiled, then looked around the room. "Now, what are we to do tonight?"

A celebration sounded perfect, but not when Thylaina had much work to do.

"I must tend to Her Ladyship once more this evening. If you wish to share a drink afterward, that would be lovely."

Bramn's grin widened. "Excellent!"

It was quiet in Tesesra's chambers. Bramn stayed in the suite with Sir Amdronus, sharing his exciting news, while Thylaina checked on Her Ladyship.

"Please leave us," she said to Quaiy. "I must concentrate." The handmaiden hesitated, as this was the first time Thylaina had ever demanded privacy for an examination. Thylaina motioned to the door. "You may wait just outside, if you wish. It shall only be a moment."

Quaiy glanced at Tesesra, then left. Once the door closed, Her Ladyship shifted her curious gaze to Thylaina. "What is this?"

"A more thorough examination that requires complete silence. Now lie back and remain still. I shall try to hear the babe's heartbeat more clearly beyond yours."

With some help from Thylaina, Tesesra did as she was told.

"Close your eyes, my lady," Thylaina said, her voice soft and steady. "Good. Now, breathe easy and deep. In… then out. Just like that. Perfect, my lady."

Shutting her eyes, she prayed in Elvish to Vynia while giving slight pressure to the sides of Tesesra's stomach. "Guide me, Great Healer. Grant me vision and show me the babe." After feeling nothing, Thylaina smoothed her hands to the top, repeating the words. Spinning clouds filled her head and her feet felt like they floated just above the floor. An image of a baby within the womb slowly formed in Thylaina's mind. Tesesra had said she was seven months pregnant, yet the child was small. However, it could be the result of Mikan's poison. Thankfully, the babe's heartbeat was now steady; all her fingers and toes were accounted for; and dark hair already covered her head. Yes. Another girl.

Thylaina stopped praying, then helped Tesesra sit up. "The babe is n'ei longer distressed."

Tears fell immediately. "Thank you," Tesesra said through a smile.

"I shall make more tea." Thylaina opened the door, shared the news with the suite's occupants, then prepared the tea. This time, she flavored it with mint, which Tesesra found more agreeable. "You should sleep through the night," Thylaina said. "If there is any trouble at all, please send for me."

"You know—" Tesesra yawned. "I'll have you moved to a closer chamber. There's no need for you to go up and down the stairs while caring for me."

Which would be perfect.

"It is greatly appreciated, Your Ladyship."

When Thylaina opened the door to leave, Nadiera rushed inside.

"Mother!" The little girl climbed onto the bed and snuggled against Tesesra's side. Her Ladyship tensed, her face skewing, but then she relaxed.

This would not do.

Arhgrim entered the chamber. His smile came and went. The backs of his fingers caressed Tesesra's cheek. "Are you well, love?"

"Just tired." Eyes closed, Tesesra rested her chin atop Nadiera's brown locks.

"Can I sleep with you tonight, Mother?"

"Of course."

"I am afraid not," Thylaina said.

Tesesra frowned, yet it flattened as she fell asleep. However, the young girl glowered at Thylaina.

"Forgive me, Lady Nadiera," Thylaina said, "but it is best this way. Especially with how often I am in and out of the room." She turned and continued explaining to the marshal. "Not to mention that should something arise, I do not want her present."

He nodded. "I agree."

"Father," Nadiera whined.

"Your mother needs rest. It's best you sleep in your chamber." He nodded again, settling the matter. "Come. You can break fast with her on the morrow."

Nadiera cast a hateful glare at Thylaina, eased off the bed, then stormed from the chamber.

Arhgrim looked from the door to Thylaina. "I'm sorry."

"I do not blame her."

"How is Tes?"

After Thylaina shared the news about the baby's condition, while withholding he was having another daughter, Quaiy sat beside the bed and resumed with her needlepoint. Arhgrim stayed, and Thylaina left with Bramn.

It was silent on their way to her room. Bramn, although excited about his upcoming marriage and improving health of the babe, seemed deep in thought. As they stepped onto the second landing, Arlin approached. His black hair was in disarray, a red welt formed near the end of his left brow, and reddened whites intensified his green irises.

"My lady," he said with a quaking voice.

"What is it?" she asked.

"I come by Raylen's request."

It was unlikely she masked her contempt. "What does he want? And why did he send you?"

"It's Captain Colmstad." The young man tugged at his collar, where more redness showed. "The priest begs for your aid."

Thylaina's chest tightened. "What has he done to the shapele?"

"N-nothing, my lady. I swear."

Bramn gripped Arlin's shirt and jerked him close. "What's happened?"

The young man's eyes watered. "The captain... He—I don't know. Something's odd. He's not acting like himself."

Thylaina patted Bramn's arm until he relaxed his hold on the squire's shirt. "He is frightened, my friend." Speaking with a soft, musical voice, she asked Arlin about his wounds.

"After leaving supper, Captain Colmstad went straight to the temple, yet he told me to wait at his house." Arlin shook his head. "But when he arrived, he was...

fury. He struck me." The young man's voice cracked. "Captain's never hit me before." Tears broke and trailed down his cheeks; he wiped them away. "I didn't know what I'd done wrong."

"Nothing," Bramn said, squeezing Arlin's shoulder. "You've done nothing." He sighed, looked at Thylaina. "Arlin, go to Kimmy and have him pour a drink for you."

"Yes, sir." Arlin wiped his eyes again, then descended to the main floor and left the mansion.

Thylaina returned to her room to collect her satchel and a shawl. There was no knowing what Raylen had done to Breydon. "Katjina, I may need your assistance."

"Yes, my lady."

Everything collected, the three headed to Breydon's home.

They came upon the herbal priest two blocks from the mansion, heading in their direction. Relief eased worry from his face as they approached. However, Bramn yanking on Raylen's robes and shouting questions left him unsettled once again.

"He demanded I give him Divine Wrath!"

Thylaina shook her head. "Shapele knows what it will do to him."

Raylen pulled his garb free, then straightened it. "His mind didn't seem true to him. He was angry, yet appeared—"

"In pain," Thylaina said.

"Yes. I believed you might know what to do."

"Do you care?" Bramn spat.

"I do." Raylen did not look away from Thylaina. "Now knowing the part I had played in Mikan's schemes, I want to right my wrongs. I want to help the captain." Sincerity weighed within his words and filled his eyes.

Thylaina nodded. "I believe you. Please tell me where the shapele is."

"Furious I wouldn't fulfill his request, he stormed from the temple." Raylen sighed. "I followed him to the vault. There, I convinced the guards to stop him from freeing Mikan. After that, he went home and struck down his squire. Once I sent Arlin to you, I posted two men at the captain's door."

Bramn charged onward; Thylaina clutched her satchel close and followed.

# Chapter Ten



**W**ithholding from Divine Wrath often exhibits an anger unknown to even the kindest of men. In my experience, one addicted to the red dust wants what is no longer available to them, so expect cruelty. Yet keep in mind they do not mean what they say nor do. Fury controls them. I have yet to discover how to help one engulfed by this ire. If ever faced with a Divine Wrath addict in great suffering—if you have the strength—reach beyond their rage and grasp the aching soul who seeks freedom from this dangerous bark. Perhaps you might find the answer I never did."—Master Eidryn, Lessons of Divine Wrath

Despite that he had never let Thylaina and her peers gain a direct understanding by tending to one ailing from an addiction to Divine Wrath, Master Eidryn shared his knowledge with his pupils. He had claimed every experience was different. And although he helped many through strenuous and horrific days of overcoming their need for Divine Wrath, Master Eidryn had yet to find a less taxing method. Even *he* needed several days of respite following the cleansing of red dust addicts. Unfortunately, there were some who failed to break free, their lives claimed by Divine Wrath. Master Eidryn sometimes referred to it as Red Death instead.

Thylaina's skills outmatched all her peers, including her cousin, Prince Valraahn. As heir to the throne, he was expected to follow his father's path to be not only the king but the nation's strongest healer. Healing came naturally to Thylaina, and she surpassed him without trying. But could *she* save Breydon from Divine Wrath?

As the small group neared the captain's home, she prayed to Vynia for guidance and strength. Her mind returned to Valraahn and his lack of faith in the Earthen Goddess during the days of their healing studies. Perhaps that was why he often sought Thylaina's aid in those years. No one needed to become a Vynist to be a successful healer, but giving honor to the goddess certainly helped. Then again, Uncle Yasontler pressed upon his son that the Vynists' path was not the king's. So why did he send Valraahn and Thylaina to Master Eidryn to enrich their healing skills? If duty as king had not demanded too much from Uncle Yasontler, perhaps he would have instructed them instead. Thinking of it all now while she should have focused on Breydon threatened the beginning of a headache. And thinking of her cousin made her heart hurt. She missed Valraahn, and would give anything at that moment for one of his light-hearted jests and infectious laughter.

Muffled shouts, thuds, and crashes sounded from the captain's abode ahead. No lights flickered from the dark windows, but Thylaina noticed movement through one of them. Then something crossed the path of one they now walked past, and a chair leg broke through. Pieces of glass burst outward, spraying to the ground below. A bellowed curse rang clear, freed by the broken pane.

Thylaina stopped abruptly and grabbed Bramn's arm. Master Eidryn's warnings had not prepared her for this.

Bramn's warm hand covered hers. "You needn't do this."

There was no other to save the captain. Thylaina set her chin and moved to the front of the house. Two sentries blocked the door, one of them holding a torch. Upon seeing the men's faces, she halted. "Gavrel?" It seemed ages had passed since last seeing him.

The dubight frowned. "My lady, what're you doing here?"

"I came to help Shapele Colmstad."

Gavrel looked from her to Bramn then to Raylen. "This is no matter for her!"

Raylen raised his hands slightly. "I can think of no one else—"

"We owe you no bloody explanations, dubight." Bramn stepped forward. "Move aside."

The muscles of Gavrel's jaw feathered. "No, sir."

Bramn's eyes widened, then narrowed. "What did you just say?"

"Didn't you see the squire?"

Pounding rattled the door. "You bastards still there?" Breydon shouted from beyond.

Thylaina jumped, stumbling backwards into Raylen's arms.

"Afraid to come in, are you?" the captain continued. "I'll slit your bloody throats!"

Gavrel had jerked from the thundering of Breydon's fists, but he and the soldier next to him did not move from their places. The dubight nodded in Thylaina's direction. "She's not going in there."

Heart beating just as hard as the captain's fist on the clattering door, Thylaina doubted she could do anything helpful.

"Come in! I dare you!" Breydon roared, his voice strained.

*I must try.* Gaze locked on the shuddering door, Thylaina approached.

Gavrel stepped into her path. "I can't let you."

"Stand aside!" Bramn's faced reddened as he also moved closer.

"Thylaina, please don't." Gavrel took her hand. "He'll hurt you."

Something heavy struck the door, seeming to shake the house. Everyone jumped and stared at it.

"To the bloody Darkness with all of you!" Breydon bellowed.

Her heart pounded no longer, it broke. It was not anger in his voice, but agony. Tears blurred her vision as she pushed past Gavrel. "I must, my friend," she whispered. *Vynia, guide me.*

"Thylai—"

She turned to see Bramn wrestling Gavrel from the entrance and tossing him into the yard. The men grappled several seconds more afore Bramn had the dubight pinned to the ground.

Katjina gaped at the scene, then turned her wide eyes to Thylaina.

"Stay here." Thylaina nodded. "I shall be fine."

"My lady!" Gavrel called, struggling from beneath Bramn. "Don't!"

She faced the door, shaking from a hard object striking it. Holding the satchel in her sweaty grasp, she raised her other hand and waited until after the next thud. She knocked. Another thud followed, then it silenced. She knocked again. "Shapele Colmstad."

Something clattered to the floor. "You shouldn't be here," Breydon said, his voice hoarse. "Why are you here?"

"I came for you."

"Leave, Lady Thylaina."

"Please let me inside." She licked her lips. Waited.

The door opened half a foot, the torch's dancing orange glow revealing a sickly man. Breydon stood in nothing but wool pants. Bruises marred a few places of his discolored flesh, and although his head was turned down, Thylaina noted darkness beneath his eyes. His chest expanded and retracted fast and erratically.

"Why are you here?" he whispered.

"I want to help you."

Stillness surrounded all in the yard. A few more soldiers and two knights joined, bringing more torches to the scene.

Breydon grimaced, closed the door until an inch of darkness remained. "Leave."

Gavrel's grunting caught her attention as he thrashed to free himself from beneath Bramn. The knight, however, was unyielding. The other men watched, some frowning. Gavrel's filthy face deepened to crimson as he cried out, "My lady!"

"I'll free him once you're inside," Bramn hollered.

Desperate, Thylaina grasped at something from earlier that day. "Breydon! When you viewed my journal this afternoon, you were not simply looking at it, were you?" The door did not close, nor did she hear him move. Switching to the Elvish Tongue, she continued. "You were reading it."

Two long seconds passed. "S'yai."

A breath rushed out as she smiled. "You speak my language?"

"On behalf of Marshal Momestid," he continued speaking in Elvish without error, although not as musically as her kin, "I am an ambassador to the xilys camps and the elven generals." His voice faded from the entrance as he spoke. "Enter, my lady."

Thylaina pushed the door open enough to slip inside, then closed it. "When were you going to share this secret with me, Captain?"

He snorted from the shadows between the fireplace and a window across the room. "You shouldn't be in here." Breydon returned to the lesser Tongue. "It's best you're not." He looked to the window, from where more torchlight entered. "Not while I'm like this."

Thylaina surveyed the room, noting the layout. It was smaller than she had expected from the outside, or so it seemed, but that could be due to the upturned table near the center, a large cushioned chair on its side adjacent to the cold hearth, and a small wooden chair with a missing leg under the opposite window from where he stood; the leg lay on the floor beside her. Other evidence of his rage decorated the floor in the forms of shattered glasses, bottles, mugs, and other items. A horrific stench struck her: vomit mixed with body odor.

She moved in Breydon's direction. "I am a healer, remember? I have seen men at their worst."

"But you've never seen *me* like this. I've—" He coughed, then groaned softly. "I felt ill."

"Does your head still ache?"

"So much it makes me dizzy." Breydon pressed the heel of his trembling hand to his temple. "Tell me, was it so difficult to speak my name?"

Thylaina's cheeks warmed, for she had not called him by his name proper until attempting to gain entrance. "How did you learn Elvish?"

"My question came first."

Watching her step, she continued toward him. There were several wet spots on the floor, obviously vomit. "N'ei, it was not."

He smiled briefly. "I love the way you say it."

"Please let me help you."

"Why? And don't tell me it's because you're a healer." He pointed at her, his arm shaking. "You've no good reason. Not after what I did to you."

Confused, she frowned. "Of what do you speak?"

Winching, he touched the side of his head. "I hurt you," he mumbled. "Gods! I tried to kill you."

"Breydon... I forgave you."

His eyes narrowed. Suddenly, he laughed. "Forgave me? Surely, you—"

"You think I lied?" Thylaina stomped toward him. "I forgave you because I—" She poked his chest, her finger slipping on flesh slick with perspiration. Forgetting what she meant to say, she wiped her hand on her skirt while staring at him.

Breydon's wet hair clung to his scalp, and dark spots had formed near his irises. The man's body quaked while he clenched his jaw. Suddenly, he grabbed her arms, squeezing hard as he pulled her closer. "I need Divine Wrath," he hushed in her ear. "Get some for me, or I might hurt you again."

No. This was not right. Breydon would not harm her. After the moments they had recently shared, it was not possible. He was not the beast she had met the first night in Caerabis, but a man who, like Thylaina, suffered loss. Breydon was deeply caring person, for it showed whenever he looked at the Momestids. He was a protector. Master Eidryn had said a red dust addict would do and say things they did not mean, and Thylaina was certain the captain had done just that. If she did not have resources beyond her master's, then what more could she do to help Breydon? The humans had different herbs, but the remedies were similar, so she doubted finding an answer with them.

Breydon wrapped his arms around her, wept within the crook of her neck. "Please, Thylaina. I need it." He shook against her.

Earlier that day, he had seemed far improved, then within hours, he was unrecognizable. This was not desire for the mind poisoning herb, but his body's need for it. There was no other explanation for Breydon's behavior and condition. With that in mind, Thylaina considered how to use the red dust to their advantage.

Mikan had abruptly increased his dosage from twice a month to every other day. Perhaps Breydon's struggle was because of the sudden surge then removal of its presence in his body. That might explain the perspiration and shaking. So withholding Divine Wrath completely could do more harm than good. If she remembered correctly, the high priest would have given him some this night.

She stroked his saturated hair. "Breydon," she said with a hint of a melody. "Cease the tears, for they will cause more pain."

"I hurt everywhere," he said against her neck.

"I will help you." As much as Thylaina hated speaking these next words, it was a promise she had to make. "I shall give you some Divine Wrath."

He pulled his head away, his nose tip grazing her cheek. His face was so close, his trembling, awful breath hot. "You will?"

The dark spots in his eyes… He must have vomited so hard that vessels broke, spilling blood into the whites. The screaming did not help either.

Remembering his question, she nodded. "S'yai."

Breydon squeezed her in a crushing embrace. "Thank you," he mumbled against her shoulder. "Thank you, Thylaina."

"I-I must get it." She palmed his cheek and smiled, then gestured to the upturned chair. "Will you sit while I retrieve the dust?"

Releasing her, he nodded the slightest, then walked backward, as if nervous to lose Thylaina from sight. "Please hurry."

"Trust that I shall do all I can."

Still gazing at Thylaina, he righted the large chair, faced it to the door, and sat. His legs bounced in anticipation or reaction to withdrawal from the red dust.

To show him she would return, Thylaina placed her healing case afore the hearth. Resting her hand reassuringly on his arm, she smiled. "Be patient."

The night air was fresh in her lungs. She had not realized how warm and stuffy it was inside. Or perhaps it was Breydon's behavior and nearness. However, respite from the strife in the captain's home was short-lived as she noticed Gavrel missing and Bramn arguing with three soldiers. Four more knights had joined the gathering in the small yard, and they stood behind Bramn, pointing and shouting at the soldiers as well.

As Thylaina stepped from the house, Katjina rushed to her. "M'lady!" The women clasped hands and drew away from the quarreling men.

"What happened?" Thylaina asked.

"Sir Bramn sent Gavrel to the vault!" Katjina shook her head, her dark hair threatening to fall from their well-placed pins. "Only moments ago. That's why they're arguing."

Thylaina tramped in Bramn's direction, but Raylen grabbed her arm.

"Did you find a remedy for Captain Colmstad?" the priest inquired.

Nodding, she guided Raylen from the commotion. "Do you still have Divine Wrath?"

He halted, disbelief wrinkling his forehead. "Did you just ask me—?"

"S'yai, I did."

Although he chuckled, there was no amusement in the sound. "Why would I after everything that just happened?"

"Because you are an herbalist and you are curious about it."

A nervous smile twisted his lips. "I-I've no reason to keep it."

"I need it for Shapele Colmstad."

The smile faded as Raylen looked away. "Why?"

"It might help to ease his body's need for it." Thylaina squeezed his hand. "Withholding it completely may have harmed him."

"Is there no other way?"

"None that I know. However, this is only a theory."

He huffed a sigh. "Very well. I'll bring it to you."

She tightened her grip. "All of it."

Raylen worked his jaw from side to side, his eyes narrowed. "You show me. Teach me what you're going to do."

Thylaina was no master, but if the herbal priest was truly willing to learn, he could help her with the other men Mikan had poisoned.

"S'yai." She let go of his hand. "Hurry."

Once he started toward the temple, she headed to the group of shouting men. "Sir Bramn!"

The voices slowly lowered, then silenced.

Bramn's leer turned on her, but at least the redness of his cheeks faded. "My lady?"

"Why is Gavrel in the jailhouse?"

His expression changed into an authoritative demeanor. Bramn did not look at her as a friend, but an intruder. "It is a matter of the knighthood." He bowed his head, ending the discussion. An unacceptable answer.

Thylaina pointed at the jailhouse. "Gavrel was worried about my wellbeing."

"It is not of your concern, my lady."

Disgust toward her friend sparked anger within, and the flame grew with each passing second that they silently stared at each other. Like a stubborn bastard, Bramn stood firm. How long had he waited for an opportunity to strike out at Gavrel?

Shaking her head, Thylaina returned to the house, stopped at the door, and looked back. "I await Raylen's return. If it is not beyond your duties to assist in this matter, *Sir Bramn*, might you be so kind to send him in?"

He squinted. Surrounded by disparaging grumbles from his comrades, Bramn bowed partially. "My lady."

She stormed into the house, slammed the door shut.

"Gods, Thylaina," Breydon mumbled, his head in his hands.

"Forgive me." She started toward him, then paused. He had once again informally addressed her.

"My head feels as if it'll burst like an overripe berry between firm fingers."

She knelt afore him and gently grasped his wrists to lower his arms.

Tears dampened his cheeks, redness swelled raw beneath his eyes, and his face had grown pallid. In the short time he had been alone, so much changed.

"It shall not be long." She patted his cheeks with her sleeve.

"How did you forgive me?"

"Is it difficult to believe you can be forgiven?"

"I don't deserve it." He sputtered a sob.

"Breydon, stop this." Thylaina caressed his hand. Even within the dimness of the room, she easily traced the scars from when he had slashed her left knuckles with the edged stick. But she felt no anger or fear toward him. That all diminished when she forgave him. Meeting Breydon's sorrowful gaze, she said, "I heard the words come from your heart. My forgiveness came from mine. What is past us is past. What is afore us is new."

He curled his fingers around hers, then rested his forehead on their clasped hands. "Thank you."

"Just do one thing for me."

Breydon breathed deep, lifted his head. "Yes?"

"Please do not apologize for that offense again." Smiling, she touched his cheek with the backs of her fingers. "If you do, it means you do not believe in my forgiveness."

Gaze locked to hers, he kissed her hand. "I promise."

Thylaina removed a mint leaf from the satchel. "Suck on this. It should help ease some of the ache in your head." *And horrible breath.* She placed it on his tongue, then massaged his shoulder, slowly circling her fingers to his nape. "Does this alleviate any pain?"

"Only a lilul," he said, the leaf clinging to his tongue.

She stood behind him and reached around the chair, continuing the massaging of his shoulders and the back of his neck. "Perhaps if we get your muscles to relax, it will help, even if only a little."

A few minutes later, she removed the mint leaf and gave him two more. "Chew on these."

"Do I swallow them?" he asked while chomping.

She considered the question, then nodded. "S'yai." Perhaps swallowing them would not only help with the awful breath, the reason she gave him two more, but ease any possible stomach upset from the Divine Wrath withdrawal.

A gentle knock sounded on the door. It opened, then Raylen peeked inside. "It's me, my lady. Captain." The priest entered.

Breydon nearly jumped from the seat, but Thylaina squeezed on his clavicle, keeping him still. The captain squirmed beneath her grip.

"You remain here," she said, her tone firm. "Raylen and I shall prepare everything."

"But I—"

Thylaina stepped around the chair, holding him with a stern expression. "If you want the red dust, you will do all that I say. Understand, Shapele?"

He swallowed the mint and sulked in the chair. "S'yai."

She met Raylen at the upturned table.

He handed her a small wooden box, then straightened the table. "What are we doing?" He took the box and set it down. Raylen then removed a key from beneath his robe and unlocked it.

"Do you know how much Mikan gave him?"

"Yes."

"Good. We shall give him half."

Breydon rose unsteadily. "You didn't tell me this."

Thylaina spun, keeping herself between him and Divine Wrath. "You must fight your need for this dust. To give you the same amount as Mikan had defeats helping you."

"It's not enough!" He kicked his foot back, knocking the chair over again.

Raylen jumped, but Thylaina remained calm.

"Breydon, to give in will lead to your death," she said.

He glowered at her. "You lie."

"Divine Wrath is not about strength. It is about one gaining control over another. But if not administered correctly, it will drive a man insane. It could kill him."

"You're a liar!"

"She's not." Raylen stepped forward. "Mikan wanted to control you."

"You know nothing!" Breydon clenched his fist, his muscles tightened. Every part of his body strained from his growing rage.

"He asked me to acquire these!" The priest did not waver under the knight's rage. "Why else was Mikan giving it to you and select others? He wanted Sir Bramn as well, but the man refused to cooperate."

"Breydon, please." Thylaina reached between them, turning the captain toward her. "If you continue on this path Mikan began, you will lose yourself. Think of those who love you. Sir Bramn, Lord Arhgrim, Ladies Tesesra and Nadiera—the ones you call your family."

His breathing eased as he stared at her. Blinking, he looked down. "Just give me some damn dust." He righted the chair once more and plopped onto it.

This warm then cold attitude was going to exhaust her.

Raylen removed a scale from the box. After he calibrated the weight, he removed a pouch from a pocket on the inside of the chest of his robe. It amazed Thylaina she had not noticed a bulge, for this pouch was surprisingly plump. He measured red dust onto the empty plate until the scale evened.

"That's not very much," Breydon rumbled.

"It is plenty." Thylaina stared at the minute red grains, curious about how something so pretty could do so much damage. "How does Mikan—?"

"A drink." Raylen scanned the room. "But it seems there's nothing to offer."

"My bedroom." Breydon pointed with his thumb to a door in the room's corner. "There are two bottles of wine at the bottom of the wardrobe."

The priest headed to the bedchamber. Breydon watched him. Once Raylen was gone, he rose, a smile twitching at the corners of his lips.

Thylaina stood in front of the scale and reached back. The pouch of Divine Wrath in her grip, she kept it behind her. "Sit, Shapele."

He swiftly moved closer, his heat striking her. "Give me the dust."

Setting her chin, she hoped to offer a solid posture. "Sit down." Damn it to Darkness, her voice faltered.

Breydon reached around her, his fingers searching. They grazed her hand, then the pouch.

Raylen was taking too long. Possibly Breydon's intent.

Thylaina's mind raced with how to stall the captain, settling on what she believed was the only option. Hopefully, the mint had worked. Just as his fingers curled around hers and the pouch, she brought her other hand forward, clutched his head, and pulled him close. She found his lips parted, likely from surprise, but a kiss ensued. Thank Vynia for mint leaves! It had freshened his mouth, making the kiss far less offensive than she had feared. Breydon abandoned the red dust, embracing her instead. Bumps rose on her flesh as her heart sprinted to catch up with the rapid pounding of his. The tiny hairs on his chin and above his mouth poked her skin, but that only added to her excitement. Thylaina thrust her fingers into his red mane, gripping the wet strands. The kiss grew deeper as he straightened, lifting her until her toes barely touched the floor. She felt so... alive.

Raylen cleared his throat. "I, uh, found the wine. Although it *wasn't* in the wardrobe."

They parted. Thylaina stared at Breydon from beneath fluttering eyelids. He was such a damn mess.

Loosening his hold, he looked at Raylen, then back to Thylaina. "Clever," he whispered, shuffling back.

She faced the table and leaned on it for support. The whole of her shook: body, soul, and mind. Everything about her had become unbalanced. She had to concentrate. "Ray—" Her voice cracked.

He opened the bottle, then poured a few swallows into a cup he brought from the bedchamber. "Wet your throat."

Thylaina nodded once, downed the wine. "Please ready this." She offered the cup, her hand still trembling.

He filled it halfway. With care, he detached the plate from the scale, then scraped the measured dust into the wine. Using his finger, he mixed the two. "Captain?"

Breydon leaned forward in the chair, elbows on his knees, gaze locked on Thylaina. Sitting up, he took the cup and drank the mixture. His eyes never left her until he finished, then he closed them and sat back. A deep breath went in, slowly came out.

Thylaina knelt beside him. She positioned his hand on the chair's arm, then felt his heartbeat within his wrist. It had been racing during that kiss, but now it increased ever faster. She bit her lip, praying she had not doomed Breydon. After a minute passed, his heart rate slowed, as did his quaking.

"He should stay in the mansion where I can watch him," she said.

Frowning, Raylen looked down and pushed debris aside with his foot. "But I can't go there, my lady, per your order. And I wish to continue giving aid."

It should not be any trouble for Thylaina to convince Arhgrim to permit the priest entry. Although she had to focus on Tesesra, it would be no bother to check on Breydon for the next few days. "I shall speak with the marshal. If he agrees, there is one thing on which I must insist."

"And that is?"

"Divine Wrath remains in my possession."

Raylen lifted the pouch, cinched it shut. "Agreed." He handed it to her.

"Excellent." She looked down at Breydon, who stared at her... again. "Let us get Sir Bramn and the other men in here to escort Shapele Colmstad to the mansion."

Her legs wobbled as she walked away from them. From *him*. She could not control the shaking that infected her, and now her stomach hurt. Even when the cold air swept over her face, there was no genuine relief. The men rushed in, and Katjina caught Thylaina as she collapsed.

"M'lady, you look dreadful."

"I-I know not why, but I feel so weak."

"I'll help you." Katjina hooked Thylaina's arm over her shoulder and walked alongside her.

The day had seen too much, and Thylaina's emotions had reached several peaks of varying degrees. All she wanted now was to sleep beneath the warm coverlet. But she must speak with Arhgrim to make arrangements for Breydon and Raylen. Not to mention explain everything that had happened. Perhaps the marshal would meet on the morrow.

"Didn't you hear me?" Bramn walked beside her, flashing a charming smile. It did not work this time.

Thylaina looked forward. "N'ei. My mind was elsewhere. And should you not be with Shapele Colmstad?"

"The other men have him." Bramn slanted in her direction and hooked her arm over his shoulder, lifting her to her tiptoes and pulling from Katjina. "I've got her."

"Yes, Sir Bramn." The handmaiden beamed at him. A lot of help *she* was.

Thylaina sighed and continued staring ahead. "What do you want?"

"I don't particularly like explaining myself again," he said. "But I want you to understand why I arrested Gavrel."

"Another time, please." Thylaina tried to pull her arm away, but he held tight. "Truly?"

"You look exhausted, my lady. In fact…" He scooped her into his arms, ignoring her yelps. "There. Now you can regain your strength *and* listen to me."

"Put me down!"

"I want you to understand why I—"

"How dare you!" Thylaina's face burned as he continued speaking over her. It did not help matters when the other knights laughed. "I said put me down now!"

"You're making this far more difficult than it needs to be."

"Sir Bramn!" Breydon bellowed.

Everyone halted, even Katjina.

Bramn turned. "Sir?"

"Stop acting like a bloody brute and set Lady Thylaina down."

Bramn faced forward again and sighed. "Yes, sir," he muttered, then gently lowered Thylaina to stand. "Forgive me, my lady. I meant no harm. Perhaps I can better explain myself when we report to Marshal Momestid."

She straightened her skirt and bodice, refusing to look at him. As Bramn continued forward, Thylaina released a heavy breath, then stretched her neck. She would rather go to bed than report to Arhgrim straight away. Breydon watched her as he neared. It was strange to see him surrounded like a prisoner.

"Sir Bramn," she called.

He stopped and spun. "Yes, my lady?"

She gestured at the men standing on each side of Breydon. "This is not necessary. He is of n'ei danger."

The knights looked at the captain, then Bramn. The latter grinned.

"If you insist." Bramn approached Breydon. "Sir, your orders?"

Breydon glanced at the men. "Thank you for your help. You may return to your homes."

"Sir," they said simultaneously, then retreated in the direction they had just come.

Breydon looked at Bramn. "You will resume your duty."

"Of course, sir."

"But you may precede us and inform Grim we must speak with him."

Bramn smirked. "As you wish, Captain." He winked at Thylaina, then increased his pace. The mansion was only a block away.

Raylen took Katjina's hand and escorted her forward.

That left Thylaina and Breydon. Alone. Hopefully, there might be no conversation at all. They had walked half a block afore he spoke. The gods were not on her side with this predicament.

"Thank you, Lady Thylaina, for what you've done for me."

She clasped her hands, wrung her fingers. "You are welcome, Shapele."

"Are we back to the formalities?"

Thylaina fought a smile. "You said it first."

He inhaled deeply, released it. "I suppose I did."

Breydon did not look at her. Was he thinking about the kiss? That foolish kiss. Yet his lips had felt so fine. Perfect. And the way he held her—crushed her to him—was as if he had always longed to know her. If Raylen had not interrupted them, Thylaina might have lost herself in Breydon's arms.

Her step faltered. *What does that mean?*

Over the past twenty-four hours, Breydon revealed to her the man about whom the others had spoken. The man they dearly loved. During her interactions with him, she came to quickly adore him just as much. While close to Breydon, she experienced a bonding, as if their souls embraced and had yet to let go. She felt it when they had shared about their mothers, when they had kissed, and now as they walked aside each other. Was this... love?

*This cannot be.* It could never be. She was going to Yeltar to begin a new life amongst her kin, not stay close to Etharell and what? Love a human? No. The nation would not accept such a bond. Perhaps her lack of experience confused her with what she now felt, which must be desire.

She gave Breydon a sidelong look and considered his behavior after taking Divine Wrath under Mikan's administrations: the captain had been aggressive and violent toward Thylaina. Yet now he remained amiable. Even protective. The kiss she shared with him had calmed his rage, and he responded with unmistakable affection.

It did not matter what the Elven Nation might think when no one there gave a bloody damn about her afore. Besides, she was no longer in Etharell. Thylaina was shaping her own destiny. And if she wanted to have a brief affair with a human, then she would.

Smiling, she slipped her hand through the crook of his arm. "Are you hungry, Breydon?"

He looked down at her and chuckled. "Starving, to be honest."

"Perhaps we can convince Marshal Momestid to meet with us in the dining hall so you can finally have your supper."

Breydon covered her hand with his. "It shall be done," he said in Elvish.

To hear him speak her language made her adore him more, and she rested her head on his arm and giggled.

Arhgrim brought everyone involved in the night's event into the feast hall to give their accounts, including Raylen, the knights Breydon had sent home and the soldier who had stood guard with Gavrel. Arlin entered the chamber and hurried to the captain's side. It amazed Thylaina that the squire apologized to Breydon. The hall silenced as Breydon stood, rested his hand on Arlin's shoulder, and spoke quietly with the young man. Thylaina heard every word as the captain assured his squire that he was not to blame.

"It is I who owes you an apology," Breydon continued. "I... I struck you." He lowered his head. "I'm sorry, Arlin. If you wish to give your service to another knight, I understand, and it will be without retribution from me."

Arlin clutched Breydon's wrist. "No, sir. I swore to serve you until I became a knight. My vow is my life."

Smiling, Breydon pulled the young man into an embrace. "You speak as a knight already, Arlin."

Those in the chamber grinned, including Thylaina. Bramn and the other present knights slammed their mugs on the table, sounding a cheer for Arlin.

"You may retire for the evening," Breydon said to the squire.

"Yes, sir."

Arhgrim nodded his approval as Breydon sat. "Let's get to tonight's events."

The marshal had agreed to allow Breydon to stay in the mansion until he recovered from Divine Wrath, and approved Raylen's admittance, but only while tending to the captain. The priest shared his account of what happened outside of and in Breydon's house. Arhgrim listened as each witness gave their report while Breydon ate.

Thylaina trembled as Bramn explained what had led to Gavrel's arrest: the dubight had slugged the back of Bramn's head. Those backing the story, including Katjina, did not help Gavrel's situation. Still, he did not deserve a fortnight of imprisonment.

"My lord," Thylaina said, gaining Arhgrim's attention. "I understand the dubight was imprudent, but his motivation was to protect me. Is a fortnight necessary?"

Bramn slammed his fist on the table. "He struck me!"

"Obviously a harmless attack." Thylaina shook her head. "He feared for my safety."

"From whom?" Arhgrim's gaze flitted from Breydon to Thylaina. "Did you feel threatened?"

Frustrated, she dropped her shoulders and leaned in his direction. "Shapele Colmstad sounded enraged, my lord. All here gave witness to the situation we came upon."

"Were you frightened of Captain Colmstad?" the marshal asked.

Lowering her gaze to her half-empty goblet, she shook her head. "I was not." She returned her attention to Arhgrim. "But that does not mean—"

"Gavrel Kedanier assaulted a knight," Arhgrim said, his voice firm. "As a dubight, he knows the consequences of such an action. The sentence stands."

She looked at the others, meeting annoyance from Bramn, surprise from Katjina, and a mix of curiosity and irritation from Breydon. "My lord," she pressed. "At Shapele Colmstad's home, we all experienced heightened emotions. It is through what we felt that we perceived the events of this evening. Although you heard everyone's witness from the moment Sir Bramn and I arrived with Raylen to the moment we departed, each telling had a slight difference."

"What's your point?" Bramn asked, his tone cold.

"That Gavrel also perceived the event differently and his telling will be varied as well. Does he not get a chance to defend himself? Or is he guilty because he is a dubight?"

Breydon released a heavy breath. The need to speak was obvious, yet he remained silent. Something troubled him. Thylaina prayed it was because he agreed with her, but withheld speaking out to avoid crossing his friend.

Arhgrim scratched behind his ear, then stared at Thylaina as if she were a pestering child with whom he must show patience. "My lady, I know not how the elves do court, but Alohrius and the knights have their ways."

She shrunk into the chair, no longer wanting to listen. There was nothing she could do.

"As a dubight, Gavrel knows his crime, and he will serve for it." The marshal lifted his goblet. "No more is to be said." After drinking, he set the cup down, then pointed at Breydon. "How long before his recovery? Do those spots affect his vision?"

Thylaina looked up at Breydon, whose gaze was on her. The blood mars around his pupils were ugly, yet she did not believe them dangerous. "He has not complained."

Breydon lowered his hand to hers, squeezed gently. "I'm fine, Grim. It doesn't hurt." He sounded tired. Worn. The man was probably as ready for bed as she was.

"It looks awful," Arhgrim said. "How does that not hurt? There's blood in your eyes."

"I said I'm fine. Just... exhausted."

"As am I," Thylaina mumbled.

"Bramn, escort Lady Thylaina to her room," Arhgrim ordered.

Breydon glared at his friend. "I'll do it."

Grinning, Bramn raised his cup to them. "Rest well."

Thylaina ignored him as she rose; Breydon pulled her chair back further.

They walked out together—with Katjina trailing—both silent, even as they ascended the stairs to the second floor. When they reached her chamber, Thylaina faced him. "Thank you, Breydon."

"It's I who owes you gratitude."

Katjina entered the room and waited inside.

Thylaina leaned against the wall beside the room's entrance. "I know not if my theory is correct. I might be mistaken." Tears threatened at the thought of hurting him.

"You're not. You've done more than you realize."

She shook her head. "But what if—?"

He took her hand and kissed it, silencing her. "You've saved my soul." He kissed it once more, then walked backwards, letting her hand slip free. "Good night, my lady."

She watched him head for the stairs to the third floor. Resting her head on the wall, she cradled her hand to her chest. "Good night... Breydon."

# Chapter Eleven

Two days later, Thylaina moved into a larger room a couple of doors from Lady Tesesra's. And like Her Ladyship's, this one had a connecting suite and a garderobe. No more chamber pots for Thylaina. Not that she opposed the pots. In fact, Thylaina had used them at the palace in Haevaun Flameral, but she loved the ingenuity of the indoor privy. What was most important was that now she could speedily attend to Tesesra, as was the purpose of the move.

Over the following week, she treated Breydon's addiction and other injuries caused by Divine Wrath, the latter by placing droplets of a new healing elixir into his nostrils each night. Improvement was visibly noticeable by his skin and eyes seeming livelier and in his charming behavior.

Thylaina and Breydon did not share another kiss, but his lips often touched her hands. When possible, they spent afternoon meals in her suite, and he sat beside her to break fast and sup in the dining hall. It seemed Breydon was at her side when not performing his duties. Although no promises or hints of something deeper passed between them, he presented Thylaina with gifts of flowers, colorful scarves, and even a new journal, all items collected from his travels to surrounding communities.

This reminded her of an old dance she had watched at the Spring Awakening Festivals over the past hundred years: The Teasing Suitor. The man led his lady of interest with the simplest steps that later turned into the most complex maneuvers, ending with them entwined, lips pressed together, and hearts beating so hard the couple trembled. Thylaina had never performed the dance with a man, but learned it with her maiden friends. Did Breydon intend to attempt those complex steps with her? She prayed not. Yet Thylaina thanked him for the gifts, indulged in the feeling of his lips on her hands and the warmth of his nearness, and fantasized about nights of passion with him, but dared not think of anything more. A friendship was all she could afford with the captain.

At least she learned more about him during their strolls in the orchard, sometimes following dinner. Breydon grew up outside of Karvorn, a large seaport in southern Alohrius; he named his Alohrian stallion Helwyn; and when Breydon concentrated, his tongue peeked from between his lips. While speaking with excitement, the man used his hands animatedly, and he stared when deep in thought. There was more to the First Captain of Caerabis, and she cherished each detail he revealed. Thylaina, however, kept much about herself secret. Thankfully, he showed no frustration about it.

Wrapped in a wool shawl, she sat beside him in one of the wide crenels of the temple rooftop. The descending honey-gold sun silhouetted the buildings into black structures, and the wispy clouds reflected a deeper orange over a darkening blue sky. Two stars peeked from the distance, promising more to come. The gargoyles at the rooftop corners did not frighten Thylaina, even as the shadows made them appear more menacing. The temple's dome blocked some of the wind, yet still blew tresses loose from her plait over her cheeks, tickling. At first, she had been nervous to sit with her feet dangling over the edge, so high above the stone terrace below. But Breydon had promised he would not let her fall. Not that she needed his assurance, for she would not let herself plummet to her death, either.

Mesmerized by the beautiful view, Thylaina pulled the shawl tighter around and shuddered. It had been too long since enjoying a sunset, and with fine company as well. Between them sat a bottle of elven wine and two half-full goblets. Again, it was a wine that should not have been in his possession, which prodded her curiosity.

"Breydon, where do you acquire the wines? The ones you have shared with me are not sold to those outside of nobility in Etharell."

A mixture of disbelief and amusement stared at her. "Your people limit wine only to the wealthy?"

"That is not what I said." Not wanting to be annoyed with him, she scowled at the city. "I do not make these wines nor sell them. But—"

"Stop." He softly squeezed her hand. "I know it's not your fault." Sitting back, his warmth slipping away from her, he sighed into the sky. "They were gifts from xilys commanders when I had been on friendlier terms with them."

"Are you healing those strained bonds?"

"I've sent messages requesting a meeting with them. Now I've just got to think of what gifts to present as peace offerings."

Pleased with the efforts he had already made, Thylaina smiled. "You need not offer anything more than a sincere apology and your friendship. Or alliance, if that is what you seek."

Breydon lowered his gaze to the dark rooftops. "I enjoyed being their friend and having their trust. I'd like to earn it back." Rubbing his thigh with long, easy strokes, he chuckled. "I suppose gifts aren't exactly earning it." His eyes rose to hers, blue irises more piercing as the sun's color deepened to fiery orange. Silent words grazed over his lips, but he said nothing.

Thylaina lifted her cup and breathed in the wine, tasting it on her tongue afore drinking it. The rich scent added to the flavor as it flooded her mouth, coursed down her throat. Red grapes, cinnamon, plum, and amber-striped fig. A rare treat, even for one of her stature.

He had watched her the whole time she drank, his gaze never leaving her face, as if taking in every muscle's movement. Courage entered with his next breath, the confidence showing in his eyes. "Thylaina, I wish you to know something."

She set the cup down, rested her hands back on the cold, rigid edge of the crenel, and gave him her full attention. "S'yai?"

"My..." He laughed nervously, his eyes dropping to the ground below. "My growing fondness for you is not because you're the... Gods! The most beautiful woman I have ever known."

Her cheeks warmed from the compliment and his bashfulness. When he looked at her, her face flushed with heat, and the wind sent another shiver down her spine. No. That was not the wind.

"It's because I've witnessed the wonderful woman you are." Seriousness overtook his visage as he continued. "You might think these past seven days are all I've had, but they're not. Despite the influence of the red dust, I still noted everything about you since the beginning. Everything."

She opened her mouth to avoid breathing heavily through her nose as his words and sincere expression struck her. "An-and what did you notice?" she whispered.

"That you're an intelligent woman. And kind." A slow smile formed. "To all those around you, whether servant, soldier, or knight, you are kind. Maybe it's because you're a healer. But I believe it's simply who you are, that you care about people, especially those in need of relief, support, or a smile to brighten their day."

No one had ever said such things to her. Ever. And it made her chest swell with a trembling breath as tears attempted to surface. She blinked them away, shaking her head to cast aside his flattery.

"I've never known anyone as forgiving." He nodded, sorrow momentarily revealed in his eyes. "I appreciate everything about you. That you immediately stepped forward to help Tes, even when many stood against you. The courage you showed was admirable."

Her chin quaked as the tears pooled, one breaking free to slide down her cheek.

Breydon's warm hand rested on her jaw, his thumb streaking the droplet away. "I... I'm enraptured with you. And there is no other maiden with whom I wish to spend every available minute away from duty."

"Gods, Breydon." Her voice was heavy with emotion; the words were barely audible. "There are things you know not about me."

"And I look forward to learn whatever you wish to share." He caressed her cheek, leaned over the wine bottle. "May I kiss you?"

A great throb rushed through her body at his request. She licked her lips as she moved closer, closed her eyes.

His mouth brushed hers, teasing. "Do you reciprocate my feelings?"

She straightened, taking him in as he remained still, waiting and wanting. "Each day, every moment spent with you, I discover more of the fine man they told me you are." She bent toward him again. "I adore being in your presence, Shapele Breydon Colmstad. You are a kind man, a dutiful knight, caring and loving to those close to you, and concerned about all in this city and beyond."

A crooked smile tugged at his fine lips. "I wish I were all of that."

"That is what *I* see." She touched her tongue tip to his bottom lip, enjoying the sound of his sharp intake of air. "That is what I feel when with you." Thylaina slid her fingers into his hair, the strands cold from the wind. "Please kiss me."

No hesitation. He grabbed her arms and pulled her close, his mouth pressing hard on hers. Desperate. Hungry. Breydon had longed for that kiss for days. He picked the perfect moment.

What a beautiful night.

Breydon had ridden eastward, gone from Caerabis for the next two days. Upon his return, Thylaina skipped to him, welcoming him home with an embrace. He removed a red sunflower from Helwyn's saddle and gave it to her. "This reminded me of our last sunset."

He then asked her to walk with him from the officers' stables. Thylaina carried the flower, thinking of that night on the temple rooftop and the sweet kiss. Only one. Then he had escorted her back to the mansion and bid her a lovely evening.

Thylaina had needed a break. Not only was she caring over Tesesra and studying Divine Wrath, but the Momestids had approved her request to grow herbs behind their home. The following day, Thylaina had three laborers at her disposal. Cleaning the areas for her future plants was the first task. Next was sending for knee holly, which had to be planted prior to the first frost. There were many herbs and plants she wanted to grow in her new garden, but were all native to Etharell. The stress of how to gain them had led to tears as she realized it would never be. So a long walk with Breydon was a welcome invitation. Besides, she wanted to be with him.

The Oaken Sun helped fight the late morning's chill, but the captain's warmth was the true victor. Her arm looped around his, she told him about the garden, then inquired about the war hammer at his side in place of the sword. That gained a wide smile and an explanation, one that left her stomach unsettled. To imagine Breydon fighting dragnols made her queasy. Although she had never seen one of the beasts from the Suflor Hills, she had done plenty of reading about them.

"I thank the gods for your safe return." She looked at the warhammer, then at his face. "But I just cannot imagine you wielding *that*."

Gaze still forward, he chuckled. "My skill with the hammer would leave you amazed if you were granted such an honor to witness."

Giggles escaped her, and she had to stop walking to laugh. "You certainly are a humble man, Shapele."

"I do favor the sword, but for when it's necessary, Helwyn carries a hammer on the saddle. It was necessary last night." He tilted his head and raised a brow. "You'd not want to get in the way of my mighty swing."

Bending forward, she laughed harder.

Breydon feigned offense. "It sounds as if you don't believe me."

Thylaina settled, caught her breath. "Thank you."

"For what?"

"For noticing I needed such merriment." She hugged his arm as they resumed walking forward. "I appreciate your care for me."

He stared down at her, a gentle smile present. It was wonderful to see the blood spots had grown minute, she could faintly see them. "You've been terribly busy while I was performing my duties. How long before the butcher's broom arrives?"

"The *knee holly* arrives in a fortnight."

He smirked. "I forgot you called it something else. But a fortnight isn't too long, considering they must dig them up and transport them from Rhigowan."

"There is more I want to do in the garden, but I have not the plants."

"And those are?"

"Oh, repenia, buraily, and yavlar—all from Etharell." She glanced at him, then added under her breath, "And insh weed."

He halted. "What?"

Thylaina licked her lips as she squinted in the sunlight to meet his gaze. "For another purpose than you imagine. As a preventative. A harmless one."

A scowl marring his handsome face retreated with her last statement. "Is that so?"

"S'yai." She tugged on his arm and resumed their stroll.

"I've never heard of repenia, bavlar, nor yaraily."

Stopping again, Thylaina laughed so hard she nearly snorted. Once she was able to speak, she said, "Yavlar and buraily."

"You're amused at my errs." He nodded. "Go on, then." Breydon looked hopelessly adorable, but then a crooked smile appeared. He had purposefully misspoken the words.

Thylaina narrowed her eyes at him.

He laughed as he pulled her along the cobblestone path amid the afternoon crowds; people performing chores, errands, and duties. A few maidens called out to Breydon, but he did not acknowledge them. It seemed no one else existed but him and Thylaina. At least not to Breydon.

Noticing his gaze grew distant, Thylaina squeezed his arm. "What is on *your* mind?"

He blinked, flashed a sad smile. "Nothing. Just... my upcoming departure."

What little she ate that morning soured in her stomach. Another damn ride out of Caerabis. She hid her disappointment behind the flower, which was as big as her head, and smelled it. Hopefully, he would not notice her battle to withhold tears. It was not only his impending absence, but that she had yet to free him of Divine Wrath. At least Arhgrim kept Breydon's travels close to Caerabis.

Breydon stopped and kissed her hand. "I'll be fine, Thylaina. You'll be too busy to worry about me. Besides, Einasa shall arrive soon, and you'll witness Bramn making a fool of himself."

"You sound as if it shall be a longer ride out."

His nose scrunched for the briefest moment. "A week, at the least."

Was Arhgrim mad? Now the tears showed.

Breydon slid one of his hands to her back, gliding it up and down in comforting strokes. "Thylaina, all will be fine."

"It is just—" She lowered her head and swung the sunflower, teasing swirls of dust from the cobblestones.

His fingers skated up to her nape, then around to her chin, and he guided her to look at him. "What is it?"

Over a week ago, such a touch from him would have had her retreating. But now, Thylaina's heart raced and goosebumps rose from excitement. At this moment, to *her*, the many passersby did not exist. It was just Thylaina and Breydon on the street, amongst the buildings, and the wind blowing about them. This was how it had been for nine days, yet for an eternity.

*I should not feel this way, but I do. Lessindra, why?* Closing her eyes, she stepped closer and rested her forehead on his chest. "I wish you were not leaving."

Breydon's protective warmth enclosed her within his arms. "I promise to return as soon as I can." His lips pressed into her hair, onto her head.

Thylaina wanted Breydon near her as much as possible—to have him within sight. It comforted her to know he was present. He *was* the finest man she had ever known. And despite the growing feelings for him, Thylaina's only intention was to use him for her pleasures. After all, he could not be part of her future.

"I didn't tell you where I'm going." He kept her close and stared into her eyes.

A horse whinnied as it trotted past, startling Thylaina from Breydon's arms.

She felt foolish, behaving like this in front of everyone on Valorius' Way, just a few doors from the temple, and standing amid several shops and knights' houses. The mansion was two blocks south of where they stood. In fact, Thylaina knew not where Breydon had been taking her.

"Where are *we* going, Shapele?"

One of his brows arched high at the address. "A stroll," he said, leading them onward.

"There are many places I have yet to see in Caerabis. Why not show me more?"

"One day."

They passed the temple and turned easterly at the next road, Steel Path. It was a wide street where the jailhouse, blacksmith, and armorer were located, as well as Breydon's home.

Seeing the jailhouse, Thylaina halted. She had not been there since the night of her arrival, but she wanted to go there now.

"Thylaina?"

"I wish to see Gavrel."

He frowned and continued beyond the steps to the entrance.

"Breydon." Thylaina pulled her hand free from his.

"No," he said flatly. A few people walking by glanced at them, but he did not look away from Thylaina. "He serves his punishment. Leave him be."

"You are demanding I desert my friend." Appalled, she shook her head. "He should not be in there for trying to protect me."

"From what?" he snapped, stepping so close, he sheltered her from the sun. "From me?"

No matter how much she wanted to be strong, the tears came, but she kept them from falling.

"You told Grim that you didn't fear me. Did you lie?"

"N'ei," she whispered. "But... it is wrong. If *you* were in there, I would come to see you."

His expression softened. "Gods, I hope so."

Breydon guided her to the shade provided by his home across the street. "Dar—" Cheeks turning red, he looked down. After a controlled breath, he met her gaze. "Thylaina, I listened to Gavrel's recounting of what had happened, to make a new decision if necessary. After hearing it, I upheld Grim's sentence."

She huffed. "Of course you did."

"My ruling wasn't influenced." Appearing hurt by her unspoken judgement, he released her hand. "Gavrel admitted to attacking Bramn from behind. His actions were unacceptable!"

"Sir Bramn had pinned him to the ground." There was no keeping the tears in check now.

"Bramn did what was necessary so you could do what you had to do. And Gavrel's pride got the best of him."

But that mattered not to her. She wiped her cheeks with the shawl, then moved closer to him. "Please, Breydon. I am begging you." Thylaina grazed his wrist with her finger. "Please take me to see him."

Turning his head toward the jailhouse, he rubbed the back of his neck. "Very well."

On the way there, and down the corridors, he explained what she could and could not do. Thylaina nodded a promise, but she had only been partly listening.

"This'll be brief," he said once again.

"I understand."

They stopped at the cell room door. He stared at her. "Please don't be angry."

Confused, she shook her head. "What?"

Breydon opened the door and stepped through. In the daylight, the cell room still looked foreboding as at night. Four torches along the lengthy wall provided the only lighting in the chamber, shadowing the prisoners' faces until they moved closer to the iron bars.

Her vision adjusted to the dim room, she entered, keeping close to the wall and away from the cells. In the first one slept a horrific-smelling man, and the second contained a familiar face, one she did not mind forgetting. Thylaina looked beyond Mikan and continued to the third cell, which held Gavrel. However, she could barely see him, for he sat on the floor in the far corner's shadows. She knelt, grabbed one of the cold bars.

"Thylaina," Breydon warned. Oh yes. He had told her not to touch the cell bars. In fact, she was not to be near them either.

Rising, she stepped back and focused on her friend. "Gavrel... How do you fare?"

He stared at her from the shadows.

Mikan rose from his cot and moved closer, his gaze locked on Breydon. "Captain." He smiled. "How much longer am I to remain here?"

"Until I say otherwise."

The priest shook his head. "Don't do this. You'll only bring harm to yourself."

"Don't threaten me," Breydon rumbled.

Hatred saturated Mikan's eyes as he looked at Thylaina, then he returned his attention to Breydon. "It's not too late, my friend. This hasn't reached Haevaun Balaeus yet. We can resume where we were interrupted."

Infuriated, Thylaina smacked Mikan in the face with the sunflower, striking more bars than flesh. Red petals floated onto the floor as he sputtered, walking backwards.

Breydon turned to her, his eyes wide and lips parted. "That was—"

"I did not want to listen to him anymore." Thylaina dropped the stem.

Mikan's face turned crimson as he glared at her. "I'm not done with you, woman."

"Enough," Gavrel said, his voice hoarse. He rose unsteadily, then walked forward, hunched and with his right hand pressed to his left side. As he drew nearer, she understood Breydon begging her not to be angry. A bruise swelled Gavrel's right eye, a split clotted the center of his bottom lip, it appeared two of his fingers were broken, and by the way he remained bent, he had other injuries she could not see.

Furious, Thylaina spun, her face burning as she tried to punch Breydon. "What have you done?"

He blocked the hit, but did not move. "I did nothing!"

"Liar!" She swung again. It hurt—her fist hitting his arm. "You expect me to believe Gavrel did that to himself?"

"It wasn't me!" Breydon snatched her wrist when she swung once more, and pulled her to the wall away from the cells. "It wasn't me," he whispered fiercely.

She fought to break from his grip, but he held fast. "Then who?"

"Others." He wrapped his arms around her when she struggled. "It's true," he said, his warm breath rushing into her ear. "Other knights learned what he did to Bramn and sought retribution. I swear it."

Thylaina pushed against his chest; he let her go. "I wish to examine him." She set her chin and straightened her dress.

"No."

Gavrel snorted a laugh as he leaned his shoulder against the bars.

"I insist." Thylaina poked Breydon's chest. "He is wounded and—"

"I'll not risk something happening to you." He headed for the exit. "We're leaving."

"N'ei." She neared the cell, slid her hand through to touch Gavrel's face. "He needs my help."

Eyes closed, the dubight rested his cheek on her palm.

"Damn it, get away!" Breydon stormed back to her.

"Ignoring his wounds could cause more harm."

Breydon yanked her from the cell. "Step away!"

"She's right, Captain," Mikan said. He then moved to the bars separating him from Gavrel. "Come to me, dubight. Let me inspect you."

Gavrel looked at Thylaina, then darted his loathe-filled gaze at Breydon. With the slightest shrug, he retreated until he was beside the priest. Mikan reached through and touched Gavrel's left side; the dubight winced. After a few minutes passed, Mikan examined the crooked fingers.

Thylaina watched intently to make sure the high priest did nothing to her friend. *She* should have been tending to him, not Mikan, but Breydon would not let her. Damn him. Damn both those men.

The priest lowered his arms. "His ribs are broken."

She faced Breydon. "I must help him."

"I'll do it," the priest said.

Gavrel shuffled to his cot and sat, releasing a slow breath.

"Please, Breydon." Thylaina gripped his arms. "You let those knights hurt him. Let me heal him."

His brows lowered and his nose wrinkled. "I didn't let them."

"Yet you did not stop them."

"You think I invited them in?" He scoffed. "Gods, Thylaina! I've been with you, not in here encouraging beatings to the bloody dubight!"

"That's why it took you so long to see me," Gavrel whispered, his focus on his broken fingers.

"Gavrel." She neared the cells, but Breydon grabbed her arm.

"Not any closer," he warned, his eyes fixed on Mikan.

The dubight rested his head against the wall and closed his eyes. "Go to the mansion, my lady. Forget about me."

"I do not *want* to forget you. You are my friend. I... I would have come sooner, but I have been taking care of Her Ladyship, the shapele, an-and—"

"You needn't worry about me." He turned his head away from her.

"Gavrel, please."

"Let me tend to him," Mikan said.

"No." In that one simple word, Breydon's voice was a mix of anger, confusion, and worry. "Raylen's a capable healer."

"Gavrel, I am sorry." A sob broke into Thylaina's words. She headed for the exit.

Mikan watched her, his gaze shifting to the dubight.

Thylaina could not reach the sun fast enough. She wanted away from this cold, horrible jailhouse. The sun's warmth did not chase away the chill and hurt living in that building.

"Thylaina!" Breydon spun her around.

She slapped him. "Damn you to Darkness. Damn all you knights."

Ignoring his shocked and pained expression, Thylaina continued toward the mansion. She pushed through gawking citizens, walking only ten feet more when she felt Breydon's grip on her elbow, yet they did not stop.

"You're not permitted to walk through Caerabis alone," he said through clenched teeth.

They spoke no further words, and upon their arrival at the mansion, Breydon escorted Thylaina to her chamber. He slammed the door shut. The last time his eyes appeared so brilliantly blue, he had tried to choke her.

Thylaina used Tesesra as an excuse to amble from him, blending the herbs at the worktable for Her Ladyship's next tea. It was a special table Arhgrim had brought into the suite for Thylaina's many herbs, bottles, and an old distiller Raylen gave her. Not enough light emitted from the low flames of the hearth, and she did not want to face Breydon, so she reached over the table and pulled the curtains to permit sunlight.

The continued silence pressed on her ears. It was without a doubt she had hurt him. But damn it to Darkness! Breydon's refusal at the jailhouse hurt as well.

"Don't leave until Bramn's here," he snapped.

The door opened, then crashed against the frame, ensuring all from the third floor to the entrance would know he was angry. Would he return for afternoon meal?

He did not. Katjina ate with Thylaina, who had little appetite in Breydon's absence. Bramn did not enter the suite, but stood on the landing. The handmaiden appeared to notice Thylaina's lack of interest in eating or sharing a conversation and offered comfort. Gods! Thylaina did not deserve such a fine friend.

Too much troubled Thylaina: Breydon, Gavrel, and Tesesra's babe. Not to mention Breydon was leaving soon, and she knew not when nor to where.

"My lady," Bramn said, breaking her from her thoughts. She had not heard him enter the room. "It's time to tend to Her Ladyship."

"S'yai. Of course."

She dropped the linen atop her unfinished meal, then gathered the healing tea mix and her journal and followed him to Tesesra's chamber. During that short walk, the First Captain consumed her mind. To have struck him was foolish. What happened to Gavrel was not Breydon's fault, yet Thylaina blamed him because he was right there to receive her fury. Tonight, when he came to take his final dose of Divine Wrath, she would make amends.

Except when he arrived that evening, he remained on the landing with Bramn. Raylen, however, came inside on Breydon's behalf to retrieve the red dust.

"Forgive me, Lady Thylaina," the herbal priest said.

She shook her head at this unacceptable behavior. "Shapele must take it in my presence."

Raylen regarded his twiddling thumbs. "He said he trusts me."

So this is what Breydon wanted? The days of joy together now debris swept away in a gale. Thylaina could be just as stubborn. "I shall give it to him."

"My lady—"

"I need only a moment."

She approached Katjina, taking her hand; the key was already in the handmaiden's palm. "Please pour some wine." Katjina walked to the decanters, while Thylaina proceeded to her worktable.

The small chest containing the red dust was under a stack of blankets in a crate beneath the table. Thylaina used the key to open the chest and remove the mind poison. Her bottom lip quivered throughout each movement. When it came to measuring the dust, focus took control of all emotions. Breydon needed very little now. And though she said this was his last time taking it, there was the possibility she might be incorrect. Thylaina had been documenting how much she gave him every other day, cutting the amount down until it was just this pinch. Tonight, perhaps tomorrow, she should know if he was truly free. If he spoke to her afterward.

While she mixed the red dust into the wine, Raylen stood beside her, babbling one sentence after another. Thylaina did not hear a word, just his voice. She was busy thinking of what to say to Breydon. Perhaps offer the goblet with a smile and tell him she missed him that afternoon. Or tell him how terribly sorry she was.

"My lady, please." Raylen touched her shoulder.

Thylaina jerked her arm back and glared at him. "I said I will give this to Shapele."

The priest lowered his gaze and nodded as he stepped aside. "Forgive me."

Goblet in hand, she hurried to the landing door. *Apologize and tell him how much you miss him.* She opened the door to find Breydon and Bramn leaned on the railing, laughing. Breydon's color looked well. Like he had not worried at all throughout the day. Apparently, he did not miss Thylaina.

Upon seeing her, he silenced and stood tall. Bramn also straightened, bowing slightly at her approach.

Thylaina shoved the goblet at Breydon. "Drink this."

A brow cocked, he looked at it. "I sent Raylen—"

"Drink it!"

He looked at Bramn, then took the cup and raised it to Thylaina. "My lady." Head tipped back, Breydon did not stop drinking until the contents were gone. Grinning, he returned the goblet back to her.

She snatched it from him and stormed into her chambers, shouldering Raylen on the way, and slammed the door shut. Leaning against it, Thylaina ignored Katjina's curious gaze and muffled her weeping behind her hand. The door pushed into her. She lunged forward, then faced it, anticipating Bramn to enter.

Breydon stepped inside, irritation replacing his amused countenance, and looked at Katjina. "Leave us." There was no kindness in his voice. The handmaiden did not check with Thylaina if that was what she wanted, but curtsied to the captain and hurried from the suite. He closed the door behind her. "You want everyone in the mansion to know you're bitter?"

Surely, he jested. Thylaina walked as gracefully to her chair as she could. There was no need to show him every fiber of her trembled with anxiety. "I see, Shapele."

Breydon's eyes twitched.

"*You* are permitted to alert the residence of the mansion that you are unhappy," she continued, "but if I behave the same, it is poor manners."

Squinting, he took three steps toward her. "You did this."

She hesitated from sitting. "I did what, Shapele?" Thylaina lowered, and crossed her ankles.

The formal use of his title appeared to sting him, for he winced again. Breydon now stood over her, anger flaring his eyes wide as he swung his hands back and forth and to the sides. "You cast everything aside! For *him!* Every effort I've made eroded to nothing in the jailhouse today when you—"

She rose abruptly, forcing him to retreat closer to the fireplace. "Of what do you speak?"

The man had the nerve to look at her as if she were a dolt. "Have you any idea?"

Huffing, she spun around the chair and approached the worktable. There was nothing to do there except escape his closeness. "I have an idea you and Sir Bramn have n'ei respect for me, Shapele."

"Stop it!" He stomped toward her. "Stop with the bloody title!"

"I will refer to you as whom you are!"

Breydon straightened and stared into her eyes as if searching for something. Hope? Shaking his head, he whispered, "I wasted my time courting you."

Her breath caught.

"Every available moment I had was spent with you. I brought you gifts, things I believed would please you." He looked down, raked his fingers through his hair. "Nothing extravagant because I... I don't have the means, nor do I know what you'd like. And I spoke the words from my heart. But..." He met her widened gaze. "You made it clear when you told the dubight your time with me was nothing but about caring over me like a bloody patient." He shook his head again. "I had believed it was greater than that between us. Now I see he means more when you reduce our last several days to something so little."

Chills invaded her body as his confessions came out one after another. Breaking from the shock, she blurted, "Breydon, please!"

"No." He walked backwards, his heels scraping the stone floor. "It hurt more than that slap and the accusation you struck me with. And I'll not tolerate more pain any further." Breydon licked his lips. A few breaths came and went while he stared at her. After a heavy sigh, he rushed to the exit and left.

Tears blurred the dancing flames.

Although she had thought of the past several days as The Teasing Suitor, she had not truly believed that was what Breydon had been doing. Then again, Thylaina had never experienced a courting. Did she understand her own feelings for him? For the past several days, she had battled every emotion beyond lust. It would be easier if the man agreed to a night of passion and remaining friends.

Yet being away from Breydon, the idea of enduring his absence, left her feeling empty. She enjoyed his company. Thylaina longed to hear his voice no matter what he spoke about, and hearing him breathe gave her a sense of comfort. Her heart thumped, her soul danced, and she felt at peace with Breydon. Was that love? Having never known love, Thylaina did not know if she could recognize it.

She dragged her feet to the chair, lowered, and locked her gaze on the fire. "No matter how much I wish, it cannot be." She folded her arms over her belly and bent forward. Sobs burst from between her lips as her heart rotted.

Three days passed, and she did not see Breydon during any of them. Arhgrim and Raylen reported his behavior seemed normal, which pleased them. Having the First Captain of Caerabis back to himself gave the marshal a sense of normalcy. Tesesra's continued improvement added to his good mood as well. And since Thylaina was the reason for the changes, the priests remained out, except Raylen, when he studied from Thylaina. Tesesra's former handmaiden, Bethlyn, was removed from the mansion permanently. It did not matter, since no one had seen her for seven days.

Bramn stood sentry behind the mansion while Thylaina continued preparing for the new herb garden. How she might obtain the desired plants, she did not yet know. The soil for the knee holly was ready, and that was the biggest project of this garden. Laborers constructed a row of herb boxes on the opposite side of the path, where sunlight would reach the plants for a few hours a day afore the apple trees interfered. The engineers were brilliant in their design to protect the soil and plants, adding rocks at the bottom of the plot boxes for drainage. The knee holly would hug the back and south side of the mansion, providing plenty of bushes for now. Thylaina could always request more if she and Viya felt the need.

Katjina exited from the scullery door, carrying a tray of fruit, cheese, and water. Thylaina and the laborers rested in the shade while they enjoyed the brief meal, but Bramn stayed near the mansion wall, being stubborn.

Thylaina approached him. "Sir Bramn."

"Yes, my lady?"

"Have we stumbled?"

He regarded her for a moment, his gaze rounding. "I hope not."

"You... We seem distant since the night at Shapele Colmstad's."

Bramn smiled reassuringly. "There has been an awful lot on my mind. With Einasa arriving soon, and—"

"Did you know what they did to Gavrel?"

He clamped his mouth shut and stared at her, the roundness replaced with squinting.

Thylaina rubbed her arms, pushed a rock off the path and into the upturned soil. "Forgive me. I was upset when I saw what the knights had done to him."

Bramn scratched the back of his head, somehow managing to keep the sandy locks within the blue ribbon. "It's what they do to teach someone a lesson. Whether it was Gavrel or another who had struck me, their fate would've been the same."

She curled her fingers into fists, her nails digging into her palms. "It is wrong."

"What you must understand is that our people do things differently. We might not like everything about the elves, yet we know it's how they are."

Mouth dropped open, she shook her head. "Tell me one vile thing elves do that disturbs you humans. I wager you cannot think of any!" Thylaina spun, ready to walk away.

"You're pompous."

Forcing a laugh, she faced him. "You call that vile?"

Bramn shrugged. "It's annoying."

She touched her fingertips to her chest and tittered. "And obviously dangerous to your people. Now if you do not mind, Sir Bramn, I must return to finishing—"

"We tire of your damn scrutiny. You elves constantly look down on us as *lesser beings* instead of treating us like equals." He glanced at the laborers beyond her, who stopped working to watch them. "We don't live centuries like you, but at least we don't waste our short lives trying to convince all Emvarr that we're more important than everyone else. We just live each day. Enjoy the sun, smell the fields, and feel the hair of one we love."

Bramn was a fool if he believed humans behaved in such a way.

Thylaina tilted her head. "You love life so much, you destroy it."

He released an irritated sigh.

"Maybe my people are self-important," she continued. "But you kill each other and those around you. You ruin nature with your carelessness, and you show little faith in the gods Who give you so much. Humans are the most selfish of all on Emvarr."

Bramn stepped closer. "During the War of the Demigods, when Alohrius needed their greatest ally, why did Etharell turn away? Warstchia was devastated because the elves abandoned us."

Cheeks burning, Thylaina seethed through her gritted teeth. "We were fighting greater beings! Demigods and immortals killed xilys warriors and villagers because of our involvement in that war. Because of Chaos!" Memories from those history lessons resulted in tears. Elves rarely thought about those days without weeping for the thousands of lives lost in the War of the Demigods.

"Chaos?" Bramn smirked. "He was in Alohrius murdering us, the newlars, and everyone else who got in his way of destroying—"

"Us!" Thylaina pushed him. "He wanted to destroy the elves, you bloody bastard!"

"And there's that self-importance." Bramn leaned back, laughing. "Captain better prepare himself before he leaves for Etharell."

Thylaina stilled. Breydon had not told her his destination. This news brought tears along with worry. Afraid of the elves finding her, she suddenly felt ill.

"What is this?" Breydon asked from the southern end of the path.

Thylaina spun, then lowered her head and wiped her sleeve over her eyes.

"Just a disagreement, Captain," Bramn said.

Breydon clasped his hands behind his back while he strolled forward, appearing to inspect the laborers' workmanship. "Sir Bramn, give us a moment. All of you leave."

Bramn bowed his head, then ushered the laborers away from Thylaina and Breydon.

Once they were alone, she found the courage to inquire about his upcoming travel. "You are going to Etharell."

He nodded while stepping beyond her.

"Why?"

"To meet with the Ormiana Commander." He looked back at her. "Not that it's your concern."

"Is it not?"

"It's not about you." He let his arms relax at his sides. "At least, not yet."

A chill spread throughout her. She desperately wanted to run to Breydon and beg him to say nothing, but she felt rooted to the ground like an ancient tree. Words could form upon her tongue, and her throat dried.

He regarded her. "You've paled."

Breath coming fast, she paused to lick her lips, then swallowed. "Shapele, please," she whispered. "I implore you, do not speak about me."

"Why?" His lips pressed into a thin line as he tilted his head back. "What have you kept secret about yourself?"

Thylaina forced her legs to move forward, and with that slight movement, she found her voice. "You know I am high born, and I left to avoid a marriage. If you say anything to the commander or the xilys, even speak my name, they will come for me."

"Perhaps that would be best," he muttered as he turned and walked on the northern path.

"Shapele!"

Breydon did not stop.

What was she to do? If he said anything to the xilys commander, Thylaina would find herself back in Haevaun Flameral, marrying Rhomasyn. She could leave, but Tesesra's babe needed her. Thylaina could not abandon them.

# Chapter Twelve

Eleven strenuous days passed. Not only did Thylaina worry about Breydon being gone four days longer than he had said the undertaking would last, but that he might reveal to the Ormiana commander about her presence in Caerabis... and she missed Breydon. Several minutes of each day replayed what he had confessed in her chamber, and it never failed to bring her to tears. Still, she pushed through each day and tended to Lady Tesesra.

Now that Her Ladyship had further improved, Arhgrim and Nadiera spent more time with her. This brought joy to the small family. Thylaina even gave Nadiera permission to spend a night or two with her mother, as long as the young girl promised to leave without resistance if anything should arise. Thankfully, no such issues had come to pass.

This morning, while Thylaina examined Tesesra, Nadiera helped Panya and Quaiy set up the morning meal for her family. Thylaina no longer administered tea while Her Ladyship broke fast, but only at night to promote healing while the woman slept. During the evening visits, she sent everyone from the room to perform a thorough exam. The mornings were far too busy with breaking fast and manor business. For the past five days, the babe's heartbeat had been steady, and the visions Vynia granted showed a healthy, although small, infant.

"My lord," the guard said loudly from the suite, warning that Arhgrim had arrived.

The marshal laughed. "You needn't shout every morning. You'll wake anyone not already out of bed."

"Sorry." Yet the guard would do it again.

Thylaina helped Tesesra sit up while Arhgrim entered, his eyes and face bright.

"Good morrow, ladies." He kissed the top of Nadiera's head, then Tesesra's cheek. "How are my two loves?"

"Panya brought corncakes, Father." Nadiera jumped up and down, staring at the flat, fluffy bread topped with butter and honey. It was as delicious as the cornbread.

"That I can't eat," Tesesra mumbled.

"I made a special one for you, m'lady." Panya presented a dish of corncakes topped with a blubbery and raspberry sauce.

"How did you sweeten it?" Thylaina asked.

The young maiden blushed. "I used juice from an apple."

Thylaina tilted her head and blinked. "May I taste it first?"

It appeared Tesesra wanted to eat, not wait for approval, but she nodded nonetheless.

Thylaina cut a small piece of cake and slid it around in the berry sauce, scooping only a couple of blueberries with it. The corncake nearly melted in her mouth, and the sauce was perfection. The apple juice was an ingenious idea.

"This is absolutely wonderful." She gave the fork to Her Ladyship. "Another superb creation of Viya's."

Panya released a breathy laugh, the tops of her cheeks rosier. "I-I created them. Viya likes it very much."

"As do I." Thylaina just wished she had an appetite.

Nadiera looked from her honey covered cakes to her mother's meal. "Can I have those instead?"

"Eat your own." Arhgrim patted her head.

Smiling, Thylaina left the family to enjoy each other's company.

The guard opened the landing door for her. "You look exhausted, my lady."

Thylaina paused, struggling to respond with a lie. There was no hiding the dark circles, which had worsened this week. "I shall be fine after I break fast."

"Food doesn't remedy lack of sleep."

She touched his arm. "I appreciate your concern."

On the landing, Bramn leaned against the rail, reading a parchment. Thylaina tapped the parchment to gain his attention. Sucking in a breath, he met her gaze. "Sorry. I was looking over Einasa's... Well, what she wants to serve at the wedding celebration. There's so much. Food, drinks, sweets, more drinks and food. This list doesn't end. The woman arrived yesterday and has already handed me demands."

Thylaina giggled as she slid her arm around his, and they walked toward the stairs. It was good to have their relationship back to normal. She had missed the comfort and conversations with him. "Is she joining us to break fast?"

"As are her friends."

Einasa's friends, three maidens Bramn had not expected her to bring to the city. Thylaina had yet to have properly met them. One of the maidens was a gorgeous blonde named Nikhia, with deeply tanned skin from working in the sun, and in need of more fabric to cover the abundant cleavage she put on display. None of the men could stop flitting their gazes at the exposed flesh, especially when she moved. Bryric! Even Thylaina could not stop glancing at Nikhia's generous bosom. The young woman was obviously fond of Breydon, for she did not cease asking question about him the night afore.

The Momestids accommodated the four women with two rooms to share on the third floor; Einasa appeared to love the pampering. However, her staying there did not promise constant time with Bramn. He had enough to do as it was: guard Thylaina, report to Arhgrim, and spend every available waking moment, little as it was, with Einasa.

"You certain you don't wish to rest?" he asked.

"I am fine."

"You've pouches under your eyes."

She yawned. If he had not said anything, it might not have ever come. Naught to do about it now.

"See? There you go. I'm taking you right to your chambers." He turned her around and proceeded to Thylaina's room.

"Well, I suppose extra rest this morning will do n'ei harm."

"Very good." He opened the door to the suite, continued to the bedroom door, where painted yellow flowers bloomed on green leafy vines. All the bedchamber doors had flowers on them, but of different colors.

"M'lady?" Katjina said upon their entry, halting her sorting through the wardrobe.

Thylaina smiled at the handmaiden, then turned to Bramn. "Thank you, my friend. I shall update my notes on Her Ladyship afor—"

"That can wait. You need rest or you'll find yourself stuck in bed for a few days from fatigue." He gestured to the comfortable mattress set within a sturdy oak bedframe.

Bramn certainly seemed desperate to get her resting. And it did not seem entirely about ensuring she had plenty of sleep.

"I promise I shall." Thylaina forced a smile. "Now, off with you."

He bowed slightly, then left the chamber.

Shaking her head, she busied herself at the worktable: entered notes on Tesesra and the babe, and measured herbs into vials. However, Bramn's behavior troubled her.

"Is something wrong, m'lady?" Katjina asked.

Thylaina corked all the vials. "Did you see the knee holly?"

"It looks lovely. Thriving well."

"It is." Thylaina sat on the bed, wondering what to do. She wished Breydon was home, but knew not what good would come of it. Their parting had not been friendly. Tears about the whole horrible situation surfaced again, and she wanted to be alone and cry.

"I'm going to retrieve aprons for this afternoon's work." Katjina gently squeezed Thylaina's arm. "I'll be back shortly."

The woman was wonderful. She often recognized when Thylaina needed a moment to herself, silence, a song, or a hair brushing to calm her nerves. Katjina could read her charge like a book and know what to do. Thylaina's previous handmaidens were oblivious to her needs. They simply performed their duties, treating her like a guest in the palace, even though she had spent most of her life there. Some had called her the Pretend Princess when they thought she could not hear. Thylaina never wanted to be the center of attention. Katjina was different. She was not just a handmaiden.

Thylaina held Katjina's hand during the length of a long breath. Calm enough to speak, she said, "Thank you, my dear friend."

"When I return, we'll do whatever you wish before beginning work in the herb garden." Katjina quietly left the room.

Once alone, Thylaina sat in the suite. She immediately imagined Breydon in the chair across from her, his eyes bright and focused, and a crooked smile pulling at his lips. She felt heat from his nearness, his scent on her tongue as his hand brushed hers, sending jolts throughout her.

Sweet Lessindra. Would he forgive her?

She wept herself to sleep, and Katjina let her be for two hours in that chair. The rest gave her enough energy to resume duties: examine Tesesra, eat a light meal, then return outside to the herb garden. There was not much to do there for now. To improve the temple's and Thylaina's future stock, Raylen agreed to acquire wormwood for stomach ailments, and anise for several remedies. Thylaina was excited about the latter. However, the seeds for both would not arrive from Brydasia until the middle of the Hawk Moon. No matter, that was the perfect timing for spring sowing.

The temperatures had dropped over the past week, meaning the first frost was close. The harvest in the city garden completed, the plots were now turned and the storage buildings filled. Which was why Einasa had to wait to come to Caerabis: to help her father, the local miller. He owned the only windmill in the region. When Einasa's father arrived with her and the other maidens, he had also delivered three wagons of flour and milled corn.

Thylaina covered the plots with burlap, inspected each knee holly bush once again—thrilled to have them arrive early—then went into the scullery to crush dried xarflas leaves and grind bossel roots.

The scullery maids sang and tossed vegetable ends at each other, all the while giggling, until Viya arrived with Bramn, Einasa, and Nikhia. The kitchen servants immediately quieted and returned to work, acting as if nothing had happened, despite the scattered evidence.

Bramn met Thylaina's gaze, then headed to her. She poured the crushed xarflas leaves through the funnel and into the large jar for later distribution.

"My lady." He rested his bottom against the table. "Did you rest well?"

"I did." Thylaina reached behind him for the bossel roots on the other side of the table. "It has given me plenty of energy to complete several tasks."

"Lady Thylaina," a woman said from behind her.

After setting the roots down, Thylaina faced Einasa.

"I'm so sorry we've yet to be properly introduced," Einasa said. "You're in the dining chamber for such a brief time; there and gone before we're finished with our discussions. Do forgive me."

The farm maiden was only an inch or two taller than Thylaina, and a long, light-brown plait rested over her solid shoulder. Her father's business might do well, but this woman put in just as much work in the fields, for strength showed with each movement. Admirable.

"N'ei apology is necessary," Thylaina said, curtsying to her. "My care over Her Ladyship limits my time in the hall. Please forgive me if it appears I have neglected your arrival."

"Oh my." Einasa's cheeks bloomed pink. "You needn't curtsy to me. Bramn? He can curtsy, but not you." Her rain cloud irises fixed on Thylaina. "Gods, you're so beautiful. I've never seen copper eyes before."

Lowering her gaze, Thylaina tilted her head down. "Thank you, my lady."

"And your accent is lovely," Nikhia said. Her voice was sweet and soft. If it were not for Thylaina's heritage, she might not have heard her amid the bustle in the scullery.

Thylaina nodded once, but said nothing.

Einasa wrapped her arms around Nikhia's. "This is the most wonderful friend I could ever pray for, Nikhia."

Thylaina forced a smile, then returned to grinding the bossel roots. She once had friends like that.

"My lady," Bramn whispered. "I'm sorry I wasn't there when you woke up."

"Listen here, Sir Bramn." Viya approached. "You've got a decision to make by this evening."

He scowled. "Why? We're not marrying until Her Ladyship has the babe."

"If you want a roasted pig or a cow, then I need to tell the butcher, and he needs to tell the farmer." Viya waggled her finger in front of his nose. "Time's something you *think* you have."

Straightening, he huffed and turned to Einasa. "What do you want, love?"

The maiden glanced at her friend, then shrugged. "I'll be far too nervous to eat. You choose."

"Whatever your decision," Viya said, "with a roasting like that, the feast'll be in the main hall. Not here."

Bramn shook his head. "I want it here."

"I've not the means to roast a whole cow or pig in this kitchen," Viya said, her eyes wide. "And I'm not doing it in the dining chamber. The last thing I want to do is burn down the Momestid's home."

"What's this about burning down Grim's home?" Breydon asked from the banded door leading outside.

While everyone else greeted him, Thylaina held her breath until it hurt. Did she dare turn to see if a squad of xilys accompanied him? Letting the air out slowly, she tried to control the quaking that overtook her.

"About time you returned," Bramn said.

"I had a lot of amending to do." Breydon's voice sounded close, right behind Thylaina. By lack of a reaction from everyone else, it was apparent he was alone. "Einasa," he said. "It's wonderful to see you again."

"It's been too long." She laughed, then sounded a humph. "Your hugs are comparable to a bear!"

"You're hugging bears now?" he slurred.

Einasa and Nikhia giggled.

Still afraid to face him, Thylaina kept her back to them. The grinding of the roots turned into a furious task.

"Nikhia? Is that you?" Breydon asked, his voice sounding awfully low.

"You remember me?"

"I could never forget." He kissed a part of her. Hopefully, her hand and not her cheek... or cleavage. "A pleasure to see you again."

"I cherish the memories, Captain. Every one of them." She released a sultry laugh. "I thought perhaps you'll walk me around Caerabis. Allow us to get reacquainted."

Thylaina frowned. Breydon had yet to show *her* the city. And why did Nikhia sound like she was trying to seduce him? Breydon needed rest after this long journey, not traipse around the whole bloody city.

He cleared his throat. "I—"

"Forgive me, Captain," Viya's gentle interruption silenced the four of them, "but I've much work to do for tonight's supper. If the reunion could move elsewhere, I'd appreciate it."

"No worries, my dear," he said. "Einasa, I look forward to dinner. Nikhia, it's truly a pleasure. We'll speak tonight."

"Oh." Disappointment weighed Nikhia's tone. "I thought we might—"

"Forgive me. I've a matter to discuss with Lady Thylaina."

Thylaina froze. She slowly peered over her shoulder at him, but he was smiling at the two maidens. A young beard adorned Breydon's face, yet it did not hide that he had missed at least two days of sleep. Heavy lids veiled his red-rimmed, teary eyes, his hair was in disarray, and he slouched. While the three wished him a fine afternoon, he swayed where he stood.

Stepping in Thylaina's direction, Nikhia wrinkled her nose. "He's been mine before," she whispered. "He'll be mine again." The woman smiled as she took Bramn's arm and left with him and Einasa.

Casting aside the woman's snide remarks, Thylaina turned to Breydon. His drooping eyelids and lack of reaction to Nikhia revealed a man too tired to note if a sparrow had splattered droppings on his head.

"Shapele, you are exhausted." She took a satchel from him and set it on the table, then touched his forehead, seeking for a temperature; he felt fine. However, his flesh was cold.

Breydon raised a brow. "I haven't slept since..." He closed his eyes and breathed deep. "Day before last."

"Two days?"

He nodded. "I wanted to come home."

Thylaina cupped his icy hand between hers to warm it. "What happened, Shapele?"

He stared at their hands for a moment, then raised his gaze to hers. "I brought something for you."

Her throat dried. Did he bring elves to take her back to Etharell? She dropped his hand and lifted the stone pestle, grinding the roots once again. "You need not have bothered yourself."

"I wanted to."

"And what is it?"

Breydon tapped the satchel she had taken from him.

Elves could not fit in the case. But a message from the commander or her brother could. *Bryric, please do not be a letter from home.*

"Open it," Breydon said, the words practically coming out as one.

Thylaina unbuckled the satchel, then slipped the leather strap free. The captain appeared too tired to notice her hands trembling. Biting her lip, she flipped the case open. Something green sprung out and flitted toward the floor. Thylaina gasped and caught it. *A buraily leaf?* Heart racing, she pulled the case closer and peeked inside. It was full of buraily leaves. A laugh escaped as she looked at Breydon.

He leaned against the table with his arms crossed, chin tucked to his chest, and his eyes closed. It was then she noticed all the scullery maidens worked as quietly as possible while Viya whispered orders or gave gestures. As much as he needed sleep, Thylaina could not leave Breydon like this.

"Shapele." She gently shook him.

He breathed in through his nose and surveyed the scullery. Blinking at Thylaina, he smacked his lips together. "Are you pleased?"

"Why did you—?"

"I told you I wanted to." He nodded at the bossel roots. "Why are you in here? Don't you have a mortar yet?"

"N'ei." Elated with his gift, she lifted another root. "Thank you for the leaves."

Breydon gently grabbed her wrist, took the root from her, and dropped it on the table, then guided her to the outside door. "Viya, please have one of the maidens finish for Lady Thylaina."

"Captain! We're busy!"

"I appreciate it, Viya!" Breydon escorted Thylaina out.

The cold Oaken air swept Thylaina's heated cheeks as she allowed him to lead her to the knee holly. "Shapele, Viya is not going to—" She halted upon seeing bundled sacks atop the burlap covers on four of the empty plots. Thylaina walked to the nearest one, scrutinizing it. "What is this?"

"Open it." His voice sounded clearer. Perhaps the fresh, chill air revived him.

"You are full of surprises, Shapele."

Breydon's expression fell flat, apparently annoyed with the formal address.

To appease him, Thylaina knelt and opened the first sack. Tears threatened to fall and her throat tightened as she viewed seven young repenia vines with the roots covered and bound in silk. "Breydon," she whispered. Two droplets fell as she raised her eyes to his. No words formed.

"Open this one." He pointed at the bundle on the plot next to him.

Clutching the repenia sack to her chest, she rose and hurried to kneel at his feet. Her hands could not move fast enough to pull the strings of the sack and pry it open. Air rushed from her. "Ashrych."

"Only two more," he said, stepping back.

Thylaina gently placed the repenias beside the ashrych, then stood. "Where did—? How did you?"

"In Etharell." He smirked, for he could not have found them elsewhere. "I asked your countrymen for aid. They questioned as to why, so I told them my herbal priest has been learning about their herbs." He lifted a sack from between two of the plots. "I'd like you to keep this close to you; whatever it is you do with them. It's insh."

"I-I know not what to say."

He scanned the small garden, then met her gaze. "You've done fine work."

It was there, staring at her. Breydon did not care about a farm maiden who apparently desired his attention. He still wanted to be with Thylaina. That much was obvious when he dismissed Nikhia from the scullery, and now shown with the longing in his eyes.

Thylaina caressed his cheek, her fingers brushing the coarse hairs. "I missed you."

His countenance softened, yet grew serious at the same time.

"I am sorry I did not understand your intentions," she continued.

He took her hand and kissed her fingers. "It's not only that." Lowering her hand, he let it go. "Gavrel is between us."

She gaped at him. Not once had the dubight crossed her mind as someone with whom to be intimate. "I wish you and Bramn would understand that Gavrel is my friend."

"And my courting you…" Breydon stepped back, rubbed his eyelids with one hand, sliding the fingers to the bridge of his nose. "I am a low born bastard, and you're beyond me."

"I am nothing and n'ei one."

It seemed he fought the urge to laugh.

"But what you must know," she continued, "is that I have never been courted."

His face scrunched. "You jest."

"N'ei."

"But you were betrothed."

"Forced. Therefore, he felt courting was not necessary." Thylaina reached for Breydon's hand, and when he gave it to her, she held it to her cheek. "This is all new to me." She met the hope in his gaze and dared not destroy it.

He pulled her closer, then cradled her face with tenderness, his thumbs gliding over her cheekbones. "I adore you, Thylaina," he whispered. "You were constantly in my thoughts."

Unable to look away from him, trapped by the affection in his eyes and aura, she smiled.

"And you *are* someone," he said. "For the Ormiana commander asked if I had heard anything about a dark-haired elf maiden with copper eyes. So you're either someone of importance, or a criminal they seek. Either one, they want you back."

Thylaina would not return to Etharell. And if using Breydon might guarantee it, then she would do what she must. Wrapping her arms around his waist, she tilted her head back, her lips brushing the hairs on his chin. "I promise you, I am n'ei a criminal."

"That's what I feared." He clutched her head and kissed her.

# Chapter Thirteen

**B**reydon made his affections for Thylaina clear to everyone, which disappointed Nikhia and Einasa. Thankfully, the latter appeared to care about Breydon's happiness, and bore no grudge. Nikhia fell silent in their presence, often eyeing Thylaina as if she wanted to make her disappear. Bramn had taken Breydon aside to speak with him, but nothing changed after that discussion, except Bramn no longer talked with Thylaina. The knight seemed to know much about elves, so must have been aware of how her people viewed intimacy afore marriage. Katjina and the Momestids—excluding Nadiera—were delighted with Breydon's relationship with Thylaina. The First Captain still behaved as if Thylaina was the only person nearby. The only one who mattered. It grew increasingly obvious that he loved her, which frightened Thylaina. She was an absolute fool to allow anything to flourish between them, yet she ignored sound reason.

Three days of bliss passed. And though Breydon returned to spending as much time with Thylaina as he could between performing his duties, she was awfully busy planting the herbs in quickly built boxes for her suite and continuing her care over Tesesra. Of the plants, her biggest concern was the repenia vines. It finally came to requesting a trellis in her chamber to help them grow through the winter months since it was too late to replant them. The first frost had arrived, the twelfth moon was soon upon them, and Tesesra's babe had moved lower.

After this morning's examination, Thylaina helped Tesesra sit up. "How are you feeling, my lady?"

Tesesra grabbed the needlepoint from the small table to her left. "I'm tired of being in bed, and I want to do something. Prepare for my child... help you with your garden."

"Which will not be ready until spring."

"I don't care! This place is collapsing around me and I can do naught about it." Frowning, Tesesra slouched.

Thylaina sat on the bed and smiled. "The mansion is far from collapsing. Quaiy delegates your commands, and all is well." She moved the needlepoint aside, then clasped Tesesra's hands. "The babe has lowered. It shall not be long now."

Her Ladyship's eyes widened, and a giggle burst forth, soon followed by laughter. Glee brightened her face, and her hips wiggled in a small dance. "How wonderful! You must tell Grim."

"Do you not wish to?"

"He's breaking fast in the hall. You tell him and the others straight away."

"If you wish, my lady."

Tesesra nodded vigorously.

"With this news, I shall be at your side more often," Thylaina said. "If not, I will be in my chambers. Always nearby."

"Excellent."

Thylaina prayed all would be well. Although things appeared fine by the visions, there was still no certainty until the babe was born. She tucked another pillow behind Tesesra, then poured a goblet of purified water for her. "There shall be n'ei more tea. With the babe positioning for birth, I do not wish to risk any reactions from the herbs."

"What about sleep?"

"If it becomes difficult, tell me. I will decide upon something then."

"Very well."

Nodding once at Quaiy, Thylaina smiled. She then joined Bramn on the landing.

He walked briskly to the stairs. "Let's be on our way." His hurry gave the suspicion that Einasa waited for him in the dining chamber.

In the entrance hall, they halted. Gavrel was at the doors, speaking with the two guards. An ill expression altered his visage as he stared at Bramn, but then he turned his attention to Thylaina, and pain showed in his eyes.

"Sir Bramn, please give me a moment," she said. Without waiting for a response, she approached the dubight. "Gavrel, how do you fare?"

He bowed partially, then kissed her hand. "I'm well, my lady. Raylen did a fine job tending to my injuries." His gaze darted to Bramn, then back. "You look lovely, as always."

Thylaina had yet to release his hand, which she now squeezed. "I had hoped to see you sooner, but I have been—"

"Occupied." Gavrel nodded. "I understand they have demanded a lot of you."

Her shoulders lowered as she stepped closer to him. "I swear to you—"

"No need to explain." He kissed her hand again. "They keep me busy as well. Don't they, Sir Bramn?" Gavrel's gaze hardened as he looked at the knight.

Saying nothing, Bramn neared them.

The dubight smirked. His brown eyes did not show kindness, and when they fixed on Thylaina again, they revealed rejection. An ache.

"I am truly sorry for not coming to see you while you were imprisoned," she said, hoping he believed her sincerity. "But I do not have the freedom to go where I wish."

"I *do* understand." His fingertips grazed her cheek. "I often forget that you're a prisoner here. One day, you'll have the freedom to do what you wish."

"My lady," Bramn said gruffly. "We must go."

Gavrel glared at him, then grinned at her. "One day."

Bramn took Thylaina's hand from him and guided her away. "Report to Captain Eilisar," he said.

"Yes, sir."

Neither man moved. Several seconds dragged afore Gavrel snorted, then turned his back to them. The guards opened the door for him, closed it after he left.

Thylaina's stomach quaked. That was not the same dubight she had met her first night here. It broke her heart to see the warmth gone from his eyes and feel it missing from his aura.

Bramn pulled her toward the hall to the dining chamber. Thylaina almost stumbled, but regained her footing. "This is why I'm not pleased about you and Breydon," he said between clenched teeth.

Scowling, she yanked her arm free and halted. "Because I care about my friend?"

"Because you're going to hurt him."

"Gavrel?"

Eyes narrowed, he shook his head. "Breydon! You don't know what he's suffered, yet you're willing to add to it."

"You assume too much." Thylaina resumed to the dining hall. "He told me about his family."

"I'm not talking about Kreysin, nor his mother." Bramn passed her, turned, and continued while walking backwards. "I speak about Iaviane."

Thylaina paused. "Who?"

"You'll ruin him. I had a promising future for him with Nikhia, but he's cast her aside for something he can't have. But you only think about what *you* want." Spinning, he stomped forward.

*Iaviane.* The name repeated in Thylaina's head. Breydon had never mentioned her. After all they had shared, he still kept too much from her. But she had no right to judge. Breydon still did not know her truth.

Thylaina eventually made it to the feast hall. She did not give Bramn the satisfaction of a glance, yet found it difficult to look at Breydon. Not even when he rose to greet her.

"Sir Bramn must've been in a hurry to leave you behind," Breydon said, then kissed her cheek. "I should reprimand him for it."

"N'ei." Flitting a smile, she sat.

Breydon remained standing for a few seconds longer afore he returned to his seat. "You'll like this morning's meal." He gestured at a plate of Panya's corncakes topped with the berry sauce. What a morning not to have an appetite. Breydon stuck his fork through two pieces, gathered a few berries, then shoved it toward her mouth. "Have a bite." Thylaina opened it to avoid having the dripping sauce all over her lips. "Delicious, isn't it?" The smile reached his eyes.

Chewing, she nodded, then viewed the others at the table. Grim ate while reading a missive; Bramn slouched in his seat, poking his meal with a fork; Einasa prattled one sentence after another about the wedding, which would come sooner than she realized; and Nikhia leaned to the side in her chair, staring at Breydon. Nadiera must have gone upstairs to join her mother, but Thylaina did not recall seeing the young girl.

Returning her attention to Breydon, she watched him eat. He truly enjoyed the corncakes and berries, for he touched nothing else nor looked from the plate, and no more steam rose from his coffee. Her heart shattered. Bramn was correct: Thylaina was going to hurt Breydon. As much as she adored the man, there was no future for them. She should let Nikhia have him. But Breydon had apparently told the young woman his heart was spoken for. Thylaina was a selfish woman.

Breydon set the fork down and wiped his mouth on a dining cloth. He drank the coffee. Grinned. He leaned close, his forehead nearly touching hers. "Love, what troubles you?" His thumb stroked her cheek, drying a teardrop.

Blinking, she straightened. "N-nothing." To drown the urge to cry, she drank some tea. "I have not much time."

He arched a brow.

Arhgrim raised his head and lowered the parchment. "Is something wrong?"

Even a deep breath could not ease the growing pain in her chest. "The babe has lowered. It shall not be much longer."

The marshal's smile came slow. His blue eyes glistened. "When?"

"Any day. At any moment."

Breydon clasped her hand and kissed her fingers. "Wonderful."

"That is lovely news," Einasa said, her glowing face making her eyes seem lighter. "Oh, Bramn! To think that all worries will soon come to an end."

He nodded, although not showing as much enthusiasm as the others.

Thylaina's stomach tightened, for that was not quite true.

"What can we do?" Arhgrim asked.

Thylaina laughed softly. "Your duties, my lord. I shall remain with her most times. If I am not in Her Ladyship's chambers, I shall be in mine. But I will always be nearby."

"Excellent." Arhgrim pounded his fist on the table, then stood. "Lady Thylaina, whatever you need, you shall have." Arhgrim's solemn expression said it all: his wife and babe took priority.

"Thank you, my lord."

"I'm going to see Tes." Arhgrim headed for the exit, his steps hurried.

"I should go as well." Thylaina rose.

Breydon stood, catching her fingers with his. "I suppose our afternoon meal is canceled?" His lips were warm on the back of her hand, then her forearm.

Bramn stood. "I'll escort you to your chambers, Lady Thylaina."

The captain seemed not to hear, for his mouth neared her shoulder. He still cared not about who was present; it was just him and Thylaina.

So why did *she* care about something that no longer concerned her? They were not in Etharell, and she had severed her blood ties to the throne and her family. As much as Thylaina loved her father and brother, they were not a part of her life.

She locked her gaze with Breydon's and palmed both sides of his face, then slid her fingers into his hair. "Shapele Breydon Colmstad."

He smiled. "S'yai?" The word was spoken in a low, breathy voice, rattling the strength in her knees.

She could say this and know without doubt she meant it. *"Et losath eywe."*

Breydon sucked in a rush of air, searched her eyes. "Is that so?"

"My lady, come," Bramn said, his tone demanding.

Thylaina rose to her tiptoes and kissed Breydon softly. "It is."

A shudder moved throughout him as a smile stretched his lips. "Thylaina." He held her tighter, bent his face closer to hers, and spoke back to her in her language. "And I love you."

Thylaina had never known a kiss to possess such passion and desire, yet feel it contained to that one act. Despite the yearning his mouth and touch relayed, it was not with need, but love. To recognize this with absolute certainty consumed her breath and threatened to burst her heart.

Noises caught her notice: giggles, chairs sliding, someone spoke, something slammed on the table, but everything was faint. Nothing was as important as that moment with Breydon and the declaration they just shared.

"Nikhia, wait!" Einasa called.

"To Darkness with this," Bramn snapped.

With the exception of Thylaina's pounding heart, it fell silent, yet the kiss continued.

Finally, Breydon straightened, drew in a deep breath. "Great Knight." He laughed. Kissed her again, but this time briefly. "Laina, you've no idea what you've done."

The shortening of her name nearly brought the wild fluttering in her stomach to a halt. The last time someone called her by that name was afore Valraahn's exile. But as Breydon's touch raised her nerves to their highest sensitivity, sending a sensation throughout her body, she swiftly forgot about the past and focused on how bloody alive she felt now. This *must* be love.

"What have I done?"

Breydon pulled her farther from the table and twirled around with her. "You've made me the happiest man in Yeuroth!"

When they stopped spinning, they kissed again. It was unbelievably exciting—being in love. This presented a whole new life for her. Yet Thylaina hoped she would remain brave enough to continue. After more than two hundred years of her father and uncle conditioning her for her future, the belief she could sever from the elvish ways sometimes seemed impossible.

In the following week, no matter Thylaina's numerous invites, Breydon refused to stay in her room. It was a strange concept for her: not being wanted. Yet he could not conceal his desire after the touches and kisses they shared. Nor could he hide the way his virility responded, growing harder and longer, sometimes damn near hurting when pressed against Thylaina. But emotionally, Breydon did not *want* her. Of course, he never said as much, but politely declined the invites or ceased her attempts to seduce him.

This night had come to an end, and they spent a few moments in her suite to wish each other an evening of peaceful sleep, the sweetest dreams, and their gods' blessings on one another. Or they would soon. Right now, sitting on her favorite chair by the fireplace, the ties at the front of her dress were loose enough to allow his hand access, and she had thrust hers into his trousers and beneath the braies. The latter took little time to get used to, considering elves rarely wore anything under their clothing. But once she heard Breydon moan when she grasped him, that he wore a garment beneath his pants was of no concern.

He turned his head, breaking their kiss. "Laina!"

She may have hesitated the first time he called her by that name, but Thylaina now adored it, and no one else was privy to use it.

A deep breath rushing between his lips, he rested his head back. "Oh, Laina." His hips moved in rhythm with her hand.

She nipped his neck, sucked on the flesh. Soft moans vibrated in her throat as her yearning intensified from him rolling her nipple under his thumb.

Hips lowering, he released her nipple and grabbed her wrist. "Stop. Please. I can't... I must go."

Not Again.

"Breydon, n'ei," she begged.

His grip tightened, ceasing the motion. "Please, Laina. I'm not ready."

A giggle sputtered from her. "You feel ready, darling."

"You know what I mean." He removed her hand from his trousers. "Not yet, love."

It still amazed her how this man could deny what he obviously wanted. She pulled the opening of her dress together, then tightened the strings enough to close it. "Your virility belies you, Breydon."

"My virility?" He looked down at his crotch. "Is that what you call it?"

"More pleasant a word than what you humans use."

Smirking, he jerked his head back. "What? Cock?"

Thylaina cringed. "It is so harsh. And you humans sprinkle that word into your conversations like a farmer sowing seeds in the fields."

Amusement flashed in his eyes. "Tell me... how many times have you heard it since your arrival?"

She stared at the hearth while scouring her mind, unable to recall a single instance.

"You haven't, have you?" Breydon laughed, then kissed the side of her head. "You're an adorable creature."

"Stop."

"It's a long word."

Brows low, she stared at him.

"Virility," he said. "Then again, it seems fitting for me." He smiled crookedly.

Pulling her skirts up, she straddled him. "S'yai, Shapele." She glided her tongue across his lips, then caught the bottom one with her teeth, tugging it.

"Gods, Laina." He clutched her buttocks, slanted his mouth over hers in a desperate kiss.

Thylaina kept her hand outside his trousers, rubbing her palm up and down his length. "I agree," she whispered. "Virility is fitting for you." She kissed him again.

There was a need to share more than her breath with him. Thylaina wanted to share everything with Breydon: her heart, soul, and life. And she could. They simply did not have to marry. There was no valid reason for her to bind herself to a human. Not even love. So she could enjoy him for as long as the gods permitted.

Thylaina turned her head, cool air brushing her face. Strange how such a warm room offered a hint of coolness, but she was overheating. Wanting. Desire and passion whirled within, waiting for Breydon to enter the dance. She had never wanted anyone so badly, but then, she had never known a proper lover, or loved someone.

"Please?" Thylaina bit his earlobe. "Breydon, please?"

His hands slid to her hips, and he gently pushed her forward. "N'ei." Sweat glistened on his face, dampened his hairline. "I must go."

She curled her fingers into his shirt, rested her cheek on his chest. Great Bryric! His heart beat rapidly. "Do not leave me."

The arms of the chair creaked beneath his grip. "Love, I must go."

Pouting, she eased off his lap.

Breydon remained still for a few minutes, his focus on the dancing fire. While he settled, Thylaina poured a drink for them, which he appreciated. Once he recovered from the fondling, he prepared to leave. The silence was odd. Thylaina was not angry with him; however, Breydon had yet to explain why he pushed her away.

He wiped his face with a cloth, then combed his hair back with his fingers. His eyes darted toward her, his gaze showing he wanted to stay. It was like this every night.

"Why?" she pressed.

He released a long, loud breath. "I knew you'd ask sooner or later."

"Why do you not wish to make love with me?"

Breydon stilled, his eyes widened. "Laina, I do. I want to spend hours appreciating every inch of you. But I'm not ready."

Scowling, she crossed her arms and leaned her bottom against the worktable. "What does that bloody mean?"

"I'm as afraid of loving you as you are of loving me."

The muscles of her face relaxed as she lowered her arms. The man understood her better than she believed. "Speak with me."

He returned to the chair and motioned for her to join him. Thylaina sat on his lap again, resting her hands on her knees. Silence returned for a few long seconds while he nibbled on his lip. Why Breydon was nervous, she knew not.

She tilted his chin up and smiled. "Speak with me, darling." His eyes revealed such love, her heart swelled.

"When I was fourteen, I had met the most wonderful maiden." The love in his eyes was not for Thylaina.

She looked down at her hands, twiddled her fingers. "Oh?"

"S'yai," he whispered. "While undergoing training for the knighthood, we agreed to marry, but before my knighting, she fell ill," Breydon continued. "Her name was Iaviane." He kept his gaze down, perhaps to prevent Thylaina from seeing the sorrow. "I loved her so bloody much." He sniffed to clear his nose, then wiped his eyes. "It didn't matter to her I wanted to marry as soon as possible, Iavi said she'd wait until the illness passed. I didn't blame her, I suppose. I was only seventeen, so I still had time."

Now understanding the sorrowful direction his tale headed, Thylaina held his hand between hers.

He looked up at her, his eyes red and wet. "How was I to know she didn't?" After a heavy breath, he continued. "I was on my way home from duty in New Portes when I received word in Perlos from her parents that..." He looked at the hearth, swallowed hard. "She had worsened." It sounded as if something blocked his voice.

Saying nothing, Thylaina squeezed his hand.

"I rode without rest. Damn near collapsed when I got to her parent's farm." Gazing at nothing, Breydon nodded. "Iavi had lost all her hair. Every auburn curl was gone. I... I've never heard of an illness doing that." Blinking, he met her gaze. "Have you?"

Thylaina shook her head slightly. "I have not."

"It wasn't only that, but she'd grown so weak in less than a month," he said. "It felt like I could've snapped her arm with little effort."

Thylaina could practically envision it, yet she knew of no illness with such ailments.

"I didn't want to touch Iavi for fear of hurting her, but she begged me to hold her." Tears finally broke free, trailed down his cheeks, and his lips quivered. "So I did." His voice softened. "I held her while she sang to me until her voice trailed and..." Breydon buried his face in Thylaina's neck and wept.

"I am so sorry." Stroking his hair, she hummed a song, hoping it might bring him comfort. To tell him she understood would do no good. Although Thylaina had lost her mother to an illness that also crippled her body, a disease that even the Elf King and Master Eidryn knew nothing about, it would give Breydon no consolation at this moment to match her experience with his. This was *his* grief. Letting him know she was there, truly present, was the best she could do.

Three-quarters through the song, he stopped crying and remained still. "Thank you," he murmured.

It still did not quite explain why they could not make love, but after this, she would not push the inquiry.

Breydon straightened, wiped his face dry. "I can't make love to you because I've not been with anyone since Iavi."

Or perhaps he would just tell her. However, what he said left Thylaina without an immediate response.

"I-I know it might sound strange, but I'm frightened of losing you," he added.

She arched a brow. "You have not been with anyone else?"

One corner of his lips rose. "That surprises you?"

Thylaina rubbed her nape, trying to find the best way to confirm her suspicions. "It was impressed upon me that there is an intimate history between you and Nikhia."

Waves formed on his forehead as he leaned his head back. "Well, it's not true. Although she had tried. Even recently."

*That* was no surprise.

"I turned her away, however, because there's only one woman with whom I wish to give myself." Breydon's fingers slid into Thylaina's hair, and he held her head with tenderness. "I love you, but I don't want to rush this with you."

This was interesting. A human not in a hurry?

Thylaina nodded. "Very well." Draping her arm across his shoulders, she drew ever closer. "Can we... perform ortia louvres?"

His eyes widened. "Oh, I've heard about that." Breydon licked his lips. "To-tonight?"

"To release our growing need, s'yai."

"What if it leads to—?"

"I shall teach you how to control yourself, darling." Hope grew into anxiety as she waited for him to answer.

His tongue tip poked out from between his teeth as he thought for a moment. Breydon shifted in the chair, his fingers curling tighter around her thigh. Thylaina imagined that tongue delving, lapping, and flicking her into ecstasy, pushing her into silent pleas to Lessindra that Breydon would agree.

Blue eyes met copper, and their smiles grew.

"Laina... show me everything."

She drew in a deep breath, her body instantly aroused and ready. "Come to my bed, and I shall share myself through ortia louvre with you." Thylaina grabbed his virility and firmly squeezed, enjoying the firmness of him. "And I look forward to tasting you."

"I'm yours," he moaned.

Ortia louvre with Breydon relieved more tension than Thylaina realized she had been containing. He learned quickly how to perform the sensual oral act, and he was a fine partner. Another joyful week passed, and though they still had not made love, they partook in ortia louvre a few more times, as well as desperate touches and kisses. Soon. She would come to know him very soon. That would wait, for more important matters gained Thylaina's attention.

She dropped her satchel at the end of Tesesra's bed and looked at Quaiy. "How long?"

The handmaiden guided a chambermaid from the room, giving instructions for more warmed water. "The blood spotted thirty minutes ago."

Tesesra wailed.

"You should have sent for me," Thylaina snapped.

"She wasn't like this then!" Quaiy wrung a cloth in the washbasin and hurried to the bedside. "There, there, Your Ladyship." She wiped the beading sweat from Tesesra's forehead. "Lady Thylaina's here now. All will be well."

Praying the handmaiden was correct, Thylaina removed the coverlet and tossed it on the chair. "Did she eat afternoon meal?"

"No. She had no appetite."

That might be helpful.

The chambermaid returned with two more servants bearing steaming kettles from the scullery.

Breydon had opened the door for them. He stared at Thylaina for a moment, darted his gaze to Tesesra, then closed the door. There was comfort knowing he was prepared to stop Arhgrim from charging in.

"Set the kettles on the vanity," Thylaina said, waving toward the mirrored table. "One of you bring me the candelabra." She looked at Quaiy. "Where is the cradle?"

"In the corner of the suite."

Tesesra shrieked. "It hurts!"

"I am here," Thylaina said calmly. "Quaiy, give the cloth to one of the other maidens. I need your help here."

"I don't know what to do, m'lady," Quaiy said from beside Thylaina.

"You will do as I say." Thylaina scanned the room. "Where is the pile of blankets I sent last week?"

"Over there." The handmaiden pointed to a stool beneath the window.

"Bring them here with the stool."

Quaiy looked at the other chambermaid. "Help me," she said, hurrying to the window.

"Your Ladyship, I am going to clean you, then examine the babe's position."

Breathing hard and fast, Tesesra nodded.

Once Quaiy brought the blankets, Thylaina spread one beneath Tesesra's legs while the chambermaid set the stool down.

Tesesra cried out again. That was closer to the last one.

Thylaina washed her hands. *Vynia, guide me. Bryric, give me strength. I am Your vessel.*

She had just begun examining Tesesra and the babe's position when she heard Arhgrim outside the door. Focused on her patient, she did not listen to the argument between the marshal and his First Captain, but thankfully, Breydon kept Arhgrim out of the bedchamber.

The babe's head was right there, crowning.

"We have not much time," Thylaina said. "My lady, prepare to push."

Tesesra nodded; the chambermaids helped her sit up.

Thylaina rested her hand on Tesesra's stomach, and they waited. Once she felt the muscles tighten, she said, "Push!"

Her Ladyship went through eight bouts of straining afore the head rested on Thylaina's palm. Honestly, it surprised her it took so much effort considering the babe's small size. No sound came forth, so she slipped her finger into the tiny mouth to clear out any gathered fluids or mucus.

"Push once more," Thylaina said. "Add heated water to the basin," she called over her shoulder.

"Yes, m'lady," the chambermaid replied.

From beside Thylaina, Quaiy wept with joy, yet Thylaina withheld any celebration.

Tesesra shouted as she gave a final push, freeing the babe at last. Whimpering, she lay back.

Thylaina turned the infant girl over and massaged her back. In Elvish, she prayed for the child to breathe. The heartbeat had been strong the womb, so why not now?

"My baby," Tesesra whispered.

Quaiy's worry weighed on Thylaina as she silently coaxed the Momestid babe to live.

Forcing Tesesra to remain bedridden, the teas, strict meals, and all else Thylaina had imposed for the sake of the baby, and she was met with this.

Taking the babe to the washbasin, Thylaina put the infant in the warmed water. Eyes closed, she spoke another prayer in her Tongue. "Vynia, although this is not earth, I call to You for aid. My devotion is to You. I am Your servant." After the prayer, she concentrated on the babe and the water. Words and a symbol formed in her mind, and a calmness filled her.

"Thylaina?" Tesesra called, sorrow swallowing her voice.

Tracing the symbol over the infant's forehead, Thylaina spoke the words she had seen. She made the symbol on the babe's throat and heart while repeating the incantation, then rested the babe on her shoulder and patted her back. Bouncing the slightest, she sang an Elvish lullaby.

The infant coughed. She hacked up a clog of mucus from her throat, then coughed some more. Fierce cries belted forth.

"Praise Valorius!" Quaiy squealed.

Tesesra wept.

Thylaina walked the infant to the chambermaid waiting with a blanket, then swaddled the babe. The warmth silenced the sweet darling. Smiling through tears, Thylaina gently placed the tiny girl in Tesesra's arms. "Your daughter, my lady."

Tesesra rocked slightly, blubbering while she stared at her daughter. "She's so small."

"But she will be strong."

"Thank you, Thylaina. Thank you."

Quaiy opened the door. "My lord!"

Arhgrim was already pushing her aside and charging into the room. "Tes!" He shoved the chair closer to the bed while practically sitting in it at the same time. His eyes watered as he stared at his new daughter. "Look at him," he whispered. "He's such a little thing."

"She," Tesesra said, her gaze still on the babe.

Arhgrim's smile remained as he touched his daughter's cheek. "She's beautiful." He kissed his wife's head. "You're the most beautiful."

Thylaina watched them, yet she still saw the incantation in her head, the words woven in her time of need. *Thank you, Goddess. I am grateful to You.*

"What's on your back?" Breydon asked, his brows low.

"Hm?" She looked at her shoulder, then giggled. "The babe's throat mucus."

His nose scrunched and his lips curled. Staring at her, he wiped his hand on his pants. "That's disgusting."

Thylaina had not felt him touch her, yet the giggles turned into laughter, which then faded.

It was finally over. The Momestids could breathe. Their babe was born, looked healthy, and was safe in their arms. Thylaina could breathe more easily as well.

# Chapter Fourteen

Spirits rose throughout the mansion and in the city. And with Telsia Momestid's arrival, plans for Bramn's wedding moved forward. Thylaina busied herself with Tesesra and the babe, and Breydon had several duties to oversee throughout the city, so their time together over the next six days had lessened. It hurt Thylaina, not feeling important to him anymore. Hopefully, it would not be like it was with Neldrid and everyone else who had been dear to her.

A snowfall welcomed the early risers on the tenth day of the twelfth month. Thylaina was not used to seeing snow until the Dalin Moon, marking the new year. Haevaun Flameral had at least another month afore soft white blanketed the ground for two weeks, although not consecutively. So she stared out Tesesra's window and delighted in the bright flakes floating down to gather atop the five inches that had fallen the prior evening.

"It is beautiful," she said, wishing to dance outside.

Quaiy added two more logs to the fireplace, then rubbed her hands. "Did m'lady hear that bloody cock crow early again this morning?"

Tesesra gazed at her nursing daughter. A moment passed afore she realized the handmaiden had addressed her. "Oh, yes. I heard him."

Thylaina closed the heavy drapes. The rooster had sung prematurely, just as he had the past three morns since Viya added him to the henhouse to increase egg production for the winter. Apparently, humans had yet to learn a rooster's only purpose was to fertilize the eggs, not encourage the hens to lay more.

"He's a lame cock," Tesesra said, stroking Telsia's cheek. "Perhaps Viya should just slaughter him for supper."

"We might get more sleep in the mornings then." Quaiy spread another blanket on the bed. "Which you and Lady Telsia need."

This handmaiden was a blessing to Her Ladyship.

Smiling, Thylaina slung the satchel strap over her shoulder and headed for the door, which opened as she neared. Arhgrim entered, his face beaming.

"Lady Thylaina, I hoped to see you before breaking fast." He guided her back toward the bed, then sat. "Quaiy, please give us a moment."

"Yes, m'lord." The handmaiden left the bedchamber, closing the door behind her.

"Is all well, my lord?" Thylaina asked.

Arhgrim kissed his wife, then his daughter's head. "We wished to have a moment with you."

She looked from him to Tesesra, hoping their concern had naught to do with Breydon.

"We owe you our deepest gratitude." Arhgrim gestured to the vanity chair. "Please join us."

Thylaina brought the chair closer to the bed and sat across from him. She could not resist adoring the dark-haired babe suckling from Tesesra's breast. The tiny girl had already won Thylaina's heart... and Breydon's and everyone else who had met her.

"We have yet to find Bethlyn," the marshal said, his voice low, and the news disheartening. With no walls around Caerabis, the former handmaiden was likely far from the city.

"And what about Mikan?" Thylaina pressed. Breydon had refused to answer her inquiries about the high priest and the pendant.

"We are gathering all information regarding what he'd done to Breydon and the other men, and Tes." Now Arhgrim's face darkened. "But once I have all witnesses accounted for, every testimony documented, a trial shall take place."

"Trial?" Thylaina shook her head. "I—" Pressing her lips together, she lowered her gaze to the babe.

"My lady?" he said.

She blinked rapidly as she raised her eyes to his. "I was found guilty and punished without a trial. Gavrel was immediately guilty. Yet this man, despite the damage he has caused, will—"

"He is a high priest and knight of Alohrius. He *shall* be granted a trial."

How bloody unfair. But there was naught she could do nor say. "Very well, my lord."

"There's another matter we wish to discuss with you." Clasping his hands together, Arhgrim leaned forward.

She tilted her head back. "And that is?"

He grinned. "After a long conversation with the First Captain and the Lady of Caerabis," he held Tesesra's hand, "I've decided it's no longer necessary to have you shadowed by a guard. You may roam the mansion without an escort."

Thylaina briefly held her breath, darted her gaze between the two.

"However," he continued, "I must insist that when you leave the premises, you have an escort with you. Understood?"

She straightened, delighted with the change, then slouched in confusion. "I am not certain that I do. Am I not a prisoner?"

Arhgrim and Tesesra smiled at each other. "We owe you so much, my lady," he said. "More than we can ever repay. You didn't have to admit the extent of your capabilities, nor come forward to help her and save our daughter. Nor did you have to save the man who wounded you so terribly, coming up with a method to relieve him and his comrades—men you did not know—from an addiction forced upon them. Yet you did all of this. And I don't believe it's all because you're a healer, my lady. I believe it's because you care. We may not know the truth of whom you really are, but you've revealed enough for us to see that truth about you. You care about us."

"And with our time spent together," Tesesra unlatched her sleeping daughter, "you've become dear to us. We now welcome you into our home not as a prisoner or a guest, but as a part of us."

Tears were suddenly there. Thylaina's breath came in sharp, leaving in soft quivers. She had been in the city for nearly two moons, and the Momestids had opened their hearts to her. Lessindra forgive her for misjudging humans, believing they could not possibly know love like the elves. As she stared at them, teardrops rolling down her cheeks, she knew the truth of her feelings. Moments had come when Thylaina could have left. It was not just the babe's life that kept her in the city, but that she *had* cared about the child and Tesesra.

"Thank you, my lord, my lady," she whispered.

Arhgrim raised his hand slightly. "With that said, let's relieve ourselves of the formalities." He rested his palm on his chest. "Grim," he gestured to his wife, "and Tes, if it pleases you."

This meant a great deal to her, for only those closest to the Momestids called them by those names. Thylaina nodded. "It pleases me." She tried not to titter with overwhelming joy. Containing it, she cleared her throat and leaned forward slightly. "Thylaina."

Grim chuckled. "Excellent!" He kissed his wife's lips, then Telsia's head again. "I'm off to break fast."

"Will you join me for afternoon meal?" Tes asked.

"Of course, love." He rose and offered his hand to Thylaina. "Will you walk with me to the hall?"

"S'yai, my lo—Grim." She stood and gripped the crook of his arm.

On their way to the dining hall, Thylaina felt like skipping.

Fire from the hearth provided the bedchamber's only light, casting shadows throughout the room, and on Breydon. When they had first entered, he kissed her with a devouring passion while untying her tunic, casting it aside. Then he led her to the vanity, cleared a few items, and sat her atop. Breydon kissed her again while pulling the shoulders of her dress down, his lips then trailing to the exposed flesh. Thylaina had believed he was finally going to make love to her, but then he sat and stared for three long minutes. His gaze seemed to burn through the fabric of her dress during his apparent contemplation.

Enough of this. Her body burned with want while he did nothing. Thylaina curled her fingers beneath the collar pressing against the rise of her right breast and slowly lowered it. His eyes widened and his lips parted. Her breast now bare, she exposed the left.

Breydon scooted the chair closer. The fingertips of his right hand grazed her collarbone, burning a path to her bosom. His touch was light, teasing.

Thylaina drew in a rush of air, pressing her breast to his hand, needing his touch. He obliged, cupping, then squeezing. Breydon rose enough to kiss her, breathed into her. Inch by inch, she bunched the skirt of her dress, hoping to hook her legs around his, but he suddenly bent and caught her nipple between his lips and sucked. Head falling back, she gasped. A blaze built within her, spreading like an uncontrolled fire. She thrust her fingers into his hair, holding him closer as his suckling intensified. He wrapped one arm around her, the other hand squeezing her left breast.

*Sweet Lessindra, yes!* Tonight, they would make love into the early morning hours.

His warm tongue lapped at her nipple, rolled it, then pulled it back into his mouth.

Thylaina could not wait to share herself with him. It would be glorious.

Pulling his head away, he let her go. "Forgive me." He panted. "I must leave."

She trapped him with her legs. "Do not go."

He swiped his hair aside. "I can't stay. Not even for ortia louvre."

Her legs fell away, freeing his. Confusion turned into ire, which no doubt skewed her expression. "Why?"

Breydon turned and exhaled hard. "I'm still not ready." The words came out soft.

After performing ortia louvre a few times and this, he was bloody ready! She pushed her skirt down and slid off the table, not caring about the perfume bottles falling over. "Your actions show you *are*."

"I'm not... ready, Laina." Shaking his head, he walked to the suite door. "Please forgive me." Then he was gone.

Thylaina bit her bottom lip, wishing he would return. He did not.

Progress to the dining hall was slow, thanks to little sleep and that blasted rooster crowing too early again. Thylaina did not even have it in her to speak with Katjina while the handmaiden dressed her and pinned her hair. She had no appetite, yet she must eat something afore performing the day's duties. Tes and Telsia needed a look in on, the herbs in the suite were thirsty, and bossel roots were ready for grinding. What she would do after that, Thylaina knew not. She was furious with Breydon, and even if she was not, he had his own duties.

Breydon. How could she sit next to him and not feel the anger rise? No matter. There was naught to do but get through the morning's meal.

Tes and the babe looked wonderful, especially with Nadiera joining them. Her Ladyship needed the young girl's presence, and Nadiera adored her little sister. It was a lovely scene in the bedchamber.

In Thylaina's room, the herbs' growth was impressive. It was difficult to give them sunlight while trying to avoid the cold air, but she positioned them on the chairs and far enough from the window—and fireplace—to open the heavy curtains. It left the suite chilled, but the blazing hearth prevented the room from becoming too cold. In a few hours, she would close the drapes and move the herbs back on the worktable.

Now to break fast with Breydon, the teasing bastard.

It was just him and Grim at the table. The many empty seats gave Thylaina a choice, but when she hesitated, Breydon looked up at her, waiting. Her displeasure from last night must have lingered on her face, for he snorted softly, then returned to his meal. She sat beside him.

"Good morrow, Grim," she said.

"Good morrow, Thylaina," his voice boomed in the empty hall. He slammed the servant caller on the table thrice. "You look tired, my dear."

"I did not sleep well." She barely glanced at Breydon, who sipped his coffee.

"That's a shame." Breydon squeezed her hand gently as if to insinuate all was well.

Thylaina narrowed her eyes at him, but he paid no mind to her upset.

A servant entered, placing tea on the table for Thylaina. Breydon moved a plate of pork strips toward her.

"I do not want any." She shoved it back.

Frowning, he bobbed his head at the small plate. "Eat something. It might be a moment longer for your porridge."

"I do not want any porridge."

He drew in a long breath, released it loudly. "Love, you always eat porridge."

Thylaina shrugged. "I have little appetite this morning."

Pulling the plate back, he grabbed a strip of pork and bit into it.

That was the longest they had sat beside each other without looking at one another since her first night at this table.

The main door opened, and Bramn and Einasa entered, having a conversation about their wedding feast. Thankfully, that event would be soon, for preparing for Mikan's trial had seemed to settle a weight of frustration on the men as of late, including Raylen. What had them most excited was the awaited arrival of Bramn's uncle, Haltrin, the high priest from Warstchia. Thylaina had been nervous about a man from a city infected with a deadly virus being near Tesesra and the babe. However, upon voicing her concerns, the others stared at her as if she was an idiot. So she did not elaborate where she had heard such rumors out of fear of being ignorant.

"I don't want the wedding at the main feast hall," Bramn said.

"But along with my small family, you've a large number of men attending along with their escorts." Sitting opposite from Thylaina, Einasa pulled her braid over her shoulder to avoid sitting on it. Mayrb'ea blossoms were tucked within the light-brown plait. "And to feed the crowd, we'll need at least one bull. Viya can't do that here."

Bramn fell heavily into his seat and sighed across the way at Breydon. "I know."

Breydon smirked.

Just afore Grim could slam the caller on the table, the scullery door opened and a servant entered with Thylaina's meal. The marshal set the wooden thumper down. "Two more," he said.

"Yes, m'lord."

Thylaina stared at the honey drizzled into a flower over her porridge, but even that could not bring a smile.

"I would love a coffee, please?" Einasa asked.

"Me as well," Bramn said.

The servant curtsied, then returned to the scullery.

Einasa stretched her neck to the side and moaned softly. "That bloody cock," she whispered. "I wish Viya would pluck his feathers and roast *him* for supper."

"He does crow awfully early," Grim mumbled.

Thylaina scooped some porridge into her mouth, then noticed Bramn raising his eyes to Breydon, one corner of his lips lifting.

"You don't suffer the cock's early calls, do you, Captain?" Bramn asked.

Dragging the spoon from her mouth, Thylaina looked at Breydon. He blinked, met Bramn's amused expression with one of his own.

"Oh, I hear the crowing of the cock, my friend. Just not nearly as loud as those near the mansion."

Thylaina's scowl darted between the two men.

Bramn relaxed in his chair, his expression purposely nonchalant. "What are your plans today, Captain?"

Breydon glanced at the approaching servant, who placed Bramn's and Einasa's coffee down. "I must inspect the men's cocks. Some of them have complained about straps needing replacement."

Einasa halted from raising her cup, and Grim paused his chewing.

Thylaina leered at Breydon, then Bramn. Were they trying to make a fool of her?

"Is that so?" Bramn nodded. "Speaking of equipment, did you hear about what happened in the Pit yesterday?"

"Do share." Breydon sat back, battling an obvious smile.

"Kimner's cock nearly broke."

"Weren't they using sparring cocks?" Breydon asked, sounding shocked.

Appalled, Thylaina's jaw dropped. They were purposefully trying to make her appear a dolt!

"Of course," Bramn said. "But Amdronus swings an excellent cock!" He sputtered a laugh, then continued. "Thank Valorius they weren't using real cocks."

*Damn them to Darkness!* Thylaina slammed her spoon on the table.

"Had they," Breydon said, as if she had not reacted, "the results would've been messy. At least Kimner didn't lose his cock. He'd never hold a cock again."

This was *not* amusing. It was absolutely ridiculous!

"Enough!" Grim pushed his plate aside. Thank goodness. At least he could control his men if they had not the sense to behave. "Your cocking is getting out of hand," he snorted, "and I don't think I can cock anymore of it!" Face red and eyes squeezed shut, he laughed until he could not breathe.

Breydon and Bramn joined him, the latter slapping the tabletop.

"I don't understand what you men are going on about," Einasa said, yet smiled in her confusion.

Thylaina stood, sliding the chair back. There was nothing to say, so she headed for the main door. In the hallway, ire heated her face, even to her ear tips. Maybe she could go outside to cool down. The fresh, chill air, birds, and knee holly might do her some good.

"Wait," Breydon called. Not wanting to speak to him, she continued. "Thylaina, wait!" He caught up in the entry hall. "Stop, damn it!" He grabbed her arm and spun her around. "I'm speaking to you."

"I am not speaking to *you*, Shapele."

Breydon frowned. "Shapele, is it?"

"S'yai. It is." Thylaina jerked free and resumed to the stairs.

Silent, like a predator, he followed right into her chambers.

Katjina gasped, nearly dropping a pitcher of water. "Forgive me, m'lady. Captain. I'll leave."

"N'ei—"

"Thank you, Katjina." Breydon held the door open for her, and the handmaiden hurried from the suite. He closed the door, then approached Thylaina. "You asked for it."

Scoffing in disbelief, she crossed her arms. "How did I ask to be humiliated?"

"Your accusation. Your assumptions. Do you ever stop believing what you were taught about us without knowing the truth?"

Licking her lips, she turned her head and… could think of nothing to say. "Well, your behavior at the table proved—"

"That you need to relax and laugh." He stepped nearer. "Besides, Einasa started the whole thing, truth be told."

Thylaina let her arms drop to her sides. "You jest!"

"She said cock first."

"She was talking about the bloody rooster!"

Brows arched high, he shrugged.

Thylaina saw it then: the mischief, humor, lessons he believed she must learn about him and his people. Breydon was a world she still needed to understand.

"You needn't be angry with me." He stepped closer, and his voice grew softer as he continued. "Not about last night, and not about this morning."

"I *am* displeased about you telling Bramn of our conversation."

"And last night?"

Thylaina *was* upset about that.

"Ah. I see." Breydon took her hand and kissed it. "Please understand, Laina, I want to be near you. I want to touch you and make love to you. But I also know how you elves are."

Breaking free from her enthrallment, she snapped her head upright. "What does that mean?"

"That while betrothed, you'll lie with another." His face paled the slightest, as if someone had given him grave news. "You love openly until you're wedded. And what if I give myself to you only to find that you willingly lay in another man's bed?"

She shook her head. "Breydon, I—"

"That's a fair question," he snapped, letting go of her hand. "You elves think we're a bunch of loveless, unfaithful idiots. Yet you're the ones who give yourselves to others, even if you're in love with your betrothed. So tell me, who are the unfaithful idiots?"

He was not wrong, but was not entirely correct, either. Both races were guilty. In fact, *he* was the result of an adulterous knight.

"Breydon, just as some humans, not all elves are like that. Many are faithful." She rested her hand right over his heart. "Since you, I have not thought of any other. I swear it."

His breath quaked within his chest. "You mean that?"

She nodded.

The kiss was deep as he crushed her against him. Thylaina hooked her arms over his shoulders, slid her fingers into his hair. It felt so good to feel his touch burn through her clothes. Their lips parted, yet they remained close.

He glided his finger up her ear to the tip, then down to the lobe. "The wedding is in less than a fortnight, and I've no escort."

"I should hope not."

He chuckled. "You think maidens haven't approached me?"

"I have n'ei doubt a particular farm maiden has made her intentions known."

Swaying, he kissed her cheek. "There's only one maiden I see."

Thylaina turned her face to his. "And she sees only you."

His lips were so fine, warm, and the kiss amazing, even with fine stubble brushing against her chin. She could get used to that.

Einasa's glowing face did not outshine Bramn's, whose cheeks were brighter than his polished ceremonial breastplate, engraved with swirls of feathers, stags, and two battling knights. His bellowing laughter displayed his joy and nervousness afore the ceremony began. Thylaina had never seen such an elated bride and bridegroom. And when Bramn began unbraiding Einasa's hair, it revealed an intimacy between a new husband and wife Thylaina now understood amid the humans. To have been a witness to this celebration was special.

Farmers, knights with their escorts, soldiers, and squires, packed the enormous feast hall a block west from the mansion. Supper now finished, dancers took up the large space between the main tables positioned in a U-shape filled with cheering onlookers. The knights surprised Thylaina with their grace in the many dances humans believed were a widespread style these past five years. She had learned them all by the time she was a hundred years old. The dances seemed to have cycles, like the shifting seasons; and someone had slightly changed a few of the moves, giving them a new name.

Thylaina tapped her foot and recalled each step, dip, spin, and clap of the dance she now observed, except these humans added a jump here or removed a turn there. She would surely look like a fool amongst them. Freed of the ceremonial breastplate, Bramn leapt into the center of them all and raised one of his arms over his head. Two knights joined him, and they interrupted the flow of spinning skirts and tunics with footwork meant for men not impeded by spirits.

Laughing, Thylaina turned her head to spot Tes bouncing Telsia. Beside her, Grim taught Nadiera an innocent dance. A few feet away, having switched the fancy breastplate for a fine tunic, Breydon stood just within the shadows of the torchlight, his gaze locked on Thylaina.

Like several other maidens, Thylaina could not help admiring him. She had seen Breydon in the leather armor he often wore around the manor, sometimes donning fine clothing with a leather jacket, and when he rode off, it was in his plate armor. At least he no longer bore the weight of the decorative breastplate. Thylaina imagined it would be quite a chore to remove... if she and Breydon ended the night together.

She had attended the wedding with him, but afore it began, he moved to Einasa's side as the bride's knight, and Grim stood beside Bramn as a witness from the knighthood. Thylaina had believed Breydon would return to her after the vows, but the Alohrians' traditions did not permit it. Not even during the feast. So Breydon often ogled her between watching the newly wedded couple like a sentry, a smile there and gone.

Despite their separation, he declined requests for dances with exceptions to Einasa and Nadiera. Thankfully, for Nikhia had asked him several times since the music began. Thylaina did not approach him, fearing she might fumble from the altered dances.

Breaking her gaze from him, she rubbed her nape and scanned the chamber. To her surprise, Gavrel stood at the front door of the hall. Was this a jest? To have him guarding at Bramn's marriage celebration was surely meant to remind him he was beneath the knights. An insult. And it was bloody ridiculous. She could at least speak with him; it had been some time since their last meeting. Perhaps she might even make him smile.

The healing satchel safe with Katjina, Thylaina sauntered to him, unable to avoid adding a sway from the fantastic performance of the minstrels. "Gavrel," she said, loud enough for him to hear. "It is wonderful to see you. I am sorry I had not come to seek you—"

"Stop." He offered a pleasant smile. "I understand Her Ladyship required your care. We're all grateful for your presence."

She grabbed his hand and squeezed. "You are always fine to me."

A flicker of sadness broke through his expression, but swiftly faded. "You deserve to be treated like a queen." Gavrel kissed her hand. "Like a goddess." His deep brown eyes revealed too much. Love, desire, and pain. The young man was aware of his situation with Thylaina, and it hurt.

"I-I knew not you were attending." She lowered her hand from his mouth. "I did not see you until now."

His jaw shifted slightly, teeth grazing along each other. "I'm on guard duty." He glided his thumb gently over her knuckles. "Although I can't take my eyes off you. You are stunning."

Thylaina had chosen a plain dress—dark green with black flowers embroidered along the hem, cuffs, and collar—hoping to avoid drawing attention from the most important woman of the event.

Shaking her head, she gestured to Einasa, who spun in a circle with Bramn, her hair flowing freely. "None outshine our bri—"

"You, my lady. No one outshines you." Gavrel nodded toward the guests. "And everyone knows it."

Thylaina did not look to affirm his comment. Despite her efforts, men still gawped at her. Such as it was for an elf amongst humans. "Your words are kind."

"I speak only the truth." He grinned, then looked toward those dancing. "I wish I could ask for a dance."

"That would be lovely." Thylaina shrugged. "But as you are on duty—"

"My lady." Arlin almost stepped between them. "Captain Colmstad wished to remind you that the dubight is performing a duty this evening."

Gavrel tilted his head back, clenched his jaw. "Of course he would," he said quietly, yet Thylaina caught it.

However, Breydon was correct, and she knew better than to disturb a working guard. She squeezed Gavrel's arm. "Be blessed, my friend."

"By your touch alone, I am."

Cheeks warm, Thylaina giggled as she shuffled back, then spun and hurried to her seat beside Katjina. Her heartbeat interfered with the music's rhythm, setting it off pace as she avoided Breydon's glare.

"My lady." A knight plopped onto the chair beside her.

Thylaina jumped, pressed her hand to her chest. "S'yai?"

"Do you have...?" He licked his lips and looked over his shoulder at a waiting maiden. Scratching his head, he smirked. "Do you have any sponishies?"

It would be that sort of evening. Bramn's and Einasa's love and joy floated like a magical mist in the chamber, infecting everyone. Even Tes and Grim stood closer, shared a touch and a knowing smile. That must be why Gavrel behaved as he had.

Over the past week, knights and maidens had approached Thylaina with requests for sponishies. Raylen had sent them to her, for he refused to provide the insh weed in any form. She did not blame them for wishing to protect themselves, but that meant demand would rise for her limited supply. However, for the night's event, Thylaina had packed two dozen vials of essence of insh and the same amount of sponishies.

Tucking her hair behind her ear, she reached her hand toward Katjina. "I do." The handmaiden passed the satchel to Thylaina, doing her best not to smile.

Thylaina removed one of the small pouches containing a sponge and a vial. "Warm the oil in a glass dish or bowl over a low flame, then let the sponge soak in it for fifteen minutes. Do not let the oil get hot."

"Yes, my lady."

"Squeeze the excess out." She gave him a pouch.

"Thank you, Lady Thylaina."

"Remember," she said, halting him from dashing off. "You can only use the sponge for two... bouts."

He drew in a long breath, glanced at the lovely maiden. "That should do."

The two disappeared.

Soon afterward, the hall depleted of guests, and Thylaina's case emptied of sponishies and oil, some couples taking more than one sponge. Thirteen knights remained, some with maidens on their laps, still drinking and shouting. Humans celebrated in strange ways. Elven events were elegant and lasted several hours longer.

"You came prepared," Breydon said from behind her.

Thylaina turned her head slightly. "I know you knights better now."

He grunted, sat in the empty chair beside her.

Katjina smiled wryly. "I'm exhausted, m'lady. May I retire?"

"Rest well." Thylaina watched her leave.

Crossing his arms, Breydon slouched. He should have been drinking and laughing with Bramn. Even as the music grew louder and faster, and Nikhia dominated the floor with an enticing dance, Breydon seemed occupied with something else. He did not appear to notice that she was dancing for him, prying the front of her dress farther apart to expose more of her bosom.

His focus now on Nikhia, he frowned. Breydon then smiled at Thylaina. "Let's leave." He stood and offered his hand.

"Where shall we go?"

The corner of his lips twitched. There it was, as like the others at the event: desire flared in his gaze. Seeing that passion afire, Thylaina's own flame soared into a blaze.

She accepted his hand and rose. After Breydon draped her fur cloak over her shoulders, then donned his own, he led her to the door. Upon their approach, she noticed Gavrel's full attention on her. The young man appeared upset. Hurt, even. But he need not worry, for there was nothing anyone could say to change Thylaina's feelings for him. Gavrel would always be dear to her.

Breydon led her carefully into the snowy night. The full Cold Moon illuminated their way down a shoveled path. Unfortunately, a light snowfall slowly dusted the slick trail, making the cobblestones slipperier. Laughter came from several directions, people still on their way to their destinations. And as she and Breydon passed the nearest tavern, more celebratory shouts and songs muffled through the glowing windows. Instead of continuing to the mansion, he turned left, toward his home at the end of this road. By the time they arrived at the door, the cold had burrowed beneath the heavy cloaks.

Thylaina shivered in the front room. This was the first time she had stood there since the night he had his withdrawal reaction from Divine Wrath. Everything was in order now, of course, the furniture straightened or replaced, and the room tidy.

Breydon dropped his cloak on the large chair near the dark fireplace. He then untied Thylaina's mantle, his fingers brushing the dampened fur collar, and it joined his own on the chair. In no time, she was in his arms, their mouths finding each other in a desperate kiss. How had they made it throughout the entire event without so much as a peck? Not even holding hands. Just glances and hungry looks. But Breydon had set that boundary.

"I'm ready now," he whispered, then kissed her again.

Those words sent a thunderous pulsation throughout her, awakening every nerve, ready to react to his lightest touch.

His fingers worked to untie the back of her dress, the garment loosening from her body. He pushed it off her shoulders until the sleeves slipped from her arms. Then the dress continued its descent, exposing her. The chilled air immediately pricked her flesh, her nipples hard. Breydon stepped back, taking in the view of her in nothing but stockings tied in place with fat green bows. Biting his lip, he came forward, bending to sweep her into his arms. Thylaina squealed, hooking her elbow over his shoulder and nibbling on the side of his neck while he carried her into his bedroom.

Heated, she remained uncovered while catching her breath, reliving their lovemaking. It was... astonishing. Admittedly, there had been a slight fear of laying with a human once the moment arrived, but Breydon had been tender and attentive. Sweet Lessindra! Adoration showed in his eyes, sounded in his voice, and flowed through his touch. Breydon had truly *shared* himself with her. And while in his arms, her heartbeat slowing, Thylaina knew love.

He pulled her close and kissed the side of her head while he tugged on the bow of her right stocking. "Want me to start a fire?"

But he had already stoked the flames within her.

She slid her leg over his, the ribbon loose from around her thigh and his hand slipping beneath the stocking. "Although I am still hot, we shall eventually need one."

"Yet I don't wish to move."

Thylaina giggled. "Nor do I wish you to leave my side."

He nuzzled his nose against her ear and released a heavy breath, warming her skin further. "You are... Great Knight, Laina, you are perfection."

Cheeks burning, she smiled.

"I didn't know elves were so bloody tight," he whispered. "I could barely control myself at first."

Thylaina had noticed his approach to a near early release. It seemed to have taken Breydon absolute concentration to keep himself hard. She slid her finger along his jaw. "Male elves' virility are slender in comparison."

He smirked. "Maybe I'm just thicker as it is."

Sighing, she rolled her eyes. "You men and your ego."

Breydon wrapped his arms around her and rolled onto his back, pulling her atop. "As long as I please you, I don't care."

Their eyes locked as they entwined their fingers.

"You please me." She slid down enough to feel his stiffening length.

"May I please you again?"

Thylaina traced the rounded edge of his human ear, then kissed him. She tasted his human lips, danced her tongue along his. Moving her hips in no hurry, she took as long as needed until his human virility was fully within her. And she shared herself with this human man.

The difference was staggering—the way her body responded. Breydon believed it was because she was an elf, but it was him; the traits between the human and elf virilities. And feeling him enter her again was just as amazing as the first time. Goosebumps rose, sending chills through every nerve and a sharp intake of air into her lungs. Her escalating heartbeat and deep breaths intensified her ecstasy. But with Breydon beneath her, he pressed deeper, reaching further into her. Overwhelmed with it all—his filling her, the motions, his squeezing her breasts and thumbing her nipples—Thylaina could not contain herself. Her moans soared with each thrust until they were both spent. Breathless.

"Gods," he whispered between pants. "You sounded beautiful."


The hearth's orange glow flickered into the Cold Moon's light beaming through the part in the curtain. No sleep had yet come, despite Thylaina's and Breydon's exhaustive endeavors. Neither could seem to get enough of each other, exploring and learning what one another enjoyed. They could have waited for future nights to learn, for there was time. However, Thylaina and Breydon indulged. A bottle of wine stood beside a goblet on the floor, the bottle half empty and the goblet nearly full. Thylaina's stockings lay in a pile next to the bottle, the green ribbons tangled, one in a knot. She would likely have to throw them out, unless if Katjina could fix them.

Thylaina's cheek rested on his rising and lowering chest, his heartbeat steady. Breydon stroked the curve of her shoulder. She tilted her head back, finding his tongue tip sticking out from between his lips. It disappeared into his mouth when he focused on her and smiled.

"What is it?" she asked.

He kissed her forehead, his fingers moving down her arm. "I love you, Laina."

Eyes closed, she released a slow breath. Thylaina reciprocated the feeling. But as much as she wanted to ignore her bloodline, it remained too much a part of her. What she shared with Breydon was perfect as it was. Thylaina could not stay in Alohrius, anyway; to remain close to Etharell was dangerous.

"We should marry," he said.

The hammering of her heart drowned out his breathing. She opened her eyes, but did not look at him. Why did he have to say that? The brief future she imagined with him was without marriage.

His fingers stilled, his heartbeat increased. "Did I say something wrong?"

Thylaina sat up, getting no resistance from him. The fire from the hearth intensified, overheating her body, interfering with her racing thoughts about her bloodline, her long life, and her many foolish choices. Thylaina's mouth dried as she tried to think of how to explain, but no words formed on her tongue. Blinking, she turned her back to him.

The bed shifted beneath as he also sat up, yet he said nothing.

The silence was too much. She had to speak. "It is... not possible."

More stillness.

"How can you say that?" Pain laced his muted voice. "After—" He huffed. "After what we've just shared, you say that. You've told me you love me. Why say this now?"

If only her dress was in the bedroom, but she had just the stockings. Arguing while naked was uncomfortable, and an argument was inevitable. Thylaina could find no other way to say what she must without revealing the deeper truth. So words just came out. "Because of who I am." She finally looked over her shoulder at him. Wished she had not.

A grimace of hurt skewed his face, his eyes glazed. "The fact you're here now has led me to believe it didn't matter I'm lowborn."

No. She had not spoken clearly. "Breydon, it does not."

"It does!" He stood, stormed around the bed to his trousers, then put them on.

"That is not what I meant."

"It doesn't matter what you meant." He pointed at her. "You're a noblewoman and I'm a bastard knight. Just a bloody good swyve for you, is that it, my lady?"

The accusations pierced like arrows, but she could not explain without revealing everything. Thylaina would not risk her safety to avoid injuring his feelings.

"Think what you wish." She grabbed the stockings, knocking the goblet over in the process, and stomped into the front room. "Bloody bastard," she said under her breath.

"If all you wanted was a hard thronging, you could've found it elsewhere," he said from the bedroom entrance.

Thylaina pulled the dress on, slid her hands into the long sleeves. There was no retying the back, nor asking for his help.

"I've no doubt *Gavrel* would've obliged."

She froze. For the briefest moment, her head spun at Breydon's attempt to hurt her. Well, Thylaina could play as well. Grabbing her cloak, she said, "If I had not been at the wedding, you would have had Nikhia in the bloody feast hall."

Breydon's brows dipped low while he fixed the collar of his blouse, then tied the front.

"She made her desires obvious when she damn near tore her dress open afore we left." Thylaina put her boots on, then headed for the door.

"You're not walking back alone."

"You need not worry about me, Shapele."

"What did I just say?" He grabbed his boots, then sat in the large chair. "You'll wait until I'm ready."

"I shall wait outside."

"Just bloody listen to me!"

She had not heard that tone since her first days in Caerabis.

Instead of grabbing his fur cloak, he opted for the long leather jacket she had seen him wear as of late. It surprised Thylaina when he fastened his weapon belt on, sheathing his broadsword in the scabbard. Breydon stood at the door and combed his fingers through his hair. He then opened it and stepped outside.

Thylaina hesitated. She did trust him. If Breydon learned whom she was, he would not bring harm upon her. He loved her and wanted to marry her. Yet being in Alohrius, so close to Etharell, kept her silent. If others somehow learned, could he protect her from them? No. It had to stay this way. As much as she adored him, Thylaina could not risk her life for him.

"Are you coming?" he barked from outside.

Swallowing the urge to weep, she joined him.

They walked in silence for half a block, their progress slow to avoid slipping. Fat flakes fell, adding to the two inches that had risen over the past few hours. The trek gave more time to think about the argument or how she could have reacted. But it was difficult with the cold swooping up her skirt and biting her bare legs and bottom. Damn it to Darkness! Thylaina left the stockings at his house. Still, she needed to clear this mess.

Wrapping the cloak tighter in a feeble attempt to keep the breeze out, she clenched her teeth. "Breydon—"

"What?" he snapped.

A long breath helped her keep focused. "Why can we not stay as we are?"

He continued looking forward and into the alleys they passed. "Because I want to marry you."

"I believed what we share was acceptable."

"I didn't think being my wife was a terrible idea."

No. In fact, it was sweet. Thylaina could fully reciprocate his affections if she was not afraid. However... "Please understand I cannot marry you."

"Then there's nothing more to say, is there?" He grabbed her arm and hurried her along. "Let's return to the mansion before you get too cold."

After she slipped a few more times, he carried her the rest of the way. That only made it harder for Thylaina, noting the tightening of his jaw while he glared forward. Yet they spoke not another word. Breydon ignored the two sentries as he set her down in the entrance hall of the mansion, bowed, then left.

Thylaina wanted to crumple right there, but pride held her upright. She made it to her warm chambers, stripped the garments off, then slid beneath the covers. Sleep did not come for nearly an hour.

"M'lady." Katjina shook her. "M'lady, you must wake." Her voice sounded strange.

Thylaina pulled the heavy coverlet over her head. "Let me sleep longer."

"Sir Bramn is here with great urgency."

Thylaina pushed the covers down and regarded the handmaiden through heavy lids. Katjina's nose was pink and her eyes red from weeping. "What is it?"

The handmaiden lifted the robe from the chair next to the bed. "Hurry. Before he comes in while you're not ready."

Thylaina slid from the bed.

Noting she was naked, Katjina grabbed a shift from the clothing chest. "Won't do you any good to rush out in only a robe," she said, the words inflected with her trembling breath.

The heartbreak in her voice added to the chill encompassing Thylaina's body, so she rubbed her arms for warmth, even after donning the robe. "Please tell me what troubles you."

"I-I can't." She rushed to the suite door and opened it. "She's ready, sir." Hand over her mouth, Katjina silenced her weeping as she stepped aside.

Bramn dashed into the room, still wearing his winter cloak. Like Katjina, it appeared something troubled him, except his face was pale, his eyes were hard, and his jaw tight. Rage darkened his blue irises, and his motions were stiff as he beckoned for Thylaina. "Come. Now."

"What is it?" She neared him, reaching to offer comfort for whatever troubled him so terribly.

Brows lowering, his breath heavier, he blinked several times as if trying to clear his vision. Or control himself. "It's Breydon."

Did Breydon do something foolish after he left her?

"Someone attacked him," Bramn continued through gritted teeth. "I'm to get you there... now."

Every nerve froze from her nape to her knees. Air balled in her chest and her body swayed back, her spine soft. It hurt to breathe. To stand.

# Chapter Fifteen

Little snow had been cleared from the streets, but men bundled in furs and wool shoveled in the chilly morning hour. In Bramn's desperation to reach the temple quickly, his horse was at the ready. Katjina had thrown the heavy fur mantel over Thylaina to cover the nightgown and robe—the satchel crossed over her torso—and in her hurry, Thylaina had put on her slippers. Amid the slick conditions, Bramn dared to race the horse against the passing minutes. Not only cold bore into Thylaina, but icy fear as she clung to him.

"What happened?" she asked, hoping loud enough for him to hear.

"I don't know. Grim sent Arlin with the news and a message to get you to the temple. I haven't been there yet." He tugged too hard on the lead, guiding the horse around a patch of ice.

Cheek squeezed to his back, she held tighter to avoid falling off the stallion as it fought to keep balance.

"Steady," he commanded. Once the horse settled into a trot afore increasing into a sprint, Bramn continued. "Arlin didn't find Breydon at home this morning, so he assumed he was with you. On his way to the mansion, he spotted drag marks in the snow leading between soldiers' houses." A rumble vibrated his bones as he growled. "Arlin investigated... and found Breydon."

Ire gave his voice strength, yet a crack faltered within those words. Bramn had yet to see Breydon and refused to believe in the worst outcome. A familiar reaction from a soldier who would deny the death of family or friend. Thylaina had seen it with Father and Neldrid.

But it could not be this way with Breydon. Surely, he only suffered an injury. However, he had left hours ago, and if Arlin found him recently, that meant far too much time had passed without those wounds receiving care.

These assumptions would weaken her. Thylaina squeezed her eyes shut and rested her forehead on Bramn's wet cloak. Everything that had happened at Breydon's home sped through her mind. She wept. Had to afore they arrived at the temple, for she needed strength. During that moment of grief, she recalled Breydon's preparation to leave his house.

"Bramn, he had his sword."

He nodded. "Still does."

"Why did Breydon not fight?"

His fingers curled tightly around hers. "He was struck from behind," he snapped. "Yet it was no thief. Whoever attacked him took nothing. Someone targeted him."

A deeper shiver coursed through her. Someone within the city hurt Breydon. No. It could not be possible. From all she had heard and seen, the men were devoted to their First Captain, just as they were to their marshal.

"You have no walls around your city," she said. "Anyone could have come into—"

"They took *nothing*, Thylaina."

A fact she could not ignore. Thankfully, the discussion ended as they arrived at the temple.

Gathered amid the snow-covered cobblestone, on the wide stairs leading to temple landing, and across the expanse of the landing itself, were nearly a hundred knights and soldiers. All of them appeared worried. Squires were in the process of positioning four enormous cauldrons at different points of the landing, while others dropped logs into the massive pots. The men expected to remain out here long enough to need the heat from the cold.

Bramn dismounted, then helped Thylaina. Back straight and expression rigid, he guided her into the crowd and to the stairs. The men parted, many offering a hand when Thylaina or Bramn slipped on a patch of ice hidden beneath the thin layer of snow. Several comments surrounded her and Bramn, most of them promising prayers for Breydon. However, there were many who sneered venomous words of retribution for whoever committed this horrific act.

Thylaina's heart could not bear the weight of hatred—fighting that battle herself already. Not only because someone had harmed Breydon, but because *she* had hurt him. Carrying that guilt might interfere with her prayers, but she could not help it. Tears blurred her vision, and she slowed, struggling to maintain control of her breathing as she tried not to crumble right there.

Bramn halted and slid his arm around her. "Thylaina, he needs your strength. We all do."

The Alohrians parted, revealing the start of a path of cloaks lain over the cobblestone and up the stairs, like a runner to a king's throne. Bramn's fingers gripped at her side and arm for the briefest moment, then he led her forward. As they ascended, men continued laying their cloaks down, the trail leading to the temple doors. They put their trust in her on that path, just as they poured prayers to their god. Thylaina was a part of those supplications.

No longer impeded, she and Bramn entered the temple within a few minutes. Captain Miryl Eilisar paced in a circle beneath the silent dome. Gray clouds above reflected the gloom of the many hearts below. Not even a sliver of sunlight penetrated the thick blanket separating the mortals from the gods. When Thylaina and Bramn entered the vestibule, Miryl stopped pacing and met Bramn's eyes. Neither man moved. Miryl gave the slightest shake of his head.

Bramn released Thylaina and hurried to the eastern corridor where the patients' rooms were located.

Thylaina gripped the satchel's strap and followed him, trying her best to ignore Miryl's tears. *Vynia, I beg of You, guide me. Do not let me fail.*

They passed several rooms, nearing a crowd of men standing outside an opened door. Heads bowed, a drone of prayers fell softly from the lips of solemn knights and priests. As Thylaina squeezed past, she heard Grim's subdued voice.

"Are you certain?"

Raylen sighed. "I don't know if he realizes we're here, nor do I—" Anguish quashed the priest's voice. He cleared his throat. "I don't believe he's truly with us anymore."

"No," Bramn whispered, then fell to his knees, his shoulders shaking as he wept. Fists clenched, he leaned back and roared, "No!" His face turned deep red from the outburst, and he slumped forward to the floor when his lungs emptied. More sobs sounded from beneath his arms.

Thylaina leaned against the man beside her to remain upright. Pulling the strap over her head, she entered the room, dropped the satchel, and neared the bed, where Arlin knelt, weeping.

From the foot of the mattress, Grim raised his red-rimmed eyes to her, tears breaking free to follow the same path as the previous droplets. "Thylaina."

She drew in a long breath, then focused on Breydon. He lay on his stomach, a cloth covering his head and face. The damage must have been so terrible, they did not wish anyone to see. A splotch of red soaked through what was obviously the back of his head by how the cloth formed against his eyes and nose. Several cloths with larger red stains piled on the floor.

"My lady, you shouldn't be here," Raylen said, directing her toward the door.

She could not take her gaze from Breydon. No. Thylaina must know. "What happened?"

The priest paused and let out a slow breath. "A blunt strike twice in the same spot. Cracked his skull."

Thylaina's knees buckled, but Raylen helped her stand.

"My lady, one of the knights shall escort you—"

"N'ei." She braced her heels to the floor to stop him from forcing her out, but the slippers slid along the marble surface.

"There's nothing to be done." Sympathy filled his eyes and voice as he cupped her hand between his. "Captain Colmstad has only minutes left."

"The result of the injury?"

"You needn't the details."

"Bloody tell me!"

The room silenced as all the men turned their attention to her and the priest.

Raylen glanced at the others, then met her gaze. "His brain swelled. I couldn't stop it."

Thylaina's eyelids fluttered, and blackness moved in. Was she breathing too fast? Or at all?

"What about Mikan?" Grim asked, the question clearing her mind like water splashed on her face.

Thylaina walked toward him. "You cannot."

"Maybe he can do what Raylen can't."

"After all he has done, you would set him free to ruin Breydon further?" she shouted.

"He's my knight!"

But Breydon was her lover. Was he not? There must be something she could do, yet no healing remedy came to mind. Thylaina needed something powerful. A spell, and she knew of only one for such dire circumstances. To do it would expose her, but in order to save the man she loved, it was worth it.

"I..." She scanned the room and faces. Too many faces. Turning to Grim, she said, "I might have the remedy, but we must move him to the temple. And we must be alone."

"You haven't time," Raylen snapped.

"Do it," Bramn said, his voice hoarse. He stepped further into the room unsteadily, his eyelids already too heavy to open fully. "Take Breydon there now."

Grim did not hide his disapproval as he looked from Bramn to Thylaina. While Bramn directed men to carry the mattress into the temple, Grim approached Thylaina. "Stop this before it goes too far," he hushed. "I'll not have you give them false hope—especially Bramn and Arlin."

"Is hope not all we have?" Although she wanted to be angry with him, the lack of faith was understandable. She had to convince Grim to have hope when Breydon was barely alive. Giving her grief and weakness to Vynia, Thylaina straightened and squared her shoulders. "Faith and hope are what I give to my goddess. Perhaps you should spare some faith for your god."

Grim's face reddened, yet no words of anger came forth.

"Move!" Bramn shoved men from the door, clearing a path for the mattress bearing Breydon. "Ensure none block our way to the temple chamber."

A priest ran ahead with two soldiers following.

"Grim." Thylaina grabbed the marshal's hand. "I cannot save Breydon without you. Your strength and prayers shall give might to my task. Stand beside me and catch me should I fall."

Raylen's frown shifted from Thylaina to Grim. Apparently, he did not agree with her actions either.

"I don't want to lose him," Grim whispered.

"Nor do I." Her eyes filled with tears as a breath rushed out. "I need you," she begged through quivering lips.

Sympathy overtook his displeasure, but Thylaina did not need his pity, just his strength.

"Then let's not dawdle," he said.

On their way out, she snatched the satchel, her mind racing with how to approach the situation. She had assisted Uncle Yasontler when he performed a divine healing to save a dear friend of his, but Thylaina had never cast the spell herself and knew not if she could. He had explained that of the royal bloodline gifted with divine magic, only *he* had enough power to call upon the gods for so great a favor, for no other could afford the fee expected from Them. But Uncle Yasontler did not save his friend, nor did he save Thylaina's mother. He was a failure, and to be truthful, Thylaina still believed that about him.

She was no Elf Queen, but she *was* of Bryric's bloodline. No matter the century that had passed since Mother's death, the words of the spell never left Thylaina. Her devotion to Vynia and Her Gifts was unbendable, so perhaps the gods might grant her Their Favors. To save Breydon, she would pay whatever Their demands.

The men had lowered the mattress at the altar, then circled around Breydon in prayer, like sentinels. Bramn knelt near Breydon's head, placed his hand on his dear friend's shoulder, and Arlin stood behind him. Thylaina neared, but stepped back and said a prayer of her own.

*Bryric, You are my strength—I lean into you. Vynia, You are my guide—I trust in You. Lessindra, You are my heart—I love through You. Valorius, You are Breydon's god—I beg of You. Hear my petition and grant us Your Graces.*

"Thylaina," Bramn said, snapping her from prayer. "Raylen said to act now."

She drew in a deep breath and viewed the sorrowful faces. "You all must leave. I need undisturbed concentration, and the presence of all these men is—"

"It is done." Grim turned to the others. "Clear the temple. Raise your voices to Valorius with those outside. Go to them now."

Bowing to Thylaina while she removed ingredients from her case, the men whispered pleas for her to succeed. Bramn lingered a moment longer, hope, and fear battling for dominance in his tear-filled eyes. After a few more words to his dying friend, he turned to Thylaina and rested his hand on her shoulder. "I trust you," he whispered.

She had not the heart to look at him, but briefly touched his hand and nodded.

Once he left, and only she and Grim remained in the massive chamber, Thylaina quickly combined the ingredients of a healing sphere, including broken barily leaves. Instead of shaping it into a ball, she made a poultice, something to press directly onto the wound and seep within. None of that mattered, really. It was for the marshal's observation she made the remedy.

"Grim, the wrappings from my case."

He snatched the wool bandages while she neared Breydon, then stood beside her, waiting.

Thylaina stared at the blood-soaked cloth, unable to speak the supplication aloud because of Grim. Hopefully, Bryric understood. *Sire, I call to You. Your Divine Energy is an honored gift. Release it through me.* The god answered with power reverberating in her chest. It then flowed throughout her as she knelt. *Bryric, You found me worthy of Your Gift. I beseech You, guide me.* Fingers trembling, she removed the cloth, exposing Breydon's ashen face and the gruesome wound. Thylaina faltered as the horrifying fact that someone had tried to kill him wavered her concentration, but the connection with Bryric remained firm. *Father of my bloodline, You live through me. Grant an open path for a divine healing.*

More than a hint of fear could collapse the prayer, and a smidgen had ebbed its way into the magic's current.

"Thylaina, did you hear me?" Grim gently squeezed her shoulder. "Are you well enough to continue?"

She could not speak, her mouth sticky. It felt as if another force had stepped into her path to break her connection with the divine. Thylaina would not let it happen, for no one else could save Breydon. Unlike her uncle, she *would not* fail. Refused to. She smacked her tongue against the roof of her mouth until enough saliva built up for her to speak one word clearly. "Grim."

"Yes?"

"You—" Her head echoed a slow pulsation that weakened with each second. Breydon's heartbeat. She was losing time. "Grim, I shall speak in an ancient language. Forgive me if it all sounds confusing, but I have not the time to explain."

His brows lowered, yet he remained silent.

Thylaina pressed the poultice to Breydon's blood-soaked hair, feeling the softened flesh and broken bone shift beneath. She had never squirmed while tending to wounds, but now her stomach nearly lurched.

"I... I shall give all my energy to these prayers. Do you understand?" She met Grim's curious gaze. "I might collapse," she whispered. "I need your strength. We both do."

Shaking his head, he lowered to his knee. "I *don't* understand. But whatever you must do, do it before we lose him."

Thylaina returned her attention to Breydon, closed her eyes, and lay her palm over the poultice. "Once I finish, wrap this against his wound. And whatever you might witness, please speak of it to n'ei other. I beg of you."

"Just do what you must."

Thylaina rolled her shoulders back, stretching the taut muscles. A slow breath filled her lungs, then eased out. When she began speaking, it was indeed an ancient language—the first ever spoken in Emvarr. She was one of the very few in Etharell who had learned Ubrasian, for many believed it a dead language. Although close to the Elvish Tongue, her people preferred to leave it in the past. Now, only the Ubrasians spoke it. But they never left their homeland, so why bother learning it? For Thylaina, it was about the magic. A connection existed between the two: Ubrasia and the Divine. Bryric had been Ubrasian. To speak His Tongue afore casting a spell, in Thylaina's opinion, honored Him and the other deities.

The plea sounded beautiful in His language. "I am nothing afore You All. Bryric, You granted me with Divine Magic. Lend Your Power to me. Lessindra, You show Your Love and Forgiveness. Please absolve all offenses and cleanse this man." Warmth filled her center, slowly expanding toward her limbs. "Vynia, I am Your Vessel. Through me, others find healing—"

"Thylaina, he's... He's gone."

The slow pulse had stopped. Tears broke through her closed eyes, but she did not cease praying. The gods were capable of many things. "Vynia, make Breydon whole," she continued in Ubrasian. "Your servant begs for Your healing powers on this wound. On this man."

"Thylaina, please," Grim's voice broke. "It's finished."

But *she* was not finished, and the Ubrasian words came out faster. "Valorius, aid Your knight. Let this not be his end. I implore You All, and willingly pay whatever Your demands."

Uncle Yasontler had made no such offer when he cast the ritual for his sister, and though he did for his friend, it resulted in no successful end. Thylaina was desperate. It was not about succeeding where the Elf King had failed. It was about Breydon's life.

The pleas ended, and the chanting began. The incantation started softly, yet the words came with conviction. Thylaina separated her emotions for Breydon to focus on the spell, and using his blood, traced a sigil on the poultice. The moment her heart untied itself from him, power balled in her chest. Divine magic as she had never experienced. She recited the lines again and again, feeding the magic until it felt like a large rock wedged beneath her ribs. If she was yelling, she knew not, for Thylaina could no longer hear her voice. The interweaving of divine magic hummed in her ears and vibrated her body from within. Then the flow began with urgency, moving from her chest, down her arm, and into her hand, leaving her and entering Breydon. But there was more. Years of her life drained—the price for the spell. The longer it took to heal him, each deity

Who answered her prayers pulled threads of her soul away. Knees wobbling, her body quaked, and the power slowly dissipated. Even with her eyes closed, she sensed blackness engulfing her, her mind spinning. Weightless, she floated. Fell. The drop did not end.

Nor did her greatest worry. Did she succeed? Or would Breydon remain at Valorius' Great Feast? Thylaina did not have the luxury of worrying for long as the deep shadows wrapped around her, dispelling all thoughts and fears.

Failure was not possible. The gods had responded to the spell with vigor. Was her soul that valuable? Of the four gods she had called upon, one did not require payment. Lessindra spoke to Thylaina during the long respite in the peaceful darkness, assuring her the love shared with Breydon was all She required. Yet it was a love Thylaina had cast aside out of panic. She could not do that again... if he chose to live; the new fear that now ebbed at her mind.

Time meant nothing in this dark veil, yet it seemed like ages had passed, which was an odd feeling for an elf. The strange sensation likely began when Thylaina's subconscious awoke within the stillness, leaving her with naught but questions about her mother's death.

Did Uncle Yasontler endure this extensive worry afore learning his sister chose not to return? Thylaina should not have troubled herself with such pondering, for Uncle Yasontler had not appeared distraught then. And although she now knew he had not failed to save her mother, Thylaina could never forgive him for being cruel to his sister for gaining Bryric's Favor. Uncle Yasontler had also treated her with disdain because Etharell had adored Princess Alihean for her kindness and for connecting with the people by marrying a soldier. It had enraged the king to see her turn away several promising suitors for Galenlyr Zorlias, even though he was highborn.

When Thylaina was fifteen years old, Mother had shared that she loved Father from the moment he introduced himself. That he had looked into her eyes, smiled charmingly, and told her he did not deserve to hear her voice nor kiss her hand, but to have held her gaze was worth living for.

In that unmoving realm, where Thylaina felt suspended, her heart ached for her father. Mother had preferred death over her family. Sadly, Father was not present for the last fourteen months she had suffered, the Second Army demanding he perform his duty. No. The Elven Nation and Her king demanded it of him. Of course, Father barely arrived in time to be with Mother when she passed, but it meant little then. He had not been there to witness her suffering, hear her cries of pain, and watch her wither into a shell of an elf. Gods! Neldrid had been present for only a fortnight of those draining months. Thylaina had been at her side, researching and studying for a cure. And the king did nothing until she had already passed. That bastard waited, believing divine healing was the only answer.

Sorrow weighed Thylaina deeper into the nothingness as she feared Breydon might also deny the chance to continue his life, and possibly at her side. She could not blame him after what had happened the night of the attack.

*Do not give in to hopelessness. It shall devour you.* It was a woman's voice, although not spoken, and not Lessindra's. A voice as old as Emvarr's soil. Sultry. *You are not in My Presence, but I am with you. I am often with you, Thylaina, My Favored Healer.*

A warm embrace offered comfort, and calm smothered the despair. Thylaina leaned into Her. *Vynia.*

*Your devotion pleases Me, Favored. It always has. Ask what you will, and if the bidding is not unreasonable, I shall provide.*

Love and joy overwhelmed Thylaina, and she rose from the deep gloom. Although still in shadows, the weight was lighter. Healing caresses grazed over her soul. *Thank you, Vynia.*

She ascended higher.


"Breydon!" Thylaina lifted her head, blinked her heavy eyelids. Fire crackled from the hearth; the room's only source of light. Just coming back from the darkest darkness she had ever known, the flames were too bright, even if several feet away. Her breath came fast and her heart raced, yet she felt solace within, even with the lingering anxiety.

"I am here," he whispered from near the fireplace.

Gasping, Thylaina sat up, turned toward his voice. His dark form leaned forward, silhouetted in the flames. Her mouth dried as her heartbeat thumped in her throat. Unable to see his details, she dared not speak for dread it was his spirit.

"What...?" He appeared to rub the back of his head. "What happened?"

It *was* Breydon! He spoke clearly, the question proof of his presence, even if she could not see his face.

"I was there... at His Feast," he continued.

Thylaina pushed the coverlet off and swung her legs over the side of the bed. Her bare feet hovered over the cold stone floor, but she willed her eyes to adjust to the shadows covering his face, desperately wanting to see him. The fire flickering in his eyes showed first, then reflected off his red hair. His jawline appeared smooth from the clean shave prior to Bramn's wedding—Oh! How fine it had felt against her cheeks, her breasts, on her belly.

"I stood before Him, Thylaina. Valorius... He spoke to me."

Her breath built in her chest as she recalled the way his heat engulfed her when he was near. How she felt while in his presence. Breydon loved her, and she loved him without any doubt.

"I saw my mother," Breydon said in a hush. Almost in disbelief. "It seems like a dream now. She was so beautiful."

Thylaina could no longer reject him and deny herself the joy she truly wanted. It mattered not that he was a human. They were in no Elven Court. Caerabis was not Haevaun Flameral, and if they were very careful, Etharell would not learn she was there. No one could force her to marry whom she did not wish to marry. The choice was hers. And she wanted to be with Breydon. That is, if he would have her once he learned the truth.

"And I saw Iavi." He nodded, then raised his eyes to Thylaina. "I held her for what felt like decades." Tears glistened until he blinked them away. "I never thought I'd ever see her as she was before that illness ruined her. To have felt her as she had been." He shook his head. "It was a gift from Valorius. All of it was."

Thylaina stilled. The warmth within quickly gave way to a wave of cold as his gaze hardened.

"Then you called to me," he said through his teeth. "Why? Why did you call after you had rejected me?"

Words failed. Thylaina had not anticipated his anger, not when he chose to come back.

"I see," he whispered. "You're a healer."

Her tongue suddenly felt thick and numb.

He stood and headed for the door.

No. She could not let him leave her. Thylaina hurried off the bed, but her legs failed her and she fell to the floor. A soft yelp escaped. "Breydon," she managed in barely a whisper. "I love you."

Did the door open and close? It was hard to know amid the silence pounding in her ears.

He was suddenly kneeling beside her, gently holding her arms. "What did you say?"

Thylaina raised her head to see his face. So close now, she noticed the tiny red hairs on his jaw. Probably a few days since he last shaved. She had slept longer than she realized.

"Thylaina?" He guided her back to the bed, sat aside her.

"I... I love you, Breydon."

The bastard laughed. "Do you?" Despite the laughter and gleam in his eyes, there was a sincere expression. Adoration. "Then why did you put me through such distress?"

Now came the truth, but telling him might ruin everything. However, if Thylaina wanted a future with Breydon, he must know whom she was. He would demand it anyway. First came the smaller truth.

"I denied even to myself what I felt for you." She held his hand. "It was never about you being from a poor farm or that you are a 'Bastard Knight'. Denying my feelings and yours was because I feared it was not possible since you are human."

Huffing a heavy breath, he turned toward the fireplace. "Valorius revealed a great deal to me—opened my eyes to the truth of what happens within this knighthood. And I must do something to stop it."

That was why Breydon returned, and not for Thylaina.

Letting go of his hand, she asked, "And what is that?"

His brows lowered as he licked his lips. "I swore to Valorius that the Three will not destroy this knighthood. I'll fight their every attempt."

An oath to his god. A promise Breydon would always put afore all else. His commitment to Valorius and the knighthood left no place for Thylaina in his life anymore.

Forcing a pleased smile, she sniffled. "They shall have quite an adversary."

"Laina, I still want you by my side for the rest of my days. Nothing has changed that." There was no lie or teasing in his tone or gaze, which remained fixed on the fire. "Your voice echoed in that hall. Even Valorius held His breath when He heard it." Breydon's cheeks glowed as he smiled wide. "He said there was such power behind your prayers. Devotion. A fierce love... for me. I-I couldn't believe it, yet knew my god wouldn't lie to me." He faced Thylaina and took her hands. "It was difficult leaving the Feast—leaving my mother and Iavi. But I couldn't deny you."

Her center surged with warmth and excitement. Breydon loved her still. She was a part of his return—a part of him. Yes. Thylaina truly wanted this.

"Breydon, I am terribly sorry about what I had said—"

"Hush." His thumb glided along her bottom lip. "I now know the truth, and that's what matters." He leaned closer, his thumb moved aside as his mouth pressed to hers.

But he did not know the truth.

Thylaina broke the kiss, lowered her head. "There is something I must tell you."

Sighing through a smile, he straightened. "You can tell me anything, Laina."

It was wonderful to hear him call her by that name again, yet she feared it would all change once he learned everything.

"What I must share with you, I wish to share with Grim as well." The marshal had witnessed enough to raise suspicion. Besides, she trusted Grim.

A mixture of confusion and concern weighed upon his brow. "If you must."

She nodded. "And it must be in a place where none can overhear what I say. No one." Thylaina gripped his hands tightly. "For fear of my safety."

Curiosity stared back at her. "There is such a place. I'll speak with Grim after we break fast, which shall be in four hours. We'll arrange a meeting as soon as possible."

She relaxed her muscles and slouched a little, her breath easing out.

"May I kiss you again?" he asked.

Thylaina smiled. There was no denying his request. And perhaps they might do more than kiss.

Thylaina thought their first night together had been intense. This time, his touches, kisses—everything about how Breydon made love with her—seized her breath. Her body burned from ecstasy, leaving her begging for more... and more. Thylaina could not get enough of Breydon, and he gave himself completely. For the first time in her life, she knew what it meant for two people to become one. But would she and Breydon remain as one after he learned the truth?

Following afternoon meal, he and Grim led Thylaina to the entry hall, then to the first corridor beyond the northern stairs. The men's steps were solid and rhythmic, as if marching. Their posture was perfectly straight, both appearing tall. Solemn. They passed several doors, including the one to the bathing room. At the end of the hallway, Grim stopped at a banded door, which seemed odd compared to the others. Why was there a fortified door here? He opened it and motioned for Thylaina and Breydon to enter.

It was a library. Not grand like at the palace, but a decent one that likely offered volumes Thylaina had never read. She doubted this room could provide protection from intrusive ears, even if there were, for some reason, two armed sentries.

Breydon continued to the eastern side of the room where the guards stood. He nodded once to them as he reached between two books, pushing one inward to the left. The shelf between the sentries slid back, then to the right, revealing stairs winding down. That explained the guards. Breydon turned to Thylaina and gestured into the darkness. "My lady."

Chuckling, Grim grabbed a lantern off a nearby table and walked ahead of her, leading the way down the steps. Thylaina followed him, and Breydon brought up the rear; the shelf closed behind them.

She expected a musty and unkempt chamber, but discovered an orderly war room. In the center was a large table with maps lined from edge to edge, and markers in various places. Against each wall were small tables containing dozens of the wooden markers representing the nations of Yeuroth, parchments, ink bottles, and quills. That explained why Grim's cabinet was bare of any strategic items; they were all hidden beneath the mansion. On the larger table in the northern corner were six crystal decanters and eight matching goblets. The scent of burnt wicks and heated oil from the wall sconces and candelabra lingered, giving the impression the room had been in recent use.

Grim lit the sconces on the wall, then the candles near the table, while Breydon repositioned three chairs.

"Have you been making plans as of late?" Thylaina asked.

Breydon darted his gaze to her and smirked. "I was down here after we parted this morning." He motioned to the single chair facing the others. "I promise no one will hear anything said within these walls."

She eyed the chair, then theirs, which were paired together. It looked as if they intended to interrogate her. Not a comfortable setting. "You did not wish to sit with me?"

"You asked to speak with both of us, and I believed it easier if you could face us at the same time."

Nodding, Thylaina sat.

Finished with lighting the chamber, Grim set the lantern on the table, then took his seat next to Breydon. The marshal remained in a straightened position, while Breydon appeared relaxed, yet nervousness touched the latter's smile.

Thylaina curled her fingers into fists on her thighs. *Where do I start?* She had no idea how to say what she must. First, she needed their promises. "You must swear to me that what I now share stays with us."

The men looked at each other, then at her.

"Of course," Grim said.

Thylaina shook her head. "I want an oath from the both of you. For me—for the sake of my life—give me a vow that you shall tell no one of what you learn in this room."

All amusement faded from Breydon's expression. "Laina, wha—?"

"Give me a knight's oath."

Gaze locked to hers, he drew in a deep breath, released it. "I swear as a knight of Alohrius, you have my word that what you share with me shall not be spoken with another. My vow is my life."

"You have my oath, Thylaina." Grim placed his hand to his heart. "What you say remains between us. My vow is my life. Not even Tes shall know what's said in this room."

Satisfied, she nodded again, and rubbed the heels of her hands on her thighs forward then back, trying to calm her nerves. The best thing to do was just say it. Get it out now and over with, yet while treating it delicately. Bryric! She really got herself into a mess. Thylaina straightened and looked at Breydon. The men remained patient while waiting for her.

"What I did at the temple to save you, only one other in Emvarr could have accomplished."

Breydon watched her. Scrutinized her eyes, facial muscles, and body language to make certain she spoke truthfully. It stung. Knowing what he did, she lowered her gaze and rounded her shoulders. At least her muscles were no longer taut.

"Who else can do it, Laina?"

She debated whether to tell him. No. There could be no debate. Thylaina must say something now, or she might never. "My uncle," she whispered. "It is because of his bloodline that I am granted such power, for it passed to me through my mother. He does not know. I-I never told him. I was afraid. My brother was not blessed with the gift, but I am."

"Who is your uncle?" Grim inquired.

Thylaina raised her head, met his curiosity. She turned to Breydon. "King Yasontler Tanagaryl."

The men froze.

"N'ei one knows I have them," she continued, the words coming out fast. "Not even in Etharell. I have been cautious here to hide the powers Bryric granted me, afraid of the wrong humans discovering. I fear what they might do should they learn I am of the Throne of Etharell."

It seemed neither man breathed. Breydon just stared at her.

"Have you determined if I speak truthfully?" she asked.

He licked his lips. Blinking, he broke free of her gaze and stood. "Gods," he hissed, turning away. "Is that why?"

"Not truly." She rose. "It really was because you are human. I did not believe it was possible to have anything more than a swyve or two. My intentions when I fled Etharell were to join my kin in Yeltar and find an acceptable husband to live out the rest of my days."

Breydon faced her, his blue eyes piercing. "And now?"

"Have I not made it clear?" She stepped toward him, but he retreated.

"You are from the Royal House of Etharell!"

"I severed that bond."

"You can't!" He spun to Grim, who still gaped at Thylaina. "What say you?"

The marshal closed his mouth, slowly looked at Breydon. "I say we've a problem on our hands."

"No doubt," Breydon snapped. "They're looking for you, Thylaina. And I denied knowing about you!"

It did not feel right when he used her name properly. Like he was putting distance between them. Well, this was not going to please them either.

"There is more you shall not like," she said.

Scowling, Breydon rested his hands on his hips and waited.

"My family name is Zorlias."

His expression flattened, swiftly shifting to recognition. "No."

"First General Neldrid Zorlias is my brother, and Second General Galenlyr Zorlias is my father."

"Gods." Grim headed to the drink table.

Breydon's eyes narrowed. "I've never met them, but rumors about your brother are unsettling."

Thylaina shrugged. "To be truthful, my brother became a stranger to me. I do not know him."

He grabbed the hair at his nape and tugged. "Gods, Laina. Neldrid Zorlias has spies all over Yeuroth. He might have them here now. And if he learns you're in Caerabis, it might start a war!"

"A war with Alohrius is the last thing my uncle wants."

Grim sat down, swilled some fruzae. "She's correct. King Yasontler is no damn fool."

"And the First General?" Breydon asked.

"My love," she said, "there is naught he nor my father can do to take me away from you."

Breydon's chest filled then emptied, and his expression shifted to worry. "Except sneak you away in the night." His voice cracked. "Don't forget I know how the xilys are."

"The Forest Army is not xilys."

"No. It's Etharell's best army led by their best general."

"I wondered, you know," Grim said, gaining their attention. "When I saw you the first night you dined with me, I recognized your face—your eyes. Just like your brother's."

"You...? You have met Neldrid?"

Grim laughed. "Of course I have. He's my ally." He finished the drink, then set the cup down. "And now I know he is of the royal bloodline. What are we to do?"

"Live as if tomorrow is another day." Thylaina spun to Breydon. "I left Etharell to experience the life I wanted, and I want that life with you."

Searching her face, he leaned against the table. Turmoil succumbed to acceptance. "With you being whom you are, the challenges we'll face shall be difficult." A slow smile lifted one corner of his lips as his eyes brightened. Love stared at her. "But together..." Breydon spread his arms. "Together we'll defeat anyone."

Giggling, Thylaina rushed into his embrace. "I love you." She tilted her head back, tightened her hold around his waist. "We are stronger than any force on Emvarr."

He delved his fingers into her hair, then rested his palm on her cheek. "Nothing and no one will ever take you from me." He kissed her softly, then deeper.

Grim cleared his throat. "Does this mean another wedding is in order?"

Thylaina heart skipped at the thought, yet she relished it. "S'yai. It does."

Breydon grinned the widest she had yet seen, and he picked her up, whirling around once. "Praise Valorius!" He set her down and kissed her hard.

This was perfect. Wonderful. And she could not wait to walk this path with him.

"I have one request of you," he said, suddenly serious.

"And that is?"

"Please keep your hair braided until our wedding night."

Thylaina recalled the moment shared between Bramn and Einasa when he released her plait. She never would have believed something such as that could be so special, so intimate, but she wanted to experience it with Breydon. "I will proudly braid my hair for you."

# Chapter Sixteen

Thylaina had hoped to see Gavrel afore the wedding, but the dubight rode out of Caerabis two days past, along with squires undergoing training for the knighthood. Although it saddened her to not have had the chance to wish him well, she was happy he was closer to achieving his goal. He would soon be an Alohrian Knight. Grim informed her Gavrel's return could be months, possibly years, but he may come back to the city as a soldier, if he came back at all.

At the moment, she and Breydon lay on the fur rug in front of his fireplace, their bodies slick with perspiration. He sat up and snatched a bottle of wine from the hearthstone. After a few swallows, he offered it to her. "There's something I'd like to know before we marry."

"What is that?" She enjoyed a deep swallow of the warmed blackberry wine.

"How old are you?"

Thylaina almost choked on the drink, but kept it to only a clearing of her throat. "You do not wish to know."

"Of course I do." He relaxed on a propped elbow. "I'll tell you my age."

She slid back down beneath him and touched his young face. "It matters not, does it?"

"You're to be my wife."

"Which is something more important we must discuss: our vows."

"What about them?"

She traced one of the longer scars on his chest, no doubt from a sword's edge. "Do you understand the elven customs?" One of the other main reasons she had hesitated to accept the possibility of marrying Breydon.

"Your marriage traditions weren't part of our teachings." He caught her hand and nibbled on her fingers, then kissed the tips.

"We marry for life."

"What does that mean?"

Thylaina tugged her hand from his mouth afore he sucked her thumb into it. "It means as it sounds. The Temple Laws state that our marriage binds us to one person—one soul—for the rest of our days. In our vows, we swear to meet our beloved when our souls arrive in Love's Garden."

He lowered her hand between them. "You mean when I die, you can't love another?"

"I cannot."

Breydon rolled to his back, his contemplation lost to the dark ceiling. It was a lot for a human to realize. To be honest, it was just as much for an elf, but in Etharell, they did not question the temple.

"You told me your mother died when you were young," he said.

"S'yai. I was only nineteen."

He turned his head to her. "How old are you now, Laina?"

Humans never realized what a horrible question that was to ask an elf. Of course, some elves did not mind answering, showing off that they lived so much longer than the lesser races. But everyone in Emvarr already knew it.

She entwined her fingers with his. "On the twenty-second day of the Hawk Moon, I shall be two hundred sixty-five." That was only four months away.

His eyes and mouth widened. "Gods," he whispered. "You were *awfully* young."

That was what his reaction was about? Not that she was far more than two centuries older than he, but because of how many years had passed since her mother's death.

"And your father has been alone since?" He looked back at the ceiling. "How could he do it all these years?"

Thylaina pressed her lips to Breydon's shoulder. How did Father endure the loneliness since Mother's death? It must have been dreadful for him.

"I don't want that for you," Breydon said.

She leaned her head back enough to see his face. "But—"

"Yet I don't expect you to say Alohrian vows, so we'll say different ones." His brows lowered for the briefest moment. He nodded. "We'll make our own."

Breydon would do that for her? Great Bryric! Thylaina loved him more now than just minutes ago.

"That sounds wonderful."

Arms firmly around her, he kissed her hard. "First thing tomorrow, we'll work on the vows. And in four days, we'll marry."

It was the most nerve-wracking morning of Thylaina's life, and it was a shame, and painful, Mother was not there to share it with her. Yet Katjina and Tes filled in as best as possible. Katjina helped Thylaina dress, braided her hair, and applied colors to her face. Tes managed the household, keeping everything in order. Nothing could go wrong. That is until Nadiera disappeared.

Knights searched where they thought the young girl might have hidden in the mansion. Tes insisted the search extend into the heavy snowfall, and everyone hurried outside, including Thylaina. The squires, Arlin and Kimmy, went to the barracks near the mansion, which stirred several soldiers into action, and they spread into the city streets. Grim, Bramn, and Breydon rode a hundred-yard perimeter around Caerabis, seeking tracks. Tes was beside herself with worry, so Katjina remained with her to attempt comfort while Quaiy cared for the babe. Amdronus helped Thylaina in the orchard, the snowfall making it difficult to determine if they saw a tree trunk or a person.

By the time Thylaina and Amdronus finished, snow and dirt soaked the dresses' bottom hem; a branch had caught on the skirt, tearing it at the back; *and* she was freezing! Thylaina had always wanted a summer wedding. But there she was on the twentieth day of the twelfth month, ready to marry a human.

"Nadiera!" Amdronus scanned the trees once more, his clouded breath billowing from his mouth.

Shivering, Thylaina hugged herself and turned for the scullery door. The fruit from the knee holly looked beautiful, the berries deep red amid the bright snow. She could not help smiling. A bush to the right of the door shook, yet there was no wind. Curious, Thylaina stepped closer, then bent forward to look beneath the snow-covered greens of the bush. Behind the row and resting against the mansion wall was a crouched form. "Nadiera?"

Steam broke between the spiny branches and wide eyes stared back at her.

"Bryric!" Thylaina straightened. "Sir Amdronus, I found her!"

The knight came bounding from the northern corner of the building. She had not realized his search had led him away. "Where is she?"

Thylaina pointed to the bushes.

He squatted and peered inside. "Lady Nadiera? What are you doing back there?"

"Darling, please come out," Thylaina said, removing the white-furred mantel Tes and Grim gifted to her that morning. "You must be cold."

"Go away." Nadiera's hushed voice quivered.

Amdronus trudged into the small gap between the two rows that permitted easier tending to the bushes. He reached into the one Nadiera hid behind.

"Sir Amdronus, this will not help," Thylaina said. "Please, let me try."

Brows furrowed, he grunted and retreated a few steps.

Thylaina held the mantel close for warmth. "I know why you are out here." No reply came. "You need not be upset, my lady." She squeezed into the gap and lowered to the ground, sitting about a foot away from the girl. A few of the thin branches caught in Thylaina's hair, but she ignored the nuisance. "Nor must you hate me."

"I *do* hate you."

A thorn pierced her heart. Thylaina had done nothing to draw such ire from her. Except...

She sighed sadly into the branches and berries in front of her face. The poor girl was too young to feel so deeply for someone, yet it explained her adverse behavior toward Thylaina. "Breydon is a fine man. A wonderful man," she said. "It is no surprise so many women come to love him."

"You don't deserve him!" Nadiera's voice broke, then she began crying. "I thought... he'd wait.. for me. But he doesn't love me."

Amdronus inched forward.

Thylaina shot him a glare and shook her head, then returned her attention to Nadiera. "I have never seen him look upon any maiden in this city with adoration and love he does with you, my lady."

The girl sniffled, darted her eyes to Thylaina. "You're lying."

"It is true." Violent shivers overtook her, the cold snow seeping through the gown and wetting her bottom. Soon, it would grow numb. "He does look at *me* that way."

Nadiera turned her head, her blue irises bright behind the mix of green, red, and white from the bushes and snow—not to mention the redness brought from her weeping. She looked so much like her father at that moment. "Are you just saying that?"

"N'ei, my lady." Thylaina shook her head, stared at the dark shapes moving closer. Three forms huddled against the snow. "Breydon's expression changes with you. A softness smooths the muscles of his face and his gaze reveals a deep love. A love he shall have for n'ei other." She smiled at the girl. "You have a special place in his heart. I believe you always shall."

"Laina, are you—?"

She raised her hand to silence Breydon.

Grim and Bramn stood on either side of him, all of them covered in white and looking miserable. Amdronus joined them, appearing just as unhappy in this unpleasant weather. At least *they* were not sitting on the cold, wet ground.

Thylaina lifted the heavy cloak. "Please join us, my lady."

"You don't want me. You hate me." Nadiera's bottom lip quaked.

"That is not true." Thylaina lowered the mantel. "I have nev—"

"You love Telsia more than me!"

Grim moved closer, snow crushing beneath his boots. "Nadiera, that's enough!"

Thylaina scowled at him.

Sighing, he rubbed his arms and bounced.

She slid her hand behind the bushes, but did not touch the girl. "It may seem that I was being cruel to you while I cared for your mother, but it was only to help your sister live. I swear it."

Nadiera stared at Thylaina's hand, then shifted her gaze to a cluster of berries.

"My lady, I would do the very same for you," Thylaina said. "You are important to me. I care very much about you."

The girl did not appear to believe her.

Cold had completely consumed Thylaina. There was no doubt Nadiera was in worse condition, considering how long she had been out there.

Thylaina twisted to her side and leaned on the building. It added to the discomfort, but Nadiera had to know Thylaina meant every word she was about to speak. "I promise you this: if anything is to befall you, I will be at your side with as much diligence as I had been with your mother. *Nothing* will stop me from making sure you are well and safe. My worry over you will be just as great."

A few quick breaths passed Nadiera quaking lips. She looked at Thylaina. "You—? You love me?"

Thylaina smiled. "Would I be sitting on this cold snow, my buttocks turning to ice, if I did not?" Maneuvering to her knees, she opened the mantel. "Please come. We shall warm ourselves. Then you can stand with me while Breydon and I speak our vows, for you are a part of us."

Tears pooled in Nadiera's eyes again. She wiped her nose, then nodded. Slowly, she moved from behind the bushes and into the waiting cloak.

Thylaina wrapped it around her and rocked. Tucking her chin over the girl's soaked hair, she hummed, then thought a prayer to Vynia. *My Goddess, please warm this child. Show her Your amazing gifts are for her as much as they were for her sister.* The mantel grew cozy and warmer within Thylaina's arms. Her heart soaring, she thanked the Earthen Goddess for answering.

"Vynia blesses you with Her Warmth, my lady," Thylaina whispered, petting Nadiera's wet hair back.

The young girl moaned softly, tipped her head back. "Is that what's happening?"

"S'yai."

"Can we go in now?" Amdronus asked.

Thylaina did not look from Nadiera. "Are you ready, my lady? It seems the men are not capable of handling the cold like us ladies."

Nadiera giggled. "Yes. We can ease their suffering."

Once Thylaina opened the cloak, Grim strode closer and took his daughter into his arms. "Gods, Nadiera. Don't frighten us like that again." He kissed the side of her head. "Let's get you inside and warmed."

Breydon helped Thylaina rise, then hurried her inside the scullery with Bramn and Amdronus following.

The scullery maidens halted their work and gawked at the party. Viya frowned, drew in a breath to speak, but said nothing to Grim as he carried his daughter through and into the feast hall.

Thylaina shook, realizing just how cold she was.

"I'm going to change," Bramn announced. "Tell Kimmy and Arlin to cancel the search."

"Yes. That's a fine idea." Amdronus followed him out.

Shaking off the wet garments was a perfect idea. Breydon led Thylaina from the kitchen, then lifted her into his arms and carried her to her chambers. He sent Katjina out until later. When the handmaiden inquired of when she should return, his only reply was a stern, "*Later.*"

Door locked, standing at the burning hearth, he stripped Thylaina of her ruined wedding gown.

"I shall have to find a new one," she said.

"Both of our marriage garments are ruined."

"Standing naked at the altar shall not do."

Breydon's brows raised high as he appreciated her body. "Well, I'm not one to share, so I suppose not." He untied his tunic and then blouse, dropping them behind him with a soft *splat*. "We're not at the altar right now, are we?"

A smile tugged at her lips as she took in what he wore underneath. "N'ei. We are not."

Thylaina had never seen Breydon wear hoses, not even for Bramn's wedding. They differed from what she donned; pulled all the way up his legs and tied to a belt, leaving his braies exposed. The elves would love such a fashion. Except elves might not wear braies to cover their virility. Why did the women tie their stockings around their thighs when the belt seemed far more ideal? She had never worn the hoses until arriving in Caerabis. Elves did not cover their legs with such thin material. They did not often wear *anything* underneath their clothing. Why was she even thinking of that while her future husband had untied his hoses and was pushing them down, soon followed by the braies?

"Breydon, you should be—"

He straightened and pulled her close. His mouth covered hers, his tongue probing. Their bodies pressed tighter as the kiss deepened. She wanted him. Wedding now or later, there was no waiting to have Breydon. Thylaina slid her hand between them and grasped his virility.

A deep moan sounded in his throat. He parted his lips from hers, yet their noses touched. "We're not yet married."

"You are mine either way." She bit his lip, then kissed him hard. "Now let us warm our bodies together."

"My thoughts exactly."

The moment was amazing, their passion fierce. And he held her afterward while watching the flames dance in the hearth. Contemplation continuously altered his expression. Unable to contain her curiosity any further, she nudged her thigh against his virility to gain his attention.

He smiled at her. "Yes?"

Thylaina caressed his face, wanting to remember it for the remainder of her long life. "Tell me what troubles your mind."

"You."

"Is that all?" She giggled. "I must be a lot to consider, for your face has displayed different emotions these past fifteen minutes."

"I'm... I'm trying to think of how to ask something of you." Concern returned, then compassion, and then sorrow.

"Just ask me afore you burst."

He chuckled. "Very well." Breydon rolled to face her, propped his head on his palm. A few hesitative breaths and several blinks. Finally, the words came out. "I want you to make another promise. One that isn't easy for me to ask, but I do this for you. Actually... there are two promises."

Interest piqued, she nodded. "Go on."

He raised her hand to his lips and kissed her fingers. "I want you to be ready, that if I should send you a message of warning, you'll gather prepared items and ride to a designated outpost at the Ormiana border."

She pulled her hand free and sat up. "Then what? Leave without you? N'ei. It shall not happen."

"I have a duty to Alohrius."

"You have a wife! Or you will." She flung the braid over her shoulder and sighed. "I shall never leave without you."

Defeated, he lay back. "I promise to do everything I possibly can to reach you at the outpost, and we'll ride into Etharell together." He looked at her. "I just want to make sure you're safe."

Thylaina could not blame him, not when she worried as well. "Acceptable. What is the other promise?"

Breydon guided her closer until she lay against him. "You'll far outlive me, my love."

Damn him. He did not need to say that. She knew what future awaited them—it was the punishment for marrying a human.

He palmed her cheek. "I can see it in your eyes you're upset, but I'm not yet finished. Gods, Laina, even your muscles tensed."

Releasing a slow breath, Thylaina relaxed her body. "Forgive me. Do continue."

He waited a moment. "The other promise I ask of you is that you *will* love again when I'm gone."

Laughter came forth as she shook her head. This was a conversation she refused to have. "We needn't talk about—"

"We do. I'm twenty-two, and I'll never live nearly as long as you. I want this assurance." He kissed her knuckles, one at a time. "And I can't bear the thought of you being alone for hundreds of years." Breydon met her gaze. "You deserve to be loved by a man worthy of you." Dropping his hand, he scowled. "I don't understand Lessindra demanding it."

Thylaina had never thought about it because she was taught not to question the law. Contemplating it now, Breydon was correct. It made no sense for Lessindra to demand one to withhold love. To the Darkness with the elven customs. Thylaina and Breydon intended to break plenty that evening when they wedded. But that he thought about her future brought on such an ache, to know he loved her that deeply. *However...* Thylaina pressed her lips together to keep them from trembling and held tears at bay. "I cannot possibly love another man as I do you."

That damn smirk formed. "I never said to do that." Breydon laughed as he embraced her. "I hope no man will ever do for you what I have, yet I want you to know great love again. Not immediately. Gods! Not even ten years after I'm gone." He leaned his head back and grinned. "Perhaps a hundred. Hm?"

She rested her forehead on his chin and giggled through tears. "S'yai. I promise."

"But I'll tell you this, Laina: if the man who takes you as his wife doesn't deserve you, I'll come from the Feast to torment him."

Snuggling as close as she could, she moaned happily. "You shall always watch over me?"

"Always."

"I love that. And I love you."

He kissed her deeply, then tapped his nose to hers. "We should prepare for our ceremony."

"I suppose."

What was to have been an early afternoon wedding turned into an evening affair. Thylaina wore a sea-blue gown with silver-threaded waterlilies along the skirt and sleeves, and a crisscrossed pattern around the neckline. It had taken nearly an hour for Katjina to redo Thylaina's braid. After choosing the dress, Thylaina sent Quaiy to find something similar for Nadiera. Thankfully, the local seamstress had one in a similar color. Stitched around the skirt were silver ripples below and above sea elves. Thylaina had never seen a sea elf in her life and doubted any human had. Yet the dress was lovely, and Nadiera loved it.

Now, Thylaina stood afore Breydon, who looked handsome in a fresh brown tunic, ivory blouse, and tan hoses. Traditionally, he should have donned his ceremonial breastplate, but since they were not quite following the customs of either nation, he dressed like a nobleman. Breydon had told Thylaina he wanted to feel he belonged aside her. Hopefully, she convinced him what he wore proved nothing. It was what they felt and shared. Besides, the fine garments were preferable to the armor.

Thylaina and Breydon wished to keep their wedding an intimate celebration. She had so few to invite—Katjina, Quaiy, Panya, and Viya. Breydon's list contained the obvious names: the Momestids, Bramn and Einasa, Amdronus, Miryl, Arlin, Raylen, and a few more knights Thylaina had yet to meet, along with their escorts.

High Priest Haltrin Jalfiasin presided over their vows. When Thylaina and Breydon approached him with their concerns about the marital oaths, he was more understanding than she had anticipated. Haltrin did not understand Etharell's ways, but he would not enforce Alohrius' traditions on her if she and Breydon did not wish. It was up to the gods on whether They would bless the union, and he had no doubt such a blessing would occur.

Knights of Alohrius did not exchange rings, yet elves did. Thylaina and Breydon agreed to come to a solution for this later. The vows were most important.

The group stood beneath the dark windows of the temple dome. Torches flickering from the sconces expanded the shadows of the nearby stone knights and other décor. Nadiera swayed with excitement between Thylaina and Bramn, and Grim beamed from behind Breydon. This was one tradition kept for the ceremony: a witness from a fellow knight to verify the authenticity of the marriage. No one could ever claim the wedding was not valid. This was what Breydon had done for Bramn. Thylaina had asked Breydon why he chose Grim and not Bramn, and his answer had left her speechless. Possibly loving him even more.

*"Grim saved your life that night at the vault... from me. He's saved me many times since Mikan began poisoning me, and never stopped fighting to keep me sane. Because of him, we are now about to become one."*

It was meant to be, however, for she could have imagined none other than Bramn as her bride knight.

Breydon and Thylaina clasped hands.

"Laina, my heart is yours. My soul is bound to you. You..." He smiled, looked down, and licked his lips. Meeting her gaze, he smirked. "You are the love of my life. I will protect you, serve you, and love you until my last breath. I swear this to Valorius and Lessindra, and before the witnesses of my promise. My vow is my life. I love you."

My vow is my life. Thylaina had quickly learned these devoted men did not speak those words lightly.

"Lady Thylaina," Haltrin said, "your vows."

"My heart is yours," she began. "And despite the promise I have already made, my soul is bound to you, Breydon Colmstad." He appeared about to protest, but she shushed him by continuing. "*You* are the love of my life." Thylaina squeezed his hands. "I will keep my promise, but I will always love you. One day, Valorius granting, I pray we will meet in Love's Garden. I will love you, serve you, and protect you until..." Her smile widened, and he grinned, until her smile faded. It was impossible to finish that promise. How could she say, *'until the end of your days'?* It was a dagger in her heart. "I am yours, and yours alone. I swear this to Lessindra and Valorius, with these witnesses to attest my oath."

Haltrin hovered his hand over theirs while he prayed to Valorius, then to Lessindra. Finished, he introduced Captain Breydon and Lady Thylaina Colmstad. "Breydon, you may unbraid her hair."

Thylaina drew in a deep breath when her husband moved behind her. A shiver rushed down her spine as he lifted her plait and pulled the sea-blue ribbon loose. With gentleness, he unwound the first braid.

"I will love you our first year," he said. Was Breydon creating something new with this tradition? With the second weave, he said, "I will love you more the next."

Her vision blurring, she looked at their friends and saw smiles from the men and tears from the ladies.

"My love grows deeper every year after," Breydon continued with the third. And with each freed braid, he promised his devotion. Moving to stand in front of her, he pulled the long black locks over her shoulders and stared into her eyes. "My love is everlasting and shall never falter."

She lunged, kissing him as hard as possible.


They snuggled beneath the covers of her bed, Breydon groaning as he stretched. Thylaina could barely move, tired from a long day and full from such a fine feast. Viya had truly outdone herself with a fantastic mix of sea fare and mutton, cornbread, vegetables in broth, and delicious tarts.

Breydon winced. "My feet bloody ache."

"I am not surprised. Not after everything we have done today."

"You know," he hooked his arm around her and pulled her even closer, "I never did thank you for helping Nadi. You did beautifully with her this afternoon, *and* this evening. I think you'll be wonderful friends now."

"I was terrified she was lost."

"As were we. With the snowfall, Grim feared her tracks would disappear and we'd never find her." Breydon kissed her head. "But you did. And you brought her back to us."

"She was behind the mansion."

"You know what I mean."

Thylaina slid her foot along the bottom of his, massaging it.

"That feels good, wife."

She noted the slight smile. "You know what else would feel good, husband?"

"Hm?"

Lifting the blanket, she slipped beneath to perform ortia louvres. His tiredness would go away soon.

# Chapter Seventeen

Thylaina had waited too long for this day, and she argued with Breydon until her throat was raw and her palms hurt from digging her nails into them. Witnessing Mikan receive justice was something she deserved. So, she stomped behind her husband as he strode to Grim's cabinet, where the high priest was to learn his fate. Her husband glanced back, sighed, then looked ahead. Upon reaching the door, he spun and put his hand out.

"This is official business of the knighthood, Laina." Without waiting, he entered and closed the door. A click sounded. The bastard locked her out.

Face burning, she gritted her teeth, doing everything not to scream. Calm settled in as she stared at the doorknob. Did he believe he could keep her out? He forgot whom he married. The spell was simple, and one of the first she had learned—taught by Valraahn when he wanted inside his father's cabinet to sneak a drink of caldin broul, the only liquor known to intoxicate an elf. Valraahn had gotten so ill, he vomited on a letter meant for his future bride's parents. The energy for the spell came from the air, which manipulated the locking mechanism. In four seconds, Thylaina opened the door and entered.

The room silenced as seven men looked in her direction. Grim, Breydon, Raylen, Mikan, and three knights eyed her as she slowly walked farther into the chamber.

Breydon's cheeks turned ruddy, and his eyes brightened. "What did I tell you?"

"I have as much of a reason to be here as everyone else." Thylaina sat in the empty chair next to Mikan, yet did not look at the high priest. "He intended for you to kill me, did he not?"

Grim exhaled slowly as he looked from her to his First Captain. "She has a—"

"No," Breydon said between his teeth. "She has nothing but demands that'll not be met by me."

"Let her stay, Captain Colmstad," Mikan said. "This might be entertaining."

"I'm not here to entertain you," Breydon snapped, then swung his gaze to Raylen.

The herbal priest shrugged. "She recognized the herbs and poisons used on Her Ladyship, you, and the other knights."

Sliding his fingers through his hair, Breydon turned his back to them all. His frustration made no sense. Raylen was correct: Thylaina had plenty of information to help ensure Mikan did not evade punishment. Unless if Breydon...

She stared at her husband in disbelief. Did he plan to let the high priest go?

He faced them. "Let's review the facts, then, shall we?"

After three hours of her and Raylen's testimonies against Mikan, they paused for afternoon meal. Breydon remained in the cabinet with Mikan, while everyone else dined in the feast hall. Thylaina disliked leaving her husband alone with the high priest, especially after some of the favorable comments Breydon had made on his behalf, even if they were true. But Grim promised her all would be well.

Having little appetite, she nibbled on her meal. "Can we not go back now?"

Grim smiled, set his goblet down. "There is naught to worry about. Breydon knows what he's doing."

"What if Mikan tries to—?"

The marshal covered her hand with his. "Trust Breydon."

During the remainder of the meal, they discussed menial things, topics of little interest to Thylaina. Getting back to her husband was all that mattered. They rose and started for the door, but it opened. Thirteen armed men donning plate armor entered.

The one leading them appeared about Breydon's age and had a strong likeness to Mikan. He stood a few inches taller than Bramn, and his blond hair flowed over his shoulders, framing a face so bloody perfect. Thylaina held her breath, enraptured. His strong jaw was smooth, his fine lips cocked in a half grin, and eyes of the clearest blue she had ever seen shifted from Grim to her as he neared. His gaze revealed nothing as he took her in from head to feet, then looked back at Grim.

"Sir Kaeleck," Bramn sneered.

The beautiful knight bowed his head to Grim. "Marshal Momestid," he said, his voice a smooth baritone. He then turned to Bramn. "You address the First Captain of Haevaun Balaeus, Sir Bramn. This is the only warning you'll receive."

Bramn snorted.

This man, Kaeleck, fixed his glare on Bramn again.

"Captain Thornsalin," Grim said, "for what reason are you in Caerabis?"

Kaeleck still did not move, did not blink, but continued the stern stare.

Bramn sighed. "Forgive me, Captain Thornsalin," he mumbled.

"I'll expect a better apology next time." Kaeleck finally gave Grim his attention. "I believe you know why I'm here."

"Let's say I do not."

Captain Thornsalin clasped his hands behind his back and glanced at his men. He chuckled. "Do you think I'm a fool, Arhgrim?"

"I said no such thing, *Captain*. And you'll address me as 'Marshal'."

Kaeleck's perfect nose curled for the quickest second. His gaze darted to Thylaina. "Rumors have reached the Three that you intend to put your city's high priest through a trial. I am here to... observe."

Cheeks shaded red, Grim said, "You mean you were sent to *free* your brother."

"What?" Thylaina stepped forward.

"Who are you?" Kaeleck asked, once again appraising her.

Grim moved to her right, and Bramn to her left. "Lady Thylaina Colmstad," Grim said. "It is my... pleasure to introduce Captain Kaeleck Thornsalin."

Kaeleck appeared to notice the hesitation and Grim's tone. He glided closer to her and gently grabbed her hand, raising it to his warm lips for a kiss. "What a delight to make your acquaintance, my lady. Did I hear correctly that he said Colmstad?"

"You did." She eased her hand from his grasp, and he did not resist. "Breydon is my husband."

Intrigue eased his dour mask. "When did you marry?"

"A few days past."

"Ah. Newly wedded." His stunning smile accentuated his beauty, yet did not hide the scrutiny in his gaze. "You did not make time for yourselves to celebrate?"

A sudden discomfort made her stomach grow queasy. "I fail to see where any of that is your concern."

Bramn gently guided her behind him. "What do you want, *Captain*?" Disrespect and loathing weighed in his tone, revealing his true feelings for the man.

Kaeleck's eyes widened. He moved so quickly, no one had a chance to react; his fist crashed on Bramn's face.

Bramn collapsed to the floor, groaning and holding his jaw. He spat, groaned some more, then spat again, leaving—a tooth?—in a small puddle of blood and saliva. Thylaina knelt beside him to examine his mouth, but he pulled away and stumbled to his feet. Raylen helped steady him, and one of the guards hurried from the room.

Kaeleck arched a brow, raised a hand to halt Grim's approach. "You'd been warned, Sir Bramn. I'll not tolerate contempt from a subordinate."

"I'm not... your bloody subordinate," Bramn rumbled, then charged.

Grim stepped into his path. "Stand down, Sir Bramn!"

Thylaina rose, glaring at Kaeleck. "Raylen, please take him to my chambers."

"Yes, my lady."

Grinning, Kaeleck shook his hand, then rubbed his knuckles. "I came for Mikan, Marshal. Hand him over to the Three for judgement."

"You forgot something, Captain." Grim waggled his finger at him. "Mikan stands trial for breaking the Code and committing crimes while in *my* city, not Haevaun Balaeus. So the bloody Three have no damn right to take him from me."

"Wrong!" Kaeleck's face darkened. Calming, he brushed his blond locks aside. "Forgive me, Marshal Momestid, but the Three have made their command."

"They do not lead the knighthood."

Silence filled the chamber. Kaeleck bobbed his head once. "You will take me to him, and *I* will hear the testimony."

Grim did not meet him eye to eye, but he certainly seemed taller at that moment. "Testimonies were already made. However, I'll allow your presence for his judgement, which will be announced upon our return. Then you and your men will leave."

"You can't make me—"

"My city, Kaeleck." Grim smiled wide.

He directed the captain's men to the tavern six blocks west, closer to the edge of the city. The three knights who had been at the trial and afternoon meal escorted Kaeleck to the cabinet. Grim walked with Thylaina. "You should go to Bramn," he said.

"I am not leaving that man with my husband," she whispered.

"I understand your concern, Thylaina, but everything will be fine."

"Who is he?"

Grim sighed. "A very powerful person. That's all I can say for now."

"Can he harm you?"

"Me? No."

"Breydon?"

The marshal laughed. "No. Now stop worrying yourself."

How could she? Kaeleck had just slugged a tooth out of Bramn's mouth!

When they reached the cabinet, Grim moved ahead of the group. He knocked five times, then opened the door.

Breydon rose from a squat, grabbed a cloth off the desk, and wiped his hand, focusing on his knuckles.

As they entered farther into the room, Thylaina spotted blood beneath Mikan's chair... and a *tooth*.

Kaeleck must have as well, for he hurried to the high priest, shoving Breydon aside. "Mikan, are you well? What the bloody Darkness happened?" He spun and pushed Breydon hard. "What did you do?"

The cloth dropped to the floor as Breydon grabbed Kaeleck by his breastplate and jerked him close. "You knocked one out of my man, so I knocked one out of yours. Sounds fair, doesn't it, *Captain*?"

It was more than a tooth. Both of Mikan's eyes were swelling, his left cheek was red and missing skin, and two of his fingers bent in the wrong direction. Thylaina was not sure whether to be appalled or impressed by her husband.

Kaeleck lunged and swung his fist at Breydon.

Breydon blocked it aside with his forearm, then hooked his elbow around Kaeleck's, locking their arms close to their sides. "Easy, Captain," he said. "We resolve nothing while behaving like this."

"I'll kill you!" Kaeleck struggled to break free of Breydon's hold.

"Enough!" Grim bellowed.

Breydon released Kaeleck, shoving him a few feet back. He glanced at Thylaina and winked. Did he find this amusing? This was no bloody game.

"Sit down, Captain Thornsalin." Grim pointed at his large chair behind the desk. When Kaeleck did not move, the marshal took one step toward him. "I will not tell you again."

Kaeleck combed his hair from his face, shouldered Breydon on his way to the chair. "Bastard knight," he mumbled.

Ire turned Breydon's cheeks crimson and lit his eyes. He bristled as he followed Kaeleck, his voice low and gravelly as he said, "What did you say?"

"Please, love," Thylaina said in Elvish as she grabbed his hand and tugged.

A moment of thick, uncomfortable silence passed while the two men leered at each other. The condescending grin Kaeleck offered revealed he had got the reaction he wanted. Now, Thylaina had to calm her husband.

"Love," she repeated, sliding her fingers between Breydon's.

He released a slow breath, then kissed the back of her hand. "All is well."

Kaeleck observed them from behind the desk, as if forming plans in his mind.

"Have you decided on the punishment, Captain Colmstad?" Grim asked.

"I have, Marshal."

A mixture of shock and anger marred Kaeleck's face as he sat up. "He has yet to be judged!"

"He's guilty," Breydon said, authority strengthening his tone. "Now you've heard the judgment." He bowed slightly to Grim, then looked at the trembling and beaten high priest. "I sentence Mikan Thornsalin to ten years for the murder of each of Lady Tesesra Momestid's two unborn babes."

Kaeleck stood. "How dare you!"

"Sit down, Captain Thornsalin!" Grim pounded his fist on the desk, his eyes watering. To have heard that judgment must have pierced his heart. Obviously, he would no longer tolerate further annoyance from this man. "You will sit, or you will leave my city. Either way, you return to Haevaun Balaeus without your brother."

Kaeleck fixed his hate-filled eyes on Breydon and lowered to the chair.

"For attempting to murder Lady Tesesra's recent babe," Breydon resumed, "I sentence you to eight years."

"To the Darkness with you!" Bloody spittle sprayed from Mikan's mouth.

"I'm not finished!" Breydon bent forward, his cheeks nearly matching his hair. "Twelve knights and myself were compromised under the influence of the red dust you gave us... Divine Wrath. You will serve another eight years for each man who suffered that mind poison."

"You're making a grave mistake," Kaeleck said.

Breydon did not look from the priest. "Think you'll live another one-hundred thirty-two years, Mikan? Five of those knights died while trying to recover from the dust." The chair's arms creaked beneath his tightening grip. "Five!" he roared in Mikan's face. After a deep breath, he whispered, "Your days end here."

"You'll die in this city," the priest said.

Breydon shrugged. "I imagine I will."

Grim turned to Kaeleck and gestured to the door. "You've got some news to deliver to the Three. Particularly the Second Marshal."

Kaeleck glowered at him, then Breydon, his forehead creasing in contemplation. One sluggish blink. Two. A slow exhale. His face no longer marred by fury, he walked to his brother. "You'll not rot here. I promise." He headed for the door.

"The trial was fair, Captain," Breydon called. "I have the witnesses' transcripts to deliver to the Council. There's nothing the Three can do."

Kaeleck opened the door, stood there for a moment, then turned, closing his hands into fists. "There's a lot they can do, Captain Colmstad. A lot *I* can do to you—to your wife—when I next return."

Breydon's muscles tightened. He bolted for Kaeleck. Captain Thornsalin laughed as he closed the door. By the time Breydon reached it, two of the knights caught up to stop him from following.

"It's what he wants," Grim warned. "Don't fall for his trap."

Breydon shook free of the knights, then paced until the rage dissipated. Thylaina had never seen him so angry. She dared not approach him, and he appeared to notice. Calmed, he embraced her. "Forgive me, Laina," he whispered. "To hear him speak such a threat... I couldn't bear it."

"I am not upset with you." She held his face, kissed him softly. "But you must be careful. He wanted you to lose control so he could gain an advantage. Do not let that happen."

Nodding, he kissed her palm. "Once again, you're correct. It *was* foolish of me."

"And we'll not ignore his threats," Grim said, pouring two glasses of fruzae.

"No. We won't." Breydon looked down at his bloodied knuckles, then at Mikan. "Can't take anything a Thornsalin says with little regard."

Thylaina disliked the priest's smirk. She took Breydon's hand and examined the minor injuries from his punishing Mikan. "Are you afraid of Captain Thornsalin?"

A gentle tug followed her question, but he did not resist her tightened grip. He laughed. "N'ei, my love. He's just a man like me. It's the power his family holds that might cause trouble. The problem is when." Receiving the offered drink from Grim, he continued. "Thornsalins slowly climbed to the position they now possess, one they'll kill to maintain. They're in no hurry to succeed. I've stood beside Kaeleck on the field before and have watched him think, scheme, and time his steps exactly where and when he wanted. He was raised to be patient. To lead." Breydon finished the fruzae in three swallows, then released a heavy breath. "He'll return just when he means to." Smiling, he winked. "But I'll be ready."

His confidence offered something of a relief.

He gestured at the priest—former high priest. "Apparently, he seduced Bethlyn, convinced her he loved her." Breydon shook his head, disgust skewing his face. "Everything she did was to please him."

Stomach succumbing to nausea, Thylaina looked at Mikan. "She was willing to harm an unborn child for that love—that lie?"

He faced forward and said nothing.

"You are a horrible person." Her lips quivered, the urge to cry over the evil the two had been willing to commit growing. "You both are."

"He doesn't know where Bethlyn is," Breydon said. "Or so he claims."

"We'll find her," Grim rumbled. "She *will* pay for her part in this."

"And where shall you imprison him?" Thylaina inquired. For Breydon's sake, she hoped somewhere far from Caerabis. Too bad they could not send him to the Spire in Etharell, a place where men like Mikan could be forgotten. "Keeping him in the jailhouse will surely encourage others to free him."

"He won't stay in the jailhou—" Grim chuckled, then ordered the knights to make sure Kaeleck and his men had been escorted beyond the farms. Once they left, he stared down at the priest. "He's not staying in the vault. We've a special place for people like Mikan. A place he's not even aware of."

"Where is that?" she pressed.

Breydon gently grabbed her elbow and led her from the room. "Can you do me a favor, love?"

"What is it you need?"

"Tend to Bramn." His countenance darkened. "I heard Kaeleck struck him hard, which is why Mikan suffered as well."

"Sweet Vynia! Absolutely." She kissed Breydon, then hurried to her chamber.

While examining Bramn's injuries and mixing bossel ointment, she shared all that had taken place in the cabinet. He laughed and groaned, and while she spread the medicine on his face, he complained about having to miss the whole event.

"I wish Breydon would've slugged a few of Kaeleck's teeth out," Bramn said, while Thylaina washed her hands. He prodded the fresh gap in his mouth and cringed. "I bloody hate that man and the whole damn Thornsalin family. They're going to ruin this knighthood."

Thylaina wiped her hands dry. "Who are these men, and how dangerous are they?"

He eyed her as if it were unwise to say anything further. Running his tongue over his teeth for the ninth—or fiftieth—time since she had tended to him, he nodded. "What do you know about the knighthood?"

She sat across from him, rested her hands on her lap, and relaxed against the back of the chair. "I know that in place of a king or queen, you have a council that oversees the country."

Bramn nodded. "It was not so for many years when Alohrius first came to be," he said. "The knighthood formed before the council, founded by men who sought to protect their community from bandits."

That missing tooth marred his handsome smile, but some women might still find it attractive. Thylaina did not mind.

"Unfortunately, some people revel in the power they think is theirs," he continued. "They began to believe they were the ones in control. Older knights brought it to a halt by calling upon those they knew could help them form a structured organization. To lay out a code and laws amid the knights and the people of Alohrius."

"The Alohrian Council, made up of common folk of Alohrius," Thylaina said. "Farmers, merchants, fisherman, and politicians."

"Even the homemakers." Bramn grinned. "A woman's voice is just as important. Just as a woman's service in the knighthood."

"Women knights? I have yet to see one here."

His expression soured. "That's because of the Three."

The Three. In Thylaina's studies of the Alohrian Nation, she had never heard about them. Since arriving in Caerabis, the Three Marshals had been an occasional subject at the feast table, often leading to arguments between knights. She had collected little information about them, most of it regarding their intentions to make changes within the knighthood. Some men supported it, while many, like Grim and Bramn, did not. Thankfully, Breydon's recent vow to Valorius disclosed his standing against them.

Curious about these powerful men, she asked, "Who are the Three?"

Bramn stood. "I'll pour us a drink and tell you everything I know. But what I share can get me into trouble with Grim." He huffed a laugh. "Breydon will cast me into the Darkness!" Amusement faded as he stared at her. "But you should know about them now that you're his wife, because he's got their attention. He's always had it."

Two cups filled with wine, Bramn returned to the chairs and handed one to her. "The Second Marshal, Salnaer Thornsalin, is Mikan and Kaeleck's father." He sat, drank a few swallows. "He lets people believe Lord Arkiem is the First Marshal, including Lord Arkiem himself, but the truth is, Salnaer is the power of the Three. And he's been trying to get Breydon into his fold since Iavi's death, but Breydon was faithful to Grim."

Thylaina still had not drunk her wine, for she had not the strength to lift the goblet. "That is why Mikan had been poisoning Breydon," she said. "To gain control of him."

Bramn raised his cup. "Until you came along. You may not realize it, Thylaina, but you've done more than save his life. You may have saved the knighthood."

# Chapter Eighteen

**O**ver the next three years, Thylaina made minor alterations to the herb garden. She moved the repenia vines on the eastern side of the scullery door to those on the west. The plants had grown so thick and healthy, and covered most of the back of the mansion, there was no longer a need for trellises this last year. Three more herb boxes were built for the kitchen and Thylaina. The most arduous work was transferring the knee holly from the wall by three feet to permit access to the repenia. Changes were needed as time moved forward. In fact, many changes came to Thylaina's life since becoming the First Captain's wife, some less important than others.

The most significant was the home Breydon had had built next to the mansion. With only thirty feet separating their houses, there was little distance from the herb gardens between her home and the Momestid's. Thylaina also imported tall bushes to provide privacy for her and Breydon, had a lovely stone path laid out to the house entrance from the cobblestone street, and a smaller path from the garden terrace on the northern side that led behind the mansion. The terrace also presented a wonderful place to break fast and enjoy afternoon meal. Her home was of modest size—for one of elven royalty.

The vestibule led into the large receiving room, which also served as a gathering place with friends and guests. Although Thylaina loved the solar, garden, and apothecary rooms, she adored this chamber the most. It was the only place in the house that truly defined her and Breydon as one. Elvish decorations complemented the simple furniture, displaying how beautifully their lives had entwined. In this room, she and Breydon were more relaxed with those closest to them, welcomed new people into their lives, toasted to good fortunes, shared the latest news, and held one another on the sofa afore the grand hearth. It was more than a greeting chamber; it was their family room. They had decided it best not to risk Thylaina's life to have a child, but Grim's and Bramn's families were theirs as well.

Breydon had been concerned about his inability to afford the construction of the home she desired, but Thylaina's jewelry and gems provided the funds and more. At first, it made him feel further inadequate to support the livelihood to which she was accustomed. However, Thylaina promised she was capable of adapting to simpler means where possible, but servants were not one of them. There was only so much she could do on her own, and she refused to dismiss Katjina. The household counted six servants, with Katjina overseeing Thylaina's needs. This included two housekeepers and Panya, the latter coming from the mansion's scullery to cook in Thylaina's. And much to Thylaina's delight, Katjina acquired two amazing gardeners to assist with the flowers, trees, and herbs. All the servants received beds and meals, along with a reasonable salary. The housekeepers shared a decent room, as did the gardeners, and Katjina and Panya had their own. None complained about the arrangements.

Life in the Colmstad Household was perfect. Blissful. More so when Breydon was home, which had not been often as of late. The knighthood—no, the people of Alohrius—called upon him to perform his duty to protect them. It often reminded her of Father and Neldrid's absence, but she came to understand.

The year following Thylaina's and Breydon's marriage, bandits struck communities between the Alohrian Downs and the Alhore Forest. During the next twelve moons, the attacks spread northward to Warstchia. It was more than a few parties of brigands, for the timing of their attacks was too close considering the distance of locations. According to Breydon, the tactics used were similar and with an organized method, much like the Southern Brigands. This left no doubt knights and soldiers were involved. The Three Marshals had made a move against

Caerabis, and it was not only about Mikan Thornsalin, but the integrity of the knighthood. A division had formed amongst the sworn protectors of Alohrius. Grim believed that was the intention of the Three ever since they claimed their titles a decade ago.

Everything Bramn had shared with Thylaina the day of Mikan's trial had frightened her, particularly the details regarding the Thornsalin men. Lord Salnaer had wanted Breydon under his wing—in his 'order'—to guide more into their fold. But when Breydon's devotion to the Code, and to Grim, revealed he would be no part of the Three's scheme to overthrow the knighthood, Salnaer resorted to using his son's herbal skills and Breydon's grief to gain control of him. The Three had nearly succeeded until Thylaina arrived. Although the marshals in Haevaun Balaeus were now aware of her presence and marriage to the First Captain of Caerabis, they remained blind to her true identity. Breydon and Grim had kept their oaths to this day, telling no one about her relation to the king of Etharell.

So while Breydon and two other captains led squads into the plains, seeking and battling the bandits plaguing the eastern half of Alohrius, Thylaina cared over those in the city who sought her healing. She worried about her husband and friends, but thankfully, knights and soldiers from Warstchia joined the hunt; however, that city had little to offer while protecting their own. The brunt of the work fell on Grim's shoulders, which meant Breydon's as well. Grim sent requests to the Council in Haevaun Balaeus for aid, but received excuses of empty words twisted to sound legitimate, the answer always coming from the same man, Lord Brevig Vantos. The men of Caerabis quickly learned Haevaun Balaeus had abandoned them, and there was an agenda behind that decision.

"They're going to remove the Council," Grim had said more than a year past.

Through her studies while growing up, Thylaina learned about the governing body of Alohrius. Not only did the Alohrian Council create laws, they oversaw the knighthood. Since her arrival in Caerabis, Thylaina had heard some men mumble their displeasure about commoners having such control. "It should be *us* having power over *them*," a few had muttered. This was no doubt a seed planted by the Three, one they hoped would flourish. Yet Grim, Breydon, and hundreds of other faithful men squashed the root placed by Second Marshal Thornsalin, caging it in a prison of which Thylaina still remained unaware. It was as if Mikan had never existed in the city.

"M'lady." One of the gardeners offered a basket of repenia leaves. "Is this enough?"

How long had she been standing beneath the late Lover's Sun, musing while the men worked? No matter. She had much to do in the apothecary. Thylaina smiled at the full basket and nodded. "Thank you. Please take them inside and prepare them for distillation."

"Yes, m'lady."

There was plenty of olesa oil to make, since she ground the dried bossel roots the day afore. She followed him to the apothecary and gathered the buraily leaves from what the servants called "the cave": a cool, damp compartment under the chamber beneath a trapdoor. Once Thylaina prepared the oil, she made a variety of sizes of healing spheres. Not that there was any hurry, but having them ready for emergencies was wise, and she never knew when one squadron might return and another ride out.

With the task finished, she grabbed her satchel and informed Katjina she was leaving for the Jalfiasin's home. Einasa had insisted on living near the city garden, where she spent much of her free time, even when she should have been resting. Hopefully today, she heeded Thylaina's instructions, which was doubtful without Bramn there to enforce them.

For the past year, Thylaina did not need an escort to walk the streets of Caerabis. Most had embraced her presence, and most importantly, her healing skills. She tended to more illnesses than the priests, and the temple did not mind, for their focus remained on caring for wounded soldiers and knights. There were times Raylen sent for Thylaina's assistance, which she gladly answered.

To be truthful, despite the horrible events in Alohrius, life in Caerabis was wonderful.

A servant welcomed Thylaina into the Jalfiasin home, then escorted her to the scullery, where Einasa labored over supper, her fully rounded belly bumping the table. Nothing stopped that woman from working, including the eighteen-month-old girl who buried her face in her mother's skirt and cried. However, Einasa was not to be exerting herself.

Thylaina rested her hands on her hips. "What do you think you are doing?"

Einasa's sweat-glistened face brightened as she swiped wisps of hair aside. "Oh, Greetings! I didn't know you were coming today."

"Every week now." Thylaina stomped into the scullery and set the satchel on the table. "And you have help in tending to these matters."

Einasa waved away Thylaina's concern. "I'm fine, love. I just needed to get some chores done." She removed Alyanna's hands from her skirt. "My sweet, please stop."

"Feeling anxious?" Thylaina asked.

"Me? No." Einasa grabbed a rag and scrubbed the table, which appeared tidy.

Thylaina turned to the nearest handmaiden. "How long has she been behaving like this?"

The young woman's eyes darted upward for a few seconds. "Since before dawn. M'lady was up and sweeping the floor."

"Blab," Einasa muttered.

Thylaina took the cloth from her friend's hand. "Let us go to your chamber for an examination."

"How much could have changed since last week?"

"This is not your first babe."

"I know, but—"

"Now, my lady."

Einasa's shoulders lowered. "There's so much to do."

Thylaina nodded toward the waiting servants. "And Bramn ensured all shall be done."

"Fine." Einasa trudged to her bedchamber, with Thylaina and Alyanna following. The little girl's hair and face shape bore a strong resemblance to Einasa, yet her eyes and facial features were perfectly Bramn's. Men would fight each other for her hand when she came of age.

The examination revealed Einasa should carry for another fortnight if she remained in bed. An unlikely event. Thylaina also learned that Bramn would have a doubly hard time with men in his future, for they would fight for the hand of his second daughter.

"Bedridden?" Einasa's rain cloud irises threatened to turn into a storm. "I can't. There's far too much—"

"To do. I know." Thylaina stroked the woman's forehead, the softest whisper passing between her lips. Once Einasa's expression relaxed, she continued. "This is about your babe. If you wish, I will have more help sent, including for the gardens. But we must care for you and yours."

Einasa curled a lock of Alyanna's hair around her finger. "Fine," she said. "I'll do as you say."

"I shall speak with the marshal about lending a servant or two." Thylaina returned lamuline ointment to the satchel, a concoction she developed a year and a half ago, combining olesa oil with water, beeswax, and lavender. Pregnant women loved it, especially since Thylaina warmed it prior to spreading it on their extended bellies. "No more chores today."

Einasa reached her hand out. "Thank you, my dear sister."

Strange how quickly their friendship had grown. Thylaina had anticipated animosity when Breydon chose her for his wife instead of Einasa's closest friend, Nikhia. But here they were, as dear as friends could be.

Nikhia. After Alyanna's birth, she married a knight from Monsor, a city near the White Plains in the far north of Alohrius. In some ways, it was nice to no longer have the lovely maiden's daggered glares toward Thylaina, and longing gazes at Breydon. Einasa missed her childhood friend, but she moved forward without her. People of Caerabis held the same great respect for her as they did Bramn.

"Does something trouble you?" she asked.

Thylaina blinked the many thoughts away and smiled. "All is well. I am considering my tasks for the day." She headed for the door. "Rest well, my friend. I shall see you after breaking fast tomorrow."

"Very well." Einasa snuggled under the blanket and closed her eyes. The poor woman had done too much already.

And Thylaina still had a long day ahead of her.

She had just finished stitching a gash on a little boy's arm, suggesting to his father the child refrain from fieldwork until she re-examined his injury in a week. His parents invited her to stay for supper, but Thylaina declined, for Panya had likely prepared dinner. She was three blocks from home when the thundering of hooves sounded from the east. Breath caught, she halted. Gathering her skirt high enough to run, she hurried toward the officers' stables on the north side of the mansion.

A rich-brown stallion trotted in her direction, his pace quickening. Aardrin was the handsomest Alohrian stallion Thylaina had ever seen. And his rider was equally attractive. Although not her husband, she was just as delighted and relieved to see the knight home safe.

"Bramn!" Thylaina squealed.

He brought the horse to a stop and dismounted, then swept her into his arms. "Thylaina."

She clung to him, grateful to Valorius that not a wound showed. "Are you well?"

"S'yai." He lowered her, a grin spread wide, revealing the small gap. "And you?"

"My night has improved significantly, Shapele." A year and a half since his promotion, and the title still felt odd on her tongue, despite how well deserved.

Tugging the lead, he guided the stallion onward to the stables. "Each step makes my night better. I can't wait to reach home."

Thylaina slipped her hand into his and smiled up at him. "Your ladies await you, Shapele."

A soft glow emanated from his face and eyes. "To hold them again... I've been looking forward to that moment since riding from here three weeks ago."

And she felt the same about Breydon's return.

"How do they fare?" he asked. "Is Einasa well? The babe?"

Thylaina patted his arm as they rounded the corner, the stables a few buildings yonder. "I have instructed her to remain in bed until the babe's arrival."

Bramn stilled, Aardrin snorting at the sudden jerk on his rein. "What's wrong?"

"Nothing, my friend." She offered a reassuring smile. "I just know that if I do not enforce limitations, your wife will push herself too much. Possibly into a condition we do not want."

Grunting, he nodded. "You know her well." They resumed to the stables. "Einasa is plenty to handle as it is," Bramn mumbled. "Alyanna is just like her, leaving my hands full with their demands and my need to please and protect them." He scratched the back of his head, his brows high as joy overcame his expression. "But I wouldn't bargain them away for all the riches of Yeuroth."

Thylaina giggled. "You think your hands are full now? Just wait until *this* girl is born."

He halted again. "Girl?" Bramn tilted his head and drew in a breath, but said nothing for a moment.

She slipped her hand free from his and backed in the direction of her home. "I must return. I imagine supper must be ready by now."

"You know?"

There was no ignoring him. He was not just her husband's closest friend; they loved Bramn as part of their family, just as his family welcomed them into theirs.

"How do you know?" He released the lead and approached her.

Thylaina slid her fingers up and down the satchel strap, her mind working quickly. "It is a gift for the most devout Vynists."

"Is it?"

Shrugging, she continued. "Some receive such a gift. I am one of a few."

"Did you know about Telsia?"

"I... I did."

Bramn stared at her, searching her face for any sign of deception.

Fool. She had learned this game with her brother decades ago. And although it had been nearly impossible to trick Neldrid, misleading this human was easy. Breydon was a different matter altogether. Her husband knew her too well.

Appearing satisfied, Bramn bobbed his head slowly. "Another daughter, is it?"

"I am fairly certain. My predictions may not be accurate." A lie.

"Have you been incorrect in the past?"

She could not withhold a small laugh. "N'ei."

He pulled her into an embrace. "This is wonderful news!" Bramn was truly happy to know he was having another daughter. It did not bother him that Einasa did not bear him a son... yet. Perhaps he intended to have a large family. Or maybe he simply loved to share a life with Einasa.

Thylaina kissed his cheek. "Get home, my dearest. But do not tell your wife of what I revealed."

"You told her nothing?"

"N'ei. It is best for the mother to learn on the birthing day."

"I'll do my best."

Thylaina spun on her heel and headed for home, but stopped and faced Bramn. "Shapele!"

He stood within the large entrance of the stables. "Yes?"

"Have you received word from Breydon?"

Bramn smirked. "A message came to me a week past. His squad camped west of Karvorn, then planned to ride toward Suflor Hills before returning home. It shouldn't be much longer."

If all was well, it would not be too long of a wait. Thylaina prayed for the safety of her husband's squad.

Four days passed, and Breydon had yet to return. Surely he could not have been too far behind Bramn's squad, not when the northern region of Suflor Hills was less than a two day's ride from Caerabis. But if Breydon had been near Karvorn, that meant he was riding along the Dred Sea shoreline, which placed him closer to the southern region of the dry hills. But what drew him to Suflor? The bandits were humans, not dragnols. Those creatures were too stupid to execute the raids that struck terror amongst the people west of the Trysk River. From the reports Bramn had gathered, not a single attack happened within the

Ullios or Alore Forests, nor eastward of them. Haevaun Balaeus kept those lands well protected. Despite their stupidity, dragnols were dangerous, and Breydon's reasons for approaching Suflor Hills better be worth risking his life and that of his squad.

Thylaina viewed the herbs behind the mansion while Telsia ran between rows of knee holly with Nadiera chasing after. The girls giggled under the sun, their brown hair bouncing. Telsia's green eyes locked on Thylaina for the briefest moment afore she turned down another lane. It was a surprise the tot was not at her father's side, seeming to favor Grim's company over Tes'. Despite his size compared to the child, Grim handled the tiny girl with such tenderness.

Heart filled with such love, Thylaina smiled. If only she and Breydon could risk having a child.

"There you are," Bramn said, startling her.

A ball of air caught in her throat as she spun to slap his arm. "Damn it to Darkness."

Chuckling, he gently blocked her hand aside. "Forgive me. I hadn't meant to frighten you."

Thylaina resumed clipping knee holly branches for the scullery. "I was not frightened. I just had not heard your approach."

"So absorbed with watching them, I see." He nodded toward the playing girls. "I understand. One day, I shall watch my daughters play like this."

She lost the battle against the urge to smile. Yes, one day Bramn would not only watch his daughters play, but he would likely join them. He was an outstanding father. "You were seeking me out?"

"Ah, yes. Einasa requests more lamuline. She said it feels like her stomach is stretching."

"I shall bring some following afternoon meal."

"Very good."

He returned his attention to the Momestid girls, who now held hands and spun in circles. "I..." A long hesitation followed a slow breath. "I know you and Breydon have discussed this, but have you reconsidered?" He bobbed his head in the girls' direction.

Thylaina's chest tightened as she straightened. Bramn knew because Breydon apparently told him. Had her husband lied when he agreed not to have children? Did it trouble him to know his bloodline ended with him? The answer stared at her as Bramn waited for a reply.

Speaking with as much patience as she would with a pestering child, Thylaina said, "I am certain he explained the dangers for me to carry his offspring. That it could kill me... and the babe as well."

Appearing unconvinced, one of Bramn's brows arched. The ass.

Thylaina sighed. "It is different for elves. Our pregnancies are shorter, unable to continue forming a half-human babe. That is why there has yet to be a successful birth resulting from your brutish knights raping our women."

Looking away, he clenched his jaw. "Not one of *our* men," he whispered. Bramn cleared his throat, then glanced at her. "Forgive me. I... I thought that with you being the greatest healer on Yeuroth, you might have the means to succeed." There was more to say—it showed in his gaze—but he bit the inside of his cheek.

Thylaina blushed. "I am flattered by your compliment more than you know. But there are two healers far more accomplished than I."

"You saved Telsia."

She met his stern expression, yet found no words.

"You've saved many lives, including babes." Taking a step back, he turned to her. "I know Breydon agreed, but I also know he has always wanted a family. He'll do what will make you happy because he loves you. I would do the same. But you? You are capable of so much—more than anyone I have ever known."

Bramn left her amid the knee holly, his last words lingering.

How dare he make her feel guilty about the decision she and Breydon had made. It was the correct decision for her sake.

Watching Nadiera and Telsia play in the orchard and herb garden, an ache filled her chest. Breydon loved the girls as if they were his own, just as he loved Alyanna. Why? Because of Thylaina. She feared giving him a child. Bramn was correct: she was a great healer. Undoubtedly far superior to the Elf King. In the past three and a half years, she had saved hundreds of lives, including those still within the womb. So why not try? Especially if she convinced the true greatest healer to aid her.

Master Eidryn cared deeply about Thylaina, and would do anything for her. She needed only to send a message to him without it leading her brother to Caerabis.

Vynia had blessed her with the power to create new medicine and new magic. Yes. Thylaina and Breydon *could* have a family together with the Earthen Goddess on their side.

She knocked on the Jalfiasin's door, surprised when Bramn answered. "Oh! I had expected a servant."

"They are tending to Einasa."

"Is she well?"

"Yes." He stepped aside and motioned for her to enter. "They're bathing her."

Thylaina gave him a jar of lamuline once he closed the door. "I imagine it makes her feel better."

"It does."

He took her hand, guiding her deeper into his modest house and to his small cabinet. Breydon's was larger, of course, he being the First Captain of Caerabis. But none of the men in this city, not even Grim, had a cabinet that could compare to Neldrid's at the palace in Haevaun Flameral. Thylaina had spent several days there, especially those she missed him most, and gazed upon her mother's portrait. Neldrid lived in that room during his rare visits, at least when he was not attempting to impress maidens and ignore Thylaina. His cabinet and bedchamber reflected him: perfection. Not a thing was ever out of place. He could not stand the slightest flaw, wrinkle, tiniest stain, or mishap, a trait gained after becoming High Captain in the Forest Army. That was when Thylaina no longer knew her brother. And the distance between them widened after Mother's passing. Neldrid never understood how much Thylaina loved him. Needed him. He was the only family since Father remained in Dragostros, commanding the Northern Army.

"I must apologize for my rudeness earlier today," Bramn said, cutting into her sad thoughts. "It wasn't my place to say anything."

Blinking away the distractions, Thylaina asked, "Einasa scold you for speaking?"

"Hm? No. I didn't dare admit that I'd made a fool of myself." Bramn's dashing smile was there and gone. "My apology is most sincere." He kissed her hand.

Thylaina stared at the floor between them. "I owe you one as well, my friend."

"What for? You did nothing to—"

"I lied." She raised her eyes to his. "There was *one* successful birth. However, we know not how she and the babe survived. We believed it was by the will of the gods."

Bramn regarded her for a moment. "No one gave her special treatment during her pregnancy?"

"N'ei. But that does not mean the same shall happen for me. There are n'ei other known half-human births."

"Known."

"Cease." She gave what she hoped was a warning look. "The mother was dear to my family, and she passed many years later. Her bastard struggled throughout his youth, and may still. The Elven Nation did not receive him with a loving embrace."

"Do you think we would cast aside your and Breydon's child?" Bramn sneered, shook his head. "We aren't elves, Thylaina. They're naught but hypocrites. Claiming they value life more than others, yet are quick to discard life because of their pretentious views. We would—"

"Enough!" Her cheeks burned, for his words were not without truth. One she had not seen until after leaving Etharell. But Alohrians were not the saviors Bramn liked to believe they were. "I know what my people are, but Alohrians are no different. They strike against brother, sister, and father. Your own mother cast you aside because of your love for Einasa. Do not dare raise your people above mine, for they are just as awful."

Anger brightened his deep blue eyes, but it dimmed as one of his handsome smiles formed. "I suppose both of our homes have places where there is such grand love that we sometimes miss the ugliness beyond. Yes. Alohrius has horrible people who do dreadful things. But know this, Thylaina... should you and

Breydon bring a child into this world, the people of Caerabis will love him or her greatly."

Thylaina threw her arms around his shoulders and squeezed. "I love you, Bramn."

"And I forgive you for lying."

Thylaina laughed.

Two more days moved at a snail's pace, dragging into the seventh month. Still no Breydon. During her time alone, Thylaina contemplated how to reach Master Eidryn. Whom could she possibly trust to deliver a message? Bramn had mentioned building a friendship with some elves in the Ormiana Xilys. Perhaps Thylaina could send a sealed message with him under the guise of a request for herbs known to grow in Etharell, and that only Master Eidryn would have. If these friends of Bramn's trusted him, they would not break the seal. However, if they were xilys doing their duty, they might. Thylaina had no other option. She had not the luxury of owning a blood falcon like the men in her family. Bramn would do this for her.

Thylaina sat at Breydon's desk and wrote a message to her former teacher. Each word carefully chosen to explain the request in a way that only a Vynist would understand. If a guard were to break the seal, they would read a plea for herbal supplies to help with typical ailments. Thylaina did not sign her name at the bottom, but what Master Eidryn had once called her when they were alone, and he spoke plainly about his beliefs of her power.

"*You are* Divine Favored. *I have no doubt. For I have never guided anyone who holds as much power as you. Thylaina, if you devote yourself to this path, you will surpass even your uncle, the king.*"

*Divine Favored* flowed from the quill. She smiled. *Vynia, You truly have blessed me, and I am grateful.*

Even if Bramn delivered this message as soon as possible, it could take weeks by the time Master Eidryn received it. So if Breydon disagreed, the supplies received would still come in useful.

She took the sealed message with her when she went to examine Einasa. Thankfully, the woman rested well, with Bramn's insistence. Afterwards, Thylaina pulled him aside and presented the tube.

He grinned. "I'm glad to assist. I leave for a post near Lake Wynland. There's a xilys camp not far from there."

"When?"

"Four days."

"Are there xilys there you trust?"

"Many."

Thylaina grabbed his hand. "Do not tell anyone about this."

"Of course not. This is between us." He looked over his shoulder, as if someone was there. Appearing satisfied that they remained alone, he asked, "Do you think Einasa will have the babe by then?"

She smiled. "Possibly, but not for certain."

"If she does, I might send another to the outpost in my stead."

"I understand. And this message can wait."

An uneasy expression passed over his face. "I'm not sure how I feel about fathering a child of the Burning Moon. I often heard they match that of the sun and moon from which they are born beneath. Am I foolish to fear such things?"

Thylaina dismissed his concern with a wave. "Stories, my dearest. Your daughter will be a wonderful reflection of her father and mother, just as is Alyanna."

Joy filling his eyes, he kissed her cheek. "You do more for us than you realize. We love you."


Thylaina wiped her face with a soft towel, then dried her hands. Supper's superb aroma of herb-buttered pheasant and roasted vegetables wafted throughout the house. After such a draining day, for her mind and body, she deserved a wonderful meal to end it. However, eating alone was not wonderful. Strange that after three years, Thylaina had still not grown accustomed to the many days and nights without her husband. Even stranger that she had not intended to marry a soldier for this very reason, suffering what Mother had suffered, yet there she was, missing her knight husband.

Just stepping from the hall leading to the master bedchamber and Breydon's cabinet, a servant maiden approached Thylaina. "M'lady, a knight awaits in the receiving room."

Anxious it was a messenger from Breydon's squad, Thylaina hurried to the front of the house. She passed the dining, garden, and solar room doors, as well as the servants' quarters afore reaching the library's double doors. Just beyond them, at the end of the hall, was the door to the receiving room where many friends and family gathered. Her heart thumped as she grasped the latch with a trembling hand. Swallowing her nervousness, she pushed it down and opened the door.

As she entered, the knight turned, his earthy eyes fixing on her. His gaze shone for the briefest moment, then pain sundered any happiness the man had once felt.

Thylaina froze. Blinked. It had been so long, she needed a moment to recognize the young man. Three years had hardened the softness of his face into sharp edges, seeming to have worn away the tenderness.

"Gavrel?" she whispered. "Or..." she stepped farther into the room, "should I say *Sir* Gavrel? I was overjoyed to hear of your swearing into the knighthood."

A hint of kindness showed as a smile smoothed the hard lines marring his former youthful face. Gavrel bowed his head. "My lady," he said, his voice deeper. "It is... a great pleasure to see you."

"Is that all you can do?" Thylaina scoffed, then hurried to embrace him. "I have missed you, my friend."

He stiffened, then slowly wrapped his arms around her, holding her tighter. "You've no inkling how much I have missed you."

She pulled her head back enough to look at his face, noting that even the dimple of his chin seemed to have deepened. Yet as he stared adoringly at her, she felt a tinge of annoyance. "Then why have you stayed away? Why no messages? I have written to you, but you never responded."

The pain returned, and he straightened, easing her hands from around his neck. Gavrel walked to the hearth and stood silently for several seconds. "I never understood," he mumbled. "I never would've hurt you, and would've done everything to protect you, yet you chose *him*. The man who harmed you in such horrific ways. Who tried to kill you."

Thylaina held her breath. "Gav—"

"Why?" He faced her. "You wrote to me, yet never mentioned your marriage to the bastard. I learned through other knights."

There was no point in getting angry about his pain. Her friend would only hear what he wanted to hear.

"I believed you understood," she said. "Breydon had been under Mikan's manipulation—under the effects of Divine Wrath. He never would have harmed me upon our first meeting."

"If he had killed you, nothing would've been done about it." A fierce scowl marred his face as he shook his head. "And he'd still be First Captain of Caerabis."

"Enough!" She crossed her arms and straightened. "I will not permit you to stand in my home and speak like this about my husband."

Chuffing, he looked toward his boots.

Silence permitted her time to consider his broken heart, and how to possibly help him understand. "Gavrel, you are dear to me." Thylaina stepped toward him. "I cannot tell you how happy and relieved I am to see you. To know you are safe. But please do not do this. Do not dig a ravine between us. I have lost too much in my life and do not wish to lose you."

He raised his head with a curious look in his eyes. No. It was hope. After a deep breath, he said, "Forgive me. I'm acting a fool. My intention was to announce my arrival, not upset you." Rubbing the back of his neck, he grimaced. "I-I know not what to say, Thylaina. I don't deserve your friendship."

She moved closer, placed her hands over his. "All is well."

"You forgive me?"

"Of course I do."

They stared at each other, his fingers curling to capture hers. After a swift kiss on her knuckles, he released her hand. "I must report to Marshal Momestid."

"Perhaps we shall speak again."

"I pray so." Gavrel bowed partially, then left.

Not the reunion she had hoped to have with him.

The next morning, Gavrel arrived with an armful of red sunflowers and another apology. Thylaina accepted both and invited him to join her in the garden room to break fast; a soft rainfall had started the day. Droplets splattered atop the ceiling panes and the outer glass walls, accompanying the meal with a relaxing song of nature. Shadows of streaks raced down Thylaina and Gavrel's faces while they ate and shared the events of the past three years. She imparted about her life as a healer in Caerabis, and he told her about his travels to Perlos, Karvorn, and other major cities in eastern Alohrius.

"When I heard about the attacks in the western region, I volunteered to bring a squad of soldiers." Gavrel dabbed the corner of his lips with a cloth. "I owe a great deal to Marshal Momestid. Besides, Caerabis is another home to me. And you're here."

Her cheeks warmed as she scooped berries smothered in a fruit glaze. "As are many wonderful people who need help."

"Certainly." Gavrel braced his arms on the table and leaned in her direction. "But I prefer to see you." His voice sounded nice. Pleasant.

"I…" She broke from his gaze and cleared her throat. "I am glad you are here, Sir Gavrel." Thylaina could not stop the smile nor the giggle that followed.

"Sir?" He nodded. "We're being formal, are we? Lady Colmstad." Her name came out too softly, as if it was difficult to speak. He turned his head and released a heavy breath. "I wish you would've told me."

But it did not matter. Nothing Gavrel might have said or done would have changed her mind. So, instead of responding, she signaled the servant to refill his teacup.

"What happens now?" Thylaina inquired. "Are you to await Breydon's return, or is Grim sending you out with the next squad?"

He shrugged. "I'm still waiting to learn."

"You'll go with me," Bramn said from the entrance, irritation heavy in his tone. "In three days."

Thylaina twisted in her seat to see him. "My dearest! Come join us."

A low growl sounded in Gavrel's throat, one Bramn likely caught with his keen hearing.

Bramn entered, his gaze locked on Gavrel. "Why are you here?"

"I'm breaking fast upon my lady's request."

A sardonic smile flashed and faded from Bramn's lips. He stepped closer, leaving a chair between them. "Not only are you alone with a wedded woman, but with the First Captain's wife. I ask again, why are you here?"

"Must I repeat myself?"

"Captain!" Bramn pounded his fist on the table; Gavrel jumped from his seat. "You address a superior, knight," Bramn said between his teeth.

Thylaina rose. "Men, please cease this. Bramn, I invited him to join me. I have not seen Sir Gavrel in years. He *is* my friend."

Bramn's sharp gaze turned on her. "Poor decision." He motioned to the door as he gave his attention to Gavrel. "Leave the premises."

Grimacing, Gavrel shook his head. "This is not your hou—"

"Get out!" Bramn's face darkened, his sandy hair appearing lighter.

Thylaina's heart beat hard, and her body trembled. "This is not necessary. I can manage my own home."

"Apparently, my lady, you cannot." Bramn did not look away from Gavrel. "I'll not order it again. Leave, or I'll make you leave."

Gavrel just... smiled. "Is this because I struck you those years back? You want to get even."

Thylaina never would have believed a person's face could turn redder than Bramn's already had, but it appeared he could burn through stone. He knocked the chair over and bent into a lunging position, and Gavrel readied.

"Stand down, Shapele!" Body tense, Thylaina grasped Bramn's wrist and slid between the men. "Gavrel, please go."

"Why do you let them control you?" he asked. "Bramn. Breydon. Grim... they all have controlled you. It never should've been this way."

She released Bramn's wrist, but remained between them. "Gavrel, you know not of what you speak."

He shook his head, disbelief overtaking his expression.

"This is the life I want," Thylaina said. "I chose to marry Breydon. I choose to be here. And I choose to be who I am. N'ei one controls me."

Bramn clenched his jaw, squinted. "He leaves now, or I drag him out."

"I'd like you to try... Captain."

Thylaina whirled around, yet did her best to keep Bramn back. "Gavrel, leave."

"As you wish, my lady." He bowed, then walked out.

A bellow erupting, Bramn kicked the downed chair, striking the glass wall and cracking it.

Thylaina jumped. "Gods, I hope your daughters' suitors are never subjected to this behavior from you."

He spun, pointing at her. "I'll never permit men like him near my daughters!"

"Why do you and Breydon despise Gavrel?" Thylaina lifted her teacup. It trembled against her lips, so she set it down after barely a sip.

"You ask *me* that?"

"There was obvious history between them, and neither of you explained anything."

Bramn rested his hands on his hips, leaned back on his leg. "Before you came to Caerabis, there was little trouble with Gavrel. He was just a soldier learning his place as a dubight. But shortly following your capture and punishment, he reported Breydon to the Three to have him removed from the knighthood." Bramn chuckled. "They weren't going to take Breydon from this city—not when they were already trying to control him. Gavrel had made a grave mistake."

"Obviously, he did not know."

"Why do you defend him?" Bramn combed his fingers through his hair. "Look, I came to escort you to my house. I hadn't expected to find him here. To be honest, I didn't even know he was in Caerabis."

"I shall get my satchel."

He grabbed her hand, halting her. "Thylaina, you should never be alone with another man. It doesn't look right. People will spread gossip throughout the city."

Things were so different between humans and elves. A married woman could entertain a male guest without suspicion from others. Perhaps elves took their marital vows more seriously than humans.

"You are here with me." Thylaina batted her eyelids as innocently as possible. "Alone."

He smirked. "It has been that way since you first arrived."

The charming bastard.

"Now," Bramn said, "as I mentioned a moment ago, I'll be leaving in three days. That means your message shall be in the hands of a trusted xilys in five." His smile widened.

The tension that had tightened every muscle in her body slowly eased. Soon, Master Eidryn should receive her request, and hopefully, he would return a positive response. "That is very good to know, my friend."

# Chapter Nineteen

Einasa remained pregnant, so Bramn kissed his favorite maidens farewell—including Thylaina—and led his squad westward to Etharell. After delivering the message there, he would then take the men northeast to Monsor, where reports of attacks had surfaced. Gavrel rode amongst the knights and soldiers, including the men he had brought to Caerabis. Thylaina could only manage a wave, for Bramn permitted no time for her to speak to Gavrel. She would have preferred a proper sending off, but humans had different notions of appropriate affection between friends. Perhaps she must still get used to their ways if she intended to continue living amongst them.

If only Breydon were home.

To prevent twisting her mind and emotions toward madness, Thylaina busied herself with the citizens of Caerabis. People always needed aid with something, whether a minor cut requiring stitches, a gash from practicing swordplay in the Pit in need of attention, or someone feeling ill. She was glad to help in any way possible. This also gave Thylaina the opportunity to expand on her ability and magic. In the past year, she had created two spells that helped mend bones. Of course, she whispered the incantations disguised as Elvish prayers and still dressed the wounds to hide her power. Although the people of Caerabis welcomed her aid, Thylaina still feared revealing the truth. The Three Marshals had spies, and to take her into their custody might endanger Uncle Yasontler and the Elven Nation. Maybe she cared about home more than she admitted.

When she had first begun tending to the citizens of Caerabis, Thylaina did not accept any form of compensation, but her funds had grown smaller. She dared not ask Breydon to supply coin toward replenishing stock from his salary, especially now that it seemed Haevaun Balaeus was cutting the roans sent to sustain the city and its forces. She certainly did not demand much from the people, for if Grim struggled to provide, then so would they. But she gathered enough supplies from the fields, and Breydon often collected wild plants and roots during his travels that Thylaina used in trading with merchants. She did well enough to care for Caerabis, and that was what mattered most.

Two days since Bramn's squad departed, and Breydon had still not returned. The Burning Sun beat upon Thylaina and her two gardeners while they gathered herbs from behind the mansion. Barely a breeze offered relief from the heat. Thylaina plucked the tiny green flowers from a row of xarflas, pausing upon the approach of dozens of horses quaking the earth. She handed the basket of flowers to one of the gardeners, her steps slow toward the corner of the mansion. Skirt lifted, she raced around the bend, bolting between the wall and the barracks and officers' stables. Several grooms ran from the latter, readying to perform their duty.

There he was, riding behind two knights. His red hair shone bright in the sun, as did his beard. Thylaina ignored the facial hair. Right now, her eyes locked on his; bright blue in the day's light. Breydon slowed his stallion to a halt, then dismounted. Just as several times in the past, Thylaina practically skipped into his arms. She laughed as he swung her in a gentle pendulum, his embrace growing tighter with each passing second.

"Laina," he whispered, his breath sweeping over her ear and into her hair. "I've missed you so bloody much."

Tears slid from beneath her closed eyelids. Words refused to come, so she breathed and held him for as long as he allowed, which was until they were the only ones standing in the stable yard. Men passed, but left their reunion in peace.

"Welcome home, my love," she finally said. Thylaina leaned her head back, scraped her fingers through the coarse hair on his face.

Breydon smiled crookedly, touched his nose to hers. "I could use a shave."

"S'yai. And we have much to discuss."

His gaze held hers. "Discussions are not what I'm thinking. I just want to hold you and know this is no dream. I'm home... with you." At last, his lips found hers, and a long, needy kiss ensued.

Sweet Lessindra, she loved this man!


The bath had been silent. A few moans of gratification from her touch accompanied the shave, and he chuckled at her teasing. But once Breydon was clean, they rested in the tub, his head upon her shoulder, his back against her breasts. It all felt perfect, especially now that his face was free of the beard. Thylaina did not mind it too much, but she preferred him without the coarse hairs hiding his handsome face. Or scratching her inner thighs, which was not always unpleasant.

He shifted his hips slightly. Then again.

Thylaina combed his hair with her fingers. "Are you well, love?"

"No." He sat up. "I haven't had a proper shite in four days."

"I would think the bath should help."

"Maybe it is." He stepped carefully out of the tub and walked to the garderobe, leaving the door open a few inches.

Thylaina finished bathing, then exited the now lukewarm water. Funny how it seemed to have cooled significantly in his absence.

"You said there was much to discuss," he called from the other side of the door.

This was not the time to talk about the message she had sent to Master Eidryn. "Not while you tend to that business."

"Fine." He grunted. "Gods."

While water droplets grew colder on her skin, she lit the sage outside the privy door. "Did you not eat well during your travel?"

"My foragers did their best, love. Although I had questioned some roots and berries they presented six days past, they had assured all was safe."

"The fruit may have been safe for eating, but still cause problems."

"I'm not sitting here all bloody night." A moment later, the door swung open, and he stomped to the water basin to wash his hands.

Thylaina finished drying her body, then focused on her hair. "I shall prepare a knee holly tea for you."

A heavy sigh sounded from him. "Very well." He wiped his hands on the towel and faced her.

Which god was she to praise while she gazed upon her husband's naked body? At that moment, Thylaina would give all glory to Fynthiar for having created someone so magnificent. Bryric for guiding her to Caerabis. Vynia for helping her save Breydon's life. And Lessindra for enriching their love. So praises to Them All.

A few seconds passed. "I'm exhausted," he said.

"I have n'ei doubt, my love."

The bath did exactly as was intended. Now he would have a fine night's rest afore reporting to Grim in the morning.

"Come to bed." Breydon offered his hand.

Thylaina dropped the towel to the floor and slid her hand into his. "Of course."

He pulled her close, crushing her body to his, and kissed her hard. Sleep fleeted from her mind, and apparently his as well.

After sharing herself with him, enjoying her husband as part of her once again, Breydon retreated to the privy for another attempt, but to no avail. So Thylaina threw on her robe, set a kettle of water over the fire in the bedchamber hearth, then went to the apothecary room to concoct a remedy for his ailment. However, by the time she returned to make the tea, he was asleep.

He stared at her, the cup of coffee raised to his chin. Breydon lowered it, nearly cracking the plate beneath. "You what?"

Thylaina ignored the irritation in his voice and expression. Surely a mistake on his part. Perhaps breaking fast in the garden instead of the garden room would have been ideal; he might have been more inclined to speak quieter. Yet, that had never seemed to deter Breydon in the past. The man often spoke his mind.

"Master Eidryn should receive the message within the fortnight, hopefully, at the latest."

"You sent a squadron of humans to deliver a message?"

"I sent Bramn." She smiled. "And only to a camp on the edge of Ormiana. He knows exactly whom to pass the request."

"I thought we decided." Although the words came out rough, there was a hint of hope in his tone... and fear. "I can't lose you, Laina." Breydon slid from the chair to kneel and take her hand. "Losing you will ruin me."

Her heart swelling with deep love for him, she caressed his smooth cheek. "I truly believe that with my and Master Eidryn's skills combined, we can succeed."

"And if you don't?"

Thylaina stared into Breydon's eyes. Would Vynia let Her Favored pass over the choice to have a child? No. The goddess would no doubt give guidance. Smiling wider, Thylaina said, "We have the Earthen Goddess on our side, my love. With Her help, we cannot fail."

He sat back on his heels, his hands free of hers. "As much as I want this, it terrifies me."

She leaned forward, clutched the sides of his head. "Trust in Vynia. Trust in Master Eidryn and me. We can bring forth a life created by our love."

He gazed at the cracked window, tracing the lines. After a long, silent moment, he nodded. "I shall trust in all of you." Breydon looked at her, tears welling in his eyes. "But if I lose you—"

Thylaina lowered to the floor and kissed him. The moment their lips parted, she said, "You will never lose me. My heart, my soul, are forever yours."

Breydon pulled her closer and kissed her deeper.

To Thylaina's surprise, Breydon allowed her to join him and Arhgrim in the war room beneath the library. So delicate was the information he had gathered from the east, he had to report it in such secrecy. Both men sat in silence after Breydon finished, Grim appearing concerned. Since Telsia's birth, more lines of worry had formed on his aging face, and not only because of having another child. It was moments like this when Thylaina appreciated the responsibilities resting on Grim's shoulders instead of Breydon's. Yet her husband refused to let his commander bear the weight all alone.

Grim's eyes flitted toward the drink table, where a variety of fruzae decanters glinted in the flickering light. The strong, fruity liquor was favored amongst human men, the choice of flavors aplenty on the market.

Thylaina poured two glasses of apple-cinnamon, one of the marshal's favorites. The men nodded in thanks, then sipped the liquor. She treated the drink like caldin broul from home: untouchable. Just the smell of it made her stomach burn. Let the men have their potent brews. Thylaina would enjoy the wine.

Grim cleared his throat as he set the glass amid the markers and maps on the table. "So their threats have weakened the Council."

"With the exception of Lord Vantos, several of the members have gone into hiding." Breydon shook his head. "The others refuse to let the Three frighten them, and Vantos has the Three's favor."

"And the orders?"

Breydon glanced at Thylaina. "Silently forming."

Straightening, she stared at him. Of what orders did he speak?

"The Three have already pinned their men with engraved badges." Breydon scoffed. "Animals."

Grim did not appear amused, only more concerned. "And...?" He looked at Thylaina, drew in a deep breath, then turned back to Breydon. "And *our* men?"

"They're right where they need to be."

"We've not the numbers!" Grim snatched the cup, spilling fruzae on the table. "How can we—?"

"We will grow." Breydon somehow remained calm, which eased Grim's worry. "Trust me, my friend. More will see the truth and join us."

Thylaina stood. "I wish you would tell me what is happening instead of speaking as if I understand." The men gave her a sidelong look. "You obviously brought me here for a reason."

Grim nodded. "For your safety, you must know what's happening." The care in his voice did not reflect the fear in his eyes.

"What is it?" Thylaina looked from one man to the other, then stepped toward Breydon. "Love, tell me."

Her husband took her hands and moved closer. "Soon, those who willingly remain stationed in Caerabis—and Warstchia—shall no longer be considered members of the knighthood." Pain came with those words. The Alohrian knighthood meant a great deal to Breydon. He, like many others, vowed their lives to serve, and now he knew not what was to become of him. He smiled. "We'll not turn our backs on Valorius, nor those we swore to protect."

And she was at this meeting because she was the Elf King's niece. "They will claim you all—knights and citizens—are traitors because of me."

"Grim and I are their targets." Breydon kissed her hands as if to assure all was well. "But no one here will believe their lies."

It did not mean Caerabis was safe while she remained.

"I see it in your eyes, Laina. But there's naught to fear at this time."

Grim relaxed in his seat. "No harm will come to you nor to our people. We'll not allow it."

Their tones, their expressions, gave solid assurance. But could they uphold such a promise?

Looking at her husband, the discussion while they broke fast came to mind. *Can I uphold my promise? Will I survive birthing a child for us?*

Six days since Bramn left, now the day of rest. Although farmers and gardeners saw no such respite, they received a grand reward at the end of the day, feasting on a long-prepared meal and sweet delights. But on this day, at the Jalfiasin home, the gardens remained empty of workers; the only action seen outside was the occasional servant running from the house with a bucket to receive water from the nearby well. Shouts and crying sounded from within. Thylaina and Katjina hurried to the door, nearly colliding with a bucket-bearing servant. A shame Bramn would not be present for the birth of his second daughter, but what elation he would have upon his return.

Alyanna whimpered in the corridor outside her mother's bedchamber.

Thylaina knelt afore the little girl. "My darling, what troubles you?"

"Mother hurts." The girl sobbed.

Thylaina pulled Alyanna into her arms. "Oh, sweet child. It is a good pain. Such that will bring your little sister into this world to be at your side."

Alyanna sniffled, looked at her with wide eyes. "Sister?"

"S'yai. I promise. But you must be a strong helper for your mother."

"H-how?"

"Please go with Katjina and gather some soft cloths and heat some water. Katjina knows exactly how warm I like it."

The handmaiden gave the herb satchel to Thylaina, then smiled as she offered her hand to the child. "I'd certainly love your help, m'lady."

Alyanna's thin brows dipped as she stared at Katjina's hand. Nodding, she said, "I'll do it."

Such a brave girl. Katjina led her to the scullery, and Thylaina entered the bedchamber.

Thankfully, she quickly brought order to the room. Thylaina removed five servants—she knew not why they were there—and calmed Einasa with little effort. The whispered chants helped, of course. Within two hours, Aella arrived, healthy and beautiful. Einasa's condition afterward promised a strong recovery. What a relief. Thylaina should not have to worry, but her patient's lack of listening to her instructions often left her with a touch of fear.

Alyanna sat gleefully on the bed, giggling at her little sister. "She's pretty."

"She looks just like you." Einasa grinned. "What will Bramn say when he learns he's another daughter? The poor man."

Thylaina withheld the laugh wishing to burst forth. A deep breath eased out as she gathered herself. "I assure you, he shall be absolutely delighted."

Einasa nodded. "I know." Then she shook her head slightly. "I just... I know he'd love a son."

"He loves you and what the two of you create together." Thylaina touched Einasa's forehead. Perfect temperature. "How do you feel now?"

"A bit peckish."

"A meal should be here soon." Thylaina brushed a damp lock of Einasa's hair aside. "Then you must rest. For you and the babe."

Einasa snatched her hand. "Thank you. For everything you've done." Tears welled in her eyes. "Truly."

A lump caught in Thylaina's throat. "I love you all."

She kissed Einasa's cheek, the top of Aella's soft head, then Alyanna's forehead. And by the gods, did Thylaina's heart thump harder as she gazed at the three ladies with deep adoration and... ache. She would one day lose them. Every single human who meant so much to her would perish.

Blinking tears away while grabbing her satchel, she laughed softly. "I shall return in the night, and then on the morrow."

Einasa sighed. "You needn't worry yourself. I've fine servants who—"

"I do not question their care, my friend." Thylaina headed for the door, opened it. "It is for my assurance that all remains well with you and Lady Aella. I would never forgive myself if something should change."

"Very well."

Thylaina admired the three once again afore leaving. On her way home, with Katjina chattering nonstop about the baby's likeness to her handsome father, Thylaina prayed Master Eidryn would receive her message very soon, and swiftly reply.

Breydon's fingertips glided over the curve of her shoulder, down to her elbow. "Are you sure you—?"

"Without a doubt." She snuggled closer, needing the tiniest of space between them gone.

The lovemaking, although always satisfying, seemed far more intense than usual. Perhaps the arrival of Bramn's child stirred something within Breydon. Desire for one of his own. Good.

"We shall succeed." She rested her chin on his chest and looked at his face. The orange from the hearth's glow aided her seeing him clearly. Turning her head, she slid her cheek down, then up his nipple. "Trust me, please."

He cupped her face, then tilted her head until their eyes met. "I trust you more than anyone."

She smiled. "Love, will you tell me about the orders? What are they and who made them?"

Breydon slid his hand to her neck, then breast, holding it while he spoke. "I spoke not about commands, my love. The Three intend to divide the knights into groups."

"Ranks?"

"No." He licked his lips, his brows dropping. "Not at first, at least. But I think that will change. Especially with Marshal Thornsalin. He and his son won't settle for anything but precision. The best. They'll expect that from anyone they bring into *their* order."

They sounded a lot like Neldrid.

"Earlier today you mentioned something about animals," she pressed.

Breydon rolled onto his back, released a heavy sigh. "They're designating the orders by animals. Each headed by the Three. More orders formed, but none as strong as the Three's."

"How do you know who belongs to which?"

"An insignia on a brooch."

"What about Grim?"

Breydon scoffed. "He'll not do any bloody animal."

"So he *will* create an order?"

He looked at her, a smile tugging at the corner of his lips. "We did a year past, my love."

Was it rage or surprise that heated the center of her chest? Not knowing how to react to Breydon hiding this, Thylaina remained still and waited.

"It wasn't distrust that kept me silent, darling." His thumb grazed her chin. "It's fear of others overhearing. Now it doesn't matter."

She lifted her head and asked in Elvish, "You believe we have spies in our home?"

"I believe it is possible," he replied in kind.

"I see." Relaxing again, she spread her fingers over his stomach, touching the trail of soft hair below his bellybutton. "What order did you and Grim create?"

"Order of the Hammer." Breydon chuckled. "For we will crush them."

Thylaina lifted the full pitcher of olesa oil and prayed while she carefully poured into each vial lined atop the table. She had finally gained some sleep since Aella's birth three days past—mother and babe were doing superbly—and had plenty of work to do in the apothecary. The blended aromas of the many herbs, oils, roots, and plants offered a sense of peace she revered. It was a place where Thylaina connected most with Vynia, for prayers often passed her lips, blessing the poultices, wraps, oils, healing spheres, teas, and all other remedies she prepared. The Earthen Goddess' presence bloomed within the room, pulsating with Her power. It flowed through Thylaina, giving grace after grace. Sometimes, it nearly brought tears to feel Her Favor envelope her.

The prayers mingled with magic, and grew slightly louder, coming out as a song. If others overheard, they should believe Thylaina sang in her language. Nothing more. She corked the vials, then slid them into the wool-pocketed bag Katjina had sewn for her. It held up to eighteen vials, but Thylaina was short of four bottles of filling it. No matter. Some leaves did not release the same amount as others during the distillation process.

All the vials put away, she turned to the eleven xarflas plants hanging from an herb wheel. They had reached the perfect dryness to remove the leaves from the stems, and the stems from the roots. Each part of the plant had exceptional healing properties; most healers only knew about the flowers and leaves. Thylaina had learned about the roots' qualities only recently, making a balm to numb injuries prior to stitching.

She had barely started when thudding shook the door. Horses neared. Thylaina smiled. That must mean Bramn had returned. Wonderful! As much as she wished to witness him seeing Aella for the first time, that moment was for his family alone. So she sighed happily and resumed with the xarflas. The roots now in a bowl, she snapped leaves from the stems, placing the wide, deep-green leaves atop each other.

The door slammed open, and she yelped, dropping the stem.

Breydon panted. Swallowed. He stormed into the room, grabbed the healing satchel and her arm. "Come. Now!"

"You are hurting me!"

"Hurry!" He dragged her toward the door, obviously not caring he had knocked bottles and bowls off the tables.

Thylaina fought his hold, but trying to twist her arm free caused more pain. "Breydon, stop!"

He continued through the door, down the short hallway to the scullery, then out the back entrance. His desperation obvious, Thylaina increased her pace to keep up and avoid losing her footing.

"Love, please ease your grip."

Breydon barely glanced at her as they bounded through the tall bushes standing between their home and the Momestid's.

Viya stood at the mansion's scullery door, keeping it wide open. Tears fell from her reddened eyes.

Worry immediately jumped Thylaina's heart into a rapid beating. She lifted her skirt and nearly stumbled on Breydon's heels. "Did something happen to one of the girls?"

Breydon sniffed, swallowed, and his chin quivered, but no words came forth.

*Vynia, grant me strength.* Thylaina tried to calm her breathing as he rushed her down the corridor. Being in control meant proper care for her patient, and she could not fail the Momestid girls.

Breydon did not lead her up the stairs to the master bedchambers, but continued to the corridor at the eastern end of the large entry room. A scattering of knights stood with their heads down, a low hum of murmurs sounding from them. One raised his damp gaze to Thylaina; soaked earthy brown surrounded by bloodshot red. Gavrel swiped his hand over his face and turned away.

Icy chills raced down Thylaina's arms and legs, her limbs suddenly stiff.

Two men stood outside the door at the end of the hall, near the exit to the officers' stables. One of them looked from Thylaina and Breydon to inside the room. "She's here, sir."

"Why?" Arhgrim asked, his voice soft.

Dread gathered in her chest, preparing her for a task she could not achieve. *No. Do not doubt yourself.*

Breydon hauled her to the bench where Bramn lay. He stared at her expectantly. "Help him."

Thylaina's knees threatened to buckle as she looked at her dear friend.

A thin film of creamy white clouded Bramn's once deep-blue irises, and flies buzzed around his nostrils, open mouth, and a gaping wound nearly severing his neck. The discolored flesh around the fatal injury had already begun rotting, and splotches of red appeared in other areas of skin exposed from someone's attempt to tear his shirt.

"Laina, please." Breydon released her arm. "Heal him."

The sheet beneath Bramn showed smudges of dried blood. There was no reason to verify what she already knew, but Thylaina curled her fingers around Bramn's hand and gently pulled. Too cold. Too stiff. "I... I cannot," she whispered.

Breydon scowled, looked from Bramn to her. "You've done it before."

"N'ei." She turned to him. "Love I have never—"

"Me!" His face darkened. "You saved me!"

"Breydon." Grim neared him. "He's gone."

"No!" Breydon gestured to Thylaina. "She can do it. She's done it before!" He looked at her again. "Bring him back."

Tears blurred her vision. "There is naught I can do. Bramn has been gone for too long. You—"

"Liar!"

"I was with you the moment you breathed your last." She reached for her husband. "Your body and blood were still warm. Bramn has been dead for more than a day."

Breydon stepped away from her. He clenched his jaw and lowered his eyes to his closest friend. "He can't be gone." Breydon's gaze returned to Thylaina and Grim. "Bramn can't be gone!"

"I'm sorry." Grim moved closer. "As much as I loved him as a brother, we can't ignore others were lost in that—"

"Don't you dare!" Breydon's hands formed into fists.

*Vynia, Lessindra, please help me.* Thylaina slid between them, glided her hands down his arms to his curled fingers. She spoke in Elvish in hopes the melody of her language might soothe him. "Darling, you know we all love Bramn. His loss hurts us. Let not your anger come onto us. We are here for you."

He closed his eyes, yet his breath still came hard. "What hurts is that you won't even try," he said through his teeth. Breydon jerked away, shot a glare at her and Grim, then stomped from the room.

Thylaina lowered her shoulders, let her taut muscles loosen. Without looking in Bramn's direction, she whispered in her language, "Farewell, my dearest." Then the realization of whom and what she had just lost struck her. Throat constricting, she bent forward and sobbed into her hands.

Grim's gentle arms pulled her close, and he rocked slightly. "We'll get past this."

They eventually would one day, but the place within her heart that Bramn had quickly filled would always be there, void of his true presence. Never would she hear his drawl again, see his charming smile, nor watch him be a wonderful father to his beautiful daughters.

And Breydon... What would this do to him?

# Chapter Twenty

**B**reydon had not been home for three days. Unable to sleep in his absence, Thylaina busied herself in the apothecary, paced in the family room, and wept in the garden room; the streaks on her cheeks adding to those from the glass ceiling and walls. Grief and worry overwhelmed every passing moment. She spent time with Arhgrim and Tesesra, needing family nearby. Nadiera, despite her grief, did not wish to be with anyone, and Telsia clung to her mother.

Grim revealed to Thylaina that the Southern Brigands had ambushed Bramn's company; Gavrel had slaughtered the rogue knight who murdered their dear friend. A bloody Alohrian knight who turned on his oath had killed Bramn. She hoped Gavrel caused that bastard immense pain.

This morning, she and Katjina gathered bread, fruit, and cheese to take to the Jalfiasin home. The house servant led them to the master bedchamber, her steps slow. Breydon stood next to Einasa's bed, fury immediately blazing within his gaze upon Thylaina's entry.

Her heart soaring to see him safe, she stepped toward him. "Breydon, it is a great relief to see—"

He rounded the bed and went straight for the door. "I shall find you later, Einasa." And he was gone.

Thylaina stared at the closed door, the painted swirls blurring behind her tears.

"I'll take that, m'lady." Katjina took the basket of bread and cheese. "Come sit."

Thylaina did not resist her handmaiden's guidance, and sat in the chair beside Einasa's bed. "Why does he hate me?" she whispered.

"No, my friend." Einasa swung her legs over the side and leaned forward, her arm across Thylaina's shoulders and her cheek atop Thylaina's head. "He doesn't hate you. Gods no." She kissed Thylaina's hair. "Breydon could never hate you. He just doesn't know how to accept Bramn's death." Her voice cracked with those last two words.

How selfish. Thylaina sat there receiving comfort from Einasa over Breydon's treatment, while their friend suffered losing her husband, lover, and father of her children. Bramn was everything to her, and yet she held herself together at that moment for Thylaina... possibly Breydon earlier. How many others behaved so selfishly in Einasa's presence?

Thylaina shook her head. "Forgive me." Her lips quivered as the wave of grief engulfed her heart. She stood and pulled Einasa close and wept with her. "I am terribly sorry. I-I could do nothing."

Einasa sniffled as she pulled back enough to look at her. "You've nothing to apologize for." The tears continued like raindrops along a glass pane. "I blame only those bloody brigands. It's a shame Breydon feels the blame goes elsewhere."

"Such as myself."

"No." Einasa shook her head. "He claims a knight had a hand in this."

Confused, Thylaina lowered her brows, for they already knew that truth. "S'yai. A traitor with the brigands."

Einasa shook her head again, although slower this time. "That's not what he says."

By Chaos' balls, what was Breydon thinking?

"He believes someone in Bramn's squad murdered him?" Thylaina asked.

Einasa sat on the bed, her shoulders slumped. This was a weight of worry she did not need.

"Never you mind." Thylaina dismissed the conversation with a flick of her wrist. "There are other matters to tend to. Tonight is meant to be a night of blessings."

Einasa bit the corner of her lip. "I know it's supposed to be, but how am I to watch my husband burn?"

Thylaina shuddered. "I truly wish they honored death differently, but this is the Alohrian custom."

"I know." Her friend drew in a deep breath, released it. "Yet I hate it."

"As do I." Thylaina sat beside her and took her hand. "I wish they would return him to Vynia and bring forth new life. Whether in a garden, amid the plains, beneath the roots of a grand tree, any place where he will enrich the earth and live."

"Oh! I should love that. For Bramn to live in a mass of plants, be it wildflowers or those I planted, or even a tree. How beautiful." Einasa's eyes watered. "I wish I could make that happen, but they would never permit it, for he was a knight."

Maybe Thylaina could convince Arhgrim and Breydon. If Breydon would speak with her.

It should not have been a surprise to find her husband with Grim, especially with Bramn's funeral hour drawing closer. The convenience made it even better. Thylaina closed Grim's office door and leaned against it. Breydon would not escape so easily.

He gave her a sidelong glance, then sighed. "We've matters to discuss that don't include you."

Grim regarded his friend in disbelief, then shook his head.

"I have something to discuss that involves both of you," Thylaina said. "And you will go n'ei where, Breydon."

Keeping his head down, he clenched his jaw.

"How can we be of service?" Grim asked.

"Einasa does not wish to set her husband afire."

Now Breydon looked at her, the anger still present. "That's no business of yours."

Although Thylaina understood his reaction, she scowled. "She already told you," she said matter-of-factly.

He stepped in her direction. "Lady Einasa is an Alohrian and knows our tradi—"

"Stop talking about her as if she is not our friend!" Thylaina's face burned, her breath trembled. "Bramn is *her* husband, and she *does not* wish to have him burnt upon a pyre."

The smirk lifting his lips sent a ripple of disgust through her. Breydon had never been so disrespectful toward her or anyone he cared about. "He was a knight first."

"Enough." Grim's face was a mix of sorrow and disappointment. "What does she want, Thylaina?"

Standing taller, she turned from her husband to her friend. "Einasa expressed she does not want to follow the knighthood traditions, but have her husband buried instead."

Breydon scoffed. "No doubt influenced by you."

Thylaina ignored him and continued. "Does she not get that choice?"

"No," her husband said.

Grim sat on the corner of his desk and folded his arms. "We've prepared everything as it is," he mumbled. "But... I can't imagine how she must feel, nor what she would feel to watch us proceed with something she doesn't desire to witness."

Breydon turned to him, his hands rising upward. "What?"

"I can't do it to her." Grim stood and met Thylaina's gaze. "We'll accommodate Einasa's desires. Find where she would like him buried, and it shall be done."

Thylaina threw herself into his arms and kissed his cheek. "Thank you."

"You can't be serious!" Breydon swung his arm out. "This is our tradition!"

"Why?" Grim shrugged faintly.

"Because we raise ourselves to Valorius."

Thylaina frowned. It made no sense, and Grim appeared to feel the same.

He rested his hand on Breydon's shoulder. "If our souls are already at the Great Feast, then why must we burn our bodies to rise to Him? It's nonsense. Someone just didn't want the duty of digging massive amounts of graves during the War of the Demigods."

It was a somber thought, considering the number of mortals slaughtered when Etharell stood beside Alohrius, until the elves had to withdraw to protect themselves. The humans of Warstchia faced Chaos' wrath and Grestin's carnage. Thylaina had heard so much blood drenched the earth, not even an elf could walk through the city without leaving a trace of their passing.

Breydon's glare darted to Thylaina afore he spun and stomped to the balcony. He had nothing more to say.

Grim took her hand with tenderness. "What are Einasa's wishes?"

"I-I do not know the exact details, but it is a garden or a tree."

"I imagine a tree." A slow smile formed as he nodded. "Did you know that is how the Yeltaran knights honor their fallen? With a tree."

"I did not."

His smile widened. "Province Woods is their cemetery. Every tree is a grave marker for a knight, whether now or in the future. When knighted, they choose their tree."

This sent a jolt of joy through her. There might be hope for the Alohrians if the Yeltarans, who also worshiped Valorius, had enough sense not to burn their dead.

Breydon looked their way, but said nothing.

Thylaina smiled at Grim. "Thank you. I shall inform Einasa so she can decide as quickly as possible." She glanced at her husband. "Come with me."

"I..." He released a heavy breath. "I have much to do."

Emptiness. Aching. Those two feelings quickly made a home within her. "Very well," she managed. "I hope you will come home tonight. I miss you terribly."

His head tilted back as he continued staring outside.

Thylaina kissed Grim's cheek, then left for Einasa's home.

Dusk set in, and the community gathered just outside the city, fifty yards beyond the Pit and the city garden, and buried Bramn. His Uncle Haltrin appeared pleased to speak prayers over a mound than a flaming pyre. At his side, the other priests showed mixed reactions, just as did the knights. None of that mattered to Thylaina while she and Breydon offered comfort to Einasa and Alyanna as they said their final farewells to Bramn. Tesesra held Aella, the week-old newborn sound asleep.

Silence fell amongst them, torches passed throughout the crowd, and heads turned to Breydon. While rocking Alyanna, he led the Prayer of the Fallen. "May his steps echo within the Great Hall, a seat prepared for him."

"Praise to Valorius," hundreds of voices recited; men and women donning the armor of knight or soldier.

"May he raise a cup with those who arrived before him. We give thanks to You," Breydon said, speaking louder, clearer.

"Glory to the Great Knight."

"May they pray for those who remain behind. We spread Your Glory."

"Praise to the Most Honorable Knight."

"Valorius, Great Knight," Breydon continued, with Grim joining, "welcome the Fallen at Your table. Grant them peace and eternal joy in Your Presence."

Then everyone, the wives, laborers, and many children included, spoke together with the knights and soldiers, "Praise Valorius, always."

To hear so many speak as one in honor of Bramn shook Thylaina to her core. Most voices were strong, some trembled, others broke, but it showed how much the words meant to the Alohrians.

Thylaina blinked new tears free, raised her gaze, and met Gavrel's. He wiped his arm over his eyes, leaving the skin around them red and barely dry, then looked down with shame. Did he take the blame? Foolish men and their egos.

"I was thinking about a Hammer Oak," Einasa's soft voice cut into Thylaina's thoughts.

"A grand tree," Breydon said gruffly. "Strong. Reliable."

Thylaina nodded, letting her sorrow free in a soft, weepy breath. "It is perfect."

Breydon gathered six knights and four laborers to accompany him to Ormiana Forest in search of a young Hammer Oak tree. They threw their tools into the back of a wagon, climbed onto their horses, and rode westward. He had offered no farewell kiss, nor even a hug. Just a nod.

It could be another week afore Breydon's return, for cutting down a young Hammer Oak could take more than a day's labor. There existed no stronger tree on all of Yeuroth. Many believed magic wove within it as well, for it was cold beneath its shadow, no matter how hot the day. Thylaina learned many Alohrian farmers had transplanted Hammer Oaks from Ormiana Forest, setting them beside their larders to keep the contents cool through the warmer months. It was brilliant since the trees survived the journey from forest to farms, showing they could live in different soil conditions. The Hammer Oak was truly remarkable. One befitting the representation of Bramn Jalfiasin.

Six days of loneliness devoured Thylaina. Would life with Breydon ever return to normal? She desperately wanted her husband back.

Sitting at his desk, she stared at the letter to Neldrid. Foolish, really. It must have been Bramn's death. Thoughts of Neldrid perishing haunted her, as did nightmares of losing Breydon. Writing about what she felt about their relationship seemed to help her release anger, pain, and worry. Her brother would never see this letter, but to have finally let everything out brought a sense of calm. Now, it would burn.

"M'lady," Katjina said, stirring Thylaina from her thoughts. The poor handmaiden had spoken so little since Bramn's death that her voice had softened to just above a whisper. "Sir Gavrel is in the gathering room."

Thylaina set the quill into the ink bottle. "I was not expecting him."

"He said as much, but insisted he must speak with you."

"Very well." The parchment curled into itself as Thylaina rose and rounded the desk.

Gavrel must have been called to ride out, for he wore plate armor and had his sword in the scabbard. He bowed his head at her approach. "My lady."

"Gavrel, are you returning to the plains?"

He drew in a deep breath, released it. "I'm…" Gavrel swallowed, looked down. "Forgive me, Thylaina. I tried to help him, but there were too many."

She hurried to embrace him. Stroking his hair as he wept, she hummed softly until he calmed. "It is not your fault, my friend."

Gavrel leaned his head back. "He believes so!" Ire brightened his tear-filled eyes. "Your husband has done nothing but spread rumors about me. He's trying to ruin me! Even after my trial, he still tells others I killed Captain Jalfiasin."

Pulling away from him, Thylaina frowned. "Trial? When?"

"It started two days following the captain's…" After several blinks to push tears back, he tugged the hair of his nape. "Despite most of the knights who witnessed the attack have confirmed my innocence, Captain Colmstad still deemed me guilty."

"What do you mean?"

He rested his hands on his hips and sneered. "The captain hoped the knights who'd been there would speak against me, but his plan to build a false account failed. Despite them telling the truth, and the Marshal's verdict of my innocence, Captain Colmstad won't relent."

Perhaps Breydon needed to blame someone, and Gavrel was the perfect target.

"Gods, he's despised me since your arrival." Lowering his arms, Gavrel sighed heavily. "His jealousy consumes him."

But was Breydon jealous? Thylaina had proclaimed her love enough for him to know her heart and soul belonged to him. Bramn's death likely muddled her husband's mind.

"I have explained your friendship is dear to me," Thylaina said. "I am sorry he—"

"The knights here listen to him—not me! They're believing his lies! And I can't endure the threats against my person any longer."

"N'ei." She pressed her fingers to her lips, then grabbed his hand. "They wish to hurt you?"

"Everyone treats me like I'm a traitor and murderer." He lowered his head, squeezed her hand gently. "Captain Colmstad's twisted the minds of the other knights, and they're plotting my death for revenge over something I'd no part in."

Breydon inciting such violence was wrong.

"They are fools! You are the one who killed Bramn's murderer."

"They'll not hear me over your husband." A mix of sorrow and frustration overtook his visage, and he dropped his voice when he continued. "I've already spoken with Marshal Momestid. I ride to Warstchia now."

Why must she lose so much? It just never ended, losing one friend after another.

"You have only just returned."

"I just wished to say farewell." Gavrel kissed her hand.

Tears instantly filled her eyes. "I do not want you to—"

He grasped her arms and kissed her cheek.

Thylaina retreated. Heat flushed her face, and her heart thundered as she straightened her bodice, dress sleeves, then stretched her shoulders back. The room had warmed. "I-I..." She met his longing gaze, praying the following words would discourage his desire. "It is a shame you must leave, Gavrel, but as you say, perhaps it is best. I shall miss you. Ride safely."

Amid the growing heat—discomfort, bitterness, and hurt—he nodded toward the floor. "And I shall miss you," he mumbled. He bowed, then spun for the door. "Farewell, my lady."

Once alone, Thylaina sat on the sofa and stared at the cold hearth. The ghost of Gavrel's grip remained, as did his lips on her skin. She rubbed her hands over her arms, then her cheek. Surely, it was simply a farewell. An elf would have done the same. But he had made his feelings for her clear, so she needed to ensure their relationship remained right where it stood. Thylaina wanted nothing more than Gavrel's friendship, and wished he could accept that. Perhaps his emotions were wrought with all that had happened, and Breydon's condemnation.

*Breydon.* She rubbed her face to ease the taut muscles. *He must never learn about this. Ever.*

"M'lady—"

Thylaina stood and whirled toward the door. "What?" she snapped.

Katjina clutched a wooden tube to her chest. "Forgive me. I hadn't meant to startle you."

Shaking her head, Thylaina approached her handmaiden and friend. "The apology is mine to give. I had not heard you enter. What have you there?"

"A rider from the Ormiana border delivered this."

Thylaina held her breath. Etched into the tube were intricate swirls and flowers of Elvish make. *Master Eidryn.*

"Thank you, Katjina. I shall read this in the cabinet."

Katjina handed the tube to her, then curtsied and exited the room.

Thylaina hurried to Breydon's cabinet, closing the door quietly behind her. She sat at the desk and shoved everything on top to the side. The tube nearly slipped from her quaking hands as she admired the cylinder, a piece of home. She unscrewed the end and tipped the parchment out, then examined it to ensure no one had tampered with the seal, which remained intact. A soft snap released the parchment. Staring at the curled letter revealed nothing, but her nerves stilled her hand. What if Master Eidryn refused to help? *Then I suppose Breydon and I shall not have a child.* Brows low, she opened the message.

> *Divine Favored,*
> *I have received your request for the rare herbs. There is one I cannot fulfill with ease, and certainly cannot just send when even one of my best pupils calls upon me.*

Her heart sank. However, there was more from her former master.

> *Therefore, I will bring the herbs myself. I shall examine the patients, learn of their ailments, and determine if the herbs remain in your care. It is not out of a lack of faith in your works, Favored, but these herbs are of great value. I must judge their use worthy.*

*Expect my arrival by the thirteenth day of the Hunter's Moon.*
*Master Eidryn*

Thylaina groaned. Once he learned she had married a human, Master Eidryn would certainly deny her request for the fertility potion. She dared not tell Breydon yet, for his heart had been stung enough.

# Chapter Twenty-One

Two days of stillness infected the city. No joy, songs, or laughter rose into the air. Even the taverns were quieter than usual. No one celebrated a damn thing while the city remained in mourning. A few of the widows had asked Thylaina if she could provide something to help them sleep. It was not sleep they wished for, but to lose their minds to nothingness. Their husbands were gone, and they could not stop grieving. The only thing Thylaina offered them was tea to relax their minds and help them rest. Sometimes she sat with them and their children, and sang Elvish songs, weaving the melodic magic into her voice to get an immediate effect. However, there was little she could do about their long-term pain. She suggested they gather and share their grief and worries, and perhaps find support from one another. A few of the wives agreed, while others faced their sorrow alone. Seeing them broken and lost tore at her heart, especially when she visited Einasa.

She prayed to Bryric and Valorius that Breydon would return home safe. He was a loss she could not bear.

Another morning of silence, but at least the young children played outside in the sun. Thylaina had been walking from a patient's home at the southern end of the city, waving at a group of tots spinning and singing, when Gavrel returned from Warstchia with a score of recruits. After losing several good knights, it was a relief to see Grim's barracks fill with men eager to serve under his leadership.

Gavrel glanced her way as he rode down the main path to the mansion, but gave no acknowledgment of having seen her. Not even a nod. Perhaps guilt still consumed him. She pushed aside thoughts about her friend and turned toward Einasa's home to examine both mother and babe. It was a brief visit, for one of the other widows was present. Good. The women needed each other.

The afternoon raced into evening by the time Thylaina arrived at home, and she had yet to eat a meal since breaking fast. Every motion felt weighted down with exhaustion and grief. While tending to her patients throughout the day, she was often in a daze. Such a dangerous state for a healer to fall into. A rosemary bath after supper should help clear her mind, for there was more work to do in the late hours.

Silence filled the house. Bramn's death and Breydon's absence affected the servants as much as Thylaina. Even Katjina's mood was subdued, and she offered little company during supper.

Thylaina smiled while memories of her first days in Caerabis flooded her mind, particularly the lovely ones of Katjina gazing at Bramn with fondness. The handmaiden had always adored him, but respectfully so, for she admired Einasa. Even when she believed Bramn had affections for Thylaina, she had shown no jealousy. What a wonderful woman Katjina truly was.

"I think I'll retire, m'lady," the handmaiden said, her voice unusually soft.

"Of course." Alone now, Thylaina stared at her barely eaten meal. Still no appetite.

She dropped the dinner cloth onto the table and stood. Some time in the apothecary afore heading to the herb garden ought to help pass time.

For five hours, Thylaina prepared repenia leaves to distill for olesa oil, ground dried bossel roots, strung up two dozen bunches of knee holly brooms to dry for Viya, and inspected the last supply of sponishies for flaws.

"M'lady," Katjina said from the doorway. "It's the twenty-second hour."

Thylaina looked up from her journal, where she needed to add one more entry about her patients of the day. "Thank you. I shall tend to the garden then go to bed."

"Do you want one of the men to help?"

"N'ei. You know I like to do it myself." Night gardening was one of her favorite times of the day. The peace of the city in slumber, the beautiful music from the nocturnal insects, and no one to interrupt her work.

"Very well. Good night, m'lady."

The door shut with a soft thud.

Thylaina finished writing about her last patient, then left the book open on the table to let the ink dry. Snatching the garden gloves and herb clippers off the table against the western wall, she mentally listed the plants to check this evening. Perhaps she might collect some herbs from behind the mansion.

In her garden, she inspected the small plots, then unrolled a gathering cloth, one-yard of light cotton, in front of three of them: ashrych, camiol, and yavlar. There was plenty of work to do tonight.

She finished clipping the oldest branches from the yavlar plants, happy to see new ones already budding from the roots. Even under the moonlight, she could see the blue veins spreading throughout the juicy brown leaves. Cutting the tiny blue flowers from the stems of the camiol plant required precision, so she bent low over them and took her time snipping each one and dropping them on the cloth.

In the distance, footsteps sounded. Casual, yet weighted. Guards.

Although there had been guards amid the city after the attack on Breydon, the number increased since the suspicion of spies. Now, following Bramn's death, more knights patrolled the streets. If the Southern Brigands would strike squads in the plains, then there might be some daring enough to enter Caerabis to cause more havoc. To be truthful, the extra sentries put Thylaina at ease, especially when she worked outside in the late nights.

She focused on the small space between the camiol bloom and the leaves. The tiny flowers dropped onto the linen.

A glow of light came from behind her.

Thylaina twisted around, the clippers out like a weapon she did not know how to use.

Gavrel stood ten feet back between two of the tall bushes and raised a lantern as he viewed her. "My lady," he whispered. "Is all well?"

Lowering the herb clippers, she released a slow breath and willed her heart to stop racing. Thylaina licked her lips and nodded. "And you?"

He glanced to the left. "Just a moment. I'll be right there." Gavrel stepped into the garden, but did not draw any closer. Apparently, his new duty did not require him to don the plate armor, but leather with a breastplate, greaves, and vambraces. "The nightmares won't stop. I... I keep seeing his eyes when that bastard killed him." Guilt forced his gaze down. "I wish I could do something for Lady Einasa, but I was told to keep away from her."

Thylaina could have guessed who made that demand. "Your desire to help is noted by Lessindra."

"It doesn't do any good. Not for any of them." His voice softened. Remorse curved his back and shoulders.

A shadow appeared between the same bushes he had stepped through. "Sir Gavrel, return to your path." The man's face came into view, revealing a knight from Breydon's squad.

Gavrel breathed deep, then released it. "I just wished to ensure you were safe, my lady."

"I do appreciate it."

"Good night."

"Good night, Sir Gavrel."

"Good night, Lady Colmstad," the other knight said.

Thylaina watched them leave, wishing she could recall the knight's name, but he was one of several with whom she never spoke.

So Grim put Gavrel on guard duty. Most of the men guarding the city at night were knights, but why Gavrel? And why on the very day he returned?

She resumed collecting the herbs. However, Thylaina did not gather any ashrych. By the time she finished with the camiol, she was ready to roll the gathering cloths and go to bed. Ashrych could wait until tomorrow night.

An uneventful afternoon passed. There were fewer patients to tend to today, so Thylaina inspected herbs in the Momestid's garden and her own, noting which ones needed her attention tonight. It mattered not how often she tried to concentrate on her tasks; the memories would not relent. And not only those of Bramn, but Breydon as well. She missed her husband, and she worried about him.

Thylaina ate supper alone. Most of her meal remained untouched, a lack of appetite still lingering. Instead, she wept. Teardrops landed on the cold fish and vegetables. She did not want to be alone anymore.

She returned to the garden in the late night to gather the ashrych, along with insh blooms, and vervain. Once she rolled the herbs into the gathering cloth, she left them near the path to the side entrance, then strolled to the back of the mansion with another rolled linen. She laid it beneath the repenia vines behind the knee holly. The deep green leaves snapped off the vines easily and floated to the waiting sheet.

She had been plucking the leaves for half an hour when she heard the approach of two men. Turning, she spotted the lantern beyond the house drawing closer. Gavrel and the same knight whispered as they neared the orchard. The former looked at her and nodded once. She returned the gesture, then resumed working. The other knight said, "Good evening, Lady Colmstad."

"Good evening." Thylaina dropped four more leaves.

Gavrel kept his eyes forward.

Their attention shifted in every direction as they walked on, but not toward her. That was fine. She just wanted to finish.

As Thylaina carried the rolled linen into the house, Master Eidryn crossed her mind. She would welcome his company right now. Or Aarosyn. Another healer, for certain. What she would give to hear from her friends and know they were well.

By the time she slipped into the cold bed, her thoughts had turned to her brother. *Bryric, please keep Neldrid safe.*

Thylaina joined the Momestids to break fast. No coaxing from Tes could get Nadiera to eat her porridge. The ten-year-old girl's gaze darted to Thylaina several times with a question and accusation. Why did Thylaina not save Bramn like she did Breydon? She had let Bramn die. The same question and accusation Breydon held against her.

Tes said little, and Grim appeared to struggle to find a subject of discussion. He asked Thylaina about her patients, the gardens, and other things he normally showed no interest in.

To be polite, Thylaina finished her porridge and tea, then pushed the dishes forward. "Grim, I noticed Sir Gavrel is amongst the night guards."

Jaw shifting side to side, he stared at her. "He is. Has he caused you trouble?"

"Of course not." She smiled to ease his suspicious expression. "He does his duty well. I was simply curious."

"We'll see if he earns his right to remain here." Grim stood, then bowed. "Have a fine day."

Well... that was the end of that conversation. However, Thylaina could not help wondering what he meant. Gavrel was an ordained knight, and like the others, he gave an oath to the people of Alohrius and his brothers. He killed the man who murdered Bramn, and Grim had been present during the testimonies that spoke on his behalf. Had Breydon influenced Grim's views on Gavrel?

"We shall persevere," Tes said, fidgeting with Telsia on her lap. She forced a smile at Thylaina, although it was saturated with sadness. "We shall."

"I know." Thylaina rose. "It is time for me to see my patients."

"Have a blessed day."

Nadiera said nothing, but her bottom lip quivered and her eyes watered.

Hurrying around the table, Thylaina knelt beside the girl and pulled her into a hug. "I am so sorry you hurt," she said, stroking Nadiera's back.

Tears soaked into the shoulder of Thylaina's dress as the girl wept. "I wish... you could've helped... him," she managed between sobs.

Pain and failure shot through Thylaina's center. Why failure when there was naught she could have done? Perhaps Uncle Yasontler had felt the same when her mother died.

"As do I," she said, rocking slightly to soothe Nadiera. "I am sorry I could not."

Tes wiped her eyes, then moved to sit beside her daughter. "No one blames you, Thylaina. So you'd better stop blaming yourself."

The woman was obviously blind to Breydon blaming her.

The lantern glowed on the tips of Thylaina's boots while she sat between the mint and the ashrych plots. Hard bumps from the ground offered no comfort, yet she did not move. She should work, but after comforting Nadiera that morning, she had walked throughout the day feeling empty. The pleasure of gardening was absent. Even preparing the remedies was with little enjoyment. Did she care anymore?

It was a foolish question. These feelings were nothing new. She had experienced them when Mother died. Tes was correct. They all would persevere because they had each other to survive this grief. But life without Bramn... It hurt as much to breathe as it did to consider finishing that thought. Those first words were enough to make her heart fracture.

Sighing, Thylaina looked at the mint. The work could wait until tomorrow, but if she put these tasks aside, she might never return to them. It was a poor habit to begin when enduring the loss of a loved one. Eyes closed, a few deep breaths of the fragrant air, and her mind cleared from troubled thoughts. At least enough to move.

She had already spread the gathering cloths at the plots needing attention. So she rolled to her knees, hummed the lullaby she often sang to Aella, and began with the mint. That task was the quickest to complete. In another week, they would be ready for picking. She then stood at the rosemary plot, looked beyond it to the xarflas, and contemplated what to do next. Several rosemary plants required trimming of their tops to encourage fuller growth, which would take nearly an hour. One of the gardeners could trim the rosemary tomorrow. The back rows of xarflas were in full bloom, indicating the perfect time for snipping the blossoms.

Removing the herb clipper from her apron pocket, she stepped around the rosemary plot, nearly tripping as the toe of her boot caught in the gathering cloth. "Damn it to Darkness," she hissed. *Calm. Relax and try to enjoy the peaceful evening.* The lullaby sounded from her throat again, and as she knelt at the xarflas, she imagined holding Aella. Would the girl grow up to look like Bramn, or be like her sister and take on her mother's physical traits? Poor Einasa would have much to deal with when the girls were of courting age. Perhaps Breydon and Grim could help her with information about the knights who approach with interest.

She had not realized she now hummed a different song, one a little more uplifting. A dancing song. With the cheerful rhythm, her hands worked faster. It seemed even the nearby insects joined in, chirping and stringing the background music to her voice.

Memories of dancing with Breydon whirled in her mind, which brought a slight smile. Then a frown. Yet she continued humming. Hopefully, he would be home very soon. Another day and night without him was more than she could bear. *I just want him—*

A cloth dropped over her head and covered her face, quickly tightening behind her.

She grabbed at the bunched end pressed against her throat and tugged, but the assailant yanked on it, forcing a choking gasp from her. *Think. Think. Think!* But terror pumped through her racing heartbeat and increased her breathing. Her vision darkened. No matter how hard Thylaina tried, she could not make a sound. Other parts of her might.

While twisting her body, which added pressure to her throat, she kicked hard and struck the wooden border of the xarflas plot. And again. Each subsequent kick weakened. The dark masses in her vision expanded and pulsed, timed with the thrumming in her ears. The burning and pain in her throat dominated all but the fear.

"Thylaina!"

Her body jerked forward as the attacker folded onto her. A moment later, he fell off. Thylaina dropped to the ground and lay still, too weak to move. The scent of dirt and a mixture of herbs entered her nose. This was the gathering cloth she had left at the rosemary. She pulled it from her throat enough to let fresh air into her mouth. Quick breaths started as she fought to remain conscious.

The shuffle of boots on dirt and hitting wood, and men's grunts, sounded behind her.

Thylaina just wanted to sleep. Something she had not done since Bramn's death and Breydon's absence. Perhaps a few hours a night, but too little, considering everything she did throughout the day. And now, it was catching up with her. When she needed to be strong, she was frail. The thought of using a spell to protect herself had not even entered her mind. Foolish.

One of the men gasped. Pain. That was death. Was it the attacker or her rescuer?

Eyes closed beneath the cloth, she waited. Prayed. The cotton lifted from her face.

"Gods." Definitely Gavrel. His fingers grazed her face. "Thylaina?"

She cracked her eyes open.

"Thank Valorius." He lifted her and hurried through the plots, and headed to the mansion. Not her home, but the Momestid's. "Stay conscious. Please."

No. Thylaina needed to sleep. And the darkness was calling to her.


"Will she drink it?" Tes asked.

"She better." That sounded like Viya. "I've told her plenty of times it'd work. Now she'll see for herself."

Thylaina slit an eye open, recognizing her old room. At least they still viewed her as a person of importance by placing her on the family floor.

"She's awake!" Viya announced. "Should I get Sir Gavrel? He wanted to know when—"

"No," Tes replied. "When Thylaina's ready, she'll speak to him."

Thylaina raised her head enough to look at Viya. "What is it you intend to give me?" she rasped. Damn, it hurt to speak.

Viya smirked and offered a teacup. "Some of *my* medicine."

It tasted awful. Viya did not bother to mask the vervain with something more pleasing. When Thylaina finished the drink, however, her throat felt improved. "Some mint would have been lovely."

"Lovely wasn't the goal." Viya snorted. "Helping you was."

"You did." Thylaina smiled. "Thank you."

A tender squeeze of the hand would have been preferable, but Viya did not seem to know when to stop, and now Thylaina's fingers ached. The head scullery maiden appeared not to notice Thylaina's wince. "You're most welcome, my dear. Now rest."

She left the bedchamber, spoke to someone in the connecting suite.

Thylaina looked at Tes. "Where is Sir Gavrel?"

"Returned to duty." Tes placed a needlepoint project on the bedside table. As much as she claimed to have hated the hobby of fine stitching, she had been doing it since Telsia's birth three years past.

"I would like to see him."

"In the morning. You still look exhausted."

Thylaina opened her mouth to argue, but yawned instead. Yes, she was far too tired. *What did Viya put in that tea?*

Thylaina entered Grim's cabinet, pleased to see Gavrel present. Steps slowing, she noted the dark circles beneath his eyes. "Sir Gavrel, you should be in bed," she said.

Smiling, he bowed. "I hoped to help Marshal Momestid identify last night's assailant."

She looked from him to Grim. "You know not whom he is?"

"Was." Grim's blue gaze darted to Gavrel. "He was killed in the scuffle."

"I had no choice," Gavrel snapped. "It was me or him... sir."

Shocked by Grim's cold stare, Thylaina touched Gavrel's arm. "I am glad you made the correct choice. And more grateful that you saved me. Thank you, my friend."

Gavrel's cheeks brightened at those last two words. Things had been strained between them since Bramn's death and Breydon's accusations. However, this should prove his loyalty to the knighthood and the people of Caerabis.

"You're welcome, my lady."

"I don't recognize the man," Grim said.

Breath caught, Thylaina turned to him. "He is not from the city?"

"No."

"Perhaps it is time to build a wall around Caerabis." She had warned three years ago the lack of a wall welcomed dangerous people.

Grim scowled. "We can't afford it. I suppose we'll have to add more men to the night watch."

There really was no other choice.

"You're dismissed," Grim said to Gavrel. "Get some sleep. You may have tonight off."

"Thank you, Marshal."

Thylaina spun to leave with him, but Grim called for her. Once the door closed, he spoke.

"Breydon will want full details—"

"I have n'ei intention of telling him about this."

He stiffened. "Why not?"

"Because he will find an excuse as to why Sir Gavrel saved me." Thylaina released a breathy laugh. "It matters not that Sir Gavrel killed Bramn's murderer and has protected me, Breydon will never see the truth. His anger distorts his view, and he pushes to make others believe him."

"You don't trust your husband?"

"I trust him more than anyone." And she meant every word. "But he is not correct all the time. Not about everything."

"Thylaina—"

"I do not want him to know," she said through her gritted teeth. "At least not until I am ready to tell him."

Disapproval stared at her. "Very well. I shall inform the others to say nothing of the matter."

"Thank you, Grim." She smiled at him. "I love you dearly. All of you."

"I know."

"Now... I have patients to see."

"I think you should also take a day of rest."

Thylaina laughed. "I know of n'ei such thing."

# Chapter Twenty-Two

Thylaina did not know if Breydon would remain cold toward her upon his return. Praise Lessindra, he seemed more himself. While men replanted the tree just beyond Bramn's grave, giving room for the roots, Breydon held Thylaina as she wept. It was a beautiful, yet awfully sad moment. Bramn was being honored by the Hammer Oak, and would now give life to the earth—to this tree, but this was truly the final farewell to their dear friend.

Breydon told her about what drew him to that particular tree, for he said it was meant to be where it now stood. "I stared at it for several minutes while the others continued inspecting the nearby oaks, but this one... I knew this one."

She sniffled, tilted her head back to see her husband's face. Tears welled in his eyes as he gazed at the tall, strong tree. "What do you mean, love?"

He squinted. "When Bramn and I traveled to the Ormiana xilys, we often camped beneath this Hammer Oak."

Thylaina rested her cheek on his shoulder and viewed the tree. "Are you certain?"

A chuckle sounded in his throat. "As strong as it is, Bramn had scarred the bark three feet from the bottom."

She guffawed. "How?"

"Swordplay." A teardrop sliding down his cheek, Breydon snorted a laugh. "Bramn broke the blade on the trunk." He dropped his arm from her shoulder, approached the tree, and ran his finger along a deep line that reached just below his hip. "Here." A crooked smile formed. "I laughed until my stomach hurt when the blade broke, for I'd warned him, but he wished to prove me wrong."

"Breydon! Thylaina!" Einasa called. She carried Aella and had Alyanna in tow.

Thylaina took the babe, a smile raising her cheeks as she cradled Aella. There was some good news to share with her husband.

Einasa rested her palm on the dark, rough bark of the tree. "Oh, Breydon, it's beautiful." She knelt and wept.

Alyanna sat beside her, looking from the tree, to her mother, to Breydon and Thylaina, the poor girl unsure of what to do.

They stayed there after the men finished planting the tree and cleaned up the gravesite. Aella suckled from her mother, then Alyanna complained about wanting supper. So Einasa wished them a good night and took her daughters home.

Thylaina's heart broke as she watched them depart. How different their home would now be in Bramn's absence. So much had already changed in *her* life, but theirs? Losing her mother had left Thylaina alone at the palace in Etharell. At least Alyanna and Aella would know and feel love every day from the people who surrounded them, and they would never know abandonment.

Also watching them, Breydon released a heavy breath.

Thylaina squeezed his hand. "There is something I must tell you."

He frowned. "Is it worrying?"

"N'ei." She smiled. "Come. I shall share this with you at home."

Thankfully, Breydon did not resist.

They stayed in the family room, which seemed fitting, and had one of the house maidens pour some rich red wine. Thylaina insisted Breydon sit beside her on the sofa, and after he had his first drink, she shared Master Eidryn's response to her request.

"Is it not wonderful?" she asked.

Breydon set the goblet on the table and sat back. "He's coming here?"

"S'yai."

"What if he doesn't come alone? What if those who come with him tell your brother about you? Or inform your uncle?"

Such thoughts had never crossed her mind, and for good reason. Thylaina caressed the top of his hand as she leaned closer to him. "Because it is not uncommon for Master Eidryn to travel to other countries, even alone. He will not endanger my happiness."

"What if he believes you're in danger?"

Breydon had to see wrong in everything lately.

Frowning, she slid her hand from his. "Master Eidryn knows me. He would never—"

"What does that bloody mean?"

"Why must you make this so difficult?" Thylaina stood and glared down at him. "What does it mean? It means he was my mentor, and I spent a great deal of time learning everything I could about Vynia and healing from him. No one in Yeuroth has a relationship with the Earthen Goddess such as he. To become as successful as I am, I gave years to his teachings. So we know each other."

Breydon nodded. "I see."

"What did you think I meant?" Thylaina widened her eyes and stepped back. "You believed I meant intimately? Gods, Breydon! Why must your mind always dart there when it comes to my relationship with other men?"

He rose, his face red. "Because you shouldn't have a relationship with other men!"

"Bramn?"

"He was different!" Breydon's irises brightened in his annoyance. "Bramn was like a brother. So don't dare use him, and don't mention Grim either!"

She let her shoulders drop, the tense muscles easing. "The priests and gardeners?"

"They're like..." He scanned the room as he pondered his response. "Peers."

Thylaina snickered. "And Gavrel?"

The ire showed in his grimace as he pointed at her. "That bastard shouldn't be near you. His affection for you makes him dangerous. *And* he's involved in Bramn's death."

There was no denying Gavrel's feelings toward her, but that did not make him dangerous toward his knight brothers nor guilty for Bramn's death.

She scowled at her husband, furious that what Gavrel had told her was true. "How dare you accuse him of such an atrocious act, when those present had testified to his innocence."

Breydon stilled. "Who told you about the trial?" When she tilted her chin and remained silent, he pressed on. "It was Gavrel, wasn't it?"

It hurt to see that fury in his gaze. Thylaina softened her voice, hoping to keep him from growing angrier. "I know Bramn's death has been difficult to endure, my love. But you cannot blame Gavrel, especially when he is innocent."

"You defend him an awful lot." Breydon clenched his jaw, then breathed deep and slow, relaxing it. "Two men said they thought he—"

"*Your* knights?"

He straightened, his face paling. "You believe I concocted it. That I'm just trying to ruin him."

"Love, I know Gavrel and Bramn were not friendly, but Gavrel is a knight who swore to defend those in need, including his brothers."

"How can you believe him over me?"

This was not about believing one or the other. It was about Breydon's poor choice as one of the city's leaders.

"Did he lie about the witnesses?" she asked.

Defeat curving his shoulders, Breydon blinked rapidly. "No," he murmured. When his eyes finally settled upon hers, strength returned. "But the two who say otherwise were more convincing."

Perhaps Gavrel was correct: Breydon envied their friendship. Maybe Breydon did not trust her. Either way, Thylaina could not support this ridiculous behavior anymore.

"If they told you he was Chaos, you would believe them." She sighed as she turned her head away. "Gods, I tire of this argument. Gavrel is my friend."

"I'm your husband… and obviously, you don't trust me. You don't believe me."

Stiffening, Thylaina fought the urge to cry.

He snatched the goblet and downed the wine. "I didn't want my return to be like this—fighting with you." Breydon released a heavy breath. "I know our people do and view things differently, but I ask this one favor of you: please don't see Gavrel again."

It ached into the depths of her, knowing he no longer believed in the vows she had made. "Does my love for you mean nothing?"

"I didn't say that."

"You have n'ei faith in me."

"Laina, that's not what I'm saying." Breydon grabbed her hands and pulled her closer, but she resisted. "I don't trust *him*."

She lowered her gaze. "At least trust *me*."

He let her hands go, scraped his heels upon the floor as he backed away. "Then at least listen to me." Breydon left the room.

The tears fell while she listened to his footsteps go farther... to their bedroom. Thank Lessindra he stayed home. Thylaina sat on the sofa and stared at her full cup of wine. So much for trying to cling onto one moment of joy amidst the grief.

The Burning Moon darkened, surrendering to the Hunter's first week. Then the second. Moods lifted slightly around the Momestid mansion as everyone returned to their routines; however, not at the Colmstad home. Thylaina and Breydon barely spoke to each other, but at least they slept in the same bed. A deep, empty chasm remained between them. It was awful to feel him so close but have him so far from her. How badly she did not want to lose her husband's precious time like this. Elves could bear grudges for years and often not worry about it, but Breydon did not have the years to lose over disagreements. Thylaina did not want to waste anymore days to silence and absence. But he left afore dawn and returned after supper, heading straight to his cabinet. She was beneath the covers and near slumber by the time he joined her.

The eighth Hunter's night, she sat at the dining table stirring vegetable broth with a chunk of bread.

"Laina."

She dropped the bread into the bowl and looked to her husband at the chamber's entrance. Catching her breath, she wiped her wrist and sleeve on the table's cloth. "You startled me."

"I wish to speak with you in my office." Breydon disappeared into the dark hallway.

Long, slow breath. Thylaina rose and followed him. When she entered the cabinet, he was already sitting in the comfortable chair behind the desk. The four wall sconces flickered, adding warmth to the room along with the small fireplace, and the lamp on the desk burned brightly. Ready to appear stoic for whatever reason he demanded her presence, Thylaina stopped in front of the desk. Her gaze fell upon the letter she had written to Neldrid, and she froze, her heartbeat increasing. In the wake of all that had happened, Thylaina had forgotten all about it. The letter must have gotten mixed with Breydon's other parchments. But that was more than a fortnight ago.

Breydon drummed his fingers along the letter's bottom, just below her signature. He slid it closer, leaned over it. "'Dear, Neldrid'," he read aloud, "'I hope you find it within yourself to forgive me after this long silence. For my absence.'"

At that moment, Thylaina wished Breydon had never learned to speak and read her language.

"'Do not believe my heart feels no pain while being far from home," he resumed. "'That I do not think of you and Father. For I do. Often you cross my mind, especially in worry. Are you safe? Are you alive? Do you miss me as much as I miss you? Do you need me like I need you?'" Breydon paused, cleared his throat. "'There are moments when I think about us and the better times we had shared. How I miss them. Gods, Neldrid. You were all I had. I needed you. But I meant so little to you—to everyone. I could easily mingle with the servants and none would notice. How long afore they told you I was gone? Did Rhomasyn even care? Did you? You cast me aside. Your sister! You left me to that pompous man, doing naught to prevent Father from forcing me into that ridiculous betrothal. Why? I despised Rhomasyn, and you knew this! But you cared not. As long as I was gone and out of the way of your courting. Why did you hate me when I loved you so bloody much? You and Father just wanted me away from you. So I am gone from you. And sometimes I wish I was not.'"

Breydon lowered the parchment, stared at those last few words for a moment. It seemed a question poised upon his lips, but he did not ask. Instead, he read on. "'Sometimes I want to be with you and Father, and be a family once more. There is so much I wish for, but know I can never have again. Most of all, I wish you are always safe from harm. Despite the pain and anger, I still love you, Neldrid.'"

Thylaina closed her eyes. This should not be difficult to explain, but when she looked upon her husband, she saw hurt staring back. "I wrote that in the wake of Bramn's death, my love."

"Do you want to go back to Etharell? Have my actions pushed you to feel this way?"

"Did you not hear me?"

"Answer." Breydon pushed the letter aside. "I've read this every night since my return. I deserve to know how you truly feel. Because if this," he motioned to the parchment, "reveals anything, it's truth. You wrote this with pure emotion."

Her husband knew her better than Thylaina had ever believed.

"I meant every word," she whispered. "I hurt from losing Bramn, and it heightened the fear of losing my brother." She nodded. "Do I want to return to Etharell? N'ei. This is my home. *You*, Breydon Colmstad, are my home. N'ei where else."

She stepped around the desk as he leaned back in the large chair, his gaze locked on hers. Thylaina lifted the letter. "I had meant to burn this, but important matters came to my attention and I forgot about it."

"Burn it before I read it?"

She released a brief laugh while lowering to his lap and resting against him. "To ensure it was never delivered. There was an urge to write my feelings at that moment."

Breydon looked toward the small hearth to their left. "Then let's burn it so it never gets into the wrong people's hands."

Thylaina kissed his cheek. Her lips lingered against the rough hairs meeting his waiting mouth. Gods! It had been so long. Her breath came fast and hard, and her heart thundered as her body sparked into life, desire ignited.

He moved the letter and other items aside, then lifted her onto the desk's top. Desperation parted the front of her dress and pushed her skirt to her hip. Breydon's heated lips left traces of kisses on her throat, chest, then her breasts as he bared them. Although a large desk, it was not a bed.

"Love... we can go to the fur on the floor," Thylaina managed between breaths.

He lifted his head from her breasts and looked at her. "Never again," he whispered, his hands busy with the strings of his trousers. "You're too refined for a floor, my love."

Breydon's lips pressed on hers, and he soon filled her. Thylaina hooked her ankles over his thighs, meeting his thrusts. Heat from the fireplace added to that which bloomed from within her, creating a sheen of perspiration on her skin. Each lunge intensified Thylaina's growing pleasure. She panted, gasped, moaned, then sang her ecstasy as his motion grew faster, harder. In the midst of her song, he joined her with his release. Wonderful. So wonderful to be with Breydon again.

While waiting for Master Eidryn's arrival, Thylaina resumed caring over ailments and injuries, and Breydon returned to overseeing the knights' duties. There were still two days until his predicted date, but it was possible he might ride in early. She should know better; Master Eidryn was always precise. The excitement of what he brought had her nearly singing to everyone she tended. The nervousness about his possible rejection had her almost in tears when she was alone. For two days, it left her emotions spiraling and Breydon cautious of what to say in her presence.

The sun burned on this thirteenth day of the eighth month, the humid air leaving the outdoor laborers' garbs soaked with perspiration. Thylaina had intended to work in the herb garden, but Breydon insisted she remain inside due to the weather. To prevent the gardeners and other workers from passing out in the heat, the overseers cycled shifts, giving them time in the shade and plenty of water. Thylaina worked in the apothecary, which remained cool despite the temperature. There were plenty of medicinal preparations to complete since she had neglected them to spend more time with Breydon. Olesa oil was low, and her experiment with xarflas flowers needed notations. Perhaps one day, she might have a healing ointment that could close wounds immediately.

Keeping her mind busy was the perfect thing to do. She knew not how much time passed while she tested six different concoctions of xarflas ointment, cutting her arm and slathering the different soothing creams over the wound. None of the injuries closed instantly, but they healed faster than other remedies she had ever used. Especially ointments two and five. She set those jars apart from the other four, corked them all, then wrote the results in the new journal.

"Laina."

She scratched the quill tip over the page, streaking ink ahead of the word she had been writing. Dropping the quill into the inkwell, she glared at her husband.

Breydon smirked. "A group of border guards approach."

Thylaina straightened, her heart stopping for the briefest second.

"And it appears they're escorting someone."

She hurried around the table and to the door, but Breydon grabbed her arm. "What?"

"We receive him here first. Once we know what is to happen, we'll decide if he meets Grim and Tes."

"Very well. Now may we go?"

"Wait in the family room." He released her arm. "I'll direct them here."

Her body trembled. "What am I to do while I wait?"

A crooked smile and gleam of amusement was his only response afore he departed. The bastard.

Thylaina called for Katjina, giving her control of the preparation. The handmaiden was quick to act. She ordered for the best bottle of wine from the cellar beneath the apothecary room, Panya to prepare a tray of cheese, fruit, and cornbread, and the gardeners to swiftly gather colorful blooms for a vase to place on the table in the gathering chamber. Although the family room was already perfect, the flowers would add a fresh scent that Eidryn might appreciate.

Thylaina started for the bedroom, but halted. "Or maybe we should meet in the garden room?"

Katjina pointed toward the front end of the house. "But the captain said—"

"S'yai, you are correct." Thylaina sighed. "Perhaps we might move to the garden room if Master Eidryn would prefer."

"If you wish, my lady."

Time dragged as she paced at the cold hearth, waiting for Breydon and Eidryn. Did her husband escort him around the perimeter of the city first? Gods! They should have been home by now.

She stilled and stared at the blank space above the fireplace. *I hate that emptiness. We need something there. A painting.*

"After your brother's failure to find you, I believed I would never see you again." Master Eidryn's voice was a pleasant tenor upon her ears. Tears forming, she faced him. "And what a vision you are, my lady." He bowed.

Thylaina rushed into his arms, wept upon his shoulders. "Master," she whispered, barely able to speak. To see him, to have a part of home so close, overwhelmed her heart.

"It is fine to be in the presence of a Favored once again."

"And it is wonderful to be in yours." She parted from him, an uncontrolled smile spreading across her cheeks. "Oh, Master! Thank you for coming."

"How could I not?" His gray eyes shone like raw iron as he stared at her. He glanced at Breydon. "Is he fluent in our language?"

Breydon chuckled. "I am," he said in Elvish. "And ever since Laina began improving my inflections, I am now exceptional with it."

The Master Healer smiled. "Then I am pleased to relax and speak in ours. The Common Tongue, although simple, can sometimes be awfully taxing." He returned his attention to Thylaina, staring at her as if she were a magical illusion. He touched her arm, her hair, then her cheek. "You truly are here," he said. "Why, my dear?"

Thylaina gestured to the sofa. "Help yourself to some fruit, cheese, and wine, and I shall tell you everything."

Breydon excused himself, leaving them alone. He returned an hour later, shortly afore she finished her tale. Not once did Master Eidryn interrupt her, but he did glance at her husband several times, appearing intrigued.

The room fell silent. He finished his wine, then stood afore her, fixing his gaze on nothing. "You married a human," he said beneath his breath. "A path I had never anticipated for you." He looked at Breydon again, then turned to Thylaina. "Although I am relieved you did not marry that pompous lord, I believed you were meant for greatness beyond that of your uncle and cousins."

Breydon shook his head and poured himself a goblet of wine.

"But I *have* gone beyond them." Gazing up at him, she grasped Master Eidryn's hand. "You look at my husband knowing that I saved him from Red Death."

He glanced at Breydon again and nodded. "Which, to be truthful, amazes me. It should not, for I knew if any could find a way, it would be you, Aarosyn, or Maelene."

Breydon lifted his cup, darted his eyes to Thylaina. "She also brought me back from a fatal injury."

Master Eidryn stiffened, his expression a mixture of shock and alarm. "You performed a divine healing?" he whispered.

Thylaina slid her hands up and down her thighs for a few seconds, finding it difficult to answer. "I-I had."

"You gave years of your so—?"

"I would give again whatever They required if I must," she said firmly. "I love Breydon. And I want to create a life with him. Please, help us."

He regarded her for a moment, then knelt and took her hand, kissing the scarred knuckles. "You know the risks." Eidryn nodded toward Breydon. "Does your husband?"

"There are no healers in all of Yeuroth as exceptional as you and I, Master," she said. "And with Vynia's Favor upon us, I have no doubt of our success."

"She has always favored you—above all others." Eidryn rose. "Beyond any pupil I have ever instructed, including the prince. Far superior than even the king," he hushed, smirking.

Thylaina's cheeks warmed beneath his compliments.

"And I will help you," he said.

Thylaina looked at Breydon, a squeal about to burst forth.

"But you must do as I say." Eidryn set his chin. "Otherwise, I leave, taking the fertility potion with me."

The room fell silent as Thylaina and Breydon stared at him. Huffing, she dropped his hand and stood with a straight spine to appear taller. "I have always followed your instruct—"

"No." His firm tone silenced her, as it had in the past. "I do this *with* you. And you *will* do what I say."

Thylaina retreated a step. This was ridiculous! Eidryn did not need to tower over her as if she was a patient! She knew how to take care of herself.

"That is exactly why I insist." He pointed at her. "Because you are stubborn. And you will work yourself frail when you must rest." Eidryn released a slow breath, lowered his hand. "If we are successful with the fertility potion, then I shall assist with your patients. When it is time for you to bedrest, which *will* happen, I shall resume caring for them and any who need help."

"Master," her voice quaked, "I am capable of—"

"Agreed." Breydon looked from Eidryn to Thylaina. "There is nothing more to say on the matter."

She curled her fingers into fists, her muscles tightening. "There absolutely is!"

"No." He motioned toward the Master Healer. "He obviously *does* know you, Laina. You are a stubborn woman who tells others to rest but will ignore that same advice. I do not want you tending to ill people while you are with child."

"I am not susceptible to your human illnesses."

"But what of our babe?"

Thylaina looked down at her fingers. It was a valid question, and one she could not answer.

"You promise to do as he says, or he leaves with the potion," Breydon said.

How could he make such demands? He wanted a child as much as Thylaina did, but to threaten her like that was awful. She fought the urge to cry. No. Neither of those men would see a teardrop from her. But truth be told, they were correct: Thylaina would do exactly as they assumed. Following Master Eidryn's terms was the best option, for it would take more than herbs to help them birth a child.

Nodding, she smoothed her bodice. "Very well. I agree."

"We work together," Eidryn repeated. "We journal every herbal remedy, ointment, potion—everything. They will be ours. Do you understand?"

Breydon crossed his arms. "She will not spend too much time in the apothecary."

"Of course, Captain." Eidryn bowed partially. "Lady Thylaina shall be treated like... royalty."

She leered at him; he grinned.

"I suppose we shall have to introduce him to Grim's family," Breydon said. "And all your patients."

Thylaina lifted a silver bell from the table beside the sofa and rang it. When Katjina entered, Thylaina gave instructions for the servants to prepare the guest bedchamber for Eidryn. Katjina blushed as she curtsied to him, then left the room.

"There is only one more thing I must demand," he said.

Thylaina tilted her head and waited. "What is that, Master?"

"Please do not call me Master anymore, my lady." His smile was warm and sweet. "For I am no longer your master, but your peer and friend."

Now she could not help hugging him.


After a wonderful feast with the Momestids, sharing with them about Thylaina's sixty years of instruction under Eidryn, she and Breydon finally had some time alone. He had been surprisingly quiet during most of supper, but his touch was constant, whether holding her hand, gliding his fingertips across her nape, or kissing her knuckles. Yet when they locked gazes, she was met with a silent question.

Afterwards in their bedroom, Breydon often glanced at her while they undressed.

She draped her dress on the changing screen, then stood naked beside the bed and waited. "What is it you wish to say?"

Finally finished enjoying the view, he smirked and pushed his trousers down, stepping out of them. "What did you give, Laina?"

That question had burned in his mind throughout the entire evening. No wonder he constantly looked her way and touched her, as if wanting her to know there was something to come tonight. Not intimacy, but this. An inquiry she did not want to answer.

Smiling, she draped her robe over the chaise next to the window. "Give?"

Head tilted, he squinted. "Don't be coy with me. You stopped Eidryn from finishing what he was saying in regards to your bringing me back." Breydon walked around the bed toward her, his steps slow. "What did you give, and to whom?"

Gods, he looked so bloody amazing. The flames danced upon his body, shadowing the contours and defining his perfection. Thylaina did not need any potions to feel a stirring for her husband.

"Laina."

She blinked away her ogling and met his intense gaze. Breydon would not accept no answer. Thylaina slid the robe on. "My soul," she whispered.

His expression went from firm to shocked concern; his voice was barely audible when he finally responded. "What?"

"It is not as dreadful as it might sound." She forced another smile. "Unless I were to do it again and again. Of which I have no intention."

He took her hand gently, led her to the chaise, and sat with her. "Why? What does that mean for you?"

One corner of her lips lifted as she placed her palm on his cheek. "Because I love you, and I could not bear my life without you."

His hand covered hers, and he turned his head to kiss the center of her palm. "Laina."

"What it means is that each god Who answered my plea to save you took a part of my soul."

He looked at her, fear saturating his eyes.

"It is the fee They require for such a favor." Thylaina nodded. "And I *would* do it again to save you, for I have many years ahead of me. That is why only elven royalty can perform such a feat." She lowered her hand. "It was believed only the king could cast the spell, but I felt Vynia's Favor that morning, and knew I could gain more aid from other gods."

"Who?"

"Does it matter?"

"I wish to know to Whom I owe great thanks."

Breydon had to be the most wonderful man in all of Yeuroth to have such devotion and gratitude, especially after all he had suffered. What had she done for the gods to bless her with him for a husband? She kissed him hard. "You are too fine, my love." Smiling, she said, "Vynia, of course. Fynthiar, Bryric, Valorius, and Lessindra. But Lessindra required nothing from me. She said my love for you was payment enough."

He paled. "Even Fynthiar?"

"Even the Father of All."

"But... why?" He raised his hands slightly. "Who am I in this vast world that *He* would grant such a favor? I am no one."

Thylaina stared at her husband. She had never considered why Fynthiar might show favor upon Breydon enough to help bring him back from death, from His own son's heavenly realm. She had heard that people from other countries and continents called Him Fate. So perhaps Fynthiar had a design for Breydon.

She lifted one shoulder toward her tilted head. "Perhaps He wanted you to fulfill your destiny."

# Chapter Twenty-Three

The temple in Haevuan Flameral would not share the fertility elixir with Eidryn without approval from the king, so he asked Vynia for Her help. That was why it took him some time to reply to Thylaina's message. When the Earthen Goddess gave him the means to create a new potion, without having to ride to the other end of Yeuroth for a key ingredient, it was Her wish for Thylaina to have a babe.

"With what are you replacing the crystal petals?" Thylaina inquired, while looking over his shoulder to peek into his herbal journal.

Eidryn closed it and faced her. "My dear, you know better than to peer into another's book."

She sighed. "It is you and me. I am not attempting to steal anything from you. I am simply curious about what you are—"

He pressed his finger to her lips, silencing her. Smiling, he lowered his hand. "Do you recall the small trees growing on the other side of the Black Graunis Mountains, along the edge of the Borial Plains?"

Thylaina shook her head.

Brows low, Eidryn continued. "Particularly south of the Peace Isles' port. I had taken you lot there for a plant found only in that region."

Those were some of Thylaina's most memorable years in Etharell. The years she was away from Haevaun Flameral and the Royal Family, except for Prince

Valraahn. At least he was not like his father. Thylaina had been amongst people who shared a love for Vynia's gifts and a desire to use them for helping others. Again, except for Valraahn. He was there because he had no choice. But he made those years special as he became more than a cousin, but her friend. The prince helped her feel comfortable with the other pupils. Eidryn cared not whom they were, for every one of them were students and nothing more than potential healers. Thylaina had made such wonderful friends during those sixty years.

"I see you remember." Eidryn chuckled. "Those were the best decades of instruction I had ever known. The lot of you..." He nodded. "I had never had more than two good students under my instruction at a time. But with your group, Vynia favored me with three exceptional healers. True healers." He opened the book and turned it toward her. "Students who were already creating their own elixirs, discovering new remedies, and showing devotion much like my own."

Thylaina smiled wide. "Aarosyn and Maelene."

"And you." Eidryn cupped her cheek. "It was a blessing. Of that, I have no doubt."

It stung for a moment, to think of her two friends. "I miss them."

"They do well in their posts." He lowered his arm and stepped back. "Aarosyn joined the Ormiana Xilys, became an Unseen to hunt the Southern Brigands, then returned to his position. He has sent me messages about new concoctions he is creating."

"He had been an Unseen?" Thylaina drew in a long breath, trying to think of why her friend had risked his life.

The Unseen were the best from an already elite force, and had trained to become invisible to their enemies. Thylaina knew not their true methods, but had heard they drove fear into the Alohrian bandits who had dared to cross into Etharell and raze villages. Once those brigands were hunted and killed, Breydon's twin amongst them, the Unseen disbanded and returned to their posts in the Ormiana and Kilstra Forests. And one of her dearest friends had been foolish enough to have joined them? He could have been killed.

Shaking her head, she snapped, "Was Aarosyn not satisfied enough to be a healer?"

"He does not simply play the part as healer, my dear." Eidryn offered a soothing smile, one that had easily comforted her in the past. "Aarosyn is a warrior and one of their best archers. He has made his mark in the xilys."

So her friend went beyond healing. How was he able to focus on both battle and healing? Aarosyn was a talented man, but to put himself in danger as an Unseen... It was all in the past now, so there was no need to worry about him.

"I see." She flipped the page of the journal, barely reading the recipes and notes. "And I know Maelene is with the Forest Army."

"She loves serving under your brother's command." Was that annoyance in Eidryn's voice? "Despite his hatred toward Vynists."

The irritation was understandable. But Thylaina did not want to discuss Neldrid.

"You have not told me what ingredient you intend to use for the elixir."

Eidryn laughed. "Forgive me. Reminiscing is something I do not often get to do." He took the journal and flipped a few pages back. "Sinzdra fruit."

She gaped at him. How could the bittersweet yet spicy fruit replace the delicate crystal petal in the fertility potion?

"After Vynia answered my prayer, I ate this odd fruit, which we have mixed with xarflas for women during their monthly bleeds and those who bled far too much." He paused when Thylaina tilted her head and widened her eyes. "And I shall tell you, my dear, I had such an appetite." Eidryn laughed. "I knew not what to do."

"You...? You craved intimacy?"

"It was a terribly rough evening." He pointed to another ingredient on the page. "Combining it with a few other herbs, particularly ginger root, will increase fertility."

"Are you certain?"

"I am." Although surety filled his voice, it did not show in his gaze.

"You have not had time to test this on anyone," Thylaina said. "You intend me to be your first subject."

"Vynia has shown me this. I trust Her."

Thylaina looked away. Truth was, she trusted Vynia and Eidryn, and knew neither would do anything to hurt her. The goddess had told Thylaina she was Her Favored, so why would She risk bringing any harm?

Nodding, she smiled. "Very well."

Eidryn instructed Thylaina on making the elixir, which was far easier than she anticipated. Breydon would partake in the drink as well, whether or not he needed. For only one of them to consume the potion would leave their mate far too exhausted to meet the demands of the other. There was no testing if she and Eidryn had made it correctly or not; Thylaina and Breydon would have to just drink it.

Eight nights later, Eidryn poured the elixir into two goblets, then added a sweet berry wine, which would blend perfectly. He offered the cups. "I shall stay to ensure this works."

Frowning, Breydon opened his mouth to speak.

"However," Eidryn said, "I will leave the moment things become... interesting."

Thylaina rolled her eyes as she took a goblet.

Breydon snatched the other, nearly spilling the precious drink. When his eyes met Thylaina's, his expression softened. "I pray for a success, and for your safety."

"And the babe's."

"Of course." Thylaina brought the cup to her mouth. "For us, my love."

Breydon hesitated, appearing he wished to say something more. Perhaps protest, but he drank instead.

The concoction tasted like a fine, exotic wine. Even Breydon appeared surprised as he stared at the empty glass with a cocked brow.

Eidryn stood near the door and waited.

Breydon glanced at him, then faced Thylaina. Disappointment showed in his eyes, which then widened. "Gods," he whispered. Beads of sweat formed along his hairline and above his lips. He set the cup on the table, but too close to the edge and it fell to the floor. That did not draw his gaze from Thylaina as he stepped closer. "I want you. I need you. Right now."

Just to hear those words and see the ravenousness way he looked at her sent a burning sensation from her breasts to her haven. And by the gods, she wanted him. Thylaina tossed the goblet onto the chair, then threw her arms around his shoulders. Their mouths met in devouring kisses. As he lifted her enough to walk to the bed, the chamber door opened and closed.

"I love you," he said against her lips, pushing her gown off her shoulders and forcing it down her body.

"Oh, Breydon." Thylaina tugged on his hoses, baring him as fast as possible.

They barely made it to the corner of the bed when he placed one of her legs over his shoulder, grabbed the other and hooked it over his hip, trying desperately to fill her. But it was never something they could do quickly. Not with him being a human and she an elf.

Breydon slowed his thrusts to how they normally began making love, and once he was fully within, the fury of desire overcame them both. He pulled her tight to him, lifting her bottom off the bed as he straightened, pushing deeper.

Making this moment memorable was not possible. Thylaina's body, mind, and desires battled with what she wanted and how to get it. Breydon was within—perfect! And she wanted him to send her to the highest point of ecstasy—which seemed was just about to happen. Too fast. It all came too damn fast. Is this how it was for all elves who partook in the fertility potion on their marriage nights?

The burning intensified as his thrusts increased. Sweet Lessindra, it was glorious!

Thylaina gave in to the release, experiencing pure rapture. And there would be two nights and one day more of this.

Thylaina awoke to someone touching her shoulder. She did not want to be touched, nor did she wish to be awake. Muscles exhausted and mind fatigued, there was only the need to sleep. But damn it to Darkness, she was hungry. She and Breydon had eaten little during their coupling.

"My dear, do remember that you must drink this," Eidryn said. What was he doing here? "Thylaina, you both must drink this. It will help you recover."

Sludge. A blend of certain herbs mixed with enough olesa oil to create a thick drink for replenishing the body and ease the aches. One still had to rest several hours, but that gave the sludge time to do what it needed to help the recipient: those recovering from nearly two days of vigorous lovemaking with practically no respite.

Thylaina sat up and took a shallow bowl from Eidryn. The drink was grainy, tasted like earth, and gave no satisfaction. Did he truly give her mud? She was too tired to care, so she gave the bowl back and slid beneath the covers.

She opened her eyes enough to see him walk around the bed, refilling the bowl to attend Breydon.

"Captain," he said, still speaking Elvish. "Drink this. Remember we spoke about it."

"Leave," Breydon mumbled.

"You shall regret it if you do not drink it."

A long groan sounded from Breydon, then he rolled over and sat up enough to drink the sludge. He coughed and hacked.

"Do not spit it out, Captain."

"That's awful."

"But it does well for your body. Now rest some more."

Eidryn quietly left.

Thylaina scooted closer to Breydon, touched her forehead to his back. "I love you."

It was silent for a few seconds.

"You are my greatest love," he whispered, then snored.

Everything Breydon and Eidryn had assumed Thylaina would attempt to do throughout the pregnancy had been accurate. She had grown larger than expected—some said she looked far too big to be walking all over the city. Breydon's frustrations with her stubbornness led to arguments, and Eidryn supporting him did not help. Thylaina was only helping others, and for once, she was teaching her former master as he assisted with her patients for four months. However, he was not only aiding her and meeting her patients, whom he would begin caring for in her stead, but he watched her like an overbearing Royal Guard. And when not taking care of the citizens of Caerabis, she and Eidryn created teas they believed would help maintain hers and the babe's health.

By the end of the first week into the pregnancy's fourth month, Thylaina experienced terrible pain in her lower abdomen. It frightened her, especially with Breydon away. Eidryn then declared she would cease work and remain in bed for the rest of the pregnancy.

She threw down the towel she just dried her hands with. "No!"

"Damn it, woman!" He crossed his arms, his gray eyes nearly silver now. "We had an agreement. And with your husband away, I shall ensure you abide by it."

"I can still help people. There is another month and a half!"

"No." His expression grew grave. "You bear a human's child, my dear. You will not complete the full pregnancy. No elf maiden ever has."

Her mouth dried. "Why did you not tell me this?"

"I had, but you disregarded it with the, '*We are the greatest healers,*' excuse to pretend all shall be fine." He directed her to the chair, then sat across from her. "This is about you and your child, Thylaina." His voice was soft and sincere, in a way she had never heard. "I do not want to lose either of you, nor does your husband."

She looked at the hearth. Breydon had lost so much as it was, and she could not do this to him. Although he had wanted a child, he would have happily gone the rest of their days without one, knowing she would be safe. But Thylaina did this, and she had to make good her promise to him and Eidryn. "Very well. I shall do as you say."

Eidryn allowed her to finish a handful of tasks in the apothecary room afore confining her to bed, as long as she remained seated. Thylaina prepared several herbs, oils, sponishies, and other remedies while she enjoyed this final moment in the room, unsure of when she would next stand there. The mixture of fragrances helped ease her mind and muscles. Eidryn accompanied her, bringing items from every end of the room. They soon broke out into a song of praise to Vynia, interrupted by a knock on the door.

Katjina entered, pausing for a moment upon meeting Eidryn's gaze. A knowing look shared between them. Something... intimate.

Thylaina did not want to further imagine her former master bedding her friend and servant. It was not upsetting, but simply unexpected. Eidryn had never seemed the sort to lay with a human. But he was unlike most elves. He truly loved life and showed respect to all. At least, until they treated him poorly. Bound to no wife, he was free to share his bed with whom he wanted. Although he had a daughter. An exceptional beauty rarely seen by others. Yaliese was no ordinary elf maiden. She was a greater being—an immortal. And Thylaina was truly thankful that Eidryn had not brought her to Caerabis, for she would have had every male within the city ignoring their duties—and wives—hoping to gain her favor. Her presence simply demanded it. Those years of studying under Eidryn, the men in Thylaina's healing group had all physically fought for Yaliese's attention.

"You are elsewhere," he said, slicing into her thoughts.

Giggling, she finished pouring insh oil into several small vials. "I was thinking about your daughter."

His face brightened, and his irises turned silver. "Thank the gods I did not bring her here. These human men would have begun dueling."

Thylaina's laughter filled the room, his quickly joining. "That is exactly what I imagined." Once they quieted, she asked, "How does she fare?"

"She despises staying in our home, but at least we have the forest." Eidryn heaved a sigh as he began wrapping another roll of linen strips. "She stalks the woods for males to sate her appetite, something I believe she inherited from her mother."

A wide smile stretched Thylaina's lips. "You truly are Vynia's Favored to have sired her child."

He looked at her, joy a beautiful expression on his handsome face. "I conceded that title to you, my lady, months ago. And I am proud to work alongside you." Eidryn returned to the wraps. "But to have loved Her were the most blessed nights and days of my life. And that She entrusted me to raise Yaliese? I am grateful. I just wish Yaliese was ready to go on her own, but she will not leave me."

"She loves you."

"She fears the mortals, and I know not why."

Thylaina considered the way her own people viewed elves like Eidryn. Like her. "Because others are not kind to those they do not understand."

He nodded once, sorrow overshadowing the joy that had been there only seconds ago. "You are correct, my dear. But one day, I shall be gone, and Yaliese must move on."

Thylaina froze, tears immediately threatening to fall. "Please do not say such things."

Eidryn dropped the linen and rounded the table to kneel afore her. "Do not worry." He kissed her hands, one at a time. "It shall be a very long time afore Death claims me."

She prayed that was true.

Thylaina despised it. Sitting in bed for two weeks and doing nothing was awful, especially while everyone celebrated the beginning of a new year. At least Breydon refused to leave for the remainder of the pregnancy. Tesesra visited, sometimes making jests about how Thylaina might want to learn needlepoint to help pass the time. Amusing, but not appreciated. In fact, many attempted to visit, but only the Momestids were permitted to see Thylaina, and only if they were well. Eidryn and Breydon would not risk her falling ill.

On the ninth Cold day, the babe was ready to enter Emvarr.

Breydon stayed at the Momestid's mansion, keeping busy with Grim. Tes and Katjina remained at Thylaina's side, and Eidryn oversaw the birth.

She had never experienced such pain, but the women offered wonderful support, and Eidryn's intense focus and calm demeanor gave an orderly environment. Then the pushing began, and Thylaina hated it.

"I swear... I am never... doing this... again!"

"Push, dear," Tes said, a hint of laughter in her voice.

Too bad she did not realize this was no comical moment. Not with an elf birthing a half-human. Despite all the care and precautions she and Eidryn did, there was no promise she and the babe would survive.

Eidryn constantly whispered prayers between instructions.

Thylaina concentrated on doing what she had to do. But after four hours of pushing with no results, fear of losing the babe weakened her heart, soul, and mind. Sobs sputtered between her lips.

"Rest for a moment, my dear," he said, moving to her side. Eidryn gently held her hand between his. "Give everything to Her. Trust Her. She did not offer us gifts for nothing. I promise you."

Thylaina closed her eyes and drew in a few deep breaths to calm herself as best as possible. *Yes. I trust You, Vynia.*

He kissed her scarred fingers, glancing at them as he rose. "Her Strength is yours."

Peace encompassed her. Comfort. Then pain. "It is time," she whispered.

Eidryn resumed the serious undertaking of guiding the birthing. Tes and Katjina continued caring for Thylaina and encouraging her. At least they did not constantly prattle words at her, but spoke softly and only occasionally, seeming to know when to speak.

*I trust You, my Goddess. I put us in Your Hands.* Thylaina pushed, grunting louder.

"That is better, my dear," Eidryn said.

Thirty minutes later, the babe cried. His body was longer than her forearm. That explained why she got so bloody big. And he took so much out of Thylaina.

Eidryn continued tending to her while she attempted to breastfeed the babe. *My son.* Tears filled her eyes. *Thank You, Vynia. Praises to You, always.*

Breydon and Grim arrived two hours later, the latter leaving with Tes shortly after. Breydon, Eidryn, and Katjina were the only ones still in the room with Thylaina and the babe. For several minutes, Breydon stared at her, speechless. Then Katjina put his freshly bathed son into his arms, which then brought him to weep.

Eidryn appeared to approve of the reaction, for he smiled faintly. "I suggest not moving Thylaina to the bedchamber just yet. Perhaps not for a day or two."

Katjina frowned. "That's ridiculous. We always move mothers to their bedchambers shortly after—"

"But those women are not an elf who just birthed a half-human." Eidryn nodded once. "I will let you know when it is safe to move her."

"It is fine," Thylaina said. "I just wish to sleep."

"You're staying with her, correct?" Breydon asked the master healer.

Eidryn grinned. "Of course, Shapele."

Breydon looked at Thylaina. "What shall we name him?"

"Let us decide later. I need rest."

"As you wish, my love."

"Brenlyr?" Breydon wrinkled his nose.

"It is part of your name and part of my father's."

He scoffed. "The father you have very little to say anything about, and when you do, it's often about how he tried to marry you off to a pompous elf lord?"

"I still love him!"

Breydon gently rocked from one foot to the other while holding their son. "I'm not saying I don't like it. I just don't know what I think about it. It's so... Elvish."

She raised a brow. "Is there something wrong with an Elvish name? His surname is human."

He smiled. "Fine." Holding the babe at arm's length to view him, he said, "Brenlyr Colmstad. Does that fit you?"

The babe's color had improved the past four days, and dark hair was more noticeable atop his scalp. What Thylaina found most adorable was the slight point of his ears. She could not help catching them between her lips when she snuggled him close.

"It fits him perfectly," she said. "A name he shall carry with great pride."

Breydon regarded his son. "I agree, my love."

# Chapter Twenty-Four

Twelve glorious years moved forward, and Thylaina and Breydon watched Brenlyr grow into a fine young squire. Two years following their son's birth, Eidryn taught Thylaina how to make a potion to reverse the effects of the fertility elixir. Although another child would have been lovely, she and Breydon decided not to risk another attempt. They already spent their days looking over their shoulders, weary of spies. It was not the fear grasping Thylaina's heart, but the promising of an end no one could stop.

Breydon continued to age slowly. Looking at him, one would believe he was still in his early twenties, when he was indeed thirty-five-years. A suspected gift from Valorius when Breydon met Him in death then lived, yet a curse to not know the extent of his longevity. Eidryn promised to seek answers. At least Breydon was there for Brenlyr. Thylaina had dreaded their son losing him too early in life. Thankfully, Breydon often had Brenlyr at his side while he was in the city, and sometimes took him to the outskirts on the plains for riding lessons.

Over the past fortnight, Breydon had been in Etharell. It was not the first time he traveled to Mystier to meet with Thylaina's brother this past decade, but this was the longest he had stayed in the Forest Army's city. He should have returned five days past; it was unlike him to be late. She had never felt as anxious as she did now. Since her husband's departure, time had moved like an hourglass full of mud instead of sand. Great Bryric, fear did awful things to one's mind and soul.

Beneath the warm Fox's Sun, Thylaina squinted as she paced along the rail of Grim's cabinet balcony. Her gaze shifted between two of the main paths leading into and out of Caerabis. The direction her life had taken since leaving Etharell was nothing as she had imagined nor planned. That she had intended to reach Yeltar was now laughed at when mentioned. Strange how her fate brought her here. From several months as a prisoner to being the wife of the First Captain of a knight city, she was the happiest she had ever been. More than she dreamed possible. And now, after nearly fifteen years of bliss, she was frightened.

Did Breydon's tongue slip about their marriage, therefore, her brother kept him prisoner? No. Breydon was no fool. Gods. If Neldrid learned about her marrying a human, he would personally haul her back to Etharell and do everything possible to revoke the marriage. But could her brother's rage destroy wedded vows? Perhaps not. However, a king's ire just might have such weight.

No. Thylaina would never permit it. She would fight Neldrid and Uncle Yasontler with all the energy flowing throughout her body. Breydon's heart was the greatest gift from Fynthiar and Lessindra. What Thylaina had done to gain such favor from the gods, especially the Father of All, she knew not. She would cherish it every moment of Breydon's life. No one—not Neldrid, Father, nor Uncle Yasontler—would take that happiness from her.

"Thylaina," Nadiera called softly from the balcony entrance. "Father said you were out here worrying yourself ill." She stepped outside, holding her infant son, Jerien. It was about time he slept. The poor babe had been suffering terrible stomach pains as of late.

Resistance was impossible; Thylaina caressed Jerien's chubby cheek. "Thank Vynia he has found sleep." The Earthen Goddess deserved praise for providing the herbs Thylaina needed to make a remedy for the poor woman standing afore her.

Nadiera showed a tired smile, appearing to have rested a little as well. "Yes. And thank *you*. That oil worked wonderfully. And now he's feeding from me instead of the nursemaid."

"Magnificent. Continue to take one drop after each meal."

"I will."

Thylaina glanced to the west, from where the pounding of hooves sounded. Not Breydon's squad. She returned her attention to Nadiera and Jerien. "You should slumber with him. You need it as much as he."

Nadiera patted the babe's back. "I know, but I wait as well."

Her husband, Sir Vhilmas Freyvlor, rode with Breydon. Days of worry and little sleep left her exhausted.

"Go on," Thylaina said. "Rest will help you produce plenty of milk for Jerien."

"As you—" Nadiera yawned. "Forgive me. I best get to bed."

Thylaina touched Jerien's cheek again. "If they arrive, I shall send for you. I promise." She directed Nadiera toward the door, where Grim now stood. "Off to bed."

The marshal kissed his daughter's head, his grandson's, then moved aside. "Sleep, love. I'm certain you'll hear plenty of commotion should they arrive." He winked at Thylaina.

Rolling her eyes, she faced the city again.

Grim stood aside her, squeezed her hand. "If only watching the path would make Breydon and the others appear."

Thylaina hugged his arm and rested her head on his shoulder. "If only."

He patted her hand. "Trust in Valorius that all is well."

"You have heard from Breydon, then?"

Grim nodded. "He's in Warstchia, and will return soon."

She pressed her lips between her teeth to stop from crying.

"One night after another, my dear," he assured.

"Another night with him gone." A teardrop overthrew her defenses. "I want my husband home."

"I assure you Breydon wishes to be here." He guided her into the cabinet, the steps slow toward the exit.

"Then why did he go to—?"

"He had his reasons." Grim smiled and opened the door.

Knights stood to attention and servants bustled up and down the stairs. Aromas of the evening's supper already wafted throughout the large chamber.

Thylaina's stomach rumbled a minor complaint; she had not eaten since breaking fast.

They descended to the first floor, and as they stepped into the foyer, he held firm to her hand. "Breydon sent his apologies," he said. Joy suddenly lit his green eyes. "That man loves you."

Promises her husband had made afore marrying, on the blessed night they spoke their vows, and several times more over the past fifteen years, repeated through her mind. Thylaina kissed Grim's cheek. "And I love him."

"I'll see you at supper."

Thylaina curtsied to the marshal, then nodded once to the guard at the entrance.

Sir Amdronus, Katjina's husband, bowed slightly and opened the door. "My lady." It was still odd to see knights guarding the mansion these days, even though it started eight years past, once suspicions of spies grew even greater. "Katjina awaits at home," he added.

"Thank you."

Thylaina glanced at the sky, determining the time near five. She had an hour to ready for dinner. Thank the gods Katjina remained with her after marrying Amdronus. The handmaiden was still reliable to complete any task, and without complaint, gossip, nor resentment. Thylaina walked next door to her home.

Brenlyr spoke at the end of the stepping-stone path with two other squires. They smiled and bowed upon her approach. "We'll finish this conversation later," Brenlyr said, dismissing them. He opened the door for Thylaina. "Any word on Father?"

She waited until they were inside. "He is in Warstchia and shall return soon."

"Warstchia?" Brenlyr frowned, looking more like Breydon. His blue eyes grew intense as his handsome face scrunched. If his hair had been red instead of black, he would be a young version of his father. "Why is he there?"

"I know not." Thylaina sighed. "I suppose he shall let us know."

Brenlyr released a heavy breath and nodded. "Are we dining with the Momestids again?"

"Unless you have other plans?" She raised a brow. "Lady Telsia shall be there, of course."

That always made him blush.

"Mother, please."

She palmed his warm cheek, her thumb grazing freckles. "Go wash."

He swiftly departed. Probably hoped to avoid any further comments about Telsia. The two would make a lovely couple. Breydon had mentioned talking to Grim about arranging a betrothal between Brenlyr and Telsia, but Thylaina opposed. Let them find love with one another if that was the path their lives led them. But that was not the life for which Telsia wished.

The young maiden had spent most of her younger years tailing her father, sitting in on the meetings he would permit, including those in the war room. She grew up with knights in her home, often accompanying her if she left the mansion. Those men became her friends, and she adored them. Instead of giving time to learn needlepoint, she pestered the knights with questions about swordplay, armor, and battles. She insisted on learning how to ride one of the stallions, although only knights could own one. The maiden even spoke with the squires, soon having them fighting over who would gain her attention most. It did not matter, for when she wanted to relax with her dearest friends, it was Brenlyr and Einasa's youngest daughter, Aella; Alyanna was too busy trying to learn how to behave like a proper lady.

Thylaina headed to her bedchamber, but redirected to the apothecary. The door closed, she relaxed in the cool air and breathed deep, tasting the fragrant herbs. Brenlyr dominated her thoughts. He seemed protective about Telsia—even more about Aella. Would he have difficulty choosing one for a bride? No reason to think such questions. There was time for them all to learn whom they were and what they wanted in life. Although, she knew what Telsia desired most.

After a moment passed and her mind calmed, Thylaina went to her bedroom.

Katjina rose from tending to the hearth. "M'lady."

Thylaina let her shoulders fall as she dragged her feet to her favorite chair. "Breydon's return is delayed."

The handmaiden frowned. "I'm sorry."

"N'ei." Thylaina waved the apology aside. "The marshal invited us to supper."

Katjina bowed her head. "I shall pick a dress."

"Thank you, dear."

The woman was immediately in motion, humming as she opened the wardrobe.

Thylaina smiled while she watched her. "I saw Amdronus at the mansion."

Katjina removed a green and marigold dress from the wardrobe. "He guards until three for the next four nights. Then he'll have two evenings off before returning for seven more."

"Dreadful shift."

"We'll adjust. He loves serving Marshal Momestid." Wrinkles formed at the corners of the handmaiden's eyes as she smiled. Nothing ever let her down.

Thylaina recalled when no such lines existed on Katjina's face, when she was in her early twenties and eager to do more than choose the perfect dresses, of which she did an excellent job. The handmaiden's life changed when Amdronus returned from Warstchia. Eight years her senior, the knight had stolen her heart shortly following his arrival. The whole affair made Katjina nervous, for she was a servant. Knights typically interacted with servants for intimate reasons, but three moons after their first dinner together, Amdronus professed his love, and they immediately married. The evenings he had off duty, he stayed with her at the Colmstad's home. Otherwise, he remained in the barracks. Katjina had hoped to have a child, but seven years had passed since making their marriage bed and she remained childless.

"M'lady?"

Thylaina raised her eyes to the handmaiden. "I was thinking of our years together."

"The best of my life." Katjina winked. "Is Jovie tending to Master Brenlyr?"

Thylaina shrugged. "I hope so."

"He has been quite lazy as of late."

"Jovie recovered from galnikath only two months ago," Thylaina said with a patience not normally needed with her handmaiden. "He is the first human to survive that illness. He does his best."

Katjina frowned. "Forgive me, m'lady. I just... Sometimes I'm angry with him when I think of how he could've infected Master Brenlyr or the captain."

Thylaina grasped her friend's hand. "And I would have saved their lives as well."

Nightmares of Brenlyr's flesh turning a pale shade of yellow while the inside of his body rotted from galnikath kept Thylaina from decent sleep. When she finally found peaceful darkness, a gentle push on her arm preceded a firm shove.

"M'lady."

Thylaina drew in a deep breath. "Katjina? What is it?"

"Captain has returned."

She sat up. "When? What time is it?" She scanned the room, finding Breydon was not there. "Where is he?"

"It's just half past the third hour." Katjina brought Thylaina's robe to her. "He returned an hour ago, but Amdronus said he came directly to the mansion. Captain's in the family room at this moment."

Thylaina stood and let the handmaiden assist with the robe. "Grim impressed his return would be a few days at the least."

"Amdronus said a messenger arrived prior to Captain. The men were all like cats prowling in the night." She retrieved Thylaina's slippers, directed her to sit at the hearth. "He said Marshal Momestid met the captain in his office. Something seemed wrong."

Thylaina lowered to the large chair. "But why did Breydon not come here?"

"I don't know, m'lady."

Thylaina's heart raced at the thought of seeing her husband. "Katjina, you may return to bed. I shall manage."

"Thank you, m'lady."

Thylaina hurried down the corridor, unable to reach the family room fast enough.

Firelight flickered wildly from beneath the door's crack. She opened it slowly, peeked inside. Breydon's head tilted back on the couch, his eyes closed, and breath deep and even. Gods, he looked ragged, especially with that beard.

Tears welled as she stared at him. Beard or not, Breydon was the most wonderful sight. Blinking her vision clear, she entered the room and neared the sofa, noting his shirt parted and the strings draped aside. Her gaze fell to the light line of red hair trailing from his belly button to beneath his leather pants. He appeared thinner.

Hard to believe her brother did not feed Breydon at all. Acquiring the best of everything to cater to Neldrid's needs included those who cooked his meals. He would impress his guests with some of the most wonderful food, like finer sea fare and sweeter dishes than at the palace; an unmet promise he had made to Thylaina decades ago. After nine years of no invitation, she knew her brother had lied to placate her. But to see Breydon a few pounds lighter was unexpected. Thylaina had waited to hear about the wonderful meals served from Neldrid's scullery. Truth be told, she wanted to learn how her brother fared.

As she neared the sofa, she spotted the tip of Breydon's tongue poking from between his lips. The man was not asleep, but deep in thought, and likely aware of her presence. As ridiculous as it looked, it was just as equally adorable. Especially since he never realized he did it.

Thylaina lifted the empty glass off the table in front of the couch and continued to the selection of drinks in the corner of the room. Something dark and smooth. Blackberry fruzae. Breydon had his preferences, all of them on this very table. Thylaina had sipped his favorite once—a blend of honey, apple, and crueberry—and found it far too strong for her liking. Wine was perfect. She poured a swill of the blackberry blend and sat beside him.

"What busies your mind, my love?"

A brow arched, but his eyes remained closed. "Is that how you greet your husband upon his return home?"

She swirled the liquor, then fitted the glass into his hand until his fingers secured around it. "How different is it than how he greets his wife?"

Breydon opened his eyes and turned his head, his voice soft as he spoke. "I didn't wish to wake you. I did, however, look upon you for several minutes." He glided the back of his finger down her cheek—a welcomed touch. "And thanked Valorius and Bryric for my safe return home."

Thylaina sat up. "What happened? Did Neldrid threaten you?"

A smile curved one corner of his lips. "N'ei. Your brother was hospitable as ever. In fact, his worry about you heightens. The search efforts have expanded across Yeuroth, and he intends to sail to Myndrose and Brydasia."

She stiffened. "He shall go so far?"

"One day." Breydon drank until the glass was empty, then set it on the table. "Neldrid's grown desperate." He shook his head as he wiped his lips with his wrist. "This is the third time I've met with him over the past eight years, and I can see that he's changed."

Thylaina turned her head toward the hearth and the blank wall above it. That would not be empty for much longer. "Is that so?"

"Regret has pierced this man."

A brief laugh escaped her, much to her husband's obvious displeasure. "A regret he would never have known should I have stayed in Haevaun Flameral and married Rhomasyn." She rose and crossed her arms. "Neldrid did not give a bloody damn what happened to me afore. I certainly do not understand why he cares now."

"Because you're his sister." Although he remained surprisingly calm, Breydon also appeared sad. "He loves you, Laina, and he wants you home safe."

"I *am* home and I *am* safe."

His shoulders lowered. "Let us go to bed, love. We'll break fast with Grim's family, then he and I shall meet."

"You met with him this evening."

"There's... more." Breydon sighed. "How's Brenlyr's training?"

Thylaina would not press for what he withheld from her. Breydon would tell her when he was ready. She looked toward the dancing flames. "You should ask him. He would love to tell you all about it."

Breydon stood and pulled her close, pressed his forehead to hers. If he did not smell of sweat, leather, armor oil, and dirt, she would not have minded his nearness. "I missed you more than you can possibly know," he said, caressing her cheek.

"I believe I do." She slid her hands behind his neck and rose to her toes. "For I ached in your absence."

Their lips met in a deep kiss, and those damn beard hairs rubbed against her skin.

"I'm exhausted," he said. "Otherwise, I'd make love to you."

Thylaina huffed a laugh. "Bathe first, my love. Then you can have me all you want."

Breydon was awake afore sunrise, writing in his cabinet. Thylaina had a bath prepared in the small bathing room shared between theirs and Brenlyr's bedchambers. She placed shaving items atop the table beside the steaming tub. Stems of rosemary floated within the rings of mint oil in the water, the blended fragrances meant to clear his mind after such a short rest.

He entered, still donning clothes from the previous night. Breydon scratched his head; the red locks an unruly mess. Eyes fixed on the table, a smirk played at the corner of his lips as he massaged his beard. "It's not even dawn."

Thylaina simpered. "I will not endure it for even one day."

He tilted his head back, his chin cradled between his finger and thumb. "I think it makes me look more... distinguished."

"Distinguished?" She pulled her belt loose and let the robe pool at her feet. "If you wish to have your face between my thighs again, you will get in the water."

His gaze lowered, irises glowing. "Shave the beard now."

Settled in the tub, Breydon relaxed against her, increasing the sensation to her already heated body. Thylaina wetted the shaving bar; a soap she had made with corn silk and special herbs. She lathered it into the rough hairs on his cheek, jaw, and throat, then let it soak.

"Why did you go to Warstchia?"

He groaned, his body feeling heavier. "There's so much, Laina." His voice was low. Irritated. "So much I wish to tell you, but I must speak with Grim first."

She tilted his head back and started an upward stroke over his throat with the shaving blade. "Tell me how my brother fares."

Breydon moaned. "How am I relaxed while you do this?"

"Because you trust me."

"Because I love feeling your body against mine," he whispered.

Thylaina smiled. "Tell me about my brother."

"I'll answer when you're finished."

Rarely had she heard a somber tone from him. It concerned her. Had something terrible befallen Neldrid?

Focusing enough to perform the task while the silence throbbed in her ears and worry busied her mind was difficult. But Thylaina managed.

Once finished, Breydon splashed his face clean, grabbed the towel from the table, and wiped dry. "I hate being in your brother's presence." He barely looked at her.

Thylaina sank slightly in the water. "Why is that?"

"Because I see you." He dunked forward and saturated his hair.

She grabbed the bathing bar and turned it until plenty of bubbles covered her hands. Rubbing it on his scalp and through his hair, she imagined Neldrid's face: elven perfection accented with rare copper eyes. Thylaina moved her hands down Breydon's nape, shoulders, and back, then grabbed a sponge and washed him, noting each scar, freckle, mole, and flexing muscle.

"General Zorlias..." Breydon shook his head. "Sometimes he frightens me. I don't know what your brother's thinking or feeling—his expressions reveal nothing. Yet when he speaks about you, he falters."

*What a shame he did not miss me afore I left.*

"Being stuck in his presence for almost two bloody weeks, seeing you in his face, it was difficult." Breydon dunked forward again, getting most of the soap from his hair. "There were times I thought I might kiss him."

Thylaina stared at the back of his head. Dropping the sponge, she hugged him; he jerked, as if expecting a different reaction. "I love you."

"Great Valorius, I thought you might hit me."

The playfulness in his voice brought a smile. Thylaina closed her eyes, rested her cheek against his wet shoulder.

"Your brother misses you. Your absence hurts him."

She opened her eyes, breathed deep, then released it. "I told you about the letter he sent to me. Neldrid wanted me out of his life." Tears came too quickly at the memory of reading those words.

*'Rhomasyn is to be your husband—something neither of us can change... Embrace your destiny just as the rest of us have.'*

There was more he had written, accusations and assumptions. But those lines had stung the most. Nothing else in Neldrid's letter emphasized his desire to have her out of his life more.

Breydon tried to reposition in the tub, but with little success. He managed to partially twist around and cram his leg against the side of the tub. But the discomfort did not stop him from palming her cheek and stroking a teardrop away with his thumb.

"I was alone," she whispered. "Everyone close to me had left Haevaun Flameral. My father and Neldrid avoided the palace—avoided me. They left me to that pompous idiot, expecting me to marry him."

"I know why you left, darling, and I understand." Breydon whirled one hand in the air, as if casting a spell. His strange gestures normally amused her, but not at this moment. "I just think you should send a letter to your brother. Let him know you're alive and safe."

Thylaina shook her head. "N'ei."

"Love—"

"He will do his best to track the letter... *here*."

"He couldn't possibly."

Strange how years ago Breydon had feared the same thing, but now? Now he had forgotten the lengths her brother would go to find her.

"Neldrid's spies are amongst the best in Yeuroth. He would use every resource available, including what my uncle might permit from the Royal Coffers." She leaned against the back of the tub. "After receiving a letter from me, Neldrid would never stop until he found me, and he would fight to take me back to Etharell."

What Thylaina spoke was the truth, yet Breydon smirked and moved closer. "They'd never take you from me. I'd call upon the gods to stop them from destroying our family."

Great Bryric, she appreciated his tenacity. However, Neldrid would kill him if he learned Breydon had hidden the truth all these years. But upon learning about Brenlyr, there would be nothing her brother could do. He could not possibly rend her family into pieces. She did not believe Uncle Yasontler, nor Father, would permit it.

"Let us finish. Grim waits." Breydon kissed her, then stood. The water streamed down his fine body.

Thylaina loved drying him after a bath: the nearness and touches. Droplets skimmed her flesh, surprisingly cold in the muggy room. Breydon took the towel from her and dropped it to the floor. "What is it you think you are doing, Shapele?"

"I'm going to dry you, my lady." He smeared water down her back to her bottom, then lowered his head to her shoulder, kissed a droplet away. The warmth of his tongue immediately followed. His arms enveloped her, holding her tight against him.

"What about your meeting with Grim?"

"It can wait." He hissed against her neck. "Great Valorius, Laina. You feel divine."

A nip on her throat sent a shiver through her, raising goosebumps.

Not the floor. Breydon was not that sort of man—never aching enough to take her to the floor. The vanity table, however, no matter that she barely fit on it, nor the mess he left on the floor from swiping the contents aside, was perfect.

Thylaina grasped the edges as he placed her knees over his shoulders, his smooth cheeks grazing the insides of her thighs. The heat of his mouth brushed against her afore his lips touched, then his tongue. She tossed her head back and sucked in a loud breath, her chest heaving. It seemed ages had passed since their last moment of passion, and his aggressive feasting proved he felt the same. Thylaina could not silence herself from the swift ecstasy. And when Breydon appeared satisfied, he slowly ventured a warm, damp trail with his tongue up her belly to her breasts. She clamped her legs around his and hugged his head while he sucked a nipple into his mouth.

After a few minutes of fondling it with his tongue, he straightened and pulled her closer. Long. Slow. Bit by bit. As always, a thrilling experience to feel him coming home. Keeping her balanced, he thrust again and again, his muscles tight, their gazes locked. Perspiration replaced the water, their bodies slicker in the heated bathing room. Already stimulated from his feasting, Thylaina peaked, yet he remained solid.

He withdrew, guided her from the table, and spun her around. His virility slid easily within. Hard. Fast.

The first time he had ever taken her in this position, she thought it dreadful. Too human. Animalistic. But the climax experienced, the pleasure *she* received, changed her view. To feel his grip on her hips tighten, hear the strain in his voice, and the change in the pace of his motion added to her excitement, and she released with him. Her legs wobbled as he held her from behind, panting into her hair.

"Gods, I love you, Laina."


They dressed, then broke fast with the Momestids. Nadiera was there with her family: Sir Vhilmas and their children, Annemie and Jerien. Their daughter had just celebrated her third birth-day a week ago, and Nadiera promised they would have a special dinner now that Vhilmas was home.

Telsia, now fifteen-years old, had plenty of attention from squires and young knights, yet brushed aside their courting attempts. But she had shared with Thylaina something she intended to reveal to her parents. It had to be soon, for time was running short for the young maiden. However, Telsia had not yet arrived to break fast.

Brenlyr was also missing. Were the two off together? This had a few speculations pass between Grim and Tes, much to Thylaina's annoyance.

As much as she adored the idea of Brenlyr and Telsia finding love, she refused to force it. Besides, there was also Aella Jalfiasin, who seemed to have taken a fancy to Brenlyr as well. But not knowing if her son would outlive his wife by decades or hundreds of years left Thylaina hesitating on suggesting any human prospects. Not that it mattered.

The meal was a loud event as laughter and chatter filled the chamber. Even the servants partook in the families' joys. Breydon, although smiling often, appeared troubled.

Nadiera laughed at something Vhilmas had whispered, almost knocking over her cup of tea. Jerien cried. She withdrew her breast from her dress, then latched the babe on.

"You look radiant, Nadiera," Thylaina said.

The young woman blushed, glanced at her husband. "Thank you."

Vhilmas tipped his head toward Thylaina. "I understand you've a hand in helping her find rest."

"Oh?" Breydon said. "Did you sleep last night?"

Thylaina slapped his arm. "That was inappropriate."

Nadiera's blush darkened, yet she fought hard to withhold a growing smile.

Vhilmas cleared his throat and grabbed his goblet of goat's milk. "Probably none more than you."

"Trust me," Breydon raised his cup of coffee, "I slept."

"That's a surprise." Vhilmas winked at Thylaina.

Scowling, Nadiera punched his arm. "That was inappropriate as well."

He rubbed his arm, frowned at her. "Not any more than what Breydon said."

Brenlyr and Telsia entered the chamber, gaining everyone's attention.

"Forgive me," Telsia said, sauntering to her chair. "I was at the temple."

Brenlyr pushed her seat in, then sat beside Thylaina. "Father, Mother." He bowed his head. "Marshal, Your Ladyship."

"Enough of that!" Tes snapped, a smile brightening her eyes. "You're amongst family." She turned to Telsia as Brenlyr lifted his spoon and scooped some porridge. "You've been at the temple quite often lately."

"There has been much to pray about." Telsia darted her gaze at Brenlyr, then Thylaina. Had they been conspiring something she knew nothing about? If so, then Telsia had not been honest with Thylaina about her intentions for her future.

"With the time you've spent at the temples," Grim began, "I've wondered if you're considering exchanging vows with one of the young priests. Marrying one of them would be acceptable, although not what I'd wished."

Telsia raised a brow. "Won't you be pleased no matter what man I marry so long as he loves me?"

"Of course we would," her mother said.

"Then why are you concerned?" Telsia asked.

"You're the marshal's daughter," Breydon said. "That alone gains the attention of several men who believe it'll help their placement in the knighthood."

The young maiden cocked her head. "No offense meant, Captain, but this is none of your affair."

Tes gasped; Nadiera's mouth fell wide open; and Arhgrim scowled at his youngest daughter.

Breydon, however, chuckled. "True, my darling girl."

Telsia looked pleadingly at Thylaina, who motioned to the marshal with a short jerk of her head.

"Father," the young girl started, but closed her mouth.

"Apologize," he said.

She looked at Breydon. "F-forgive me, Captain."

"I wish you wouldn't call me that." Breydon gazed at Telsia. "I've known you since you were a babe. Even held you after you were born." He grinned wide and winked. "I'll forgive you if you drop the formality nonsense."

She minded her fingers, which she practically knotted. "I find it difficult."

"Why?" Tes asked. "Breydon is part of our family."

"Because..." Telsia raised her eyes to Thylaina.

Thylaina smiled and nodded once.

Sitting upright, the young woman set her chin, then faced her father. "I wish to join the knighthood."

The chamber fell silent.


Breydon stared at Thylaina while they changed into the fine attire they had not donned in three weeks, the last time they met with the Brydasian artist. The white blouse's collar peeked from beneath his brown leather jacket, the neutral color revealing the few white strands attempting to hide within his hair. Would the artist include the hints of his aging?

Thylaina lowered her gaze from his head to his piercing eyes. Katjina lacing the back of the dark-green gown pulled at her, but she smirked at him, then looked in the mirror. Yes. Everything was just as the previous sittings.

"Why do I have the feeling you knew?" he asked.

"Telsia told me moons ago."

"And you never thought to share this with me?"

"I promised her I would say nothing." Thylaina smiled at Katjina. "Thank you, dear. Please tell Mezadie we shall be there shortly."

Katjina curtsied, then left.

Breydon sat in the chair near the hearth and grabbed a pair of polished black boots. Groaning, he put them on. "Why are we doing this?"

"We never finished." Thylaina checked her hair. It was precisely as it should be. "This will be the last session."

"Never should've had a first," he mumbled.

She squinted at him through the reflection. "You promised."

"I'm getting ready, aren't I?"

"You shall not regret it." She approached him and offered her hand. "It will be a memory."

Ignoring her hand, he sat back with a sorrowful expression. "For you, you mean."

Thylaina let her arm fall to her side. It was not what she had meant. Not at all. "For us, Breydon."

"It will be around longer than I."

That bitter truth stung every bloody time he mentioned it. She hated him for it.

"And Brenlyr's not included," he added. "I know your reason, but I still—"

Thylaina hurried for the door. "If you do not wish to be a part of it, then I shall have her finish without you!"

Tears fell without permission as pain choked her. She could barely breathe by the time she reached the family room. But damn it, a beautiful portrait would hang over the fireplace, even if Breydon did not stand with her for the last session.

Mezadie had sailed to Yeuroth to spread her fame throughout Emvarr. Thylaina learned about the foreigner from Vhilmas' sister, who had the artist to paint a portrait of their father afore he passed. After seeing Mezadie's work, Thylaina hired her to do one of her and Breydon. It had taken longer to complete because of Breydon's duties.

The Brydasian smiled, which faltered upon seeing Thylaina. "My lady," she said, her words drawing out slightly as she fought to lessen her accent. "What's the trouble? Where is the captain?"

Thylaina searched the room for something to wipe her face dry, but found nothing.

Mezadie offered a cloth from her satchel. "He is coming, yes?"

"I am afraid we shall have to finish without him." Thylaina blinked away the frustration, annoyance, and hurt. Why did Breydon have to be difficult with this one thing she wanted of him?

"I suppose I can paint him from memory," Mezadie said. "He has a memorable face, yes?"

"That won't be necessary." Breydon closed the door.

"Oh. Excellent." Relief eased wrinkles from the woman's forehead. "I hoped you would make this easy for me." She clapped.

Thylaina turned away as he approached.

"Darling," he said. Soft. Pleading. "You know me. I wasn't—Look, I didn't mean to upset you." He rested his hands on her shoulders. So warm. Thylaina could melt into his heat.

"That is what this painting is about," she whispered.

"What's that, love?"

"To always be a part of each other."

Breydon stepped around to stand afore her. He removed one of the two gold chains connected by two pendants from around his neck. An intricate warhammer was fixed within a circle. Simple, yet lovely. The knights did not exchange wedding rings like elves did, so this was what Thylaina and Breydon wore instead. The hammer for the forging of their love, and the circle for their eternal bond. Whenever he left the city, the pendants were connected and either he or Thylaina wore them. At this moment, he pried them apart, then placed the necklace with the circle around her neck. "The portrait wouldn't look the same if you weren't wearing this."

She sniffled. Nodded.

"Forgive me," he said.

"Only if we finish this today."

"It's just... It wasn't how I imagined spending my first day with you."

Thylaina stared up at him. "I want it done so we can free Mezadie and ourselves of this tediously precious undertaking."

"Tedious?" Breydon arched a brow. "I've tried my best to make it enjoyable."

"My work is good, yes?" Mezadie called from the other side of the canvas.

"I'm certain it's wonderful," Breydon shouted back. "But we'll know once we finally see it," he said under his breath.

He gently took Thylaina's hands and kissed them. "I love you. And there's nothing and no one more important to me than you and Brenlyr and your happiness. I want the rest of our days filled with creating wonderful memories for you."

Thylaina slid her arms over his shoulders. "I want to create memories *with* you."

"Then let's finish this timeless memory." He pulled her close and kissed her tenderly.

She did not let go, and the kiss grew deeper.

"I wish I could paint *this*," Mezadie said. "It would be splendid, yes?"



Following Telsia's announcement, Arhgrim had been beside himself with what to say or do. The number of women knights had dwindled in the wake of the Three Marshals' growing power. Even Breydon appeared troubled by Telsia's desire to join the ranks. Since Grim would not permit discussions about it at the table, very little was said at all.

Perhaps something uplifting would lighten the mood.

"Mezadie completed our portrait," Thylaina said. "She promised to send it once she found the perfect frame."

A few glanced at her and Breydon, offering a brief smile.

"She will have it wrapped for a special unveiling." Thylaina continued, her voice faltering. "We shall love to have you all present. I truly cannot wait to see it."

"I'm sure it's lovely," Tes said, barely looking at her.

They must have learned she had known about Telsia's wish to join the knighthood. That explained their evading eye contact.

Grim excused himself at the end of dinner, saying he was in no mood to have a drink afterward.

Breydon appeared to understand. So, he and Thylaina returned home. Katjina retired to her room, and Breydon took Thylaina to theirs. He made love to her. Sweet Lessindra, it was glorious. Then he held her close, skating his fingers down her arm with his thoughts obviously lost in the darkness above them; his teeth had captured his tongue again, leaving it peeking between his lips.

"Speak with me, darling," she said.

He slipped his tongue back into his mouth and smiled at her, then returned his attention to the shadowed ceiling. "You're correct about your brother's spies."

Breydon's brows lowered. "General Zorlias somehow knows about the decaying roots within the knighthood. And he told me what he's learned."

Thylaina turned further onto her side to see his face clearly. "What is it?"

"The reason I went to Warstchia, and why I met with Grim upon my return, was because of what Neldrid revealed to me." Breydon shook his head. "Why am I finding out about these events from my allies instead of my knight brothers?"

She waited. It was not the time to speak.

"The Three have completed building their orders." Breydon sighed heavily. "The bastards are moving into position to take full control."

Thylaina shook her head. "They cannot possibly sway all the knights."

"They've convinced the newly ordained and younger knights that factions led by individual marshals can build a stronger organization. In truth, it will divide and weaken the knighthood." Breydon licked his lips, his gaze still fixed on the darkness. "Marshal Arkiem Korda leads the Order of the Stag, Salnaer Thornsalin, the Order of the Griffon, and Frindor Cyle, the Order of the Bear... And Telsia wants to join. That's what troubles Grim. Truly the only reason. He fears what might happen to his daughter should she get tangled in this mess."

"Why has the Council not put a stop to this?"

Breydon's frown deepened, and his voice softened. "They no longer exist."

Her heart palpitated. "What happened?"

"Threats to their lives grew worse, and Lord Vantos did nothing but support the Three. Most members rescinded their seats while others stood strong, defying Lord Vantos." He swallowed hard, stared back at the ceiling. "Two of those who had remained vigilant against the Three were found dead. One by a *mugging* and the other, the baker's wife..." Breydon drew in a deep breath, held it for a moment. "Their shop burned down while she was inside. The ovens apparently broke while in use. And she *could not* escape?" He shook his head again. "The bloody lying Three."

Thylaina trembled at the image of the deaths of the poor Council members. "This is wrong. What shall the people do about it?"

"The people of Haevaun Balaeus see tragedy. And now that the other Council members have handed the knighthood to the Three Marshals upon Lord Vantos' urging, there's naught to be done."

And there was no more to be said. The Three had finally set everything in motion. Breydon had warned her the Thornsalins were men of precision. That they would strike at the time they intended, and not when others expected. But Grim and Breydon had prepared for this upon learning about the orders and attempts to seize the knighthood from the Council. Breydon was to have been a part of the Three's plans, but—thank the gods—Thylaina came into his life.

She rested her head on his chest, listened to his thumping heart, and wept for the lives lost, and more to be lost, for this overthrow.

It was silent for a few minutes. "Have you...?" Breydon cleared his throat. "Have you heard from Sir Gavrel?"

Not for some time. Years passing, his relocating to Rhigowan, and the behavior between him and Breydon seemed to have affected the bond she once shared with her friend. And she hated it.

"Laina?"

"N'ei, darling. I have not seen him in years."

"I asked if you've heard from him."

She smiled at his patient tone. "The last message Gavrel sent was two years past. Why do you ask?"

"Curious." He repositioned his arm to her lower back. "It's best he stays from Caerabis."

"You mean away from me."

"That as well."

Frowning, she shook her head. "He and I have always been friends."

"He's a bloody nuisance. And I don't want to talk about him anymore."

"You mentioned him."

"Now I'm ending the discussion."

"Fine."

It was better anyway. Breydon always grew cross about Gavrel; his jealousy and accusations had never diminished.

"Remember the promise you made before we married?" Breydon asked. "If any sign of danger comes to Caerabis, you'll go to Ormiana—take Brenlyr with you."

"And wait for you, s'yai."

"Keep that promise, Laina. Even if you must use magic, get to Ormiana. And... and don't wait for me to cross into Etharell."

How could she leave Caerabis without her greatest love? No. It was an impossible request.

"Laina, I mean it. Make this new promise with me." He held her closer. "I just want you both safe."

This was not about just her, but their son. She had to protect Brenlyr.

"S'yai, love. I promise."

The Momestids, Nadiera's family, and Einasa and her daughters gathered with the Colmstad's in their family room. It was not often Thylaina entertained so many in her home, for most celebrations were held at the mansion. Usually, she only had one or two guests for tea, or a couple priests who sat with her after collecting herbs from the garden. But this occasion was special. One she wanted to share with those she considered her family.

Servants poured wine, laughter filled the room, and Thylaina stood beside the covered portrait that Breydon nervously glanced at. She smiled, hoping to calm him. Once everyone gathered at the draped item, she nodded to Katjina, who appeared just as eager as Thylaina.

The handmaiden viewed the many faces, then grabbed the gray cloth. "I'm so very proud to present my lady and lord immortalized." Katjina gently pulled the cloth from the painting.

Thylaina held her breath as tears pooled. She could barely see the vibrant colors and amazing details.

Vhilmas snorted. "What was going through your head while you smiled at the painter, Breydon? Must've been many amusing thoughts, because she got that crooked grin perfectly."

Not only had Mezadie captured Breydon's devious smirk, but she had preserved the mischievous glint often in his gaze. This was her husband when he was in a playful mood. What in the bloody Darkness *had* he been thinking during those many sittings?

Breydon shook his head, muttering, "Damn Brydasian."

The corners of Grim's lips twitched. "I, uh... I noticed she added a line or two of white in your hair." The marshal looked at Breydon, seeming to focus on his head. "Never mind. That apparently was no mistake." He and Vhilmas bellowed in laughter, Einasa giggled, and Nadiera shook her head.

While bouncing Jerian, Nadiera said, "I think it's absolutely beautiful."

"It's nice." Brenlyr nodded as he gazed at it. Telsia, Alyanna, and Aella voiced agreement from aside him. Although his sentiment was simple, Brenlyr's expression as he studied the painting revealed a deeper emotion: adoration.

Warmth filling and surrounding her, Thylaina returned her attention to the portrait and wiped her eyes.

"Why didn't you include Brenlyr?" Tes asked.

Thylaina combed her fingers through her son's dark hair. "We shall wait until he is older, for he will change much from such a young age."

"True," Nadiera said, a woman who, as a child, had golden hair like her mother's, but now grew dark-brown waves.

"I suppose I understand." Yet Tes looked sadly upon Brenlyr, as if he had been denied something special.

Truth was, he understood. And the young man would have absolutely dreaded the sitting more than his father had.

Breydon pulled Thylaina close. "See the pendants?"

Mezadie had done such marvelous work. The hammer and circle, and even the gold chains, shone as if real.

Thylaina hugged him. "Thank you for doing this for me," she said, trying to contain herself. "I love this."

"It's fine work indeed." Grim's tone was firm. Serious. "Definitely deserves its placement above the hearth."

Einasa nodded. "Lovely, my dearests," she said, her voice tight and eyes glistening with tears. Alyanna and Aella looked from the portrait to Brenlyr, both appearing as if they might weep. Perhaps they all missed Bramn. But the way the girls kept looking at Brenlyr showed something else. They likely needed to share an important matter with him, yet feared it as well. Aella's gaze dropped to a flower in her hand. Definitely from Thylaina's garden. Brenlyr must have given it to her.

Nadiera bumped her hip into Vhilmas. "We should hire Mezadie."

He glanced at Breydon, who chuckled.

Thylaina rested her head on her husband's arm. "I truly love it."

"We'll hang it right this moment."

The men set to work, mixed instructions directing Breydon until he had the painting placed perfectly above the fireplace. He wiped sweat from his face, then drank a glass of fruzae with Grim and Vhilmas. Telsia, Alyanna, and Aelle rained plenty of attention on Brenlyr. Thylaina sat with the women, and half-listened to them while she watched Einasa continuously battle tears.

When the event ended, the Momestids said good night. Thylaina and Breydon returned to the family room, finding Einasa and her daughters whispering on the sofa. Brenlyr rubbed his tired eyes, but smiled at his mother and father. Breydon patted the boy's shoulder, then approached Einasa. Thylaina followed with Brenlyr close behind.

"What is it, Einasa?" Breydon asked.

She looked from him to her daughters, then to Brenlyr.

Thylaina took her son's hand. "Please take Alyanna and Aelle to the garden room for tea."

"Yes, Mother." Brenlyr bowed slightly and motioned to the door. "My ladies, if you will."

Aella's lips trembled as she stepped forward, covering her mouth as she exited the room.

Once Brenlyr closed the door, Breydon looked at Thylaina, then Einasa. "What troubles the girls?"

Her eyes immediately filled with tears, falling like raindrops from gray clouds. "I hope you'll forgive me." Shaking her head, she fussed with her skirt. "But we must move forward. It's time for us to leave Caerabis."

Breydon jerked back, as if struck. "You can't mean that."

"It isn't easy to say, but—"

"Look at me, Einasa." Now his tone was firm. Hurt. When her tear-filled gaze met his, he scowled. "Where are you going?"

Thylaina sat beside the struggling woman and held her hand. "Breathe easy, my sister."

That did not help.

Einasa leaned into her and wept. "The girls... They're upset, yet they understand. I'm so alone—and he's a good man. A fine knight." She lifted her head, stared at Breydon. "I promise he is."

"You're marrying again," he said. "Why didn't you tell me?"

"You've too much—"

"Don't," he snapped. "I would never turn you or the girls away. You're our family." He stood and paced. "And now you're leaving."

"N'ei!" Brenlyr shouted from down the hall.

Thylaina straightened, then headed toward the door. By the time she reached it, he had entered the room, Aella's hand clasped in his. The poor girl was blubbering.

"Tell me it's not true." The redness of his eyes intensified his blue irises, and his ruddy cheeks made the freckles prominent. He stomped toward Einasa. "You cannot go!"

Breydon hurried to him, reached out. "Son, she does what she must for her family."

Brenlyr released Aella's hand and pushed past his father. "N'ei!" He pointed at Einasa. "Leaving is not the answer."

Aella walked to her sister at the room's entrance, quick breaths sputtering her sobbing. Alyanna embraced her, tears falling into Aella's hair.

"You cannot take her away!" Brenlyr gestured at the girls. "Can't you see they don't wish to go?"

Einasa looked from her daughters to him, her heart visibly breaking. "I'm to wed a fine knight in Warstchia. You'll see each other again. I promise."

"Don't lie to me!" Brenlyr stormed from the room.

Aelle spun and clung to her sister, crying louder.

Thylaina regarded Einasa. The poor woman had withstood nearly thirteen years of loneliness. How had Father managed two hundred? Gods. The temple in Haevaun Flameral must be wrong to insist that one could not love again after losing their spouse. When she shifted her gaze to her husband's, she recalled the other promise she had made him. As much as she questioned the temple, the thought to love another man after Breydon was gone seemed impossible.

# Chapter Twenty-Five

**B**renlyr grew into a fine young knight. For seven years, the maidens' notice of him spread as they reached courting age. Longing gazes sought his attention, but Brenlyr barely glanced at the women with anything other than a courteous greeting, polite conversation, and kind farewells. And when new knights arrived to swear loyalty to the Order of the Hammer, their daughters were instantly smitten by Brenlyr's beauty. His elvish heritage developed further as he reached his sixteenth birth-day; his blue eyes slanted slightly more and his ears grew pointier, although not as high as Thylaina's. Now nineteen, Brenlyr's inherited human features shared his father's build, jawline, and brow. The brawny lad had grown into a muscular man who could loose a bow well and swing a sword with the grace and lethality of an elf, yet with the force of a human. Much to Thylaina's dismay, he had grown his hair to hide his ears beneath the thick, black waves.

Three moons following his sixteenth birth-day, Thylaina noticed traces of divine power while he trained with the healing herbs. It was then she revealed to him the truth of his elven bloodline. Understanding the danger it would pose to him and Thylaina, Brenlyr swore to speak of it with no one, and she promised to teach him spells that would aid in healing his companions, or protect him in dire need. The young man's dedication resembled her dear friend Aarosyn: intelligent and innovative with the herbs. Brenlyr's mind constantly sought other uses that she had yet discovered. Sometimes he spent time in the apothecary with her instead of sparring at the Pit.

That changed after his nineteenth birth-day. Breydon pushed him to take the knighthood with more devotion, and begin considering a future bride. The maidens fawned over Brenlyr at every opportunity to gain his favor. Despite their attention, his gazes and touches lingered upon only one: Telsia Momestid.

After Einasa moved her daughters to Warstchia and married, Brenlyr often wrote letters to Aella. There was one recent response that had drawn him into a fortnight of depression and bitterness. Even Telsia had difficulty comforting him. What had Aella said? It broke Thylaina's heart to see her son still aching over the maiden in Warstchia when Telsia was right there. But he had never stopped loving Aella, even as he grew closer to Telsia, who remained unwedded despite passing her courting age.

The marshal's daughter focused on her career as an Alohrian captain, yet she spent a great deal of her free time with Brenlyr. The adoration shone in her blue gaze when she looked upon him, but sorrow often overtook her expression. Something battled within her.

There was no doubt Brenlyr loved both Aella and Telsia and always had. It was amazing neither woman seemed to hold animosity toward him nor each other over his divided heart. When they were younger, jealousy did not exist in their relationship. The three shared an understanding they were too young—or should have been—to grasp.

Four days ago, while gathering herbs behind the house, Thylaina overheard Brenlyr reading a letter to Telsia announcing Aella's betrothal to an unnamed knight. Telsia comforted him as he wept. Could it be someone Brenlyr knew? A brother he disliked, or worse... a friend? To sour the air further, the marriage was to happen in less than two weeks in Caerabis. Aella wanted her father's Uncle Haltrin to perform the ceremony. Or did she want one last chance to see Brenlyr afore she made vows to another man?

Perhaps Breydon should have taken Brenlyr on patrol to avoid contact with Aella. But it was not Thylaina's place to interfere. Her son might need to say his piece with the young maiden, or wish her a heartfelt blessing upon her marriage.

No. Thylaina was no meddler. She had let Brenlyr make his own decisions thus far, and would do her best to avoid the same path Father and Uncle Yasontler had taken when making choices about her life.

On the Lover's eighteenth dawn, Thylaina stood with her son, Telsia, and two other knights outside the mansion, their attention on the approaching carriage. Brenlyr watched with anxious anticipation as it drew nearer; Telsia slid her fingers between his. The touch appeared to calm him... somewhat. He smiled at her, then looked back to the dark horses and shadowed coach trailed by a billowing of road dust, his brows lowering. What thoughts consumed him at that moment? He had not seen Aella in seven years and had never released her from his heart. Hopefully, she had freed him from hers.

As the carriage rounded the cobblestone path to the mansion steps, Thylaina prayed to Lessindra that Aella had in fact moved forward. It would allow Brenlyr to breathe a little easier, after the heavier, more painful breaths. Thylaina would be there for him, of course, but he was a strong young man and would survive an expected heartbreak.

The knights stood tall as the groom opened the carriage door and placed the coach stairs down. "My lady," he said, offering his hand.

Einasa climbed out, dressed in a simple yet lovely blue gown. She smiled brightly as she threw her arms around Thylaina's shoulders. "My dearest."

The warmth of her hug filled Thylaina with such love and pain, Einasa's absence over the past seven years striking her at that moment. Thylaina held her a little longer, fighting the urge to weep. "I have missed you, my friend—my sister."

Einasa parted from her and shook her head. "I do wish we could've stayed, but..." She sighed happily. "We're doing well in Warstchia."

"I am pleased for you." Thylaina noticed neither daughter had yet to leave the carriage. "Are Alyanna and Aella well?"

Einasa glanced back. "Yes. Yes, they are." She leaned inside and snapped, "Come now. Don't keep our hosts waiting."

"Yes, Mother," one of them responded. It was difficult to know which daughter, for it had been so long since hearing their voices.

Brenlyr drew in a deep breath, his gaze locked on the open coach door.

The groom offered his hand as one of the young maidens reached out. Alyanna. Since her sixth year, she had taken on more of Einasa's physical traits. A quick glance darted toward Brenlyr afore she hugged Thylaina. "Auntie, you are as beautiful as ever."

"Thank you, love." Thylaina took the young woman in. "You have grown so much. And you look more like your mother. Am I to understand you are to wed as well?"

"Yes." She leaned in close and whispered, "However, my betrothed is performing a secret task in Yeltar, and we must postpone until his return."

"Enough." Einasa rolled her eyes. "You needn't tell *her*. She probably knows more than you."

Actually, Breydon did not share everything of the Hammer's doings with Thylaina.

She smiled politely at the young maiden. "I pray he returns home safe, Alyanna."

"Thank you."

Brenlyr stepped forward, guiding the groom aside. "I shall assist Lady Aella."

Einasa stiffened, drew in a breath to protest, but Alyanna squeezed her mother's arm and shook her head.

There she was, a beauty who could still the breath of even an elven man. Aella was a soft and elegant reflection of her father. Even the smirk playing at her lips as she stepped down from the carriage was reminiscent of Bramn. The two other male knights released gasps of awe, and Telsia stared at her childhood friend with admiration. The young girl had grown tall, standing four to five inches higher than her mother and sister.

Gazes locked, Brenlyr and Aella did not speak. Finally, he kissed her hand. "It is... ever so fine to see you, Lady Aella."

Her eyelids lowered slightly as a full smile formed and her head tilted. The bloody tease. "I've missed you, Sir Brenlyr."

That was all he apparently needed to hear. He pulled her close and pressed his face to her neck; Aella wrapped her arms around him and held him tight.

"This is inappropriate," Einasa seethed.

Alyanna rested her hand on her mother's shoulder. "They've not seen each other in years."

The effort to calm Einasa did not work. "She is promised to another."

Telsia stepped up and joined the embrace. "We're back together again," she whispered. "At least, for a little."

Aella giggled. "For a little."

Thylaina's keen hearing caught it all, including Brenlyr's gentle, "I love you. Both of you. You know that, s'yai?"

What was she to do?

Plans for the marriage ceremony dominated the conversation during the feast at the Momestid's; however, it appeared Brenlyr, Aella, and Telsia had their own discussions at their end of the table. Perhaps they were sharing everything that had transpired over the past several years, for laughter often sounded from them throughout the meal. It took many attempts for others to gain their attention. This agitated Einasa, who then reminded Aella that her betrothed would join them in two days. Brenlyr fell somber afterward.

"You have yet to tell us the blessed knight's name," Thylaina said, breaking the silence.

Einasa looked amongst the diners, then at her daughter, who remained quiet. Sighing at Aella's lack of reply, she smiled at everyone and said, "Sir Rhodrin Vantos."

Breydon and Grim straightened, glanced at one another, then at Einasa.

"Lord Brevig Vantos' son?" Grim asked.

Thylaina had heard that name plenty of times. The one Council member who had helped the Three dismantle the Alohrian Council. A traitor.

Einasa dabbed her lips with the dinner cloth, pride brightening her face. "The very same."

Neither man responded, but their displeasure was openly displayed.

Nervousness overthrew Einasa's sure demeanor, and she grabbed her goblet and drank deeply beneath the men's heavy stares. The cup thumped on the table, and she regained her composure as she glared back at them. "Sir Rhodrin is a respected knight."

"Sir Brenlyr," Grim said. "Please escort the ladies to the orchard for a walk. The fragrance is wonderful at this hour."

Einasa tilted her head back as she leered at Brenlyr. "That's not necessary."

"I insist." Grim leaned forward. "I would like a moment with you, Lady Einasa."

Brenlyr rose, bowed to Einasa, then Alyanna and Aella. "My ladies, please accompany me to the orchard."

Telsia stood. "I shall go with them."

That did not ease Einasa's annoyance, but she gave no further protests. Grim would not permit it anyway. She watched while her daughters left with Brenlyr and Telsia.

Breydon nodded at his new squire, who then went to the two knights standing near the mosaic windows and whispered to them. The knights followed Brenlyr and the maidens, which still did not appear to give Einasa any further comfort.

She pointed at Grim. "You've no right—"

"I didn't want to make them uncomfortable with my inquiries," he said.

Einasa breathed deeply, preparing for whatever it was Grim wished to discuss. "Sir Rhodrin is a fine knight."

"And his father is close with Marshals Thornsalin and Korda," Breydon said, gaining her attention. "He betrayed his fellow Council members."

The corner of Einasa's lips twitched. "However, Sir Rhodrin doesn't agree with his father nor the man's actions. Nor does he support the Three." She rose, swinging her irritation at Grim. "I chose strong names to protect my daughters—to keep them safe from the danger you now thrust your order into." Blinking the sudden arrival of tears away, Einasa looked at Thylaina. "My denying Brenlyr's request for Aella's hand was not personal. I... I just want to keep my daughters safe."

So, that was what had upset Brenlyr a month ago. And now Einasa was quickly marrying her daughters off.

Thylaina shook her head. "I knew nothing of his proposal."

"I'm sorry, just the same." Einasa glanced at Breydon, then back to Thylaina. "It was one of the hardest letters I had ever written. I love Brenlyr." A sad smile added to her sorrowful expression. "He was almost like one of my own. I could've easily accepted him as a son-by-law if the Three weren't looming over us like a dark storm."

Breydon squeezed Thylaina's knee.

She turned her head to find him stiff, clenching his jaw while he stared at Einasa. Thylaina curled her fingers around his, returned her attention to their friend, who now regarded Breydon.

"I must do what is best for Alyanna and Aella," Einasa said. "What Bramn would've wanted me to do. And I believe I am."

The hem of her skirt swept over the floor as she exited the hall. No one moved, not even to lift their cup. A dreadfully silent moment passed.

"I-I cannot blame her." Tes nodded once. "I'm frightened as well."

"We have Valorius on our side," Breydon said.

Grim grabbed his goblet, finished the drink, and then slammed the cup down. "Einasa said Sir Rhodrin shall arrive in two days." He smirked. "That gives us plenty of time to prepare."

"It certainly does," Breydon said.

Thylaina leaned to the side and regarded her husband. "What is it you to plan to do?"

"We shall meet with him," Grim said. "And learn just how dedicated he is to the Hammer."

"I find it hard to believe he'd go against his father." Breydon scoffed. Nose wrinkled, he looked at Grim. "How did Brevig's son end up in Warstchia?"

"We'll soon find out."


The Lover's Moon showed half its light at the first hour, providing enough for late gardening. Thylaina knelt at the plot of ramgwolf, a plant she had added to the garden eight years ago. It flourished like weeds throughout the southern half of Yeuroth, so humans, therefore, believed it *was* a weed. A shame they often discarded and trampled it in their ignorance. Four months prior to its addition to her herb garden, Eidryn had sent a pouch full of them in complete form to her with a note explaining her old friend and peer, Aarosyn, believed the plant contained healing properties, as well as having ill-effects if misused. And if Aarosyn thought he discovered something, then he likely had. Although an impressive xilys warrior, he was a far more remarkable healer. Nearly equal to Thylaina in skill without the divine power. So everything she learned about ramgwolf, she noted and sent to Eidryn, knowing he would share with Aarosyn.

Afore now, the only use she had found for the plant was to help those suffering from galnikath: a horrible human virus that, until seven years past, had no cure. With ramgwolf and yavlar, Thylaina concocted a base recipe to mix with other ingredients, all depending on the individual patient. Ever since creating this cure, she had saved twenty-three human lives, including Nadiera's.

The best time to gather ramgwolf was during the darkest hours of the night. She would have preferred snuggling close to Breydon after such a dreadfully long evening, but her mind remained busy. Why had Brenlyr kept his proposition to Einasa secret from Thylaina and Breydon? It hurt that her son had not shared his intentions with her.

She busied her mind with the task at hand. Cutting the leaves away was time-consuming, with the fat foliage getting in the way. Forty-minutes had passed when Thylaina gathered plenty to fold in havir leaves, another gift from Eidryn. He had brought the long, wide leaves from his latest travel to the east, promising she would love them, and she truly did. For three years she had sought methods to keep certain herbs in their original moist state during out-of-season months, and the havir did just that, as long as she drizzled water over them once every fortnight. Now she could keep a supply of many herbs throughout the year.

Footsteps sounded behind the mansion.

After setting the basket by the back entrance of the house, she tip-toed between the tall bushes, across the walking path between her home and the Momestid's, and toward the back corner leading to the orchard, the trees' sweet fragrances reaching her.

Aella stood beneath one of the apple trees, a cloak draped over her robe and nightgown. Her sandy-blonde hair was bound in a thick plait, a few loose strands floating over her eyes as she watched the northern path. Good. She would not see Thylaina while awaiting someone to join her.

No reason to question whom that might be when the answer was so bloody obvious. What was Brenlyr planning to do?

He arrived five minutes later, properly dressed and with his sword at his side. A true knight did not leave home without their weapon.

Thylaina ducked behind the corner and listened, not wanting to witness her son's foolishness. Yet she could not leave. If he made a poor choice, she must interfere.

"You're late," Aella whispered.

"And we're imprudent to meet here."

"You refused to take me to your house." Hurt sounded in her voice. Maybe Brenlyr was not such an idiot. "Don't you want to be with me?"

"You know I do."

"Then..."

It was quiet for too long. Thylaina peeked around the corner to see Aella in Brenlyr's arms, the young maiden's lips too close to his.

"Please take me home." She kissed him. Of course, having a swyve with another man afore marriage would be acceptable in Etharell, but Aella was not an elf, and this was Alohrius.

Face burning, Thylaina curled her fingers into fists. No, she could not permit her son to be hurt like this. Just as she was about to step out and speak, Brenlyr retreated.

"Aella, don't do this." His eyes watered, and his voice wavered. "I... I can't."

"But I want you to be the first man I know. Not *him*."

Thylaina froze. This was not the Aella she had imagined. To use Brenlyr to sate her carnal desires while knowing he loved her was wrong. And Thylaina had to say something, but his response kept her still.

"No." He raised his hand to halt Aella's nearing. "You're promised to one of my brothers."

"You are half-elven." She sniffled. "Elves love freely until they wed, don't they?"

Brenlyr lowered his hand, his jaw flexing. "S'yai. But I am an Alohrian knight who made vows. My oath is my life. And I will not sneak away in the night with a brother's betrothed."

She turned away.

"I love you, Aella," he whispered. "I will love you for the rest of my days. But I must honor the bond that is now between you and Sir Rhodrin."

"What bond?" She drew in a deep breath, then cleared her throat and raised her chin. "Good night, Sir Brenlyr." She stomped to the scullery door and knocked twice. Whoever waited inside, possibly her handmaiden, struggled to pull the door open, so Brenlyr helped. Aella disappeared inside, the door closed, and Brenlyr remained outside, staring at it.

A heavy breath expelled, he turned his head toward Thylaina, but she hid behind the corner. Too slow. Brenlyr approached. "How often do you spy on me, Mother?" he asked in the Elvish Tongue.

Sighing, she shook her head. "I was not spying on you. Well, not intentionally." She stepped nearer, grazed her fingers along his smooth jaw. "Are you—?"

"I am fine." He scanned the area, then frowned. "Why are you out here?"

Thylaina bobbed her head in the direction of home. "Gathering ramgwolf."

"I see." Brenlyr glanced back at the scullery door. "I... I must go. It has been an exhausting day." He leered at her. "And you need not ensure I find my way."

There was no reason for him to strike at her because he hurt. Thylaina had not caused his pain; however, she understood. He was young and had not yet experienced heartbreak.

She rested her hand on his shoulder and squeezed. "Find rest, Son. I love you."

He nodded once. "Good night, Mother."

Brenlyr walked the northern path, heading to the house that had once been his father's.

Thylaina took her time returning home, Aella's proposition replaying in her mind. This was not the same young maiden she had known seven years ago.

Thankfully, Einasa kept Aella too busy with wedding plans to give the maiden time to harass Brenlyr with temptations. He spent extra hours in the Pit practicing the bow and accepting as many spar challenges as possible. Requests for Thylaina's healing skills distracted her from preparing herbs for upcoming squad departures, for her son's ire had led to many injuries. Breydon must speak to him soon.

Then the day of Sir Rhodrin's arrival dawned. Breydon and Grim waited in the marshal's cabinet, preparing for their meeting with the knight, while Einasa and her daughters, Thylaina, Brenlyr, Vhilmas, and Telsia waited outside for the approaching squad.

Rhodrin rode amid a small group of knights, pushing his horse forward to meet his future bride. The man sat proudly atop the steed, his straight brown hair barely brushing his shoulders, and his brown eyes fixed upon only one person at the bottom of the mansion steps. A slight bump near the bridge of his nose revealed a break that had not healed correctly and slightly marred his decent looks. Yet nothing could ruin the joy that brightened his face as he dismounted and neared Aella.

The maiden, however, forced a smile as he kissed her hand, no joy reflecting in her blank gaze, which darted to Brenlyr.

Thylaina turned her head toward her son, who stood stoically to the side, watching Rhodrin like a predator.

"My lady," Rhodrin said, his voice surprisingly deep. It did not fit his kind face, which, if Thylaina guessed correctly, aged him near thirty. "I've been counting the days. My heart beats faster as each passes, knowing you shall soon be my wife."

"Y-you are very kind." Aella sucked her lips between her teeth, refusing to look him in the eyes.

"I... I brought gifts." Rhodrin released her hand and hurried back to his horse; the other knights had dismounted and walked to the northern stables, only a few remaining behind. He returned with a lovely wooden box and held it outward for Aella to open.

Alyanna's cheeks turned pink. "How wonderful," she squealed.

Aella gave her sister a sidelong look, then lifted the box's lid. She removed a book of poems, set it back inside, then a bottle of apple and cherry mead, giggling at the sweet scent.

"The merchant allowed me to sample a taste." Rhodrin's grin stretched. "I believe your mother and sister will enjoy this with you."

The charmer.

Aella rested the bottle back into the box, then removed a small pouch. From within, she pulled out a piece of dark chocolate.

Thylaina gasped. "Gods." It had been decades since she had last tasted the creamy delicacy.

Rhodrin looked at her. "You know what this is, my lady?"

She nodded. "A delight from Myndrose. It has been difficult to acquire such fine goods from the Northern Continent these past two decades."

"It has, but we happened upon a merchant from Vhormos who sails often to Myndrose." Knobby nose or not, Rhodrin had a handsome smile, especially when his focus returned to Aella. "And the chocolates are for you alone—if you wish, that is. Of course, if you'd like to share with your mother and sister, then do as you please."

"These are wonderful, Sir Rhodrin," Einasa said.

"Yes," Alyanna added.

The gifts were indeed impressive. And the only time Rhodrin had looked away was when he addressed Thylaina. He stared at Aella with great care and affection. Now Thylaina's heart ached for *him* as well.

"Forgive me, Sir Rhodrin." Telsia moved forward. "Marshal Momestid wishes to meet with you immediately. You'll be escorted to your accommodations afterward."

He finally broke free of his enchantment, looking from Aella to Telsia. "As the marshal commands." Rhodrin kissed Aella's hand once again and promised to join her for supper. He gently gave the box to her, then followed Telsia and Vhilmas to the mansion doors.

Telsia offered Brenlyr an apologetic half-smile, then ascended the stairs. Brenlyr dropped his gaze to the cobblestones.

"Come," Einasa said. "We're off to the seamstress. She must pin the dress and discuss the changes you want."

Gripping the box of gifts, Aella swallowed hard, then followed her mother and sister down the street and to the shops.

Thylaina approached Brenlyr. "Are you well?"

He nodded.

Just as she raised her hand to touch him, he spun and stomped eastward, toward the Pit. More men would face his wrath, and Thylaina would have to heal them.

A few knights walked nearby, but one from the newly arrived squad remained behind. He stared at Thylaina.

She began turning for the mansion, but his grin brought her to a halt. Her breath rushed out as she whirled to face him.

The dimple in his chin deepened as his smile grew broad. "My lady." He bowed slightly, yet his earthy eyes never strayed.

To hear his voice after five years brought tears to surface. He was there. Gavrel was right there, grinning at her. And it was wonderful to see him. "Gavrel," she said, barely hearing herself. Thylaina willed her feet to move, but they refused.

Chuckling, he stepped closer, his arms suddenly tight around her. "I have missed you," he said into her hair.

Thylaina pushed away and punched his chest, which slightly hurt her hand. "Bloody liar!"

He frowned and dropped his arms to his sides. "Not the welcoming I had expected."

"You have not sent a letter in several years." She pointed at him. "So do not dare tell me you missed me."

Hurt overcame his expression. "You've no inkling of the loneliness I've known while away from… here. Forgive me for not writing, but please understand all that I have endured—things you don't realize."

She crossed her arms. "Such as?"

Gavrel licked his lips, then scanned the curved cobblestone path. "Might we share a drink?" If he had just arrived with Rhodrin's squad, he was likely hungry, and afternoon meal was near.

Thylaina nodded. "Join me in my garden."

"I would be honored."

She did not take him into the house, but led him to the side garden instead. Katjina appeared shocked and displeased upon seeing Gavrel; however, she performed her duty perfectly as usual and ensured a wonderful afternoon meal was served.

Gavrel shared very little about what he had been doing since his last visit to Caerabis. It sounded like mostly performing his duties at the port city of Karvorn occupied his time. "I watch ships sail past, inspect those who dock, and arrest those who cause trouble." He shrugged. "I just watch and listen."

Curious, she bent forward. "For what do you watch and listen?"

He leaned in to whisper, but breathed in as if tasting her scent, his eyelids lowering half-shut, like his mind whirled. "Anything that might be dangerous to the knighthood," he hushed.

Thylaina sat back, putting distance between them, and fidgeted with the teacup's handle. "The knighthood is precious to us all."

A slanted smile forming as he straightened, Gavrel nodded. "That it is."

He removed a dark pouch from his belt. "I have a gift for you." The pouch was identical to the one Rhodrin had given Aella. "My dearest."

Thylaina hesitated, but then snatched the silky pouch from him and greedily opened it. The delightful scent of dark chocolate emerged, bringing a soft, delighted sigh from her. "Gavrel, how did—?"

"The merchant was convincing while he spoke to Sir Rhodrin." He shrugged, nodded toward the pouch. "He mentioned it was considered a rare delicacy amongst elves, so I believed you might be pleased."

She removed a small piece and ate it, moaning from the rich, bittersweet flavor. "Thank you, Gavrel. I am more than pleased."

His smile widened as he took her hand and kissed it. "I wish to please you and more."

Nervousness quickly set in as desire flared in his gaze. She had written it to him several times in the past, but perhaps he needed to hear it from her. "You are my friend, and I care deeply about you."

"I know." Amusement fled from his eyes as he shifted his attention to the flowers and green leaves. "I care about you more than you realize," he murmured.

Sometimes Thylaina hated that she could hear clearly. Ignoring his admittance, she continued. "I adore our friendship and how much we have grown. It is perfect. I do not wish to jeopardize it with poor choices."

He sucked in a breath as he turned his head, released it. His teeth grazed each other. "There was only one poor choice, in my opinion."

"Please stop." She looked down and shook her head. "This..." She sighed. "This is what hurts us. Your refusal to accept where our paths have taken us."

"The path you chose. And I still don't understand."

"Does it matter? The knighthood is your first concern, is it not?"

Never had Gavrel appeared so serious. His gaze hardened, his posture stiffened, and his face was unreadable. "Thylaina," he said, her name coming out softer than she anticipated. "My loyalty is to the knighthood. I will defend and protect it, my oath, and those I care about most."

She nibbled on her lip afore asking the thought aloud. "You have been away for years, yet here you are. Why?"

He took her left hand and kissed it, his warm lips lingering longer than they should have. The scars. He kissed the scars. Finally looking at her, he said, "I'm here because I've come to speak to Marshal Momestid." Gavrel cupped her cheek, his gaze softening. "And because I had to see you."

Katjina stepped forward. "My lady, you are to see Sir Amdronus this afternoon."

Gavrel's gaze slowly rose to the handmaiden, ire burning within.

"Blessed Vynia!" Thylaina used her best palace performance as she looked from Katjina to the knight. "I had forgotten. Please retrieve my satchel." That definitely sounded convincing.

Brows drawn close, Gavrel rose. "I suppose I'll take my leave."

"Forgive me." Thylaina squeezed his hand. "It truly is wonderful to see you again. I hope we have more time to share all that has changed these many years. Except Breydon." She giggled. "He is much the same."

Gavrel cringed. The man did not even hide his difficulty with Thylaina's marriage.

"And our son is a fine knight," she added, pride strengthening her voice.

"I have heard." He bowed his head. "Perhaps we shall meet again soon."

"Have a blessed day." Thylaina kissed his cheek. Why had she done that? Certainly, she had kissed Bramn's, Grim's, and even Vhilmas' cheeks, for they were like family. However, since her marriage to Breydon, she had never touched her lips to Gavrel's. Perhaps the act was simply her natural reaction with a friend. Afore she could retreat, he grabbed her arms and kept her close, resting his head against hers.

"Gods, woman," he said, his breath coming fast. "Why do you do this to me?"

"I-I must go." She broke free and hurried toward the house's back door. A prayer accompanied each step, hoping her folly went unnoticed.


Breydon did not question Thylaina at supper, nor did anyone ask about her afternoon with Gavrel. So why was she on edge? At least it waned throughout the evening as Sir Rhodrin drew most of the attention. He sat beside Aella, often smiling at her and asking questions about the past fortnight. Although it seemed she attempted to dislike his grazing touches, his lips pressed to her fingers, and genuinely fawning over her, Aella's gaze brightened when meeting Rhodrin's. There were moments when the maiden could not withhold a smile for him.

And Brenlyr's expression darkened as the feast continued. As dessert was served, he rose. "I've an early morning at the temple," he said, addressing Grim. "If I have your leave, Marshal."

Grim's brow dropped for the slightest second. "Of course, Sir Brenlyr."

"Thank you, my lord." Brenlyr's eyes swept over the others, stopping on his father. "Good night."

Telsia turned in her chair, watching him, as did Aella. Thylaina nearly stood, but Breydon squeezed her hand. There was nothing she could do to help at this moment. Brenlyr needed time alone.

Breydon dropped his dinner linen on the table. "Forgive me, Grim, but I must retire as well."

Thylaina watched as her husband wished everyone a good evening, then left. She almost followed, but Breydon squeezing her hand had been a signal. Brenlyr wanted *him*, not her. This was a moment for a father to speak with his son, and she needed to give them that. Hopefully, Breydon could help.

Aella remained subdued for the rest of the night. The others might not have realized Rhodrin noticed, for he did not make it obvious, but Thylaina caught the anxiousness in his tone and body language.

After supper, he walked Aella to the stairs in the entry hall, where Thylaina awaited her escort. "Lady Aella, I hope your night is full of rest and your dreams are nearly as wonderful as you." Rhodrin kissed her hand. "I'll see you in the morning to break fast."

Aella curtsied. "Good night, Sir Rhodrin." Her ascension to the third floor was sluggish, as if weighted by her emotions for the two men.

Thylaina looked away as he faced her.

"Lady Thylaina," Rhodrin said, nearing. "May I have the honor of escorting you home?"

There was no harm in learning more about the man who was to marry Bramn's youngest daughter.

"I should like that."

The walk was slow, their conversation light. Rhodrin chuckled most of the way while speaking about his travel from northern Yeltar, from where he had acquired Aella's gifts.

They stopped outside her front door.

"Are you familiar with Sir Gavrel?" she asked.

Waves formed on his forehead as his eyes turned upward in thought. "I met him and a few other knights on Trysk Pass." He grinned. "They said they were coming here to give their oaths to the Hammer. So I welcomed them into my squad."

Thylaina held her breath. Why did Gavrel not tell her the truth? Perhaps he wished to surprise her. But the tension between him and Breydon might cause problems within the city.

"Is something wrong, my lady?"

"Oh... N'ei. I-I am pleased to learn of this."

"He seems an outstanding knight." Rhodrin nodded.

"That he is."

Thylaina opened the door, but he tugged on her hand.

"My lady, I know about your history with Lady Aella's family, that her father was a dear friend to you and Captain Colmstad." He looked away and licked his lips, nervousness overtaking the confidence that had emanated from him throughout most of the night. "I promise Aella will want for nothing. I'll treat her like a queen."

Warmth filled Thylaina's center, and light chills spread over her upper arms. It felt good to know the depth of this man's devotion... and love. "You are smitten with her."

A breathy laugh escaped Rhodrin. "I am. She is such a fine maiden. Intelligent—witty!" He laughed louder. "Her wit is amazing." Nodding, his smile faded. "And she's caring. I see how much she cares about her mother and sister, and others around her. People in Warstchia adore Aella."

Tears surfaced in Thylaina's eyes. Rhodrin looked beyond Aella's beauty to see the maiden. Thylaina truly liked him. "You are a fine knight, Sir Rhodrin," she said. "And your marriage shall be a blessed one."

He looked down at his boots. "When she... If she comes to love me."

Thylaina palmed his cheek in reassurance. "She is partly there. I saw it during supper."

Hope bloomed in his eyes. "Thank you, my lady." He kissed her hand, then returned to the mansion.

Thylaina entered the house. Chances were, Breydon and Brenlyr would consume fruzae until drunkenness claimed them.

Katjina approached as Thylaina stepped into the main corridor. "M'lady, where's the captain?"

"He shall be out for the evening." Thylaina headed for the bedroom. "Let us get me into a comfortable dress, then the apothecary. There is work to do."

While Katjina untied the back of the dress, Thylaina stared into the mirror and thought about Gavrel and why he had hidden his intentions from her.

Breydon did not return by the time she readied for bed. It was unlike him to stay out late without sending a message, and though he had been with Brenlyr, it did not mean they were still together. Thylaina paced at the bedchamber hearth, worry gnawing her insides as horrifying memories from years ago consumed her. What if someone attacked him once again, and he lay in a dark alley, dying?

Katjina brought some tea to help Thylaina relax, but sleep was not easily found.

Dreadful scenes played out in her mind like a performance, leading her into a gruesome nightmare. Breydon lay afore her, his skull crushed and bleeding and his arms broken, but she could do nothing to save him. His blue eyes clouded to white as his flesh rotted far too quickly.

Thylaina sat up, struggling to breathe into her aching lungs. Sobs overtook her, each intake of air hurting.

Fingers grazed her shoulder. "Laina?"

She twisted around, gasping.

Breydon sat upright, swiped his hand down his face, then focused on her. "Love, what is it? Are you well?"

Moving slowly so as not to frighten the spirit away, she raised her hand to touch his face. Real flesh and bone, and warm as well. The tension in her chest lessened, each breath finding passage easier. But damn him. Thylaina slapped Breydon's cheek as hard as she could. Her palm and fingers stung and throbbed as he gaped at her. At least she felt a little better for it.

"What the bloody Darkness was that for?" he griped.

Shoulders lowering, she let a rush of air go, the muscles loosening further. "You should have sent a message." Thylaina frowned. "I was worried when you did not return."

Realization showed in his eyes, as did guilt. "I'm sorry. I thought nothing about it since you knew I was with Brenlyr."

She pulled her knees up and rested her arms and head on them. "It did not relieve the worry," Thylaina said into the pocket formed with the blanket.

His hand slid up and down her back in comforting strokes. "I'm terribly sorry. It'll never happen again. I promise." He kissed her arm, shoulder, then head. Pulling her close, he rocked gently. "I love you, Laina."

Solace surrounded her in that embrace, and she rested against him—melted into him. There was no one with whom she had ever felt such a connection. The rocking slowed to a stop, and they sank back beneath the covers. Their breaths came and went together. Perfect.

Thylaina rested her hand over his heart. "You are my greatest love."

Breydon awoke with an appetite and vigor of which a human his age should not have been capable, yet they made love for nearly an hour. Exhausted, they panted aside each other, their bodies cooling, and heart rates easing. His body, his face, even his hair... How did Breydon still look so young? The man displayed the energy of one in his twenties, not forty-two! Would this all catch up with him one day and age him suddenly?

"I don't know what Brenlyr's going to do," he said. "But Sir Rhodrin has proven himself a respectable man. And he's devoted to the Hammer. It surprised me and Grim to learn of his dissent from his father. Rhodrin wants naught to do with the Three and their intentions with the knighthood. To be honest, we are glad of it. He'll do well within our ranks."

"It is a comfort to hear you say." Thylaina slid her fingers between his and raised their hands, staring at them as their fingers curled. "What can Brenlyr do?" Huffing, she lowered their hands. "Why did he not tell us about the proposal?"

Breydon turned and caressed her cheek. "Because of what happened. He did not want us disappointed or angry with Einasa."

"I am not either of those with her."

"Nor am I. But he feared it nonetheless." His toes slid along her foot. "And Telsia is not a future for him."

"She could marry him if he becomes a shapele. And he would make a fine shapele."

Breydon smiled, pride showing in his eyes. "He certainly would. But it'll take some time."

"It did not take time for Telsia."

"She excelled faster than anyone I had ever seen. Even me." He nodded. "The girl spied on us every bloody chance she had since she was a tot. So unlike her sister." Breydon chuckled as he slid his fingertips down Thylaina's shoulder. "I'm relieved we had a boy."

She frowned. "You believe daughters are more difficult?"

"After watching those closest to me with their daughters? Yes." He let go of her hand and rolled away, sitting up at the edge of the bed. "Mostly, I'm glad not to have to endure suitors. Gods! I don't think I could stand men approaching me for my daughter's hand."

"You would not force her into a betrothal?"

He looked at her from over his shoulder. "Never."

If it were possible to love that man more than she already did, it happened at that moment.

Shortly after breaking fast, Breydon left to meet with Grim. Thylaina sat in the apothecary, writing notes in her newest Healer's Journal. This was the twelfth in the collection, and the binding was a different color than the others. Brenlyr had bought the book from an Aubrasnan merchant, and even had one of his own.

The young man was just as interested in gaining knowledge about healing as he was about learning to use the bow, spear, and sword.

"M'lady," Katjina said from the entrance. "Sir Rhodrin is here."

Thylaina cocked her head, then nodded once. "I shall join him in the family room."

"Yes, m'lady."

She finished writing the notes on the recent experiments with the fertility stone Brenlyr had prompted—likely for his benefit—on whether it could determine the fertility of a man as it did a woman. His inquiry had piqued her curiosity, and she immediately had him drop his pants and sit, then handed him the yellow stone for placement. It turned gray within five seconds, a sign of dormant fertility. That evening, Thylaina had placed the stone on Breydon's bollocks, much to his discomfort, and the stone turned white, signifying his fruitful condition. Their son had taken on the elven trait. If he had been truly infertile, the stone would have turned black. Which led to Thylaina's next question: could the fertility potion cure one who was barren? Breydon's recovery from the elixir was enough to frighten her from considering such an experiment on the lesser race. Thylaina may never learn if it would ever work on one who could not bear a child.

"M'lady, he awaits." Katjina's voice cut into her pondering.

Thylaina spread pounce on the notes, then left for the family room.

Sir Rhodrin was not in his armor, but like any other knight, his sword was sheathed at his side. "Lady Thylaina." He bowed.

"Your visit is unexpected, Sir Rhodrin." She gestured to the sofa. "Please sit."

"Actually, Sir Brenlyr asked me to meet him." His eyes darted about the room, ending on the portrait above the hearth. "I was admiring that while I waited. It's truly magnificent."

Thylaina's cheeks warmed. "Thank you. It took several sittings with the artist, and I absolutely adore it."

"Why is Sir Brenlyr not in the painting?" Rhodrin sat, one brow cocked in curiosity.

"He was quite young." Thylaina walked to the drink table. "Fruzae?"

"Thank you."

"Any particular blend?"

He blinked, his eyes darting toward the ceiling. "Do you have…" he looked at her, "apple honey?"

She giggled. "A shapele's house would not be proper without it." Thylaina lifted the rectangular decanter with the intricate cuts into the glass and half-filled a cup.

"Forgive me for asking," he began, "but what is a shapele?"

Thylaina handed him the drink and smiled. "The apology is mine, Sir Rhodrin. It is Elvish for 'captain', and one of my native words I often use without thought."

"No worries, my lady. I imagine those around you are used to hearing it." He sipped the fruzae, his cheeks turning rosy afterward. "Gods, that's delicious. Sometimes, you find a blend far superior to others."

"Some make it with greater care."

Rhodrin's posture eased. He was nervous to meet with Brenlyr, who had just opened the door. Aella's betrothed jerked his head toward him, his muscles stiffening, and set the glass on the table. He stood. "Sir Brenlyr."

It was strange to see a man who held several years in the knighthood over her son behave as if he were of lower rank. But this meeting, she was sure, had naught to do with the knighthood.

"Sir Rhodrin." Brenlyr approached Thylaina. "Mother." He kissed her cheek, then nodded toward the door. "Thank you for entertaining him while awaiting my arrival."

"It was a pleasure." She gestured to the bell beside Rhodrin's drink. "If you need anything, please call Katjina. I shall return to the apothecary."

Rhodrin grinned. "I heard you rarely ceased your work. Admirable. Truly, it is." He bowed at the waist. "Thank you for your hospitality, my lady."

He seemed a man raised to show respect and gratitude, and it was difficult to believe his father was one of whom to be concerned. Perhaps Rhodrin's mother had guided him down a better path, just as Thylaina's did for her.

"The pleasure was mine." She curtsied, then turned to Brenlyr and kissed his cheek.

Curiosity gnawed at her mind for nearly an hour. Thylaina busied herself in the herb garden behind the house—speaking with the help, then sitting in the side garden for a refreshing drink—all while she wondered what her son was doing. Hopefully, nothing that would lead him into trouble.

She lifted the journal from the table and reviewed the notes, realizing she had forgotten to include why she believed the fertility potion was too potent for human consumption. Breydon had nearly gone mad with lust, and it took longer for the elixir's effects to fade from him than it did her. Afterward, he did not wish to touch her for a fortnight.

"Might I join you?" Brenlyr pulled a chair from the table.

Thylaina nearly stood abruptly, but swiftly recovered from his sudden presence. So deep in thought, she had not heard him. "Of course, darling."

He sat and motioned for the servant to pour him a drink. A quiet minute passed while he finished the blend of fruit juices, a concoction created by Panya. He set the glass down, glanced at Thylaina.

"Is all well, Brenlyr?"

He nodded. "I asked a great favor of him."

Thylaina set the journal down and leaned toward her son, placing her hand atop his.

Brenlyr blinked several times, opened his mouth, then closed it. Clearing his throat, he met her gaze. "He shall take Aella from Warstchia after they wed. To Haevaun Balaeus, where he will swear loyalty to one of the Three."

It was not the promise she had expected. Maybe that Rhodrin would love her greatly and care for her as if she were a goddess, but not take Aella to the other side of Alohrius. To the very pit where the vipers nested.

She squeezed his hand. "Darling, why would you do such a thing?"

Tears shimmering in his eyes, he straightened, withdrawing his hand from hers. "Because Einasa is correct: the Three hover over us like a bloody storm. And I want Aella safe. Rhodrin's name holds power, and if he aligns with one of the Three, danger will not touch her." He nodded slightly. "She'll be safe there."

Her heart broke to hear his voice tremor. Brenlyr was doing all he could to keep himself in one piece.

"You might never see her again," she said.

The tears broke free, and his bottom lip quivered. "I know," he whispered.

Thylaina rose and hugged his head. "Darling, I am sorry."

# Chapter Twenty-Six

**D**isappointment dominated Aella's visage as she scanned the guests on the way to her awaiting bridegroom. The one person she sought was not present. Brenlyr had left Caerabis with a squad the afternoon afore. Thylaina had asked if it was what he truly wished to do, and he claimed it was. Understandable. How could he witness her marriage to another? He would not return for at least five days, and Aella and Sir Rhodrin shall ride for Warstchia by then to pack her belongings for a new life in Haevaun Balaeus.

Three days left of the sixth month, one of the most dreadfully taxing Lover's Moon Thylaina had ever experienced.

The celebration proved as joyous as could be. Aella smiled often, Rhodrin constantly. Thylaina distributed sponishies, as she often did on such occasions, and gazed at her husband, who once again had stood as the bride's knight. Soon, he would shake off his responsibility and join her for a dance or two, then take her to bed.

"If you're not too busy, might I have the honor to share this dance with you?"

Thylaina turned to Gavrel, unable to respond. "I... I had not expected to see you."

"Sir Rhodrin and I became quickly acquainted, and he invited me." Gavrel winked. "And since I've never been a guest to one of these momentous occasions,

I find myself with the opportunity to do something that I never have: dance with you."

A solid truth, yet one that could not be fulfilled. Not with her husband glaring from seventy feet away.

"Please, my lady?" Gavrel offered his hand. "I may never have this opportunity again."

Another truth.

Over the years, Thylaina had danced with Bramn, Grim, and other friends. So why would Gavrel be any different?

*Because of Breydon.* She worked up a smile, knowing no joy touched upon it, and said, "Forgive me, but I cannot."

His hand lowered, his gaze darted toward Breydon, then back. "So he still controls you?"

It sounded just as ridiculous as the first time he had made that accusation.

Thylaina shook her head as she stood. "The answer is mine. I am sorry, but—"

He grabbed her hand and swept her onto the floor, spinning her. "A dance between friends is forbidden, is it?"

Thylaina pushed on his chest, but he held too tightly, turning them in circles as he moved them deeper within the crowd.

"Take your hands off her!" Breydon gripped Thylaina's arm and yanked her away. The music continued playing, despite that everyone now stilled. Fierce gaze locked on Gavrel, Breydon rumbled, "Leave now."

Scratching the back of his head, Gavrel chuckled. "Seeing as I'm Sir Rhodrin's guest, you've no authority to remove me."

Eyes brightened in his fury, Breydon curled his hands into fists. "I'll not say it again."

The music slowly halted, murmurs passed between the guests, and Aella and Rhodrin stared with horrified expressions.

Great Bryric! Why did Gavrel and Breydon behave like this?

Thylaina gently touched Breydon's arm. "Love, we shall leave."

He shook off her hand, but never looked away from Gavrel. "We're not the ones leaving. *He* is."

Grim broke from the gathered crowd, his eyes darting toward the approaching guards. "Knights, this is not how we honor one of our brothers."

Gavrel looked from them to Thylaina. "How in Valorius' name did you ever forgive him for splitting your flesh?"

Gasps echoed throughout the chamber, as did many growls as more men closed in to defend their captain.

Shocked and appalled, Thylaina stood speechless. It had been thirty-three years since the horrible night she first met Breydon. To mention it now, when she had granted forgiveness and life moved forward, was meant to draw the dreadful reaction Gavrel intended.

Jaw clenched hard, Breydon's face turned crimson. "Get out," he said through his teeth.

But Gavrel remained fixed on Thylaina. "I never understood how you could forgive a man who assaulted you as the good captain had?" He shook his head. "It amazes me still after these many years. I just don't understand how you came to love the beast who tried to bust your fingers."

Her flesh chilled upon his words.

"That's enough!" Grim bellowed, but it was too late.

There was no stopping Breydon, a raging stallion ready to trample. He grabbed Gavrel by the collar and jerked him close. "I'll bust your jaw until it's on the floor."

Laughing, Gavrel clutched Breydon's wrists. "Haven't seen that temper in some time, Captain. I believe the day you condemned her a thief."

Breydon threw him down, then bent over Gavrel with his fist back, and landed a solid punch.

Women shrieked, men hollered, and Grim shouted orders.

"Cease!" Thylaina tried to grab Breydon's arm, but missed.

Blood trailed from Gavrel's nose, yet he laughed as Breydon struck him again.

"Stop!" She attempted to grab his arm again, but a guard pulled her back and another moved in, grappling Breydon off Gavrel.

"This is unacceptable!" Grim shouted as two knights assisted Gavrel off the floor. "We do not behave with such a lack of decorum. Not toward our brothers!"

With the exception of Aella's weeping and Breydon's heavy breathing, the hall fell silent.

"No knight in my city causes disruption such as this," Grim continued. "We'll not tolerate it!"

Gavrel smirked at Grim as he swiped his hand over his face, leaving a line of blood from his nose to his ear. "You'd let him finish what he never got to those many years ago." He looked at Thylaina. "Unless the good captain now leaves marks on her where none can see them."

A rush of air made it halfway down her throat as she froze.

Breydon roared as he broke from the guard's hold and charged at Gavrel. Thankfully, other knights got in the way to intercept.

"Escort him out," Grim ordered, his sharp glare frightening Thylaina.

Gavrel wiped at the blood again, then nodded. "Very well."

The guards walked him toward the door, passing Thylaina. He swiftly spun around them and snatched Thylaina's hand. Kissed it. "Farewell, my lady."

Two knights twisted their arms around Breydon, containing him as his shouts reverberated off the walls and windows.

Shaken by the spectacle, Thylaina stood motionless, then she battled the growing need to sob. Breydon and Gavrel may have exchanged hostile words in the past, but they had never fought.

Once it seemed Breydon had settled, the guards released him. He glowered at everyone.

Grim neared him. "Take her home," he said. "I'll have extra sentries active tonight."

Breydon's dark gaze turned to her. "Yes, sir."

He took her by the elbow and guided her to the door. Four guards followed, keeping about twenty feet behind. No words passed between Thylaina and Breydon as they headed down the street from the Great Hall, their pace fast to reach home.

"I don't ever want him in your company again," Breydon said, his voice gravelly.

Everything that had just happened spun in her mind. Confusion dominated her emotions, for nothing made sense.

"I... I do not understand," she whispered. "Why did he—?"

"You bloody well know his feelings for you!" Breydon jerked her arm slightly. "Gods! Do you enjoy adding this strain to my mind?" He swung his arm in the opposite direction. "To his?"

She huffed in disbelief. "I have *always* made it clear that he is naught more than my friend."

"Which should never be necessary." He let go of her and rubbed his reddened knuckles. "Keep away from him, Laina."

"He was not himself," she said. "Perhaps he had too much to drink."

Breydon stopped, his face dark. "Bloody listen to me!"

It was quiet for several seconds. Seemed like minutes.

The tears finally broke free and would not stop. Not even as they resumed the trek home.


While breaking fast the next morning, Breydon did not eat—only sipped his coffee and glared at Thylaina. "Shall there be any troubles with understanding my demand?"

His demand. It certainly sounded like he was controlling her. But what Gavrel had done was wrong. His horrible words repeated in her mind throughout the night. She tried to touch Breydon, to let him know all was well between them, but he turned his back to her.

He slammed his fist on the table. "Why do you ignore me?" His voice ricocheted off the glass walls and ceiling, rang off her ears. "Have I asked too much of you to stay away from that man?"

"I do not have to suffer this!" She rose and threw the linen on her unfinished porridge. "I am not pleased with his actions, but I can only believe something was not well last night."

Breydon scoffed as he looked away and shook his head.

"Gavrel has been my friend since I first arrived to this city." Thylaina straightened and crossed her arms. "And I tire of this foolish jealousy over a simple friendship."

Lowering his head into his hands, he groaned. Breydon massaged his scalp, then ran his fingers through his hair. He sighed heavily as he sat back and stared at her. "I don't bloody trust Gavrel. I fear for your safety when he's near you."

"Fear? He has done nothing to me."

Breydon stood abruptly. "He murdered Bramn!"

"That is a bloody lie and you know it!" Thylaina shook her head. "Why do you insist on spreading such horrible gossip about Gavrel? He tried to save Bramn—men witnessed it."

His jaw shifted left to right. "He's the one who struck me that night I was killed."

She gaped at him, her brows slowly lowering. "How could you say that?" Thylaina walked away, then paced near the glass wall in the sun's warmth. This argument was insane.

"Gavrel had every reason to want me dead."

She halted, regarded him as if he ignored vital facts. "So did every man loyal to Mikan."

"You didn't even tell me he was in the city!" Breydon's face darkened further.

Hopefully, guilt was not a mask on her face. "I saw no purpose," she said. "We shared a drink in the garden, and spoke about the events of the past years. It was lovely to see my friend."

Muscles tightened throughout his body. After staring at her for a silent moment, he headed for the door.

"I never told you that you could not remain friends with Nikhia, did I?" she called out.

He stopped and faced her. "She's not a threat to either of us, nor did she kill you." He resumed his exit.

There went any hope for reconciliation.

Thylaina hated when they shared little interaction over several days, or even a few. Two passed since Aella's wedding and Breydon still barely spoke with her. He lay in bed, yet did not hold her. She woke up close to him, but then he slipped away to begin his day. This morning, however, his behavior would not continue.

"Do you not love me anymore?" she asked, as he dressed in the garb worn under the chain armor. Was he going somewhere today?

Breydon stilled. "How could you ask me that?"

"You act as if I am not here. Not touching or—" The air caught in her chest, hurting. It ached to think of how she felt at that moment, and the past few days. "Not speaking to me or touching me, as if the thought disgusts you."

Shame was an expression he rarely bore, but it weighed upon him now as he neared her. "I just wish you'd understand, Laina. I wish you would listen to my concerns." He grasped the hair at his nape. "This never-ending argument about him frustrates me. I-I feel like he's more important than I am, and I don't know what to do anymore."

Her husband felt less than another in her eyes. The reasons might seem foolish to her, but it was how Breydon saw them.

Thylaina took his hand, thankful he did not recoil. "You are my greatest and only love," she said in Elvish. "There is none who can claim my heart and soul." She smirked. "Well, except Brenlyr."

Breydon laughed softly. It died as quickly as it came.

"I love you." She stepped close enough to feel his body heat. "And shall never love another as I do you." Thylaina skimmed her fingertips over his jaw, cheekbone, then into his hair. "I am sorry for causing this strain upon your mind and spirit."

He blinked. Stared at her as if surprised by her response. "I forgive you, my love. I just... I can't choose your friends. You don't even like all of mine." Whatever he had to say, it was not with amusement, for a smirk did not grace his lips. "But if Gavrel ever touches you like that again, I'll bloody kill him."

Three days after the wedding, on the second day of the new Burning Moon, Sir Rhodrin, Aella, and her family readied to ride to Warstchia. Deciding to remove Gavrel from the city, Grim ordered him and five other knights to escort the carriage. Breydon spoke with his former squire, Sir Arlin, who would lead the squad, while Thylaina approached Einasa's family to say farewell. Still furious about Gavrel's actions at the wedding, she ignored him as she passed him by. She hugged Einasa and Alyanna, Rhodrin, then Aella. Brenlyr was still away, as he had intended, and Aella appeared hurt by his absence. Thylaina hugged her longer, for she would likely never see Aella again.

"Be well and safe, my dear," she whispered. "We shall pray for you often. Both of you."

Aella's breath trembled as she wept softly. "Thank you."

Whether the tears were from Brenlyr keeping away or that she was aware of where Rhodrin would soon take her, Thylaina knew not. But she let the maiden weep a while longer afore she released her and stepped back.

"Mount up!" Arlin ordered.

Thylaina did not look toward Gavrel, but hooked her arm around Breydon's waist and leaned closer to him. It was difficult holding in the hurt her friend had caused, but Breydon gently stroking her back gave the comfort she needed, and she smiled. They waved as the carriage departed, the knights riding on each side.

Just afore they were out of sight, she looked at Gavrel's back and prayed for him.

A fortnight had passed when a letter arrived from Warstchia. Thylaina expected word from Einasa that Rhodrin had finally made his announcement to leave for Haevuan Balaeus, but it was a message from Gavrel.

*Lady Thylaina,*
*I know I'm the last person you wish to receive any correspondence from, but I've been in misery since leaving Caerabis. It is not only because you shunned me, but because I know I had hurt you. I beg for your forgiveness. I had consumed far too much drink, and found courage to say awful things. It was terrible and wrong of me. Upsetting and hurting you is the last thing I wish to do.*
*If you do not respond, I will understand that to mean our friendship is truly lost at no other's fault but my own. I pray you will forgive me.*
*Faithfully your friend,*
*Sir Gavrel Kedanier*

She frowned at the letter. Annoyed, she grabbed a parchment and the quill.

*Sir Gavrel,*
*I appreciate your apology. It takes a great deal of humility to admit your actions were wrong and hurtful. But I am not the only one to whom an apology is owed. Am I?*
*The things you said to my husband were offensive and cruel. I forgave him of his transgressions years ago. Things he did while controlled by another. If I have the strength and compassion to forgive him for what he did to me, then perhaps you can find it in yourself as well.*
*Your efforts to reconcile our friendship depend on what you do next.*
*I hope you make the wise decision.*
*Lady Thylaina Colmstad*

That letter was sent with the next rider going to Warstchia.

On the fifth day of the Hunter's Moon, a message from Gavrel arrived, the parchment addressed to Breydon. Thank Lessindra he realized his wrongdoing and was willing to make amends.

However, after Breydon read the letter, he crumpled it, then added it to the burning logs in the fireplace.

Thylaina wrung her fingers as she neared him, her hopes faltering. "What did he say?"

Breydon smirked at her from over his shoulder, then returned to watching the parchment burn. "He apologized."

Frustration rushed from her lungs in a huff as she dropped her hands to her sides. "And you will not accept it?"

"No." No hesitation. No consideration.

"*I* did."

Breydon spun, his gaze dark within the shadowed firelight. "Of course you did!"

"It takes a lot for a person to ask forgiveness. You know that as well as anyone."

He stepped closer. "He sent one to Grim as well."

Thylaina straightened. "As he should have."

"At least that one sounded more sincere than the shite he sent me." Breydon spat toward the hearth. "That bastard will get nothing from me."

Her heart sunk. "But... That is not Lessindra's Way."

He took her hand, not letting her jerk it from him. "Laina, I'm sorry. But I'll never forgive that man for everything he's done. Ever."

# Chapter Twenty-Seven

Thylaina would have believed she knew delicate peace while growing up in the palace, an environment so fragile, one had to tread carefully and whisper. Especially with so many years spent with a temperamental princess like Valrae. But the storm Einasa had worried about grew darker over the next eleven years as the Three gained further control of the knighthood. Marshals Korda, Thornsalin, and Cyle had convinced the community that transferring power from the Council to them was a necessity to keep order and balance, lest the country appear frail to their enemies. "The sanctity of the organization belongs in the hands of those who hold it in high regard," Marshal Korda had said. Those hands were the men who had given their lives, blood, and oaths to Alohrius. Men who knew what was best for the knighthood. Marshals. And not just any marshals, but the three highest ranked... like him.

Few of the smaller orders spoke against this change, particularly the Hammer, led by Arhgrim. Their numbers were not enough to be heard over the vast quantity of knights supporting the Three. However, as the weaker sects swore to stand beside the Order of the Hammer, the Three could not remove them from the knighthood—not with Grim standing at the helm with Breydon at his side. The smaller orders had not violated the Code.

Thylaina had asked Breydon why they wished to stay under the rule of the Three Marshals, who could do so much harm.

"To fight them from within," he had replied. "More join our order every week. We'll defeat the corruption of the Three and restore our knighthood."

Knights from all over Alohrius arrived, swearing loyalty to Marshal Momestid and the Order of the Hammer. And with the Three outlawing women from the knighthood, the female knights came to Caerabis to continue their sworn duties. Not only did the Three diminish women from the organization, but prohibited them from learning to use weapons, or even a bow to hunt. Learning many in Haevaun Balaeus supported these decisions shocked the women of Caerabis. How could their lady-kin give in so easily?

Breydon spoke to a gathered crowd of nearly two thousand consisting of knights, soldiers, shopkeepers, farmers, and servants, all from the surrounding communities, giving them strength to fight for their beliefs and love of Alohrius.

"Do not look down upon your brothers and sisters to the east," he had bellowed toward the mass standing on the plains outside the city. "Over the years, the Three have whispered lies and deceit, confusing our kin and reshaping their thinking. We can help them!"

The people cheered.

"Do not hate them!" His face turned nearly as red as his hair. "But pray for them. For all of them!"

Hands waved as more cheered, and many others dried their tears. Like Breydon and the men of the Hammer, they did not want this impending war nor the death of the knights. Too much blood had already been spilt, and with little talk between the leaders. None of the Three had yet come to Caerabis, a long-anticipated visit since the day of Mikan Thornsalin's imprisonment. Missives came from Haevaun Balaeus demanding the former high priest's release, but Grim nor Breydon sent a reply.

Breydon often led squads into the plains to protect the people from forces sent by the Three, sometimes taking Brenlyr's contingent along if in need of more men. He rarely sent Brenlyr's squad on missions without him. Despite their son showing apt capability as a captain, Breydon could not bear the thought of something happening and not being there to help. No doubt Bramn's death had a part in that fear, but mainly because of the Three. However, Breydon trusted Brenlyr's safety in Telsia's hands.

Of course, Brenlyr resented the over protectiveness, or coddling, as he once called it. He did not understand, not even when Thylaina tried to explain. And although Breydon already knew his son secretly held divine power, no amount of begging prevented him from letting Brenlyr lead on his own. It was a serrated blade for Thylaina. She wanted to see her son soar into the incredible captain he could be, yet she feared for him every time he rode out, just as she did for her husband. The missions that kept Breydon away beyond a week's time were more than she could bear.

Her husband appeared two decades younger than his fifty-three years, and maintained a fit physique, so exhaustion was not a concern—he was not Grim. The poor marshal was excusing himself to bed earlier at night or falling asleep in the war room, leaving the plans in the First Captain's hands. But the Three had a target on Breydon for breaking free from their clutches and for imprisoning Mikan. However, Breydon was not their only focus.

When the Three learned about Brenlyr's existence, shortly after his promotion to Captain, his squad's missions on the plains and in the Downs grew more dangerous, for it seemed the attacks had grown doubly concentrated on him. That was when Breydon no longer permitted Brenlyr to ride without his or Telsia's forces. Thylaina had never imagined her son becoming a target of the Three, and she now wished he was no longer a captain. But Brenlyr would not let the knighthood or the peoples of Alohrius down.

Sadly, after his promotion, no marriage ceremony followed, as some had hoped; however, Brenlyr and Telsia maintained their intimate relationship. Tes and Grim were just as displeased as Thylaina, but Telsia, as much as she loved Brenlyr, was too devoted to the knighthood to settle into a marriage. At least the two seemed happy with their life together.

For the next two years, attacks increased as the Order of the Hammer continued leading resistance against the Three. More families moved from the eastern side of the Trysk River, which practically split Alohrius in half, and they settled amongst the plains between Caerabis and Warstchia. More farms producing crops and livestock were established to meet the demands for the growing population. Trade with merchants from Etharell, Vhormos, Aubrasna, and imports from harbors also increased to help maintain a stable economy. Unfortunately, Arhgrim had to instill more taxes to sustain the Hammer's coffers, for knights and soldiers needed to support themselves and their families. Some complained, but nothing worthy of note.

Life moved forward for most. When a homestead on the plains suffered from a bandit attack, the Order of the Hammer helped them recover. Grim and Breydon never turned their backs on anyone. With Grim's aging, he often said Breydon should take over as the marshal of Caerabis, but Breydon assured they were right where Valorius meant them to be. The people loved Arhgrim Momestid, and with Breydon as his First Captain, the two headed a remarkable order. Caerabis was strong, and the people were safe.

Something was terribly wrong. Something Breydon seemed reluctant to share with Thylaina.

Pressing her bare flesh against his, she strummed his ribs with her fingertips. "Darling."

He jerked, sucked in a quick breath. "Yes?"

"Forgive me for waking you." Thylaina stilled her hand, snuggled her cheek on his chest, and listened to his strong heartbeat.

"I was barely asleep." He laughed softly.

"What troubles you and Grim?"

"What makes you—?"

"I know you." Thylaina pushed upward and stared down at him. "Do not think you can fool me."

More white showed in his hair now, and a few wrinkles formed on his face, but those blue eyes and that damn crooked smile still made her heart spring.

"I could never fool you." Breydon rose enough to kiss her neck, then lay back down. "You've been around too bloody long to even try."

Thylaina squinted. "Are you jesting about my age?"

He scanned her face, then her bare torso. "As fine as you are, you think *I* would dare jest about *your* age?" He glided his calloused hands up her side, cupped her breast. Sitting up, he kissed her hard.

Sweet Lessindra, the man had never lost the ability to touch Thylaina how she liked, kiss her favorite places, nor love her perfectly.

Lips in constant contact, she straddled him. It took a little time for Breydon to be ready, and she sank upon his virility. Thylaina loved feeling him within her. Being one with him.

After making love, she opened the bedroom window to cool their bodies. The air flowed in, providing instant relief. She stared at the first glow of the coming dawn; the fifteenth day of the Hawk Moon. A week from now, Thylaina would celebrate her two-hundred-ninety-fourth birth-day. Great Bryric, she was nearly three centuries old!

Crossing her arms to grasp her shoulders, she turned from the chilled spring air and regarded her husband while he slept. During Eidryn's last visit ten years past, he revealed that Breydon's standing in Valorius' presence was the reason his aging had slowed.

*"People like you are called Ageless," Eidryn had said. "They are not immortals, for they still age, as is evident with you. It just takes decades longer... or perhaps hundreds of years."*

*The wine glass Thylaina had been holding nearly slipped from her grasp as she gaped at her friend for a long moment, trying to understand, while Breydon just stared in disbelief. His death and return left one thought: was he meant to die and stand afore his god so he and Thylaina could share a long life together?*

*"How did you learn of this?" she inquired.*

*Eidryn straightened, his smile spreading wider. "Because I... I am an Ageless as well, from my time spent with Vynia."*

*She set the goblet down, yet her eyes did not shift from him. "If you knew this, why did you wait to tell us?"*

*He lowered beside her on the sofa, clasped her hands, then flashed a grin at Breydon. "Because I had to learn from Vynia if I was permitted to share this with you. Gaining an audience with Her is not as easy as you might believe, even for Her former Favored."*

*Tears had pooled and fell at the knowledge that she and Breydon would have more years together than they expected. A blessing. Thank Valorius.*

These days, another question sometimes pestered Thylaina when she looked upon her son: would it affect Brenlyr being the offspring of an Ageless and an elf? At thirty years, he still appeared seventeen by human standards. No scholar in Etharell knew the life expectancy of a half-elf since only one had survived birth.

She poured a glass of water and drank a few swallows while pondering it all again. Then she sat beside Breydon and played with his hair. "You must wake, my love."

He groaned. "You've exhausted me."

Breydon had avoided her question, which she could not let go unanswered.

"Tell me what truly concerns you and Grim."

He rubbed his eyes, glanced at her, then curled under the blanket. "Darling, with everything we face, much concerns us."

"There is more." Thylaina leaned close and kissed his cheek. "I can make you tell me if you will not do so willingly."

He smirked. "You're a terrible liar."

But she *could* make him. Thylaina would just have difficulty using such magic on her husband.

Breydon appeared to take her silence as annoyance. Sighing, he rolled onto his back and rested his hand on her thigh. "There's... I need a new promise from you." His gaze and voice lacked the playfulness they held earlier.

"And what promise is that?" Her tone came out sharper than she had intended.

"When I command it, you leave Caerabis."

Thylaina stared at him. Did he forget how much had changed since the promise after Brenlyr's birth? They had a family now. The people of Caerabis needed her as much as they needed Breydon. And this time, he mentioned nothing about waiting for him to join her. Shaking her head, she said, "Never."

He sat up and grasped her hand. "I'm not saying now, but I fear the time shall come soon. Etharell is the safest place for you—"

"Not without you." Thylaina tugged her hand free and bolted from the bed. She stomped to the basin to splash water on her face, but gripped the basin instead. "I... I cannot go without you, nor Brenlyr."

"Damn it, Laina, it's about your safety!" The reddening of his face intensified his irises.

Fist on her hips, she faced him. "What have you learned? What are you not telling me?"

Breydon's visage softened. "Although we have a strong force, their collective orders outnumber us. Rhodrin's last report informed of their intentions to lay siege upon the city." He met her gaze, held it. "You have worried for years of what might happen if they learned the truth about you, but I fear so much more. It's what they'll do to you if they get you in their clutches." Tears filled his eyes, one breaking free to leave a trail down his cheek. "They say Marshal Salnaer Thornsalin rides toward Caerabis, and his son is already in the region. Kaeleck now bears the title Marshal. Rhodrin claims the man's viciousness outdoes that of his father, and he's expected to claim one of the Three posts in the future. Salnaer had been training him for it." He swiped his hands over his face, drying it. "To protect Aella and Rhodrin, I ordered him to cease the reports. I can't risk his life anymore. If they learn his oath was false," he shook his head, "they'll brand him a traitor, torture him, then drag his body through the city."

Thylaina shuddered at the image. How correct Breydon was about her concerns regarding the Three Marshals, and Kaeleck Thornsalin's presence in the Alohrian Plains was indeed disturbing news, but relieving Rhodrin of his spying duties eased worries for his and Aella's safety. "What if they learn about Rhodrin's past actions against them?"

Breydon arched a brow. "His father did," he whispered. "But Brevig doesn't want anything to happen to his son and daughter-by-law, nor their children, whom he adores. He begged Salnaer to remove Rhodrin from the ranks and keep him in the city."

"And what happened?" She stepped closer.

"Salnaer put Rhodrin in charge of the city vault." Breydon rubbed the back of his neck as he looked down. "It's an insult to put a knight in such a position."

Perhaps it was, yet she would rather Rhodrin and Aella were out of danger's path than threatened.

But this changed nothing of how Thylaina felt about Breydon's request—his demand. All who remained in Caerabis after the forming of the Order of the Hammer had expected the dangers for standing against the Three, and they stayed anyway. Why would she leave?

She fought the growing urge to weep. "Breydon, I cannot leave without you or Brenlyr. I refuse."

"I can't make him go!" He splayed his arms in frustration. "Brenlyr is devoted to his oath. Besides, he'll never leave Telsia."

"He can bring her." Tears blurred her vision and her throat fought every breath. "You think they will not do anything to him if they capture him?" she shouted.

Breydon's eyes widened. Obviously, the thought had never occurred to him. After a long exhale, he relaxed. "He will die fighting for his beliefs. That is the sort of man we raised together."

Images of Brenlyr bleeding on the plains, gashes spreading his flesh wide, invaded her mind. Thylaina crumpled to the floor, sobbing. It could not be this way.

Breydon's arms enveloped her. "If I could protect you both, I would, but I can only give my best to you now. And I'm begging you to ride to the Ormiana outpost when I give the word." His fingers curled into her hair and his lips pressed to her head. "Wait two days for me, unless something seems suspicious. Then ride or run into Etharell, to the nearest xilys post." Leaning back, he held her face and stared into her eyes. "We will meet again. I promise you."

A promise he would wait for her if he never made it to Etharell; their souls would reunite in Love's Garden. A reminder of their vows.

She had no choice. Breydon would not let this go until she agreed. And Thylaina was a woman of her word. "Very well," she whispered.

"What was that?"

"I promise." Bryric! She hated those words at that moment.

# Chapter Twenty-Eight

Events on the southern plains and at the Downs remained consistent for a fortnight. Squads came and went, many wounded or dead returning. Then Marshal Kaeleck Thornsalin attacked on the eastern plains, the assaults increasing the month that followed. Aid from Warstchia lessened as Marshal Salnaer Thornsalin camped an army outside the city walls, blocking not only reinforcements, but supplies. Contingents from Monsor rounded Warstchia, sometimes battling against other orders to reach Caerabis. Thankfully, those men brought food, herbs, and weaponry to continue their fight against the Three. Although the Hammer did not have the numbers to defeat the Three Marshals, it did not stop Telsia from leading an elite calvary to aid their struggling allies. Her squad gave the edge needed, and forced Salnaer to withdraw his army and retreat.

A week later, Breydon's focus was drawn southward, for two enemy units attacked farmers on the plains, homesteads along Bendeus Highway, then headed toward Alohrian Downs north of the Suflor Hills. He led his squad out with Brenlyr's force to halt that assault, both men coming home victorious, although with casualties and too many wounded. Unfortunately, Breydon left shortly after his return, taking a fresh squad from Monsor with him.

Thylaina worked tirelessly with the temple to mend the wounded, including farmers caught amid the battles. Brenlyr walked behind her, a mixture of concern and anger skewing his handsome face as he viewed the many wounded and dying men and women in the temple's main hall. The young man had a minor injury that he had tended to on their way back to Caerabis. His healing skills were astounding, much like hers.

He stopped at the bed of Kyr Deanna, one of the eight women remaining in the knighthood. Kyr was the title given to the ordained women. The knighthood believed referring to them as 'Lady' denied them what they had worked hard to attain. Thylaina had heard Kyr was the name of Valorius' first immortal daughter. Whether that was true, she knew not, nor did she care at that moment.

She lifted the blood-stained blanket and viewed the wounds: a gash in the knight's side and a severed left hand. Both healed wonderfully. "Kyr Deanna, how do you feel?"

Deanna blinked slowly, then turned her head to Thylaina. "Empty," she rasped.

The woman would never swing a sword again, but it did not mean her life was over.

Brenlyr rested his hand on Deanna's shoulder. "You saved four comrades and seven innocents. Be not empty, but proud of your deeds."

She focused on him, her gaze clearing. "Yes, Captain. Thank you."

"Valorius blesses you this day." Brenlyr nodded once, then stepped away, glancing at Thylaina.

She followed him to one of the empty corridors, sensing his need to speak with her. "What is it?"

"Have you heard from Telsia? Anything about her cavalry?"

Thylaina wiped her hands on the stained apron. "She defends farms to the northeast from a faction of the Stag."

Brenlyr held his breath momentarily.

Knights of the Stag, like those of the Griffon, had a reputation of fierce battle tactics and lack of mercy. These men took pleasure in destroying the farmhouses, crops, and slaughtering the livestock. Such senseless waste.

Brenlyr cleared his throat as he leaned against the wall, his gaze setting on the shadows above. "She'll return, s'yai?"

Thylaina squeezed his arm. "Of course she will. Telsia is an exceptional leader."

"That she is." Sighing, he lowered his eyes to her. "And Father?"

Her stomach twisted upon his question. "I had hoped you learned something."

He barely shook his head and straightened. "I must go."

Nodding, she headed to the hallway's exit and viewed the many patients. "I need to gather herbs and return to the apothecary. There is so much to prepare."

Brenlyr kissed her cheek, then rested his forehead above her ear. "You need to rest."

Thylaina turned, then held his hand, her gazed dropping to it. After speaking a prayer in Elvish, they parted. He returned to his squad, and she went home. Each step carried the weight of every patient and worry for her family and the Momestids.

"Where are you off to?" a man dressed in travel leathers asked.

She continued walking without looking at him. There was too much on her mind. "The herb garden."

"Might I accompany you?"

His voice was awfully familiar, and one she had not heard in years.

Thylaina froze. Heart thumping, she whirled around. "Gavrel?"

He chuckled as he neared her, his arms wide. "My lady."

Had she moved into his embrace? She must have, for he held her close. Perhaps it was the joy of his presence lifting all the worries, even if for a brief time, but Thylaina needed this. She hugged her friend tightly, tears breaking from the corners of her eyes.

"It's so bloody fine to see you," he said. "And even better to know you're safe."

Stepping back, Thylaina giggled. "You are here! How?"

"I came with the force from Monsor. It took a lot of battling to reach Caerabis, but we finally made it. Thank Valorius." The years had done him well, his age maturing him into quite a handsome man of fifty-three, even with the gray hairs mixed within the brown strands on his head and goatee.

"When did you arrive?"

"This morning. I had to report to Marshal Momestid, then claim a bed in the barracks." Gavrel laughed softly. "I would've thought I'd gained a house by now."

"Are you—?" She tilted her head as she stared at him. "Are you staying here from now on?"

"For as long as they'll keep me."

At least Grim had accepted Gavrel's apology years ago, and admitted to needing the help of every available knight willing to fight the corrupted Three.

"What are you to do now?" she asked.

"I'm settling in." He nodded. "And I'm bored. It'd be fantastic if Marshal Momestid would send me out there now, but he must decide which squad to place me in. Certainly not *your* husband's."

And it likely would not be Brenlyr either. The smartest choice was Telsia, but Gavrel would have to prove himself an exceptional fighter on horseback.

"I hope you find the perfect squad," Thylaina said. "I should move on. There is work to do in the herb garden."

"Allow me to help."

As much as she adored the idea to learn all he had to share, it would not do to have him at her home. And Gavrel appeared to notice her hesitation.

"Forget the offer," he said. "I understand it'd be best that I—"

"Nonsense." What was she doing? She was willing to upset Breydon to avoid hurting Gavrel. And why? Because they had not seen each other in over a decade. But it was too late to rescind the invitation without looking like a fool. "It is only the garden."

"Are you certain?"

"Of course. I must change from these garments first." She motioned to the bloodied apron.

He nodded once. "Understandable."

Thylaina left him in the family room while Katjina helped her change into a summer gardening outfit. It was a light blouse and a long skirt. Usually, the late spring months still provided cool days in this region, but the temperatures had been warmer lately, and the thinner material was preferable while working under the high sun. The Lover's Moon would soon arrive with the hotter days accompanying it.

"How long is he staying?" Venom touched upon Katjina's tone.

Thylaina sighed at the handmaiden. "He is helping me in the garden. Nothing more."

Katjina frowned, yet bobbed her head. "Of course, m'lady."

Thylaina headed for the family room to retrieve Gavrel. He stood at the hearth, staring at the painting of her and Breydon. A somber expression had overtaken his face.

She neared him. "What is it?"

"It's..." He looked down at her. "It's fine work."

Thylaina stopped beside him and took in the details of her husband's face in the painting. "The artist was a delight. And she did an outstanding job."

"She did," he whispered.

Thylaina tugged on his arm. "Let us get work done afore it grows too hot outside."

He remained still. "What might I have done differently?"

The following silence nearly stifled her. There was naught Gavrel could have done to change their fates. Thylaina was where Bryric directed her. Where Lessindra led her and Breydon. There was nowhere else she wished to be.

Finally, he offered a forced smile and followed her outside.

It was quiet for the first half hour. Thylaina could not take it anymore, so she sang. It appeared to relax Gavrel, and he hummed along while extracting the roots and plants faster. After an hour passed, it seemed all was well enough to chat. Topics evaded her as she considered her friend. But there was something that surprised her, considering the years that had passed and the fine man he was.

"Gavrel?"

"Yes?"

"Why have you never married?"

He ceased pulling a ramgwolf from the large plot, kept his eyes cast down. "Because my heart already yearns for someone." He yanked the plant out. "Someone I can't have." Gavrel tossed it behind him.

It was a foolish question, and she wished she had not inquired. Truth was, Thylaina could not understand why he held on to something he knew could never be. Perhaps she might convince him to move forward.

She sat back on her heels. "Surely, there must be a woman who—"

"Please stop." Gavrel stilled again, wiped sweat from his forehead. "Unless you say you're done with him, and that you'll be mine, don't say anymore on the matter."

Her heart throbbed in her ears. "F-forgive me," she whispered.

He finally looked at her. "Always, Thylaina."

They gathered plenty of ramgwolf, bossel root, repenia, and lavender, then headed to the apothecary, where they washed. She splashed water on him from the basin. It was nice to hear him laugh.

Katjina waited in the hallway, glared at Gavrel when he left the room. "M'lady, Sir Amdronus awaits in the gathering room."

Thylaina tilted her head. She was not expecting him nor any knight to visit. But for Katjina to name her own husband in a formal manner was odd. Perhaps it was because another knight was present. But when Thylaina looked at Gavrel to apologize for having to end their visit, she understood. Once again, Katjina was excusing him from the house with a lie. Which meant no one was waiting for her. But she could not expose her handmaiden—her dearest friend.

"I must tend to Sir Amdronus," she said.

Gavrel bowed his head. "I understand."

They walked toward the vestibule. Thylaina could have entered through there to say farewell again, but she did not want to risk him seeing no one waited for her. So she faced him at the library door. "Have a blessed day."

He took her hand and kissed it. "Thank you for a lovely afternoon. It makes Caerabis more welcoming than ever." Brushing past Katjina as she gestured to the vestibule door, he left.

Thylaina entered the library, then continued to the family room, planning to have a drink while she stared at the portrait. But someone *was* in there, and it was not Amdronus. Her heartbeat increased as excitement soared throughout her. But it swiftly deflated, and she shrunk into herself.

Breydon's gaze bore into Thylaina as his jaw muscles feathered. He sank the last of the fruzae in his glass, then slammed it on the table. "In our home?" he asked, his voice awfully quiet. Subdued.

Thylaina wrung her fingers as she watched his tense body move stiffly to the drink table, where he refilled the glass. She had been waiting for his return, but it could not have happened at the worst moment. There was no intention of being sneaky with Gavrel; she would not have gardened with him outside if that were the truth. Perhaps Breydon would realize that as well.

"He helped me gather herbs, love. That was all."

He spun, spilling the liquor on the floor. "He was in *our* home! That bastard was here!"

Startled by the outburst, she jumped and retreated a step. "Nothing inappropriate happened."

"You never bloody listen, do you?" Another swirl of dark fruzae went down his throat. "I thought you understood. What am I to think, Laina?"

It seemed the entire house fell silent as she stared at her husband, wondering what exactly he implied. "Is there something *to* think?" She bit down on her quivering lip to prevent him from seeing she was on the verge of sobbing. But her voice betrayed her. "I did *nothing*!"

"No." He neared her, anger distorting his handsome face. "You did plenty. And I've had enough."

Breydon left through the gathering room door that led to the vestibule. That one and the outer door slammed shut upon his exits.

Thylaina crumped to the sofa and blubbered into her hands.

Katjina entered a few minutes later and sat beside her, offering comfort. "Forgive me, m'lady. His return surprised me, and I believed it was best he didn't come upon you two together. So I begged him to wait—"

"We did nothing inappropriate!" She pulled from Katjina. "Sir Gavrel helped me, that was all. There was naught to—"

"But he was in your home." The handmaiden stood abruptly. "And I know that's against the captain's wishes." She stormed toward the door, apparently deciding there was nothing more to say. It was a rare moment to see Katjina like that. "I came to inform you more injured soldiers and knights arrived and need your attention." She left.

Thylaina sighed loudly, wiped her face dry, then headed for the apothecary. Perhaps helping someone would distract her from the argument with Breydon. She collected a clean apron and the herbal box Eidryn had given her. There would likely be wounds to retreat and redress as well.

Three hours passed, supper had come and gone, but Thylaina was too busy to even nibble on the fruit and cheese Katjina brought. The handmaiden offered it to others who gazed at the food with obvious hunger. After finishing with the wounded, speaking with the priests for half an hour, Thylaina and Katjina headed home. The evening's temperature was pleasant and a whisper of a breeze kissed their cheeks.

The tall street lanterns flickered, and outdoor torches burned on walls of several structures. Too bad it was not a full moon, for it would have been a truly beautiful night.

As they came upon the barracks next to the mansion, someone stepped from the building's shadows and walked toward them. Katjina's grip tightened on Thylaina's arm. Thylaina knew not why, for there was never a time the handmaiden had ever seemed uncomfortable around the knights and soldiers.

"My lady," Gavrel said, his voice rough.

"Good night," Katjina snapped afore Thylaina could respond.

He did not look at the handmaiden, but stepped closer to Thylaina, the firelight shadowing his face. Except, what she thought were shadows were swelling bruises and a split lip.

Thylaina sucked in a rush of air as she slipped her arm from Katjina. "Gavrel... what happened to you?"

His gaze lowered as his tongue tip touched the split. After a curt nod, he raised his eyes to her. "Captain Colmstad came to me this afternoon. And he... He attacked me."

Brows low, she shook her head. "Why?"

Gavrel shrugged, sorrow overtaking his bruised face. "He told me to keep away from you. Even after I promised nothing questionable had happened."

As she stepped forward to touch his cheek, Katjina jerked her back. "M'lady," she seethed. "We must go."

Thylaina drew in a deep breath, then returned her attention to Gavrel. "I am terribly sorry about this. And it *will* be addressed."

He bowed partially. "I just wished to make sure you remained unharmed." Then he spun on his heel and stomped back to the barracks.

Remained unharmed. Those two words spoke clearly to her. Gavrel still believed Breydon might hurt her. A foolish belief.

Thylaina hurried the rest of the way home. Breydon was not there.

After Katjina entered the house, Thylaina ordered a bath.

The reunion with Breydon was not what Thylaina had hoped for; no loving embraces or kisses. No outpouring words of affection. After hearing nothing about him for days, she had worried for his safety, wanting him home in her arms. Not this. And for the first time, she was furious with Katjina. She wept again; the teardrops mingled with the bathwater.

Despite the day's events, Katjina washed the stress from Thylaina's muscles and hummed a song she had often sung to Brenlyr when he was a tot. Then she sat beside the tub and cleaned the dirt and blood from beneath Thylaina's nails with a dull knife.

A knock sounded on the door, then it immediately started to open.

Thylaina sat up. "N'ei! You stay out!"

The door stilled, then closed.

"Darling," Breydon said. "Might I come in?"

Thylaina drew in a deep breath, recalling his expression while he yelled accusations at her that afternoon, and then what he had done to Gavrel. "N'ei."

"I must speak with you."

"I saw what you did to Sir Gavrel!"

Katjina sat back, removing the knife from near Thylaina's hand.

"Gods, Breydon! It hurts to know you do not trust me. But for you to seek one of your brothers and leave him as you did—All because of your bloody jealousy! I..." She released a heavy breath. "I do not wish to speak with you at this moment."

After a long pause of silence, Breydon finally answered. "Very well. I... I love you, Laina. I'm sorry I hurt you."

She listened to his slow, hesitating retreat. Then his steps increased. Faded.

Katjina resumed her task. "Are you certain you don't wish to speak with him, m'lady? I can fetch the captain before he's gone."

Thylaina closed her eyes and envisioned that afternoon. "I am."

Several minutes later, the front door opened and closed. Breydon was probably heading to the Momestid's now.

The bath had not offered any real comfort, and Thylaina had no appetite for supper afterward. She just wanted to go to her bedroom and curl beneath the blankets. Perhaps tomorrow would bring a better day.

A folded parchment on her bedside table caught her notice. Beside it lay two gold chains with interlocked pendants: the hammer and the circle.

> *Laina,*
>
> *Grim received warning of another anticipated attack along Bendeus Highway. We fear more strikes may also come from the east. To remove one of these threats before the other advances gives us a better defense.*
>
> *I had hoped for a proper parting, however, you were in no mind to receive me. I wasn't myself this afternoon. No disrespect toward you was intended. Please forgive me.*
>
> *I wish you understood how much Sir Gavrel makes me uneasy. And you know for certain of his feelings for you. It's never been about jealousy toward your friendship. I do trust you.*
>
> *You are my greatest love, Laina.*
>
> *May Bryric, Valorius, and Lessindra keep you safe.*
>
> *Breydon*

She dropped the letter on the table and caught the chains with her fingertips, then dragged the pendants along the surface. Breydon was gone. Her hurt and anger prevented them from saying farewell. No embrace. No kiss.

Thylaina slid the necklaces over her head. He had worn them while he was last away. Now it was her turn. A silly thing perhaps, but it was their little sense of closeness when parted from one another.

Eyes closed, she prayed to those three gods: Bryric, the God of the Elves; Valorius, the Great Knight of the Humans; and Lessindra, Goddess of Love, Forgiveness, and Mercy. *Please hold Breydon and his force in Your Safekeeping. Guide them in strength, victory, and mercy. Bring my husband home.*

A lonely fortnight passed terribly slow. Breydon sent no messages, and no one had heard from him. At least, none shared any reports that might have come into the city. Brenlyr's squad joined Breydon's, so Thylaina could not ask him for any news. It hurt, made her stomach cramp almost constantly to worry about them both. But to have not said farewell, nor even kissed Breydon afore he left, wrung her insides.

Thylaina looked upon the repenia vines on the mansion's back wall. All the gardens shared a wonderful fragrance in the summer nights, some herbs giving a stronger aroma. Particularly the vines. She smiled sadly, recalling the day Breydon brought the original plants to her, which began the repenia wall on the mansion. The succulent leaves were the key ingredient to many potions, which Raylen also took an interest in creating. Sadly, he was still the only herbal priest in the city, for none of the three young priests showed interest to learn how to use the herbs. What need was there when Raylen and Thylaina were present? Her concern was that Raylen—and Haltrin—were aged, and the newer priests did not have the same devotion as the two older men. From what Thylaina had heard, the numbers of those swearing vows to the temples had dwindled significantly. Caerabis was blessed to have three young priests join their temple.

The battle of power within the knighthood had caused a disruption of faith in Valorius. Even the younger men in the city displayed skepticism. Of course, there were hundreds who still showed dedication to Valorius, men like Breydon and

Arhgrim, but the Three Marshalls had succeeded in planting doubt in the god they swore to serve.

*Sad.* Thylaina plucked a handful of leaves from one of the vines. *Their faith could help them conquer the Three.*

"My lady?"

Gasping, she spun to face Gavrel. Pressing her palm to her chest, she eased her breath. "What are you doing here?"

"Investigating the noise you're making." He stepped further between the trees. "I'm pleased it's you and not someone sneaking into the mansion."

She smiled about his devotion, but it faded as she thought about Breydon. Pain revisited, so she returned to the leaves, noting Gavrel donned regular garments. "I see you are off duty tonight."

"A few hours back. I just had ale with a friend." He leaned against a trunk, catching her gaze with his, and holding it. "You shouldn't be out here alone. Not when you don't know who are enemies of the Hammer."

Appreciation returned a smile to her lips, which he then reflected. Thylaina shoved the leaves into a pouch. "I feel safe in Caerabis. Even more now that you are with me."

His smile faltered. "You'll push me down a path of insanity."

She dropped her focus to the sack's drawstrings, tugged it closed.

"Need assistance?" he asked.

"I am finished." She brushed past him.

Gavrel caught her arm. "Will you walk with me? It's a gorgeous Lover's evening, and I can think of no one else with whom I wish to spend it."

Thylaina should have gone home. The repenia leaves needed cleaning for distilling, prayers must be said, but... She wanted something positive to distract her from worry. She did not want to be alone.

Her fingers gripping the crook of his arm, she said, "I would enjoy that."

They stayed in the garden, but headed toward where it connected to Thylaina's. Neither spoke for the first five minutes as they listened to the crickets' song and bats clicking high above.

Gavrel appeared older under the moonlight. And paler. The moon tended to do that to people.

"You seem worried," he said.

"There is silence from the plains." She stepped over the root of a pear tree. "Not even Arhgrim has heard from Breydon."

"Nothing from the good captain?"

"I wish you would not call him that." Thylaina released his arm, but he placed his hand over hers and held it in place.

"Forgive me. I—" Gavrel looked ahead. "I hope he and the others are well."

She ducked a branch of the orchard's last tree afore her yard. "I am terribly concerned. And I wonder if I should—" Thylaina bit her lip.

"Should what?"

Sighing, she glanced at him. Could she trust Gavrel? To be truthful with herself, she knew not why Breydon insisted he was untrustworthy. Gods! Her husband still claimed the man had a hand in Bramn's death, even after the trial over a decade past. Gavrel showed humility when he sent the letters of apology, and courage when he finally returned to offer his sword to Grim. Turning against the Three was dangerous, yet here he was. Yes. She could trust him.

"Come," she said, guiding him into her garden. When they reached the flowering bushes, she stepped between them, pulling Gavrel along.

A brow arched, he chuckled. "You have something in mind?"

Thylaina squinted. "Gavrel, you are my friend and I care about you. I trust you."

Seriousness swiftly took over his expression. "I am truly honored, Thylaina."

"I had made a promise to Breydon to meet him at the outpost in Ormiana Forest upon the first sign of trouble. From there, we shall cross into Etharell." She closed her eyes and shook her head. "I wonder if I should ride to the outpost now." Opening her eyes, she noted deep concern weighed Gavrel's brow. "You have been on the plains and have seen more than I of what happens. They do not tell me everything. Are the outlooks so grim I should leave now?"

He scanned the surrounding foliage, appearing to make certain they were alone. Gavrel then lowered his mouth to her ear and whispered, "If he was waiting for you, or believed your life was in jeopardy, surely he would've sent a message."

"I have considered that as well." Thylaina moved closer to him in an already tight enclosure. "Something is wrong. I feel it."

"Who else knows about this plan?"

"Brenlyr and Grim, of course."

Gavrel nodded. "Wait another day or two. Maybe they're riding back now. If you've not heard anything, *I'll* take you to the outpost."

For the first time in several days, a sense of security eased into her mind. "I am grateful. Thank you." She raised on her toes and kissed his cheek. As she lowered to step back, his hand rested on her waist, stilling her. "Gavrel," she whispered. "I-I must go inside."

"These things you do—what you sometimes say..." He released her and straightened. "I have always cared deeply about you, Thylaina. For that reason, I'll do all I can to protect you. Taking you to the outpost isn't for his sake. It's for you." Gavrel bowed. "Rest well, my lady."

She watched him depart. There had been no intention of stirring strong emotions in him. Thylaina had only wished to show gratitude. After thirty-three years, she still did not quite understand humans.

Three nights later, Tesesra invited Thylaina to have supper with them. Their company was much needed, so she accepted and walked with Katjina and Amdronus, who had arrived to escort them.

"I think I'll retire this autumn," he said.

Katjina sent an irritated glance his way. Her slight tremble alerted they had already made a decision. They were going to leave Caerabis.

Thylaina expected this would soon come. Though Katjina still performed as wonderfully as three decades ago, the poor woman grew tired faster.

Why did humans have to age so quickly? However, this was the life Thylaina had chosen, to surround herself with people who lived such short lives. It broke her heart. And even more now that she was about to lose one of her dearest friends. But not right now. There was too much already on her mind with Breydon's absence and their horrible parting. She did not need to have this weight on her heart as well.

Thylaina pretended not to have heard Amdronus as she walked up the steps to the mansion's front door. Hopefully there would be some good news to raise her spirits.

It was a delight to see Telsia present, looking splendid in her armor. Rare was it to see her donning anything else. Many claimed she slept in the chain and plate pieces. But to have her safely home was a gift from Valorius.

"Lady Thylaina," Telsia bowed her head. "It's a pleasure to see you."

"It is wonderful to see you, my dear." Thylaina hugged her as best she could with the chair's high back in the way. "Have you heard anything from my men?"

"I'm afraid not." She glanced at her father, then minded her plate.

Just as Thylaina sat, she noticed more guards present than usual. She smiled at Arhgrim and Tesesra, then welcomed the servant bringing a bowl of broth and a plate of bread.

Discussions were light, subjects jumping from gardening, the temple, and the weather. Anything but the current situation with the knighthood and the battles on the plains. Thylaina wanted to yell, demanding to learn what they knew. The gazes shared between the Momestids revealed they were aware of something.

She was just about to slap her hand upon the table and insist they tell her, but the servant filling her wineglass discreetly placed a folded parchment on her empty plate. Thylaina raised her eyes to Grim, his irises so blue beneath thick gray hair.

He bobbed his head once, his expression solemn.

Her heart thudded fast. Hands shaking, she reached for the paper.

*Laina,*

*Pack your healing case and food. Nothing more. Leave for the outpost as soon as possible. If I'm not there within two days' time, cross into*

*Etharell. Wait for me at the nearest xilys post. Please don't stall.*
*I love you. May the gods keep you safe.*
*Breydon*

She looked at Grim. "What—?"

He placed his finger to his lips and shook his head once. They had found spies in the mansion afore, and he must be concerned about more.

Thylaina breathed slow, shaky.

Telsia looked around her chair, jerked her head in Thylaina's direction. Two guards stepped forward.

Hoping to present a strong voice, Thylaina said, "I must prepare the repenia leaves I collected last night." She forced a smile, fought the tears blurring her vision as she looked at people who had been family for more than thirty years. Swallowing the sob constricting her, she nodded slightly. "There is much... to do for extracting the oil."

"You are always so busy with your remedies," Tes said, a teardrop lining down her cheek.

"Do you need any help?" Grim asked.

"N'ei. It is simple work for me. Likely complicated for you humans." Thylaina did her best to giggle. It sounded awful.

"Maybe you can teach me," Telsia said.

"Come to the house when you have a moment."

Telsia tilted her head back, nodded once.

Thylaina tucked the letter in the bodice of her dress, then headed for the door; the two guards followed. She had barely walked ten feet when she halted and ran back to Grim's chair. Arms tight around him, she rested her head on his shoulder. Thylaina had never wept so quietly in her long life. "I love you," she whispered. "All of you."

He patted her arm and uttered, "And we you." His eyes were as red as hers felt. "Be safe."

She hurried for the door, stopping at it. A final look back was the only farewell she could afford. The hug was risky as it was. Breydon waited for her... she prayed.

The guards remained outside the house while she filled the healing satchel, gathered some food in a sack, and filled a wine skin. Thylaina changed into a riding outfit Breydon had set aside for this very plan. The pants and blouse fit her to form, yet allowed easy movement. He had not wanted her in garments that might snag on low branches.

She exited the bedchamber, picked up the satchel and food sack from the kitchen, then rushed to the family room.

The portrait. She wanted to take it with her, but there was no time. Setting the items down, Thylaina wrote a note asking Katjina to take the painting to the mansion.

*I shall soon see Breydon. That is most important.* Thylaina gathered her items and left through the garden door. *Hopefully, Brenlyr will join us.*

Upon entering the garden, she halted, her heart skipping a few beats as her mind verified who was present. Gavrel stood where the guards should have been. He was armed and in traveling leather that bore no order insignia.

She surveyed the bushes and each garden path as she stepped toward him. "Where are they? And Captain Momestid?"

Gavrel partially bowed. "The Three sent reinforcements." Brows low, he shook his head. "Marshal Momestid sent the captain's squad to battle them. Her cavalry may turn the tide in our favor." He offered his hand. "I promised to take you to Ormiana."

Of course, Telsia's elite force could bring victory once again. But where were the knights who awaited her?

She swept her arm to the side, indicating the garden. "Where are the men who—?"

"We must travel alone."

"But..." Thylaina gripped the satchel strap. "Gavrel—"

"Listen to me." He stepped closer, his voice low and soft. "If we have too many riding out of here, it will draw suspicion from the spies. Yes, there are spies within the city. And your little display of hugging the marshal before leaving didn't go unnoticed. So we must do our best to leave without gaining further attention. Two people have a better chance than four."

*Damn it to Darkness!* Thylaina clenched her jaw, furious with herself.

Gavrel gently squeezed her shoulders. "I know the plains well, and I *will* get you to that outpost safely."

Thylaina nodded as she turned in the direction of the stables, but he grabbed her arm.

"There's no time. Mine's behind the house." The Alohrian stallions were the largest horses on Yeuroth, and could ride for several hours longer than the elven breeds, all while bearing the heavier weight of humans and their gear. "We'll walk around the orchard, then head for the forest," he said, as he led her behind her home.

Starting north of Caerabis was a wise route. They could skirt any fighting from the Downs in the south that might have spilled into the western plains.

Gavrel moved quietly, alert of every sound and motion. Thylaina often held her breath, waiting for an enemy spy or knight to leap from a shadow. When they reached the northern end of the orchard, some relief eased the tightness in her chest.

Sweet Vynia, she was going to miss the fragrances of this place.

"You're so light," Gavrel grasped her waist, shocking her from her thoughts, and lifted her to the saddle, "Hallendel won't even notice you."

Thylaina forced a smile. Too much worry about being caught and whether Breydon and Brenlyr were alive consumed her to find any sort of amusement.

Gavrel climbed on behind her, pulled her partially onto his legs, then grabbed the reins with his free hand. "I'll get you there. I promise."

As they rode westward with no signs of being followed, she relaxed slightly. Every move she had made since reading Breydon's letter recounted in her mind, right to leaving the orchard. She did not want to believe all they had feared had indeed come to pass. At least there was comfort that Gavrel was with her.

# Chapter Twenty-Nine

**D**ark farmhouses offered no welcome or warmth, especially under the moon's cold light. Hallendel's hooves thudded as he galloped amid the eerie plains. During six hours of riding, Gavrel had permitted bouts of cantering to give the stallion rest, but they did not stop. Thylaina was tired. The forest loomed ahead, yet seemed too far away, solace just out of reach.

"Lean upon me if you wish," Gavrel said, his breath heavy in her ear.

She accepted his suggestion and relaxed against him. As they rode toward their destination, she glanced in each direction, watching for approach from patrols. Fear of capture left her tense and unable to slumber. And there was still the curiosity that the knight bore no insignia, which could cause trouble.

Thylaina shifted slightly, her shoulders rubbing his chest. "Gavrel, why do you not wear an emblem?"

"I believed it was best not to should we come upon enemy knights."

Thylaina frowned in thought. "But they would still question your loyalty."

"Yes." He directed Hallendel around a shadowed dip in the ground that could have left the horse lame. "If that were to happen, I'll tell them just what I said to you."

"And if they question my being with you?"

"Thylaina, rest. I'm trying to pay attention to our surroundings."

"I just wished to know."

He slowed the stallion to a halt, scanned the fields, then drank from the waterskin. "I'd tell them I'm following the marshal's orders, and taking you somewhere safe."

"And if they are our enemy?"

"I'm taking you to the marshal."

She turned her head enough to see him. "You would lie?"

Gavrel's expression was solemn. "I'd do everything possible to get you to that outpost. I swear it."

A knight's vow was his life. Thylaina could count on her friend to help. She returned to resting against him. "Thank you."

"You're welcome." He commanded the horse forward at a faster pace.

The jouncing did not offer much comfort, but Thylaina closed her eyes and thought about his warmth and security. Exhaustion finally took its toll, and she fell into slumber.


A sudden jerking, Gavrel's weight briefly pressing upon her, and the horse's harsh grunting stirred Thylaina. They had entered Ormiana Forest. He dismounted, then led the way through the moon-dappled woodland. The outpost was located toward the northeastern side of Lake Wynland. Riding the path would have been easier, but perhaps Gavrel had his reasons to avoid it.

After stumbling seven times from dips and branches hidden beneath the leaves, he drew his sword and hacked at an innocent bush, curses hissing through his teeth.

"Do you wish to stop?" Thylaina asked. "You must be tired. Besides, can you see in this darkness as well as I?"

"I'm fine." Yet he sounded winded and frustrated.

"Please, Gavrel. Twenty minutes of respite, for your sake."

He scanned the area. "For Hallendel as well," he said, patting the stallion's neck. "Good boy."

Gavrel continued ten yards, finding a suitable place to rest.

Thylaina provided him some fruit, cheese, and wine, and fed Hallendel two apples and a carrot. She spoke to the horse, wishing she had received the gift of communicating with animals. There were few elves who could, and she knew none of them.

After Gavrel ate, he leaned against a tree and closed his eyes.

Nibbling on some fruit, Thylaina lowered beside him.

The forest was quiet, save for the expected sounds: an owl, night rodents scampering on the ground, crickets chirping, the wind passing through the leaves.

Prayers repeated in her mind while she listened for the approach of a horse, or many. Any sign of Breydon's arrival. Regret nipped at her heart. Why was their last moment together a terrible one? Thylaina should have welcomed him into the bathing room. Rarely did she and Breydon fight, and when they did, the anger lingered for little time. But she had clung to bitterness over his behavior toward her friend.

There was no telling how many hours had passed while she relived that evening. Gavrel snored softly, and Thylaina hated to wake him, but she had to reach the outpost. What if Breydon was already there?

She shook him. "Gavrel, we must go."

He bolted upright, reaching for his sword. Eyes wild, he stared at her. He blinked a few times, then relaxed. "Forgive me."

She returned to the saddle and used her elven sight to guide Gavrel onward.

Nearly three hours passed when they arrived at the outpost. Dawn's first lights could not yet touch this deep into the forest, so two bullseye lanterns hung outside the large wooden structure, and one man stood at the door.

"Hail," Gavrel called, slowing as they neared. He helped Thylaina off Hallendel.

"Hail, sir."

Thylaina straightened her blouse, then approached. "Is First Captain Colmstad here? Or Captain Brenlyr Colmstad?"

The soldier's gaze flitted to Gavrel. "No, my lady." He adjusted his cloak, covering his left shoulder where the order insignia should have been. There was no pin. The Hammer brooch should have been on the man's cloak. But he was not...

Thylaina stepped back, bumping into Gavrel.

"What is it?" he asked.

"Something is... amiss." She noted the soldier's nostrils curling. "This man is not one of ours."

Gavrel pulled her behind him, then advanced upon the soldier. He slugged the man to the ground. Spinning, he nodded to the horse. "Get on!"

Thylaina attempted to hook her foot in the stirrup, but she could not focus. Pounding in her ears nearly deafened her, the pulsation rushing to her head.

Men charged from the building and the trees—far too many men. They surrounded Thylaina and Gavrel.

He pulled his weapon and yanked her behind him again. "Keep back." He pointed the sword at the soldier in front of him. The men rushed forward, only a few with weapons drawn. Hands clutched at Thylaina, dragging her from Gavrel's protection. A bellow erupted from him, and his eyes widened with a maniacal expression. He swung his blade at those holding Thylaina, striking one man's arm and another's side afore the other men grappled him from behind, taking him to the ground. One of them slammed his head to the earth twice. Her friend lay still.

"Gavrel!" Thylaina screamed. Something hard struck her head. So much pain. Warmth oozed from her scalp. The branches above spun. Nausea set in. Then she felt nothing.

The bedroom was familiar, but not hers. Although it had been once afore. The Momestid's mansion. This was the room she had occupied prior to marrying Breydon.

Thylaina sat up, touching the painful lump on her head, which caused more hurt.

"M'lady?" Katjina said from the chair at the vanity. The handmaiden hurried over and sat on the bed. "Are you well? Gods! I was worried."

"What happened?"

Katjina held Thylaina's hands, tears trailing one after another. "Their forces entered the city from every direction. It happened so quickly—Marshal Momestid had no time to get the defenses in motion. I overheard something said about traitors from within striking our barracks and guardhouses."

Chills spread down Thylaina's arms, raising bumps on her flesh. "Is the family safe?"

"Yes. However, they're locked in the mansion. Even Amdronus."

"Breydon and Brenlyr?"

Katjina shook her head. "No one has seen them."

Heart plunging into her stomach, Thylaina wanted to vomit. Swallowing that urge, and withholding the building sob, she whispered, "Do you know what happened to Sir Gavrel?"

The handmaiden frowned. "I... I haven't seen him."

Her heart broke further. "They must have killed him at the outpost." Tears blurred her vision. "Why did not Grim prepare? They suspected spies. An-and Breydon's letter should have been a warning."

Katjina's shoulders sagged, the sorrow and strain overwhelming her face. "I don't know, m'lady. Something was troubling the marshal. Something that had gone wrong. They were talking about you."

"Me?" Thylaina wiped her eyes and cheeks dry. "Afore the attack?"

"Yes. Captain Momestid was furious about plans going awry."

"Cap—" Thylaina straightened, shook her head. "She led her cavalry into the plains."

Katjina blinked, confusion wrinkling her forehead. "She left for your house, then came back saying you were already gone."

No. Gavrel would not have betrayed the Momestids, and certainly not Thylaina. He took her to the outpost. The men there attacked him—likely killed him. It made no sense.

A knock sounded, then the door opened without a response from either woman. A knight bearing a brooch of the Griffon entered. "Good. You're awake. Marshal Salnaer Thornsalin is ready to receive you."

He was in Caerabis? The Second Marshal of Alohrius must have led the attack into the city. The chances that Breydon was still alive grew slimmer.

Tears quickly pooled as the realization of his demise set in. Thylaina had likely lost her husband and son to the Griffons. She covered her mouth to silence her weeping.

Katjina squared her shoulders with the knight. "I must prepare m'lady before she is seen by anyone."

He sneered. "You have fifteen minutes." The door closed, and his heavy steps faded.

The handmaiden hugged Thylaina until the crying ended, then wiped the teardrops away. "Time for afternoon meal."

"Was I unconscious for that long?"

Katjina nodded. "They permitted me to retrieve a dress from the house. Marshal Thornsalin wants you presentable."

"It seems I have n'ei choice."

Katjina quickly washed Thylaina, then dressed her. They did not bother with colorful facial powders. Neither cared about making her *that* presentable for Marshal Thornsalin.

Thirty minutes later, the knight returned with a comrade. He instructed Katjina to remain in the room, then escorted Thylaina to the dining chamber, leaving his companion with the handmaiden. A prayer accompanied each step to the feast hall that no harm would befall her dearest friend.

Thylaina had expected to find Salnaer in Grim's chair, but the man appeared to concede the master of the house his proper place, and sat to Grim's right. To her surprise, the whole family was present, including Nadiera's husband, Vhilmas, and their son, Jerien; Annemie had married a knight and moved to Monsor six years past. They all had dressed in fine garb and appeared unarmed. It was the first time in over ten years Thylaina had seen Telsia in anything but armor.

Knights bearing pins of the Griffon on their cloaks stood along the wall and windows. Possibly two dozen men.

Everyone rose when Thylaina approached the table. The knight escorting her pulled back the chair to Grim's left—across from Marshal Thornsalin, and waited for her to sit.

Thylaina locked gazes with Salnaer.

He was tall, possibly six-and-a-half feet. It was difficult to tell with the leather armor and the griffon decorated breastplate, but he appeared strong and young for his age, which was close to Grim's mid-sixtieth years. Short blond hair showed signs of whitening, and his piercing blue eyes shone bright. It was easy to see the likeness shared with his son, Kaeleck.

"Lady Thylaina." He bowed his head, his voice deep. "It's a pleasure to finally meet you."

Keeping her full attention on him, she sat. "I cannot share the sentiment, Marshal Thornsalin."

A crooked smile was his only reply. He looked to the Momestids and gestured to their chairs. "Sit. Please."

Once the others lowered to their seats, he did as well, his gaze on Thylaina; she shifted to a more comfortable position beneath his scrutiny.

The Momestid family barely moved. The silence within the large chamber had more life than those within. Servants bustled into the room, bringing steaming bowls of broth, platters of flat breads and fruit, and decanters of wine. The family eyed the meal, but none reached for their food.

Chuckling, Salnaer broke some bread and dipped it in the broth, biting into the soaked bread. He grunted an approval. "Fine cooks, Grim. May I still call you Grim?"

"We're not friends." Grim's voice was low. Subdued.

Salnaer smiled wryly again, darted his gaze to Thylaina. "You're not eating, my lady."

She wrinkled her nose. "I have n'ei appetite."

He hesitated. "You shall need your strength for the coming days." Marshal Thornsalin dropped the bread onto the table, then motioned at her meal. "I insist."

Jerien, who had been inducted into the knighthood two years past, was the first of the Momestids to begin eating. Nadiera tried to stop him, but he ignored her.

"Very good." Salnaer grinned, his attention rarely straying from Thylaina. When Tesesra asked a servant to pour wine, his face brightened. "That's more like it."

Thylaina remained ignored the food and drink.

"So," Salnaer paused as an attendant filled his glass, "you're a spy for the Elven Nation."

Snorting, Thylaina looked away from him.

"You've been in Caerabis long enough to give your people information about the knighthood, therefore, endangering my countrymen."

"I have done n'ei such thing." She gritted her teeth.

"Do not speak your language in my presence." It was the first time the man did not smile, nor show amusement. He looked dangerous. "'No' is simple enough for even you to accomplish."

For the Momestid's sake, she did her best to avoid using any Elvish words. "I have done nothing to compromise the people of Alohrius."

"That is for me to judge."

"Shall you judge fairly?"

"Pah!" Grim bellowed. "Salnaer Thornsalin a fair man? I'd win a wager if I bet against that."

"Grim," Tesesra said, her expression begging.

He waved his hand in Salnaer's direction. "I'll not tolerate this bastard storming into my city and holding my family captive!"

"You will tolerate me questioning your loyalty to the knighthood you swore to uphold, Arhgrim." Salnaer sipped from his cup.

"I uphold it," Grim said, his tone full of loathing. "It's you Three who've twisted it to your desires—corrupting the Law and Code. Your greed for power swayed the weak and like-minded into following your path!"

"Enough." Salnaer had remained calm throughout Grim's tirade. "We've heard this nonsense before. Your order broke from the knighthood, and you convinced the others that your way was the true way. Yet here you were for thirty years with an enemy spy in your midst."

Jerien slammed his hand on the table and stood. "She's no bloody spy! Lady Thylaina is a healer."

"I've heard, Sir Jerien." Salnaer nodded once. "Now take your seat." He returned his attention to Thylaina. "I've also learned she concocts potions that can charm... and poison."

"Ridiculous," Telsia said under her breath. "She's never done any such thing."

"No?" Salnaer scanned the glowering faces at the table. "Did she not marry Captain Breydon Colmstad after he deemed her a thief? And was she not guilty of the accusation?"

Watching her fidgeting fingers, Thylaina bit her lip.

"As I'm certain you recall, she saved Breydon's life," Grim said, "from your *son's* poison."

Salnaer abruptly rose. "Do not dare accuse Mikan of such deeds!"

"Then don't accuse Lady Thylaina." Grim's voice remained steady, and not a bead of sweat formed upon his calm demeanor. "We witnessed what that man did to Breydon, and the deaths of other men in my ranks."

The Second Marshal released a long breath, returned to sitting. "The knighthood would never take the word of an elf spy—"

"But it accepted the testimony of a priest and Mikan's victims. Enough to charge him." Grim smiled now, although it appeared forced. "If it had not been for Lady Thylaina, I would've lost my First Captain. She's not guilty of poisoning anyone."

Salnaer lifted his glass. "She's certainly bewitched many." He drank, then looked at Thylaina. "What is it they call people like you? Vynist witches?"

She scrunched her face. "I have never heard of such a thing. A Vynist, perhaps, but never a witch."

"That's what *we* call your kind." He lowered the cup. "And now that you've admitted to being a Vynist, I've no more questions on that matter." He looked around the table, let out a humph. "Aren't you hungry?"

The others still hadn't touched their meal.

"Very well." Salnaer smiled at Thylaina. "Pour a glass of fruzae for Marshal Momestid and me, will you?"

"I am n'e..." She calmed, reminded herself to speak the weaker Tongue. "I am no servant."

"I find it hard to believe you've never poured a drink for your darling husband. Or is it traitorous knight?"

"Breydon is no traitor." Grim pointed at him, his face red and eyes bright. "And you bloody know it!"

"He married a spy and gave her information to share with her people—our enemy. He's a traitor." Salnaer's voice tremored, his face darkened. "And they created a bloody abomination together."

"When did Etharell become our enemy?" Telsia asked. "They've been our allies for hundreds of years. At least, until you Three deemed them our foe."

"While your father's made a bed with the elves," Salnaer said, "Haevaun Balaeus has carefully watched their actions. Attacks on our people—"

"They attacked us first!" Thylaina hated these lies.

Marshal Thornsalin piercing gaze stilled her. She did not want to breathe while he pressed his hatred into her soul.

"They've killed knights simply for walking near the border, my lady," he said. "We have witnesses. Survivors. Men who suffer nightmares. And your king, generals, and xilys must answer for it. All of it."

She tilted her head, confused. None of that made sense. These were not actions of her people—a race who loved life. "You are lying."

His jaw clenched and unclenched. "Pour the drinks, woman."

Her chair was suddenly dragged back; she grabbed the arms to hold steady.

"Get up," the knight who had escorted her commanded.

Huffing, Thylaina stomped to the table in the room's corner. There was only one bottle on it, so she poured two glasses.

"Would anyone else—?"

"Just two," Salnaer said. "This is a special blend meant for men like Arhgrim and me."

The idea to bash the decanter on the Second Marshal's head crossed her mind, but with the family unarmed and the knights present, it would do no good.

She returned, set a glass afore each man. "Anything else, *my lord*?"

Salnaer chuffed. "Amusing woman." He nodded across the way. "Take your seat."

Walking slowly, Thylaina considered that magic might be their way out of this situation. But if the spell failed to affect all the men of the Griffon, the consequences could be dire for some of the family members. Word might reach Haevaun Balaeus that kin to the king of Etharell had been living in Caerabis all these years. Alohrians might view the Momestids as traitors. The action could also endanger Aella's family in Haevaun Balaeus. No, she could not risk it. Thylaina fell into her seat, defeated.

Grinning, Salnaer raised his glass. "Remember the old days, Arhgrim? You and I used to share a glass of honey-apple fruzae after a long day in the sun."

"You mean the days when you weren't such a self-important ass?"

Marshal Thornsalin tilted his head back, appearing offended. "Self-important? I was at your side when you offered your proposition to Tesesra's father. We shared a drink after he accepted."

Grim looked at his wife. "Like I said, when you weren't self-important." He lifted the glass. "You were devoted to the knighthood. Loved it." He drank a few swallows. "Great Valorius, Salnaer, you were bound for such greatness then."

"I'm bound for greatness now. As is my bloodline." His gaze flitted around the table. "Mine shall live for ages."

Thylaina froze. Her lips chilled at the thought of the Momestid family dying horrible deaths at the hands of the men in the chamber. She looked at Salnaer and the fruzae he had yet to drink.

Marshal Thornsalin smiled at Arhgrim. "To you and yours." He drank until the golden liquor was gone.

Finished with his drink, Grim set the cup down.

Relieved Salnaer had also partaken in the spirits, Thylaina relaxed.

"Now," the Second Marshal said. "Let's return to our discussion about this elf wom—"

Grim coughed hard. Scratchy. Dry. His face turned red.

Thylaina reached for him. "Grim?"

Salnaer tugged at his breastplate, pulling it from his throat. His face also darkened, and his eyes watered. He began coughing.

Grim worsened. Tears trailed from the corners of his eyes as his coughing grew louder and into hacking.

"Grim!" Tes ran around the table toward him.

"Thylaina, help!" Nadiera shouted.

Grim spewed blood. It landed on the table, slid down his chin and onto his shirt. He would not stop coughing.

Thylaina jumped from her seat and turned him over the chair's arm. "Try to breathe."

What was she saying? He was obviously poisoned. As was Salnaer, for he was on his hands and knees, spitting blood on the floor between violent heaves.

Two knights hurried to Salnaer and lay him on his side. "Help him," one of them demanded of her.

Thylaina returned her focus to Grim. The blood would not cease, but now, chunks came with it.

"Grim!" Tes screamed.

Vhilmas joined Thylaina, while Jerien held Nadiera back, and despite the fear reigning her visage, Telsia tried to calm her mother.

Thylaina attempted to identify Arhgrim's symptoms to learn what poison he had consumed, but she had never seen anything act so quickly. Without her satchel, she had no remedies available. Not knowing what else to do, she thrust her fingers down his throat, hoping to force him into vomiting.

He only gagged and produced more thick blood.

One of the knights copied her, gaining success. Marshal Thornsalin purged his body of food and drink and small amounts of blood.

Grim had not eaten a thing.

Tes pushed away from Telsia and dropped to her knees beside her husband. She petted his hair back as he heaved breaths in. The whites of his eyes appeared nearly purple.

Then he stopped. Everything. Vomiting, breathing, living.

Thylaina trembled as she stared at him—this man she dearly loved like an older brother. He had taken her into his home, treated her as family. And she let him die.

"You bitch," Salnaer rasped. "You poisoned us."

Thylaina blinked. Looked from Grim to Salnaer. What did he just say? The words came again and again. She grasped onto them. Understood. "N'ei," she whispered.

"You tried to kill us!" He groaned, pressed his hand to his throat.

Jerien shook his head. "Thylaina would never. *Never.* She loves us. Loves my grandsire."

"Love?" A knight pointed at Grim. "He's dead!"

Tes raised her reddened eyes to Thylaina. "You could've saved him."

"I-I tried. I swear I—"

"Why didn't you save him?" Tes shouted. Turning to Salnaer, she screamed, "Get out! All of you!"

"Tesesra," Marshal Thornsalin whispered. "Listen to me—"

"You did this." The flow of tears did not stop as her rage grew, her face turning darker from her agonizing outbursts. "You bastard! All of you!" Tesesra swung her arm in a sweeping motion, indicating Salnaer and his men. "Get out of my home!"

Blubbering into her hands, Nadiera knelt beside her mother. "Father."

The marshal rubbed at his throat while he stared at Tes. His gaze shifted to Thylaina. "Take her."

As knights stepped toward Thylaina, Telsia moved into their path. Swords slid from sheaths.

"No." Tes rushed to stand in front of her youngest daughter. "Telsia, I'll not lose you as well."

"Mother." Nadiera stumbled to her feet to protect Tes.

Jerian and Vhilmas also stood between Salnaer's knights and the Momestid women.

Telsia shook her head. "You're not taking Lady Thylaina."

"She killed him." Marshal Thornsalin nodded at Grim's body. "Just as she tried to kill me."

Thumping pounded in Thylaina's head and shook her body as she looked from Salnaer to Grim, then to the rest of the family.

Nadiera and Telsia glanced at one another while the marshal wiped blood from his chin. There was no denying Salnaer had been poisoned. How could Thylaina and the Momestids prove her innocence?

"Take her to the vault," he said.

"No." Telsia stepped from behind her family and moved toward Thylaina.

"If any of you interfere," Salnaer's eyes narrowed, "*all* of you go to the vault."

"Stand down," Tes said, shame and guilt adding to the grief already weighing within her voice.

The family was suffering too much as it was, and Thylaina could not increase Tes' anguish with another lost life on her behalf. She kissed Grim's forehead. Determination was the only thing giving her the strength to rise and face them—her family. "Be strong, for him and everyone." Hopefully, they knew she spoke about Breydon and Brenlyr. "I love you all." Meeting Tes' tear-filled eyes, Thylaina added, "Forgive me."

The Momestids huddled close to Grim and watched as the knights led Thylaina from the feast hall.

"I'll never forget you!" Telsia called as the doors closed.


The knight slapped her again—no doubt her lip split that time. Hours of abuse had passed. They punched her in the stomach, as well as tore the back of her dress to burn her flesh. Her body could take no more, but they did not stop. Through it all, the divine power was beyond her reach, for they had bound her. Even if it was possible, doing so risked further endangerment for herself and Brenlyr... if he still lived.

Once the torture ended, the men dumped her into a jailhouse cell.

"Just wait until Captain Arnadha arrives," one said. "He'll enjoy a bout with you."

Their laughter faded as they left the cell room, closing the door behind them.

Thylaina curled, stopping when the scorching pain spread over her back. Hot tears rolled down her cheeks. She finally relaxed on her stomach, rested her head on her folded arms. Sleep might never come, but there was nothing else to do.

Was Bryric punishing her for leaving Etharell? No. The question made no sense. He would have served punishment sooner than thirty years. Or would He have? Maybe Bryric wanted Thylaina to experience joy, then take it from her. Make her believe life would have been better for everyone if she had stayed home. However, Bryric was not that sort of god... was He?

And Lessindra. How could the Goddess of Love, Forgiveness, and Mercy permit such anguish upon Her devoted? Thylaina and Breydon were faithful to Her and Valorius.

The Great Knight... He turned His bloody back on the devoted knights of the Hammer: Breydon, Arhgrim, and the others who surely fell while fighting those from the Order of the Griffon. Perhaps even Brenlyr.

*Please, Vynia... not my son.*

Why were the men who followed Salnaer Thornsalin rewarded?

She sputtered a sob. "Breydon... I am so sorry."

"Oh no. Gods no," someone whispered. Touched her with tenderness. Breydon. "What did they do to you?" His handling of her was gentle as he helped her sit up. "Darling."

She sucked in a breath. "Brey—"

He covered her mouth. "Hush." Breydon lowered his hand and kissed her.

Tears of overwhelming joy and ache fell. She wanted to hold him, but it hurt her back to raise her arms. "Love, I thought you were dead."

"We evaded the drift of Griffons." His nose wrinkled and brows lowered. "I went to the outpost and found the place a bloody mess." He assisted her to rise. "What happened? You were supposed to ride with Telsia."

"Gavrel came for me."

"Gavrel?" Breydon's face turned crimson, and his grip on her arm tightened. "I told you to stay away from him. Gods! Don't you ever listen to me?" He swiped his fingers through his hair. "Damn it, Laina. I told you I had my reasons. But you always thought it was jealousy."

"That is not why I left with him."

He looked toward the door. "We must go. It's not safe." Viewing her back, he clenched his teeth. "I'll kill them."

After checking the jail keeper's room, he pulled her inside. Two of his men waited by the outside door. They nodded once, then left the building.

"Where is Brenlyr?" she asked.

He looked at her, deep worry a horrid mask. "They have him." Those three words broke as he spoke them.

Thylaina's knees lost strength, and everything around her whirled with shadows. She could barely breathe.

"Love," Breydon said, holding her up.

Everything hurt her back, his touch, and her muscles tight from her sobbing, but she could only think of Brenlyr. "N'ei."

"Laina, listen to me." Breydon leaned against a wall, using it to help him keep her steady.

Thylaina fell into him, welcoming any pain it brought.

"Laina, I've heard he's unharmed."

"We must go to him."

"Not until you're out of this city."

"N'ei. We go to him now."

Hands on her hips, he pulled her closer. "We will save him, but I must get you to safety first. I promise you, love. Brenlyr will not remain a prisoner here, nor will you."

Her body trembled as she wept. Could this nightmare end afore she lost anyone else dear to her heart? The pain resurfaced, as did the memory of Grim's death and her helplessness. It ached to breathe again as the need to sob harder overwhelmed her. Control. There would be no escaping if she did not gain control of herself.

Sniffling, she turned her head. "Grim's dead."

"I know." Breydon swallowed. "Telsia told me."

"You have spoken with the family?"

"We helped them escape the mansion—Katjina and Amdronus went with them. They ride to Monsor as we speak. That's how Salnaer's men caught Brenlyr."

Another crack in her heart upon those words. Brenlyr... They had to save him. "What happened?" she asked.

"He charged a squad of Griffons to halt their spotting the Momestid's escape." Breydon nodded at his waiting men, then gently directed Thylaina back to their path. "Telsia nearly went with him, but she had given her word to protect her family."

Brenlyr had foolishly put himself in danger knowing that if the Alohrian leaders learned about his bloodline, they might use such information against Etharell to their advantage. Still, she could not blame him for protecting the people he loved. At least he saved the Momestids, where she had failed to save Grim.

Thylaina tugged on Breydon's arm. "I did not kill Grim."

Halting, he stared down at her. "I know you'd never hurt them."

"I do not understand how Marshal Thornsalin survived." Thylaina shook her head. "The poison seemed so strong. It affected Grim—"

"The bastard's clever. Likely built a tolerance to it."

Thylaina stiffened. *Of course. That was why Salnaer had lesser of a reaction.* Her stomach hurt at the realization. There was nothing she could have done. Salnaer had planned it perfectly. Grim was going to die while he survived. Breydon had warned her that these men took action at the precise moments, and by the gods! Salnaer's every move was planned perfectly.

Breydon and the knights stopped and looked toward the barracks at the edge of the city. "Let's go."

She snapped from the revelation and followed her husband around the storage building, then to the other side of the privy.

"Don't go too far!" someone shouted from atop the nearby storage building, then laughed.

Men guarding along the perimeter spun, bows nocked.

Breydon drew his hammer, and the two knights pulled their swords. He pushed her between the structures and charged. "Run, Laina!"

Panic left her searching for a path or friendly face with an opened door, but no such thing presented itself.

Men immediately surrounded Breydon, yet he fought.

No, she could not let him fall. Lightning magic immediately came to mind. Thylaina stood between two houses and concentrated on the earth and roots beneath her. Currents flickered through her body, power throbbing from her core. Pulsating, it grew, prickling to her outstretched hands, ready to consume her enemies. The incantation danced upon her tongue, waiting for her to speak. "*Chan—*"

Something struck her back—a boot—kicked her forward and knocked the wind from her lungs. Pain spread from the burn wounds. She stumbled to her stomach, her face smacking the cobblestone. Heaviness rested between her shoulder blades. So damn heavy, keeping her on the ground. Someone grabbed her hair, wrenched her head back, then slammed her face to the stone again.

Breydon held her close and caressed her face with his fingertips. "Remember your promise, Laina." Pooled tears fled from his eyes. "Remember what you promised tonight."

Scowling, she stared at him. What did he mean?

He smirked as he grabbed her hand and kissed it. "We made more than just marital vows."

Their wedding night. How were they here again? Thylaina would not complain to share this moment with Breydon once more. He looked just as handsome now as he had then, even with his hair disheveled. To see him so young again, despite that he had aged slowly, was wonderful. She welcomed this memory.

"Keep that promise, Laina."

She sighed. "Must we speak of it now?"

"Yes." Pain skewed his face. "I won't be with you for long, darling."

Thylaina held tight to him. "I will not let you go. Breydon... you are my greatest love."

"I shall wait for you. I will." He cradled her face, rested his forehead on hers. "I love you, Laina." His lips felt so fine against hers. Perfect. "Keep yourself safe. Don't let them learn the truth."

"But... I could—"

"Laina, no." His grip tightened. "They'll hurt you *and* Brenlyr."

She squeezed her eyes shut. Gods, Thylaina had forgotten the Griffons captured Brenlyr. There was no risking his life.

Nodding as best she could within Breydon's hold, she said, "I promise."

"What do you swear?"

"I will not threaten Brenlyr's safety, nor my own." Tears fell as her lips quivered, the words getting harder to speak. "And I will love again."

Breydon kissed her forehead. "Thank you."

Why were the gods doing this to her family?

"Laina."

What act had she committed to suffer this?

"Laina." Breydon's voice scratched.

Why was everything hurting?

"Laina," he rasped.

"Silence!" It was a different man's voice, and a thud sounded, like pounding on flesh.

Breydon screamed in anguish.

Thylaina opened her eyes. Dried blood caked her right brow and temple.

Numerous torches and candles brightened the chamber, causing her to blink several times, squinting until she could see clearly enough.

Six men were in front of her. One was shirtless and on his knees, bent forward with his arms forced up behind him from ropes fastened to hooks on the walls. Blood surfaced from several places on his body. The other men laughed while another struck the bound one four times with a sword hilt.

Breydon hollered.

"N'ei," she murmured.

His hair was a mixture of pink and red—blood-red. Cuts and bruises riddled his face, his eyes swelled shut, and his bottom lip was missing one corner.

Thylaina would not have recognized him were it not for his voice. She could not find hers to speak.

They paused their torture upon noticing her consciousness.

"Just in time, my lady." One of them stepped forward and bowed. He was tall and heavyset. "I'm Captain Slatin Arnadha. Marshal Thornsalin has put this... situation in my hands." He laughed. "Of which I'm quite pleased. Breydon and I have known each other for years."

She stared at her husband.

"I'm speaking to you," Captain Arnadha said.

"Breydon," was all she could muster.

"I see." The captain walked behind Breydon. "I understand you attempted to murder Marshal Thornsalin."

Gritting her teeth, she raised her eyes to him. "N'ei."

The man smiled, as if that was the answer for which he had hoped. "Spread them."

Two of the men went to the hooks and pulled the ropes, forcing Breydon's arms farther apart.

Breydon groaned, which soon turned into a cry of pain.

Captain Arnadha placed his booted foot where Breydon's right shoulder and arm met. In one swift motion, he bent the other leg and... hopped down on Breydon.

Thylaina screamed at the same time as her husband, just as his arm twisted to the side, snapping from the shoulder. She tried to lurch forward, but she was bound to a chair. A prickling sensation moved throughout her body. She could not feel the ropes.

"Watch, my lady," the captain said.

Thylaina dropped her head, shaking it.

"You must witness what we do to traitors of the knighthood."

"N'ei," she whispered.

"Help her."

Pain jolted through her scalp as someone yanked her hair, forcing her head back.

"That's better." Captain Arnadha already had his foot positioned in the same spot on Breydon's left shoulder. "I love the feeling of the bone separating beneath my foot." Then he did it again.

Breydon bellowed his agony until only air passed his swollen lips.

Thylaina shrieked, tried to move. Nothing happened.

The knights maintained their hold on the ropes, keeping Breydon in the vulnerable position. It looked... horrific.

Captain Arnadha lifted the sword they had been striking Breydon with. "This is his," he said. "And he shall receive a traitor's death by this blade."

Thylaina held her breath, looked from her husband to the captain. "I beg you. He is n'ei a traitor!"

"Oh, but he is. He helped you plan Marshal Momestid's death, and the attempt on the Second Marshal's life." The man grinned. "We have a letter stating concern about such devious acts. A letter signed by Lady Tesesra Momestid."

She shook her head. "Lies."

"Laina," Breydon whispered so softly, Thylaina was certain only she heard him. "You... are the love... of my life."

"Did he just say something?" Captain Arnadha asked.

"I don't think so, sir."

"No matter." The captain moved behind Breydon and positioned the sword's point beneath Breydon's ribs.

"Wait," someone said from the room's entrance. "This death is mine."

The captain sneered, but dropped the expression as he turned. "Of course, Mikan. I imagine revenge would taste exquisite right now."

Thylaina held her breath as Mikan Thornsalin came into view. She had not seen him in over thirty years, after Breydon and Grim sent him to a prison of which she knew nothing. Fear choked her as he neared Breydon.

Mikan was gangly and pale, his hair appearing freshly cut. Darkness surrounded his sunken eyes, and a yellow gap-toothed sneer shifted from Thylaina to Breydon.

*Vynia, help me.*

He took the sword from Captain Arnadha, positioned the point on the left side of Breydon's back. "This will be a slow and painful death, Captain Colmstad," he said, giving enough pressure to break the skin.

Another bloody mark upon Breydon's beautiful flesh. What have they done?

*Vynia, please. Help us.*

Movement slowed as warmth worked its way up Thylaina's legs and to her center. The divine magic sparked a new spell. Thylaina fought the growing sob to focus on the flow of power and the one word that formed in her mind. She drew her gaze from the sword to the top of Breydon's head, unable to see his face.

"I love you," she said. "For the rest of my days."

Shouting, Mikan plunged the sword into Breydon's back.

At that very moment, Thylaina whispered, "*Endoc.*"

Breydon would not endure the death these men wanted; he had suffered enough. He instantly fell limp. No breath passed. No moaning of agony. He was free.

Captain Arnadha looked from Breydon to Thylaina. "Did you just say something?"

Through tears, she stared at her broken husband. Blood trailed down his side and dripped to the floor in a rhythm that matched her racing heart.

The captain clutched her chin and jerked it, forcing her to look at him. "I heard you whisper."

"An Elvish word," she said through trembling lips. "A farewell prayer."

Mikan leered at her from behind Slatin.

Captain Arnadha slapped her hard; a stinging burn spread over her cheek. "Lying bitch! You think *your* suffering is finished? I assure you it's not!"

Mikan dropped the sword, wincing as it clattered. He spun and left the room.

A few hours passed afore the captain had Thylaina dragged from the jailhouse. They marched her to the top step of the marshal's mansion, where Salnaer waited, then faced her to the main road. The morning sun caused her head to hurt, far too bright in her eyes.

She laced her fingers together, wishing they would at least have the courtesy to loosen the binding on her wrists. A drink of water as well.

A group of soldiers walked toward them, dragging and pushing another. As they neared, the faces became clearer, and the one being abused was not one of them, but Brenlyr. Bruises and cuts marred his face, but he appeared otherwise unharmed. When he saw Thylaina, tears filled his eyes, and his lips quaked.

Had they told him about his father?

They marched Brenlyr to Salnaer's other side, keeping him from Thylaina's reach.

Heavy breaths came and went, and she kept looking toward him. She twitched, wanting to hold her son. To speak to him. But Salnaer's imposing presence silenced and stilled her.

Captain Arnadha walked up the stairs, a ridiculous smile spreading his thin lips. "I hope you'll enjoy what I have planned for you, my lady."

Eyes burning, Thylaina squinted. She was so bloody tired and cried out and in pain. Every part of her. Body, soul, and heart.

Thumping of an approaching horse pounded in her ears, spreading to her head. She scowled and turned toward the rider.

A knight neared, dust rising behind him. Odd. Most of the roads in the city were of cobblestones. It would take something with weight to cause the dirt between the stones to stir in such a way. The rider halted ten feet from the mansion and stared at Thylaina.

"Are you ready?" Captain Arnadha whispered in her ear.

She was ready to lie down and never wake up.

He nodded to the rider. "Go on, then!"

The knight bowed his head to Thylaina. He commanded the horse to run straight down the road, dragging Breydon's naked corpse behind it, the mangled arms flopping.

Thylaina collapsed to the steps. Her heart wanted to burst, especially as Brenlyr's agonizing screams filled her ears, each word drawn out in heartrending grief. "No! Father! No!"

The rider stopped at the end of the road, from where a tall pole had been erected. He tossed the free end of the rope over the crossbar, tied it to the saddle, then ordered the horse to walk.

Breydon's body rose high, hanging upside down.

"Everyone shall see and know what befalls those who betray the knighthood," Salnaer said.

Captain Arnadha chuckled, as did those nearby.

"Take him back," the marshal ordered.

"Mother! Mother!" Brenlyr's shouts faded.

She could not blink—could not look away from Breydon.

"Now, get up," Salnaer said.

Brenlyr's voice was gone.

Rough hands hauled Thylaina to her feet, then dragged her into the mansion. She could not recall anything else, but she now lay on her old bed. Grabbing the pillow, she screamed into it until her throat was raw and blackness filled her head. Then Thylaina sobbed until the pillow was soaked.

An elder woman she did not know entered. "It's time to wash."

There was no care or gentleness in how the woman handled her; wounds reopened, flesh tore from the burns, and everything hurt more.

"I have longed for this moment," the woman said. "To see you suffer... I Praise Chaos for this gift."

*Chaos?* Why would the woman offer thanks to the evil demigod? Only fools would think to do such a thing. And who was she? Thylaina did not know her.

The woman straightened, her plump and wrinkly face coming into focus.

No. Thylaina knew her from somewhere, but she could not recall.

"There's a few of us who've waited for this day. Escany amongst them, but he passed four years ago." The woman stood, a menacing smile spread wide. "But another waits in the hall."

Thylaina crossed her arms to clutch her shoulders, giving no warmth to her shivering body as the woman walked to the door. Escany, the former master gardener, had hated Thylaina. Thankfully, her interactions with him were so few. She knew he had died, but thought nothing of his passing. The man had been cruel to her.

"You ruined our lives," the woman said as she grasped the handle. "It's only right to see yours destroyed. All of you." She opened the door and motioned for another woman to enter. "Come, Bethlyn, We've not much time."

Thylaina gasped. An icy chill raced from her shoulders to her elbows, and down half her back.

Tes' former handmaiden entered with the aid of a cane. Bethlyn was thinner than afore Telsia's birth. Hatred burned in her eyes as she neared Thylaina. "I have waited ages for this day," she said. "I hid among the servants of the farms for years, slowly working my way back to the city as another's handmaiden. And I did my part to aid my lords. To see the city fall from the Momestid's reign, and watch you suffer all the pain you deserve, is more than I could've wished for."

Spies.

Thylaina looked at the other woman. "Ardella," she whispered.

"So you *do* remember me." The woman cackled.

When Thylaina returned her attention to Bethlyn, the woman's cane was crashing down on her head.

Two knights escorted Thylaina to the marshal's cabinet. Salnaer did not sit at Arhgrim's desk, but his son, Kaeleck, did. He was more imposing than the first time she had met him. The man seemed even larger, his eyes sharp like his father's, and his presence demanded respect and obedience. Kaeleck's mien gave no indication of his thoughts. It was like coming face to face with Neldrid. And it frightened her.

In one of the chairs afore the desk, was... Gavrel. The man was bathed, his jaw smooth from a clean shave.

Thylaina froze. She squeezed her eyes shut, then opened them again. He was still there. "Gavrel?"

He rose, set a glass of fruzae on the desk, then bowed. "Gods, what have they done to you?" Gavrel walked to her, but she retreated a few steps. He now bore the brooch of a Griffon.

Shaking her head, she stepped back again, Breydon's words echoing in her head.

*"I told you I had my reasons. But you always thought it was jealousy."*

His reasons. Breydon never trusted Gavrel, and yes, Thylaina believed it was because of jealousy. But it truly never was. He did not trust Gavrel because he believed the man was a...

"Traitor," she spat.

He licked his lips, then drew in a breath, but said nothing.

"You betrayed us."

He cocked his head. "I remained faithful to the knighthood."

"You betrayed *us!*" She lunged, punching his chest several times. Her whole body throbbed in pain from trying to cause him harm. None of it did any good. "The gods damn you to Darkness." She stepped away from him, weeping. "They murdered Breydon!"

"They punished a traitor," he said. "That's different."

She stilled.

Kaeleck watched with obvious amusement; leaned back in the chair, his arms behind his head.

"You bastard. All of you are bastards!" Thylaina turned for the door.

"You're going nowhere." Kaeleck sat forward, drank his liquor. "We've something to discuss."

Gavrel motioned to the other chair. "Please?"

"N'ei."

Kaeleck tilted his head and raised a brow. "My lady, do not speak your language in front of me."

"I do not bloody care!" She pointed at him. "What else can you possibly do?"

"More." That one word spoke clearly, especially as his piercing blue eyes bore into her, much like his father's did. "Your son is in our custody."

*I must protect him.* Still staring at Kaeleck, she said, "Tell me how he did it."

"Did what?"

"The poison."

The faintest smile played upon his lips.

"It was not immunity," she said. "Not with his reaction."

"Immunity wasn't possible with this poison." Kaeleck lifted the glass again. "Trained tolerance? Yes. And no matter how much you might try to poison me or my father, you'll fail. We've both trained our bodies to tolerate them all and at several dosages."

"Damn you." She wiped the tears from her cheeks, not even realizing she had shed any. "Grim was a good man."

"That he was." At least the marshal appeared to mean it. "But it was a shame he went against us."

Kaeleck looked at Gavrel, then at Thylaina. "It seems a reward's in order," he said. "If it were not for Sir Gavrel's exhaustive efforts, we never would've met our goals. Bringing our men into Caerabis, learning the position of the squads, their leaders, when and where *you* were going, and the precise time to strike the city, is all with gratitude to Sir Gavrel."

Thylaina faced the knight. Despite that he tried to present some sense of pride, guilt showed in Gavrel's face as he stared back. She slugged him. It hurt, but she had to.

The marshal laughed.

Thylaina held her curled hand to her chest and wept some more.

"Enough of this," Kaeleck said, his laughter settling. "I've plenty to do today, so let's move forward."

"What do you want?" she snapped.

"It's not what I want." He gestured to Gavrel.

She did not wish to look at him again. But did.

Gavrel stood straight, ran his fingers through his graying hair. "Thylaina… In two weeks' time I return to Rhigowan. I have a modest home I want to share with you for the rest of my days."

Silence followed his request as she stared at him, dumbfounded. "You cannot mean that," she whispered.

"You see, my lady," Marshal Thornsalin said, "I promised him a reward for his assistance. And though I want to keep you imprisoned here, I decided to grant him this one wish. But you *will* return once he passes." The bastard smiled.

"I can provide you with a fine life and be a good husband."

"I had a fine life and a wonderful husband!" She shoved him back. "You took it all from me."

"It's a good offer," Kaeleck said.

"It is." Gavrel mustered a sincere expression. "I'll treat you well. I've loved you since we met, Thylaina. You know this. And I'll love you the rest of my days." The man meant it. They had just slaughtered her husband, dragged him through the city, and strung him up.

Thylaina drew in a deep breath. With as much conviction as she could give, she said, "I would rather suffer Caerabis the rest of my days than one moment with you."

Gavrel widened his eyes, parted his lips.

Heavier silence passed for a few seconds, accentuating her pounding heartbeat in her ears.

"It seems she's made her decision," Kaeleck said.

Gavrel turned. "Sir, I ask that you—"

"You gave the offer, and she made her choice." The marshal shifted his gaze to Thylaina. "You shall remain imprisoned in Caerabis for the rest of your days for the murder of Marshal Arhgrim Momestid, amongst other deaths we shall claim you caused."

She shook her head. "N'e—No."

"This is what shall be."

Gavrel squeezed his fingers into tight fists.

"As for you, Sir Gavrel..." Kaeleck sat back and smiled. "As you're here for the next fortnight," he swung his gaze to Thylaina, "she's yours until you leave."

Ice bolting throughout her, she looked at Gavrel. He appeared a stranger. A very cold stranger. Thylaina stepped backward, toward the door. "N'ei."

Gavrel faced her fully, advanced.

"Gavrel, n'ei!"

He grasped her wrists and pulled her close, his breath billowing upon her face. "I told you that you'd lead us down this path."

"Do not do this to me—to us!"

"There is no us, Thylaina. You've made that clear."

The knight at the door opened it as Gavrel approached, dragging Thylaina with him.

She dug her heels into the floor, trying to stop him. Her screams echoed in the entry hall, up and down the stairs.

Gavrel continued, yanked painfully on her arm. Even when she fell to the floor, he kept pulling. Nearing one of the bedchambers, he pointed with his free hand and shouted at the nearest servant, "Open that door!"

Thylaina scratched his face. Slapped. Punched. Fought as hard as she could. During all of this, no one tried to help.

Gavrel pushed her into the room. "It never needed to be like this. But you chose it."

When the door slammed shut, her nightmare continued.

# Chapter Thirty

She hated him. Everything about Gavrel. The pungent odor of sweat and filth emanating from him, spreading on her. His voice. Gods, she despised his voice. Those earthy eyes staring at her with love—something he knew naught about. And that damn dimple on his chin... Thylaina hated that, too. More than anything, she loathed his touch. Wished she could go numb to it all. To have left this world with Breydon. But now, she was forced to listen to Gavrel weep from the edge of the bed.

Since the moment he shoved her into this room, the seconds had felt like minutes, lost like days cast into a bottomless well. How much time had passed since that first invasion? When she had tried to escape into memories. It happened again and again, and seemed his invasions would never end. She hurt as never afore. Shades of purple marked the tender places of her body. And her back—Oh gods, her back! Gavrel thought nothing of it, not even after he saw the burn marks. But now? Now he wept.

He blew his nose on the bedsheets, rose, and splashed water from the basin on his face. After drying, he dressed.

Thylaina could not move. She did not want to.

Her torn dress landed across her stomach.

"Put that on." Gavrel turned away. "Do it now."

It took fifteen painful minutes to don the garment. Thylaina tied it as best she could, including the ripped ends. No thoughts came to mind, just focusing on the task.

"Salnaer took your son to Haevaun Balaeus."

She stopped moving and slowly raised her head. "Why?" she rasped, her throat raw from shouting and screaming, all of it ignored by the guards outside the door.

"They believed it was best to have him as far from here as possible." Gavrel nodded. "Closer to them should they need to act against you."

Them. The Three. Brenlyr truly was in danger. Perhaps it was wise Thylaina had not brought harm upon Gavrel. She had nearly burned and blinded him, but stilled her tongue and finger motions. Instead, she suffered his carnal desires.

*Breydon, forgive me.*

Gavrel walked to the window and stared outside. The weight of a decision made filled the room.

Beneath the pain and whatever his decision was, Thylaina moved slowly while slipping her shoes on.

"Breydon was correct about Bramn's death," he said. "I did it."

Still bent over, she froze. A chill rippled down her arms as memories of the last time she saw her dear friend returned. Never did Thylaina forget the dreadful throat wound and lifeless eyes, nor the heartbreak that overtook hundreds within Caerabis. Particularly Bramn's family.

"Arhgrim and Breydon were fools. Their focus was on the mansion and spies within it, that they never considered the knights and soldiers." Gavrel turned enough to look at her. "Since my being knighted, every time I rode into this city with a squad, it was with men devoted to the Three. As long as the marshal and captain believed the knights came from Warstchia or Monsor, they thought nothing of it."

Thylaina straightened, the iciness spreading down her back and flaring over her arms again. In the marshal's cabinet, she had been in shock at seeing Gavrel alive and learning he played a part in the demise of Caerabis and those she loved, that she had paid little attention to what Kaeleck had said. It was true. She recalled men always accompanying Gavrel with his every return. The Three had infiltrated the city for years, waiting for the precise moment to attack.

"We worked our way into the force here," he continued, "and Arhgrim suspected nothing." Gavrel released a breathy laugh. "So when I rode out with Bramn, most of the men in the squad had been mine. Only two of the survivors were loyal to Marshal Momestid, but they didn't understand what happened. They saw one of our knights turn traitorous and attack the captain. And when I charged forward to help, it couldn't have been more perfect."

She closed her eyes, wishing the memory of Bramn's death would disappear. But as Gavrel continued speaking, her friend's dead gaze remained fixed on hers.

"I can still see it all," Gavrel chuffed. "Bramn had bent forward to dodge the other knight's blade, and that's when I brought my sword to his throat. His expression of realization that I wasn't there to help him was exhilarating. To see his flesh part and blood spill... Gods! I wish I could experience that again." Gavrel bared a malicious smile. "But what I relive most was watching his horror before I turned on the knight beside me and killed him, making sure everyone witnessed *that* strike. Bramn couldn't say a damn thing to expose me."

Swallowing several times to re-wet her drying mouth, she built the strength to whisper, "Why?"

"He pushed me too far. He *and* Breydon. And the Three wanted him gone."

Gavrel became a blurred form through the burning tears. Breydon. Was he correct about both accusations?

"Did you—?" She licked her lips and found her voice again. "Did you attack Breydon the night of Bramn's marriage?"

Gavrel lowered his head and nodded. "I saw you with him... through the slit of his bedroom curtain." His breath trembled, then his voice as he said, "And at that moment, I decided to kill him. But you stopped it, which saved my life." The man had the nerve to laugh.

Anger mixed with the pain as she fought to control herself. The desire to rain fire on him grew stronger while he resumed speaking.

"The Three learned quickly about that attack on the good captain, and had sent someone to seek retribution. But because Breydon lived, I suffered less punishment for going beyond their command." He shook his head. "I never crossed the Three again."

Breydon had been correct about Gavrel all along. And Thylaina was the biggest fool for believing this man truly was her friend.

*Forgive me, Breydon.* She slouched forward and wept.

"I'll give you some time for that," Gavrel said. "But not much. We must go. I... I cannot do this to you anymore."

No. He would not leave this city alive. He would not leave this room.

Thylaina breathed deep, calling upon the divine power. Vynia answered. This man killed her husband, and he slaughtered Bramn. He betrayed everyone dear to her. There would be no mercy. With Vynia at her side—always at her side—Thylaina rose and approached Gavrel.

He glanced over her ragged attire, then gestured to the door. "Let us go."

Thrusting her hand forward, she struck his chest with her palm, right over his heart. At that very moment, she spoke the word, "*Estogpa!*"

Gavrel's eyes widened, as did his mouth. Sharp gasps escaped him as he stumbled back, clutching at his chest. He collapsed, then writhed on the floor.

Thylaina felt the pounding grow harder, then slow until it ceased.

Gavrel lay motionless, unblinking.

She sat on the bed, recalled those two horrible moments when he had taken life away, and wished his suffering could have lasted so much longer. The gods forgive her, she had just killed a man. While staring at him, she nodded. Gavrel deserved death, but so did she. Because of her choices to believe him, to trust him, her husband was dead, Grim was dead, and everyone else was gone. At least the rest of the Momestids were safe. Brenlyr... His fate was her fault as well. Now she had to concoct a convincing story about Gavrel's death.

Thylaina removed his clothes, then dragged him onto the bed. Divine power aided with this task, for he was too heavy. Vynia must have forgiven her, but could Lessindra? She dismissed that question, for where was the Goddess of Love, Mercy, and Forgiveness when Thylaina and Breydon needed her? She toed her shoes off, then untied the dress. While rushing to the door, she slapped her cheeks to redden them and panted heavily, increasing her heart's beating. The door felt heavy as she swung it open. It took a moment for her to find her voice and call for help.

Two nearby guards hurried into the room and viewed the scene. They asked no questions, just grabbed her by the arms and dragged her to the marshal's cabinet.

Kaeleck was there, of course, but Mikan and Captain Slatin Arnadha were with him. They all turned as the guards dragged her toward them, their gazes shifting to Thylaina. Slatin smirked.

Marshal Thornsalin gave his attention to the guards, annoyance apparent in his leer. "What is this?"

One of them shoved Thylaina forward, and she stumbled into the back of a chair facing the desk. "Sir Gavrel is dead," the guard announced.

Slatin snorted, then bellowed a laugh. "After three days of cock-ramming the witch, I'm not surprised!"

That was how long Gavrel kept her in that damn bedchamber? For three days she had endured his body, lips, and declarations of love. He had begged her to change her mind and return to Rhigowan with him, but she said nothing. Thylaina did all she could to escape from the nightmare that bastard had forced on her.

Kaeleck's eyes darted from Thylaina to Slatin. "Enough."

Slatin silenced.

The marshal stepped toward her. "What happened?"

Thylaina's head spun and her ears throbbed. She could barely hold on to the back of the chair, let alone keep the torn dress together within her curled fingers, the knuckles white.

Rough hands clutched her arms, guided her to sit. It hurt to do anything. Even to think.

"Answer me, witch," Kaeleck said.

"He... He was having his way with me," she managed. She opened her eyes and looked up at the marshal. "Suddenly, he sounded as if he hurt. I asked him about it, but he could not speak. Then he died. I believe his heart stopped."

Mikan scrutinized her for a moment. "I'll examine him."

"Go on then." Kaeleck sat on the desk, his gaze fixed on Thylaina.

Nothing was said in the former high priest's absence, but the men shifting their positions while waiting for his return prevented uncomfortable silence. Slatin started to speak, however, Kaeleck's glare quieted him.

Mikan returned fifteen minutes later. "It appears Sir Gavrel's heart stopped."

"Perhaps he enjoyed himself too much." Slatin chuckled.

Mikan scowled at the captain, then turned to his brother. "Now what?"

Rubbing his chin, Kaeleck sighed. "She's out of our hands and is now in Slatin's."

Every nerve rose as cold rushed down Thylaina's body. She refused to look at the captain.

Mikan motioned to her. "What are your intentions, Marshal Arnadha?"

The gods have mercy. He was to oversee Caerabis now.

"Don't worry, my lord," Slatin said, a hint of laughter dancing upon his gravelly voice. "She'll suffer."

More?

Mikan nodded. "Make sure that she does."


Kaeleck and Mikan stayed long enough to watch the spectacle Marshal Slatin Arnadha had planned for Thylaina. Outside the mansion, his men stripped her of the raggedy dress, then marched her to the jailhouse, a three-block walk. Knights and soldiers had lined the cobblestone road, some shouting hateful accusations about her being a witch and attempting to assassinate Second Marshal Salnaer Thornsalin. Other men threw rocks at her. Slatin's laughter followed each successful blow as he trailed from a safe distance.

When the temple came into view, she looked toward it, hoping one of the priests might come to her aid. But there was no help to be had, for hanging from gallows on the landing were High Priest Haltrin Jalfiasin and the herbal priest, Raylen. Their bodies swayed slightly, their blue tongues clinging to the corners of their mouths, eyes bulging out. They were meant to have died a slow death.

Thylaina's knees gave, and she crumpled to the street. Why did the priests have to die? They were loyal to Valorius!

The men cheered, and more rocks struck her. Then Ardella's words echoed in her memory.

*"I praise Chaos for this gift."*

These knights were not men of Valorius.

"Get back! Take your hands off her!" a man shouted.

"That's enough!" bellowed another.

"What do you think you're doing, Dubight?" a different man asked.

"I said enough!"

The men's voices pounded on her ears as hard as the rocks on her body.

"My lady." Hands slid beneath her arms and gently helped her rise. "Walk with me." His voice seemed kind, even with the panicked tremble.

"Get back!" the other man roared.

Most of the laughter faltered, only a few continuing as if they knew not what now happened.

"I asked you, Dubight," the third man pressed, "what do you think you're doing?"

Thylaina looked back at the loud one, the dubight, expecting to see a young Gavrel. Could she trust him?

The stocky soldier pointed at Slatin. "We'll not allow anymore of this, Captain." His eyes darted toward the two marshals. "Punish us. I don't care." Without waiting for a response, he lifted Thylaina and carried her to the jailhouse. The other helpful man followed, watching the onlookers.

"I'm sorry if I hurt you," the dubight whispered.

"Take me from here," she managed. The first thing she had said since the cabinet. Sweet Vynia, her throat hurt.

"If only that I could."

The other man, a knight by the armor he wore, opened the jailhouse door. "What are we doing? Gods! They're going to beat the life out of us."

"Then they do." The dubight lowered Thylaina to a chair. He went into another room, returning with a blanket for her, then took a scrap of cloth from a nearby table and pressed it to her head. "Hold that there."

The two paced the room, mumbling to each other about the death they now likely faced.

"Damn you to Darkness," the dubight snapped, slapping the other's hand away. "You told me the Griffon was a respectable order. It's naught but corruption!"

The knight's shoulders lowered. "My brother convinced me. I'm sorry." He nodded in Thylaina's direction. "I knew nothing about her." He then rested his hands on the dubight's shoulders. "But they want you in their ranks. Kaeleck isn't going to let this ruin your chances."

"How do you know?"

"Because he would've killed you in the street."

Thylaina lowered the cloth. "Why?"

The men looked at her, then the knight laughed. "You haven't yet learned?" he asked.

"Why did you help me?"

The dubight sighed. Staring at his friend, he said with conviction, "Because it's all wrong. And I don't care how much Thornsalin wants me, I'll resist until I die."

There had been enough bloodshed on her behalf. Thylaina could not let another lose his life because of her. However, to hear one already within the rotted knighthood speak as such gave some hope. Perhaps one of them might become her savior.

The rhythmic thudding of heavy footsteps neared. The two men turned toward the door just as it swung open. Marshal Slatin Arnadha stood there, accompanied by three knights. Slatin smirked as he looked from the dubight to Thylaina.

"Put her in a cell," he ordered, and his two knights advanced.

The dubight squared his shoulders. "I'll not let you hurt her."

"You!" Slatin's roar and fierce expression brought everyone to a halt. "You're to leave now. Marshal Thornsalin awaits your immediate arrival with his company."

The dubight frowned. "What?"

Slatin's heavy exhale filled the room. He jerked his head toward Thylaina, and the knights resumed toward her. "You're both going to Haevaun Balaeus," he said.

"What if I refuse?"

"Don't," his friend begged.

Marshal Arnadha laughed. "Then you'll hang next to the priests."

Thylaina retreated from the approaching knights and reached for the young man. "Please go, Dubight."

He spun, charged between her and the two men. "Not a chance."

Thylaina touched his shoulder. "I will not have your blood on my hands."

"Nor will I have yours on mine."

"Please," she whispered, as the knights drew their blades. "They will not kill me."

"Can you make that promise?"

"S'yai. I do."

Seeming defeated, his taut muscles slackened, and his shoulders fell. "Fine."

"Wise decision," Slatin said. "Now get to Marshal Thornsalin. That's an order."

The dubight faced Thylaina. "I'll never forget this day."

"Tell me your name."

He glanced over his shoulder at Slatin, then took her hand and kissed it. "Elgier Constine."

"Thank you, Elgier."

He bowed his head, then spun on his heel and stomped from the chamber, his friend following. Elgier offered no salute or respectful parting words to Slatin.

The knights grabbed Thylaina and forced her into the cell room. Slatin had the blanket taken away afore they pushed her into a cell.

"You'll stay here until you're useful," he said, then spread his arms. "This is your new bedchamber."

The four of them laughed as they exited.

Torchlight flickered from across the cell. Another glowed fifteen feet toward the path's dead end.

Thylaina stared at the flames, wishing she could feel warmth within this cold chamber. Were there others like Elgier who might help her? She had to hope that one day men like him would save her and Brenlyr from the knighthood. Hope was all she had left to grasp on to.

Emvarr's calendar year consists of twelve thirty-day months, often referred to as 'moons'. Each month is named after its moon. The order is:

Dalin (Wolf)
Amber
Stallion
Hawk
Blossom
Lover's
Burning
Hunter's
Fox
Harvest
Oaken
Cold

## Alohrius

Aella (*Ī-la*) – A child in Caerabis.

Alyanna (*Al-**yan**-a*) – A child in Caerabis.

Amdronus (***Am**-dre-nes*) – Tesesra's personal guard.

Ardella (*Ar-**del**-a*) – Head mansion servant.

Arkiem Korda (*Ar-**kē**-em **Kōr**-da*) – The First Marshall.

Arlin (***Ar**-lin*) – Breydon's squire.

Bethlyn (***Beth**-lin*) – Tesesra's handmaiden.

Brevig Vantos (***Bre**-vig **Van**-tōs*) – Member of the Alohrian Council.

Einasa (*Ī-**nes**-a*) – Maiden from the southern farmsteads.

Elgier Constine (*El-**gē**-ir Kon-**stēn***) – A dubight in Caerabis.

Escany (***Es**-kin-ē*) – Master Gardener.

Frindor Cyle (***Frin**-dōr **Sī**-el*) – The Third Marshal.

Iaviane (*Ī-**u**-vē-an*) – Breydon's lost love.

Jerien (***Jeer**-ē-in*) – A child in Caerabis.

Kaeleck Thornsalin (***Kā**-lek*) – Captain of Haevaun Balaeus.

Kreysin (***Krā**-sin*) – Breydon's twin brother.

Mezadie (*Mez-u-**dē***) – An artist from Brydasia.

Miryl Eilisar (***Mī**-ril **Ā**-li-sar*) – A Captain of Caerabis.

Nikhia (*Ni-**kē**-u*) – Einasa's closest friend.

Panya (***Pan**-ya*) – A scullery maiden.

Quaiy (***Kwā**-ē*) – Tesesra's chambermaid.

Raylen (***Rā**-lin*) – Herbal Priest at the temple.

Rhodrin (***Rō**-drin*) – Knight of Warstchia. Son of Brevig Vantos.

Salnaer Thornsalin (***Sal**-neer*) – The Second Marshal.

Slatin Arnadha (***Slat**-in Ar-**na**-da*) – Captain of Haevaun Balaeus.

Vhilmas Freyvlor (***Vil***-*mes **Frā**-vlor*) – Knight of Caerabis.

Viya (***Vī**-a*) – Head of the scullery.


## **Etharell**

Eidryn (***Ī**-drin*) – Etharell's Master Healer and Thylaina's instructor.

Galenlyr (***Gal**-in-leer*) – Thylaina's father.

Neldrid (***Nel**-drid*) – Thylaina's brother.

Rhomasyn Draphise (***Rō**-ma-sin **Dra**-fĕs*) – Thylaina's betrothed.

Valraahn (***Val**-ron*) and Valrae Tanagaryl (***Val**-rā Tan-a-ga-**ril***) – Thylaina's cousins. Prince and Princess of Etharell.

Yasontler (*Yu-**sont**-ler*) and Lilisa Tanagaryl (***Lu**-li-sa*) – Thylaina's uncle and aunt. King and Queen of Etharell.

Aarosyn (***Air**-ō-sin*), Lailynne (***Lā**-u-lin*), Leisyn (***Lā**-sin*), and Rainsala (*Rān-**sa**-la*) – Thylaina's dearest friends from Etharell.


## **Places**

Aubrasna (*Aw-**bra**-sna*) – Small country north of Alohrius. Home of the Aubrasnans, kin to the elves.

Brydasia (*Bri-**dā**-sha*) – The Eastern Continent of Emvarr.

Myndrose (***Min**-drōs*) – The Northern Continent of Emvarr.

Mystier (***Mis**-tē-eer*) – City where First General Neldrid Zorlias oversees the Forest Army of Etharell.

New Portes (*New **Pōr**-tez*) – Yeuroth's largest seaport.

Suflor Hills (***Su**-flōr*) – Dry hills between the Alohrian Downs and the Dred Sea. Home of the Dragnols.

Ubrasia (*Ū-**brā**-sha*) – The Western Continent of Emvarr.

Yeltar (***Yel**-tar*) – Third largest country of Yeuroth. Home of the Yeltaran Knighthood.

Yeuroth (***Yer**-uth*) – The Southern Continent of Emvarr.

<u>**Miscellaneous**</u>

*Shapele* (**Sha**-pel) – Elvish for 'Captain'.

*S'yai* (**Sē**-ā) – Elvish for 'Yes'.

*N'ei* (Nē-**ī**) – Elvish for 'No'.

*Et losath eywe* (Et lō-**sahth** ī-**wē**) – Elvish for 'I love you'.

*Endoc* (**En**-dōk) – Spell to quickly end a life without touching.

*Estogpa* (**Es**-tōg-pa) – A spell to stop one's heart by touch.

*Falishia* (Fa-lu-**shē**-a) – Magic word for 'sleep'.


<u>The Ageless</u> – Mortals whose natural lives are extended through interaction with the divine, whether while alive or through death.

<u>The Council</u> – Five Alohrians selected by their peers to oversee the laws of Alohrius and its knighthood.

<u>Dragnols</u> (***Drag***-*nuls*) – Large beasts from Suflor Hills.

<u>Dubight</u> (*Doo*-***bīt***) – A soldier training for the Alohrian Knighthood.

<u>Southern Brigands</u> – Groups of bandits consisting of knights, soldiers, and criminals.

<u>The Three Marshals</u> – The three leaders of the Alohrian knighthood.

<u>The Unseen</u> – An elite group of xilys warriors formed to defeat the Southern Brigands.

<u>Vynist</u> (***Vin***-*yist*) – One who shows deep devotion to the Earthen Goddess, Vynia.

<u>Xilys</u> (***Zī***-*lus*) – The elite force that guards the Etharell borders.


<u>Ashrych</u> (***Ash***-*rich*) – A small bush with tiny pink flowers with red edges. Helps calm before bed or lessen their anxieties.

<u>Bariy</u> (***Bar***-*ē*) – Tree from where buraily leaves come.

<u>Beidira</u> (*Bī*-***deer***-*a*) – A tree in Myndrose with thick black bark that is processed into a red dust with mind-altering effects. Known as Divine Wrath.

<u>Bossel</u> (***Bah***-*sul*) – A pale root found throughout Yeuroth, often used for basic healing remedies.

<u>Buraily</u> (*Bur*-***ā***-*lē*) – A deep green leaf with whitish veins containing strong

healing properties.

Camiol (**Kam**-ē-ōl) – Tiny blue flowers with green centers used as a sleep aid.

Crueberry (**Kroo**-beer-ē) – Dark-red, tart berries from the crueberry bush. Often used in drinks and sweets.

Havir (**Ha**-vir) – Leaves from the havir trees found in the tropical forests of Garhlas, used to keep items damp or supple.

Insh Oil – Oil distilled from insh weed used as a preventative from pregnancies.

Insh Weed (*insh*) – A tall plant with purple petals that forms a bulb used to end pregnancies.

Lamuline (**La**-moo-lēn) – An ointment to soothe the skin of a pregnant woman's stomach.

Mayrb'ei (**Mar**-bē-ī) – Long-stemmed flowers with sprays of small red blossoms and raspberry-like scent.

Olesa (Ō-**les**-a) – Oil with mild healing qualities made from repenia leaves. Mainly used as a potion base or to soak bossel roots.

Ramgwolf (**Ram**-wulf) – Long rooted plant with seven to eight fat leaves, often mistaken as a weed.

Repenia (Re-**pēn**-ya) – A vine with deep green leaves used to make Olesa Oil.

Sinzdra (**Sinz**-dra) – A small fruit the size of an infant's hand. Used in elixirs as an aphrodisiac and to increase fertility.

Vervain (Ver-**vān**) – A plant with clusters of mauve flowers and jagged leaves. Used for several ailments.

Xarflas (**Zar**-fles) – A dark green plant with light green flowers. All parts of this plant have powerful healing properties.

Yavlar (**Yav**-lar) – A juicy brown leaf with blue veins, and has an awful taste.


Fruzae (Froo-**zā**) – A strong liquor made of fermented fruit and often times honey. Favored amongst humans.

Ortia Louvres (**Or**-sha **Loo**-vray) – A sensual oral act to offer sexual release or to share intimacy.

Sponishies (Spon-**ē**-shēs) – A pregnancy preventative paired with insh oil.

Thring, Throng, Swyve (**Swīv**) – Sexual intercourse.

*Acknowledgements*

There are so many to thank for their part in this novel. My husband, Scott, most of all. I wouldn't be doing what I love if it weren't for him. His love and support surpass everything. To my Beta Readers, Ronald, Erica, Crystal, Tyler, and EP, thank you for your time and honest feedback. It's more valuable than you may realize. To Amanda and Ben, your name suggestions helped immensely, even if for side characters. Amanda, yours became far more important than I had intended. Erica has done wonderfully with the maps and artworks—exactly what I wanted. Ronald G Bellar's professional input has, once again, helped me liven some scenes. Thank you for always being available for author talk. I'm grateful for the support from my family and fellow indie-authors. And last but not least, Secretary Maggie and Miss Milla, I love having you with me every step of the way.

## About the Author

Mary J Nichols began short story writing in 2003, expanding into novels in 2007. She published her first novel, For Duty & For Love, in 2021. Introduced to Dungeons & Dragons at a young age, and still an active player, Mary developed a love for fantasy books and arts. After years of writing short stories in several genres, she found her niche in romantic fantasy. Writers such as Margaret Weis, Tracy Hickman, Terry Brooks, and Richard Knaak, Dean Koontz, as well as Guy Gavriel Kay's 'The Fionavar Tapestry', have been inspiring works. When not writing, Mary adores spending time with her family, especially playing various types of games and watching movies. In the rare moments she's alone, she listens to music while reading with either one or both of her mini dachshunds curled up with her.

You can sign up for Mary's Newsletter at her website: maryjnichols.com
And find her on these social media platforms
Facebook: facebook.com/FatesOfEmvarr
TikTok: maryjnichols_author

**<u>Fates of Emvarr Novels by Mary J Nichols:</u>**

For Duty & For Love

An Unsought Destiny

Mockingbird & Vulture

The Misfortunate Maiden